THE MODERN LIBRARY
OF THE WORLD'S BEST BOOKS

SHE *and* KING SOLOMON'S MINES

SHE
&
KING
SOLOMON'S
MINES

by **H. RIDER HAGGARD**

With an Introduction

by ORVILLE PRESCOTT

THE MODERN LIBRARY, NEW YORK

Random House IS THE PUBLISHER OF *The Modern Library*

BENNETT CERF · DONALD S. KLOPFER

Manufactured in the United States of America by H. Wolff

Introduction

by Orville Prescott

THE RAILWAY compartment was occupied by two brothers who were traveling up to London together. One of them said that he didn't think Robert Louis Stevenson's *Treasure Island* was anything so very remarkable. "Well," replied the other, "I'd like to see you write anything half as good—bet you a bob you can't."

"Done," said Henry Rider Haggard, and within the next six weeks he wrote *King Solomon's Mines*. That was in 1885. Haggard was only twenty-nine, the author of two unsuccessful novels and of a book about the Zulu war in Africa. The story he wrote so casually, "only a tale of adventure" as he himself called it, was not as good as *Treasure Island*. Nevertheless, it is a great deal more than half as good and an acknowledged masterpiece of its kind. Anyone who did not read it in his early teens missed one of the thrills of his lifetime and should try to atone for the error by presenting a copy to someone who is in his early teens.

King Solomon's Mines became one of the world's great best sellers and is beloved to this day in every corner of the English-speaking world. Two years later, also in a six-week interval, Haggard wrote another immensely popular tale of adventure, *She*. The two books have delighted hundreds of thousands of readers and in their several film versions millions of movie-goers. What is the secret of their undying appeal to the young in heart, to all those fortunate enough not to have lost their ability to delight in tales of romantic adventure?

The answer lies in the character of the man who wrote them. Haggard was a Victorian English gentleman, bearded, distinguished-looking, the author of more than fifty novels which won him the critical admiration and personal friendship of Rudyard Kipling, Andrew Lang, and Theodore Roosevelt. He was born in 1856. In 1875, when he was only nineteen, he went out to Africa as a member of the staff of the governor of Natal.

During the next few years young Haggard reveled in the great experience of his life. He hunted big game, journeyed across the veldt by oxcart and on horseback, and personally hoisted the flag which marked the annexation of the Transvaal. Before, during, and after the Zulu war he studied the Zulu people with admiration and affection, listening with rapt attention to tales told by old men with long memories. When he settled down briefly on an ostrich farm in Natal near the Transvaal border he found himself in the thick of the First Boer War, which England lost.

For the rest of his life Haggard's imagination was kindled by the memory of the stirring events in which he had played a part; by the very idea of the vast African wilderness and the romantic possibilities which lay in its still unexplored interior; by the barbaric splendor of Zulu impies tossing their plumed headdresses and rattling their spears against their shields. Africa was the match that set his creative imagination on fire.

But his own special cast of mind shaped the romances he wrote. A born storyteller with a remarkable gift for spinning a grand yarn, Haggard had no interest in the subtleties of literary art. He was an honorable gentleman, a champion of the British Empire, and also a mystic. He believed in the transmigration of souls and that in earlier incarnations he had been an ancient Egyptian, a Norse Viking, and a Zulu. He had studied those peoples, of course, but he *knew* about them from personal experience, or thought he did. His instinctive sympathy for primitive societies and violent ways of life gave an extra dimension to his best books.

Which are these?

Three generations of men and boys have preferred the two romances now republished in this volume. The reason for their enthusiasm, I think, is that in both *King Solomon's Mines* and *She* the narrators speak for their creator and express his personality. And it is Haggard's appealing personality and ideas, as well as his fine accounts of perilous journeys, lost civilizations, and epic feats of arms, which endear him to his readers.

A few critics have admired other Haggard novels more, notably *Nada the Lily*, a tremendous tale of blood and slaughter among the Zulus before the white men came, and *Eric Bright Eyes*, a marvelously successful effort to recapture the spirit of the Icelandic sagas in a story of love and vengeance before Christianity came to Iceland. But in those books Haggard eliminated his own personality and with it the source of much of his enduring charm.

Allan Quatermain, hero of *King Solomon's Mines*, experienced imaginary adventures; but, Haggard admitted, Allan's thoughts were the author's. Allan is modest, courageous, tolerant, and honorable, respectful of the culture of primitive peoples and humble before the mysteries of life. It is not surprising that so good and yet so likable a man became an object of hero worship to hordes of readers. Like Sherlock Holmes, whose popularity forced Conan Doyle to restore him to life after his official demise, Allan Quatermain reappeared in a dozen more books after his official death. Several of those books are as good as *King Solomon's Mines*, and Haggard's trilogy about the decline and fall of the Zulu kingdom (*Marie, Child of Storm* and *Finished*) is even better.

Nevertheless, the best introduction to Haggard will always be *King Solomon's Mines*. Here is "something new out of Africa," romantic action for its own sake with a superb account of a native kingdom, a fiendish witch, and a battle between native armies which once read will never be forgotten. This is pure Haggard with all his characteristic qualities and typical material present in abundance. If you like it, you will want more. If you don't, you are too sophisticated in your literary taste, too accustomed to psychological novels about complex problems, too far from your youth and from youth's appetite for the strange and marvelous.

She is similar to *King Solomon's Mines*, but more extravagant in its imaginative fantasy. A gloomy and exciting thriller told in a rhetorically old-fashioned prose, it is a romance about a dead civilization in Africa, a mysterious queen, "She-who-must-be-obeyed," and the queen's miraculous patience while she waited two thousand years for her lover to be born again. Sublimely beautiful, wise, passionate, and gifted with supernatural powers, Haggard's heroine is a somewhat awkward symbol of his ideas about love and power, time and eternity.

Even if *She* seems a trifle too preposterous for modern tastes, it is still a wonderfully imaginative romance crammed with gruesome episodes and amazing adventures. Its narrator shares many of Allan Quatermain's attractive qualities.

Rider Haggard was knighted in 1912. He continued to write with unimpaired prodigality of invention until shortly before his death in 1925. A storyteller in a great tradition, he only wanted to entertain and to express some of the awe and reverence he felt before the mysteries of human existence. He did so with enormous success and thoroughly deserves this opportunity to be introduced to a new generation of readers.

SHE ◆

A History of Adventure

In earth and skie and sea
strange thynges ther be

Doggerel couplet from the Sherd of Amenartas

Introduction

IN GIVING to the world the record of what, looked at as an adventure only, is I suppose one of the most wonderful and mysterious experiences ever undergone by mortal men, I feel it incumbent on me to explain what my exact connection with it is. And so I may as well say at once that I am not the narrator but only the editor of this extraordinary history, and then go on to tell how it found its way into my hands.

Some years ago I, the editor, was stopping with a friend, *"vir doctissimus et amicus meus,"* at a certain university, which for the purposes of this history we will call Cambridge, and was one day much struck with the appearance of two people whom I saw going arm-in-arm down the street. One of these gentlemen was I think, without exception, the handsomest young fellow I have ever seen. He was very tall, very broad, and had a look of power and a grace of bearing that seemed as native to him as it is to a wild stag. In addition his face was almost without flaw —a good face as well as a beautiful one, and when he lifted his hat, which he did just then to a passing lady, I saw that his head was covered with little golden curls growing close to the scalp.

"Good gracious!" I said to my friend, with whom I was walking, "why, that fellow looks like a statue of Apollo come to life. What a splendid man he is!"

"Yes," he answered, "he is the handsomest man in the

university, and one of the nicest too. They call him 'the Greek god'; but look at the other one, he's Vincey's (that's the god's name) guardian, and supposed to be full of every kind of information. They call him 'Charon.'"
I looked, and found the older man quite as interesting in his way as the glorified specimen of humanity at his side. He appeared to be about forty years of age, and was I think as ugly as his companion was handsome. To begin with, he was shortish, rather bow-legged, very deep chested, and with unusually long arms. He had dark hair and small eyes, and the hair grew right down on his forehead, and his whiskers grew right up to his hair, so that there was uncommonly little of his countenance to be seen. Altogether he reminded me forcibly of a gorilla, and yet there was something very pleasing and genial about the man's eye. I remember saying that I should like to know him.

"All right," answered my friend, "nothing easier. I know Vincey; I'll introduce you," and he did, and for some minutes we stood chatting—about the Zulu people, I think, for I had just returned from the Cape at the time. Presently, however, a stoutish lady, whose name I do not remember, came along the pavement, accompanied by a pretty fair-haired girl, and these two Mr. Vincey, who clearly knew them well, at once joined, walking off in their company. I remember being rather amused because of the change in the expression of the elder man, whose name I discovered was Holly, when he saw the ladies advancing. He suddenly stopped short in his talk, cast a reproachful look at his companion, and, with an abrupt nod to myself, turned and marched off alone across the street. I heard afterwards that he was popularly supposed to be as much afraid of a woman as most people are of a mad dog, which accounted for his precipitate retreat. I cannot say, however, that young Vincey showed much aversion to feminine society on this occasion. Indeed, I remember laughing, and remarking to my friend at the time that he was not the sort of man whom it would be desirable to introduce to the lady one was going to marry, since it is exceedingly probable that the acquaintance would end in a transfer of her affections. He was altogether too good-looking, and, what is more, he had none of that consciousness and conceit about him which usually afflicts handsome men, and makes them deservedly disliked by their fellows.

That same evening my visit came to an end, and this was the last I saw or heard of "Charon" and "the Greek god" for many a long day. Indeed, I have never seen either of them from that hour to this, and do not think it probable that I shall. But a month ago I received a letter and two packets, one of manuscript, and on opening the first found that it was signed "Horace Holly," a name that at the moment was not familiar to me. It ran as follows:

—— *College, Cambridge, May 1, 18—*

My Dear Sir,

You will be surprised, considering the very slight nature of our acquaintance, to get a letter from me. Indeed, I think I had better begin by reminding you that we once met, now some five years ago, when I and my ward Leo Vincey were introduced to you in the street at Cambridge. To be brief and come to my business. I have recently read with much interest a book of yours describing a Central African adventure. I take it that this book is partly true, and partly an effort of the imagination. However this is, it has given me an idea. It happens, how you will see in the accompanying manuscript (which together with the Scarab, the "Royal Son of the Sun," and the original sherd, I am sending to you by hand), that my ward, or rather my adopted son, Leo Vincey and myself have recently passed through a real African adventure, of a nature so much more marvelous than the one which you describe, that to tell you the truth I am almost ashamed to submit it to you for fear lest you should disbelieve my tale. You will see it stated in this manuscript that I, or rather we, had made up our minds not to make this history public during our joint lives. Nor should we alter our determination were it not for a circumstance which has recently arisen. We are for reasons that, after perusing this manuscript, you may be able to guess, going away again, this time to Central Asia, where, if anywhere upon this earth, wisdom is to be found, and we anticipate that our sojourn there will be a long one. Possibly we shall not return. Under these altered conditions it has become a question whether we are justified in withholding from the world an account of a phenomenon which we believe to be of unparalleled interest, merely because our private life is involved, or because we are afraid of ridicule and doubt being cast upon our statements. I hold one view about this matter, and Leo holds another, and finally, after much discussion, we have come to a compromise, namely, to send the history to you, giving you full leave to publish it if you think fit, the only stipulation being that you shall disguise our real names, and as much concerning our personal identity as is consistent with the maintenance of the *bona fides* of the narrative.

And now what am I to say further? I really do not know beyond once more repeating that everything is described in the accompanying manuscript exactly as it happened. As regards *She* herself I have nothing to add. Day by day we have greater occasion to regret that we did not better avail ourselves of our opportunities to obtain more information from that marvelous woman. Who was she?

How did she first come to the Caves of Kôr, and what was her real religion? We never ascertained, and now, alas, we never shall, at least not yet. These and many other questions arise in my mind, but what is the good of asking them now?

Will you undertake the task? We give you complete freedom, and as a reward you will, we believe, have the credit of presenting to the world the most wonderful history, as distinguished from romance, that its records can show. Read the manuscript (which I have copied out fairly for your benefit), and let me know.

Believe me, very truly yours,

L. Horace Holly

P.S.—Of course, if any profit results from the sale of the writing should you care to undertake its publication, you can do what you like with it, but if there is a loss I will leave instructions with my lawyers, Messrs. Geoffrey and Jordan, to meet it. We entrust the sherd, the scarab, and the parchments to your keeping till such time as we demand them back again.—L. H. H.

This letter, as may be imagined, astonished me considerably, but when I came to look at the MS., which the pressure of other work prevented me from doing for a fortnight, I was still more astonished, as I think the reader will be also, and at once made up my mind to press on with the matter. I wrote to this effect to Mr. Holly, but a week afterwards received a letter from that gentleman's lawyers, returning my own, with the information that their client and Mr. Leo Vincey had already left this country for Tibet, and they did not at present know their address.

Well, that is all I have to say. Of the history itself the reader must judge. I give it him, with the exception of a very few alterations, made with the object of concealing the identity of the actors from the general public, exactly as it has come to me. Personally I have made up my mind to refrain from comments. At first I was inclined to believe that this history of a woman on whom, clothed in the majesty of her almost endless years, the shadow of Eternity itself lay like the dark wing of Night, was some gigantic allegory of which I could not catch the meaning. Then I thought that it might be a bold attempt to portray the possible results of practical immortality, informing the substance of a mortal who yet drew her strength from Earth, and in whose human bosom passions yet rose and fell and beat as in the undying world around her the winds and the tides rise and fall and beat unceasingly. But as I went on I abandoned that idea also. To me the story seems to bear the stamp of truth upon its face. Its explanation I must leave to others, and with this slight preface, which circumstances make necessary, I introduce the world to Ayesha and the Caves of Kôr.

THE EDITOR

P.S.—There is on consideration one circumstance that, after a reperusal of this history, struck me with so much force that I cannot resist calling the attention of the reader to it. He will observe that so far as we are made acquainted with him there appears to be nothing in the character of Leo Vincey which in the opinion of most people would have been likely to attract an intellect so powerful as that of Ayesha. He is not even, at any rate to my view, particularly interesting. Indeed, one might imagine that Mr. Holly would under ordinary circumstances have easily outstripped him in the favor of *She*. Can it be that extremes meet, and that the very excess and splendor of her mind led her by means of some strange physical reaction to worship at the shrine of matter? Was that ancient Kallikrates nothing but a splendid animal beloved for his hereditary Greek beauty? Or is the true explanation what I believe it to be—namely, that Ayesha, seeing further than we can see, perceived the germ and smoldering spark of greatness which lay hid within her lover's soul, and well knew that under the influence of her gift of life, watered by her wisdom, and shone upon with the sunshine of her presence, it would bloom like a flower and flash out like a star, filling the world with light and fragrance?

Here also I am not able to answer, but must leave the reader to form his own judgment on the facts before him, as detailed by Mr. Holly in the following pages.

1 ♦

My Visitor

THERE ARE some events of which each circumstance and surrounding detail seems to be graven on the memory in such fashion that we cannot forget it, and so it is with the scene that I am about to describe. It rises as clearly before my mind at this moment as though it had happened yesterday.

It was in this very month something over twenty years ago that I, Ludwig Horace Holly, was sitting one night in my rooms at Cambridge, grinding away at some mathematical work, I forget what. I was to go up for my fellowship within a week, and was expected by my tutor and my college generally to distinguish myself. At last, wearied out, I flung my book down, and, going to the mantelpiece, took down a pipe and filled it. There was a candle burning on the mantelpiece, and a long, narrow glass at the back of it; and as I was in the act of lighting the pipe I caught sight of my own countenance in the glass, and paused to reflect. The lighted match burned away till it scorched my fingers, forcing me to drop it; but still I stood and stared at myself in the glass, and reflected.

"Well," I said aloud, at last, "it is to be hoped that I shall be able to do something with the inside of my head, for I shall certainly never do anything by the help of the outside."

This remark will doubtless strike anybody who reads it

as being slightly obscure, but I was in reality alluding to my physical deficiencies. Most men of twenty-two are endowed at any rate with some share of the comeliness of youth, but to me even this was denied. Short, thick-set, and deep-chested almost to deformity, with long sinewy arms, heavy features, deep-set gray eyes, a low brow half overgrown with a mop of thick black hair, like a deserted clearing on which the forest had once more begun to encroach; such was my appearance nearly a quarter of a century ago, and such, with some modification, is it to this day. Like Cain, I was branded—branded by Nature with the stamp of abnormal ugliness, as I was gifted by Nature with iron and abnormal strength and considerable intellectual powers. So ugly was I that the spruce young men of my college, though they were proud enough of my feats of endurance and physical prowess, did not even care to be seen walking with me. Was it wonderful that I was misanthropic and sullen? Was it wonderful that I brooded and worked alone, and had no friends—at least, only one? I was set apart by Nature to live alone, and draw comfort from her breast, and hers only. Women hated the sight of me. Only a week before I had heard one call me a "monster" when she thought I was out of hearing, and say that I had converted her to the monkey theory. Once, indeed, a woman pretended to care for me, and I lavished all the pent-up affection of my nature upon her. Then money that was to have come to me went elsewhere, and she discarded me. I pleaded with her as I have never pleaded with any living creature before or since, for I was caught by her sweet face, and loved her; and in the end by way of answer she took me to the glass, and stood side by side with me, and looked into it.

"Now," she said, "if I am Beauty, who are you?" That was when I was only twenty.

And so I stood and stared, and felt a sort of grim satisfaction in the sense of my own loneliness; for I had neither father, nor mother, nor brother; and as I did so there came a knock at my door.

I listened before I went to open it, for it was nearly twelve o'clock at night, and I was in no mood to admit any stranger. I had but one friend in the college, or, indeed, in the world—perhaps it was he.

Just then the person outside the door coughed, and I hastened to open it, for I knew the cough.

A tall man of about thirty, with the remains of great personal beauty, came hurrying in, staggering beneath the weight of a massive iron box which he carried by a handle with his right hand. He placed the box upon the table, and then fell into an awful fit of coughing. He coughed and coughed till his face became quite purple, and at last he sank into a chair and began to spit up blood. I poured out some whisky into a tumbler, and gave it to him. He drank it, and seemed better; though his better was very bad indeed.

"Why did you keep me standing there in the cold?" he asked pettishly. "You know the drafts are death to me."

"I did not know who it was," I answered. "You are a late visitor."

"Yes; and I verily believe it is my last visit," he answered, with a ghastly attempt at a smile. "I am done for, Holly. I am done for. I do not believe that I shall see tomorrow!"

"Nonsense!" I said. "Let me go for a doctor."

He waved me back imperiously. "It is sober sense; but I want no doctors. I have studied medicine, and I know all about it. No doctors can help me. My last hour has come! For a year past I have only lived by a miracle. Now listen to me as you never listened to anybody before; for you will not have the opportunity of getting me to repeat my words. We have been friends for two years; now tell me how much do you know about me?"

"I know that you are rich, and have had a fancy to come to college long after the age that most men leave it. I know that you have been married, and that your wife died; and that you have been the best, indeed almost the only friend I ever had."

"Did you know that I have a son?"

"No."

"I have. He is five years old. He cost me his mother's life, and I have never been able to bear to look upon his face in consequence. Holly, if you will accept the trust, I am going to leave you that boy's sole guardian."

I sprang almost out of my chair. "*Me!*" I said.

"Yes, you. I have not studied you for two years for nothing. I have known for some time that I could not last, and since I realized the fact I have been searching for someone to whom I could confide the boy and this," and he tapped the iron box. "You are the man, Holly; for, like a rugged tree, you are hard and sound at core. Listen; the boy will be the only representative of one of the most ancient families in the world, that is, so far as families can be traced. You will laugh at me when I say it, but one day it will be proved to you beyond a doubt, that my sixty-fifth or sixty-sixth lineal ancestor was an Egyptian priest of Isis, though he was himself of Grecian extraction, and was called Kallikrates.[1] His father was one of the Greek mercenaries raised by Hak-Hor, a Mendesian pharaoh

[1] The Strong and Beautiful, or, more accurately, the Beautiful in Strength.

of the twenty-ninth dynasty, and his grandfather, I believe, was that very Kallikrates mentioned by Herodotus.[2]
In or about the year 339 before Christ, just at the time
of the final fall of the Pharaohs, this Kallikrates (the
priest) broke his vows of celibacy and fled from Egypt
with a princess of royal blood who had fallen in love
with him, and was finally wrecked upon the coast of
Africa, somewhere, as I believe, in the neighborhood
of where Delagoa Bay now is, or rather to the north of
it, he and his wife being saved, and all the remainder
of their company destroyed in one way or another. Here
they endured great hardships, but were at last entertained
by the mighty queen of a savage people, a white woman
of peculiar loveliness, who, under circumstances which I
cannot enter into, but which you will one day learn, if you
live, from the contents of the box, finally murdered my
ancestor, Kallikrates. His wife, however, escaped, how I
know not, to Athens, bearing a child with her, whom she
named Tisisthenes, or the Mighty Avenger. Five hundred
years or more afterwards the family migrated to Rome
under circumstances of which no trace remains, and here,
probably with the idea of preserving the idea of vengeance

[2] The Kallikrates here referred to by my friend was a Spartan, spoken of
by Herodotus (Herod. ix. 72) as being remarkable for his beauty. He fell
at the glorious battle of Plataea (September 22, B.C. 479), when the La-
cedaemonians and Athenians under Pausanias routed the Persians, putting
nearly 300,000 of them to the sword. The following is a translation of the
passage: "For Kallikrates died out of the battle, he came to the army the
most beautiful man of the Greeks of that day—not only of the Lacedae-
monians themselves, but of the other Greeks also. He when Pausanias was
sacrificing was wounded in the side by an arrow; and then they fought, but
on being carried off he regretted his death, and said to Arimnestus, a Plataean,
that he did not grieve at dying for Greece, but at not having struck a blow,
or, although he desired so to do, performed any deed worthy of himself."
This Kallikrates, who appears to have been as brave as he was beautiful, is
subsequently mentioned by Herodotus as having been buried among the
ἰρέ̄νες (young commanders), apart from the other Spartans and the Helots.
—L. H. H.

which we find set out in the name of Tisisthenes, they appear to have pretty regularly assumed the cognomen of Vindex, or Avenger. Here, too, they remained for another five centuries or more, till about 770 A.D., when Charlemagne invaded Lombardy, where they were then settled, whereon the head of the family seems to have attached himself to the great Emperor, and to have returned with him across the Alps, and finally to have settled in Brittany. Eight generations later his lineal representative crossed to England in the reign of Edward the Confessor, and in the time of William the Conqueror was advanced to great honor and power. From that time till the present day I can trace my descent without a break. Not that the Vinceys—for that was the final corruption of the name after its bearers took root in English soil—have been particularly distinguished—they never came much to the fore. Sometimes they were soldiers, sometimes merchants, but on the whole they have preserved a dead level of respectability, and a still deader level of mediocrity. From the time of Charles II till the beginning of the present century they were merchants. About 1790 my grandfather made a considerable fortune out of brewing, and retired. In 1821 he died, and my father succeeded him, and dissipated most of the money. Ten years ago he died also, leaving me a net income of about two thousand a year. Then it was that I undertook an expedition in connection with *that*"—and he pointed to the iron chest—"which ended disastrously enough. On my way back I traveled in the South of Europe, and finally reached Athens. There I met my beloved wife, who might well also have been called the 'Beautiful,' like my old Greek ancestor. There I married her, and there, a year afterwards, when my boy was born, she died."

He paused awhile, his head sunk upon his hand, and

then continued, "My marriage had diverted me from a project which I cannot enter into now. I have no time, Holly—I have no time! One day, if you accept my trust, you will learn all about it. After my wife's death I turned my mind to it again. But first it was necessary, or, at least, I conceived that it was necessary, that I should attain to a perfect knowledge of Eastern dialects, especially Arabic. It was to facilitate my studies that I came here. Very soon, however, my disease developed itself, and now there is an end of me." And as though to emphasize his words he burst into another terrible fit of coughing.

I gave him some more whisky, and after resting he went on: "I have never seen my boy, Leo, since he was a tiny baby. I never could bear to see him, but they tell me that he is a quick and handsome child. In this envelope"—and he produced a letter from his pocket addressed to myself— "I have jotted down the course I wish followed in the boy's education. It is a somewhat peculiar one. At any rate, I could not entrust it to a stranger. Once more, will you undertake it?"

"I must first know what I am to undertake," I answered.

"You are to undertake to have the boy, Leo, to live with you till he is twenty-five years of age—not to send him to school, remember. On his twenty-fifth birthday your guardianship will end, and you will then, with the keys that I give you now"—and he placed them on the table—"open the iron box, and let him see and read the contents, and say whether or no he is willing to undertake the quest. There is no obligation on him to do so. Now, as regards terms. My present income is two thousand two hundred a year. Half of that income I have secured to you by will for life contingent on your undertaking the guardianship—that is, one thousand a year remuneration to yourself, for you will have to give up your life to it, and one hundred a year to pay for the board of the boy. The rest is to accumulate till Leo is twenty-five, so that there may be a sum in hand should he wish to undertake the quest of which I spoke."

"And suppose I were to die?" I asked.

"Then the boy must become a ward of Chancery and take his chance. Only be careful that the iron chest is passed on to him by your will. Listen, Holly, don't refuse me. Believe me, this is to your advantage. You are not fit to mix with the world—it would only embitter you. In a few weeks you will become a fellow of your college, and the income that you will derive from that combined with what I have left you will enable you to live a life of learned leisure, alternated with the sport of which you are so fond, such as will exactly suit you."

He paused and looked at me anxiously, but I still hesitated. The charge seemed so very strange.

"For my sake, Holly. We have been good friends, and I have no time to make other arrangements."

"Very well," I said, "I will do it, provided there is nothing in this paper to make me change my mind," and I touched the envelope he had put upon the table by the keys.

"Thank you, Holly, thank you. There is nothing at all. Swear to me by God that you will be a father to the boy, and follow my directions to the letter."

"I swear it," I answered solemnly.

"Very well, remember that perhaps one day I shall ask for the account of your oath, for though I am dead and forgotten, yet shall I live. There is no such thing as death, Holly, only a change, and, as you may perhaps learn in time to come, I believe that even here that change could under certain circumstances be indefinitely postponed," and again he broke into one of his dreadful fits of coughing.

"There," he said, "I must go. You have the chest, and my will will be found among my papers, under the authority of which the child will be handed over to you. You will be well paid, Holly, and I know that you are honest, but if you betray my trust, by heaven I will haunt you."

I said nothing, being, indeed, too bewildered to speak.

He held up the candle, and looked at his own face in the glass. It had been a beautiful face, but disease had wrecked it. "Food for the worms," he said. "Curious to think that in a few hours I shall be stiff and cold—the journey done, the little game played out. Ah me, Holly, life is not worth the trouble of life, except when one is in love—at least, mine has not been; but the boy Leo's may be if he has the courage and the faith. Good-by, my friend!" and with a sudden access of tenderness he flung his arm about me and kissed me on the forehead, and then turned to go.

"Look here, Vincey," I said, "if you are as ill as you think, you had better let me fetch a doctor."

"No, no," he said earnestly. "Promise me that you won't. I am going to die, and, like a poisoned rat, I wish to die alone."

"I don't believe that you are going to do anything of the sort," I answered. He smiled, and, with the word "Remember" on his lips, was gone. As for myself, I sat down and rubbed my eyes, wondering if I had been asleep. As this supposition would not bear investigation I gave it up, and began to think that Vincey must have been drinking. I knew that he was, and had been, very ill, but still it seemed impossible that he could be in such a condition as to be able to know for certain that he would not outlive the night. Had he been so near dissolution surely he would scarcely have been able to walk, and carry a heavy iron box with him. The whole story, on reflection, seemed to me utterly incredible, for I was not then old enough to be aware how many things happen in this world that the common sense of the average man would set down as so improbable as to be absolutely impossible. This is a fact that I have only recently mastered. Was it likely that a man would have a son five years of age whom he had never seen since he was a tiny infant? No. Was it likely that he could foretell his own death so accurately? No. Was it likely that he could trace his pedigree for more than three centuries before Christ, or that he would suddenly confide the absolute guardianship of his child, and leave half his fortune, to a college friend? Most certainly not. Clearly Vincey was either drunk or mad. That being so, what did it mean? And what was in the sealed iron chest?

The whole thing baffled and puzzled me to such an extent that at last I could stand it no longer, and determined to sleep over it. So I jumped up, and having put the keys and the letter that Vincey had left away into my dispatch box, and stowed the iron chest in a large port-manteau, I turned in, and was soon fast asleep.

As it seemed to me, I had only been asleep for a few minutes when I was awakened by somebody calling me. I sat up and rubbed my eyes; it was broad daylight—eight o'clock, in fact.

"Why, what is the matter with you, John?" I asked of the gyp who waited on Vincey and myself. "You look as though you had seen a ghost!"

"Yes, sir, and so I have," he answered, "leastways I've seen a corpse, which is worse. I've been in to call Mr. Vincey, as usual, and there he lies stark and dead!"

2 ♦

The Years Roll By

OF COURSE, poor Vincey's sudden death created a great stir in the college; but, as he was known to be very ill, and a satisfactory doctor's certificate was forthcoming, there was no inquest. They were not so particular about inquests in those days as they are now; indeed, they were generally disliked, as causing a scandal. Under all these circumstances, as I was asked no questions, I did not feel called upon to volunteer any information about our interview of the night of Vincey's decease, beyond saying that he had come into my rooms to see me, as he often did. On the day of the funeral a lawyer came down from London and followed my poor friend's remains to the grave, and then went back with his papers and effects, except, of course, the iron chest which had been left in my keeping. For a week after this I heard no more of the matter, and, indeed, my attention was amply occupied in other ways, for I was up for my fellowship, a fact that had prevented me from attending the funeral or seeing the lawyer. At last, however, the examination was over, and I came back to my rooms and sank into an easy chair with a happy consciousness that I had got through it very fairly.

Soon, however, my thoughts, relieved of the pressure that had crushed them into a single groove during the last few days, turned to the events of the night of poor Vincey's death, and again I asked myself what it all meant, and

pon the health and management of children, and read
hem, first to myself, and then aloud to Job—that was the
young man's name—and waited.

At length the child arrived in the charge of an elderly
person, who wept bitterly at parting with him, and a
beautiful boy he was. Indeed, I do not think that I ever
saw such a perfect child before or since. His eyes were
gray, his forehead broad, and his face, even at that early
age, clean cut as a cameo, without being pinched or thin.
But perhaps his most attractive point was his hair, which
was pure gold in color and tightly curled over his shapely
head. He cried a little when his nurse finally tore herself
away and left him with us. Never shall I forget the scene.
There he stood, with the sunlight from the window playing
upon his golden curls, his fist screwed in one eye, while
he took us in with the other. I was seated in a chair, and
stretched out my hand to him to induce him to come to
me, while Job, in the corner, was making a sort of clucking
noise, which, arguing from his previous experience, or from
the analogy of the hen, he judged would have a soothing
effect, and inspire confidence in the youthful mind, and
running a wooden horse of peculiar hideousness backwards
and forwards in a way that was little short of inane. This
went on for some minutes, and then all of a sudden the lad
stretched out both his little arms and ran to me.

"I like you," he said. "You is ugly, but you is good."

Ten minutes afterwards he was eating large slices of
bread and butter, with every sign of satisfaction; Job
wanted to put jam on them, but I sternly reminded him
of the excellent works we had read, and forbade it.

In a very little while (for, as I expected, I got my fellowship) the boy became the favorite of the whole college—
where, all orders and regulations to the contrary notwith-

wondered if I should hear anything more of the matter, and
if I did not, what it would be my duty to do with the curious
iron chest. I sat there and thought and thought till I began
to grow quite disturbed over the whole occurrence: the
mysterious midnight visit, the prophecy of death so shortly
to be fulfilled, the solemn oath that I had taken, and which
Vincey had called on me to answer to in another world than
this. Had the man committed suicide? It looked like it.
And what was the quest of which he spoke? The circumstances were almost uncanny, so much so that, though I
am by no means nervous, or apt to be alarmed at anything
that may seem to cross the bounds of the natural, I grew
afraid, and began to wish I had had nothing to do with it.
How much more do I wish it now, over twenty years afterwards!

As I sat and thought, there was a knock at the door,
and a letter, in a big blue envelope, was brought in to me.
I saw at a glance that it was a lawyer's letter, and an instinct told me that it was connected with my trust. The
letter, which I still have, runs thus:

Sir,
Our client, the late M. L. Vincey, Esq., who died on
the 9th instant in —— College, Cambridge, has left
behind him a Will, of which you will please find copy
enclosed, and of which we are the executors. By this Will
you will perceive that you take a life interest in about half
of the late Mr. Vincey's property, now invested in Consols,
subject to your acceptance of the guardianship of his only
son, Leo Vincey, at present an infant, aged five. Had we
not ourselves drawn up the document in question in obedience to Mr. Vincey's clear and precise instructions, both
personal and written, and had he not then assured us that
he had very good reasons for what he was doing, we are

bound to tell you that its provisions seem to us of so unusual a nature, that we should have felt bound to call the attention of the Court of Chancery to them, in order that such steps might be taken as seemed desirable to it, either by contesting the capacity of the testator or otherwise, to safeguard the interest of the infant. As it is, knowing that the testator was a gentleman of the highest intelligence and acumen, and that he has absolutely no relations living to whom he could have confided the guardianship of the child, we do not feel justified in taking this course.

Awaiting such instructions as you please to send us as regards the delivery of the infant and the payment of the proportion of the dividends due to you,

We remain, Sir, faithfully yours.

Geoffrey and Jordan

I put down the letter, and ran my eye through the will, which appeared, from its utter unintelligibility, to have been drawn on the strictest legal principles. So far as I could discover, however, it exactly bore out what my friend had told me on the night of his death. So it was true after all. I must take the boy. Suddenly I remembered the letter which he had left with the chest. I fetched it and opened it. It only contained such directions as he had already given to me as to opening the chest on Leo's twenty-fifth birthday, and laid down the outlines of the boy's education, which was to include Greek, the higher Mathematics, and Arabic. At the bottom there was a postscript to the effect that if the boy died under the age of twenty-five, which, however, he did not believe would be the case, I was to open the chest, and act on the information I obtained if I saw fit. If I did not see fit, I was to destroy all

the contents. On no account was I to pass t... stranger.

As this letter added nothing material to my k... and certainly raised no further objection in my min... dertaking the task I had promised my dead friend to... take, there was only one course open to me—name... write to Messrs. Geoffrey and Jordan, and express my re... ness to enter on the trust, stating that I should be will... to commence my guardianship of Leo in ten days' tim... This done I proceeded to the authorities of my college, and, having told them as much of the story as I considered desirable, which was not very much, after considerable difficulty succeeded in persuading them to stretch a point, and, in the event of my having obtained a fellowship, which I was pretty certain I had done, allow me to have the child to live with me. Their consent, however, was only granted on the condition that I vacated my rooms in college and took lodgings. This I did, and with some difficulty succeeded in obtaining very good apartments quite close to the college gates. The next thing was to find a nurse. And on this point I came to a determination. I would have no woman to lord it over me about the child, and steal his affections from me. The boy was old enough to do without female assistance, so I set to work to hunt up a suitable male attendant. With some difficulty I succeeded in hiring a most respectable round-faced young man, who had been a helper in a hunting stable, but who said that he was one of a family of seventeen and well accustomed to the ways of children, and professed himself quite willing to undertake the charge of Master Leo when he arrived. Then, having taken the iron box to town, and with my own hands deposited it at my banker's, I bought some books standing, he was continually in and out—a sort of chartered libertine, in whose favor all rules were relaxed. The offerings made at his shrine were simply without number, and I had a serious difference of opinion with one old resident Fellow, now long dead, who was usually supposed to be the crustiest man in the university, and to abhor the sight of a child. And yet I discovered, when a frequently recurring fit of sickness had forced Job to keep a strict lookout, that this unprincipled old man was in the habit of enticing the boy to his rooms and there feeding him upon unlimited quantities of brandy balls, and making him promise to say nothing about it. Job told him that he ought to be ashamed of himself, "at his age, too, when he might have been a grandfather if he had done what was right," by which Job understood had got married, and thence arose the row.

But I have no space to dwell upon those delightful years, round which memory still fondly hovers. One by one they went by, and as they passed we two grew dearer and yet more dear to each other. Few sons have been loved as I love Leo, and few fathers know the deep and continuous affection that Leo bears to me.

The child grew into the boy, and the boy into the young man, as one by one the remorseless years flew by, and as he grew and increased so did his beauty and the beauty of his mind grow with him. When he was about fifteen they used to call him Beauty about the college, and me they nicknamed the Beast. Beauty and the Beast was what they called us when we went out walking together, as we used to do every day. Once Leo attacked a great strapping butcher's man, twice his size, because he sang it out after us, and thrashed him, too—thrashed him fairly. I walked on and pretended not to see, till the combat got too exciting, when

I turned round and cheered him on to victory. It was the chaff of the college at the time, but I could not help it. Then when he was a little older the undergraduates got fresh names for us. They called me Charon and Leo the Greek god! I will pass over my own appellation with the humble remark that I was never handsome, and did not grow more so as I grew older. As for his, there was no doubt about its fitness. Leo at twenty-one might have stood for a statue of the youthful Apollo. I never saw anybody to touch him in looks, or anybody so absolutely unconscious of them. As for his mind, he was brilliant and keen-witted, but not a scholar. He had not the dullness necessary for that result. We followed out his father's instructions as regards his education strictly enough, and on the whole the results, especially so far as the Greek and Arabic went, were satisfactory. I learned the latter language in order to help to teach it to him, but after five years of it he knew it as well as I did—almost as well as the professor who instructed us both. I always was a great sportsman—it is my one passion—and every autumn we went away somewhere shooting or fishing, sometimes to Scotland, sometimes to Norway, once even to Russia. I am a good shot, but even in this he learned to excel me.

When Leo was eighteen I moved back into my rooms, and entered him at my own college, and at twenty-one he took his degree—a respectable degree, but not a very high one. Then it was that I, for the first time, told him something of his own story, and of the mystery that loomed ahead. Of course he was very curious about it, and of course I explained to him that his curiosity could not be gratified at present. After that, to pass the time away, I suggested that he should get himself called to the bar;

and this he did, reading at Cambridge, and only going up to London to eat his dinners.

I had only one trouble about him, and that was that every young woman who came across him, or, if not every one, nearly so, would insist on falling in love with him. Hence arose difficulties which I need not enter into here, though they were troublesome enough at the time. On the whole, he behaved fairly well; I cannot say more than that.

And so the time went by till at last he reached his twenty-fifth birthday, at which date this strange and, in some ways, awful history really begins.

3 ♦

The Sherd of Amenartas

On the day preceding Leo's twenty-fifth birthday we both proceeded to London, and extracted the mysterious chest from the bank where I had deposited it twenty years before. It was, I remember, brought up by the same clerk who had taken it down. He perfectly remembered having hidden it away. Had he not done so, he said, he should have had difficulty in finding it, it was so covered up with cobwebs.

In the evening we returned with our precious burden to Cambridge, and I think that we might both of us have given away all the sleep we got that night and not have been much the poorer. At daybreak Leo arrived in my room in a dressing gown, and suggested that we should at once proceed to business. I scouted the idea as showing an unworthy curiosity. The chest had waited twenty years, I said, so it could very well continue to wait until after breakfast. Accordingly at nine—an unusually sharp nine—we breakfasted; and so occupied was I with my own thoughts that I regret to state that I put a piece of bacon into Leo's tea in mistake for a lump of sugar. Job, too, to whom the contagion of excitement had, of course, spread, managed to break the handle off my Sèvres china teacup, the identical one I believe that Marat had been drinking from just before he was stabbed in his bath.

At last, however, breakfast was cleared away, and Job, at my request, fetched the chest, and placed it upon the table in a somewhat gingerly fashion, as though he mistrusted it. Then he prepared to leave the room.

"Stop a moment, Job," I said. "If Mr. Leo has no objection, I should prefer to have an independent witness to this business, who can be relied upon to hold his tongue unless he is asked to speak."

"Certainly, Uncle Horace," answered Leo; for I had brought him up to call me uncle—though he varied the appellation somewhat disrespectfully by calling me "old fellow," or even "my avuncular relative."

Job touched his head, not having a hat on.

"Lock the door, Job," I said, "and bring me my dispatch box."

He obeyed, and from the box I took the keys that poor Vincey, Leo's father, had given me on the night of his death. There were three of them: the largest a comparatively modern key, the second an exceedingly ancient one, and the third entirely unlike anything of the sort that we had ever seen before, being fashioned apparently from a strip of solid silver, with a bar placed across to serve as a handle, and some nicks cut in the edge of the bar. It was more like a model of some antediluvian railway key than anything else.

"Now are you both ready?" I said, as people do when they are going to fire a mine. There was no answer, so I took the big key, rubbed some salad oil into the wards, and after one or two bad shots, for my hands were shaking, managed to fit it, and shoot the lock. Leo bent over and caught the massive lid in both his hands, and with an effort, for the hinges had rusted, leaned it back. Its removal revealed another case covered with dust. This we extracted from the iron chest without any difficulty, and removed the accumulated filth of years from it with a clothes brush.

It was, or appeared to be, of ebony, or some such close-grained black wood, and was bound in every direction with flat bands of iron. Its antiquity must have been extreme, for the dense heavy wood was actually in parts commencing to crumble away from age.

"Now for it," I said, inserting the second key.

Job and Leo bent forward in breathless silence. The key turned, and I flung back the lid, and uttered an exclamation, as did the others; and no wonder, for inside the ebony case was a magnificent silver casket, about twelve inches square by eight high. It appeared to be of Egyptian work-manship, for the four legs were formed of Sphinxes, and the dome-shaped cover was also surmounted by a Sphinx. The casket was of course much tarnished and dinted with age, but otherwise in fairly sound condition.

I drew it out and set it on the table, and then, in the midst of the most perfect silence, I inserted the strange-looking silver key, and pressed this way and that until at last the lock yielded, and the casket stood open before us. It was filled to the brim with some brown shredded ma-terial, more like vegetable fiber than paper, the nature of which I have never been able to discover. This I care-fully removed to the depth of some three inches, when I came to a letter enclosed in an ordinary modern-looking envelope, and addressed in the handwriting of my dead friend Vincey: "*To my son Leo, should he live to open this casket.*" I handed the letter to Leo, who glanced at the envelope, and then put it down upon the table, making a motion to me to go on emptying the casket.

The next thing that I found was a parchment carefully rolled up. I unrolled it, and seeing that it was also in Vincey's handwriting, and headed "Translation of the Uncial Greek Writing on the Potsherd," put it down by the letter. Then followed another ancient roll of parchment, that had become yellow and crinkled with the passage of years. This I also unrolled. It was likewise a translation of the same Greek original, but into black-letter Latin this time, which at the first glance appeared to me from the style and character to date from somewhere about the beginning of the sixteenth century. Immediately beneath this roll was something hard and heavy, wrapped up in yellow linen, and reposing upon another layer of the fibrous material. Slowly and carefully we unrolled the linen, exposing to view a very large but undoubtedly ancient potsherd of a dirty yellow color! This potsherd had in my judgment once been a part of an ordinary amphora of medium size. For the rest, it measured ten and a half inches in length by seven in width, was about a quarter of an inch thick, and densely covered on the convex side that lay towards the bottom of the box with writing in the later uncial Greek character, faded here and there, but for the most part perfectly legible, the inscription having evidently been executed with the greatest care, and by means of a reed pen, such as the ancients often used. I must not forget to mention that in some remote age this wonderful fragment had been broken in two, and rejoined by means of cement and eight long rivets. Also there were numerous inscriptions on the inner side, but these were of the most erratic character, and had clearly been made by different hands and in many different ages, and of them, together with the writings on the parchments, I shall have to speak presently.

"Is there anything more?" asked Leo, in a kind of excited whisper.

I groped about, and produced something hard, done up in a little linen bag. Out of the bag we took first a very beautiful miniature done upon ivory, and, secondly, a small chocolate-colored composition scarabaeus, marked thus:

symbols which, we have since ascertained, mean "Suten se Rā," which is being translated the "Royal Son of Rā or the Sun." The miniature was a picture of Leo's Greek mother —a lovely, dark-eyed creature. On the back of it was written, in poor Vincey's handwriting, "My beloved wife."

"That is all," I said.

"Very well," answered Leo, putting down the miniature, at which he had been gazing affectionately; "and now let us read the letter," and without further ado he broke the seal, and read aloud as follows:

"My Son Leo,
When you open this, if you ever live to do so, you will have attained to manhood, and I shall have been long enough dead to be absolutely forgotten by nearly all who knew me. Yet in reading it remember that I have been, and for anything you know may still be, and that in it, through this link of pen and paper, I stretch out my hand to you across the gulf of death, and my voice speaks to you from the unutterable silence of the grave. Though I am dead, and no memory of me remains in your

mind, yet am I with you in this hour that you read. Since your birth to this day ·I have scarcely seen your face. Forgive me this. Your life supplanted the life of one whom I loved better than women are often loved, and the bitterness of it endureth yet. Had I lived I should in time have conquered this foolish feeling, but I am not destined to live. My sufferings, physical and mental, are more than I can bear, and when such small arrangements as I have to make for your future well-being are completed it is my intention to put a period to them. May God forgive me if I do wrong. At the best I could not live more than another year."

"So he killed himself," I exclaimed. "I thought so."

"And now," Leo went on, without replying, "enough of myself. What has to be said belongs to you who live, not to me, who am dead, and almost as much forgotten as though I had never been. Holly, my friend (to whom, if he will accept the trust, it is my intention to confide you), will have told you something of the extraordinary antiquity of your race. In the contents of this casket you will find sufficient to prove it. The strange legend that you will find inscribed by your remote ancestress upon the potsherd was communicated to me by my father on his deathbed, and took a strong hold upon my imagination. When I was only nineteen years of age I determined, as, to his misfortune, did one of our ancestors about the time of Elizabeth, to investigate its truth. Into all that befell me I cannot enter now. But this I saw with my own eyes. On the coast of Africa, in a hitherto unexplored region, some distance to the north of where the Zambesi falls into the sea, there is a headland, at the extremity of which a peak towers up, shaped like the head of a Negro, similar to that of which the writing speaks. I landed there, and learned from a wandering native, who had been cast out by his people because of some crime which he had committed, that far inland are great mountains, shaped like cups, and caves surrounded by measureless swamps. I learned also that the people there speak a dialect of Arabic, and are ruled over by a *beautiful white woman* who is seldom seen by them, but who is reported to have power over all things living and dead. Two days after I had ascertained this the man died of fever contracted in crossing the swamps, and I was forced by want of provisions and by symptoms of an illness which afterwards prostrated me to take to my dhow again.

"Of the adventures that befell me after this I need not now speak. I was wrecked upon the coast of Madagascar, and rescued some months afterwards by an English ship that brought me to Aden, whence I started for England, intending to prosecute my search as soon as I had made sufficient preparations. On my way I stopped in Greece, and there, for *Omnia vincit amor,* I met your beloved mother, and married her, and there you were born and she died. Then it was that my last illness seized me, and I returned hither to die. But still I hoped against hope, and set myself to work to learn Arabic, with the intention, should I ever get better, of returning to the coast of Africa, and solving the mystery of which the tradition has lived so many centuries in our family. But I have not got better, and, so far as I am concerned, the story is at an end.

"For you, however, my son, it is not at an end, and to you I hand on these the results of my labor, together with the hereditary proofs of its origin. It is my intention to provide that they shall not be put into your hands until you have reached an age when you will be able to judge for yourself whether or no you will choose to investigate what, if it is true, must be the greatest mystery in the world. or to put it by as an idle fable, originating in the first place in a woman's disordered brain.

"I do not believe that it is a fable; I believe that if it can only be rediscovered there is a spot where the vital forces of the world visibly exist. Life exists; why therefore should not the means of preserving it indefinitely exist also? But I have no wish to prejudice your mind about the matter. Read and judge for yourself. If you are inclined to undertake the search, I have so provided that you will not lack for means. If, on the other hand, you are satisfied that the whole thing is a chimera, then, I adjure you, destroy the potsherd and the writings, and let a cause of troubling be removed from our race forever. Perhaps that will be wisest. The unknown is generally taken to be terrible, not as the proverb would infer, from the inherent superstition of man, but because it so often is terrible. He who would tamper with the vast and secret forces that animate the world may well fall a victim to them. And if the end were attained, if at last you emerged from the trial ever beautiful and ever young, defying time and evil, and lifted above the natural decay of flesh and intellect, who shall say that the awesome change would prove a happy one? Choose, my son, and may the Power who rules all things, and who says 'thus far shalt thou go, and thus much shalt thou learn,' direct the choice to your own happiness and the happiness of the world, which, in the event of your success, you would one day certainly rule by the pure force of accumulated experience.—Farewell!"

Thus the letter, which was unsigned and undated, abruptly ended.

"What do you make of that, Uncle Holly?" said Leo, with a sort of gasp, as he replaced it on the table. "We have been looking for a mystery, and we certainly seem to have found one."

"What do I make of it? Why, that your poor dear

father was off his head, of course," I answered testily. "I guessed as much that night, twenty years ago, when he came into my room. You see he evidently hurried his own end, poor man. It is absolute balderdash."

"That's it, sir!" said Job solemnly. Job was a most matter-of-fact specimen of a matter-of-fact class.

"Well, let's see what the potsherd has to say, at any rate," said Leo, taking up the translation in his father's writing, and commencing to read:

"I, Amenartas, of the Royal House of the Pharaohs of Egypt, wife of Kallikrates (the Beautiful in Strength), a Priest of Isis whom the gods cherish and the demons obey, being about to die, to my little son Tisisthenes (the Mighty Avenger). I fled with thy father from Egypt in the days of Nectanebes,[1] causing him through love to break the vows that he had vowed. We fled southward, across the waters, and we wandered for twice twelve moons on the coast of Libya (Africa) that looks towards the rising sun, where by a river is a great rock carven like the head of an Ethiopian. Four days on the water from the mouth of a mighty river were we cast away, and some were drowned and some died of sickness. But us wild men took through wastes and marshes, where the sea fowl hid the sky, bearing us ten days' journey till we came to a hollow mountain, where a great city had been and fallen, and where there are caves of which no man hath seen the end; and they brought us to the Queen of the people who place pots upon the heads of strangers, who is a magician having a knowledge of all things, and life and loveliness that does not die. And she cast eyes of love upon thy father, Kallikrates, and would have slain me, and taken him to husband, but he loved me and feared her, and would not.

[1] Nekht-nebf, or Nectanebo II., the last native Pharaoh of Egypt fled from Ochus to Ethiopia, B.C. 339.—EDITOR.

Then did she take us, and lead us by terrible ways, by means of dark magic, to where the great pit is, in the mouth of which the old philosopher lay dead, and showed to us the rolling Pillar of Life that dies not, whereof the voice is as the voice of thunder; and she did stand in the flames, and come forth unharmed, and yet more beautiful. Then did she swear to make thy father undying even as she is, if he would but slay me, and give himself to her, for me she could not slay because of the magic of my own people that I have, and that prevailed thus far against her. And he held his hand before his eyes to hide her beauty, and would not. Then in her rage did she smite him by her magic, and he died; but she wept over him, and bore him thence with lamentations: and being afraid, me she sent to the mouth of the great river where the ships come, and I was carried far away on the ships where I gave thee birth, and hither to Athens I came at last after many wanderings. Now I say to thee, my son, Tisisthenes, seek out the woman, and learn the secret of Life, and if thou mayest find a way slay her, because of thy father Kallikrates; and if thou dost fear or fail, this I say to all of thy seed who come after thee, till at last a brave man be found among them who shall bathe in the fire and sit in the place of the Pharaohs. I speak of those things, that though they be past belief, yet I have known, and I lie not."

"May the Lord forgive her for that," groaned Job, who had been listening to this marvelous composition with his mouth open.

As for myself, I said nothing, my first idea being that my poor friend, being demented, had composed the whole thing, though it scarcely seemed likely that such a story could have been invented by anybody. It was too original. To solve my doubts I took up the potsherd and began to read the close uncial Greek writing on it; and very good

Greek of the period it is, considering that it came from
the pen of an Egyptian born. Here is an exact transcript
of it:

ΑΜΕΝΑΡΤΑΣΤΟΥΒΑΣΙΛΙΚΟΥΓΕΝΟΥΣΤΟΥΑ
ΙΓΥΓΤΙΟΥΗΤΟΥΚΑΛΛΙΚΡΑΤΟΥΣΙΣΙΔΟΣΙΕΡ
ΕΩΣΗΝΟΙΜΕΝΘΕΟΙΤΡΕΦΟΥΣΙΤΑΔΕΔΑΙΜΟ
ΝΙΑΥΓΟΤΑΣΣΕΤΑΙΗΔΗΤΕΛΕΥΤΩΣΑΤΙΣΙΣ
ΘΕΝΕΙΤΩΓΑΙΔΙΕΓΙΣΤΕΛΛΕΙΤΑΔΕΣΥΝΕΦΥΓΟ
ΝΓΑΡΓΟΤΕΕΚΤΗΣΑΙΓΥΓΤΙΑΣΕΓΙΝΕΚΤΑΝΕΒ
ΟΥΜΕΤΑΤΟΥΣΟΥΓΑΤΡΟΣΔΙΑΤΟΝΕΡΩΤΑΤΟ
ΝΕΜΟΝΕΓΙΟΡΚΗΣΑΝΤΟΣΦΥΓΟΝΤΕΣΔΕΓΡΟ
ΣΝΟΤΟΝΔΙΑΓΟΝΤΙΟΙΚΑΙΚΔΜΗΝΑΣΚΑΤΑΤΑ
ΓΑΡΑΘΑΛΑΣΣΙΑΤΗΣΛΙΒΥΗΣΤΑΓΡΟΣΗΛΙΟΥ
ΑΝΑΤΟΛΑΣΓΛΑΝΗΘΕΝΤΕΣΕΝΘΑΓΕΡΓΕΤΡΑ
ΤΙΣΜΕΓΑΛΗΓΛΥΓΤΟΝΟΜΟΙΩΜΑΑΙΘΙΟΓΟΣ
ΚΕΦΑΛΗΣΕΙΤΑΗΜΕΡΑΣΔΑΓΟΣΤΟΜΑΤΟΣΓΟ
ΤΑΜΟΥΜΕΓΑΛΟΥΕΚΓΕΣΟΝΤΕΣΟΙΜΕΝΚΑΤΕ
ΓΟΝΤΙΣΘΗΜΕΝΟΙΔΕΝΟΣΩΙΑΓΕΘΑΝΟΜΕΝΤ
ΕΛΟΣΔΕΥΓΑΓΡΙΩΝΑΝΘΡΩΓΩΝΕΦΕΡΟΜΕΘΑ
ΔΙΑΕΛΕΩΝΤΕΚΑΙΤΕΝΑΓΕΩΝΕΝΘΑΓΕΡΓΤΗΝ
ΩΝΓΛΗΘΟΣΑΓΟΚΡΥΓΤΕΙΤΟΝΟΥΡΑΝΟΝΗΜ
ΕΡΑΣΙΕΩΣΗΛΘΟΜΕΝΕΙΣΚΟΙΛΟΝΤΙΟΡΟΣΕΝ
ΘΑΓΟΤΕΜΕΓΑΛΗΜΕΝΓΟΛΙΣΗΝΑΝΤΡΑΔΕΑΓ
ΕΙΡΟΝΑΗΓΑΓΟΝΔΕΩΣΒΑΣΙΛΕΙΑΝΤΗΝΤΩΝΞ
ΕΝΟΥΣΧΥΤΡΑΙΣΣΤΕΦΑΝΟΥΝΤΩΝΗΤΙΣΜΑΓΕ
ΙΑΜΕΝΕΧΡΗΤΟΕΓΙΣΤΗΜΗΔΕΓΑΝΤΩΝΚΑΙΔ
ΗΚΑΙΚΑΛΛΟΣΚΑΙΡΩΜΗΝΑΓΗΡΩΣΗΝΗΔΕΚΑ
ΛΛΙΚΡΑΤΟΥΣΤΟΥΣΟΥΓΑΤΡΟΣΕΡΑΣΘΕΙΣΑΤ
ΟΜΕΝΓΡΩΤΟΝΣΥΝΟΙΚΕΙΝΕΒΟΥΛΕΤΟΕΜΕΔ
ΕΑΝΕΛΕΙΝΕΓΕΙΤΑΩΣΟΥΚΑΝΕΓΕΙΘΕΝΕΜΕΓΑ
ΡΥΓΕΡΕΦΙΛΕΙΚΑΙΤΗΝΞΕΝΗΝΕΦΟΒΕΙΤΟΑΓΗ
ΓΑΓΕΝΗΜΑΣΥΓΟΜΑΓΕΙΑΣΚΑΘΟΔΟΥΣΣΦΑΛ
ΕΡΑΣΕΝΘΑΤΟΒΑΡΑΘΡΟΝΤΟΜΕΓΑΟΥΚΑΤΑΣ
ΤΟΜΑΕΚΕΙΤΟΟΓΕΡΩΝΟΦΙΛΟΣΟΦΟΣΤΕΘΝΕ
ΩΣΑΦΙΚΟΜΕΝΟΙΣΔΕΔΕΙΞΕΦΩΣΤΟΥΒΙΟΥΕΥ
ΘΥΟΙΟΝΚΙΟΝΑΕΛΙΣΣΟΜΕΝΟΝΦΩΝΗΝΙΕΝΤ
ΑΚΑΘΑΓΕΡΒΡΟΝΤΗΣΕΙΤΑΔΙΑΓΥΡΟΣΒΕΒΗΚ
ΥΙΑΑΒΛΑΒΗΣΚΑΙΕΤΙΚΑΛΛΙΩΝΑΥΤΗΕΑΥΤΗΣ
ΕΞΕΦΑΝΗΕΚΔΕΤΟΥΤΩΝΩΜΟΣΕΚΑΙΤΟΝΣΟ

ΝΓΑΤΕΡΑΑΘΑΝΑΤΟΝΑΓΟΔΕΙΞΕΙΝΕΙΣΥΝΟΙΚ
ΕΙΝΟΙΒΟΥΛΟΙΤΟΕΜΕΔΕΑΝΕΛΕΙΝΟΥΓΑΡΟΥ
ΝΑΥΤΗΑΝΕΛΕΙΝΙΣΧΥΕΝΥΓΟΤΩΝΗΜΕΔΑΓΩ
ΝΗΝΚΑΙΑΥΤΗΕΧΩΜΑΓΕΙΑΣΟΔΟΥΔΕΝΤΙΜΑ
ΛΛΟΝΗΘΕΛΕΤΩΧΕΙΡΕΤΩΝΟΜΜΑΤΩΝΓΡΟΙ
ΣΧΩΝΙΝΑΔΗΤΟΤΗΣΓΥΝΑΙΚΟΣΚΑΛΛΟΣΜΗ
ΟΡΩΗΕΓΕΙΤΑΟΡΓΙΣΘΕΙΣΑΚΑΤΕΓΟΗΤΕΥΣΕΜ
ΕΝΑΥΤΟΝΑΓΟΛΟΜΕΝΟΝΜΕΝΤΟΙΚΛΑΟΥΣΑ
ΚΑΙΟΔΥΡΟΜΕΝΗΕΚΕΙΘΕΝΑΓΗΝΕΓΚΕΝΕΜΕΔ
ΕΦΟΒΩΙΑΦΗΚΕΝΕΙΣΣΤΟΜΑΤΟΥΜΕΓΑΛΟΥΓ
ΟΤΑΜΟΥΤΟΥΝΑΥΣΙΓΟΡΟΥΓΟΡΡΩΔΕΝΑΥΣΙ
ΝΕΦΩΝΓΕΡΓΛΕΟΥΣΑΕΤΕΚΟΝΣΕΑΓΟΓΛΕΥΣ
ΑΣΑΜΟΛΙΣΓΟΤΕΔΕΥΡΟΑΘΗΝΑΖΕΚΑΤΗΓΑΓ
ΟΜΗΝΣΥΔΕΩΤΙΣΙΣΘΕΝΕΣΩΝΕΓΙΣΤΕΛΛΩΜ
ΗΟΛΙΓΩΡΕΙΔΕΙΓΑΡΤΗΝΓΥΝΑΙΚΑΑΝΑΖΗΤΕΙ
ΝΗΝΓΩΣΤΟΤΟΥΒΙΟΥΜΥΣΤΗΡΙΟΝΑΝΕΥΡΗ
ΣΚΑΙΑΝΑΙΡΕΙΝΗΝΓΟΥΓΑΡΑΣΧΗΔΙΑΤΟΝΣΟ
ΝΓΑΤΕΡΑΚΑΛΛΙΚΡΑΤΗΝΕΙΔΕΦΟΒΟΥΜΕΝΟ
ΣΗΔΙΑΑΛΛΟΤΙΑΥΤΟΣΛΕΙΓΕΙΤΟΥΕΡΓΟΥΓΑ
ΣΙΤΟΙΣΥΣΤΕΡΟΝΑΥΤΟΤΟΥΤΟΕΓΙΣΤΕΛΛΩΕ
ΩΣΓΟΤΕΑΓΑΘΟΣΤΙΣΓΕΝΟΜΕΝΟΣΤΩΓΥΡΙΛ
ΟΥΣΑΣΘΑΙΤΟΛΜΗΣΕΙΚΑΙΤΑΑΡΙΣΤΕΙΑΕΧΩΝ
ΒΑΣΙΛΕΥΣΑΙΤΩΝΑΝΘΡΩΓΩΝΑΓΙΣΤΑΜΕΝΔ
ΗΤΑΤΟΙΑΥΤΑΛΕΓΩΟΜΩΣΔΕΑΑΥΤΗΕΓΝΩΚ
ΑΟΥΚΕΨΕΥΣΑΜΗΝ

For general convenience in reading, I have here accurately transcribed this inscription into the cursive character:

Ἀμενάρτας, τοῦ βασιλικοῦ γένους τοῦ Αἰγυπτίου, ἡ
τοῦ Καλλικράτους Ἴσιδος ἱερέως, ἣν οἱ μὲν θεοὶ τρέφουσι
τὰ δὲ δαιμόνια ὑποτάσσεται, ἤδη τελευτῶσα Τισισθένει τῷ
παιδὶ ἐπιστέλλει τάθε· συνέφυγον γάρ ποτε ἐκ τῆς Αἰγυ-
πτίας ἐπὶ Νεκτανέβου μετὰ τοῦ σοῦ πατρός, διὰ τὸν ἔρωτα
τὸν ἐμὸν ἐπιορκήσαντος. φυγόντες δὲ πρὸς νότον διαπόντιοι

καὶ κ´δ´ μῆνας κατὰ τὰ παραθαλάσσια τῆς Λιβύης τὰ πρὸς
ἡλίου ἀνατολὰς πλανηθέντες, ἔνθα πέτρα τις μεγάλη, γλυπτὸν
ὁμοίωμα Αἰθίοπος κεφαλῆς, εἶτα ἡμέρας δ´ ἀπὸ στόματος
ποταμοῦ μεγάλου ἐκπεσόντες, οἱ μὲν κατεποντίσθημεν, οἱ
δὲ νόσῳ ἀπεθάνομεν· τέλος δὲ ὑπ᾽ ἀγρίων ἀνθρώπων ἐφε-
ρόμεθα διὰ ἑλέων τε καὶ τεναγέων ἔνθαπερ πτηνῶν πλῆθος
ἀποκρύπτει τὸν οὐρανόν, ἡμέρας ι, ἕως ἤλθομεν εἰς κοῖλόν
τι ὄρος, ἔνθα ποτὲ μεγάλη μὲν πόλις ἦν, ἄντρα δὲ ἀπείρονα·
ἤγαγον δὲ ὡς βασίλειαν τὴν τῶν ξένους χύτραις στεφανούντων, ἥτις μαγείᾳ μὲν ἐχρῆτο ἐπιστήμῃ δὲ πάντων καὶ δὴ καὶ
κάλλος καὶ ῥώμην ἀγήρως ἦν· ἡ δὲ Καλλικράτους τοῦ σοῦ
πατρὸς ἐρασθεῖσα τὸ μὲν πρῶτον συνοικεῖν ἐβούλετο ἐμὲ
δὲ ἀνελεῖν· ἔπειτα, ὡς οὐκ ἀνέπειθεν, ἐμὲ γὰρ ὑπερεφίλει καὶ
τὴν ξένην ἐφοβεῖτο, ἀπήγαγεν ἡμᾶς ὑπὸ μαγείας καθ᾽ ὁδοὺς
σφαλερὰς ἔνθα τὸ βάραθρον τὸ μέγα, οὗ κατὰ στόμα ἔ-
κειτο ὁ γέρων ὁ φιλόσοφος τεθνεώς, ἀφικομένοις δ᾽ ἔδειξε
φῶς τοῦ βίου εὐθύ, οἷον κίονα ἑλισσόμενον φώνην ἱέντα κα-
θάπερ βροντῆς, εἶτα διὰ πυρὸς βεβηκυῖα ἀβλαβὴς καὶ ἔτι
καλλίων αὐτὴ ἑαυτῆς ἐξεφάνη, ἐκ δὲ τούτων ὤμοσε καὶ τὸν
σὸν πατέρα ἀθάνατον ἀποδείξειν, εἰ συνοικεῖν οἱ βούλοιτο
ἐμὲ δε ἀνελεῖν, οὐ γὰρ οὖν αὐτὴ ἀνελεῖν ἴσχυεν ὑπὸ τῶν ἡ-
μεδαπῶν ἦν καὶ αὐτὴ ἔχω μαγείας. ὁ δ᾽ οὐδέν τι μᾶλλον ἤθε-
λε, τὼ χεῖρε τῶν ὀμμάτων προΐσχων ἵνα δὴ τὸ τῆς γυναικὸς
κάλλος μὴ ὁρῴη· ἔπειτα ὀργισθεῖσα κατεγοήτευσε μὲν αὐτόν,
ἀπολόμενον μέντοι κλάουσα καὶ ὀδυρομένη ἐκεῖθεν ἀπή-
νεγκεν, ἐμὲ δὲ φόβῳ ἀφῆκεν εἰς στόμα τοῦ μεγάλου ποταμοῦ
τοῦ ναυσιπόρου, πόρρω δὲ ναυσίν, ἐφ᾽ ὧνπερ πλέουσα ἔτεκόν
σε, ἀποπλεύσασα μόλις ποτὲ δεῦρο ᾽Αθήνάζε κατηγαγόμην.
σὺ δέ, ὦ Τισίσθενες, ὧν ἐπιστέλλω μὴ ὀλιγώρει· δεῖ γὰρ τὴν
γυναῖκα ἀναζητεῖν ἥν πως τὸ τοῦ βίου μυστήριον ἀνεύρῃς,
καὶ ἀναιρεῖν, ἥν που παρασχῇ, διὰ τὸν σὸν πατέρα Καλλι-

κράτην. εἰ δὲ φοβούμενος ἢ διὰ ἄλλο τι αὐτὸς λείπει τοῦ ἔργου, πᾶσι τοῖς ὕστερον αὐτὸ τοῦτο ἐπιστέλλω, ἕως ποτὲ ἀγαθός τις γενόμενος τῷ πυρὶ λούσασθαι τολμήσει καὶ τὰ ἀριστεῖα ἔχων βασιλεῦσαι τῶν ἀνθρώπων· ἄπιστα μὲν δὴ τὰ τοιαῦτα λέγω, ὅμως δὲ ἃ αὐτὴ ἔγνωκα οὐκ ἐψευσάμην.

The English translation was, as I discovered on further investigation, and as the reader may easily see by comparison, both accurate and elegant.

Besides the uncial writing on the convex side of the sherd at the top, painted in dull red, on what had once been the lip of the amphora, was the cartouche already mentioned as being on the scarabaeus, which we had also found in the casket. The hieroglyphics or symbols, however, were reversed, just as though they had been pressed on wax. Whether this was the cartouche of the original Kallikrates,[2] or of some Prince or Pharaoh from whom his wife Amenartas was descended, I am not sure, nor can I tell if it was drawn upon the sherd at the same time that the uncial Greek was inscribed, or copied on more recently from the Scarab by some other member of the family. Nor was this all. At the foot of the writing, painted in the same dull red, was the faint outline of a somewhat rude drawing of the head and shoulders of a Sphinx wearing two feathers, symbols of majesty, which, though common enough upon the effigies of sacred bulls and gods, I have never before met with on a Sphinx.

Also on the right-hand side of this surface of the sherd, painted obliquely in red on the space not covered by the

---

[2] The cartouche, if it be a true cartouche, cannot have been that of Kallikrates, as Mr. Holly suggests. Kallikrates was a priest and not entitled to a cartouche, which was the prerogative of Egyptian royalty, though he might have inscribed his name or title upon an oval.—EDITOR.

uncial, and signed in blue paint, was the following quaint inscription:

IN EARTH AND SKIE AND SEA
STRANGE THYNGES THER BE.
HOC FECIT
DOROTHEA VINCEY

Perfectly bewildered, I turned the relic over. It was covered from top to bottom with notes and signatures in Greek, Latin, and English. The first, in uncial Greek, was by Tisisthenes, the son to whom the writing was addressed. It was, "I could not go. Tisisthenes to his son, Kallikrates." Here it is in facsimile with its cursive equivalent:

ΟΥΚΑΝΔΥΝΑΙΜΗΝΓΟΡΕΥΕϹΘΑΙΤΙϹΙϹΘΕΝΗ
ϹΚΑΛΛΙΚΡΑΤΕΙΤΩΙΓΑΙΔΙ

οὐκ ἂν δυναίμην πορεύεσθαι.
Τισισθένης Καλλικράτει τῷ παιδί.

This Kallikrates (probably, in the Greek fashion, so named after his grandfather) evidently made some attempt to start on the quest, for his entry, written in very faint and almost illegible uncial, is, "I ceased from my going, the gods being against me. Kallikrates to his son." Here it is also:

ΤΩΝΘΕΩΝΑΝΤΙϹΤΑΝΤΩΝΕΓΑΥϹΑΜΗΝΤΗϹ
ΓΟΡΕΙΑϹΚΑΛΛΙΚΡΑΤΗϹΤΩΙΓΑΙΔΙ

τῶν θεῶν ἀντιστάντων ἐπαυσάμην τῆς πορείας.
Καλλικράτης τῷ παιδί.

Between these two ancient writings—the second of which was inscribed upside down and was so faint and worn that, had it not been for the transcript of it executed by Vincey, I should scarcely have been able to read it, since, owing to its having been written on that portion of the tile which had, in the course of ages, undergone the most handling, it was nearly rubbed out—was the bold, modern-looking signature of one Lionel Vincey, "Aetate sua 17," which was written thereon, I think, by Leo's grandfather. To the right of this were the initials "J. B. V.," and below came a variety of Greek signatures, in uncial and cursive character, and what appeared to be some carelessly executed repetitions of the sentence "τῷ παιδι" (to my son), showing that the relic was religiously passed on from generation to generation.

The next legible thing after the Greek signatures was the word "ROMAE, A.U.C.," showing that the family had now migrated to Rome. Unfortunately, however, with the exception of its termination (cvi), the date of their settlement there is forever lost, for just where it had been placed a piece of the potsherd is broken away.

Then followed twelve Latin signatures, jotted about here and there, wherever there was a space upon the tile suitable to their inscription. These signatures, with three exceptions only, ended with the name "Vindex" or "the Avenger," which seems to have been adopted by the family after its migration to Rome as a kind of equivalent to the Grecian "Tisisthenes," which also means an avenger. Ultimately, as might be expected, this Latin cognomen of

Vindex was transformed first into De Vincey, and then into the plain, modern Vincey. It is very curious to observe how the idea of revenge, inspired by an Egyptian before the time of Christ, is thus, as it were, embalmed in an English family name.

A few of the Roman names inscribed upon the sherd I have actually since found mentioned in history and other records. They were, if I remember right,

> MVSSIVS. VINDEX
> SEX. VARIVS. MARVLLVS
> C. FVFIDIVS. C. F. VINDEX

and

> LABERIA POMPEIANA. CONIVX. MACRINI. VINDICIS

the last being, of course, the name of a Roman lady.

The following list, however, comprises all the Latin names upon the sherd:

> C. CAECILIVS VINDEX
> M. AIMILIVS VINDEX
> SEX. VARIVS. MARVLLVS
> Q. SOSIVS PRISCVS SENECIO VINDEX
> L. VALERIVS COMINIVS VINDEX
> SEX. OTACILIVS. M. F.
> L. ATTIVS. VINDEX
> MVSSIVS VINDEX
> C. FVFIDIVS. C. F. VINDEX
> LICINIVS FAVSTVS
> LABERIA POMPEIANA CONIVX MACRINI VINDICIS
> MANILIA LVCILLA CONIVX MARVLLI VINDICIS

After the Roman names there is evidently a gap of very
many centuries. Nobody will ever know now what was the
history of the relic during those dark ages, or how it came
to have been preserved in the family. My poor friend Vincey
had, it will be remembered, told me that his Roman ancestors finally settled in Lombardy, and when Charlemagne
invaded it, returned with him across the Alps, and made
their home in Brittany, whence they crossed to England
in the reign of Edward the Confessor. How he knew this
I am not aware, for there is no reference to Lombardy or
Charlemagne upon the tile, though, as will presently be
seen, there is a reference to Brittany. To continue: the
next entries on the sherd, if I may except a long splash
of either blood or red coloring matter of some sort, consist of two crosses drawn in red pigment, and probably
representing Crusaders' swords, and a rather neat mono-
gram ("D. V.") in scarlet and blue, perhaps executed by
that same Dorothea Vincey who wrote, or rather painted,
the doggerel couplet. To the left of this, inscribed in faint
blue, were the initials A. V., and after them a date, 1800.

Then came what was perhaps as curious an entry as anything upon this extraordinary relic of the past. It is executed in black letter, written over the crosses or Crusaders'
swords, and dated fourteen hundred and forty-five. As
the best plan will be to allow it to speak for itself, I here
give the black-letter facsimile, together with the original
Latin without the contractions, from which it will be seen
that the writer was a fair medieval Latinist. Also we
discovered what is still more curious, an English version of
the black-letter Latin. This, also written in black letter,
we found inscribed on a second parchment that was in
the coffer, apparently somewhat older in date than that

on which was inscribed the medieval Latin translation of the uncial Greek of which I shall speak presently. This I also give in full.

Facsimile of Black-Letter Inscription on the Sherd of Amenartas

𝕴𝖘𝖙𝖆 reliquia est valde misticū et myrificv opus q̄d maiores mei ex Armorica ſſ Brittania miore secū cōvehebāt et q̄dm ſc̄s cleriĉs sēper p̄ri meo in manv ferebat q̄d p̄itus illvd destrueret affirmās q̄d esset ab ipſo sathana cōſſatv preſtigioſa et dyabolica arte q̄re p̄ter mevs cōfregit illvd ī dvas p̄tes q̄s q̄dm ego Johs de Uīceto salvas servavi et adaptavi sicvt apparet die lūe p̄x poſt feſt beate Marie virg̃ anni gr̃e mccccrlv

Expanded Version of the above Black-Letter Inscription

ISTA reliquia est valde misticum et myrificum opus, quod majores mei ex Armorica, scilicet Britannia Minore, secum convehebant; et quidam sanctus clericus semper patri meo in manu ferebat quod penitus illud destrueret, affirmans quod esset ab ipso Sathan conflatum prestigiosa et dyabolica arte, quare pater meus confregit illud in duas partes, quas quidem ego Johannes de Vinceto salvas servavi et adaptavi sicut apparet die lune proximo post festum beate Marie Virginis anni gratie MCCCCXLV.

Facsimile of the Old English Black-Letter Translation of the above Latin Inscription from the Sherd of Amenartas found inscribed upon a parchment

Thys rellike ys a ryghte mistycall worke
    & a marveylous ye whyche myne aun=
ceteres afore tyme dyd conveighe hider wt ym
ffrom Armoryke why ys to seien Britayne ye
lesse & a certayne holye clerke shoulde allweyes
beare my ffadir on honde yt he owghte vtterly
ffor to ffrusshe ye same affirmynge yt yt was
ffourmnd & coufflatyd off sathanas hym selffe
by arte magike & dauellysshe wherefore my
ffadir dyd take ye same & to brast yt yn tweyne
but I Iohn de Vincey dyd save whool ye tweye
ptes therof & topeecnd ym togydder agayne soe
as yee se on ys deye mondaye next ffolowynge
after ye ffeeste of seynte Marye ye blessed
vyrgyne yn ye yeere of salvacioun ffowertene
hundreth & ffyve & ffowrti。

*Modernized Version of the above Black-Letter Transla-
tion*

THYS rellike ys a ryghte mistycall worke and a marvaylous,
ye whyche myne aunceteres aforetyme dyd conveigh hider with
them from Armoryke which ys to seien Britaine ye Lesse and
a certayne holye clerke should allweyes beare my fadir on honde

that he owghte uttirly for to frusshe ye same, affyrmynge that yt was fourmed and conflatyd of Sathanas hym selfe by arte magike and dyvellysshe wherefore my fadir dyd take ye same and tobrast yt yn tweyne, but I, John de Vincey, dyd save whool ye tweye partes therof and topeecyd them togydder agayne soe as yee se, on this daye mondaye next followynge after ye feeste of Seynte Marye ye Blessed Vyrgyne yn ye yeere of Salvacioun fowertene hundreth and fyve and fowerti.

The next and, save one, last entry was Elizabethan, and dated 1564, "A most strange historie, and one that did cost my father his life; for in seekynge for the place upon the east coast of Africa, his pinnace was sunk by a Portuguese galleon off Lorenzo Marquez, and he himself perished.—JOHN VINCEY."

Then came the last entry, apparently, to judge by the style of writing, made by some representative of the family in the middle of the eighteenth century. It was a misquotation of the well-known lines in *Hamlet*, and ran thus: "There are more things in Heaven and earth than are dreamt of in your philosophy, Horatio." [3]

And now there remained but one more document to be examined—namely, the ancient black-letter translation into medieval Latin of the uncial inscription on the sherd. As will be seen, this translation was executed and subscribed in the year 1495, by a certain "learned man," Edmundus de Prato (Edmund Pratt) by name, licentiate in Canon Law,

---

[3] Another thing that makes me fix the date of this entry at the middle of the eighteenth century is that, curiously enough, I have an acting copy of *Hamlet*, written about 1740, in which these two lines are misquoted almost exactly in the same way, and I have little doubt but that the Vincey who wrote them on the potsherd heard them so misquoted at that date. Of course, the lines really run:

> There are more things in heaven and earth, Horatio,
> Than are dreamt of in your philosophy.—L. H. H.

of Exeter College, Oxford, who had actually been a pupil of Grocyn, the first scholar who taught Greek in England.[4] No doubt on the fame of this new learning reaching his ears, the Vincey of the day, perhaps that same John de Vincey who years before had saved the relic from destruction and made the black-letter entry on the sherd in 1445, hurried off to Oxford to see if perchance it might avail to solve the secret of the mysterious inscription. Nor was he disappointed, for the learned Edmundus was equal to the task. Indeed, his rendering is so excellent an example of medieval learning and Latinity that, even at the risk of sating the learned reader with too many antiquities, I have made up my mind to give it in facsimile, together with an expanded version for the benefit of those who find the contractions troublesome. The translation has several peculiarities on which this is not the place to dwell, but I would in passing call the attention of scholars to the passage *"dux-erunt autem nos ad reginam* advenaslasaniscoronantium,"* which strikes me as a delightful rendering of the original, " ἤγαγον δὲ ὡς βασίλειαν τὴν τῶν ξένους χύτραις στεφανούντων."

Medieval Black-Letter Latin Translation of the Uncial Inscription on the Sherd of Amenartas

𝕬menartas e gen. reg. Egyptu vror Cal: lireratis sacerdoť Isidis quā dei fovēt demonia attēdūt filioľ suo Tisisthem iā mori: būda ita mādat: Effugi quōdā ex Egypto regnāte Nectanebo cū patre tuo, ꝑpter met

---

[4] Grocyn, the instructor of Erasmus, studied Greek under Chalcondylas the Byzantine at Florence, and first lectured in the Hall of Exeter College, Oxford, in 1491.—EDITOR.

amorē pejerato. Fvgiētes autē v'sus Notū
trans mare et xxiiij mēses p'r litora Libye
v'sus Oriētē errant vbi est petra quedā mgna
scvlpta instar Ethiop capit, deinde dies iiij ab
ost ssum mgni eiecti p'tim submersi sumus
p'tim morbo mortui sum: in sine autē a fer
hōibs portabamur pr palvo et vada. vbi aviū
m'titvdo celū obūbrat dies x. donec advenim ad
cavū quedā montē, ubi olim mgna vrbs erat,
cauerne quoq imēse: dvrerūt autē nos ad reginā
Advenaslasaniscoronātiū que magic vtebair et
peritia omniū rex et saltē pvlcrit et vigore
isecscribil' erat. Hec mgno patr tui amore
pcvlssa p'mū q'dē ei coūubiū michi mortē
parabat. postea v'ro recvsāte Callicrate amore
mei et timore regine affecto nos pr magicā
abdurit p'r vias horribil' vbi est putcus ille
psūdus, cuius iurta aditū iacebat seniox philosophi cadauer, et advēiētib mōstrabit ssamā
Uite erectā, istar columne volutātis, voces
cmittētē qsi tonitrvs: tūc pr igne ipetu nociuo
expers trāsiit et iā ipa sese formosior visa est.

Quib saci iuravit se patrē tuū quoq imor-
talē ostēsurā esse, si me prius occisa regine
cōtvberniū mallet; neq eni ipsa me occidere
valuit, ppter nostratū mgicā cuius egomet
ptem habeo Ille vero nichil huius geū
maluit, manib ante ocut passis ne mulier

formositatē adſpiceret: poſtea eū ſigica ꝑcuſſit
arte, at mortuū efferebat īde cū ſletib et vagitib,
me ꝑr timorē expulit ad oſtiū ſigni ſlumiū
velmoſi porro in nave in qua te peperi, uir
poſt dies hvc Athenas invecta ſū. At tu, O
Tiſiſtheū, ne q'd quorū mādo nauci fac neceſſe
enī eſt mulierē exqvirere ſi qva Uite myſteriū
īpetres et vidicare, qvātū in te eſt, patrē tuū
Callicraſ in regine morte. Sin timore ſeu aliq
cabſa rē reliqvis īſectā, hoc ipſū oīb poſterꝰ
mādo dū bonvs ꝗs inveniatur qvi ignis lauacrū
nō ꝑrhorreſcet et ꝑtentia digū dōiabit hōiū.

Talia dico incredibilia ꝗdē at miīe ficta de
reb michi cognitis.

Hec Grece ſcripta Latine reddidit vir
doctus Edmōds de Prato, in Decretis Licenciatus e Coll. Exon· Oxon· doctiſſimi
Groepni quondam e pupillis, Id Apr Aº
Dūi. MCCCCLXXXXUº.

*Expanded Version of the above Medieval Latin
Translation*

AMENARTAS, e genere regio Egyptii, uxor Callicratis, sacer-
dotis Isidis, quam dei fovent demonia attendunt, filiolo suo
Tisistheni jam moribunda ita mandat: Effugi quondam ex
Egypto, regnante Nectanebo, cum patre tuo, propter mei
amorem pejerato. Fugientes autem versus Notum trans mare,
et viginti quatuor menses per litora Libye versus Orientem
errantes, ubi est petra quedam magna sculpta instar Ethiopis

capitis, deinde dies quatuor ab ostio fluminis magni ejecti partim submersi sumus partim morbo mortui sumus: in fine autem a feris hominibus portabamur per paludes et vada, ubi avium multitudo celum obumbrat, dies decem, donec advenimus ad cavum quendam montem, ubi olim magna urbs erat, caverne quoque immense; duxerunt autem nos ad reginam Advenaslasaniscoronantium, que magica utebatur et peritia omnium rerum, et saltem pulcritudine et vigore insenescibilis erat. Hec magno patris tui amore perculsa, primum quidem ei connubium michi mortem parabat; postea vero, recusante Callicrate, amore mei et timore regine affecto nos per magicam abduxit per vias horribiles ubi est puteus ille profundus, cujus juxta aditum jacebat senioris philosophi cadaver, et advenientibus monstravit flammam Vite erectam, instar columne volutantis, voces emittentem quasi tonitrus: tunc per ignem impetu nocivo expers transiit et jam ipsa sese formosior visa est.

Quibus factis juravit se patrem tuum quoque immortalem ostensuram esse, si me prius occisa regine contubernium mallet; neque enim ipsa me occidere valuit, propter nostratum magicam cujus egomet partem habeo. Ille vero nichil hujus generis malebat, manibus ante oculos passis, ne mulieris formositatem adspiceret: postea illum magica percussit arte, at mortuum efferebat inde cum fletibus et vagitibus, at me per timorem expulit ad ostium magni fluminis, velivoli, porro in nave, in qua te peperi, vix post dies huc Athenas vecta sum. At tu, O Tisisthenes, ne quid quorum mando nauci fac: necesse enim est mulierem exquirere si qua Vite mysterium impetres et vindicare, quantum in te est, patrem tuum Callicratem in regine morte. Sin timore seu aliqua causa rem relinquis infectam, hoc ipsum omnibus posteris mando, dum bonus quis inveniatur qui ignis lavacrum non perhorrescet, et potentia dignus dominabitur hominum.

Talia dico incredibilia quidem at minime ficta de rebus michi cognitis.

Hec Grece scripta Latine reddidit vir doctus Edmundus de Prato, in Decretis Licenciatus, e Collegio Exoniensi Oxoniensi doctissimi Grocyni quondam e pupillis, Idibus Aprilis Anno Domini MCCCCLXXXXV°.

"Well," I said, when at length I had read out and carefully examined these writings and paragraphs, at least those of them that were still easily legible, "that is the conclusion of the whole matter, Leo, and now you can form your own opinion on it. I have already formed mine."

"And what is it?" he asked, in his quick way.

"It is this. I believe that potsherd to be perfectly genuine, and that, wonderful as it may seem, it has come down in your family from since the fourth century before Christ. The entries absolutely prove it, and therefore, however improbable it may seem, it must be accepted. But there I stop. That your remote ancestress, the Egyptian princess, or some scribe under her direction, wrote that which we see on the sherd I have no doubt, nor have I the slightest doubt but that her sufferings and the loss of her husband had turned her head, and that she was not right in her mind when she did write it."

"How do you account for what my father saw and heard there?" asked Leo.

"Coincidence. No doubt there are bluffs on the coast of Africa that look something like a man's head, and plenty of people who speak bastard Arabic. Also, I believe that there are lots of swamps. Another thing is, Leo, and I am sorry to say it, but I do not believe that your poor father was quite right when he wrote that letter. He had met with a great trouble, and also he had allowed this story to prey on his imagination, and he was a very imaginative man. Anyway, I believe that the whole thing is the most unmitigated rubbish. I know that there are curious things and forces in nature which we rarely meet with, and, when we do meet them, cannot understand. But until I see it with my own eyes, which I am not likely to, I never will believe that there is any means of avoiding death, even for a time, or that there is or was a white sorceress living in the heart of an African swamp. It is bosh, my boy, all bosh! What do you say, Job?"

"I say, sir, that it is a lie, and, if it is true, I hope Mr. Leo won't meddle with no such things, for no good can't come of it."

"Perhaps you are both right," said Leo very quietly. "I express no opinion. But I say this. I am going to set the matter at rest once and for all, and if you won't come with me I will go by myself."

I looked at the young man, and saw that he meant what he said. When Leo means what he says he always puts on a curious look about the mouth. It has been a trick of his from a child. Now, as a matter of fact, I had no intention of allowing Leo to go anywhere by himself, for my own sake, if not for his. I was far too much attached to him for that. I am not a man of many ties or affections. Circumstances have been against me in this respect, and men and women shrink from me—or at least I fancy they do, which comes to the same thing—thinking, perhaps, that my somewhat forbidding exterior is a key to my character. Rather than endure this, I have, to a great extent, secluded myself from the world, and cut myself off from those oppor- tunities which with most men result in the formation of relations more or less intimate. Therefore Leo was all the world to me—brother, child, and friend—and until he wearied of me, where he went there I should go too. But, of course, it would not do to let him see how great a hold he had over me; so I cast about for some means whereby I might let myself down easy.

"Yes, I shall go, Uncle; and if I don't find the 'rolling Pillar of Life,' at any rate I shall get some first-class shooting."

Here was my opportunity, and I took it.

"Shooting?" I said. "Ah, yes; I never thought of that. It must be a very wild stretch of country, and full of big game. I have always wanted to kill a buffalo before I die. Do you know, my boy, I don't believe in the quest, but I do believe in big game, and really, on the whole, if, after thinking it over, you make up your mind to go, I will take a holiday, and come with you."

"Ah," said Leo, "I thought that you would not lose such a chance. But how about money? We shall want a good lot."

"You need not trouble about that," I answered. "There is all your income that has been accumulating for years, and besides that I have saved two-thirds of what your father left to me, as I consider, in trust for you. There is plenty of cash."

"Very well, then, we may as well stow these things away and go up to town to see about our guns. By the way, Job, are you coming too? It's time you began to see the world."

"Well, sir," answered Job stolidly, "I don't hold much with foreign parts, but if both you gentlemen are going you will want somebody to look after you, and I am not the man to stop behind after serving you for twenty years."

"That's right, Job," said I. "You won't find out anything wonderful, but you will get some good shooting. And now look here, both of you. I won't have a word said to a living soul about this nonsense," and I pointed to the potsherd. "If it got out, and anything happened to me, my next of kin would dispute my will on the ground of insanity, and I should become the laughingstock of Cambridge."

That day three months we were on the ocean, bound for Zanzibar.

4 ◆

The Squall

How DIFFERENT is the scene that I have now to tell from that which has just been told! Gone are the quiet college rooms, gone the wind-swayed English elms and cawing rooks, and the familiar volumes on the shelves, and in their place there rises a vision of the great calm ocean gleaming in shaded silver lights beneath the beams of the full African moon. A gentle breeze fills the huge sail of our dhow, and draws us through the water that ripples musically against our sides. Most of the men are sleeping forward, for it is near midnight, but a stout swarthy Arab, Mahomed by name, stands at the tiller, lazily steering by the stars. Three miles or more to our starboard is a low dim line. It is the eastern shore of Central Africa. We are running to the southward, before the Northeast Monsoon, between the mainland and the reef that for hundreds of miles fringes that perilous coast. The night is quiet, so quiet that a whisper can be heard fore and aft the dhow; so quiet that a faint booming sound rolls across the water to us from the distant land.

The Arab at the tiller holds up his hand, and says one word: "*Simba* [lion]!"

We all sit up and listen. Then it comes again, a slow, majestic sound that thrills us to the marrow.

"Tomorrow by ten o'clock," I say, "we ought, if the Captain is not out in his reckoning, which I think very

57

probable, to make this mysterious rock with a man's head, and begin our shooting."

"And begin our search for the ruined city and the Fire of Life," corrected Leo, taking his pipe from his mouth, and laughing a little.

"Nonsense!" I answered. "You were airing your Arabic with that man at the tiller this afternoon. What did he tell you? He has been trading (slave-trading probably) up and down these latitudes for half of his iniquitous life, and once landed on this very "man" rock. Did he ever hear anything of the ruined city or the caves?"

"No," answered Leo. "He says that the country is all swamp behind, and full of snakes, especially pythons, and game, and that no man lives there. But then there is a belt of swamp all along the East African coast, so that does not go for much."

"Yes," I said, "it does—it goes for malaria. You see what sort of an opinion these gentry have of the country. Not one of them will go with us. They think that we are mad, and upon my word I believe that they are right. If ever we see old England again I shall be astonished. However, it does not greatly matter to me at my age, but I am anxious for you, Leo, and for Job. It's a Tom Fool's business, my boy."

"All right, Uncle Horace. So far as I am concerned, I am willing to take my chance. Look! What is that cloud?" and he pointed to a dark blotch upon the starry sky, some miles astern of us.

"Go and ask the man at the tiller," I said.

He rose, stretched his arms, and went. Presently he returned.

"He says it is a squall, but it will pass far on one side of us."

Just then Job came up, looking very stout and English in his shooting suit of brown flannel, and with a sort of perplexed appearance upon his honest round face that had been very common with him since he got into these strange waters.

"Please, sir," he said, touching his sun hat, which was stuck on to the back of his head in a somewhat ludicrous fashion, "as we have got all those guns and things in the whaleboat astern, to say nothing of the provisions in the lockers, I think it would be best if I got down and slept in her. I don't like the looks"—here he dropped his voice to a portentous whisper—"of these black gentry; they have such a wonderful thievish way about them. Supposing now that some of them were to slip into the boat at night and cut the cable, and make off with her? That would be a pretty go, that would."

The whaleboat, I may explain, was one specially built for us at Dundee, in Scotland. We had brought it with us, as we knew that this coast was a network of creeks, and that we might require something to navigate them with. She was a beautiful boat, thirty feet in length, with a center-board for sailing, copper-bottom to keep the worm out of her, and full of water-tight compartments. The captain of the dhow had told us that when we reached the rock, which he knew, and which appeared to be identical with the one described upon the sherd and by Leo's father, he would probably not be able to run up to it on account of the shallows and breakers. Therefore we had employed three hours that very morning, while we were totally becalmed, the wind having dropped at sunrise, in transferring most of our goods and chattels to the whaleboat, and placing the guns, ammunition, and preserved provisions in the water-tight lockers specially prepared for them, so that when we did sight the fabled rock we should have nothing to do but step into the boat, and run her ashore. Another reason that induced us to take this precautionary step was that Arab captains are apt to run past the point that they are making, either from carelessness or owing to a mistake in its identity. Now, as sailors know, it is quite impossible for a dhow which is only rigged to run before the monsoon to beat back against it. Therefore we got our boat ready to row for the rock at any moment.

"Well, Job," I said, "perhaps it would be as well. There are lots of blankets there, only be careful to keep out of the moon, or it may turn your head or blind you."

"Lord, sir! I don't think it would much matter if it did; it is that turned already with the sight of these blackamoors and their filthy, thieving ways. They are only fit for muck, they are; and they smell bad enough for it already."

Job, it will be perceived, was no admirer of the manners and customs of our dark-skinned brothers.

Accordingly we hauled up the boat by the tow rope till it was right under the stern of the dhow, and Job bundled into her with all the grace of a falling sack of potatoes. Then we returned and sat down on the deck again, and smoked and talked in little gusts and jerks. The night was so lovely, and our brains were so full of suppressed excitement of one sort and another, that we did not feel inclined to turn in. For nearly an hour we sat thus, and then, I think, we both dozed off. At least I have a faint recollection of Leo sleepily explaining that the head was not a bad place to hit a buffalo, if you could catch him exactly between the horns, or send your bullet down his throat, or some nonsense of the sort.

Then I remember no more; till suddenly—a frightful

roar of wind, a shriek of terror from the awakening crew, and a whiplike sting of water in our faces. Some of the men ran to let go the halyards and lower the sail, but the parrel jammed and the yard would not come down. I sprang to my feet and hung on to a rope. The sky aft was dark as pitch, but the moon still shone brightly ahead of us and lit up the blackness. Beneath its sheen a huge white-topped breaker, twenty feet high or more, was rushing onto us. It was on the break—the moon shone on its crest and tipped its foam with light. On it rushed beneath the inky sky, driven by the awful squall behind it. Suddenly, in the twinkling of an eye, I saw the black shape of the whaleboat cast high into the air on the crest of the breaking wave. Then—a shock of water, a wild rush of boiling foam, and I was clinging for my life to the shroud, ay, swept straight out from it like a flag in a gale.

We were pooped.

The wave passed. It seemed to me that I was under water for minutes—really it was seconds. I looked forward. The blast had torn out the great sail, and high in the air it was fluttering away to leeward like a huge wounded bird. Then for a moment there was comparative calm, and in it I heard Job's voice yelling wildly, "Come here to the boat."

Bewildered and half drowned as I was, I had the sense to rush aft. I felt the dhow sinking under me—she was full of water. Under her counter the whaleboat was tossing furiously, and I saw the Arab Mahomed, who had been steering, leap into her. I gave one desperate pull at the tow rope to bring the boat alongside. Wildly I sprang also, and Job caught me by one arm and I rolled into the bottom of the boat. Down went the dhow bodily, and as she did so Mahomed drew his curved knife and severed the fiber rope by which we were fast to her, and in another second we were driving before the storm over the place where the dhow had been.

"Great God!" I shrieked, "where is Leo? *Leo! Leo!*"

"He's gone, sir, God help him!" roared Job into my ear; and such was the fury of the squall that his voice sounded like a whisper.

I wrung my hands in agony. Leo was drowned, and I was left alive to mourn him.

"Look out!" yelled Job. "Here comes another."

I turned; a second huge wave was overtaking us. I half hoped that it would drown me. With a curious fascination I watched its awful advent. The moon was nearly hidden now by the wreaths of the rushing storm, but a little light still caught the crest of the devouring breaker. There was something dark on it—a piece of wreckage. It was on us now, and the boat was nearly full of water. But she was built in air-tight compartments—heaven bless the man who invented them!—and lifted up through it like a swan. Through the foam and turmoil I saw the black thing on the wave hurrying right at me. I put out my right arm to ward it from me, and my hand closed on another arm, the wrist of which my fingers gripped like a vice. I am a very strong man, and had something to hold to, but my arm was nearly torn from its socket by the strain and weight of the floating body. Had the rush lasted another two seconds I must either have let go or gone with it. But it passed, leaving us up to our knees in water.

"Bail out! Bail out!" shouted Job, suiting the action to the word.

But I could not bail just then, for as the moon went out and left us in total darkness, one faint, flying ray of light lit upon the face of the man I had gripped, who was now half lying, half floating in the bottom of the boat.

It was Leo. Leo brought back by the wave—back, dead or alive, from the very jaws of death.

"Bail out! Bail out!" yelled Job. "Or we shall founder."

I seized a large tin bowl with a handle to it, which was fixed under one of the seats, and the three of us bailed away for dear life. The furious tempest drove over and round us, flinging the boat this way and that; the wind and the storm wreaths and the sheets of stinging spray blinded and bewildered us; but through it all we worked like demons with the wild exhilaration of despair, for even depair can exhilarate. One minute! Three minutes! Six minutes! The boat began to lighten, and no fresh wave swamped us. Five minutes more, and she was fairly clear. Then, suddenly, above the awful shriekings of the hurricane came a duller, deeper roar. Great heavens! It was the voice of breakers!

At that moment the moon began to shine forth again— this time behind the path of the squall. Far out across the torn bosom of the ocean shot the ragged arrows of her light, and there, half a mile ahead of us, was a white line of foam, then a little space of open-mouthed blackness, and then another line of white. It was the breakers, and their roar grew clearer and yet more clear as we sped down upon them like a swallow. There they were, boiling up in snowy spouts of spray, smiting and gnashing together like the gleaming teeth of hell.

"Take the tiller, Mahomed!" I roared in Arabic. "We must try and shoot them." At the same moment I seized an oar, and got it out, motioning to Job to do likewise.

Mahomed clambered aft and got hold of the tiller,

and with some difficulty Job, who had sometimes pulled a tub upon the homely Cam, got out his oar. In another minute the boat's head was straight on to the ever nearing foam, towards which she plunged and tore with the speed of a racehorse. Just in front of us the first line of breakers seemed a little thinner than to the right or left—there was a gap of rather deeper water. I turned and pointed to it.

"Steer for your life, Mahomed!" I yelled. He was a skillful steersman, and well acquainted with the dangers of this most perilous coast, and I saw him grip the tiller and bend his heavy frame forward, and stare at the foaming terror till his big round eyes looked as though they would start out of his head. The send of the sea was driving the boat's head round to starboard. If we struck the line of breakers fifty yards to starboard of the gap we must sink. It was a great field of twisting, spouting waves. Mahomed planted his foot against the seat before him, and, glancing at him, I saw his brown toes spread out like a hand with the weight he put upon them as he took the strain of the tiller. She came round a bit, but not enough. I roared to Job to back water, whilst I dragged and labored at my oar. She answered now, and none too soon.

Heavens, we were in them! And then followed a couple of minutes of heartbreaking excitement such as I cannot hope to describe. All I remember is a shrieking sea of foam, out of which the billows rose here, there, and everywhere like avenging ghosts from their ocean grave. Once we were turned right round, but either by chance, or through Mahomed's skillful steering, the boat's head came straight again before a breaker filled us. One more—a monster. We were through it or over it—more through than over—and then, with a wild yell of exultation from the Arab, we shot out into the comparatively smooth water of the mouth of sea between the teeth-like lines of gnashing waves.

But we were half full of water again, and not more than half a mile ahead was the second line of breakers. Again we set to and bailed furiously. Fortunately the storm had now quite gone by, and the moon shone brightly, revealing a rocky headland running half a mile or more out into the sea, of which this second line of breakers appeared to be a continuation. At any rate, they boiled around its foot. Probably the ridge that formed the headland ran out into the ocean, only at a lower level, and made the reef also. This headland was terminated by a curious peak that seemed not to be more than a mile away from us. Just as we got the boat pretty clear for the second time, Leo, to my immense relief, opened his eyes and remarked that the clothes had tumbled off the bed, and that he supposed it was time to get up for chapel. I told him to shut his eyes and keep quiet, which he did without in the slightest degree realizing our position. As for myself, his reference to chapel made me reflect, with a sort of sick longing, on my comfortable rooms at Cambridge. Why had I been such a fool as to leave them? This is a reflection that has several times recurred to me since, and with ever increasing force.

But now again we were drifting down on the breakers, though with lessened speed, for the wind had fallen, and only the current or the tide (it afterwards turned out to be the tide) was driving us.

Another minute, and with a sort of howl to Allah from the Arab, a pious ejaculation from myself, and something that was not pious from Job, we were in them. And then the whole scene, down to our final escape, repeated itself, only not quite so violently. Mahomed's skillful steering and the air-tight compartments saved our lives. In five minutes we were through, and drifting—for we were too exhausted to do anything to help ourselves except keep the boat's head straight—with the most startling rapidity round the headland which I have described.

Round we went with the tide, until we got well under the lee of the point, and then suddenly the speed slackened, we ceased to make way, and finally appeared to be in dead water. The storm had entirely passed, leaving a clean-washed sky behind it; the headland intercepted the heavy sea that had been occasioned by the squall, and the tide, which had been running so fiercely up the river (for we were now in the mouth of a river), was sluggish before it turned, so we floated quietly, and before the moon went down managed to bail out the boat thoroughly and get her a little shipshape. Leo was sleeping profoundly, and on the whole I thought it wise not to wake him. It was true he was sleeping in wet clothes, but the night was now so warm that I thought (and so did Job) that they were not likely to injure a man of his unusually vigorous constitution. Besides, we had no dry ones at hand.

Presently the moon went down and left us floating on the waters, now only heaving like some troubled woman's breast, giving us leisure to reflect upon all that we had gone through and all that we had escaped. Job stationed himself at the bow, Mahomed kept his post at the tiller, and I sat on a seat in the middle of the boat close to where Leo was lying.

The moon went slowly down in chastened loveliness, she departed like some sweet bride into her chamber, and long veil-like shadows crept up the sky through which the stars peeped shyly out. Soon, however, they too began to pale before a splendor in the east, and then the quivering footsteps of the dawn came rushing across the new-born blue, and shook the planets from their places. Quieter and yet more quiet grew the sea, quiet as the soft mist that brooded on her bosom, and covered up her troubling, as the illusive wreaths of sleep brood upon a pain-racked mind, causing it to forget its sorrow. From the east to the west sped the angels of the dawn, from sea to sea, from mountain top to mountain top, scattering light with both their hands. On they sped out of the darkness, perfect, glorious, like spirits of the just breaking from the tomb; on, over the quiet sea, over the low coastline, and the swamps beyond, and the mountains beyond them; over those who slept in peace, and those who woke in sorrow; over the evil and the good; over the living and dead; over the wide world and all that breathes or has breathed thereon.

It was a wonderfully beautiful sight, and yet sad, per-haps from the very excess of its beauty. The arising sun; the setting sun! There we have the symbol and the type of humanity, and all things with which humanity has to do. The symbol and the type, yes, and the earthly be-ginning, and the end also. And on that morning this came home to me with a peculiar force. The sun that rose to-day for us had set last night for eighteen of our fellow-voyagers!—had set forever for eighteen whom we knew!

The dhow had gone down with them, they were tossing about now among the rocks and seaweed, so much human drift on the great ocean of death! And we four were saved. But one day a sunrise will come when we shall be among those who are lost, and then others will watch those glorious rays, and grow sad in the midst of beauty, and dream of death in the full glow of arising life!

For this is the lot of man.

5 ♦

The Head of the Ethiopian

AT LENGTH the heralds and forerunners of the royal sun had done their work, and, searching out the shadows, had caused them to flee away. Then up he came in glory from his ocean bed, and flooded the earth with warmth and light. I sat there in the boat listening to the gentle lapping of the water and watched him rise, till presently the slight drift of the boat brought the odd-shaped rock, or peak, at the end of the promontory which we had weathered with so much peril, between me and the majestic sight, and blotted it from my view. I still continued to stare at the rock, however, absently enough, till presently it became edged with the fire of the growing light behind it, and then I started, as well I might, for I perceived that the top of the peak, which was about eighty feet high by one hundred and fifty thick at its base, was shaped like a Negro's head and face, whereon was stamped a most fiendish and terrifying expression. There was no doubt about it; there were the thick lips, the fat cheeks, and the squat nose standing out with startling clearness against the flaming background. There, too, was the round skull, washed into shape perhaps by thousands of years of wind and weather, and, to complete the resemblance, there was a scrubby growth of weeds or lichen upon it, which against the sun looked for all the world like the wool on a colossal Negro's head. It certainly was very odd; so odd that now I believe that it is not a mere freak of nature but a gigantic monument fashioned, like the well-known Egyptian Sphinx, by a forgotten people out of a pile of rock that lent itself to their design, perhaps as an emblem of warning and defiance to any enemies who approached the harbor. Unfortunately we were never able to ascertain whether or not this was the case, inasmuch as the rock was difficult of access from both the land and the water side, and we had other things to attend to. Myself, considering the matter by the light of what we afterwards saw, I believe that it was fashioned by man, but whether or not this is so, there it stands, and sullenly stares from age to age out across the changing sea—there it stood two thousand years and more ago, when Amenartas, the Egyptian princess, and the wife of Leo's remote ancestor Kallikrates, gazed upon its devilish face—and there I have no doubt it will still stand when as many centuries as are numbered between her day and our own are added to the year that bore us to oblivion.

"What do you think of that, Job?" I asked of our retainer, who was sitting on the edge of the boat, trying to get as much sunshine as possible, and generally looking uncommonly wretched, and I pointed to the fiery and demoniacal head.

"Oh Lord, sir," answered Job, who now perceived the object for the first time, "I think that the Old Gentleman must have been sitting for his portrait on them rocks."

I laughed, and the laugh woke up Leo.

"Hullo," he said, "what's the matter with me? I am all stiff—where is the dhow? Give me some brandy, please."

"You may be thankful that you are not stiffer, my boy," I answered. "The dhow is sunk, and everybody on board her is drowned, with the exception of us four, and your own life was only saved by a miracle"; and while Job,

now that it was light enough, searched about in a locker
for the brandy for which Leo asked, I told him the history
of our night's adventure.

"Great heavens!" he said, faintly. "And to think that
we should have been chosen to live through it!"

By this time the brandy was forthcoming, and we all
had a good pull at it, and thankful enough we were for it.
Also the sun was beginning to get strength, and warm our
chilled bones, for we had been wet through for five hours
or more.

"Why," said Leo with a gasp, as he put down the
brandy bottle, "there is the head the writing talks of, the
'rock carven like the head of an Ethiopian.'"

"Yes," I said, "there it is."

"Well, then," he answered, "the whole thing is true."

"I don't at all see that that follows," I answered. "We
knew this head was here, your father saw it. Very likely
it is not the same head that the writing talks of; or if it
is, it proves nothing."

Leo smiled at me in a superior way. "You are an un-
believer, Uncle Horace," he said. "Those who live will see."

"Exactly so," I answered, "and now perhaps you will
observe that we are drifting across a sandbank into the
mouth of the river. Get hold of your oar, Job, and we will
row in and see if we can find a place to land."

The river mouth which we were entering did not appear
to be a very wide one, though as yet the long banks of
steaming mist that clung about its shores had not lifted
sufficiently to enable us to see its exact width. There was,
as is the case with nearly every East African river, a considerable bar at the mouth, which, no doubt, when the
wind was on shore and the tide running out, was absolutely

impassable even for a boat drawing only a few inches. But as things were it was manageable enough, and we did not ship a cupful of water. In twenty minutes we were well across it, with but slight assistance from ourselves, and being carried by a strong though somewhat variable breeze, well up the harbor. By this time the mist was being sucked up by the sun, which was getting uncomfortably hot, and we saw that the mouth of the little estuary was here about half a mile across, and that the banks were very marshy, and crowded with crocodiles lying about on the mud like logs. About a mile ahead of us, however, was what appeared to be a strip of firm land, and for this we steered. In another quarter of an hour we were there, and making the boat fast to a beautiful tree with broad shining leaves, and flowers of the magnolia species, only they were rose-colored and not white,[1] which hung over the water, we disembarked. This done we undressed, washed ourselves, and spread our clothes and the contents of the boat in the sun to dry, which they very quickly did. Then, taking shelter from the sun under some trees, we made a hearty breakfast off a "Paysandu" potted tongue, of which we had brought a good quantity with us from the Army and Navy Stores, congratulating ourselves loudly on our good fortune in having loaded and provisioned the boat on the previous day, before the hurricane destroyed the dhow. By the time that we had finished our meal our clothes were quite dry, and we hastened to get into them, feeling not a little refreshed. Indeed, with the exception of weariness and a few bruises, none of us were the worse for the terrifying adventure which had been fatal to all our

---

[1] There is a known species of magnolia with pink flowers. It is indigenous in Sikkim, and known as *Magnolia Campbellii.*—Editor.

companions. Leo, it is true, had been half-drowned, but that is no great matter to a vigorous young athlete of five-and-twenty.

After breakfast we started to look about us. We were on a strip of dry land about two hundred yards broad by five hundred long, bordered on one side by the river, and on the other three by endless desolate swamps that stretched as far as the eye could reach. This strip of land was raised about twenty-five feet above the plain of the surrounding swamps and the river level: indeed, it had every appearance of having been made by the hand of man.

"This place has been a wharf," said Leo dogmatically.

"Nonsense," I answered. "Who would be stupid enough to build a wharf in the middle of these dreadful marshes in a country inhabited by savages, that is if it is inhabited at all?"

"Perhaps it was not always marsh, and perhaps the people were not always savage," he said drily, looking down the steep bank, for we were standing by the river. "Look there," he went on, pointing to a spot where the hurricane of the previous night had torn up one of the magnolia trees, which had grown on the extreme edge of the bank just where it sloped down to the water, by the roots, and lifted a large cake of earth with them. "Is not that stonework? If not, it is very like it."

"Nonsense," I said again, and we clambered down to the spot, and got between the upturned roots and the bank.

"Well?" he said.

But I did not answer this time. I only whistled. For there, laid bare by the removal of the earth, was an undoubted facing of solid stone laid in large blocks and bound together with brown cement, so hard that I could make no impression on it with the file in my shooting knife. Nor was this all; seeing something projecting through the soil at the bottom of the bared patch of walling, I removed the loose earth with my hands, and revealed a huge stone ring, a foot or more in diameter, and about three inches thick. This fairly staggered me.

"Looks rather like a wharf where good-sized vessels have been moored, does it not, Uncle Horace?" said Leo with an excited grin.

I tried to say "Nonsense" again, but the word stuck in my throat—the ring spoke for itself. In some past age vessels *had* been moored there, and this stone wall was undoubtedly the remnant of a solidly constructed wharf. Probably the city to which it had belonged lay buried beneath the swamp behind it.

"Begins to look as though there were something in the story after all, Uncle Horace," said the exultant Leo; and reflecting on the mysterious Negro's head and the equally mysterious stonework, I made no direct reply.

"A country like Africa," I said, "is sure to be full of the relics of long dead and forgotten civilizations. Nobody knows the age of the Egyptian civilization, and very likely it had offshoots. Then there were the Babylonians and the Phoenicians, and the Persians and all manner of people, all more or less civilized, to say nothing of the Jews, whom everybody 'wants' nowadays. It is possible that they, or any one of them, may have had colonies or trading stations about here. Remember those buried Persian cities that the consul showed us at Kilwa." [2]

[2] Near Kilwa, on the east coast of Africa, about four hundred miles south of Zanzibar, is a cliff which has been recently washed by the waves. On the top of this cliff are Persian tombs known to be at least seven centuries old by the dates still legible upon them. Beneath these tombs is a layer of debris representing a city. Further down the cliff is a second layer represent-

"Quite so," said Leo, "but that is not what you said before."

"Well, what is to be done now?" I asked, turning the conversation.

As no answer was forthcoming we proceeded to the edge of the swamp, and looked over it. It was apparently boundless, and vast flocks of every sort of waterfowl came flying from its recesses, till it was sometimes difficult to see the sky. Now that the sun was getting high it drew thin sickly-looking clouds of poisonous vapor from the surface of the marsh and from the scummy pools of stagnant water.

"Two things are clear to me," I said, addressing my three companions, who stared at this spectacle in dismay: "first, that we can't go across there"—I pointed to the swamp—"and, secondly, that if we stop here we shall certainly die of fever."

"That's as clear as a haystack, sir," said Job.

"Very well, then; there are two alternatives before us. One is to 'bout ship, and try and run for some port in the whaleboat, which would be a sufficiently risky proceeding, and the other to sail or row on up the river, and see where we come to."

"I don't know what you are going to do," said Leo, setting his mouth, "but I am going up that river."

Job turned up the whites of his eyes and groaned, and the Arab murmured, "Allah," and groaned also. As for me, I remarked sweetly that as we seemed to be between the

---

ing an older city, and further down still a third layer, the remains of yet another city of vast and unknown antiquity. Beneath the bottom city were recently found some specimens of glazed earthenware, such as are occasionally to be met with on that coast to this day. I believe that they are now in the possession of Sir John Kirk.—EDITOR.

devil and the deep sea, it did not much matter where we went. But in reality I was as anxious to proceed as Leo. The colossal Negro's head and the stone wharf had excited my curiosity to an extent of which I was secretly ashamed, and I was prepared to gratify it at any cost. Accordingly, having carefully fitted the mast, restowed the boat, and got out our rifles, we embarked. Fortunately the wind was blowing on shore from the ocean, so we were able to hoist the sail. Indeed, we afterwards found out that as a general rule the wind set on shore from daybreak for some hours, and off shore again at sunset, and the explanation that I offer of this is that when the earth is cooled by the dew and the night the hot air rises, and the draft rushes in from the sea till the sun has once more heated it through. At least that appeared to be the rule here.

Taking advantage of this favoring wind, we sailed merrily up the river for three or four hours. Once we came across a school of hippopotami, which rose, and bellowed dreadfully at us within ten or a dozen fathoms of the boat, much to Job's alarm, and, I will confess, to my own. These were the first hippopotami that we had ever seen, and, to judge by their insatiable curiosity, I should judge that we were the first white men that they had ever seen. Upon my word, I once or twice thought that they were coming into the boat to gratify it. Leo wanted to fire at them, but I dissuaded him, fearing the consequences. Also we saw hundreds of crocodiles basking on the muddy banks, and thousands upon thousands of waterfowl. Some of these we shot, and among them was a wild goose, which, in addition to the sharp curved spurs on its wings, had a spur about three-quarters of an inch long growing from the skull just between the eyes. We never shot another like it, so I do not know if it was a "sport" or a distinct species. In the latter case this incident may interest naturalists. Job named it the Unicorn Goose.

About midday the sun grew intensely hot, and the stench drawn up by it from the marshes which the river drains was something too awful, and caused us instantly to swallow precautionary doses of quinine. Shortly afterwards the breeze died away altogether, and as rowing our heavy boat against the stream in the heat was out of the question, we were thankful enough to get under the shade of a group of trees—a species of willow—that grew by the edge of the river, and lie there and gasp till at length the approach of sunset put a period to our miseries. Seeing what appeared to be an open space of water straight ahead of us, we determined to row there before settling what to do for the night. Just as we were about to loosen the boat, however, a beautiful waterbuck, with great horns curving forward, and a white stripe across the rump, came down to the river to drink, without perceiving us hidden away within fifty yards under the willows. Leo was the first to catch sight of it, and being an ardent sportsman, thirsting for the blood of big game, about which he had been dreaming for months, he instantly stiffened all over, and pointed like a setter dog. Seeing what was the matter, I handed him his express rifle, at the same time taking my own.

"Now then," I whispered, "mind you don't miss."

"Miss!" he whispered back contemptuously. "I could not miss it if I tried."

He lifted the rifle, and the roan-colored buck, having drunk his fill, raised his head and looked out across the river. He was standing right against the sunset sky on a little eminence, or ridge of ground, which ran across the swamp, evidently a favorite path for game, and there was something very beautiful about him. Indeed, I do not think that if I live to a hundred I shall ever forget that desolate and yet most fascinating scene: it is stamped upon my memory. To the right and left were wide stretches of lonely, death-breeding swamp, unbroken and unrelieved so far as the eye could reach, except here and there by ponds of black and peaty water that, mirror-like, flashed up the red rays of the setting sun. Behind us and before stretched the vista of the sluggish river, ending in glimpses of a reed-fringed lagoon, on the surface of which the long lights of the evening played as the faint breeze stirred the shadows. To the west loomed the huge red ball of the sinking sun, now vanishing down the vapory horizon, and filling the great heaven, high across whose arch the cranes and wild fowl streamed in line, square, and triangle, with flashes of flying gold and the lurid stain of blood. And then ourselves—three modern Englishmen in a modern English boat—seeming to jar upon and looking out of tone with that measureless desolation; and in front of us the noble buck limned out upon a background of ruddy sky.

Bang! Away he goes with a mighty bound. Leo has missed him. *Bang!* right under him again. Now for a shot. I must have one, though he is going like an arrow, and a hundred yards away and more. By Jove! Over and over and over! "Well, I think I've wiped your eye there, Master Leo," I say, struggling against the ungenerous exultation that in such a supreme moment of one's existence will rise in the best-mannered sportsman's breast.

"Confound you, yes," growled Leo; and then, with that quick smile that is one of his charms lighting up his handsome face like a ray of light, "I beg your pardon, old fellow. I congratulate you; it was a lovely shot, and mine were vile."

We got out of the boat and ran to the buck, which was shot through the spine and stone dead. It took us a quarter of an hour or more to clean it and cut off as much of the best meat as we could carry, and, having packed this away, we had barely light enough to row up into the lagoon-like space, into which, there being a hollow in the swamp, the river here expanded. Just as the light vanished we cast anchor about thirty fathoms from the edge of the lake. We did not dare to go ashore, not knowing if we should find dry ground to camp on, and greatly fearing the poisonous exhalations from the marsh, from which we thought we should be freer on the water. So we lighted a lantern, and made our evening meal off another potted tongue in the best fashion that we could, and then prepared to go to sleep, only, however, to find that sleep was impossible. For, whether they were attracted by the lantern, or by the un-accustomed smell of a white man, for which they had been waiting for the last thousand years or so, I know not; but certainly we were presently attacked by tens of thousands of the most bloodthirsty, pertinacious, and huge mosquitoes that I ever saw or read of. In clouds they came, and pinged and buzzed and bit till we were nearly mad. Tobacco smoke only seemed to stir them into a merrier and more active life, till at length we were driven to covering ourselves with blankets, head and all, and sitting to slowly stew and con-tinually scratch and swear beneath them. And as we sat, suddenly rolling out like thunder through the silence came the deep roar of a lion, and then of a second lion, moving among the reeds within sixty yards of us.

"I say," said Leo, sticking his head out from under his blanket, "lucky we ain't on the bank, eh, Avuncular?" (Leo sometimes addressed me in this disrespectful way.)

"Curse it! A mosquito has bitten me on the nose," and the head vanished again.

Shortly after this the moon came up, and notwithstanding every variety of roar that echoed over the water to us from the lions on the banks, we began, thinking ourselves perfectly secure, to gradually doze off.

I do not quite know what it was that made me poke my head out of the friendly shelter of the blanket; perhaps I did so because I found that the mosquitoes were biting right through it. Anyhow, as I did so I heard Job whisper, in a frightened voice, "Oh, my stars, look there!"

Instantly we all of us looked, and this was what we saw in the moonlight. Near the shore were two wide and ever widening circles of concentric rings rippling away across the surface of the water, and in the heart and center of the circles were two dark moving objects.

"What is it?" asked I.

"It is those damned lions, sir," answered Job, in a tone which was an odd mixture of a sense of personal injury, habitual respect, and acknowledged fear, "and they are swimming here to *h*eat us," he added, nervously picking up an "h" in his agitation.

I looked again, there was no doubt about it; I could catch the glare of their ferocious eyes. Attracted either by the smell of the newly killed waterbuck or of ourselves, the hungry beasts were actually storming our position.

Leo already had his rifle in his hand. I called to him to wait till they were nearer, and meanwhile grabbed my own. Some fifteen feet from us the water shallowed on a bank to the depth of about fifteen inches, and presently the first of them—it was the lioness—got onto it and shook herself and roared. At that moment Leo fired, and the bullet went right down her open mouth and out at the back of her neck, and down she dropped, with a splash, dead. The other lion—a full-grown male—was some two paces behind her. At this second he got his forepaws onto the bank, when a strange thing happened. There was a rush and disturbance of the water, such as one sees in a pond in England when a pike takes a little fish, only a thousand times fiercer and larger, and suddenly the lion gave a most terrific snarling roar and sprang forward onto the bank, dragging something black with him.

"Allah!" shouted Mahomed. "A crocodile has got him by the leg!" And sure enough he had. We could see the long snout with its gleaming lines of teeth and the reptile body behind it.

And then followed an extraordinary scene indeed. The lion managed to get well onto the bank, the crocodile half standing and half swimming, still nipping his hind leg. He roared till the air quivered with the sound, and then, with a savage, shrieking snarl, turned round and clawed hold of the crocodile's head. The crocodile shifted his grip, having, as we afterwards discovered, had one of his eyes torn out, and slightly turned over, and instantly the lion got him by the throat and held on, and then over and over they rolled upon the bank struggling hideously. It was impossible to follow their movements, but when next we got a clear view the tables had turned, for the crocodile, whose head seemed to be a mass of gore, had got the lion's body in his iron jaws just above the hips, and was squeezing him and shaking him to and fro. For his part the tortured brute, roaring in agony, was clawing and biting madly at his enemy's scaly head, and fixing his great hind claws in the crocodile's, comparatively speaking, soft throat, ripping it open as one would rip a glove.

Then, all of a sudden, the end came. The lion's head fell forward on the crocodile's back, and with an awful groan he died, and the crocodile, after standing for a minute motionless, slowly rolled over onto his side, his jaws still fixed across the carcass of the lion, which we afterwards found he had bitten almost in halves.

This duel to the death was a wonderful and a shocking sight, and one that I suppose few men have seen—and thus it ended.

When it was all over, leaving Mahomed to keep a lookout, we managed to spend the rest of the night as quietly as the mosquitoes would allow.

6 ◆

An Early Christian Ceremony

NEXT MORNING, at the earliest blush of dawn, we rose, performed such ablutions as circumstances would allow, and generally made ready to start. I am bound to say that when there was sufficient light to enable us to see each other's faces I, for one, burst out into a roar of laughter. Job's fat and comfortable countenance was swollen out to nearly twice its natural size from mosquito bites, and Leo's condition was not much better. Indeed, of the three I had come off much the best, probably owing to the toughness of my dark skin, and to the fact that a good deal of it was covered by hair, for since we started from England I had allowed my naturally luxuriant beard to grow at its own sweet will. But the other two were, comparatively speaking, clean shaved, which of course gave the enemy a larger extent of open country to operate on, though as for Mahomed the mosquitoes, recognizing the taste of a true believer, would not touch him at any price. How often, I wonder, during the next week or so did we wish that we were flavored like an Arab!

By the time that we had done laughing as heartily as our swollen lips would allow, it was daylight, and the morning breeze was coming up from the sea, cutting lanes through the dense marsh mists, and here and there rolling them before it in great balls of fleecy vapor. So we set our sail, and having first taken a look at the two dead lions and the dead crocodile, which we were of course unable to skin, being destitute of means of curing the pelts, we started, and, sailing through the lagoon, followed the course of the river on the farther side. At midday, when the breeze dropped, we were fortunate enough to find a convenient piece of dry land on which to camp and light a fire, and here we cooked two wild duck and some of the waterbuck's flesh—not in a very appetizing way, it is true, but still, sufficiently. The rest of the buck's flesh we cut into strips and hung in the sun to dry into "biltong," as I believe the South African Dutch call flesh thus prepared. On this welcome patch of dry land we stopped till the following dawn, and, as before, spent the night in warfare with the mosquitoes, but without other troubles. The next day or two passed in similar fashion, and without noticeable adventures, except that we shot a specimen of a peculiarly graceful hornless buck, and saw many varieties of water lilies in full bloom, some of them blue and of exquisite beauty, though few of the flowers were perfect, owing to the prevalence of a white water maggot with a green head that fed upon them.

It was on the fifth day of our journey, when we had traveled, so far as we could reckon, about one hundred and thirty-five to a hundred and forty miles westwards from the coast, that the first event of any real importance occurred. On that morning the usual wind failed us about eleven o'clock, and after pulling a little way we were forced to halt more or less exhausted at what appeared to be the junction of our stream with another of a uniform width of about fifty feet. Some trees grew near at hand—the only trees in all this country were along the banks of the river, and under these we rested, and then, the land being fairly dry just here, walked a little way along the edge of the river

to prospect, and shoot a few waterfowl for food. Before
we had gone fifty yards we perceived that all hopes of
getting further up the stream in the whaleboat were at an
end, for not two hundred yards above where we had stopped
were a succession of shallows and mudbanks, with not six
inches of water over them. It was a watery cul-de-sac.

Turning back, we walked some way along the banks
of the other river, and soon came to the conclusion, from
various indications, that it was not a river at all, but
an ancient canal, like the one which is to be seen above
Mombasa, on the Zanzibar coast, connecting the Tana River
with the Ozy, in such a way as to enable the shipping coming down the Tana to cross to the Ozy, and reach the sea by
it, and thus avoid the very dangerous bar that blocks the
mouth of the Tana. The canal before us had evidently
been dug out by man at some remote period of the world's
history, and the results of his digging still remained in the
shape of the raised banks that had no doubt once formed
towing-paths. Except here and there, where they had been
hollowed out or fallen in, these banks of stiff binding clay
were at a uniform distance from each other, and the depth
of the water also appeared to be uniform. Current there
was little or none, and, as a consequence, the surface of the
canal was choked with vegetable growth, intersected by little
paths of clear water, made, I suppose, by the constant passage of waterfowl, iguanas, and other vermin. Now, as it
was evident that we could not proceed up the river, it
became equally evident that we must either try the canal or
else return to the sea. We could not stop where we were,
to be baked by the sun and eaten up by the mosquitoes,
till we died of fever in that dreary marsh.

"Well, I suppose that we must try it," I said; and the
others assented in their various ways—Leo as though it

were the best joke in the world; Job in respectful disgust; and Mahomed with an invocation to the Prophet and a comprehensive curse upon all unbelievers and their ways of thought and travel.

Accordingly, as soon as the sun got low, having little or nothing more to hope for from our friendly wind, we started. For the first hour or so we managed to row the boat, though with great labor; but after that the weeds got too thick to allow it, and we were obliged to resort to the primitive and most exhausting resource of towing her. For two hours we labored, Mahomed, Job, and I, who was supposed to be strong enough to pull against the two of them, on the bank, while Leo sat in the bow of the boat, and brushed away the weeds which collected round the cutwater with Mahomed's sword. At dark we halted for some hours to rest and enjoy the mosquitoes, but about midnight we went on again, taking advantage of the comparative cool of the night. At dawn we rested for three hours, and then started once more, and labored on till about ten o'clock, when a thunderstorm, accompanied by a deluge of rain, overtook us, and we spent the next six hours practically under water.

I do not know that there is any necessity for me to describe the next four days of our voyage in detail, further than to say that they were, on the whole, the most miserable that I ever spent in my life, forming one monotonous record of heavy labor, heat, misery, and mosquitoes. All the way we passed through a region of almost endless swamp, and I can only attribute our escape from fever and death to the constant doses of quinine and purgatives which we took, and the unceasing toil which we were forced to undergo. On the third day of our journey up the canal we had sighted a round hill that loomed dimly through the vapors of the marsh, and on the evening of the fourth night, when we camped, this hill seemed to be within five-and-twenty or thirty miles of us. We were by now utterly exhausted, and felt as though our blistered hands could not pull the boat a yard further, and that the best thing that we could do would be to lie down and die in that dreadful wilderness of swamp. It was an awful position, and one in which I trust no other white man will ever be placed; and as I threw myself down in the boat to sleep the sleep of utter exhaustion, I bitterly cursed my folly in ever having been a party to such a mad undertaking, which could, I saw, only end in our death in this ghastly land. I thought, I remember, as I slowly sank into a doze, of what the appearance of the boat and her unhappy crew would be in two or three months' time from that night. There she would lie, with gaping seams and half filled with fetid water, which, when the mist-laden wind stirred her, would wash backwards and forwards through our moldering bones, and that would be the end of her, and of those in her who would follow after myths and seek out the secrets of nature.

Already I seemed to hear the water rippling against the desiccated bones and rattling them together, rolling my skull against Mahomed's, and his against mine, till at last Mahomed's stood straight up upon its vertebrae, and glared at me through its empty eyeholes, and cursed me with its grinning jaws, because I, a dog of a Christian, disturbed the last sleep of a true believer. I opened my eyes, and shuddered at the horrid dream, and then shuddered again at something that was not a dream, for two great eyes were gleaming down at me through the misty darkness. I struggled up, and in my terror and confusion shrieked, and shrieked again, so that the others sprang up too, reeling, and drunken with sleep and fear. And then all of a sudden there was a flash of cold steel, and a great spear was held against my throat, and behind it other spears gleamed cruelly.

"Peace," said a voice, speaking in Arabic, or rather in some dialect into which Arabic entered very largely. "Who are ye who come hither swimming on the water? Speak or ye die," and the steel pressed sharply against my throat, sending a cold chill through me.

"We are travelers, and have come hither by chance," I answered in my best Arabic, which appeared to be understood, for the man turned his head, and, addressing a tall form that towered up in the background, said, "Father, shall we slay?"

"What is the color of the men?" said a deep voice in answer.

"White is their color."

"Slay not," was the reply. "Four suns since was the word brought to me from 'She-who-must-be-obeyed,' 'White men come; if white men come, slay them not.' Let them be brought to the land of 'She-who-must-be-obeyed.' Bring forth the men, and let that which they have with them be brought forth also."

"Come," said the man, half leading and half dragging me from the boat, and as he did so I perceived other men doing the same kind office to my companions.

On the bank were gathered a company of some fifty men. In that light all I could make out was that they were armed with huge spears, were very tall, and strongly built, comparatively light in color, and nude, save for a leopard skin tied round the middle.

Presently Leo and Job were bundled out and placed beside me.

"What on earth is up?" said Leo, rubbing his eyes.

"Oh, Lord, sir, here's a rum go," ejaculated Job; and just at that moment a disturbance ensued, and Mahomed came tumbling between us, followed by a shadowy form with an uplifted spear.

"Allah! Allah!" howled Mahomed, feeling that he had little to hope from man. "Protect me! Protect me!"

"Father, it is a black one," said a voice. "What said 'She-who-must-be-obeyed' about the black one?"

"She said naught; but slay him not. Come hither, my son."

The man advanced, and the tall shadowy form bent forward and whispered something.

"Yes, yes," said the other, and chuckled in a rather blood-curdling tone.

"Are the three white men there?" asked the form.

"Yes, they are there."

"Then bring up that which is made ready for them, and let the men take all that can be brought from the thing which floats."

Hardly had he spoken when men came running up, carrying on their shoulders neither more nor less than palanquins—four bearers and two spare men to a palanquin —and in these it was promptly indicated we were expected to stow ourselves.

"Well!" said Leo. "It is a blessing to find anybody to carry us after having to carry ourselves so long."

Leo always takes a cheerful view of things.

There being no help for it, after seeing the others into theirs I tumbled into my own litter, and very comfortable I found it. It appeared to be manufactured of cloth woven from grass fiber, which stretched and yielded to every motion after the body, and, being bound top and bottom to the bearing pole, gave a grateful support to the head and neck.

Scarcely had I settled myself when, accompanying their steps with a monotonous song, the bearers started at a swinging trot. For half an hour or so I lay still, reflecting on the very remarkable experiences that we were going through, and wondering if any of my eminently respectable fossil friends down at Cambridge would believe me if I were to be miraculously set at the familiar dinner table for the purpose of relating them. I don't want to convey any disrespectful notion or slight when I call those good and learned men fossils, but my experience is that people are apt to fossilize even at a university if they follow the same paths too persistently. I was getting fossilized myself, but of late my stock of ideas has been very much enlarged. Well, I lay and reflected, and wondered what on earth would be the end of it all, till at last I ceased to wonder, and went to sleep.

I suppose I must have slept for seven or eight hours, getting the first real rest that I had had since the night before the loss of the dhow, for when I woke the sun was high in the heavens. We were still journeying on at a pace of about four miles an hour. Peeping out through the mistlike curtains of the litter, which were ingeniously fixed to the bearing pole, I perceived to my infinite relief that we had passed out of the region of eternal swamp, and were now traveling over swelling grassy plains towards a cup-shaped hill. Whether or not it was the same hill that we had seen from the canal I do not know, and have never since been able to discover, for, as we afterwards found out, these people will give little information upon such points. Next I glanced at the men who were bearing me. They were of a magnificent build, few of them being under six feet in height, and yellowish in color. Generally their appearance had a good deal in common with that of the East African Somali, only their hair was not frizzed up, and hung in thick black locks upon their shoulders. Their features were aquiline, and in many cases exceedingly handsome, the teeth being especially regular and beautiful. But notwithstanding their beauty, it struck me that, on the whole, I had never seen a more evil-looking set of faces. There was an aspect of cold and sullen cruelty stamped upon them that revolted me, and which in some cases was almost uncanny in its intensity.

Another thing which struck me about them was that they never seemed to smile. Sometimes they sang the monoto-nous song of which I have spoken, but when they were not singing they remained almost perfectly silent, and the light of a laugh never came to brighten their somber and evil countenances. Of what race could these people be? Their language was a bastard Arabic, and yet they were not Arabs; I was quite sure of that. For one thing they were too dark, or rather yellow. I could not say why, but I know that their appearance filled me with a sick fear of which I felt ashamed. While I was still wondering another litter came up alongside of mine. In it—for the curtains were drawn—sat an old man, clothed in a whitish robe, made apparently from coarse linen, that hung loosely about him, who, I at once jumped to the conclusion, was the shadowy figure who had stood on the bank and been ad-dressed as "Father." He was a wonderful-looking old man, with a snowy beard, so long that the ends of it hung over the sides of the litter, and he had a hooked nose, above which flashed out a pair of eyes as keen as a snake's, while his whole countenance was instinct with a look of wise and sardonic humor impossible to describe on paper.

"Art thou awake, stranger?" he said in a deep and low voice.

"Surely, my father," I answered courteously, feeling certain that I should do well to conciliate this ancient Mammon of Unrighteousness.

He stroked his beautiful white beard, and smiled faintly.

"From whatever country thou camest," he said, "and by the way it must be from one where somewhat of our language is known, they teach their children courtesy there, my stranger son. And now wherefore comest thou unto this land, which scarce an alien foot has pressed from the time that man knoweth? Art thou and those with thee weary of life?"

"We came to find new things," I answered boldly. "We are tired of the old things; we have come up out of the sea to know that which is unknown. We are of a brave race who fear not death, my very much respected father— that is, if we can get a little fresh information before we die."

"Humph!" said the old gentleman. "That may be true; it is rash to contradict, otherwise I should say that thou wast lying, my son. However, I dare say that '*She-who-must-be-obeyed*' will meet thy wishes in the matter."

"Who is '*She-who-must-be-obeyed*'?" I asked curiously.

The old man glanced at the bearers, and then answered, with a little smile that somehow sent my blood to my heart, "Surely, my stranger son, thou wilt learn soon enough, if it be her pleasure to see thee at all in the flesh."

"In the flesh?" I answered. "What may my father wish to convey?"

But the old man only laughed a dreadful laugh, and made no reply.

"What is the name of my father's people?" I asked.

"The name of my people is Amahagger" (the People of the Rocks).

"And if a son might ask, what is the name of my father?"

"My name is Billali."

"And whither go we, my father?"

"That shalt thou see," and at a sign from him his bearers started forward at a run till they reached the litter in which Job was reposing (with one leg hanging over the side). Apparently, however, he could not make much out of Job, for presently I saw his bearers trot forward to Leo's litter.

And after that, as nothing fresh occurred, I yielded to the pleasant swaying motion of the litter, and went to sleep again. I was dreadfully tired. When I woke I found that we were passing through a rocky defile of a lava formation with precipitous sides, in which grew many beautiful trees and flowering shrubs.

Presently this defile took a turn, and a lovely sight unfolded itself to my eyes. Before us was a vast cup of green from four to six miles in extent, of the shape of a Roman amphitheater. The sides of this great cup were rocky, and clothed with bush, but the center was of the richest meadow land, studded with single trees of magnificent growth, and watered by meandering brooks. On this rich plain grazed herds of goats and cattle, but I saw no sheep. At first I could not imagine what this strange spot could be, but presently it flashed upon me that it must represent the crater of some long-extinct volcano, which had afterwards been a lake, and was ultimately drained in some unexplained way. And here I may state that from my subsequent experience of this and a much larger, but otherwise similar spot, which I shall have occasion to describe by and by, I have every reason to believe that this conclusion was correct. What puzzled me, however, was that, although there were people moving about herding the goats and cattle, I saw no signs of any human habitation. Where did they all live? I wondered. My curiosity was soon destined to be gratified. Turning to the left the string of litters followed the cliffy sides of the crater for a distance of about half a mile, or perhaps a little less, and then halted. Seeing the old gentleman, my adopted "father," Billali, emerge from his litter, I did the same, and so did Leo and Job. The first thing I saw was our wretched Arab companion, Mahomed, lying exhausted on the ground. It appeared that he had not been provided with a litter, but had been forced to run the entire distance, and, as he was already quite worn out when we started, his condition now was one of great prostration.

On looking round we discovered that the place where we had halted was a platform in front of the mouth of a great cave, and piled upon this platform were the entire contents of the whaleboat, even down to the oars and sail. Round the cave stood groups of the men who had escorted us, and other men of a similar stamp. They were all tall and all handsome, though they varied in their degree of darkness of skin, some being as dark as Mahomed, and some as yellow as a Chinese. They were naked, except for the leopard skin round the waist, and each of them carried a huge spear.

There were also some women among them, who, instead of the leopard skin, wore a tanned hide of a small red buck, something like that of the oribé, only rather darker in color. These women were, as a class, exceedingly good-looking, with large, dark eyes, well-cut features, and a thick bush of curling hair—not crisped like a Negro's—ranging from black to chestnut in hue, with all shades of intermediate color. Some, but very few of them, wore a yellowish linen garment, such as I have described as worn by Billali, but this, as we afterwards discovered, was a mark of rank, rather than an attempt at clothing. For the rest, their appearance was not quite so terrifying as that of the men, and they sometimes, though rarely, smiled. As soon as we had alighted they gathered round us and examined us with curiosity, but without excitement. Leo's tall, athletic form and clear-cut Grecian face, however, evidently excited their attention, and when he politely lifted his hat to them, and showed his curling yellow hair, there was a slight murmur of admiration. Nor did it stop there; for, after regarding him critically from head to foot, the handsomest of the young women—one wearing a robe, and with hair of a shade between brown and chestnut—deliberately advanced to him, and, in a way that would have been winning had it not been so determined, quietly put her arm round his neck, bent forward, and kissed him on the lips.

I gave a gasp, expecting to see Leo instantly speared; and Job ejaculated, "The hussy—well, I never!" As for Leo, he looked slightly astonished; and then, remarking that we had got into a country where they clearly followed the customs of the early Christians, deliberately returned the embrace.

Again I gasped, thinking that something would happen; but to my surprise, though some of the young women showed traces of vexation, the older ones and the men only smiled slightly. When we came to understand the customs of this extraordinary people the mystery was explained. It then appeared that, in direct opposition to the habits of almost every other savage race in the world, women among the Amahagger are not only upon terms of perfect equality with the men, but are not held to them by any binding ties. Descent is traced only through the line of the mother, and while individuals are as proud of a long and superior female ancestry as we are of our families in Europe, they never pay attention to, or even acknowledge, any man as their father, even when their male parentage is perfectly well known. There is but one titular male parent of each tribe, or, as they call it, "household," and he is its elected and immediate ruler, with the title of "father." For instance, the man Billali was the father of this "household," which consisted of about seven thousand individuals all told, and no other man was ever called by that name. When a woman took a fancy to a man she signified her preference by advancing and embracing him publicly, in the same way that this handsome and exceedingly prompt young lady, who was called Ustane, had embraced Leo. If he kissed her back it was a token that he accepted her, and the arrangement continued till one of them wearied of it. I am bound, however, to say that the change of husbands was not nearly so frequent as might have been expected. Nor did quarrels arise out of it, at least among the men, who, when their wives deserted them in favor of a rival, accepted the whole thing much as we accept the income tax or our marriage laws, as something not to be disputed, and as tending to the good of the community, however disagreeable they may in particular instances prove to the individual.

It is very curious to observe how the customs of mankind on this matter vary in different countries, making morality an affair of latitude, and what is right and proper in one place wrong and improper in another. It must, however, be understood that, as all civilized nations appear to accept it as an axiom that ceremony is the touchstone of morality, there is, even according to our canons, nothing immoral about this Amahagger custom, seeing that the interchange of the embrace answers to our ceremony of marriage, which, as we know, justifies most things.

7 ♦

Ustane Sings

WHEN THE kissing operation was finished—by the way, none of the young ladies offered to pet me in this fashion, though I saw one hovering round Job, to that respectable individual's evident alarm—the old man Billali advanced, and graciously waved us into the cave, whither we went, followed by Ustane, who did not seem inclined to take the hints I gave her that we liked privacy.

Before we had gone five paces it struck me that the cave that we were entering was none of Nature's handiwork, but, on the contrary, had been hollowed by the hand of man. So far as we could judge it appeared to be about one hundred feet in length by fifty wide, and very lofty, resembling a cathedral aisle more than anything else. From this main aisle opened passages at a distance of every twelve or fifteen feet, leading, I supposed, to smaller chambers. About fifty feet from the entrance of the cave, just where the light began to get dim, a fire was burning, which threw huge shadows upon the gloomy walls around. Here Billali halted, and asked us to be seated, saying that the people would bring us food, and accordingly we squatted ourselves down upon the rugs of skins which were spread for us, and waited. Presently the food, consisting of goat's flesh boiled, fresh milk in an earthenware pot, and boiled cobs of Indian corn, was brought by young girls. We were almost starving, and I do not think that I ever in my life before ate with such satisfaction. Indeed, before we had finished we literally ate up everything that was set before us.

When we had done, our somewhat saturnine host, Billali, who had been watching us in perfect silence, rose and addressed us. He said that it was a wonderful thing that had happened. No man had ever known or heard of white strangers arriving in the country of the People of the Rocks. Sometimes, though rarely, black men had come here, and from them they had heard of the existence of men much whiter than themselves, who sailed on the sea in ships, but for the arrival of such there was no precedent. We had, however, been seen dragging the boat up the canal, and he told us frankly that he had at once given orders for our destruction, seeing that it was unlawful for any stranger to enter here, when a message had come from "She-who-must-be-obeyed," saying that our lives were to be spared, and that we were to be brought hither.

"Pardon me, my father," I interrupted at this point; "but if, as I understand, 'She-who-must-be-obeyed' lives yet farther off, how could she have known of our approach?"

Billali turned, and seeing that we were alone—for the young lady, Ustane, had withdrawn when he had begun to speak—said, with a curious little laugh, "Are there none in your land who can see without eyes and hear without ears? Ask no questions; She knew."

I shrugged my shoulders at this, and he proceeded to say that no further instructions had been received on the subject of our disposal, and this being so he was about to start to interview "She-who-must-be-obeyed," generally spoken of, for the sake of brevity, simply as "Hiya" or She, who he gave us to understand was the Queen of the Ama- hagger, and learn her wishes.

I asked him how long he proposed to be away, and he said that by traveling hard he might be back on the fifth day, but there were many miles of marsh to cross before he came to where *She* was. He then said that every arrangement would be made for our comfort during his absence, and that, as he personally had taken a fancy to us, he sincerely trusted that the answer he should bring from *She* would be one favorable to the continuation of our existence, but at the same time he did not wish to conceal from us that he thought this doubtful, as every stranger who had ever come into the country during his grandmother's life, his mother's life, and his own life, had been put to death without mercy, and in a way that he would not harrow our feelings by describing; and this had been done by the order of *She* herself, at least he supposed it was by her order. At any rate, she never interfered to save them.

"Why," I said, "but how can that be? You are an old man, and the time you talk of must reach back three men's lives. How therefore could *She* have ordered the death of anybody at the beginning of the life of your grandmother, seeing that she herself would not have been born?"

Again he smiled—that same faint, peculiar smile—and with a deep bow departed, without making any answer; nor did we see him again for five days.

When he had gone we discussed the situation, which filled me with alarm. I did not at all like the accounts of this mysterious Queen, *"She-who-must-be-obeyed,"* or more shortly *She*, who apparently ordered the execution of any unfortunate stranger in a fashion so unmerciful. Leo, too, was depressed about it, but proceeded to console himself by triumphantly pointing out that this *She* was undoubtedly the person referred to in the writing on the potsherd and in his father's letter, in proof of which he advanced Billali's allusions to her age and power. I was by this time so overwhelmed with the whole course of events that I had not even got the heart left to dispute a proposition so absurd, so I suggested that we should try and go out and get a bath, of which we all stood sadly in need.

Accordingly, having indicated our wish to a middle-aged individual of an unusually saturnine cast of countenance, even among this saturnine people, who appeared to be deputed to look after us now that the father of the hamlet had departed, we started in a body—having first lit our pipes. Outside the cave we found quite a crowd of people evidently watching for our appearance, but when they saw us come out smoking they vanished this way and that, calling out that we were great magicians. Indeed, nothing about us created so great a sensation as our tobacco smoke—not even our firearms.[1] After this we succeeded in reaching a stream that had its source in a strong ground spring, and taking our bath in peace, though some of the women, not excepting Ustane, showed a decided inclination to follow us even there.

By the time that we had finished this most refreshing bath the sun was setting; indeed, when we got back to the big cave it had already set. The cave itself was full of people gathered round fires—for several more had now been lighted—and eating their evening meal by their lurid light, and by that of various lamps which were set about or hung upon the walls. These lamps were of a rude manufacture of baked earthenware, and of all shapes, some of them

[1] We found tobacco growing in this country as it does in every other part of Africa, and, although they are so absolutely ignorant of its other blessed qualities, the Amahagger use it habitually in the form of snuff, and also for medicinal purposes.—L. H. H.

graceful enough. The larger ones were formed of big red earthenware pots, filled with clarified melted fat, and having a reed wick stuck through a wooden disk which filled the top of the pot, and this sort of lamp required the most constant attention to prevent its going out whenever the wick burned down, as there were no means of turning it up. The smaller hand lamps, however, which were also made of baked clay, were fitted with wicks manufactured from the pith of a palm tree, or sometimes from the stem of a very handsome variety of fern. This kind of wick was passed through a round hole at the end of the lamp, to which a sharp piece of hard wood was attached wherewith to pierce and draw it up whenever it showed signs of burning low.

For a while we sat down and watched this grim people eating their evening meal in silence as grim as themselves, till at length, getting tired of contemplating them and the huge moving shadows on the rocky walls, I suggested to our new keeper that we should like to go to bed.

Without a word he rose, and, taking me politely by the hand, advanced with a lamp to one of the small passages that I had noticed opening out of the central cave. This we followed for about five paces, when it suddenly widened out into a small chamber, about eight feet square, and hewn out of the living rock. On one side of this chamber was a stone slab, about three feet from the ground, and running its entire length like a bunk in a cabin, and on this slab he intimated that I was to sleep. There was no window or air hole to the chamber, and no furniture; and, on looking at it more closely, I came to the disturbing conclusion (in which, as I afterwards discovered, I was quite right) that it had originally served for a sepulcher for the dead rather than a sleeping place for the living, the slab being designed to receive the corpse of the departed. The thought made me shudder in spite of myself; but, seeing that I must sleep somewhere, I got over the feeling as best I might, and returned to the cavern to get my blanket, which had been brought up from the boat with the other things. There I met Job, who, having been inducted to a similar apartment, had flatly declined to stop in it, saying that the look of the place gave him the horrors, and that he might as well be dead and buried in his grandfather's brick grave at once, and expressed his determination of sleeping with me if I would allow him. This, of course, I was only too glad to do.

The night passed very comfortably on the whole. I say on the whole, for personally I went through a most horrible nightmare of being buried alive, induced, no doubt, by the sepulchral nature of my surroundings. At dawn we were aroused by a loud trumpeting sound, produced, as we afterwards discovered, by a young Amahagger blowing through a hole bored in its side into a hollowed elephant tusk, which was kept for the purpose.

Taking the hint, we got up and went down to the stream to wash, after which the morning meal was served. At breakfast one of the women, no longer quite young, advanced, and publicly kissed Job. I think it was in its way the most delightful thing (putting its impropriety aside for a moment) that I ever saw. Never shall I forget the respectable Job's abject terror and disgust. Job, like myself, is a bit of a misogynist—I fancy chiefly owing to the fact of his having been one of a family of seventeen—and the feelings expressed upon his countenance when he realized that he was not only being embraced publicly, and without authorization on his own part, but also in the presence of his masters, were too mixed and painful to admit of accurate description. He sprang to his feet, and pushed the woman, a buxom person of about thirty, from him.

"Well, I never!" he gasped, whereupon, probably thinking that he was only coy, she embraced him again.

"Be off with you! Get away, you minx!" he shouted, waving the wooden spoon, with which he was eating his breakfast, up and down before the lady's face. "Beg your pardon, gentlemen, I am sure I haven't encouraged her. Oh, Lord! She's coming for me again. Hold her, Mr. Holly! Please hold her! I can't stand it; I can't, indeed. This has never happened to me before, gentlemen, never. There's nothing against my character," and here he broke off, and ran as hard as he could go down the cave, and for once I saw the Amahagger laugh. As for the woman, however, she did not laugh. On the contrary, she seemed to bristle with fury, which the mockery of the other women about only served to intensify. She stood there literally snarling and shaking with indignation, and, seeing her, I wished Job's scruples had been at Jericho, forming a shrewd guess that his admirable behavior had endangered our throats. Nor, as the sequel shows, was I wrong.

The lady having retreated, Job returned in a great state of nervousness, and keeping his weather eye fixed upon every woman who came near him. I took an opportunity to explain to our hosts that Job was a married man, and had had very unhappy experiences in his domestic relations, which accounted for his presence here and his terror at the sight of women, but my remarks were received in grim silence, it being evident that our retainer's behavior was considered as a slight to the "household" at large, although the women, after the manner of some of their more civilized sisters, made merry at the rebuff of their companion.

After breakfast we took a walk and inspected the Ama-hagger herds, and also their cultivated lands. They have two breeds of cattle, one large and angular, with no horns, but yielding beautiful milk; and the other, a red breed, very small and fat, excellent for meat, but of no value for milking purposes. This last breed closely resembles the Norfolk red-pole strain, only it has horns which generally curve forward over the head, sometimes to such an extent that they have to be cut to prevent them from growing into the bones of the skull. The goats are long-haired, and are used for eating only, at least I never saw them milked. As for the Amahagger cultivation, it is primitive in the extreme, being all done by means of a spade made of iron, for these people smelt and work iron. This spade is shaped more like a big spear head than anything else, and has no shoulder to it on which the foot can be set. As a consequence, the labor of digging is very great. It is, however, all done by the men, the women, contrary to the habits of most savage races, being entirely exempt from manual toil. But then, as I think I have said elsewhere, among the Amahagger the weaker sex has established its rights.

At first we were much puzzled as to the origin and constitution of this extraordinary race, points upon which they were singularly uncommunicative. As the time went on— for the next four days passed without any striking event —we learned something from Leo's lady friend Ustane, who, by the way, stuck to that young gentleman like his own shadow. As to origin, they had none, at least, so far as she was aware. There were, however, she informed us, mounds of masonry and many pillars near the place where *She* lived, which was called Kôr, and which the wise said had once been houses wherein men lived, and it was suggested that they were descended from these men. No one, however, dared go near these great ruins, because they were haunted: they only looked on them from a distance. Other similar ruins were to be seen, she had heard, in various parts of the country, that is, wherever one of the mountains rose above the level of the swamp. Also, the caves in which they lived had been hollowed out of the rocks by men, perhaps the same who built the cities. They themselves had no written laws, only custom, which was, however, quite as binding as law. If any man offended against the custom, he was put to death by order of the father of the "household." I asked how he was put to death, and she only smiled, and said that I might see one day soon.

They had a queen, however. *She* was their queen, but she was very rarely seen, perhaps once in two or three years, when she came forth to pass sentence on some offenders, and when seen was muffled up in a big cloak, so that nobody could look upon her face. Those who waited upon her were deaf and dumb, and therefore could tell no tales, but it was reported that she was lovely as no other woman was lovely, or ever had been. It was rumored also that she was immortal, and had power over all things, but she, Ustane, could say nothing of all that. What she believed was that the Queen chose a husband from time to time, and as soon as a female child was born this husband, who was never again seen, was put to death. Then the female child grew up and took the place of the Queen when its mother died, and had been buried in the great caves. But of these matters none could speak for certain. Only *She* was obeyed throughout the length and breadth of the land, and to question her command was certain death. She kept a guard, but had no regular army, and to disobey her was to die.

I asked what size the land was, and how many people lived in it. She answered that there were ten "households," like this that she knew of, including the big "household," where the Queen was, that all the "households" lived in caves, in places resembling this stretch of raised country, dotted about in a vast extent of swamp, which was only to be threaded by secret paths. Often the "households" made war on each other until *She* sent word that it was to stop, and then they instantly ceased. That and the fever which they caught in crossing the swamps prevented their numbers from increasing too much. They had no connection with any other race, indeed, none lived near them, or were able to thread the vast swamps. Once an army from the direction of the great river (presumably the Zambesi) had attempted to attack them, but they got lost in the marshes, and at night, seeing the great balls of fire that move about there, tried to come to them, thinking that they marked the enemy's camp, and half of them were drowned. As for the rest, they soon died of fever and starvation, not a blow being struck at them. The marshes, she told us, were absolutely impassable except to those who knew the paths, adding, what I could well believe, that we should never have reached this place where we then were had we not been brought thither.

These and many other things we learned from Ustane during the four days' pause before our real adventures began, and, as may be imagined, they gave us considerable cause for thought. The whole thing was exceedingly remarkable, almost incredibly so, indeed, and the oddest part of it was that so far it did more or less correspond to the ancient writing on the sherd. And now it appeared that there was a mysterious queen clothed by rumor with dread and wonderful attributes, and commonly known by the impersonal but, to my mind, rather awesome title of *She*. Altogether, I could not make it out, nor could Leo, though of course he was exceedingly triumphant over me because I had persistently mocked at the whole thing. As for Job, he had long since abandoned any attempt to call his reason his own, and left it to drift upon the sea of circumstance. Mahomed, the Arab, who was, by the way, treated civilly indeed, but with chilling contempt, by the Amahagger, was, I discovered, in a great fright, though I could not quite make out what he was frightened about. He would sit crouched up in a corner of the cave all day long, calling upon Allah and the Prophet to protect him. When I pressed him about it, he said that he was afraid because these people were not men and women at all, but devils, and that this was an enchanted land; and, upon my word, once or twice since then I have been inclined to agree with him. And so the time went on, till the night of the fourth day after Billali had left, when something happened.

We three and Ustane were sitting round a fire in the cave just before bedtime, when suddenly the woman, who had been brooding in silence, rose, and laid her hand upon Leo's golden curls, and addressed him. Even now, when I shut my eyes, I can see her proud, imperial form, clothed alternately in dense shadow and the red flickering of the fire, as she stood, the wild center of as weird a scene as I ever witnessed, and delivered herself of the burden of her thoughts and forebodings in a kind of rhythmical speech that ran something as follows:

> *Thou art my chosen—I have waited for thee from the beginning!*
> *Thou art very beautiful. Who hath hair like unto thee, or skin so white?*

Who hath so strong an arm, who is so much a man?

Thine eyes are the sky, and the light in them is the stars.

Thou art perfect and of a happy face, and my heart turned itself towards thee.

Ay, when mine eyes fell on thee I did desire thee,—

Then did I take thee to me—thou, my Beloved,

And hold thee fast, lest harm should come unto thee.

Ay, I did cover thine head with mine hair, lest the sun should strike it;

And altogether was I thine, and thou wast altogether mine.

And so it went for a little space, till Time was in labor with an evil Day;

And then what befell on that day? Alas! my Beloved, I know not!

But I, I saw thee no more—I, I was lost in the blackness.

And she who is stronger did take thee; ay, she who is fairer than Ustane.

Yet didst thou turn and call upon me, and let thine eyes wander in the darkness.

But, nevertheless, she prevailed by Beauty, and led thee down horrible places,

And then, ah! then my Beloved——

Here this extraordinary woman broke off her speech, or chant, which was so much musical gibberish to us, for all that we understood of what she was talking about, and seemed to fix her flashing eyes upon the deep shadow before her. Then in a moment they acquired a vacant, terrified stare, as though they were striving to realize some half-seen horror. She lifted her hand from Leo's head, and pointed into the darkness. We all looked, and could see nothing; but she saw something, or thought she did, and something evidently that affected even her iron nerves, for, without another sound, down she fell senseless between us.

Leo, who was growing really attached to this remarkable young person, was in a great state of alarm and distress, and I, to be perfectly candid, was in a condition not far removed from superstitious fear. The whole scene was an uncanny one.

Presently, however, she recovered, and sat up with an extraordinary convulsive shudder.

"What didst thou mean, Ustane?" asked Leo, who, thanks to years of tuition, spoke Arabic very prettily.

"Nay, my chosen," she answered with a little forced laugh. "I did but sing unto thee after the fashion of my people. Surely, I meant nothing. How could I speak of that which is not yet?"

"And what didst thou see, Ustane?" I asked, looking her sharply in the face.

"Nay," she answered again; "I saw naught. Ask me not what I saw. Why should I fright ye?" And then, turning to Leo with a look of the most utter tenderness that I ever saw upon the face of a woman, civilized or savage, she took his head between her hands, and kissed him on the forehead as a mother might. "When I am gone from thee, my chosen; when at night thou stretchest out thine hand and canst not find me, then shouldst thou think at times of me, for of a truth I love thee well, though I be not fit to wash thy feet. And now let us love and take that which is given us, and be happy; for in the grave there is no love and no warmth, nor any touching of the lips. Nothing perchance, or perchance but bitter memories of what might have been. Tonight the hours are our own, how know we to whom they shall belong tomorrow?"

The Feast, and After!

ON THE DAY following this remarkable scene—a scene calculated to make a deep impression upon anybody who beheld it, more because of what it suggested and seemed to foreshadow than of what it revealed—it was announced to us that a feast would be held that evening in our honor. I did my best to get out of it, saying that we were modest people, and cared little for feasts, but my remarks being received with the silence of displeasure, I thought it wisest to hold my tongue.

Accordingly, just before sundown, I was informed that everything was ready, and, accompanied by Job, went into the cave, where I met Leo, who was, as usual, followed by Ustane. These two had been out walking somewhere, and knew nothing of the projected festivity till that moment. When Ustane heard of it I saw an expression of horror spring up upon her handsome features. Turning, she caught a man who was passing up the cave by the arm, and asked him something in an imperious tone. His answer seemed to reassure her a little, for she looked relieved, though far from satisfied. Next she appeared to attempt some remonstrance with the man, who was a person in authority, but he spoke angrily to her, and shook her off, and then changing his mind, led her by the arm, and sat her down between himself and another man in the circle

110

round the fire, and I perceived that for some reason of her own she thought it best to submit.

The fire in the cave was an unusually big one that night, and in a large circle round it were gathered about thirty-five men and two women, Ustane and the woman to avoid whom Job had played the role of another Scriptural character. The men were sitting in perfect silence, as was their custom, each with his great spear stuck upright behind him, in a socket cut in the rock for that purpose. Only one or two wore the yellowish linen garment of which I have spoken, the rest had nothing on except the leopard's skin about the middle.

"What's up now, sir?" said Job doubtfully. "Bless us and save us, there's that woman again. Now, surely, she can't be after me, seeing that I have given her no encouragement. They give me the creeps, the whole lot of them, and that's a fact. Why, look, they have asked Mahomed to dine, too. There, that lady of mine is talking to him in as nice and civil a way as possible. Well, I'm glad it isn't me, that's all."

We looked up, and sure enough the woman in question had risen, and was escorting the wretched Mahomed from the corner, where, overcome by some acute prescience of horror, he had been seated, shivering, and calling on Allah. He appeared unwilling enough to come, if for no other reason perhaps because it was an unaccustomed honor, for hitherto his food had been given to him apart. Anyway I could see that he was in a state of great terror, for his tottering legs would scarcely support his stout, bulky form, and I think it was rather owing to the resources of barbarism behind him, in the shape of a huge Amahagger with a proportionately huge spear, than to the seduction of the lady who led him by the hand, that he consented to come at all.

"Well," I said to the others, "I don't at all like the look of things, but I suppose that we must face it out. Have you fellows got your revolvers on? Because, if so, you had better see that they are loaded."

"I have, sir," said Job, tapping his Colt, "but Mr. Leo has only got his hunting knife, though that is big enough, surely."

Feeling that it would not do to wait while the missing weapon was fetched, we advanced boldly, and seated ourselves in a line, with our backs against the side of the cave.

As soon as we were seated, an earthenware jar was passed round containing a fermented fluid, of by no means unpleasant taste, though apt to turn upon the stomach, made of crushed grain—not Indian corn, but a small brown grain that grows upon the stem in clusters, not unlike that which in the southern part of Africa is known by the name of Kafir corn. The vase in which this liquid was handed round was very curious, and as it more or less resembled many hundreds of others in use among the Amahagger I may as well describe it. These vases are of a very ancient manufacture, and of all sizes. None such can have been made in the country for hundreds, or rather thousands, of years. They are found in the rock tombs, of which I shall give a description in their proper place, and my own belief is that, after the fashion of the Egyptians, with whom the former inhabitants of this country may have had some connection, they were used to receive the viscera of the dead. Leo, however, is of opinion that, as in the case of Etruscan amphorae, they were placed there for the spiritual use of the deceased. They are mostly two-handled, and of all sizes, some being nearly three feet in height, and running from that down to as many inches. In shape they vary, but are all exceedingly beautiful and graceful, being made of a very fine black ware, not lustrous, but slightly rough. On this groundwork were inlaid figures much more graceful and lifelike than any others I have seen on antique vases. Some of these inlaid pictures represented love scenes with a child-like simplicity and freedom of manner which would not commend itself to the taste of the present day. Others again were pictures of maidens dancing, and yet others of hunting scenes. For instance, the very vase from which we were then drinking had on one side a most spirited drawing of men, apparently white in color, attacking a bull elephant with spears, while on the reverse was a picture, not quite so well done, of a hunter shooting an arrow at a running antelope, I should say from the look of it either an eland or a koodoo.

This is a digression at a critical moment, but it is not too long for the occasion, for the occasion itself was very long. With the exception of the periodical passing of the vase, and the movement necessary to throw fuel onto the fire, nothing happened for the best part of a whole hour. Nobody spoke a word. There we all sat in perfect silence, staring at the glare and glow of the large fire, and at the shadows thrown by the flickering earthenware lamps (which, by the way, were not ancient). On the open space between us and the fire lay a large wooden tray, with four short handles to it, exactly like a butcher's tray, only not hollowed out. By the side of the tray was a great pair of long-handled iron pincers, and on the other side of the fire was a similar pair. Somehow I did not at all like the appearance of this tray and the accompanying pincers. There I sat and stared at them and at the silent circle of the fierce moody faces of the men, and reflected that it was all very awful, and that we were absolutely in the power of this alarming people, who, to me at any rate, were all the more formidable because their true character was still very much of a mystery to us. They might be better than I thought them, or they might be worse. I feared that they were worse, and I was not wrong. It was a curious sort of a feast, I reflected, in appearance, indeed, an entertainment of the Barmecide stamp, for there was absolutely nothing to eat.

At last, just as I was beginning to feel as though I were being mesmerized, a move was made. Without the slightest warning, a man from the other side of the circle called out in a loud voice, "Where is the flesh that we shall eat?"

Thereon everybody in the circle answered in a deep measured tone, and stretching out the right arm towards the fire as he spoke: *"The flesh will come."*

"Is it a goat?" said the same man.

"It is a goat without horns, and more than a goat, and we shall slay it," they answered with one voice, and turning half round they one and all grasped the handles of their spears with the right hand, and then simultaneously let them go.

"Is it an ox?" said the man again.

"It is an ox without horns, and more than an ox, and we shall slay it," was the answer, and again the spears were grasped, and again let go.

Then came a pause, and I noticed, with horror and a rising of the hair, that the woman next to Mahomed began to fondle him, patting his cheeks, and calling him by names of endearment, while her fierce eyes played up and down his trembling form. I do not know why the sight frightened me so, but it did frighten us all dreadfully, especially Leo.

The caressing was so snakelike, and so evidently a part of some ghastly formula that had to be gone through.[1] I saw Mahomed turn white under his brown skin, sickly white with fear.

"Is the meat ready to be cooked?" asked the voice more rapidly.

"It is ready; it is ready."

"Is the pot hot to cook it?" it continued, in a sort of scream that echoed painfully down the great recesses of the cave.

"It is hot; it is hot."

"Great heavens!" roared Leo. "Remember the writing, *'The people who place pots upon the heads of strangers.'* "

As he said the words, before we could stir, or even take the matter in, two great ruffians jumped up, and, seizing the long pincers, plunged them into the heart of the fire, and the woman who had been caressing Mahomed suddenly produced a fiber noose from under her girdle or moocha, and, slipping it over his shoulders, ran it tight, while the men next him seized him by the legs. The two men with the pincers gave a heave, and, scattering the fire this way and that upon the rocky floor, lifted from it a large earthenware pot, heated to a white heat. In an instant, almost with a single movement, they had reached the spot where Mahomed was struggling. He fought like a fiend, shrieking in the abandonment of his despair, and notwithstanding the noose round him, and the efforts of the men who held his legs, the advancing wretches were for the moment unable to accomplish their purpose, which, horrible and

[1] We afterwards learned that its object was to pretend to the victim that he was the object of love and admiration, and so to soothe his injured feelings, and cause him to expire in a happy and contented frame of mind. —L. H. H.

incredible as it seems, was *to put the red-hot pot upon his head*.

I sprang to my feet with a yell of horror, and drawing my revolver fired it by a sort of instinct straight at the diabolical woman who had been caressing Mahomed, and was now gripping him in her arms. The bullet struck her in the back and killed her, and to this day I am glad that it did, for, as it afterwards transpired, she had availed herself of the anthropophagous customs of the Amahagger to organize the whole thing in revenge of the slight put upon her by Job. She sank down dead, and as she did so, to my terror and dismay, Mahomed, by a superhuman effort, burst from his tormentors, and, springing high into the air, fell dying upon her corpse. The heavy bullet from my pistol had driven through the bodies of both, at once striking down the murderess, and saving her victim from a death a hundred times more horrible. It was an awful and yet a most merciful accident.

For a moment there was a silence of astonishment. The Amahagger had never heard the report of a firearm before, and its effects dismayed them. But the next a man close to us recovered himself, and seized his spear preparatory to making a lunge with it at Leo, who was the nearest to him.

"Run for it!" I shouted, setting the example by starting up the cave as hard as my legs would carry me. I would have made for the open air if it had been possible, but there were men in the way, and, besides, I had caught sight of the forms of a crowd of people standing out clear against the skyline beyond the entrance to the cave. Up the cave I went, and after me came the others, and after them thundered the whole crowd of cannibals, mad with fury at the death of the woman. With a bound I cleared the prostrate form of Mahomed. As I flew over him I felt the heat from the red-hot pot, which was lying close by, strike upon my legs, and by its glow saw his hands—for he was not quite dead—still feebly moving. At the top of the cave was a little platform of rock three feet or so high by about eight deep, on which two large lamps were placed at night. Whether this platform had been left as a seat, or as a raised point afterwards to be cut away when it had served its purpose as a standing-place from which to carry on the excavations, I do not know—at least, I did not then. At any rate, we all three reached it, and, jumping on it, prepared to sell our lives as dearly as we could. For a few seconds the crowd that was pressing on our heels hung back when they saw us face round upon them. Job was on one side of the rock to the left, Leo in the center, and I to the right. Behind us were the lamps. Leo bent forward, and looked down the long lane of shadows, terminated in the fire and lighted lamps, through which the quiet forms of our would-be murderers flitted to and fro with the faint light glinting on their spears, for even their fury was silent as a bulldog's. The only other thing visible was the red-hot pot still glowing angrily in the gloom. There was a curious light in Leo's eyes, and his handsome face was set like a stone. In his right hand was his heavy hunting knife. He shifted its thong a little up his wrist, and then put his arm round me and gave me a good hug.

"Good-by, old fellow," he said, "my dear friend—my more than father. We have no chance against those scoundrels; they will finish us in a few minutes, and eat us afterwards, I suppose. Good-by. I led you into this. I hope you will forgive me. Good-by, Job."

"God's will be done," I said, setting my teeth, as I prepared for the end. At that moment, with an exclamation,

Job lifted his revolver and fired, and hit a man—not the man he had aimed at, by the way: anything that Job shot *at* was perfectly safe.

On they came with a rush, and I fired too as fast as I could, and checked them—between us, Job and I, besides the woman, killed or mortally wounded five men with our pistols before they were emptied. But we had no time to reload, and they still came on in a way that was almost splendid in its recklessness, seeing that they did not know but that we could go on firing forever.

A great fellow bounded up upon the platform, and Leo struck him dead with one blow of his powerful arm, sending the knife right through him. I did the same by another, but Job missed his stroke, and I saw a brawny Amahagger grip him by the middle and whirl him off the rock. The knife, not being secured by a thong, fell from Job's hand as he did so, and, by a most happy accident for him, lit upon its handle on the rock, just as the body of the Amahagger, being undermost, hit upon its point and was transfixed upon it. What happened to Job after that I am sure I do not know, but my own impression is that he lay still upon the corpse of his deceased assailant, "playing 'possum" as the Americans say. As for myself, I was soon involved in a desperate encounter with two ruffians who, luckily for me, had left their spears behind them; and for the first time in my life the great physical power with which Nature has endowed me stood me in good stead. I had hacked at the head of one man with my hunting knife, which was almost as big and heavy as a short sword, with such vigor that the sharp steel had split his skull down to the eyes, and was held so fast by it that as he suddenly fell sideways the knife was twisted right out of my hand.

Then it was that the two others sprang upon me. I

saw them coming, and got an arm round the waist of each, and down we all fell upon the floor of the cave together, rolling over and over. They were strong men, but I was mad with rage, and that awful lust for slaughter which will creep into the hearts of the most civilized of us when blows are flying, and life and death tremble on the turn. My arms were round the two swarthy demons, and I hugged them till I heard their ribs crack and crunch up beneath my grip. They twisted and writhed like snakes, and clawed and battered at me with their fists, but I held on. Lying on my back there, so that their bodies might protect me from spear thrusts from above, I slowly crushed the life out of them, and as I did so, strange as it may seem, I thought of what the amiable head of my college at Cambridge (who is a member of the Peace Society) and my brother fellows would say if by clairvoyance they could see me, of all men, playing such a bloody game. Soon my assailants grew faint, and almost ceased to struggle, their breath had failed them, and they were dying, but still I dared not leave them, for they died very slowly. I knew that if I relaxed my grip they would revive. The other ruffians probably thought—for we were all three lying in the shadow of the ledge—that we were all dead together; at any rate they did not interfere with our little tragedy.

I turned my head, and as I lay gasping in the throes of that awful struggle I could see that Leo was off the rock now, for the lamplight fell full upon him. He was still on his feet, but in the center of a surging mass of struggling men, who were striving to pull him down as wolves pull down a stag. Up above them towered his beautiful pale face crowned with its bright curls (for Leo is six feet two high), and I saw that he was fighting with a desperate abandonment and energy that was at once splendid and hideous to behold. He drove his knife through one man—they were so close to him and mixed up with him that they could not get at him to kill him with their big spears, and they had no knives or sticks. The man fell, and then somehow the knife was wrenched from his hand, leaving him defenseless, and I thought the end had come. But no; with a desperate effort he broke loose from them, seized the body of the man he had just slain, and lifting it high in the air hurled it right at the mob of his assailants, so that the shock and weight of it swept some five or six of them to the earth. But in a minute they were all up again, except one, whose skull was smashed, and had once more fastened upon him. And then slowly, and with infinite labor and struggling, the wolves bore the lion down. Once even then he recovered himself, and felled an Amahagger with his fist, but it was more than man could do to hold his own for long against so many, and at last he came crashing down upon the rock floor, falling as an oak falls, and bearing with him to the earth all those who clung about him. They gripped him by his arms and legs, and then cleared off his body.

"A spear," cried a voice, "a spear to cut his throat, and a vessel to catch his blood."

I shut my eyes, for I saw the man coming with a spear, and myself, I could not stir to Leo's help, for I was growing weak, and the two men on me were not yet dead, and a deadly sickness overcame me.

Then suddenly there was a disturbance, and involuntarily I opened my eyes again, and looked towards the scene of murder. The girl Ustane had thrown herself on Leo's prostrate form, covering his body with her body, and fastening her arms about his neck. They tried to drag her from him, but she twisted her legs round his, and hung on like a bulldog, or rather like a creeper to a tree, and they could not. Then they tried to stab him in the side without hurting her, but somehow she shielded him, and he was only wounded.

At last they lost patience.

"Drive the spear through the man and the woman together," said a voice, the same voice that had asked the questions at that ghastly feast, "so of a verity shall they be wed."

Then I saw the man with the weapon straighten himself for the effort. I saw the cold steel gleam on high, and once more I shut my eyes.

As I did so I heard the voice of a man thunder out in tones that rang and echoed down the rocky ways: *"Cease!"*

Then I fainted, and as I did so it flashed through my darkening mind that I was passing down into the last oblivion of death.

A Little Foot

WHEN I OPENED my eyes again I found myself lying on a skin mat not far from the fire round which we had been gathered for that dreadful feast. Near me lay Leo, still apparently in a swoon, and over him was bending the tall form of the girl Ustane, who was washing a deep spear wound in his side with cold water preparatory to binding it up with linen. Leaning against the wall of the cave behind her was Job, apparently uninjured, but bruised and trembling. On the other side of the fire, tossed about this way and that, as though they had thrown themselves down to sleep in some moment of absolute exhaustion, were the bodies of those whom we had killed in our frightful struggle for life. I counted them: there were twelve besides the woman, and the corpse of poor Mahomed, who had died by my hand, which, the fire-stained pot at its side, was placed at the end of the irregular line. To the left a body of men were engaged in binding the arms of the surviving cannibals behind them, and then fastening them two and two. The villains were submitting with a look of sulky indifference upon their faces which accorded ill with the baffled fury that gleamed in their somber eyes. In front of these men, directing the operations, stood no other than our friend Billali, looking rather tired, but particularly patriarchal with his flowing beard, and as cool and unconcerned as though he were superintending the cutting up of an ox.

Presently he turned, and perceiving that I was sitting up advanced to me, and with the utmost courtesy said that he trusted that I felt better. I answered that at present I scarcely knew how I felt, except that I ached all over.

Then he bent down and examined Leo's wound.

"It is a nasty cut," he said, "but the spear has not pierced the entrails. He will recover."

"Thanks to thy arrival, my father," I answered. "In another minute we should all have been beyond the reach of recovery, for those devils of thine would have slain us as they would have slain our servant," and I pointed towards Mahomed.

The old man ground his teeth, and I saw an extraordinary expression of malignity light up his eyes.

"Fear not, my son," he answered. "Vengeance shall be taken on them such as would make the flesh twist upon the bones merely to hear of it. To *She* shall they go, and her vengeance shall be worthy of her greatness. That man" —pointing to Mahomed—"I tell thee that man would have died a merciful death to the death these hyena men shall die. Tell me, I pray of thee, how it came about."

In a few words I sketched what had happened.

"Ah, so," he answered. "Thou seest, my son, here there is a custom that if a stranger comes into this country he may be slain by 'the pot,' and eaten."

"It is hospitality turned upside down," I answered feebly. "In our country we entertain a stranger, and give him food to eat. Here ye eat him, and are entertained."

"It is a custom," he answered with a shrug. "Myself I think it an evil one; but then," he added as an afterthought, "I do not like the taste of strangers, especially after they have wandered through the swamps and lived on wildfowl. When 'She-who-must-be-obeyed' sent orders that ye were to be saved alive she said naught of the black man, therefore, being hyenas, these men lusted after his flesh, and the woman it was, whom thou didst rightly slay, who put it into their evil hearts to hot-pot him. Well, they will have their reward. Better for them would it be if they had never seen the light than that they should stand before *She* in her terrible anger. Happy are those of them who died by your hands.

"Ah," he went on, "it was a gallant fight that ye fought. Knowest thou, that thou, long-armed old baboon that thou art, hast crushed in the ribs of those two who are laid out there as though they were but as the shell on an egg? And the young one, the lion, it was a beautiful stand that he made—one against so many—three did he slay outright, and that one there"—and he pointed to a body that was still moving a little—"will die anon, for his head is cracked across, and others of those who are bound are hurt. It was a gallant fight, and thou and he have made a friend of me by it, for I love to see a well-fought fray. But tell me, my son, the baboon—and now I think of it thy face, too, is hairy, and altogether like a baboon's—how was it that ye slew those with a hole in them? Ye made a noise, they say, and slew them—they fell down on their faces at the noise?"

I explained to him as well as I could, but very shortly— I was terribly wearied, and only persuaded to talk at all through fear of offending one so powerful if I refused to do so—what were the properties of gunpowder, and he instantly suggested that I should illustrate what I said by operating on the person of one of the prisoners. One, he said, never would be counted, and it would not only be very interesting to him, but would give me an opportunity of an installment of revenge. He was greatly astounded when I told him that it was not our custom to avenge ourselves in cold blood, and that we left vengeance to the law and a higher power, of which he knew nothing. I added, however, that when I recovered I would take him out shooting with us, and he should kill an animal for himself, and at this he was as pleased as a child at the promise of a new toy.

Just then Leo opened his eyes beneath the stimulus of some brandy (of which we still had a little) that Job had poured down his throat, and our conversation came to an end.

After this we managed to get Leo, who was in a very poor way indeed, and only half-conscious, safely off to bed, supported by Job and that brave girl Ustane, to whom, had I not been afraid she might resent it, I would certainly have given a kiss for her splendid behavior in saving my dear boy's life at the risk of her own. But Ustane was not the sort of young person with whom one would care to take liberties unless one were perfectly certain that they would not be misunderstood, so I repressed my inclinations. Then, bruised and battered, but with a sense of safety in my breast to which I had for some days been a stranger, I crept off to my own little sepulcher, not forgetting before I lay down in it to thank Providence from the bottom of my heart that it was not a sepulcher indeed, as were it not for a merciful combination of events that I can only attribute to its protection, it would certainly have been for me that night. Few men have been nearer their end and yet escaped it than we were on that dreadful day.

I am a bad sleeper at the best of times, and my dreams that night when at last I got to rest were not of the pleasantest. The awful vision of poor Mahomed struggling to escape the red-hot pot would haunt them, and then in the background, as it were, a veiled form was always hovering, which, from time to time, seemed to draw the coverings from its body, revealing now the perfect shape of a lovely blooming woman, and now again the white bones of a grinning skeleton, and which, as it veiled and unveiled, uttered the mysterious and apparently meaningless sentence: *"That which is alive hath known death, and that which is dead yet can never die, for in the Circle of the Spirit life is naught and death is naught. Yea, all things live forever, though at times they sleep and are forgotten."*

The morning came at last, but when it came I found that I was too stiff and sore to rise. About seven Job arrived, limping terribly, and with his face the color of a rotten apple, and told me that Leo had slept fairly, but was very weak. Two hours afterwards Billali (Job called him "Billy-goat," to which, indeed, his white beard gave him some resemblance, or more familiarly "Billy") came too, bearing a lamp in his hand, his towering form reaching nearly to the roof of the little chamber. I pretended to be asleep, and through the cracks of my eyelids watched his sardonic but handsome old face. He fixed his hawklike eyes upon me, and stroked his glorious white beard, which, by the way, would have been worth a hundred a year to any London barber as an advertisement.

"Ah!" I heard him mutter (Billali had a habit of muttering to himself), "he is ugly—ugly as the other is beautiful—a very Baboon, it was a good name. But I like the man. Strange now, at my age, that I should like a man. What says the proverb—'Mistrust all men, and slay him whom thou mistrustest overmuch; and as for women, flee from them, for they are evil, and in the end will destroy thee.' It is a good proverb, especially the last part of it: I think it must have come down from the ancients. Nevertheless I like this Baboon, and I wonder where they taught him his tricks, and I trust that *She* will not bewitch him. Poor Baboon! He must be wearied after that fight. I will go lest I should awake him."

I waited till he had turned and was nearly through the entrance, walking softly on tiptoe, and then I called after him.

"My father," I said, "is it thou?"

"Yes, my son, it is I; but let me not disturb thee. I did but come to see how thou didst fare, and to tell thee that those who would have slain thee, my Baboon, are by now well on their road to *She*. *She* said that ye also were to come at once, but I fear ye cannot yet."

"Nay," I said, "not till we have recovered a little; but have me borne out into the daylight, I pray thee, my father. I love not this place."

"Ah, no," he answered, "it hath a sad air. I remember when I was a boy I found the body of a fair woman lying where thou liest now, yes, on that very bench. She was so beautiful that I was wont to creep in hither with a lamp and gaze upon her. Had it not been for her cold hands, almost could I think that she slept and would one day awake, so fair and peaceful was she in her robes of white. White was she, too, and her hair was yellow and lay down her almost to the feet. There are many such still in the tombs at the place where *She* is, for those who set them there had a way I know naught of, whereby to keep their beloved out of the crumbling hand of Decay, even when Death had slain them. Ay, day by day I came hither, and gazed on her till at last—laugh not at me, stranger, for I was but a silly lad—I learned to love that dead form, that shell which once had held a life that no more is. I would creep up to her and kiss her cold face, and wonder how many men had lived and died since she was, and who had loved her and embraced her in the days that long had passed away. And, my Baboon, I think I learned wisdom from that dead one, for of a truth it taught me of the littleness of life, and the length of Death, and how all things that are under the sun go down one path, and are forever forgotten. And so I mused, and it seemed to me that wisdom flowed into me from the dead, till one day my mother, a watchful woman, but hasty-minded, seeing I was changed, followed me, and saw the beautiful white one, and feared that I was bewitched, as, indeed, I was. So half in dread, and half in anger, she took the lamp, and standing the dead woman up against the wall there, set fire to her hair, and she burned fiercely, even down to the feet, for those who are thus kept burn excellently well.

"See, my son, there on the roof is yet the smoke of her burning."

I looked up doubtfully, and there, sure enough, on the roof of the sepulcher, was a peculiarly unctuous and sooty mark, three feet or more across. Doubtless it had in the course of years been rubbed off the sides of the little cave, but on the roof it remained, and there was no mistaking its appearance.

"She burned," he went on in a meditative way, "even to the feet, but the feet I came back and saved, cutting the burned bone from them, and hid them under the stone bench there, wrapped up in a piece of linen. Surely, I re-member it as though it were but yesterday. Perchance they are there if none have found them, even to this hour. Of a truth I have not entered this chamber from that time to this very day. Stay, I will look," and, kneeling down, he groped about with his long arm in the recess under the stone bench. Presently his face brightened, and with an exclamation he pulled something forth that was caked in dust; which he shook onto the floor. It was covered with the remains of a rotting rag, which he undid, and revealed to my astonished gaze a beautifully shaped and almost white woman's foot, looking as fresh and as firm as though it had but now been placed there.

"Thou seest, my son, the Baboon," he said, in a sad voice, "I spake the truth to thee, for here is yet one foot remaining. Take it, my son, and gaze upon it."

I took this cold fragment of mortality in my hand and looked at it in the light of the lamp with feelings which I cannot describe, so mixed up were they between astonishment, fear, and fascination. It was light, much lighter I should say than it had been in the living state, and the flesh to all appearance was still flesh, though about it there clung a faintly aromatic odor. For the rest it was not shrunk or shriveled, or even black and unsightly, like the flesh of Egyptian mummies, but plump and fair, and, except where it had been slightly burned, perfect as on the day of death—a very triumph of embalming.

Poor little foot! I set it down upon the stone bench where it had lain for so many thousand years, and wondered whose was the beauty that it had upborne through the pomp and pageantry of a forgotten civilization—first as a merry child's, then as a blushing maid's, and lastly as a perfect woman's. Through what halls of Life had its soft step echoed, and in the end, with what courage had it trodden down the dusty ways of Death! To whose side had it stolen in the hush of night when the black slave slept upon the marble floor, and who had listened for its stealing? Shapely little foot! Well might it have been set upon the proud neck of a conqueror bent at last to woman's beauty, and well might the lips of nobles and of kings have been pressed upon its jeweled whiteness.

I wrapped up this relic of the past in the remnants of the old linen rag which had evidently formed a portion of its owner's graveclothes, for it was partially burned, and put it away in my Gladstone bag, which I had bought at the Army and Navy Stores—a strange combination, I thought. Then with Billali's help I staggered off to see Leo. I found him dreadfully bruised, worse even than myself, perhaps owing to the excessive whiteness of his skin, and faint and weak with the loss of blood from the flesh wound in his side, but for all that cheerful as a cricket, and asking for some breakfast. Job and Ustane got him onto the bottom, or rather the sacking of a litter, which was removed from its pole for that purpose, and with the aid of old Billali carried him out into the shade at the mouth of the cave, from which, by the way, every trace of the slaughter of the previous night had now been removed, and there we all breakfasted, and indeed spent that day, and most of the two following ones.

On the third morning Job and myself were practically recovered. Leo also was so much better that I yielded to Billali's often expressed entreaty, and agreed to start at once upon our journey to Kôr, which we were told was the name of the place where the mysterious She lived, though I still feared for its effects upon Leo, and especially lest the motion should cause his wound, which was scarcely skinned over, to break open again. Indeed, had it not been for Billali's evident anxiety to get off, which led us to suspect that some difficulty or danger might threaten us if we did not comply with it, I would not have consented to go.

10 ♦

Speculations

WITHIN AN HOUR of our finally deciding to start, five litters were brought up to the door of the cave, each accompanied by four regular bearers and two spare hands, also a band of about fifty armed Amahagger, who were to form the escort and carry the baggage. Three of these litters, of course, were for us, and one for Billali, who, I was immensely relieved to hear, was to be our companion, while the fifth I presumed was for the use of Ustane.

"Does the lady go with us, my father?" I asked of Billali, as he stood superintending things generally.

He shrugged his shoulders as he answered, "If she wills. In this country the women do what they please. We worship them, and give them their way, because without them the world could not go on; they are the source of life."

"Ah," I said, the matter never having struck me quite in that light before.

"We worship them," he went on, "up to a certain point, till at last they get unbearable, which," he added, "they do about every second generation."

"And then what do you do?" I asked with curiosity.

"Then," he answered with a faint smile, "we rise, and kill the old ones as an example to the young ones, and to show them that we are the strongest. My poor wife was killed in that way three years ago. It was very sad, but to

131

tell thee the truth, my son, life has been happier since, for my age protects me from the young ones."

"In short," I replied, quoting the saying of a great man whose wisdom has not yet lightened the darkness of the Amahagger, "thou hast found thy position one of greater freedom and less responsibility."

This phrase puzzled him a little at first from its vagueness, though I think my translation hit off its sense very well, but at last he saw it, and appreciated it.

"Yes, yes, my Baboon," he said, "I see it now, but all the 'responsibilities' are killed, at least some of them are, and that is why there are so few old women about just now. Well, they brought it on themselves. As for this girl," he went on, in a graver tone, "I know not what to say. She is a brave girl, and she loves the Lion [Leo]; thou sawest how she clung to him, and saved his life. Also, she is, according to our custom, wed to him, and has a right to go where he goes, unless," he added significantly, "*She* would say her no, for her word overrides all rights."

"And if *She* bade her leave him, and the girl refused? What then?"

"If," he said with a shrug, "the hurricane bids the tree to bend, and it will not, what happens?"

And then, without waiting for an answer, he turned and walked to his litter, and in ten minutes from that time we were all well under way.

It took us an hour and more to cross the cup of the volcanic plain, and another half hour or so to climb the edge on the farther side. Once there, however, the view was a very fine one. Before us was a long steep slope of grassy plain, broken here and there by clumps of trees mostly of the thorn tribe. At the bottom of this gentle slope, some nine or ten miles away, we could make out a dim sea of marsh, over which the foul vapors hung like smoke about a city. It was easy going for the bearers down the slopes, and by midday we had reached the borders of the dismal swamp. Here we halted to eat our midday meal, and then, following a winding and devious path, plunged into the morass. Presently the path, at any rate to our unaccustomed eyes, grew so faint as to be almost indistinguishable from those made by the aquatic beasts and birds, and it is to this day a mystery to me how our bearers found their way across the marshes. Ahead of the cavalcade marched two men with long poles, which they now and again plunged into the ground before them, the reason of this being that the nature of the soil frequently changed from causes with which I am not acquainted, so that places which might be safe enough to cross one month would certainly swallow the wayfarer the next. Never did I see a more dreary and depressing scene. Miles on miles of quagmire, varied only by bright green strips of comparatively solid ground, and by deep and sullen pools fringed with tall rushes, in which the bitterns boomed and the frogs croaked incessantly: miles on miles of it without a break, unless the fever fog can be called a break. The only life in this great morass was that of the aquatic birds, and the animals that fed on them, of both of which there were vast numbers. Geese, cranes, ducks, teal, coot, snipe, and plover swarmed all around us, many being of varieties that were quite new to me, and all so tame that one could almost have knocked them over with a stick. Among these birds I especially noticed a very beautiful variety of painted snipe, almost the size of woodcock, and with a flight more resembling that bird's than an English snipe's. In the pools, too, was a species of small alligator or enormous iguana,

I do not know which, that fed, Billali told me, upon the waterfowl, also large quantities of a hideous black water snake, of which the bite is very dangerous, though not, I gathered, so deadly as a cobra's or a puff adder's. The bull-frogs were also very large, and with voices proportionate to their size; and as for the mosquitoes—the "musqueteers," as Job called them—they were, if possible, even worse than they had been on the river, and tormented us greatly. Undoubtedly, however, the worst feature of the swamp was the awful smell of rotting vegetation that hung about it, which was at times positively overpowering, and the malarious exhalations that accompanied it, which we were of course obliged to breathe.

On we went through it all, till at last the sun sank in sullen splendor just as we reached a spot of rising ground about two acres in extent—a little oasis of dry in the midst of the miry wilderness—where Billali announced that we were to camp. The camping, however, turned out to be a very simple process, and consisted, in fact, in sitting down on the ground round a scanty fire made of dry reeds and some wood that had been brought with us. However, we made the best we could of it, and smoked and ate with such appetite as the smell of damp, stifling heat would allow, for it was very hot on this low land, and yet, oddly enough, chilly at times. But, however hot it was, we were glad enough to keep near the fire, because we found that the mosquitoes did not like the smoke. Presently we rolled ourselves up in our blankets and tried to go to sleep, but so far as I was concerned the bullfrogs, and the extraordinary roaring and alarming sound produced by hundreds of snipe hovering high in the air, made sleep an impossibility, to say nothing of our other discomforts. I turned and looked at Leo, who was next me; he was dozing, but his face had a flushed appearance that I did not like, and by the flickering firelight I saw Ustane, who was lying on the other side of him, raise herself from time to time upon her elbow, and look at him anxiously enough.

However, I could do nothing for him, for we had all already taken a good dose of quinine, which was the only preventive we had; so I lay and watched the stars come out by thousands, till all the immense arch of heaven was sewn with glittering points, and every point a world! Here was a glorious sight by which man might well measure his own insignificance! Soon I gave up thinking about it, for the mind wearies easily when it strives to grapple with the Infinite, and to trace the footsteps of the Almighty as he strides from sphere to sphere, or deduce His purpose from His works. Such things are not for us to know. Knowledge is to the strong, and we are weak. Too much wisdom would perchance blind our imperfect sight, and too much strength would make us drunk, and overweight our feeble reason till it fell, and we were drowned in the depths of our own vanity. For what is the first result of man's increased knowledge interpreted from Nature's book by the persistent effort of his purblind observation? Is it not but too often to make him question the existence of his Maker, or indeed of any intelligent purpose beyond his own? The truth is veiled, because we could no more look upon her glory than we can upon the sun. It would destroy us. Full knowledge is not for man as man is here, for his capacities, which he is apt to think so great, are indeed but small. The vessel is soon filled, and, were one-thousandth part of the unutterable and silent wisdom that directs the rolling of those shining spheres, and the force which makes them roll, pressed into it, it would be shattered into fragments. Perhaps in some other place and time it may be otherwise, who can tell? Here the lot of man born of the flesh is but to endure midst toil and tribulation, to catch at the bubbles blown by fate, which he calls pleasures, thankful if before they burst they rest a moment in his hand, and when the tragedy is played out, and his hour comes to perish, to pass humbly whither he knows not.

Above me, as I lay, shone the eternal stars, and there at my feet the impish marsh-born balls of fire rolled this way and that, vapor-tossed and earth-desiring, and methought that in the two I saw a type and image of what man is, and what perchance man may one day be, if the living Force who ordained him and them should so ordain this also. Oh, that it might be ours to rest year by year upon that high level of the heart to which at times we momentarily attain! Oh, that we could shake loose the prisoned pinions of the soul and soar to that superior point, whence, like to some traveler looking out through space from Darien's giddiest peak, we might gaze with the spiritual eyes of noble thoughts deep into Infinity!

What would it be to cast off this earthy robe, to have done forever with these earthy thoughts and miserable desires; no longer, like those corpse candles, to be tossed this way and that, by forces beyond our control; or which, if we can theoretically control them, we are at times driven by the exigencies of our nature to obey! Yes, to cast them off, to have done with the foul and thorny places of the world; and, like to those glittering points above me, to rest on high wrapped forever in the brightness of our better selves, that even now shines in us as fire faintly shines within those lurid balls, and lay down our littleness in that wide glory of our dreams, that invisible but surrounding good, from which all truth and beauty comes!

These and many such thoughts passed through my

mind that night. They come to torment us all at times. I say to torment, for, alas, thinking can only serve to measure out the helplessness of thought. What is the use of our feeble crying in the awful silences of space? Can our dim intelligence read the secrets of that star-strewn sky? Does any answer come out of it? Never any at all, nothing but echoes and fantastic visions. And yet we believe that there is an answer, and that upon a time a new Dawn will come blushing down the ways of our enduring night. We believe it, for its reflected beauty even now shines up continually in our hearts from beneath the horizon of the grave, and we call it Hope. Without Hope we should suffer moral death, and by the help of Hope we yet may climb to Heaven, or at the worst, if she also prove but a kindly mockery given to hold us from despair, be gently lowered into the abysses of eternal sleep.

Then I fell to reflecting upon the undertaking on which we were bent, and what a wild one it was, and yet how strangely the story seemed to fit in with what had been written centuries ago upon the sherd. Who was this extraordinary woman, queen over a people apparently as extraordinary as herself, and reigning amidst the vestiges of a lost civilization? And what was the meaning of this story of the Fire that gave unending life? Could it be possible that any fluid or essence should exist which might so fortify these fleshy walls that they should from age to age resist the mines and batterings of decay? It was possible, though not probable. The indefinite continuation of life would not, as poor Vincey said, be so marvelous a thing as the production of life and its temporary endurance. And if it were true, what then? The person who found it could no doubt rule the world. He could accumulate all the wealth in the world, and all the power, and all the wisdom that is power. He might give a lifetime to the study of each art or science. Well, if that were so, and this *She* were practically immortal, which I did not for one moment believe, how was it that, with all these things at her feet, she preferred to remain in a cave among a society of cannibals? This surely settled the question. The whole story was monstrous, and only worthy of the superstitious days in which it was written. At any rate I was very sure that *I* would not attempt to attain unending life. I had had far too many worries and disappointments and secret bitternesses during my forty-odd years of existence to wish that this state of affairs should be continued indefinitely. And yet I suppose that my life has been, comparatively speaking, a happy one.

And then, reflecting that at the present moment there was far more likelihood of our earthly careers being cut exceedingly short than of their being unduly prolonged, I at last managed to get to sleep, a fact for which anybody who reads this narrative, if anybody ever does, may very probably be thankful.

When I woke again it was just dawning, and the guard and bearers were moving about like ghosts through the dense morning mists, getting ready for our start. The fire had died quite down, and I rose and stretched myself, shivering in every limb from the damp cold of the dawn. Then I looked at Leo. He was sitting up, holding his hands to his head, and I saw that his face was flushed and his eye bright, and yet yellow round the pupil.

"Well, Leo," I said, "how do you feel?"

"I feel as though I were going to die," he answered hoarsely. "My head is splitting, my body is trembling, and I am as sick as a cat."

I whistled, or if I did not whistle I felt inclined to—

Leo had got a sharp attack of fever. I went to Job and asked him for the quinine, of which fortunately we had still a good supply, only to find that Job himself was not much better. He complained of pains across the back, and dizziness, and was almost incapable of helping himself. Then I did the only thing it was possible to do under the circumstances—gave them both about ten grains of quinine, and took a slightly smaller dose myself as a matter of precaution. After that I found Billali, and explained to him how matters stood, asking at the same time what he thought had best be done. He came with me, and looked at Leo and Job (whom, by the way, he had named the Pig on account of his fatness, round face, and small eyes).

"Ah," he said, when we were out of earshot, "the fever! I thought so. The Lion has it badly, but he is young, and he may live. As for the Pig, his attack is not so bad; it is the 'little fever' which he has; that always begins with pains across the back, it will spend itself upon his fat."

"Can they go on, my father?" I asked.

"Nay, my son, they must go on. If they stop here they will certainly die; also, they will be better in the litters than on the ground. By tonight, if all goes well, we shall be across the marsh and in good air. Come, let us lift them into the litters and start, for it is very bad to stand still in this morning fog. We can eat our meal as we go."

This we accordingly did, and with a heavy heart I once more set out upon our strange journey. For the first three hours all went as well as could be expected, and then an accident happened that nearly lost us the pleasure of the company of our venerable friend Billali, whose litter was leading the cavalcade. We were going through a particularly dangerous stretch of quagmire, in which the bearers sometimes sank up to their knees. Indeed, it was a mystery to me how they contrived to carry the heavy litters at all over such ground as that which we were traversing, though the two spare hands, as well as the four regular ones, had of course to put their shoulders to the pole.

Presently, as we blundered and floundered along, there was a sharp cry, then a storm of exclamations, and, last of all, a most tremendous splash, and the whole caravan halted.

I jumped out of my litter and ran forward. About twenty yards ahead was the edge of one of those sullen peaty pools of which I have spoken, the path we were following running along the top of its bank, which, as it happened, was a steep one. Looking towards this pool, to my horror I saw that Billali's litter was floating on it, and as for Billali himself, he was nowhere to be seen. To make matters clear I may as well explain at once what had happened. One of Billali's bearers had unfortunately trodden on a basking snake, which had bitten him in the leg, whereon he had, not unnaturally, let go of the pole, and then, finding that he was tumbling down the bank, grasped at the litter to save himself. The result of this was what might have been expected. The litter was pulled over the edge of the bank, the bearers let go, and the whole thing, including Billali and the man who had been bitten, rolled into the slimy pool. When I got to the edge of the water neither of them was to be seen, and, indeed, the unfortunate bearer never was seen again. Either he struck his head against something, or got wedged in the mud, or possibly the snake bite paralyzed him. At any rate, he vanished. But though Billali was not to be seen, his whereabouts was clear enough from the agitation of the floating litter, in the bearing cloth and curtains of which he was entangled.

"He is there! Our father is there!" said one of the men, but he did not stir a finger to help him, nor did any of the others. They simply stood and stared at the water.

"Out of the way, you brutes," I shouted in English, and throwing off my hat I took a run and sprang well out into the horrid slimy-looking pool. A couple of strokes took me to where Billali was struggling beneath the cloth.

Somehow, I do not quite know how, I managed to push this free of him, and his venerable head, all covered with green slime, like that of a yellowish Bacchus with ivy leaves, emerged upon the surface of the water. The rest was easy, for Billali was an eminently practical individual, and had the common sense not to grasp hold of me as drowning people often do, so I got him by the arm and towed him to the bank, through the mud of which we were with difficulty dragged. Such a filthy spectacle as we presented I have never seen before or since, and it will perhaps give some idea of the almost superhuman dignity of Billali's appearance when I say that, coughing, half-drowned, and covered with mud and green slime as he was, with his beautiful beard coming to a dripping point, like a Chinaman's freshly oiled pigtail, he still looked venerable and imposing.

"Ye dogs," he said, addressing the bearers, as soon as he had sufficiently recovered to speak, "ye left me, your father, to drown. Had it not been for this stranger, my son the Baboon, assuredly I should have drowned. Well, I will remember it," and he fixed them with his gleaming though slightly watery eye, in a way I saw they did not like, though they tried to appear sulkily indifferent.

"As for thee, my son," the old man went on, turning towards me and grasping my hand, "rest assured that I am thy friend through good and evil. Thou hast saved my life: perchance a day may come when I shall save thine."

After that we cleaned ourselves as best we could, fished out the litter, and went on, minus the man who had been drowned. I do not know if it was owing to his being an unpopular character, or from native indifference and selfishness of temperament, but I am bound to say that nobody seemed to grieve much over his sudden and final disappearance, unless, perhaps, it was the men who had to do his share of the work.

11 ♦

The Plain of Kôr

ABOUT AN HOUR before sundown we at last, to my
unbounded gratitude, emerged from the great belt of marsh
onto land that swelled upwards in a succession of rolling
waves. Just on the hither side of the crest of the first wave
we halted for the night. My first act was to examine Leo's
condition. It was, if anything, worse than in the morning,
and a new and very distressing feature, vomiting, set in,
and continued till dawn. Not one wink of sleep did I get
that night, for I passed it in assisting Ustane, who was one
of the most gentle and indefatigable nurses I ever saw,
to wait upon Leo and Job. However, the air here was warm
and genial without being too hot, and there were no mosquitoes to speak of. Also, we were above the level of the
marsh mist, which lay stretched beneath us like the dim
smoke pall over a city, lit up here and there by the wandering globes of fen fire. Thus it will be seen that we were,
speaking comparatively, in clover.

By dawn on the following morning Leo was quite light-
headed, and fancied that he was divided into halves. I
was dreadfully distressed, and began to wonder with a sort
of sick fear what the termination of the attack would be.
Alas! I had heard but too much of how these attacks generally terminate. As I was doing so Billali came up and
said that we must be getting on, more especially as, in his
opinion, if Leo did not reach some spot where he could be

143

quiet, and have proper nursing, within the next twelve hours, his life would only be a matter of a day or two. I could not but agree with him, so we got him into the litter, and started on, Ustane walking by Leo's side to keep the flies off him, and see that he did not throw himself out onto the ground.

Within half an hour of sunrise we had reached the top of the rise of which I have spoken, and a most beautiful view broke upon our gaze. Beneath us was a rich stretch of country, verdant with grass and lovely with foliage and flowers. In the background, at a distance, so far as I could judge, of some eighteen miles from where we then stood, a huge and extraordinary mountain rose abruptly from the plain. The base of this great mountain appeared to consist of a grassy slope, but rising from this, I should say, from subsequent observation, at a height of about five hundred feet above the level of the plain, was a most tremendous and absolutely precipitous wall of bare rock, quite twelve or fifteen hundred feet in height. The shape of the mountain, which was undoubtedly of volcanic origin, was round, and of course, as only a segment of its circle was visible, it was difficult to estimate its exact size, which was enormous. I afterwards discovered that it could not cover less than fifty square miles of ground. Anything more grand and imposing than the sight presented by this great natural castle, starting in solitary grandeur from the level of the plain, I never saw, and I suppose I never shall. Its very solitude added to its majesty, and its towering cliffs seemed to kiss the sky. Indeed, generally speaking, they were clothed in clouds that lay in fleecy masses upon their broad and level battlements.

I sat up in my hammock and gazed out across the plain

at this thrilling and majestic sight, and I suppose that Billali noticed it, for he brought his litter alongside.

"Behold the House of '*She-who-must-be-obeyed*'!" he said. "Had ever a queen such a throne before?"

"It is wonderful, my father," I answered. "But how do we enter? Those cliffs look hard to climb."

"Thou shalt see, my Baboon. Look now at the plain below us. What thinkest thou that is? Thou art a wise man. Come, tell me."

I looked, and saw what appeared to be the line of roadway running straight towards the base of the mountain, though it was covered with turf. There were high banks on each side of it, broken here and there, but fairly continuous on the whole, the meaning of which I did not understand. It seemed so very odd that anybody should embank a roadway.

"Well, my father," I answered, "I suppose that it is a road, otherwise I should have been inclined to say that it was the bed of a river, or rather," I added, observing the extraordinary directness of the cutting, "of a canal."

Billali—who, by the way, was none the worse for his immersion of the day before—nodded his head sagely as he replied, "Thou art right, my son. It is a channel cut out by those who were before us in this place to carry away water. Of this am I sure: within the rocky circle of the great mountain whither we journey was once a great lake. But those who were before us, by wonderful arts of which I know naught, hewed a path for the water through the solid rock of the mountain, piercing even to the bed of the lake. But first they cut the channel that thou seest across the plain. Then, when at last the water burst out, it rushed down the channel that had been made to receive it, and crossed this plain till it reached the low land behind the rise, and there, perchance, it made the swamp through which we had come. Then when the lake was drained dry, the people whereof I speak built a mighty city, whereof naught but ruins and the name of Kôr yet remaineth, on its bed, and from age to age hewed the caves and passages that thou wilt see."

"It may be," I answered; "but if so, how is it that the lake does not fill up again with the rains and the water of the springs?"

"Nay, my son, the people were a wise people, and they left a drain to keep it clear. Seest thou the river to the right?" and he pointed to a fair-sized stream that wound away across the plain, some four miles from us. "That is the drain, and it comes out through the mountain wall where this cutting goes in. At first, perhaps, the water ran down this canal, but afterwards the people turned it, and used the cutting for a road."

"And is there then no other place where one may enter into the great mountain," I asked, "except through the drain?"

"There is a place," he answered, "where cattle and men on foot may cross with much labor, but it is secret. A year mightest thou search and shouldst never find it. It is only used once a year, when the herds of cattle that have been fatting on the slopes of the mountain, and on this plain, are driven into the space within."

"And does *She* live there always?" I asked, "or does she come at times without the mountain?"

"Nay, my son, where she is, there she is."

By now we were well onto the great plain, and I was examining with delight the varied beauty of its semitropical flowers and trees, the latter of which grew singly, or at most in clumps of three or four, much of the timber being of large size, and belonging apparently to a variety of evergreen oak. There were also many palms, some of them more than one hundred feet high, and the largest and most beautiful tree ferns that I ever saw, about which hung clouds of jeweled honeysuckers and great-winged butterflies. Wandering about among the trees or crouching in the long and feathered grass were all varieties of game, from rhinoceros down. I saw rhinoceros, buffalo (a large herd), eland, quagga, and sable antelope, the most beautiful of all the bucks, not to mention many smaller varieties of game, and three ostriches which scudded away at our approach like white drift before a gale. So plentiful was the game that at last I could stand it no longer. I had a single-barrel sporting Martini with me in the litter, the express being too cumbersome, and espying a beautiful fat eland rubbing himself under one of the oaklike trees, I jumped out of the litter, and proceeded to creep as near to him as I could. He let me come within eighty yards, and then turned his head, and stared at me, preparatory to running away. I lifted the rifle, and taking him about midway down the shoulder, for he was side on to me, fired. I never made a cleaner shot or a better kill in all my small experience, for the great buck sprang right up into the air and fell dead. The bearers, who had all halted to see the performance, gave a murmur of surprise, an unwonted compliment from these sullen people, who never appear to be surprised at anything, and a party of the guard at once ran off to cut the animal up. As for myself, though I was longing to have a look at him, I sauntered back to my litter as though I had been in the habit of killing eland all my life, feeling that I had gone up several degrees in the estimation of the Amahagger, who looked on the whole thing as a very high-class manifestation of witchcraft. As a matter of fact, however, I had never seen an eland in a wild state before. Billali received me with enthusiasm.

"It is wonderful, my son the Baboon," he cried; "wonderful! Thou art a very great man, though so ugly. Had I not seen, surely I would never have believed. And thou sayest that thou wilt teach me to slay in this fashion?"

"Certainly, my father," I said airily; "it is nothing."

But all the same I firmly made up my mind that when "my father" Billali began to fire I would without fail lie down or take refuge behind a tree.

After this little incident nothing happened of any note till about an hour and a half before sundown, when we arrived beneath the shadow of the towering volcanic mass that I have already described. It is quite impossible for me to describe its grim grandeur as it appeared to me while my patient bearers toiled along the bed of the ancient watercourse towards the spot where the rich brown-clad cliff shot up from precipice to precipice till its crown lost itself in cloud. All I can say is that it almost awed me by the intensity of its lonesome and most solemn greatness. On we went up the bright and sunny slope, till at last the creeping shadows from above swallowed up its brightness, and presently we began to pass through a cutting hewn in the living rock. Deeper and deeper grew this marvelous work, which must, I should say, have employed thousands of men for many years. Indeed, how it was ever executed at all without the aid of blasting powder or dynamite I cannot to this day imagine. It is and must remain one of the mysteries of that wild land. I can only suppose that these cuttings and the vast caves that had been hollowed out of the rocks they pierced were the state undertakings of the people of Kôr, who lived here in the dim lost ages of the world, and, as in the case of the Egyptian monuments, were executed by the forced labor of tens of thousands of captives, carried on through an indefinite number of centuries. But who were the people?

At last we reached the face of the precipice itself, and found ourselves looking into the mouth of a dark tunnel that forcibly reminded me of those undertaken by our nineteenth-century engineers in the construction of railway lines. Out of this tunnel flowed a considerable stream of water. Indeed, though I do not think that I have mentioned it, we had followed this stream, which ultimately developed into the river I have already described as winding away to the right, from the spot where the cutting in the solid rock commenced. Half of this cutting formed a channel for the stream, and half, which was placed on a slightly higher level—eight feet, perhaps—was devoted to the purposes of a roadway. At the termination of the cutting, however, the stream turned off across the plain and followed a channel of its own. At the mouth of the cave the cavalcade was halted, and, while the men employed themselves in lighting some earthenware lamps they had brought with them, Billali, descending from his litter, informed me politely but firmly that the orders of *She* were that we were now to be blindfolded, so that we should not learn the secret of the paths through the bowels of the mountains. To this I, of course, assented cheerfully enough, but Job, who was now very much better, notwithstanding the journey, did not like it at all, fancying, I believe, that it was but a preliminary step to being hot-potted. He was, however, a little consoled when I pointed out to him that there were no hot pots at hand, and, so far as I knew, no fire to heat them in. As for poor Leo, after turning restlessly for hours, he had, to my deep thankfulness, at last dropped off into a sleep or stupor, I do not know which, so there was no need to blindfold him. The blind-folding was performed by binding a piece of the yellowish linen—whereof those of the Amahagger who condescended to wear anything in particular made their dresses—tightly round the eyes. This linen I afterwards discovered was taken from the tombs, and was not, as I had at first supposed, of native manufacture. The bandage was then knotted at the back of the head, and finally brought down again and the ends bound under the chin to prevent its slipping. Ustane was, by the way, also blindfolded, I do not know why, unless it was from fear that she should impart the secrets of the route to us.

This operation performed, we started on once more, and soon, by the echoing sound of the footsteps of the bearers and the increased noise of the water caused by reverbera-tion in a confined space, I knew that we were entering into the bowels of the great mountain. It was an eerie sensation, being borne along into the dead heart of the rock we knew not whither, but I was getting used to eerie sensations by this time, and by now was pretty well pre-pared for anything. So I lay still, and listened to the tramp, tramp of the bearers and the rushing of the water, and tried to believe that I was enjoying myself. Presently the men set up the melancholy little chant that I had heard on the first night when we were captured in the whaleboat, and the effect produced by their voices was very curious, and quite indescribable on paper. After a while the air began to get exceedingly thick and heavy, so much so, indeed, that I felt as though I were going to choke, till at length the litter took a sharp turn, then another and another, and the sound of the running water ceased. After this the air got fresher again, but the turns were con-tinuous, and to me, blindfolded as I was, most bewildering.

I tried to keep a map of them in my mind in case it might ever be necessary for us to try and escape by this route, but, needless to say, failed utterly. Another half hour or so passed, and then suddenly I became aware that we were once more in the open air. I could see the light through my bandage and feel its freshness on my face. A few more minutes and the caravan halted, and I heard Billali order Ustane to remove her bandage and undo ours. Without waiting for her attentions I got the knot of mine loose, and looked out.

As I anticipated, we had passed right through the precipice, and were now on the farther side, and immediately beneath its beetling face. The first thing I noticed was that the cliff was not nearly so high here, not so high I should say by five hundred feet, which proved that the bed of the lake, or rather of the vast ancient crater in which we stood, was much above the level of the surrounding plain. For the rest, we found ourselves in a huge rock-surrounded cup, not unlike that of the first place where we had sojourned, only ten times the size. Indeed, I could only just make out the frowning line of the opposite cliffs. A great portion of the plain thus enclosed by nature was cultivated, and fenced in with walls of stone placed there to keep the cattle and goats, of which there were large herds about, from breaking into the gardens. Here and there rose great grass mounds, and some miles away towards the center I thought that I could see the outline of colossal ruins. I had no time to observe anything more at the moment, for we were instantly surrounded by crowds of Amahagger, similar in every particular to those with whom we were already familiar, who, though they spoke little, pressed round us so closely as to obscure the view to a person lying in a hammock. Then all of a sudden a number of armed men arranged in companies, and marshaled by officers who held ivory wands in their hands, came running swiftly towards us, having, so far as I could make out, emerged from the face of the precipice like ants from their burrows. These men as well as their officers were all robed in addition to the usual leopard skin, and, as I gathered, formed the bodyguard of *She* herself.

Their leader advanced to Billali, saluted him by placing his ivory wand transversely across his forehead, and then asked some question which I could not catch, and Billali having answered him the whole regiment turned and marched along the side of the cliff, our cavalcade of litters following in their track. After going thus for about half a mile we halted once more in front of the mouth of a tremendous cave, measuring about sixty feet in height by eighty wide, and here Billali descended finally, and requested Job and myself to do the same. Leo, of course, was far too ill to do anything of the sort. I did so, and we entered the great cave, into which the light of the setting sun penetrated for some distance, while beyond the reach of the light it was faintly illuminated with lamps which seemed to me to stretch away for an almost immeasurable distance, like the gas lights of an empty London street. The first thing that I noticed was that the walls were covered with sculptures in bas-relief, of a sort, pictorially speaking, similar to those that I have described upon the vases: love scenes principally, then hunting pictures, pictures of executions, and the torture of criminals by the placing of a presumably red-hot pot upon the head, showing whence our hosts had derived this pleasant practice. There were very few battle pieces, though many of duels, and men running and wrestling, and from this fact I am led to believe that this people was not much subject to attack by exterior foes, either on account of the isolation of its position or because of its great strength. Between the pictures were columns of stone characters of a formation absolutely new to me; at any rate they were neither Greek, nor Egyptian, nor Hebrew, nor Assyrian—that I am sure of. They looked more like Chinese writings than any other that I am acquainted with. Near the entrance of the cave both pictures and writings were worn away, but further in they were in many cases absolutely fresh and perfect as the day on which the sculptor had ceased work upon them.

The regiment of guards did not come further than the entrance to the cave, where they formed up to let us pass through. On entering the place itself we were, however, met by a man robed in white, who bowed humbly, but said nothing, which, as it afterwards appeared that he was a deaf mute, was not very wonderful.

Running at right angles to the great cave, at a distance of some twenty feet from the entrance, was a smaller cave or wide gallery that was pierced into the rock both to the right and to the left of the main cavern. In front of the gallery to our left stood two guards, from which circumstance I argued that it was the entrance to the apartments of *She* herself. The mouth of the right-hand gallery was unguarded, and along it the mute indicated that we were to proceed. Walking a few yards down this passage, which was lighted with lamps, we came to the entrance to a chamber having a curtain made of some grass material, not unlike a Zanzibar mat in appearance, hung over the doorway. This the mute drew back with another profound obeisance, and led the way into a good-sized apartment, hewn, of course, out of the solid rock, but to my great delight lighted by means of a shaft pierced in the face of the precipice. In this room was a stone bedstead, pots full of water for washing, and beautifully tanned leopard skins to serve as blankets.

Here we left Leo, who was still sleeping heavily, and with him stopped Ustane. I noticed that the mute gave her a very sharp look, as much as to say, "Who are you, and by whose orders do you come here?" Then he conducted us to another similar room, which Job took, and then to two more that were respectively occupied by Billali and myself.

12 ♦
"She"

THE FIRST care of Job and myself, after seeing to Leo, was to wash ourselves and put on clean clothing, for what we were wearing had not been changed since the loss of the dhow. Fortunately, as I think that I have said, by far the greater part of our personal baggage had been packed into the whaleboat, and was therefore saved—and brought hither by the bearers—although all the stores laid in by us for barter and presents to the natives were lost. Nearly all our clothing was made of a well-shrunk and very strong gray flannel, and excellent I found it for traveling in these places, because though a Norfolk jacket, shirt, and pair of trousers of it only weighed about four pounds, a great consideration in a tropical country, where every extra ounce tells on the wearer, it was warm, and offered a good resistance to the rays of the sun, and best of all to chills, which are so apt to result from sudden changes of temperature.

Never shall I forget the comfort of the "wash and brush-up," and of those clean flannels. The only thing that was wanting to complete my joy was a cake of soap, of which we had none.

Afterwards I discovered that the Amahagger, who do not include dirt among their many disagreeable qualities, use a kind of burned earth for washing purposes, which, though unpleasant to the touch till one gets accustomed to it, forms a very fair substitute for soap.

By the time that I was dressed, and had combed and trimmed my black beard, the previous condition of which was certainly sufficiently unkempt to give weight to Billali's appellation for me, the "Baboon," I began to feel most uncommonly hungry. Therefore I was by no means sorry when, without the slightest preparatory sound or warning, the curtain over the entrance to my cave was flung aside, and another mute, a young girl this time, announced to me by signs that I could not misunderstand—that is, by opening her mouth and pointing down it—that there was something ready to eat. Accordingly I followed her into the next chamber, which we had not yet entered, where I found Job, who had also, to his great embarrassment, been conducted thither by a fair mute Job had never got over the advances the former lady had made towards him, and suspected every girl who came near to him of similar designs.

"These young parties have a way of looking at one, sir," he would say apologetically, "which I don't call respectable."

This chamber was twice the size of the sleeping caves, and I saw at once that it had originally served as a refectory, and also probably as an embalming room for the Priests of the Dead; for I may as well say at once that these hollowed-out caves were nothing more or less than vast catacombs, in which for tens of ages the mortal remains of the great extinct race whose monuments surrounded us had been first preserved, with an art and a completeness that has never since been equaled, and then hidden away for all time. On each side of this particular rock chamber was a long and solid stone table, about three feet wide by three feet six in height, hewn out of the living rock, of which it had formed part, and was still attached to at the base. These tables were slightly hollowed out or curved inward, to give room for the knees of anyone sitting on the stone ledge that had been cut for a bench along the side of the cave at a distance of about two feet from them. Each of them, also, was so arranged that it ended right under a shaft pierced in the rock for the admission of light and air. On examining them carefully, however, I saw that there was a difference between them that had at first escaped my attention, viz., that one of the tables, that to the left as we entered the cave, had evidently been used, not to eat upon, but for the purposes of embalming. That this was beyond all question the case was clear from five shallow depressions in the stone of the table, all shaped like a human form, with a separate place for the head to lie in, and a little bridge to support the neck, each depression being of a different size, so as to fit bodies varying in stature from a full-grown man's to a small child's, and with little holes bored at intervals to carry off fluid. And, indeed, if any further confirmation was required, we had but to look at the wall of the cave above to find it. For there, sculptured all round the apartment, and looking nearly as fresh as the day it was done, was the pictorial representation of the death, embalming, and burial of an old man with a long beard, probably an ancient king or grandee of this country.

The first picture represented his death. He was lying upon a couch which had four short curved posts at the corners coming to a knob at the end, in appearance something like a written note of music, and was evidently in the very act of expiring. Gathered round the couch were women and children weeping, the former with their hair hanging down their back. The next scene represented the embalmment of the body, which lay nude upon a table with depressions in it, similar to the one before us; probably, indeed, it was a picture of the same table. Three men were employed at the work—one superintending, one holding a funnel shaped exactly like a port wine strainer, of which the narrow end was fixed in an incision in the breast, no doubt in the great pectoral artery; while the third, who was depicted as standing straddle-legged over the corpse, held a kind of large jug high in his hand, and poured from it some steaming fluid which fell accurately into the funnel. The most curious part of this sculpture is that both the man with the funnel and the man who poured the fluid are drawn holding their noses, either I suppose because of the stench arising from the body, or more probably to keep out the aromatic fumes of the hot fluid which was being forced into the dead man's veins. Another curious thing which I am unable to explain is that all three men were represented as having a band of linen tied round the face with holes in it for the eyes.

The third sculpture was a picture of the burial of the deceased. There he was, stiff and cold, clothed in a linen robe, and laid out on a stone slab such as I had slept upon at our first sojourning place. At his head and feet burned lamps, and by his side were placed several of the beautiful painted vases that I have described, which were perhaps supposed to be full of provisions. The little chamber was crowded with mourners, and with musicians playing on an instrument resembling a lyre, while near the foot of the corpse stood a man with a sheet, with which he was preparing to cover it from view.

These sculptures, looked at merely as works of art, were so remarkable that I make no apology for describing them rather fully. They struck me also as being of surpassing interest as representing, probably with studious accuracy, the last rites of the dead as practiced among an utterly lost people, and even then I thought how envious some antiquarian friends of my own at Cambridge would be if ever I got an opportunity of describing these wonderful remains to them. Probably they would say that I was exaggerating, notwithstanding that every page of this history must bear so much internal evidence of its truth that it would obviously have been quite impossible for me to have invented it.

To return. As soon as I had hastily examined these sculptures, which I think I omitted to mention were executed in relief, we sat down to a very excellent meal of boiled goat's flesh, fresh milk, and cakes made of meal, the whole being served upon clean wooden platters.

When we had eaten, Job and I returned to see how poor Leo was getting on, Billali going to wait upon *She* and hear her commands. On reaching Leo's room we found the poor boy in a very bad way. He had woke up from his torpor, and was altogether off his head, babbling about some boat race on the Cam, and was inclined to be violent. Indeed, when we entered the room Ustane was holding him down. I spoke to him, and my voice seemed to soothe him; at any rate he grew much quieter, and was persuaded to swallow a dose of quinine.

I had been sitting with him for an hour, perhaps—at any rate I know that it was getting so dark that I could only just make out his head lying like a gleam of gold upon the pillow we had extemporized out of a bag covered with a blanket—when suddenly Billali arrived with an air of great importance, and informed me that *She* herself had deigned to express a wish to see me—an honor, he added, accorded to but very few. I think that he was a little horrified at my cool way of taking the honor, but the fact was that I did not feel overwhelmed with gratitude at the prospect of seeing some savage, dusky queen, however absolute and mysterious she might be, more especially as my mind was full of dear Leo, for whose life I began to have great fears. However, I rose to follow him, and as I did so I caught sight of something bright lying on the floor, which I picked up. Perhaps the reader will remember that with the potsherd in the casket was a composition scarabaeus marked with a round O, a goose, and another curious hieroglyphic, the meaning of which signs is "Suten se Rā," or "Royal Son of the Sun." This scarab, which is a very small one, Leo had insisted upon having set in a massive gold ring, such as is generally used for signets, and it was this very ring that I now picked up. He had pulled it off in the paroxysm of his fever, at least I suppose so, and flung it down upon the rock floor. Thinking that if I left it about it might get lost, I slipped it onto my own little finger, and then followed Billali, leaving Job and Ustane with Leo.

We passed down the passage, crossed the great aisle-like cave, and came to the corresponding passage on the other side, at the mouth of which the guards stood like two statues. As we came they bowed their heads in salutation, and then lifting their long spears placed them transversely across their foreheads, as the leaders of the troop that had met us had done with their ivory wands. We stepped between them, and found ourselves in an exactly similar gallery to that which led to our own apartments, only this passage was, comparatively speaking, brilliantly lighted. A few paces down it we were met by four mutes— two men and two women—who bowed low and then arranged themselves, the women in front and the men behind of us, and in this order we continued our procession past

several doorways hung with curtains resembling those leading to our own quarters, and which I afterwards found
opened out into chambers occupied by the mutes who
attended on *She*. A few paces more and we came to another doorway facing us, and not to our left like the
others, which seemed to mark the termination of the passage. Here two more white-, or rather yellow-robed guards
were standing, and they too bowed, saluted, and let us
pass through heavy curtains into a great antechamber,
quite forty feet long by as many wide, in which some eight
or ten women, most of them young and handsome, with
yellowish hair, sat on cushions working with ivory needles
at what had the appearance of being embroidery frames.
These women were also deaf and dumb. At the farther
end of this great lamp-lit apartment was another doorway
closed in with heavy Oriental-looking curtains, quite unlike
those that hung before the doors of our own rooms, and
here stood two particularly handsome girl mutes, their
heads bowed upon their bosoms and their hands crossed in
an attitude of the humblest submission. As we advanced
they each stretched out an arm and drew back the curtains.
Thereupon Billali did a curious thing. Down he went,
that venerable-looking old gentleman—for Billali is a gentleman at the bottom—down onto his hands and knees, and
in this undignified position, with his long white beard trail-
ing on the ground, he began to creep into the apartment
beyond. I followed him, standing on my feet in the usual
fashion. Looking over his shoulder he perceived it.

"Down, my son; down, my Baboon; down onto thy hands
and knees. We enter the presence of *She*, and, if thou art
not humble, of a surety she will blast thee where thou
standest."

I halted, and felt scared. Indeed, my knees began to

give way of their own mere motion; but reflection came to my aid. I was an Englishman, and why, I asked myself, should I creep into the presence of some savage woman as though I were a monkey in fact as well as in name? I would not and could not do it, that is, unless I was absolutely sure that my life or comfort depended upon it. If once I began to creep upon my knees I should always have to do so, and it would be a patent acknowledgment of inferiority. So, fortified by an insular prejudice against kowtowing, which has, like most of our so-called prejudices, a good deal of common sense to recommend it, I marched in boldly after Billali. I found myself in another apartment, considerably smaller than the anteroom, of which the walls were entirely hung with rich-looking curtains of the same make as those over the door, the work, as I subsequently discovered, of the mutes who sat in the antechamber and wove them in strips, which were afterwards sewn together. Also, here and there about the room, were settees of a beautiful black wood of the ebony tribe, inlaid with ivory, and all over the floor were other tapestries, or rather rugs. At the top end of this apartment was what appeared to be a recess, also draped with curtains, through which shone rays of light. There was nobody in the place except ourselves.

Painfully and slowly old Billali crept up the length of the cave, and with the most dignified stride that I could command I followed after him. But I felt that it was more or less of a failure. To begin with, it is not possible to look dignified when you are following in the wake of an old man writhing along on his stomach like a snake, and then, in order to go sufficiently slowly, either I had to keep my leg some seconds in the air at every step, or else to advance with a full stop between each stride, like Mary

Queen of Scots going to execution in a play. Billali was not good at crawling, I suppose his years stood in the way, and our progress up that apartment was a very long affair. I was immediately behind him, and several times I was sorely tempted to help him on with a good kick. It is so absurd to advance into the presence of savage royalty after the fashion of an Irishman driving a pig to market, for that is what we looked like, and the idea nearly made me burst out laughing then and there. I had to work off my dangerous tendency to unseemly merriment by blowing my nose, a proceeding which filled old Billali with horror, for he looked over his shoulder and made a ghastly face at me, and I heard him murmur, "Oh, my poor Baboon!"

At last we reached the curtains, and here Billali collapsed flat onto his stomach, with his hands stretched out before him as though he were dead, and I, not knowing what to do, began to stare about the place. But presently I clearly felt that somebody was looking at me from behind the curtains. I could not see the person, but I could distinctly feel his or her gaze, and, what is more, it produced a very odd effect upon my nerves. I was frightened, I do not know why. The place was a strange one, it is true, and looked lonely, notwithstanding its rich hangings and the soft glow of the lamps—indeed, these accessories added to, rather than detracted from its loneliness, just as a lighted street at night has always a more solitary appearance than a dark one. It was so silent in the place, and there lay Billali like one dead before the heavy curtains, through which the odor of perfume seemed to float up towards the gloom of the arched roof above. Minute grew into minute, and still there was no sign of life, nor did the curtain move; but I felt the gaze of the unknown being sinking through and through me, and filling me with a nameless terror, till the perspiration stood in beads upon my brow.

At length the curtain began to move. Who could be behind it? Some naked savage queen, a languishing Oriental beauty, or a nineteenth-century young lady, drinking afternoon tea? I had not the slightest idea, and should not have been astonished at seeing any of the three. I was getting beyond astonishment. The curtain agitated itself a little, then suddenly between its folds there appeared a most beautiful white hand (white as snow), and with long tapering fingers, ending in the pinkest nails. The hand grasped the curtain, and drew it aside, and as it did so I heard a voice, I think the softest and yet most silvery voice I ever heard. It reminded me of the murmur of a brook.

"Stranger," said the voice in Arabic, but much purer and more classical Arabic than the Amahagger talk, "stranger, wherefore art thou so much afraid?"

Now I flattered myself that in spite of my inward terrors I had kept a very fair command of my countenance, and was, therefore, a little astonished at this question. Before I had made up my mind how to answer it, however, the curtain was drawn, and a tall figure stood before us. I say a figure, for not only the body, but also the face was wrapped up in soft white, gauzy material in such a way as at first sight to remind me most forcibly of a corpse in its grave-clothes. And yet I do not know why it should have given me that idea, seeing that the wrappings were so thin that one could distinctly see the gleam of the pink flesh beneath them. I suppose it was owing to the way in which they were arranged, either accidentally, or more probably by design. Anyhow, I felt more frightened than ever at this ghostlike apparition, and my hair began to rise upon my head as the feeling crept over me that I was in the presence of something that was not canny. I could, however, clearly distinguish that the swathed mummy-like form before me was that of a tall and lovely woman, instinct with beauty in every part, and also with a certain snake-like grace which I had never seen anything to equal before. When she moved a hand or foot her entire frame seemed to undulate, and the neck did not bend, it curved.

"Why art thou so frightened, stranger?" asked the sweet voice again—a voice which seemed to draw the heart out of me, like the strains of softest music. "Is there that about me that should affright a man? Then surely are men changed from what they used to be!" And with a little coquettish movement she turned herself, and held up one arm, so as to show all her loveliness and the rich hair of raven blackness that streamed in soft ripples down her snowy robes, almost to her sandaled feet.

"It is thy beauty that makes me fear, O Queen," I answered humbly, scarcely knowing what to say, and I thought that as I did so I heard old Billali, who was still lying prostrate on the floor, mutter, "Good, my Baboon, good."

"I see that men still know how to beguile us women with false words. Ah, stranger," she answered, with a laugh that sounded like distant silver bells, "thou wast afraid because mine eyes were searching out thine heart, therefore wast thou afraid. But being but a woman, I forgive thee for the lie, for it was courteously said. And now tell me how came ye hither to this land of the dwellers among caves—a land of swamps and evil things and dead old shadows of the dead? What came ye for to see? How is it that ye hold your lives so cheap as to place them in the hollow of the hand of Hiya, into the hand of '*She-who-must-be-obeyed*'? Tell me also how come ye to know the tongue I talk. It is an ancient tongue, that sweet child of the old Syriac. Liveth it yet in the world? Thou seest I dwell among the caves and the dead, and naught know I of the affairs of men, nor have I cared to know. I have lived, O stranger, with my memories, and my memories are in a grave that mine own hands hollowed, for truly hath it been said that the child of man maketh his own path evil," and her beautiful voice quivered, and broke in a note as soft as any wood bird's. Suddenly her eye fell upon the sprawling frame of Billali, and she seemed to recollect herself.

"Ah! Thou art there, old man. Tell me how it is that things have gone wrong in thine household. Forsooth, it seems that these my guests were set upon. Ay, and one was nigh to being slain by the hot pot to be eaten of those brutes, thy children, and had not the others fought gallantly they too had been slain, and not even I could have called back the life which had been loosed from the body. What means it, old man? What hast thou to say that I should not give thee over to those who execute my vengeance?"

Her voice had risen in her anger, and it rang clear and cold against the rocky walls. Also, I thought I could see her eyes flash through the gauze that hid them. I saw poor Billali, whom I had believed to be a very fearless person, positively quiver with terror at her words.

"O Hiya! O *She!*" he said, without lifting his white head from the floor. "O *She*, as thou art great be merciful, for I am now as ever thy servant to obey. It was no plan or fault of mine, O *She*, it was those wicked ones who are called my children. Led on by a woman whom thy guest the Pig had scorned, they would have followed the ancient custom of the land, and eaten the fat black stranger who came hither with these thy guests the Baboon and the

Lion who is sick, thinking that no word had come from thee about the black one. But when the Baboon and the Lion saw what they would do, they slew the woman, and slew also their servant to save him from the horror of the pot. Then those evil ones, ay, those children of the Wicked One who lives in the Pit, they went mad with the lust of blood, and flew at the throats of the Lion and the Baboon and the Pig. But gallantly they fought. O Hiya! They fought like very men, and slew many, and held their own, and then I came and saved them, and the evildoers have I sent on hither to Kôr to be judged of thy greatness, O *She*, and here they are."

"Ay, old man, I know it, and tomorrow will I sit in the great hall and do justice upon them, fear not. And for thee, I forgive thee, though hardly. See that thou dost keep thine household better. Go."

Billali rose upon his knees with astonishing alacrity, bowed his head thrice, and, his white beard sweeping the ground, crawled down the apartment as he had crawled up it, till he finally vanished through the curtains, leaving me, not a little to my alarm, alone with this terrible but most fascinating person.

13 ♦

Ayesha Unveils

"There," said *She*, "he has gone, the white-bearded old fool! Ah, how little knowledge does a man acquire in his life. He gathereth it up like water, but like water it runneth through his fingers, and yet, if his hands be but wet as though with dew, behold a generation of fools call out, 'See, he is a wise man!' Is it not so? But how call they thee? 'Baboon,' he says," and she laughed; "but that is the fashion of these savages who lack imagination, and fly to the beasts they resemble for a name. How do they call thee in thine own country, stranger?"

"They call me Holly, O Queen," I answered.

"Holly," she answered, speaking the word with difficulty, and yet with a most charming accent; "and what is 'Holly'?"

" 'Holly' is a prickly tree," I said.

"So. Well, thou hast a prickly and yet a treelike look. Strong art thou, and ugly, but, if my wisdom be not at fault, honest at the core, and a staff to lean on. Also one who thinks. But stay, O Holly, stand not there, enter with me and be seated by me. I would not see thee crawl before me like those slaves. I am aweary of their worship and their terror; sometimes when they vex me I could blast them for very sport, and to see the rest turn white, even to the heart." And she held the curtain aside with her ivory hand to let me pass in.

168

I entered, shuddering. This woman was very terrible. Within the curtains was a recess, about twelve feet by ten, and in the recess was a couch and a table whereon stood fruit and sparkling water. By it, at its end, was a vessel like a font cut in carved stone, also full of pure water. The place was softly lit with lamps formed out of the beautiful vessels of which I have spoken, and the air and curtains were laden with a subtle perfume. Perfume too seemed to emanate from the glorious hair and white, clinging vestments of *She* herself. I entered the little room, and there stood uncertain.

"Sit," said *She*, pointing to the couch. "As yet thou hast no cause to fear me. If thou hast cause, thou shalt not fear for long, for I shall slay thee. Therefore let thy heart be light."

I sat down on the end of the couch near to the fontlike basin of water, and *She* sank down softly onto the other end.

"Now, Holly," she said, "how comest thou to speak Arabic? It is my own dear tongue, for Arabian am I by my birth, even 'al Arab al Ariba' [an Arab of the Arabs], and of the race of our father Yárab, the son of Kâhtan, for in that fair and ancient city Ozal was I born, in the province of Yaman the Happy. Yet dost thou not speak it as we used to speak. Thy talk doth lack the music of the sweet tongue of the tribes of Hamyar which I was wont to hear. Some of the words too seemed changed, even as among these Amahagger, who have debased and defiled its purity, so that I must speak with them in what is to me another tongue." [1]

---

[1] Yárab the son of Kâhtan, who lived some centuries before the time of Abraham, was the father of the ancient Arabs, and gave its name Araba to the country. In speaking of herself as "al Arab al Ariba," *She* no doubt meant to convey that she was of the true Arab blood as distinguished from

"I have studied it," I answered, "for many years. Also, the language is spoken in Egypt and elsewhere."

"So it is still spoken, and there is yet an Egypt? And what pharaoh sits upon the throne? Still one of the spawn of the Persian Ochus, or are the Achaemenians gone, for far is it to the days of Ochus?"

"The Persians have been gone from Egypt for nigh two thousand years, and since then the Ptolemies, the Romans, and many others have flourished and held sway upon the Nile, and fallen when their time was ripe," I said, aghast. "What canst thou know of the Persian Artaxerxes?"

She laughed, and made no answer, and again a cold chill went through me. "And Greece," she said; "is there still a Greece? Ah, I loved the Greeks. Beautiful were they as the day, and clever, but fierce at heart and fickle, notwithstanding."

"Yes," I said, "there is a Greece; and, just now, is it once more a people. Yet the Greeks of today are not what the Greeks of the old time were, and Greece herself is but a mockery of the Greece that was."

"So! The Hebrews, are they yet at Jerusalem? And does the Temple that the wise king built stand, and if so, what God do they worship therein? Is their Messiah come, of whom they preached so much and prophesied so loudly, and doth He rule the earth?"

"The Jews are broken and gone, and the fragments of their people strew the world, and Jerusalem is no more. As for the temple that Herod built—"

"Herod!" she said. "I know not Herod. But go on."

the naturalized Arabs, the descendants of Ismael, the son of Abraham and Hagar, who were known as "al Arab al mostáreba." The dialect of the Koreish was usually called the clear or "perspicuous" Arabic, but the Hamaritic dialect approached nearer to the purity of the mother Syriac.
—L. H. H.

"The Romans burned it, and the Roman eagles flew across its ruins, and now Judea is a desert."

"So, so! They were a great people, those Romans, and went straight to their end—ay, they speed to it like Fate, or like their own eagles on their prey!—and left peace be-·hind them."

"*Solitudinem faciunt, pacem appellant*," I suggested.

"Ah, thou canst speak the Latin tongue, too!" she said, in surprise. "It hath a strange ring in my ears after all these days, and it seems to me that thy accent does not fall as the Romans put it. Who was it wrote that? I know not the saying, but it is a true one of that great people. It seems that I have found a learned man—one whose hands have held the water of the world's knowledge. Knowest thou Greek also?"

"Yes, O Queen, and something of Hebrew, but not to speak them well. They are all dead languages now."

She clapped her hands in childish glee. "Of a truth, ugly tree that thou art, thou growest the fruits of wisdom, O Holly," she said, "but of those Jews whom I hated, for they called me 'heathen' when I would have taught them my philosophy. Did their Messiah come, and doth He rule the world?"

"Their Messiah came," I answered with reverence; "but He came poor and lowly, and they would have none of Him. They scourged Him, and crucified Him upon a tree, but yet His words and His works live on, for He was the Son of God, and now of a truth He doth rule half the world, but not with an Empire of the World."

"Ah, the fierce-hearted wolves," she said, "the followers of Sense and of many gods—greedy of gain and faction-torn. I can see their dark faces yet. So they crucified their Messiah? Well can I believe it. That he was a Son of the

Living Spirit would be naught to them, if indeed He was so, and of that we will talk afterwards. They would care naught for any God if he came not with pomp and power. They, a chosen people, a vessel of Him they call Jehovah, ay, and a vessel of Baal, and a vessel of Astoreth, and a vessel of the gods of the Egyptians—a high-stomached people, greedy of aught that brought them wealth and power. So they crucified their Messiah because He came in lowly guise—and now are they scattered about the earth. Why, if I remember, so said one of their prophets that it should be. Well, let them go—they broke my heart, those Jews, and made me look with evil eyes across the world, ay, and drove me to this wilderness, this place of a people that was before them. When I would have taught them wisdom in Jerusalem they stoned me, ay, at the Gate of the Temple whose white-bearded hypocrites and rabbis hounded the people on to stone me! See, here is the mark of it to this day!" and with a sudden move she pulled up the gauzy wrapping on her rounded arm, and pointed to a little scar that showed red against its milky beauty.

I shrank back horrified.

"Pardon me, O Queen," I said, "but I am bewildered. Nigh upon two thousand years have rolled across the earth since the Jewish Messiah hung upon His cross at Golgotha. How then canst thou have taught thy philosophy to the Jews before He was? Thou art a woman, and no spirit. How can a woman live two thousand years? Why dost thou befool me, O Queen?"

She leaned back on the couch, and once more I felt the hidden eyes playing upon me and searching out my heart.

"O man!" she said at last, speaking very slowly and deliberately, "it seems that there are still things upon the earth of which thou knowest naught. Dost thou still believe that all things die, even as those very Jews believed? I tell thee that naught really dies. There is no such thing as Death, though there be a thing called Change. See," and she pointed to some sculptures on the rocky wall. "Three times two thousand years have passed since the last of the great race that hewed those pictures fell before the breath of the pestilence which destroyed them, yet are they not dead. E'en now they live; perchance their spirits are drawn towards us at this very hour," and she glanced round. "Of a surety it sometimes seems to me that my eyes can see them."

"Yes, but to the world they are dead."

"Ay, for a time; but even to the world are they born again and again. I, yes I, Ayesha[2]—for that is my name, stranger—I say to thee that I wait now for one I loved to be born again, and here I tarry till he finds me, knowing of a surety that hither he will come, and that here, and here only, shall he greet me. Why, dost thou suppose that I, who am all powerful, I, whose loveliness is more than the loveliness of the Grecian Helen, of whom they used to sing, and whose wisdom is wider, ay, far more wide and deep than the wisdom of Solomon the Wise—I, who know the secrets of the earth and its riches, and can turn all things to my uses—I, who have even for a while overcome Change, that ye call Death—why, I say, O stranger, dost thou think that I herd here with barbarians lower than the beasts?"

"I know not," I said humbly.

"Because I wait for him I love. My life has perchance been evil, I know not—for who can say what is evil and what good?—so I fear to die even if I could die, which I cannot until mine hour comes, to go and seek him where he is; for between us there might rise a wall I could not

[2] Pronounced Assha.—L. H. H.

climb, at least, I dread it. Surely easy would it be also to lose the way in seeking in those great spaces wherein the planets wander on forever. But the day will come, it may be when five thousand more years have passed, and are lost and melted into the vault of Time, even as the little clouds melt into the gloom of night, or it may be tomorrow, when he, my love, shall be born again, and then, following a law that is stronger than any human plan, he shall find me *here*, where once he knew me, and of a surety his heart will soften towards me though I sinned against him; ay, even though he know me not again, yet will he love me, if only for my beauty's sake."

For a moment I was dumfounded, and could not answer. The matter was too overpowering for my intellect to grasp.

"But even so, O Queen," I said at last, "even if we men be born again and again, that is not so with thee, if thou speakest truly"—here she looked up sharply, and once more I caught the flash of those hidden eyes—"thou," I went on hurriedly, "who hast never died?"

"That is so," she said; "and it is so because I have, half by chance and half by learning, solved one of the great secrets of the world. Tell me, stranger: life is—why therefore should not life be lengthened for a while? What are ten or twenty or fifty thousand years in the history of life? Why in ten thousand years scarce will the rain and storms lessen a mountain top by a span in thickness? In two thousand years these caves have not changed, nothing has changed, but the beasts and man, who is as the beasts. There is naught that is wonderful about the matter, couldst thou but understand. Life is wonderful, ay, but that it should be a little lengthened is not wonderful. Nature hath her animating spirit as well as man, who is Nature's child, and he who can find that spirit, and let it breathe upon him, shall live with her life. He shall not live eternally, for Nature is not eternal, and she herself must die, even as the nature of the moon hath died. She herself must die, I say, or rather change and sleep till it be time for her to live again. But when shall she die? Not yet, I ween, and while she lives, so shall he who hath all her secret live with her. All I have not, yet have I some, more perchance than any who were before me. Now, to thee I doubt not that this thing is a great mystery, therefore I will not overcome thee with it now. Another time will I tell thee more if the mood be on me, though perchance I shall never speak thereof again. Dost thou wonder how I knew that ye were coming to this land, and so saved your heads from the hot pot?"

"Ay, O Queen," I answered feebly.

"Then gaze upon that water," and she pointed to the fontlike vessel, and then, bending forward, held her hand over it.

I rose and gazed, and instantly the water darkened. Then it cleared, and I saw as distinctly as I ever saw anything in my life—I saw, I say, our boat upon that horrible canal. There was Leo lying at the bottom asleep in it, with a coat thrown over him to keep off the mosquitoes, in such a fashion as to hide his face, and myself, Job, and Mahomed towing on the bank.

I started back aghast, and cried out that it was magic, for I recognized the whole scene—it was one which had actually occurred.

"Nay, nay, O Holly," she answered, "it is no magic; that is a fiction of ignorance. There is no such thing as magic, though there is such a thing as a knowledge of the secrets of Nature. That water is my glass; in it I see what passes if I care to summon up the pictures, which is not often. Therein I can show thee what thou wilt of the past, if it be anything to do with this country and with what I have known, or anything that thou, the gazer, hast known. Think of a face if thou wilt, and it shall be reflected from thy mind upon the water. I know not all the secret yet—I can read nothing in the future. But it is an old secret; I did not find it. In Arabia and in Egypt the sorcerers knew it centuries ago. So one day I chanced to bethink me of that old canal—some twenty centuries ago I sailed upon it, and I was minded to look thereon again. And so I looked, and there I saw the boat and three men walking, and one, whose face I could not see, but a youth of a noble form, sleeping in the boat, and so I sent and saved ye. And now farewell. But stay, tell me of this youth— the Lion, as the old man calls him. I would look upon him, but he is sick, thou sayest—sick with the fever, and also wounded in the fray."

"He is very sick," I answered sadly; "canst thou do nothing for him, O Queen who knowest so much?"

"Of a surety I can. I can cure him; but why speakest thou so sadly? Doth thou love the youth? Is he perchance thy son?"

"He is my adopted son, O Queen. Shall he be brought in before thee?"

"Nay. How long hath the fever taken him?"

"This is the third day."

"Good; then let him lie another day. Then will he perchance throw it off by his own strength, and that is better than that I should cure him, for my medicine is of a sort to shake the life in its very citadel. If, however, by tomorrow night, at that hour when the fever first took him, he doth not begin to mend, then will I come to him and cure him. Stay, who nurses him?"

"Our white servant, him whom Billali names the Pig; also"—and here I spoke with some little hesitation—"a woman named Ustane, a very handsome woman of this country, who came and embraced him when first she saw him, and hath stayed by him ever since, as I understand is the fashion of thy people, O Queen."

"My people! Speak not to me of my people," she answered hastily; "these slaves are no people of mine, they are but dogs to do my bidding till the day of my deliverance comes; and as for their customs, naught have I to do with them. Also, call me not Queen—I am sick of flattery and titles—call me Ayesha; the name hath a sweet sound in mine ears, it is an echo from the past. As for this Ustane, I know not. I wonder if it be she against whom I was warned, and whom I in turn did warn? Hath she—stay, I will see," and, bending forward, she passed her hand over the font of water and gazed intently into it. "See," she said quietly, "is that the woman?"

I looked into the water, and there, mirrored upon its placid surface, was the silhouette of Ustane's stately face. She was bending forward, with a look of infinite tenderness upon her features, watching something beneath her, and with her chestnut locks falling onto her right shoulder.

"It is she," I said, in a low voice, for once more I felt much disturbed at this most uncommon sight. "She watches Leo asleep."

"Leo!" said Ayesha in an absent voice. "Why, that is 'lion' in the Latin tongue. The old man hath named happily for once. It is very strange," she went on speaking to herself, "very. So like—but it is not possible!" With an impatient gesture she passed her hand over the water once more. It darkened, and the image vanished as silently and mysteriously as it had risen, and once more the lamplight, and the lamplight only, shone on the placid surface of that limpid, living mirror.

"Hast thou aught to ask me before thou goest, O Holly?" she said after a few moments' reflection. "It is but a rude life that thou must live here, for these people are savages, and know not the ways of cultivated man. Not that I am troubled thereby, for, behold my food," and she pointed to the fruit upon the little table. "Naught but fruit doth ever pass my lips—fruit and cakes of flour, and a little water. I have bidden my girls to wait upon thee. They are mutes, thou knowest, deaf are they and dumb, and therefore the safest of servants, save to those who can read their faces and their signs. I bred them so—it hath taken many centuries and much trouble; but at last I have triumphed. Once I succeeded before, but the race was too ugly, so I let it die away; but now, as thou seest, they are otherwise. Once, too, I reared a race of giants, but after a while Nature would no more of it, and it died away. Hast thou aught to ask of me?"

"Ay, one thing, O Ayesha," I said boldly; but feeling by no means as bold as I trust I looked. "I would gaze upon thy face."

She laughed out in her bell-like notes. "Bethink thee, Holly," she answered; "bethink thee. It seems that thou knowest the old myths of the gods of Greece. Was there not one Actaeon who perished miserably because he looked on too much beauty? If I showed thee my face, perchance thou wouldst perish miserably also; perchance thou wouldst eat out thy heart in impotent desire; for know I am not for thee—I am for no man, save one, who hath been, but is not yet."

"As thou wilt, Ayesha," I said. "I fear not thy beauty.

I have put my heart away from such vanity as woman's loveliness, that passes like a flower."

"Nay, thou errest," she said; "that does *not* pass. My beauty endures even as I endure; still, if thou wilt, oh rash man, have thy will; but blame not me if passion mount thy reason, as the Egyptian breakers used to mount a colt, and guide it whither thou wilt not. Never may the man to whom my beauty hath been unveiled put it from his mind, and therefore even with these savages do I go veiled, lest they vex me, and I should slay them. Say, wilt thou see?"

"I will," I answered, my curiosity overpowering me.

She lifted her white and rounded arms—never had I seen such arms before—and slowly, very slowly, withdrew some fastening beneath her hair. Then all of a sudden the long, corpselike wrappings fell from her to the ground, and my eyes traveled up her form, now robed only in a garb of clinging white that did but serve to show its perfect and imperial shape, instinct with a life that was more than life, and with a certain serpentlike grace that was more than human. On her little feet were sandals, fastened with studs of gold. Then came ankles more perfect than ever sculptor dreamed of. About the waist her white kirtle was fastened by a double-headed snake of solid gold, above which her gracious form swelled up in lines as pure as they were lovely, till the kirtle ended on the snowy argent of her breast, whereon her arms were folded. I gazed above them at her face, and—I do not exaggerate—shrank back blinded and amazed. I have heard of the beauty of celestial beings, now I saw it; only this beauty, with all its awful loveliness and purity, was *evil*—at least, at the time, it struck me as evil. How am I to describe it? I cannot—simply, I cannot! The man does not live whose pen could convey a sense of what I saw. I might talk of the great changing eyes of deepest, softest black, of the tinted face, of the broad and noble brow, on which the hair grew low, and delicate, straight features. But, beautiful, surpassingly beautiful as they all were, her loveliness did not lie in them. It lay rather, if it can be said to have had any fixed abiding place, in a visible majesty, in an imperial grace, in a godlike stamp of softened power, which shone upon that radiant countenance like a living halo. Never before had I guessed what beauty made sublime could be—and yet, the sublimity was a dark one—the glory was not all of heaven—though none the less was it glorious. Though the face before me was that of a young woman of certainly not more than thirty years, in perfect health, and the first flush of ripened beauty, yet it had stamped upon it a look of unutterable experience, and of deep acquaintance with grief and passion. Not even the lovely smile that crept about the dimples of her mouth could hide this shadow of sin and sorrow. It shone even in the light of the glorious eyes, it was present in the air of majesty, and it seemed to say: "Behold me, lovely as no woman was or is, undying and half-divine; memory haunts me from age to age, and passion leads me by the hand—evil have I done, and with sorrow have I made acquaintance from age to age, and from age to age evil I shall do, and sorrow shall I know till my redemption comes."

Drawn by some magnetic force which I could not resist, I let my eyes rest upon her shining orbs, and felt a current pass from them to me that bewildered and half-blinded me.

She laughed—ah, how musically!—and nodded her little

head at me with an air of sublimated coquetry that would have done credit to a Venus Victrix.

"Rash man!" she said. "Like Actaeon, thou hast had thy will; be careful lest, like Actaeon, thou too dost perish miserably, torn to pieces by the ban-hounds of thine own passions. I too, O Holly, am a virgin goddess, not to be moved of any man, save one, and it is not thou. Say, hast thou seen enough?"

"I have looked on beauty, and I am blinded," I said hoarsely, lifting my hand to cover up my eyes.

"So! What did I tell thee? Beauty is like the lightning; it is lovely, but it destroys—especially trees, O Holly!" And again she nodded and laughed.

Suddenly she paused, and through my fingers I saw an awful change come over her countenance. Her great eyes suddenly fixed themselves into an expression in which horror seemed to struggle with some tremendous hope arising through the depths of her dark soul. The lovely face grew rigid, and the gracious, willowy form seemed to erect itself.

"Man," she half whispered, half hissed, throwing back her head like a snake about to strike, "man, where didst thou get that scarab on thy hand? Speak, or by the Spirit of Life I will blast thee where thou standest!" And she took one light step towards me, and from her eyes there shone such an awful light—to me it seemed almost like a flame—that I fell, then and there, on the ground before her, babbling confusedly in my terror.

"Peace," she said, with a sudden change of manner, and speaking in her former soft voice, "I did affright thee! Forgive me! But at times, O Holly, the almost infinite mind grows impatient of the slowness of the very finite, and I am tempted to use my power out of pure vexation—very nearly wast thou dead, but I remembered— But the scarab—about the scarabaeus!"

"I picked it up," I gurgled feebly as I got onto my feet again, and it is a solemn fact that my mind was so disturbed that at the moment I could remember nothing else about the ring except that I had picked it up in Leo's cave.

"It is very strange," she said, with a sudden access of womanlike trembling and agitation which seemed out of place in this awful woman, "but once I knew a scarab like that. It—hung round the neck—of one I loved," and she gave a little sob, and I saw that after all she was only a woman, although she might be a very old one.

"There," she went on, "it must be one like it, and yet never did I see one like it, for thereto hung a history, and he who wrote it prized it much.[3] But the scarab that I knew was not set thus in the bezel of a ring. Go now, Holly, go, and, if thou canst, try to forget that thou hast looked upon Ayesha's beauty," and, turning from me, she flung herself on her couch, and buried her face in the cushions.

As for me, I stumbled from her presence, and I do not remember how I reached my own cave.

[3] I am informed by a renowned and most learned Egyptologist, to whom I have submitted this very interesting and beautifully finished scarab, "Suten se Rā," that he has never seen one resembling it. Although it bears a title frequently given to Egyptian royalty, he is of opinion that it is not necessarily the cartouche of a pharaoh, on which either the throne or personal name of the monarch is generally inscribed. What the history of this particular scarab may have been we can now, unfortunately, never know, but I have little doubt but that it played some part in the tragic story of the Princess Amenartas and her lover Kallikrates, the forsworn priest of Isis.—EDITOR.

14 ♦

A Soul in Hell

It was nearly ten o'clock at night when I cast myself
down upon my bed, and began to gather my scattered wits,
and reflect upon what I had seen and heard. But the
more I reflected the less I could make of it. Was I mad,
or drunk, or dreaming, or was I merely the victim of a
gigantic and most elaborate hoax? How was it possible
that I, a rational man, not unacquainted with the leading
scientific facts of our history, and hitherto an absolute and
utter disbeliever in all the hocus-pocus that in Europe
goes by the name of the supernatural, could believe that
I had within the last few minutes been engaged in conversation with a woman two thousand and odd years old?
The thing was contrary to the experience of human nature,
and absolutely and utterly impossible. It must be a hoax,
and yet, if it were a hoax, what was I to make of it? What,
too, was to be said of the figures on the water, of the
woman's extraordinary acquaintance with the remote past,
and her ignorance, or apparent ignorance, of any subsequent history? What, too, of her wonderful and awful loveliness? This, at any rate, was a patent fact, and beyond the
experience of the world. No merely mortal woman could
shine with such a supernatural radiance. About that she
had, at any rate, been in the right—it was not safe for
any man to look upon such beauty. I was a hardened vessel
in such matters, having, with the exception of one painful

experience of my green and tender youth, put the softer
sex (I sometimes think that this is a misnomer) almost
entirely out of my thoughts. But now, to my intense horror, I *knew* that I could never put away the vision of those
glorious eyes; and, alas, the very *diablerie* of the woman,
whilst it horrified and repelled, attracted in even a greater
degree. A person with the experience of two thousand
years at her back, with the command of such tremendous
powers and the knowledge of a mystery that could hold off
death, was certainly worth falling in love with, if ever
woman was. But alas, it was not a question of whether
or no she was worth it, for so far as I could judge, not being
versed in such matters, I, a fellow of my college, noted
for what my acquaintances are pleased to call my misogyny,
and a respectable man now well on in middle life, had
fallen absolutely and hopelessly in love with this white
sorceress. Nonsense; it must be nonsense! She had warned
me fairly, and I had refused to take the warning. Curses
on the fatal curiosity that is ever prompting man to draw
the veil from woman, and curses on the natural impulse
that begets it! It is the cause of half—ay, and more than
half—of our misfortunes. Why cannot man be content to
live alone and be happy, and let the women live alone
and be happy too? But perhaps they would not be happy,
and I am not sure that we should either. Here was a nice
state of affairs. I, at my age, to fall a victim to this modern
Circe! But then she was not modern, at least she said not.
She was almost as ancient as the original Circe.

I tore my hair, and jumped up from my couch, feeling
that if I did not do something I should go off my head.
What did she mean about the scarabaeus too? It was
Leo's scarabaeus, and had come out of the old coffer
that Vincey had left in my rooms nearly one-and-twenty

years before. Could it be, after all, that the whole story was true, and the writing on the sherd was *not* a forgery, or the invention of some crack-brained, long-forgotten individual? And if so, could it be that *Leo* was the man that *She* was waiting for—the dead man who was to be born again? Impossible again! The whole thing was gibberish! Who ever heard of a man being born again?

But if it were possible that a woman could exist for two thousand years, this might be possible also—anything might be possible. I myself might, for aught I knew, be a reincarnation of some other forgotten self, or perhaps the last of a long line of ancestral selves. Well, *vive la guerre!* why not? Only, unfortunately, I had no recollection of these previous conditions. The idea was so absurd to me that I burst out laughing, and, addressing the sculptured picture of a grim-looking warrior on the cave wall, called out to him aloud, "Who knows, old fellow? Perhaps I was your contemporary. By Jove! perhaps I was you and you are I," and then I laughed again at my own folly, and the sound of my laughter rang dismally along the vaulted roof, as though the ghost of the warrior had uttered the ghost of a laugh.

Next I bethought me that I had not been to see how Leo was, so, taking up one of the lamps which was burning at my bedside, I slipped off my shoes and crept down the passage to the entrance of his sleeping cave. The draft of the night air was lifting his curtain to and fro gently, as though spirit hands were drawing and redrawing it. I slid into the vaultlike apartment and looked round. There was a light by which I could see that Leo was lying on the couch, tossing restlessly in his fever, but asleep. At his side, half-lying on the floor, half-leaning against the stone couch, was Ustane. She held his hand in one of hers, but she too was dozing, and the two made a pretty, or rather a pathetic, picture. Poor Leo! His cheek was burning red, there were dark shadows beneath his eyes, and his breath came heavily. He was very, very ill; and again the horrible fear seized me that he might die, and I be left alone in the world. And yet if he lived he would perhaps be my rival with Ayesha; even if he were not the man, what chance should I, middle-aged and hideous, have against his bright youth and beauty? Well, thank Heaven, my sense of right was not dead. *She* had not killed that yet; and, as I stood there, I prayed to the Almighty in my heart that my boy, my more than son, might live—ay, even if he proved to be the man.

Then I went back as softly as I had come, but still I could not sleep; the sight and thought of dear Leo lying there so ill had but added fuel to the fire of my unrest. My wearied body and overstrained mind awakened all my imagination into preternatural activity. Ideas, visions, almost inspirations, floated before it with startling vividness. Most of them were grotesque enough, some were ghastly, some recalled thoughts and sensations that had for years been buried in the debris of my past life. But behind and above them all hovered the shape of that awful woman, and through them gleamed the memory of her entrancing loveliness. Up and down the cave I strode—up and down.

Suddenly I observed what I had not noticed before, that there was a narrow aperture in the rocky wall. I took up the lamp and examined it; the aperture led to a passage. Now I was still sufficiently sensible to remember that it is not pleasant, in such a situation as ours was, to have passages running into one's bedchamber from no one knows where. If there are passages, people can come up them; they can come up when one is asleep. Partly to see where it went to, and partly from a restless desire to be doing something, I followed the passage. It led to a stone stair, which I descended; the stair ended in another passage, or rather tunnel, also hewn out of the bedrock, and running, so far as I could judge, exactly beneath the gallery that led to the entrance of our rooms, and across the great central cave. I went on down it: it was as silent as the grave, but still, drawn by some sensation or attraction that I cannot describe, I followed on, my stockinged feet falling without noise on the smooth and rocky floor. When I had traversed some fifty yards of space, I came to another passage running at right angles, and here an awful thing happened to me: the sharp draft caught my lamp and extinguished it, leaving me in utter darkness in the bowels of that mysterious place. I took a couple of strides forward so as to clear the bisecting tunnel, being terribly afraid lest I should turn up it in the dark if once I got confused as to the direction, and then paused to think. What was I to do? I had no match; it seemed awful to attempt that long journey back through the utter gloom, and yet I could not stand there all night, and, if I did, probably it would not help me much, for in the bowels of the rock it would be as dark at midday as at midnight. I looked back over my shoulder—not a sight or a sound. I peered forward down the darkness: surely, far away, I saw something like the faint glow of fire. Perhaps it was a cave where I could get a light—at any rate, it was worth investigating. Slowly and painfully I crept along the tunnel, keeping my hand against its wall, and feeling at every step with my foot before I put it down, fearing lest I should fall into some pit. Thirty paces—there was a light, a broad light that came and went, shining through curtains! Fifty paces—it was close at hand! Sixty—oh, great heaven!

I was at the curtains, and they did not hang close, so I could see clearly into the little cavern beyond them. It had all the appearance of being a tomb, and was lit up by a fire that burned in its center with a whitish flame and without smoke. Indeed, there, to the left, was a stone shelf with a little ledge to it three inches or so high, and on the shelf lay what I took to be a corpse; at any rate, it looked like one, with something white thrown over it. To the right was a similar shelf, on which lay some broidered coverings. Over the fire bent the figure of a woman; she was sideways to me and facing the corpse, wrapped in a dark mantle that hid her like a nun's cloak. She seemed to be staring at the flickering flame. Suddenly, as I was trying to make up my mind what to do, with a convulsive movement that somehow gave an impression of despairing energy, the woman rose to her feet and cast the dark cloak from her.

It was *She* herself!

She was clothed, as I had seen her when she unveiled, in the kirtle of clinging white, cut low upon her bosom, and bound in at the waist with the barbaric double-headed snake, and, as before, her rippling black hair fell in heavy masses down her back. But her face was what caught my eye, and held me as in a vice, not this time by the force of its beauty, but by the power of fascinated terror. The beauty was still there, indeed, but the agony, the blind passion, and the awful vindictiveness displayed upon those quivering features, and in the tortured look of the upturned eyes, were such as surpass my powers of description.

For a moment she stood still, her hands raised high above her head, and as she did so the white robe slipped from her down to her golden girdle, baring the blinding loveliness of her form. She stood there, her fingers clenched, and the awful look of malevolence gathered and deepened on her face.

Suddenly, I thought of what would happen if she discovered me, and the reflection made me turn sick and faint. But even if I had known that I must die if I stopped, I do not believe that I could have moved, for I was absolutely fascinated. But still I knew my danger. Supposing she should hear me, or see me through the curtain, supposing I even sneezed, or that her magic told her that she was being watched—swift indeed would be my doom.

Down came the clenched hands to her sides, then up again above her head, and, as I am a living and honorable man, the white flame of the fire leaped up after them, almost to the roof, throwing a fierce and ghastly glare upon *She* herself, upon the white figure beneath the covering, and every scroll and detail of the rockwork.

Down came the ivory arms again, and as they did so she spoke, or rather hissed, in Arabic, in a note that curdled my blood, and for a second stopped my heart.

"Curse her, may she be everlastingly accursed."

The arms fell and the flame sank. Up they went again, and the broad tongue of fire shot up after them; then again they fell.

"Curse her memory—accursed be the memory of the Egyptian."

Up again, and again down.

"Curse her, the fair daughter of the Nile, because of her beauty."

"Curse her, because her magic hath prevailed against me."

"Curse her, because she kept my beloved from me."

And again the flame dwindled and shrank.

She put her hands before her eyes, and, abandoning the

hissing tone, cried aloud: "What is the use of cursing? She prevailed, and she is gone."

Then she recommenced with an even more frightful energy:

"Curse her where she is. Let my curses reach her where she is and disturb her rest.

"Curse her through the starry spaces. Let her shadow be accursed.

"Let my power find her even there.

"Let her hear me even there. Let her hide herself in the blackness.

"Let her go down into the pit of despair, because I shall one day find her."

Again the flame fell, and again she covered her eyes with her hands.

"It is no use—no use," she wailed; "who can reach those who sleep? Not even I can reach them."

Then once more she began her unholy rites.

"Curse her when she shall be born again. Let her be born accursed.

"Let her be utterly accursed from the hour of her birth until sleep finds her.

"Yea, then, let her be accursed: for then shall I overtake her with my vengeance, and utterly destroy her."

And so on. The flame rose and fell, reflecting itself in her agonized eyes; the hissing sound of her terrible maledictions—and no words of mine, especially on paper, can convey how terrible they were—ran round the walls and died away in little echoes, and the fierce light and deep gloom alternated themselves on the white and dreadful form stretched upon that bier of stone.

But at length she seemed to wear herself out, and ceased. She sat herself down upon the rocky floor, and shook the dense cloud of her beautiful hair over her face and breast, and began to sob terribly in the torture of a heart-rending despair.

"Two thousand years," she moaned, "two thousand years have I waited and endured; but though century doth still creep on to century, and time give place to time, the sting of memory hath not lessened, the light of hope doth not shine more bright. Oh, to have lived two thousand years, with my passion eating at my heart, and with my sin ever before me! Oh, that for me life cannot bring forgetfulness! Oh, for the weary years that have been and are yet to come, and evermore to come, endless and without end!

"My love! My love! My love! Why did that stranger bring thee back to me after this sort? For five hundred years I have not suffered thus. Oh, if I sinned against thee, have I not wiped away the sin? When wilt thou come back to me who have all, and yet without thee have naught? What is there that I can do? What? What? What? And perchance she—perchance that Egyptian doth abide with thee where thou art, and mock my memory. Oh, why could I not die with thee, I who slew thee? Alas, that I cannot die! Alas! Alas!" And she flung herself prone upon the ground, and sobbed and wept till I thought her heart must burst.

Suddenly she ceased, raised herself to her feet, rearranged her robe, and, tossing back her long locks impatiently, swept across to where the figure lay upon the stone.

"Oh Kallikrates," she cried, and I trembled at the name, "I must look upon thy face again, though it be agony. It is a generation since I looked upon thee whom I slew— slew with mine own hand," and with trembling fingers she seized the corner of the sheetlike wrapping that covered the form upon the stone bier, and then paused. When she spoke again, it was in a kind of awed whisper, as though her idea were terrible even to herself.

"Shall I raise thee," she said, apparently addressing the corpse, "so that thou standest there before me, as of old? I *can* do it," and she held out her hands over the sheeted dead, while her whole frame became rigid and terrible to see, and her eyes grew fixed and dull. I shrank in horror behind the curtain, my hair stood up upon my head, and whether it was my imagination or a fact I am unable to say, but I thought that the quiet form beneath the covering began to quiver, and the winding sheet to lift as though it lay on the breast of one who slept. Suddenly she withdrew her hands, and the motion of the corpse seemed to me to cease.

"What is the use?" she said gloomily. "Of what use is it to recall the semblance of life when I cannot recall the spirit? Even if thou stoodest before me thou wouldst not know me, and couldst but do what I bid thee. The life in thee would be *my* life, and not *thy* life, Kallikrates."

For a moment she stood there brooding, and then cast herself down on her knees beside the form, and began to press her lips against the sheet, and weep. There was something so horrible about the sight of this awe-inspiring woman letting loose her passion on the dead—so much more horrible even than anything that had gone before, that I could no longer bear to look at it, and, turning, began to creep, shaking as I was in every limb, slowly along the pitch-dark passage, feeling in my trembling heart that I had had a vision of a soul in Hell.

On I stumbled, I scarcely know how. Twice I fell, once I turned up the bisecting passage, but fortunately found out my mistake in time. For twenty minutes or more

I crept along, till at last it occurred to me that I must have passed the little stair by which I descended. So, utterly exhausted, and nearly frightened to death, I sank down at length there on the stone flooring, and sank into oblivion.

When I came to I noticed a faint ray of light in the passage just behind me. I crept to it, and found it was the little stair down which the weak dawn was stealing. Passing up it I gained my chamber in safety, and, flinging myself on the couch, was soon lost in slumber or rather stupor.

15 ♦

Ayesha Gives Judgment

THE NEXT THING that I remember is opening my eyes and perceiving the form of Job, who had now practically recovered from his attack of fever. He was standing in the ray of light that pierced into the cave from the outer air, shaking out my clothes as a makeshift for brushing them, which he could not do because there was no brush, and then folding them up neatly and laying them on the foot of the stone couch. This done, he got my traveling dressing case out of the Gladstone bag, and opened it ready for my use. First, he stood it on the foot of the couch also, then, being afraid, I suppose, that I should kick it off, he placed it on a leopard skin on the floor, and stood back a step or two to observe the effect. It was not satisfactory, so he shut up the bag, turned it on end, and, having rested it against the foot of the couch, placed the dressing case on it. Next, he looked at the pots full of water, which constituted our washing apparatus. "Ah," I heard him murmur, "no hot water in this beastly place. I suppose these poor creatures only use it to boil each other in," and he sighed deeply.

"What is the matter, Job?" I said.

"Beg pardon, sir," he said, touching his hair. "I thought you were asleep, sir; and I am sure you look as though you want it. One might think from the look of you that you had been having a night of it."

I only groaned by way of answer. I had, indeed, been

having a night of it, such as I hoped never to have again.

"How is Mr. Leo, Job?"

"Much the same, sir. If he don't soon mend, he'll end, sir; and that's all about it; though I must say that that there savage, Ustane, do do her best for him, almost like a baptized Christian. She is always hanging round and looking after him, and if I ventures to interfere, it's awful to see her; her hair seems to stand on end, and she curses and swears away in her heathen talk—at least I fancy she must be cursing from the look of her."

"And what do you do then?"

"I make her a perlite bow, and I say, 'Young woman, your position is one that I don't quite understand, and can't recognize. Let me tell you that I has a duty to perform to my master as is incapacitated by illness, and that I am going to perform it until I am incapacitated too,' but she don't take no heed, not she—only curses and swears away worse than ever. Last night she put her hand under that sort of nightshirt she wears and whips out a knife with a kind of a curl in the blade, so I whips out my revolver, and we walks round and round each other till at last she bursts out laughing. It isn't nice treatment for a Christian man to have to put up with from a savage, however handsome she may be, but it is what people must expect as is *fools* enough"—Job laid great emphasis on the "fools"—"to come to such a place to look for things no man is meant to find. It's a judgment on us, sir—that's my opinion; and I, for one, is of opinion that the judgment isn't half done yet, and when it is done, we shall be done too, and just stop in these beastly caves with the ghosts and the corpseses for once and all. And now, sir, I must be seeing about Mr. Leo's broth, if that wildcat will let me; and, perhaps, you would like to get up, sir, because it's past nine o'clock."

Job's remarks were not of an exactly cheering order to a man who had passed such a night as I had; and, what is more, they had the weight of truth. Taking one thing with another, it appeared to me to be an utter impossibility that we should escape from the place where we were. Supposing that Leo recovered, and supposing that *She* would let us go, which was exceedingly doubtful, and that she did not "blast" us in some moment of vexation, and that we were not hot-potted by the Amahagger, it would be quite impossible for us to find our way across the net-work of marshes which, stretching for scores and scores of miles, formed a stronger and more impassable fortification round the various Amahagger households than any that could be built or designed by man. No, there was but one thing to do—face it out; and, speaking for my own part, I was so intensely interested in the whole weird story that, so far as I was concerned, notwithstanding the shattered state of my nerves, I asked nothing better, even if my life paid forfeit to my curiosity. What man for whom physiology has charms could forbear to study such a character as that of this Ayesha when the opportunity of doing so presented itself? The very terror of the pursuit added to its fascination, and besides, as I was forced to own to myself even now in the sober light of day, she herself had attractions that I could not forget. Not even the dreadful sight which I had witnessed during the night could drive that folly from my mind; and alas, that I should have to admit it, it has not been driven thence to this hour.

After I had dressed myself I passed into the eating, or rather embalming chamber, and had some food, which was as before brought to me by the girl mutes. When I had finished I went and saw poor Leo, who was quite off his head, and did not even know me. I asked Ustane how she thought he was; but she only shook her head and began to cry a little. Evidently her hopes were small; and I then and there made up my mind that, if it were in any way possible, I would get *She* to come and see him. Surely she would cure him if she chose—at any rate she said she could. While I was in the room, Billali entered, and also shook his head.

"He will die at night," he said.

"God forbid, my father," I answered, and turned away with a heavy heart.

" '*She-who-must-be-obeyed*' commands thy presence, my Baboon," said the old man as soon as we got to the curtain; "but oh, my dear son, be more careful. Yesterday I made sure in my heart that *She* would blast thee when thou didst not crawl upon thy stomach before her. She is sitting in the great hall even now to do justice upon those who would have smitten thee and the Lion. Come on, my son; come swiftly."

I turned and followed him down the passage, and when we reached the great central cave saw that many Amahagger, some robed, and some merely clad in the sweet simplicity of a leopard skin, were hurrying up it. We mingled with the throng, and walked up the enormous and, indeed, almost interminable cave. All the way its walls were elaborately sculptured, and every twenty paces or so passages opened out of it at right angles, leading, Billali told me, to tombs, hollowed in the rock by "the people who were before." Nobody visited those tombs now, he said; and I must say that my heart rejoiced when I thought of the opportunities of antiquarian research which opened out before me.

At last we came to the head of the cave, where there was a rock dais almost exactly similar to the one on which we had been so furiously attacked, a fact that proved to me that these daises must have been used as altars, probably for the celebration of religious ceremonies, and more especially of rites connected with the interment of the dead. On either side of this dais were passages leading, Billali informed me, to other caves full of dead bodies. "Indeed," he added, "the whole mountain is full of dead, and nearly all of them are perfect."

In front of the dais were gathered a great number of people of both sexes, who stood staring about in their peculiar gloomy fashion, which would have reduced Mark Tapley himself to misery in about five minutes. On the dais was a rude chair of black wood inlaid with ivory, having a seat made of grass fiber, and a footstool formed of a wooden slab attached to the framework of the chair.

Suddenly there was a cry of "Hiya! Hiya!" ("*She! She!*"), and thereupon the entire crowd of spectators instantly precipitated itself upon the ground, and lay still as though it were individually and collectively stricken dead, leaving me standing there like some solitary survivor of a massacre. As it did so a long string of guards began to defile from a passage to the left, and ranged themselves on either side of the dais. Then followed about a score of male mutes, then as many women mutes bearing lamps, and then a tall white figure, swathed from head to foot, in whom I recognized *She* herself. She mounted the dais and sat down upon the chair, and spoke to me in Greek, I suppose because she did not wish those present to understand what she said.

"Come hither, O Holly," she said, "and sit thou at my feet, and see me do justice on those who would have slain thee. Forgive me if my Greek doth halt a lame man; it is so long since I have heard the sound of it that my tongue it stiff, and will not bend rightly to the words."

I bowed, and, mounting the dais, sat down at her feet.

"How didst thou sleep, my Holly?" she asked.

"I slept not well, O Ayesha!" I answered with perfect truth, and with an inward fear that perhaps she knew how I had passed the heart of the night.

"So," she said with a little laugh. "I, too, have not slept well. Last night I had dreams, and methinks that thou didst call them to me, O Holly."

"Of what didst thou dream, Ayesha?" I asked indifferently.

"I dreamed," she answered quickly, "of one I hate and one I love," and then, as though to turn the conversation, she addressed the captain of her guard in Arabic: "Let the men be brought before me."

The captain bowed low, for the guard and her attendants did not prostrate themselves but had remained standing, and departed with his underlings down a passage to the right.

Then came a silence. *She* leaned her swathed head upon her hand and appeared to be lost in thought, while the multitude before her continued to grovel upon their stomachs, only screwing their heads round a little so as to get a view of us with one eye. It seemed that their queen so rarely appeared in public that they were willing to undergo this inconvenience, and even graver risks, to have the opportunity of looking on her, or rather on her garments, for no living man there except myself had ever seen her face. At last we caught sight of the waving of lights, and heard the tramp of men coming along the passage, and in filed the guard, and with them the survivors of our would-be murderers to the number of twenty or more, on whose countenances the natural expression of sullenness struggled with the terror that evidently filled their savage hearts. They were ranged in front of the dais, and would have cast themselves down on the floor of the cave like the spectators, but *She* stopped them.

"Nay," she said in her softest voice, "stand; I pray you stand. Perchance the time will soon be when ye shall grow weary of being stretched out," and she laughed melodiously.

I saw a cringe of terror run along the rank of the poor doomed wretches, and, wicked villains as they were, I felt sorry for them. Some minutes, perhaps two or three, passed before anything fresh occurred, during which *She* appeared from the movement of her head—for, of course, we could not see her eyes—to be slowly and carefully examining each delinquent. At last she spoke, addressing herself to me in a quiet and deliberate tone.

"Dost thou, O my guest, who art known in thine own country by the name of the Prickly Tree, recognize these men?"

"Ay, O Queen, nearly all of them," I said, and I saw them glower at me as I said it.

"Then tell to me, and this great company, the tale whereof I have heard."

Thus adjured, I, in as few words as I could, related the history of the cannibal feast, and of the attempted torture of our poor servant. The narrative was received in perfect silence, both by the accused and by the audience, and also by *She* herself. When I had done, Ayesha called upon Billali by name, and, lifting his head from the ground, but without rising, the old man confirmed my story. No further evidence was taken.

"Ye have heard," said *She* at length, in a cold, clear

voice, very different from her usual tones—indeed, it was one of the most remarkable things about this extraordinary creature that her voice had the power of suiting itself in a wonderful manner to the mood of the moment. "What have ye to say, ye rebellious children, why vengeance should not be done upon you?"

For some time there was no answer, but at last one of the men, a fine, broad-chested fellow, well on in middle-life, with deep-graven features and an eye like a hawk's, spoke, and said that the orders that they had received were not to harm the white men; nothing was said of their black servant, so, egged on thereto by a woman who was now dead, they proceeded to try to hot-pot him after the ancient and honorable custom of their country, with a view of eating him in due course. As for their attack upon ourselves, it was made in an access of sudden fury, and they deeply regretted it. He ended by humbly praying that mercy might be extended to them; or, at least, that they might be banished into the swamps, to live or die as it might chance; but I saw it written on his face that he had but little hope of mercy.

Then came a pause, and the most intense silence reigned over the whole scene, which, illuminated as it was by the flicker of the lamps striking out broad patterns of light and shadow upon the rocky walls, was as strange as any I ever saw, even in that unholy land. Upon the ground before the dais were stretched scores of the corpselike forms of the spectators, till at last the long lines of them were lost in the gloomy background. Before this outstretched audience were the knots of evildoers, trying to cover up their natural terrors with a brave appearance of unconcern. On the right and left stood the silent guards, robed in white and armed with great spears and daggers, and men and women mutes watching with hard curious eyes. Then, seated in her barbaric chair above them all, with myself at her feet, was the veiled white woman, whose loveliness and awesome power seemed to visibly shine about her like a halo, or rather like the glow from some unseen light. Never have I seen her veiled shape look more terrible than it did in that space, while she gathered herself up for vengeance.

At last it came.

"Dogs and serpents," *She* began in a low voice that gradually gathered power as she went on, till the place rang with it. "Eaters of human flesh, two things have ye done. First, ye have attacked these strangers, being white men, and would have slain their servant, and for that alone death is your reward. But that is not all. Ye have dared to disobey me. Did I not send my word unto you by Billali, my servant, and the father of your household? Did I not bid you to hospitably entertain these strangers, whom now ye have striven to slay, and whom, had not they been brave and strong beyond the strength of men, ye would cruelly have murdered? Hath it not been taught to you from childhood that the law of *She* is an ever fixed law, and that he who breaketh it by so much as one jot or tittle shall perish? And is not my lightest word a law? Have not your fathers taught you this, I say, while as yet ye were but children? Do ye not know that as well might ye bid these great caves to fall upon you, or the sun to cease its journeying, as to hope to turn me from my courses, or make my word light or heavy, according to your minds? Well do ye know it, ye wicked ones. But ye are all evil—evil to the core—the wickedness bubbles up in you like a fountain in the springtime. Were it not for me, generations since had ye ceased to be, for of your own evil way had ye destroyed each other. And now, because ye have done this thing, because ye have striven to put these men, my guests, to death, and yet more because ye have dared to disobey my word, this is the doom that I doom you to. That ye be taken to the cave of torture,[1] and given over to the tormentors, and that on the going down of tomorrow's sun those of you who yet remain alive be slain, even as ye would have slain the servant of this my guest."

She ceased, and a faint murmur of horror ran round the cave. As for the victims, as soon as they realized the full hideousness of their doom, their stoicism forsook them, and they flung themselves down upon the ground, and wept and implored for mercy in a way that was dreadful to behold. I, too, turned to Ayesha, and begged her to spare them, or at least to mete out their fate in some less awful way. But she was as hard as adamant about it.

"My Holly," she said, again speaking in Greek, which, to tell the truth, although I have always been considered a better scholar of that language than most men, I found it rather difficult to follow, chiefly because of the change in the fall of the accent. Ayesha, of course, talked with the accent of her contemporaries, whereas we have only tradition and the modern accent to guide us as to the exact pronunciation. "My Holly, it cannot be. Were I to show mercy to those wolves, your lives would not be safe among this people for a day. Thou knowest them not. They are

[1] I afterwards saw this dreadful place, also a legacy from the prehistoric people who lived in Kôr. The only objects in the cave itself were slabs of rock arranged in various positions to facilitate the operations of the torturers. Many of these slabs, which were of a porous stone, were stained quite dark with the blood of ancient victims that had soaked into them. Also in the center of the room was a place for a furnace, with a cavity wherein to heat the historic pot. But the most dreadful thing about the cave was that over each slab was a sculptured illustration of the appropriate torture being applied. These sculptures were so awful that I will not harrow the reader by attempting a description of them.—L. H. H.

tigers to lap blood, and even now they hunger for your lives. How thinkest thou that I rule this people? I have but a regiment of guards to do my bidding, therefore it is not by force. It is by terror. My empire is of the imagination. Once in a generation mayhap I do as I have done but now, and slay a score by torture. Believe not that I would be cruel, or take vengeance on anything so low. What can it profit me to be avenged on such as these? Those who live long, my Holly, have no passions, save where they have interests. Though I may seem to slay in wrath, or because my mood is crossed, it is not so. Thou hast seen how in the heavens the little clouds blow this way and that without a cause, yet behind them is the great wind sweeping on its path whither it listeth. So is it with me, O Holly. My moods and changes are the little clouds, and fitfully these seem to turn; but behind them ever blows the great wind of my purpose. Nay, the men must die; and die as I have said."

Then, suddenly turning to the captain of the guard: "As my word is, so be it!"

16 ♦

The Tombs of Kôr

AFTER THE PRISONERS had been removed Ayesha waved her hand, and the spectators turned round and began to crawl off down the cave like a scattered flock of sheep. When they were a fair distance from the dais, however, they rose and walked away, leaving the Queen and myself alone, with the exception of the mutes and the few remaining guards, most of whom had departed with the doomed men. Thinking this a good opportunity, I asked *She* to come and see Leo, telling her of his serious condition; but she would not, saying that he certainly would not die before the night, as people never died of that sort of fever except at nightfall or dawn. Also she said that it would be better to let the sickness spend its course as much as possible before she cured it. Accordingly, I was rising to leave, when she bade me follow her, as she would talk with me, and show me the wonders of the caves.

I was too much involved in the web of her fatal fascinations to say her no, even if I had wished, which I did not. She rose from her chair, and, making some signs to the mutes, descended from the dais. Thereupon four of the girls took lamps and ranged themselves two in front and two behind us, but the others went away, as also did the guards.

"Now," she said, "wouldst thou see some of the wonders of this place, O Holly? Look upon this great cave. Sawest thou ever the like? Yet was it, and many more

205

like it, hollowed by the hands of the dead race that once lived here in the city on the plain. A great and a wonderful people must they have been, those men of Kôr, but, like the Egyptians, they thought more of the dead than of the living. How many men, thinkest thou, working for how many years, did it need to the hollowing out this cave and all the galleries thereof?"

"Tens of thousands," I answered.

"So, O Holly. This people was an old people before the Egyptians were. A little can I read of their inscriptions, having found the key thereto—and, see thou here, this was one of the last of the caves that they hollowed," and, turning to the rock behind her, she motioned the mutes to hold up the lamps. Carven over the dais was the figure of an old man seated in a chair, with an ivory rod in his hand. It struck me at once that his features were exceedingly like those of the man who was represented as being embalmed in the chamber where we took our meals. Beneath the chair, which, by the way was shaped exactly like the one in which Ayesha had sat to give judgment, was a short inscription in the extraordinary characters of which I have already spoken, but which I do not remember sufficient of to illustrate. It looked more like Chinese writing than any other that I am acquainted with. This inscription Ayesha proceeded, with some difficulty and hesitation, to read aloud and translate. It ran as follows:

> In the year four thousand two hundred and fifty-nine from the founding of the City of imperial Kôr was this cave [or burial place] completed by Tisno, King of Kôr, the people thereof and their slaves having labored thereat for three generations, to be a tomb for their citizens of rank who shall come after. May the blessing of the heaven

above the heaven rest upon their work, and make the sleep
of Tisno, the mighty monarch, the likeness of whose
features is graven above, a sound and happy sleep till the
day of awakening,[1] and also the sleep of his servants, and
of those of his race who, rising up after him, shall yet lay
their heads as low.

"Thou seest, O Holly," she said, "this people founded
the city, of which the ruins yet cumber the plain yonder,
four thousand years before this cave was finished. Yet,
when first mine eyes beheld it two thousand years ago,
was it even as it is now. Judge, therefore, how old must
that city have been! And now, follow thou me, and I will
show thee after what fashion this great people fell when
the time was come for it to fall," and she led the way
down to the center of the cave, stopping at a spot where a
round rock had been let into a kind of large manhole in
the flooring, accurately filling it just as the iron plates fill
the spaces in the London pavements down which the coals
are thrown. "Thou seest," she said. "Tell me, what is it?"

"Nay, I know not," I answered; whereon she crossed to
the left-hand side of the cave (looking towards the entrance) and signed to the mutes to hold up the lamps.
On the wall was something painted with a red pigment
in similar characters to those hewn beneath the sculpture
of Tisno, King of Kôr. This inscription she proceeded to
translate to me, the pigment still being quite fresh enough
to show the form of the letters. It ran as follows:

I, Junis, a priest of the Great Temple of Kôr, write
this upon the rock of the burying place in the year four
thousand eight hundred and three from the founding of

[1] This phrase is remarkable, as seeming to indicate a belief in a future state.—EDITOR.

Kôr. Kôr is fallen! No more shall the mighty feast in her halls, no more shall she rule the world, and her navies go out to commerce with the world. Kôr is fallen! And her mighty works and all the cities of Kôr, and all the harbors that she built and the canals that she made, are for the wolf and the owl and the wild swan, and the barbarian who comes after. Twenty and five moons ago did a cloud settle upon Kôr, and the hundred cities of Kôr, and out of the cloud came a pestilence that slew her people, old and young, one with another, and spared not. One with another they turned black and died—the young and the old, the rich and the poor, the man and the woman, the prince and the slave. The pestilence slew and slew, and ceased not by day or by night, and those who escaped from the pestilence were slain of the famine. No longer could the bodies of the children of Kôr be preserved according to the ancient rites, because of the number of the dead, therefore were they hurled into the great pit beneath the cave through the hole in the floor of the cave. Then at last, a remnant of this the great people, the light of the whole world, went down to the coast and took ship and sailed northwards; and now am I, the Priest Junis, who write this, the last man left alive of this great city of men, but whether there be any yet left in the other cities I know not. This do I write in misery of heart before I die, because Kôr the Imperial is no more, and because there are none to worship in her temple, and all her palaces are empty, and her princes and her captains and her traders and her fair women have passed off the face of the earth.

I gave a sigh of astonishment—the utter desolation depicted in this rude scrawl was so overpowering. It was terrible to think of this solitary survivor of a mighty people recording its fate before he too went down into darkness. What must the old man have felt as, in ghastly terrifying solitude, by the light of one lamp feebly illumining a little space of gloom, he in a few brief lines daubed the history of his nation's death upon the cavern wall? What a subject for the moralist, or the painter, or indeed for anyone who can think!

"Doth it not occur to thee, O Holly," said Ayesha, laying her hand upon my shoulder, "that those men who sailed north may have been the fathers of the first Egyptians?"

"Nay, I know not," I said; "it seems that the world is very old."

"Old? Yes, it is old indeed. Time after time have nations, ay, and rich and strong nations, learned in the arts, been and passed away and been forgotten, so that no memory of them remains. This is but one of several; for Time eats up the works of man, unless, indeed, he digs in caves like the people of Kôr, and then mayhap the sea swallows them, or the earthquake shakes them in. Who knows what hath been on the earth, or what shall be? There is no new thing under the sun, as the wise Hebrew wrote long ago. Yet were not these people utterly destroyed, as I think. Some few remained in the other cities, for their cities were many. But the barbarians from the south, or perchance my people, the Arabs, came down upon them, and took their women to wife, and the race of the Amahagger that is now is a bastard brood of the mighty sons of Kôr, and behold it dwelleth in the tombs with its fathers' bones.[2] But I know not: who can know? My arts cannot pierce so far into the blackness of Time's night. A great people were they. They

[2] The name of the race Amahagger would seem to indicate a curious mingling of races such as might easily have occurred in the neighborhood of the Zambesi. The prefix "ama" is common to the Zulu and kindred races, and signifies "people," while "hagger" is an Arabic word meaning a stone.— EDITOR.

conquered till none were left to conquer, and then they dwelt at ease within their rocky mountain walls, with their man servants and their maid servants, their minstrels, their sculptors, and their concubines, and traded and quarreled, and ate and hunted and slept and made merry till their time came. But come, I will show thee the great pit beneath the cave whereof the writing speaks. Never shall thine eyes witness such another sight."

Accordingly I followed her to a side passage opening out of the main cave, then down a great number of steps, and along an underground shaft which cannot have been less than sixty feet beneath the surface of the rock, and was ventilated by curious borings that ran upward, I do not know where. Suddenly the passage ended, and she halted and bade the mutes hold up the lamps, and, as she had prophesied, I saw a scene such as I was not likely to see again. We were standing in an enormous pit, or rather on the edge of it, for it went down deeper—I do not know how much— than the level on which we stood, and was edged in with a low wall of rock. So far as I could judge, this pit was about the size of the space beneath the dome of St. Paul's in London, and when the lamps were held up I saw that it was nothing but one vast charnel house, being literally full of thousands of human skeletons, which lay piled up in an enormous gleaming pyramid, formed by the slipping down of the bodies at the apex as fresh ones were dropped in from above. Anything more appalling than this jumbled mass of the remains of a departed race I cannot imagine, and what made it even more dreadful was that in this dry air a considerable number of the bodies had simply become desiccated with the skin still on them, and now, fixed in every conceivable position, stared at us out of the mountain of white bones, grotesquely horrible caricatures of humanity. In my astonishment I uttered an ejaculation, and the echoes of my voice ringing in the vaulted space disturbed a skull that had been accurately balanced for many thousands of years near the apex of the pile. Down it came with a run, bounding along merrily towards us, and of course bringing an avalanche of other bones after it, till at last the whole pit rattled with their movement, even as though the skeletons were getting up to greet us.

"Come," I said, "I have seen enough. These are the bodies of those who died of the great sickness, is it not so?" I added, as we turned away.

"Yes. The people of Kôr ever embalmed their dead, as did the Egyptians, but their art was greater than the art of the Egyptians, for whereas the Egyptians disemboweled and drew the brain, the people of Kôr injected fluid into the veins, and thus reached every part. But stay, thou shalt see," and she halted at haphazard at one of the little doorways opening out of the passage along which we were walking, and motioned to the mutes to light us in. We entered into a small chamber similar to the one in which I had slept at our first stopping place, only instead of one there were two stone benches or beds in it. On the benches lay figures covered with yellow linen,[3] on which a fine and impalpable dust had gathered in the course of ages but nothing like to the extent that one would have anticipated, for in these deep-hewn caves there is no material to turn to dust. About the bodies on the stone shelves and floor of the tomb were many painted vases, but I saw very few ornaments or weapons in any of the vaults.

"Uplift the cloths, O Holly," said Ayesha, but when I

[3] All the linen that the Amahagger wore was taken from the tombs, which accounted for its yellow hue. If it was well washed, however, and properly rebleached, it acquired its former snowy whiteness, and was the softest and best linen I ever saw.—L. H. H.

put out my hand to do so I drew it back again. It seemed like sacrilege, and to speak the truth I was awed by the dread solemnity of the place, and of the presences before us. Then, with a little laugh at my fears, she drew them herself, only to discover other and yet finer cloths lying over the forms upon the stone bench. These also she withdrew, and then for the first time for thousands upon thousands of years did living eyes look upon the face of that chilly dead. It was a woman; she might have been thirty-five years of age, or perhaps a little less, and had certainly been beautiful. Even now her calm clear-cut features, marked out with delicate eyebrows and long eyelashes which threw little lines of the shadow of the lamplight upon the ivory face, were wonderfully beautiful. There, robed in white, down which her blue-black hair was streaming, she slept her last long sleep, and on her arm, its face pressed against her breast, there lay a little babe. So sweet was the sight, although so awful, that—I confess it without shame—I could scarcely withhold my tears. It took me back across the dim gulf of the ages to some happy home in dead Imperial Kôr, where this winsome lady girt about with beauty had lived and died, and dying taken her last-born with her to the tomb. There they were before us, mother and babe, the white memories of a forgotten human history speaking more eloquently to the heart than could any written record of their lives. Reverently I replaced the grave-clothes, and, with a sigh that flowers so fair should, in the purpose of the Everlasting, have bloomed only to be gathered to the grave, I turned to the body on the opposite shelf, and gently unveiled it. It was that of a man in advanced life, with a long grizzled beard, and also robed in white, probably the husband of the lady, who, after surviving her many years, came at last to sleep once more for good and all beside her.

We left the place and entered others. It would be too long to describe the many things I saw in them. Each one had its occupants, for the five-hundred-odd years that had elapsed between the completion of the cave and the destruction of the race had evidently sufficed to fill these catacombs, numberless as they were, and all appeared to have been undisturbed since the day when they were placed there. I could fill a book with the description of them, but to do so would only be to repeat what I have said, with variations.

Nearly all the bodies, so masterly was the art with which they had been treated, were as perfect as on the day of death thousands of years before. Nothing came to injure them in the deep silence of the living rock: they were beyond the reach of heat and cold and damp, and the aromatic drugs with which they had been saturated were evidently practically everlasting in their effect. Here and there, however, we saw an exception, and in these cases, although the flesh looked sound enough externally, if one touched it it fell in, and revealed the fact that the figure was but a pile of dust. This arose, Ayesha told me, from these particular bodies having, either owing to haste in the burial or to other causes, been soaked in the preservative,[4]

[4] Ayesha afterwards showed me the tree from the leaves of which this ancient preservative was manufactured. It is a low bushlike tree that to this day grows in wonderful plenty upon the sides of the mountains, or rather upon the slopes leading up to the rocky walls. The leaves are long and narrow, a vivid green in color, but turning a bright red in the autumn, and not unlike those of a laurel in general appearance. They have little smell when green, but if boiled the aromatic odor from them is so strong that one can hardly bear it. The best mixture, however, was made from the roots, and among the people of Kôr there was a law, which Ayesha showed me alluded to on some of the inscriptions, to the effect that under heavy penalties no one under a certain rank was to be embalmed with the drugs prepared from the roots. The object and effect of this was, of course, to preserve the trees from extermination. The sale of the leaves and roots was a government monopoly, and from it the kings of Kôr derived a large proportion of their private revenue.—L. H. H.

instead of its being injected into the substance of the flesh.

About the last tomb we visited I must, however, say one word, for its contents spoke even more eloquently to the human sympathies than those of the first. It had but two occupants, and they lay together on a single shelf. I withdrew the grave-clothes, and there, clasped heart to heart, were a young man and a blooming girl. Her head rested on his arm, and his lips were pressed against her brow. I opened the man's linen robe, and there over his heart was a dagger wound, and beneath the girl's fair breast was a like cruel stab, through which her life had ebbed away. On the rock above was an inscription in three words. Ayesha translated it. It was *"Wedded in Death."*

What was the life history of these two, who, of a truth, were beautiful in their lives, and in their death were not divided?

I closed my eyelids, and imagination, taking up the thread of thought, shot its swift shuttle back across the ages, weaving a picture on their blackness so real and vivid in its detail that I could almost for a moment think that I had triumphed o'er the Past, and that my spirit's eyes had pierced the mystery of Time.

I seemed to see this fair girl form—the yellow hair streaming down her, glittering against her garments snowy white, and the bosom that was whiter than the robes, even dimming with its luster her ornaments of burnished gold. I seemed to see the great cave filled with warriors, bearded and clad in mail, and, on the lighted dais where Ayesha had given judgment, a man standing, robed, and surrounded by the symbols of his priestly office. And up the cave there came one clad in purple, and before him and behind him came minstrels and fair maidens, chanting a wedding song. White stood the maid against the altar, fairer than the fairest there—purer than a lily, and more cold than the dew that glistens in its heart. But as the man drew near she shuddered. Then out of the press and throng there sprang a dark-haired youth, and put his arm about this long-forgotten maid, and kissed her pale face in which the blood shot up like lights of the red dawn across the silent sky. And next there was turmoil and uproar, and a flashing of swords, and they tore the youth from her arms, and stabbed him, but with a cry she snatched the dagger from his belt, and drove it into her snowy breast, home to the heart, and down she fell, and then, with cries and wailing, and every sound of lamentation, the pageant rolled away from the arena of my vision, and once more the past shut to its book.

Let him who reads forgive the intrusion of a dream into a history of fact. But it came so home to me—I saw it all so clear in a moment, as it were; and, besides, who shall say what proportion of fact, past, present, or to come, may lie in the imagination? What is imagination? Perhaps it is the shadow of the intangible truth, perhaps it is the soul's thought.

In an instant the whole thing had passed through my brain, and *She* was addressing me.

"Behold the lot of man," said the veiled Ayesha, as she drew the winding sheets back over the dead lovers, speaking in a solemn, thrilling voice, which accorded well with the dream that I had dreamed. "To the tomb, and to the forgetfulness that hides the tomb, must we all come at last! Ay, even I who live so long. Even for me, O Holly, thousands upon thousands of years hence; thousands of years after thou hast gone through the gate and been lost in the mists, a day will dawn whereon I shall die, and be even as thou art and these are. And then what will it avail that

I have lived a little longer, holding off death by the knowledge I have wrung from Nature, since at last I too must
die? What is a span of ten thousand years, or ten times ten
thousand years, in the history of time? It is as naught—
it is as the mists that roll up in the sunlight; it fleeth away
like an hour of sleep or a breath of the Eternal Spirit.
Behold the lot of man! Certainly it shall overtake us, and
we shall sleep. Certainly, too, we shall awake, and live again
and again shall sleep, and so on and on, through periods,
spaces, and times, from eon unto eon, till the world is
dead, and the worlds beyond the world are dead, and
naught liveth save the Spirit that is Life. But for us twain
and for these dead ones shall the end of ends be Life, or
shall it be Death? As yet Death is but Life's Night, but out
of the night is the Morrow born again, and doth again
beget the Night. Only when Day and Night, and Life and
Death, are ended and swallowed up in that from which
they came, what shall be our fate, O Holly? Who can see
so far? Not even I!"

And then, with a sudden change of tone and manner:
"Hast thou seen enough, my stranger guest, or shall I
show thee more of the wonders of these tombs that are
my palace halls? If thou wilt, I can lead thee to where
Tisno, the mightiest and most valorous king of Kôr, in
whose day these caves were ended, lies in a pomp that
seems to mock at nothingness, and bid the empty shadows
of the past do homage to his sculptured vanity!"

"I have seen enough, O Queen," I answered. "My heart
is overwhelmed by the power of the present Death. Mortality is weak, and easily broken down by a sense of the companionship that waits upon its end. Take me hence, O
Ayesha!"

17 ♦

The Balance Turns

In a few minutes, following the lamps of the mutes, which, held out from the body as a bearer holds water in a vessel, had the appearance of floating down the darkness by themselves, we came to a stair which led us to *She*'s ante-room, the same that Billali had crept up upon all fours on the previous day. Here I would have bid the Queen adieu, but she would not.

"Nay," she said, "enter with me, O Holly, for of a truth thy conversation pleaseth me. Think, O Holly: for two thousand years have I had none to converse with save slaves and my own thoughts, and though of all this thinking hath much wisdom come, and many secrets been made plain, yet am I weary of my thoughts, and have come to loathe mine own society, for surely the food that memory gives to eat is bitter to the taste, and it is only with the teeth of hope that we can bear to bite it. Now though thy thoughts are green and tender, as becometh one so young, yet are they those of a thinking brain, and in truth thou dost bring back to my mind certain of those old philosophers with whom in days bygone I have disputed at Athens, and at Becca in Arabia, for thou hast the same crabbed air and dusty look, as though thou hadst passed thy days in reading ill-writ Greek, and been stained dark with the grime of manuscripts. So draw the curtain, and sit here by my side, and we will eat fruit, and talk of

217

pleasant things. See, I will again unveil to thee. Thou
hast brought it on thyself, O Holly; fairly have I warned
thee—and thou shalt call me beautiful as even those old
philosophers were wont to do. Fie upon them, forgetting
their philosophy!"

And without more ado she stood up and shook the
white wrappings from her, and came forth shining and
splendid like some glittering snake when she has cast her
slough; ay, and fixed her wonderful eyes upon me—more
deadly than any Basilisk's—and pierced me through and
through with their beauty, and sent her light laugh ringing through the air like chimes of silver bells.

A new mood was on her, and the very color of her
mind seemed to change beneath it. It was no longer torture-
torn and hateful, as I had seen it when she was cursing her
dead rival by the leaping flames, no longer icily terrible as
in the judgment hall, no longer rich, and somber, and splendid, like a Tyrian cloth, as in the dwellings of the dead.
No, her mood now was that of Aphrodite triumphing. Life
—radiant, ecstatic, wonderful—seemed to flow from her
and round her. Softly she laughed and sighed, and swift her
glances flew. She shook her heavy tresses, and their perfume
filled the place; she struck her little sandaled foot upon the
floor, and hummed a snatch of some old Greek epithalamium. All the majesty was gone, or did but lurk and faintly
flicker through her laughing eyes, like lightning seen through
sunlight. She had cast off the terror of the leaping flame,
the cold power of judgment that was even now being done,
and the wise sadness of the tombs—cast them off and put
them behind her, like the white shroud she wore, and now
stood out the incarnation of lovely tempting womanhood,
made more perfect—and in a way more spiritual—than
ever woman was before.

"There, my Holly, sit there where thou canst see me. It is by thine own wish, remember—again I say, blame me not if thou dost spend the rest of thy little span with such a sick pain at the heart that thou wouldst fain have died before ever thy curious eyes were set upon me. There, sit so, and tell me, for in truth I am inclined for praises—tell me, am I not beautiful? Nay, speak not so hastily; consider well the point; take me feature by feature, forgetting not my form, and my hands and feet, and my hair, and the whiteness of my skin, and then tell me truly hast thou ever known a woman who in aught, ay, in one little portion of her beauty, in the curve of an eyelash even, or the modeling of a shell-like ear, is justified to hold a light before my loveliness? Now, my waist! Perchance thou thinkest it too large, but of a truth it is not so; it is this golden snake that is too large, and doth not bind it as it should. It is a wise snake, and knoweth that it is ill to tie in the waist. But see, give me thy hands—so—now press them round me, there, with but a little force, thy fingers touch, O Holly."

I could bear it no longer. I am but a man, and she was more than a woman. Heaven knows what she was— I do not! But then and there I fell upon my knees before her, and told her in a sad mixture of languages—for such moments confuse the thoughts—that I worshiped her as never woman was worshiped, and that I would give my immortal soul to marry her, which at that time I certainly would have done, and so, indeed, would any other man, or all the race of men rolled into one. For a moment she looked a little surprised, and then she began to laugh, and clap her hands in glee.

"Oh, so soon, O Holly!" she said. "I wondered how many minutes it would need to bring thee to thy knees. I have not seen a man kneel before me for so many days, and, believe me, to a woman's heart the sight is sweet, ay, wisdom and length of days take not from that dear pleasure which is our sex's only right.

"What wouldst thou? What wouldst thou? Thou dost not know what thou doest. Have I not told thee that I am not for thee? I love but one, and thou art not the man. Ah, Holly, for all thy wisdom—and in a way thou art wise—thou art but a fool running after folly. Thou wouldst look into mine eyes—thou wouldst kiss me! Well, if it pleaseth thee, *look*," and she bent herself towards me, and fixed her dark and thrilling orbs upon my own; "ay, and *kiss* too, if thou wilt, for, thanks be given to the scheme of things, kisses leave no marks, except upon the heart. But if thou dost kiss, I tell thee of a surety wilt thou eat out thy breast with love of me, and die!" and she bent yet further towards me till her soft hair brushed my brow, and her fragrant breath played upon my face, and made me faint and weak. Then of a sudden, even as I stretched out my arms to clasp, she straightened herself, and a quick change passed over her. Reaching out her hand, she held it over my head, and it seemed to me that something flowed from it that chilled me back to common sense, and a knowledge of propriety and the domestic virtues.

"Enough of this wanton play," she said with a touch of sternness. "Listen, Holly. Thou art a good and honest man, and I fain would spare thee; but, oh, it is so hard for a woman to be merciful. I have said I am not for thee, therefore let thy thoughts pass by me like an idle wind, and the dust of thy imagination sink again into the depths —well, of despair, if thou wilt. Thou dost not know me, Holly. Hadst thou seen me but ten hours past when my passion seized me, thou hadst shrunk from me in fear and trembling. I am a woman of many moods, and, like the water in that vessel, I reflect many things; but they pass, my Holly; they pass, and are forgotten. Only the water is the water still, and I still am I, and that which maketh the water maketh it, and that which maketh me maketh me, nor can my quality be altered. Therefore, pay no heed to what I seem, seeing that thou canst not know what I am. If thou troublest me again I will veil myself, and thou shalt behold my face no more."

I rose, and sank on the cushioned couch beside her, yet quivering with emotion, though for a moment my mad passion had left me, as the leaves of a tree quiver still, although the gust be gone that stirred them. I did not dare to tell her that I *had* seen her in that deep and hellish mood, muttering incantations to the fire in the tomb.

"So," she went on, "now eat some fruit; believe me, it is the only true food for man. Oh, tell me of the philosophy of that Hebrew Messiah, who came after me, and whom thou sayest doth now rule Rome, and Greece, and Egypt, and the barbarians beyond. It must have been a strange philosophy that He taught, for in my day the peoples would have naught of our philosophies. Revel and lust and drink, blood and cold steel, and the shock of men gathered in the battle—these were the canons of their creeds."

I had recovered myself a little by now, and, feeling bitterly ashamed of the weakness into which I had been betrayed, I did my best to expound to her the doctrines of Christianity, to which, however, with the single exception of our conception of Heaven and Hell, I found that she paid but faint attention, her interest being all directed towards the Man who taught them. Also, I told her that among her own people, the Arabs, another prophet, one

Mohammed, had arisen and preached a new faith to which many millions of mankind now adhered.

"Ah!" she said. "I see—two new religions! I have known so many, and doubtless there have been many more since I knew aught beyond these caves of Kôr. Mankind asks ever of the skies to vision out what lies behind them. It is terror for the end, and but a subtler form of selfishness —this it is that breeds religions. Mark, my Holly, each religion claims the future for its followers; or, at the least, the good thereof. The evil is for those benighted ones who will have none of it, seeing the light the true believers worship as the fishes see the stars, but dimly. The religions come and the religions pass, and the civilizations come and pass, and naught endures but the world and human nature. Ah, if man would but see that hope is from within and not from without—that he himself must work out his own salvation! He is there, and within him is the breath of life and a knowledge of good and evil as good and evil is to him. Thereon let him build and stand erect, and not cast himself before the image of some unknown God, modeled like his poor self, but with a bigger brain to think the evil thing; and a longer arm to do it."

I thought to myself, which shows how old such reasoning is, being, indeed, one of the recurring quantities of theological discussion, that her argument sounded very like some that I have heard in the nineteenth century, and in other places than the caves of Kôr, and with which, by the way, I totally disagree, but I did not care to try and discuss the question with her. To begin with, my mind was too weary with all the emotions through which I had passed, and, in the second place, I knew that I should get the worst of it. It is weary work enough to argue with an ordinary materialist, who hurls statistics and whole strata of geological facts at your head, while you can only buffet him with deductions and instincts and the snowflakes of faith, that are, alas, so apt to melt in the hot embers of our troubles. How little chance, then, should I have against one whose brain was supernaturally sharpened, and who had two thousand years of experience, besides all manner of knowledge of the secrets of Nature at her command! Feeling that she would be more likely to convert me than I should to convert her, I thought it best to leave the matter alone, and so sat silent. Many a time since then have I bitterly regretted that I did so, for thereby I lost the only opportunity I can remember having had of ascertaining what Ayesha *really* believed, and what her "philosophy" was.

"Well, my Holly," she continued, "and so those people of mine have also found a prophet, a false prophet thou sayest, for he is not thine own, and, indeed, I doubt it not. Yet in my day was it otherwise, for then we Arabs had many gods. Allât there was, and Saba, the Host of Heaven, Al Uzza, and Manah the stony one, for whom the blood of victims flowed, and Wadd and Sawâ, and Yaghûth the Lion of the dwellers in Yaman, and Yäûk the Horse of Morad, and Nasr the Eagle of Hamyar; ay, and many more. Oh, the folly of it all, the shame and the pitiful folly! Yet when I rose in wisdom and spoke thereof, surely they would have slain me in the name of their outraged gods. Well, so hath it ever been—but, my Holly, art thou weary of me already, that thou dost sit so silent? Or dost thou fear lest I should teach thee my philosophy? For know I have a philosophy. What would a teacher be without her own philosophy? And if thou dost vex me overmuch, beware, for I will have thee learn it, and thou shalt be my disciple, and we twain will found a faith that shall swallow up all others. Faithless man! And but half an hour since thou

wast upon thy knees—the posture does not suit thee, Holly
—swearing that thou didst love me. What shall we do?
Nay, I have it. I will come and see this youth, the Lion,
as the old man Billali calls him, who came with thee, and
who is so sick. The fever must have run its course by
now, and if he is about to die I will recover him. Fear
not, my Holly, I shall use no magic. Have I not told thee
that there is no such thing as magic, though there is such
a thing as understanding and applying the forces which
are in Nature? Go now, and presently when I have made
the drug ready I will follow thee." [1]

Accordingly I went, only to find Job and Ustane in a
great state of grief, declaring that Leo was in the throes
of death, and that they had been searching for me everywhere. I rushed to the couch and glanced at him: clearly
he was dying. He was senseless, and breathing heavily,
but his lips were quivering, and every now and again a
little shudder ran down his frame. I knew enough of
doctoring to see that in another hour he would be beyond
the reach of earthly help—perhaps in another five minutes.
How I cursed my selfishness and the folly that had kept
me lingering by Ayesha's side while my dear boy lay
dying! Alas and alas! How easily the best of us are lighted
down to evil by the gleam of a woman's eyes! What
a wicked wretch was I! Actually, for the last half hour I
had scarcely thought of Leo, and this, be it remembered,
of the man who for twenty years had been my dearest
companion, and the chief interest of my existence. And
now, perhaps it was too late!

[1] Ayesha was a great chemist, indeed, chemistry appears to have been her
only amusement and occupation. She had one of the caves fitted up as a
laboratory, and, although her appliances were necessarily rude, the results
that she attained were, as will become clear in the course of this narrative,
sufficiently surprising.—L. H. H.

I wrung my hands, and glanced round. Ustane was sitting by the couch, and in her eyes burned the dull light of despair. Job was blubbering—I am sorry I cannot name his distress by any more delicate word—audibly in the corner. Seeing my eye fixed upon him he went outside to give way to his grief in the passage. Obviously the only hope lay in Ayesha. She, and she alone—unless, indeed, she was an impostor, which I could not believe—could save him. I would go and implore her to come. As I started to do so, however, Job came flying into the room, his hair literally standing on end with terror.

"Oh, God help us, sir!" he ejaculated in a frightened whisper. "Here's a corpse acoming sliding down the passage!"

For a moment I was puzzled, but presently, of course, it struck me that he must have seen Ayesha, wrapped in her gravelike garment, and been deceived by the extraordinary undulating smoothness of her walk into a belief that she was a white ghost gliding towards him. Indeed, at that very moment the question was settled, for Ayesha herself was in the apartment, or rather cave. Job turned and saw her sheeted form, and then, with a convulsive howl of "Here it comes!" sprang into a corner and jammed his face against the wall, and Ustane, guessing whose the dread presence must be, prostrated herself upon her face.

"Thou comest in a good time, Ayesha," I said, "for my boy lies at the point of death."

"So," she said softly; "provided he be not dead, it is no matter, for I can bring him back to life, my Holly. Is that man there thy servant, and is that the method wherewith thy servants greet strangers in thy country?"

"He is frightened of thy garb—it hath a deathlike air," I answered.

She laughed. "And the girl? Ah, I see now. It is her of whom thou didst speak to me. Well, bid them both to leave us, and we will see to this sick Lion of thine. I love not that underlings should perceive my wisdom."

Thereon I told Ustane in Arabic and Job in English both to leave the room; an order which the latter obeyed readily enough, and was glad to obey, for he could not in any way subdue his fear. But it was otherwise with Ustane.

"What does *She* want?" she whispered, divided between her fear of the terrible queen and her anxiety to remain near Leo. "It is surely the right of a wife to be near her husband when he dieth. Nay, I will not go, my lord, the Baboon."

"Why doth not that woman leave us, my Holly?" asked Ayesha from the other end of the cave, where she was engaged in carelessly examining some of the sculptures on the wall.

"She is not willing to leave Leo," I answered, not knowing what to say. Ayesha wheeled round, and, pointing to the girl Ustane, said one word, and one only, but it was quite enough, for the tone in which it was said meant volumes.

"Go!"

And then Ustane crept past her on her hands and knees, and went.

"Thou seest, my Holly," said Ayesha with a little laugh, "it was needful that I should give these people a lesson in obedience. That girl went nigh to disobeying me, but then she did not learn this morn how I treat the disobedient. Well, she has gone; and now let me see the youth," and she glided towards the couch on which Leo lay, with his face in the shadow and turned toward the wall.

"He hath a noble shape," she said, as she bent over him to look upon his face.

Next second her tall and willowy form was staggering back across the room, as though she had been shot or stabbed, staggering back till at last she struck the cavern wall, and then there burst from her lips the most awful and unearthly scream that I ever heard in all my life.

"What is it, Ayesha?" I cried. "Is he dead?"

She turned and sprang towards me like a tigress.

"Thou dog!" she said in her terrible whisper, which sounded like the hiss of a snake, "why didst thou hide this from me?" And she stretched out her arm, and I thought that she was about to slay me.

"What?" I ejaculated in the most lively terror. "What?"

"Ah," she said, "perchance thou didst not know. Learn, my Holly, learn: there lies—there lies my lost Kallikrates. Kallikrates, who has come back to me at last, as I knew he would, as I knew he would." And she began to sob and to laugh, and generally to conduct herself like any other lady who is a little upset, murmuring "Kallikrates, Kallikrates!"

"Nonsense," thought I to myself, but I did not like to say it; and, indeed, at that moment I was thinking of Leo's life, having forgotten everything else in that terrible anxiety. What I feared now was that he should die while she was "carrying on."

"Unless thou art able to help him, Ayesha," I put in by way of a reminder, "thy Kallikrates will soon be far beyond thy calling. Surely he dieth even now."

"True," she said with a start. "Oh, why did I not come before! I am unnerved—my hand trembles, even mine—and yet it is very easy. Here, thou Holly, take this phial," and she produced a tiny jar of pottery from the folds of her garment, "and pour the liquid in it down his throat. It will cure him if he be not dead. Swift, now! Swift! The man dies!"

I glanced towards him; it was true enough, Leo was in his death struggle. I saw his poor face turning ashen, and heard the breath begin to rattle in his throat. The phial was stoppered with a little piece of wood. I drew it with my teeth, and a drop of the fluid within flew out upon my tongue. It had a sweet flavor, and for a second made my head swim, and a mist gather before my eyes, but happily the effect passed away as swiftly as it had arisen.

When I reached Leo's side he was plainly expiring—his golden head was slowly turning from side to side, and his mouth was slightly open. I called to Ayesha to hold his head, and this she managed to do, though the woman was quivering from head to foot, like an aspen leaf or a startled horse. Then, forcing the jaw a little more open, I poured the contents of the phial into his mouth. Instantly a little vapor arose from it, as happens when one disturbs nitric acid, and this sight did not increase my hopes, already faint enough, of the efficacy of the treatment.

One thing, however, was certain, the death throes ceased—at first I thought because he had got beyond them, and crossed the awful river. His face turned to a livid pallor, and his heartbeats, which had been feeble enough before, seemed to die away altogether—only the eyelid still twitched a little. In my doubt I looked up at Ayesha, whose head wrapping had slipped back in her excitement when she went reeling across the room. She was still holding Leo's head, and, with a face as pale as his own, watching his countenance with such an expression of agonized anxiety as I have never seen before. Clearly she did not know if he would live or die. Five minutes slowly passed, and I saw that she was abandoning hope; her lovely oval face seemed to fall in and grow visibly thinner beneath the pressure of a mental agony whose pencil drew black lines about the hollows of her eyes. The coral faded even from her lips, till they were as white as Leo's face, and quivered pitifully. It was shocking to see her: even in my own grief I felt for hers.

"Is it too late?" I gasped.

She hid her face in her hands, and made no answer, and I too turned away. But as I did so I heard a deep-drawn breath, and looking down perceived a line of color creeping up Leo's face, then another and another, and then, wonder of wonders, the man we had thought dead turned over on his side.

"Thou seest," I said in a whisper.

"I see," she answered hoarsely. "He is saved. I thought we were too late—another moment—one little moment more—and he had been gone!" And she burst into an awful flood of tears, sobbing as though her heart would break, and yet looking lovelier than ever as she did it. At last she ceased.

"Forgive me, my Holly—forgive me for my weakness," she said. "Thou seest after all I am a very woman. Think—now think of it! This morning didst thou speak of the place of torment appointed by this new religion of thine. Hell or Hades thou didst call it—a place where the vital essence lives and retains an individual memory, and where all the errors and faults of judgment, and unsatisfied passions and the unsubstantial terrors of the mind wherewith it hath at any time had to do, come to mock and haunt and gibe and wring the heart forever and forever with the vision of its own hopelessness. Thus, even thus, have I lived for full two thousand years—for some six and sixty generations, as ye reckon time—in a hell, as thou callest it—tormented by the memory of a crime, tortured day and night with an unfulfilled desire—without companionship, without comfort, without death, and led on down my dreary road only by the marsh lights of hope, which though they flickered here and there, and now glowed strong, and now were not, yet, as my skill told me, would one day lead unto my deliverer.

"And then—think of it still, O Holly, for never shalt thou hear such another tale, or see such another scene, nay, not even if I give thee ten thousand years of life—and thou shalt have it in payment if thou wilt—think: at last my deliverer came—he for whom I had watched and waited through the generations—at the appointed time he came to seek me, as I knew that he must come, for my wisdom could not err, though I knew not when or how. Yet see how ignorant I was! See how small my knowledge, and how faint my strength! For hours he lay here sick unto death, and I felt it not—I who had waited for him for two thousand years—I knew it not. And then at last I see him, and behold, my chance is gone but by a hair's breadth even before I have it, for he is in the very jaws of death; whence no power of mine can draw him. And if he die, surely must the hell be lived through once more—once more must I face the weary centuries, and wait, and wait till the time in its fullness shall bring my beloved back to me. And then thou gavest him the medicine, and that five minutes dragged along before I knew if he would live or die, and I tell thee that all the sixty generations that are gone were not so long as that five minutes. But they passed at length, and still he showed no sign, and I knew that if the drug works not then, so far as I have had knowledge, it works not at all. Then thought I that he was once more dead, and all the tortures of all the years gathered themselves into a single venomed spear, and pierced me through and through, because once again I had lost Kallikrates! And then, when all was done, behold! he sighed, behold! he lived, and I knew that he would live, for none die on whom the drug takes hold. Think of it now, my Holly—think of the wonder of it! He will sleep for twelve hours, and then the fever will have left him!"

She stopped, and laid her hand upon the golden head, and then bent down and kissed the brow with a chastened abandonment of tenderness that would have been beautiful to behold had not the sight cut me to the heart—for I was jealous!

18 ♦

Go, Woman!

THEN FOLLOWED a silence of a minute or so, during which *She* appeared, if one might judge from the almost angelic rapture of her face—for she looked angelic sometimes—to be plunged in a happy ecstasy. Suddenly, however, a new thought struck her, and her expression became the very reverse of angelic.

"Almost had I forgotten," she said, "that woman, Ustane. What is she to Kallikrates—his servant, or—" and she paused, and her voice trembled.

I shrugged my shoulders. "I understand that she is wed to him according to the custom of the Amahagger," I answered; "but I know not."

Her face grew dark as a thunder cloud. Old as she was, Ayesha had not outlived jealousy.

"Then there is an end," she said; "she must die, even now!"

"For what crime?" I asked, horrified. "She is guilty of naught that thou art not guilty of thyself, oh Ayesha. She loves the man, and he has been pleased to accept her love: where, then, is her sin?"

"Truly, O Holly, thou art foolish," she answered, almost petulantly. "Where is her sin? Her sin is that she stands between me and my desire. Well, I know that I can take him from her—for dwells there a man upon this earth, O Holly, who could resist me if I put out my strength?

Men are faithful for so long only as temptations pass them by. If the temptation be but strong enough, then will the man yield, for every man, like every rope, hath his breaking strain, and passion is to men what gold and power are to women—the weight upon their weakness. Believe me, ill will it go with mortal women in that heaven of which thou speakest, if only the spirits be more fair, for their lords will never turn to look upon them, and their heaven will become their hell. For man can be bought with woman's beauty, if it be but beautiful enough; and woman's beauty can be ever bought with gold, if only there be gold enough. So was it in my day, and so it will be to the end of time. The world is a great mart, my Holly, where all things are for sale to him who bids the highest in the currency of our desires."

These remarks, which were as cynical as might have been expected from a woman of Ayesha's age and experience, jarred upon me, and I answered testily that in our heaven there was no marriage or giving in marriage.

"Else would it not be heaven, dost thou mean?" she put in. "Fie upon thee, Holly, to think so ill of us poor women! Is it, then, marriage that marks the line between thy heaven and thy hell? But enough of this. This is no time for disputing and the challenge of our wits. Why dost thou always dispute? Art thou also a philosopher of these latter days? As for this woman, she must die; for though I can take her lover from her, yet, while she lived, might he think tenderly of her, and that I could not away with. No other woman shall dwell in my lord's thoughts; my empire shall be all my own. She hath had her day, let her be content; for better is an hour with love than a century of loneliness—now the night shall swallow her."

"Nay, nay," I cried, "it would be a wicked crime; and from a crime naught comes but what is evil. For thine own sake do not this deed."

"Is it, then, a crime, O foolish man, to put away that which stands between us and our ends? Then is our life one long crime, my Holly; for day by day we destroy that we may live, since in this world none save the strongest can endure. Those who are weak must perish; the earth is to the strong, and the fruits thereof. For every tree that grows a score shall wither, that the strong ones may take their share. We run to place and power over the dead bodies of those who fail and fall; ay, we win the food we eat from out the mouths of starving babes. It is the scheme of things. Thou sayest, too, that a crime breeds evil, but therein thou dost lack experience; for out of crimes come many good things, and out of good grows much evil. The cruel rage of the tyrant may prove a blessing to thousands who come after him, and the sweet-heartedness of a holy man may make a nation slaves. Man doeth this and doeth that from the good or evil of his heart; but he knoweth not to what end his moral sense doth prompt him; for when he striketh he is blind to where the blow shall fall, nor can he count the airy threads that weave the web of circumstance. Good and evil, love and hate, night and day, sweet and bitter, man and woman, heaven above and the earth beneath—all these things are necessary one to the other, and who knows the end of each? I tell thee that there is a hand of Fate that twines them up to bear the burden of its purpose, and all things are gathered in that great rope to which all things are needful. Therefore doth it not become us to say this thing is evil and this good, or the dark is hateful and the light lovely; for to other eyes than ours the evil may be the good and the darkness more beautiful than the day, or all alike be fair. Hearest thou, my Holly?"

I felt it was hopeless to argue against casuistry of this nature, which, if it were carried to its logical conclusion, would absolutely destroy all morality, as we understand it. But her talk gave me a fresh thrill of fear; for what may not be possible to a being who, unconstrained by human law, is also absolutely unshackled by a moral sense of right and wrong, which, however partial and conventional it may be, is yet based, as our conscience tells us, upon the great wall of individual responsibility that marks off mankind from the beasts?

But I was deeply anxious to save Ustane, whom I liked and respected, from the dire fate that overshadowed her at the hands of her mighty rival. So I made one more appeal.

"Ayesha," I said, "thou art too subtle for me; but thou thyself hast told me that each man should be a law unto himself, and follow the teaching of his heart. Hath thy heart no mercy towards her whose place thou wouldst take? Bethink thee, as thou sayest—though to me the thing is incredible—him whom thou desirest has returned to thee after many ages, and but now thou hast, as thou sayest also, wrung him from the jaws of death. Wilt thou celebrate his coming by the murder of one who loved him, and whom perchance he loved—one, at the least, who saved his life for thee when the spears of thy slaves would have made an end thereof? Thou sayest also that in past days thou didst grievously wrong this man, that with thine own hand thou didst slay him because of the Egyptian Amenartas whom he loved."

"How knowest thou that, O stranger? How knowest thou that name? I spoke it not to thee," she broke in with a cry, catching at my arm.

"Perchance I dreamed it," I answered; "strange dreams do hover about these caves of Kôr. It seems that the dream was, indeed, a shadow of the truth. What came to thee of thy mad crime? Two thousand years of waiting, was it not? And now wouldst thou repeat the history? Say what thou wilt, I tell thee that evil will come of it; for to him who doeth, at the least, good breeds good and evil evil, even though in after days out of evil cometh good. Offenses must needs come; but woe to him by whom the offense cometh. So said that Messiah of whom I spoke to thee, and it was truly said. If thou slayest this innocent woman, I say unto thee that thou shalt be accursed, and pluck no fruit from thine ancient tree of love. Also, what thinkest thou? How will this man take thee red-handed from the slaughter of her who loved and tended him?"

"As to that," she answered, "I have already answered thee. Had I slain thee as well as her, yet should he love me, Holly, because he could not save himself therefrom any more than thou couldst save thyself from dying, if by chance I slew thee, O Holly. And yet maybe there is truth in what thou dost say; for in some way it presseth on my mind. If it may be, I will spare this woman; for have I not told thee that I am not cruel for the sake of cruelty? I love not to see suffering, or to cause it. Let her come before me—quick now, before my mood changes," and she hastily covered her face with its gauzy wrapping.

Well pleased to have succeeded even to this extent, I passed out into the passage and called to Ustane, whose white garment I caught sight of some yards away, huddled up against one of the earthenware lamps that were placed at intervals along the tunnel. She rose and ran towards me.

"Is my lord dead? Oh, say not he is dead," she cried, lifting her noble-looking face, all stained as it was with tears, up to me with an air of infinite beseeching that went straight to my heart.

"Nay, he lives," I answered. "*She* hath saved him. Enter."

She sighed deeply, entered, and fell upon her hands and knees, after the custom of the Amahagger people, in the presence of the dread *She*.

"Stand," said Ayesha in her coldest voice, "and come hither."

Ustane obeyed, standing before her with bowed head.

Then came a pause, which Ayesha broke.

"Who is this man?" she said, pointing to the sleeping form of Leo.

"The man is my husband," she answered in a low voice.

"Who gave him to thee for a husband?"

"I took him according to the custom of our country, O *She*."

"Thou hast done evil, woman, in taking this man, who is a stranger. He is not a man of thine own race, and the custom fails. Listen: perchance thou didst this thing through ignorance, therefore, woman, do I spare thee, otherwise hadst thou died. Listen again. Go from hence back to thine own place, and never dare to speak to or set thine eyes upon this man again. He is not for thee. Listen a third time. If thou breakest this my law, that moment thou diest. Go."

But Ustane did not move.

"Go, woman!"

Then she looked up, and I saw that her face was torn with passion.

"Nay, O *She*, I will not go," she answered in a choked voice. "The man is my husband, and I love him—I love him, and I will not leave him. What right hast thou to command me to leave my husband?"

I saw a little quiver pass down Ayesha's frame, and shuddered myself, fearing the worst.

"Be pitiful," I said in Latin; "it is but Nature working."

"I am pitiful," she answered coldly in the same language; "had I not been pitiful she had been dead even now." Then addressing Ustane: "Woman, I say to thee, go before I destroy thee where thou art!"

"I will not go! He is mine—mine!" she cried in anguish. "I took him, and I saved his life! Destroy me, then, if thou hast the power! I will not give thee my husband—never—never!"

Ayesha made a movement so swift that I could scarcely follow it, but it seemed to me that she lightly struck the poor girl upon the head with her hand. I looked at Ustane, and then staggered back in horror, for there upon her hair, right across her bronzelike tresses, were three fingermarks *white as snow*. As for the girl herself, she had put her hands to her head, and was looking dazed.

"Great heavens!" I said, perfectly aghast at this dreadful manifestation of inhuman power; but *She* did but laugh a little.

"Thou thinkest, poor ignorant fool," she said to the bewildered woman, "that I have not power to slay. Stay, there lies a mirror," and she pointed to Leo's round shaving glass that had been arranged by Job with other things upon his portmanteau. "Give it to this woman, my Holly, and let her see that which lies across her hair, and whether or no I have power to slay."

I picked up the glass and held it before Ustane's eyes.

She gazed, then felt at her hair, then gazed again, and then sank upon the ground with a sort of sob.

"Now, wilt thou go, or must I strike a second time?" asked Ayesha, in mockery. "Look, I have set my seal upon thee so that I may know thee till thy hair is all as white as it. If I see thy face here again, be sure, too, that thy bones shall soon be whiter than my mark upon thy hair."

Utterly awed and broken down, the poor creature rose, and, marked with that awful mark, crept from the room sobbing bitterly.

"Look not so frightened, my Holly," said Ayesha when she had gone. "I tell thee I deal not in magic—there is no such thing. 'Tis only a force that thou dost not understand. I marked her to strike terror to her heart, else must I have slain her. And now I will bid my servants bear my lord Kallikrates to a chamber near mine own, that I may watch over him, and be ready to greet him when he wakes; and thither, too, shalt thou come, my Holly, and the white man, thy servant. But one thing remember at thy peril. Naught shalt thou say to Kallikrates as to how this woman went, and as little as may be of me. Now, I have warned thee!" and she slid away to give her orders, leaving me more absolutely confounded than ever. Indeed, so bewildered was I, and racked and torn with such a succession of various emotions, that I began to think that I must be going mad. However, perhaps fortunately, I had but little time to reflect, for presently the mutes arrived to carry the sleeping Leo and our possessions across the central cave, so for a while all was bustle. Our new rooms were situated immediately behind what we used to call Ayesha's boudoir— the curtained space where I had first seen her. Where she herself slept I did not then know, but it was somewhere quite close.

That night I passed in Leo's room, but he slept through it like the dead, never once stirring. I also slept fairly well, as, indeed, I needed to do, but my sleep was full of dreams of all the horrors and wonders I had undergone. Chiefly, however, I was haunted by that frightful piece of *diablerie* by which Ayesha left her fingermarks upon her rival's hair. There was something so terrible about the swift, snakelike movement, and the instantaneous blanching of that three-fold line, that, if the results to Ustane had been much more tremendous, I doubt if they would have impressed me so deeply. To this day I often dream of that awful scene, and see the weeping woman, bereaved, and marked like Cain, cast a last look at her lover, and creep from the presence of her dread Queen.

Another dream that troubled me originated in the huge pyramid of bones. I dreamed that they all stood up and marched past me in thousands and tens of thousands—in squadrons, companies, and armies—with the sunlight shining through their hollow ribs. On they rushed across the plain to Kôr, their imperial home; I saw the drawbridges fall before them, and heard their bones clank through the brazen gates. On they went, up the splendid streets, on past fountains, palaces, and temples such as the eye of man never saw. But there was no man to greet them in the market place, and no woman's face appeared at the windows—only a bodiless voice went before them, calling: "*Fallen is Imperial Kôr! Fallen! Fallen! Fallen!*" On, right through the city, marched those gleaming phalanxes, and the rattle of their bony tread echoed through the silent air as they pressed grimly on. They passed through the city and climbed the wall, and marched along the great roadway that was made upon the wall, till at length they once more reached the drawbridge. Then, as the sun was sinking, they returned again towards their sepulcher, and luridly his light shone in the sockets of their empty eyes, throwing gigantic shadows of their bones that stretched away, and crept and crept like huge spider's legs as their armies wound across the plain. Then they came to the cave, and once more one by one flung themselves in unending files through the hole into the pit of bones, and I awoke, shuddering, to see *She*, who had evidently been standing between my couch and Leo's, glide like a shadow from the room.

After this I slept again, soundly this time, till morning, when I awoke much refreshed, and got up. At last the hour drew near at which, according to Ayesha, Leo was to awake, and with it came *She* herself, as usual, veiled.

"Thou shalt see, O Holly," she said; "presently shall he awake in his right mind, the fever having left him."

Hardly were the words out of her mouth when Leo turned round and stretched out his arms, yawned, opened his eyes, and, perceiving a female form bending over him, threw his arms round her and kissed her, mistaking her for Ustane. He said in Arabic, "Hullo, Ustane, why have you tied your head up like that? Have you got the tooth-ache?" and then, in English, "I say, I'm awfully hungry. Why, Job, you old son of a gun, where the deuce have we got to now—eh?"

"I am sure I wish I knew, Mr. Leo," said Job, edging suspiciously past Ayesha, whom he still regarded with the utmost disgust and horror, being by no means sure that she was not an animated corpse; "but you mustn't talk, Mr. Leo, you've been very ill, and given us a great deal of hanxiety, and, if this lady"—looking at Ayesha—"would be so kind as to move, I'll bring you your soup."

This turned Leo's attention to the "lady," who was standing by in perfect silence. "Hullo!" he said; "that is not Ustane—where is Ustane?"

Then, for the first time, Ayesha spoke to him, and her first words were a lie. "She has gone from hence upon a visit," she said; "and, behold, in her place am I here as thine handmaiden."

Ayesha's silver notes seemed to puzzle Leo's half-awakened intellect, as also did her corpselike wrappings. However, he said nothing at the time, but drank off his soup greedily enough, and then turned over and slept again till the evening. When he woke for the second time he saw me, and began to question me as to what had happened, but I had to put him off as best I could till the morrow, when he awoke almost miraculously better. Then I told him something of his illness and of my doings, but as Ayesha was present I could not tell him much except that she was the queen of the country, and well disposed towards us, and that it was her pleasure to go veiled; for, though of course I spoke in English, I was afraid that she might understand what we were saying from the expression of our faces, and besides, I remembered her warning.

On the following day Leo got up almost entirely recovered. The flesh wound in his side was healed, and his constitution, naturally a vigorous one, had shaken off the exhaustion consequent on his terrible fever with a rapidity that I can only attribute to the effects of the wonderful drug which Ayesha had given to him, and also to the fact that his illness had been too short to reduce him very much. With his returning health came back full recollection of all his adventures up to the time when he had lost consciousness in the marsh, and of course of Ustane also, to whom I had discovered he had grown considerably attached. Indeed, he overwhelmed me with quetsions about the poor girl, which I did not dare to answer, for after Leo's first wakening *She* had sent for me, and again warned me solemnly that I was to reveal nothing of the story to him, delicately hinting that if I did it would be the worse for me. She also, for the second time, cautioned me not to tell Leo anything more than I was obliged about herself, saying that she would reveal herself to him in her own time.

Indeed, her whole manner changed. After all that I had seen I had expected that she would take the earliest opportunity of claiming the man she believed to be her old-world lover, but this, for some reason of her own, which was at the time quite inscrutable to me, she did not do. All that she did was to attend to his wants quietly, and with a humility which was in striking contrast with her former imperious bearing, addressing him always in a tone of something very like respect, and keeping him with her as much as possible. Of course his curiosity was as much excited about this mysterious woman as my own had been, and he was particularly anxious to see her face, which I had, without entering into particulars, told him was as lovely as her form and voice. This in itself was enough to raise the expectations of any young man to a dangerous pitch, and had it not been that he had not as yet completely shaken off the effects of illness, and was much troubled in his mind about Ustane, of whose affection and brave devotion he spoke in touching terms, I have no doubt that he would have entered into her plans, and fallen in love with her by anticipation. As it was, however, he was simply wildly curious, and also, like myself, considerably awed, for though no hint had been given to him by Ayesha of her extraordinary age, he not unnaturally came to identify her with the woman spoken of on the potsherd. At last, quite driven into a corner by his continual questions, which he showered on me while he was dressing on this third morning, I referred him to Ayesha, saying, with perfect truth, that I did not know where Ustane was. Accordingly, after Leo had eaten a hearty breakfast, we adjourned into *She*'s presence, for her mutes had orders to admit us at all hours.

She was, as usual, seated in what, for want of a better term, we called her boudoir, and on the curtains being drawn she rose from her couch and, stretching out both hands, came forward to greet us, or rather Leo; for I, as may be imagined, was now quite left in the cold. It was a pretty sight to see her veiled form gliding towards the sturdy young Englishman, dressed in his gray flannel suit; for though he is half a Greek in blood, Leo is, with the exception of his hair, one of the most English-looking men I ever saw. He has nothing of the supple form or slippery manner of the modern Greek about him, though I presume that he got his remarkable personal beauty from his foreign mother, whose portrait he resembles not a little. He is very tall and big-chested, and yet not awkward, as so many big men are, and his head is set upon him in such a fashion as to give him a proud and vigorous air, which was well translated in his Amahagger name of the "Lion."

"Greeting to thee, my young stranger lord," she said in her softest voice. "Right glad am I to see thee upon thy feet. Believe me, had I not saved thee at the last, never wouldst thou have stood upon those feet again. But the danger is done, and it shall be my care"—and she flung a world of meaning into the words—"that it doth return no more."

Leo bowed to her, and then, in his best Arabic, thanked

her for all her kindness and courtesy in caring for one unknown to her.

"Nay," she answered softly, "ill could the world spare such a man. Beauty is too rare upon it. Give me no thanks, who am made happy by thy coming."

"Humph! Old fellow," said Leo aside to me in English, "the lady is very civil. We seem to have tumbled into clover. I hope that you have made the most of your opportunities. By Jove, what a pair of arms she has got!"

I nudged him in the ribs to make him keep quiet, for I caught sight of a gleam from Ayesha's veiled eyes, which were regarding me curiously.

"I trust," went on Ayesha, "that my servants have attended well upon thee; if there can be comfort in this poor place, be sure it waits on thee. Is there aught that I can do for thee more?"

"Yes, O *She*," answered Leo hastily. "I would fain know whither the young lady who was looking after me has gone to."

"Ah," said Ayesha. "The girl—yes, I saw her. Nay, I know not; she said that she would go, I know not whither. Perchance she will return, perchance not. It is wearisome waiting on the sick, and these savage women are fickle."

Leo looked both sulky and distressed at this intelligence.

"It's very odd," he said to me in English; and then addressing *She*, "I cannot understand," he said; "the young lady and I—well—in short, we had a regard for each other."

Ayesha laughed a little, very musically, and then turned the subject.

"Give Me a Black Goat!"

THE CONVERSATION after this was of such a desultory order that I do not quite recollect it. For some reason, perhaps from a desire to keep her identity and character in reserve, Ayesha did not talk freely, as she usually did. Presently, however, she informed Leo that she had arranged a dance that night for our amusement. I was astonished to hear this, as I fancied that the Amahagger were much too gloomy a folk to indulge in any such frivolity; but, as will presently more clearly appear, it turned out that an Amahagger dance has little in common with such fantastic festivities in other countries, savage or civilized. Then, as we were about to withdraw, she suggested that Leo might like to see some of the wonders of the caves, and as he gladly assented thither we departed, accompanied by Job and Billali. To describe our visit would only be to repeat a great deal of what I have already said. The tombs we entered were indeed different, for the whole rock was a honeycomb of sepulchers,[1] but the contents were nearly always similar. Afterwards we visited the pyramid of bones that had haunted my dreams on the previous night, and from thence went down a long passage to one of the great

[1] For a long while it puzzled me to know what could have been done with the enormous quantities of rock that must have been dug out of these vast caves; but I afterwards discovered that it was for the most part built into the walls and palaces of Kôr, and also used to line the reservoirs and sewers.—L. H. H.

vaults occupied by the bodies of the poorer citizens of Imperial Kôr. These bodies were not nearly so well preserved as were those of the wealthier classes. Many of them had no linen covering on them, also they were buried from five hundred to one thousand in a single large vault, the corpses in some instances being thickly piled one upon another, like a heap of slain.

Leo was of course intensely interested in this stupendous and unequaled sight, which was, indeed, enough to awake all the imagination a man had in him into the most active life. But to poor Job it did not prove attractive. His nerves—already seriously shaken by what he had undergone since we had arrived in this terrible country—were, as may be imagined, still further disturbed by the spectacle of these masses of departed humanity, whereof the forms still remained perfect before his eyes, though their voices were forever lost in the eternal silence of the tomb. Nor was he comforted when old Billali, by way of soothing his evident agitation, informed him that he should not be frightened of these dead things, as he would soon be like them himself.

"There's a nice thing to say of a man, sir," he ejaculated, when I translated this little remark; "but there, what can one expect of an old man-eating savage? Not but what I dare say he's right," and Job sighed.

When we had finished inspecting the caves, we returned and had our meal, for it was now past four in the afternoon, and we all—especially Leo—needed some food and rest. At six o'clock we, together with Job, waited on Ayesha, who set to work to terrify our poor servant still further by showing him pictures on the pool of water in the fontlike vessel. She learned from me that he was one of seventeen children, and then bade him think of all his brothers and sisters, or as many of them as he could, gathered together in his father's cottage. Then she told him to look in the water, and there, reflected from its stilly surface, was that dead scene of many years gone by, as it was recalled to our retainer's brain. Some of the faces were clear enough, but some were mere blurs and splotches, or with one feature grossly exaggerated; the fact being that, in these instances, Job had been unable to recall the exact appearances of the individuals, or remembered them only by a peculiarity of his tribe, and the water could only reflect what he saw with his mind's eye. For it must be remembered that *She*'s power in this matter was strictly limited; she could apparently, except in very rare instances, only photograph upon the water what was actually in the mind of someone present, and then only by his will. But if she was personally acquainted with a locality, she could, as in the case of ourselves and the whaleboat, throw its reflection upon the water, and also it seems the reflection of anything extraneous that was passing there at the time. This power, however, did not extend to the minds of others. For instance, she could show me the interior of my college chapel, as I remembered it, but not as it was at the moment of reflection; for, where other people were concerned, her art was strictly limited to the facts or memories present to *their* consciousness at the moment. So much was this so, that when we tried, for her amusement, to show her pictures of noted buildings, such as St. Paul's or the Houses of Parliament, the result was most imperfect; for, of course, though we had a good general idea of their appearance, we could not recall all the architectural details, and therefore the minutiae necessary to a perfect reflection were wanting. But Job could not be got to understand this, and far from accepting a natural explanation of the matter, which was after all, though strange enough in all conscience, nothing more than an instance of glorified and perfected telepathy, he set the whole thing down as a manifestation of the blackest magic. I shall never forget the howl of terror which he uttered when he saw the more or less perfect portraits of his long-scattered brethren staring at him from the quiet water, or the merry peal of laughter with which Ayesha greeted his consternation. As for Leo, he did not altogether like it either, but ran his fingers through his yellow curls, and remarked that it gave him the creeps.

After about an hour of this amusement, in the latter part of which Job did *not* participate, the mutes by signs indicated that Billali was waiting for an audience. Accordingly he was told to "crawl up," which he did as awkwardly as usual, and announced that the dance was ready to begin if *She* and the white strangers would be pleased to attend. Shortly afterwards we all rose, and Ayesha having thrown a dark cloak (the same, by the way, that she had worn when I saw her cursing by the fire) over her white wrappings, we started. The dance was to be held in the open air, on the smooth rocky plateau in front of the great cave, and thither we made our way. About fifteen paces from the mouth of the cave we found three chairs placed, and here we sat and waited, for as yet no dancers were to be seen. The night was almost, but not quite, dark, the moon not having risen as yet, which made us wonder how we should be able to see the dancing.

"Thou wilt presently understand," said Ayesha, with a little laugh, when Leo asked her; and we certainly did. Scarcely were the words out of her mouth when from every point we saw dark forms rushing up, each bearing with him what we at first took to be an enormous flaming torch. Whatever they were they were burning furiously, for the flames stood out a yard or more behind each bearer.

On they came, fifty or more of them, carrying their flaming burdens and looking like so many devils from hell. Leo was the first to discover what these burdens were.

"Great heavens!" he said. "They are corpses on fire!"

I stared and stared again. He was perfectly right—the torches that were to light our entertainment were human mummies from the caves!

On rushed the bearers of the flaming corpses, and, meeting at a spot about twenty paces in front of us, built their ghastly burdens crossways into a huge bonfire. Heavens, how they roared and flared! No tar barrel could have burned as those mummies did. Nor was this all. Suddenly I saw one great fellow seize a flaming human arm that had fallen from its parent frame, and rush off into the darkness. Presently he stopped, and a tall streak of fire shot up into the air, illumining the gloom, and also the lamp from which it sprang. That lamp was the mummy of a woman tied to a stout stake let into the rock, and he had fired her hair. On he went a few paces and touched a second, then a third, and a fourth, till at last we were surrounded on all three sides by a great ring of bodies flaring furiously, the material with which they were preserved having rendered them so inflammable that the flames would literally spout out of the ears and mouth in tongues of fire a foot or more in length.

Nero illuminated his gardens with live Christians soaked in tar, and we were now treated to a similar spectacle, probably for the first time since his day, only happily our lamps were not living ones.

But although this element of horror was fortunately wanting, to describe the awful and hideous grandeur of the spectacle thus presented to us is, I feel, so absolutely beyond my poor powers, that I scarcely dare attempt it.

To begin with, it appealed to the moral as well as the physical susceptibilities. There was something very terrible, and yet very fascinating, about the employment of the remote dead to illumine the orgies of the living; in itself the thing was a satire on both the living and the dead. Caesar's dust—or is it Alexander's?—may stop a bunghole, but the functions of these dead Caesars of the past was to light up a savage fetish dance. To such base uses may we come, of so little account may we be in the minds of the eager multitudes that we shall breed, many of whom, so far from revering our memory, will live to curse us for begetting them into such a world of woe.

Then there was the physical side of the spectacle, and a weird and splendid one it was. Those old citizens of Kôr burned as, to judge from their sculptures and inscriptions, they had lived, very fast, and with the utmost liberality. What is more, there were plenty of them. As soon as ever a mummy had burned down to the ankles, which it did in about twenty minutes, the feet were kicked away, and another one put in its place. The bonfire was kept going on the same generous scale, and its flames shot up, with a hiss and a crackle, twenty or thirty feet into the air, throwing great flashes of light far out into the gloom, through which the dark forms of the Amahagger flitted to and fro like devils replenishing the infernal fires. We all stood and stared aghast—shocked, and yet fascinated at so strange a spectacle, and half-expecting to see the spirits those flaming forms had once enclosed come creeping from the shadows to work vengeance on their desecrators.

"I promised thee a strange sight, my Holly," laughed Ayesha, whose nerves alone did not seem to be affected; "and, behold, I have not failed thee. Also, it hath its lesson. Trust not to the future, for who knows what the future may bring! Therefore, live for the day, and endeavor not to escape the dust which seems to be man's end. What thinkest thou those long-forgotten nobles and ladies would have felt had they known that they should one day flare to light the dance or boil the pot of savages? But see, here come the dancers; a merry crew, are they not? The stage is lit—now for the play."

As she spoke, we perceived two lines of figures, one male and the other female, to the number of about a hundred, each advancing round the human bonfire, arrayed only in the usual leopard and buck skins. They formed up, in perfect silence, in two lines, facing each other between us and the fire, and then the dance—a sort of infernal and fiendish cancan—began. To describe it is quite impossible, but, though there was a good deal of tossing of legs and double-shuffling, it seemed to our untutored minds to be more of a play than a dance, and, as usual with this dreadful people, whose minds seem to have taken their color from the caves in which they live, and whose jokes and amusements are drawn from the inexhaustible stores of preserved mortality with which they share their homes, the subject appeared to be a most ghastly one. I know that it represented an attempted murder first of all, and then the burial alive of the victim and his struggling from the grave; each act of the abominable drama, which was carried on in perfect silence, being rounded off and finished with a furious and most revolting dance round the supposed victim, who writhed upon the ground in the red light of the bonfire.

Presently, however, this pleasing piece was interrupted. Suddenly there was a slight commotion, and a large powerful woman, whom I had noted as one of the most vigorous of the dancers, came, made mad and drunken with unholy excitement, bounding and staggering towards us, shrieking out as she came: "I want a black goat, I must have a black goat, bring me a black goat!" and down she fell upon the rocky floor foaming and writhing, and shrieking for a black goat, about as hideous a spectacle as can well be conceived.

Instantly most of the dancers came up and got round her, though some still continued their capers in the background.

"She has got a Devil," called out one of them. "Run and get a black goat. There, Devil, keep quiet! Keep quiet! You shall have the goat presently. They have gone to fetch it, Devil."

"I want a black goat, I must have a black goat!" shrieked the foaming rolling creature again.

"All right, Devil, the goat will be here presently; keep quiet, there's a good Devil!"

And so on till the goat taken from a neighboring kraal did at last arrive, being dragged bleating onto the scene by its horns.

"Is it a black one, is it a black one?" shrieked the possessed.

"Yes, yes, Devil, as black as night." Then, aside, "Keep it behind thee, don't let the Devil see that it has got a white spot on its rump and another on its belly. In one minute, Devil. There, cut his throat quick. Where is the saucer?"

"The goat! The goat! The goat! Give me the blood of my black goat! I must have it, don't you see I must have it? Oh! Oh! Oh! Give me the blood of the goat."

At this moment a terrified *bah!* announced that the poor goat had been sacrificed, and the next minute a woman ran up with a saucer full of the blood. This the possessed creature, who was then raving and foaming her wildest,

seized and drank, and was instantly recovered, and without
a trace of hysteria, or fits, or being possessed, or whatever
dreadful thing it was she was suffering from. She stretched
her arms, smiled faintly, and walked quietly back to the
dancers, who presently withdrew in a double line as they
had come, leaving the space between us and the bonfire
deserted.

I thought that the entertainment was now over, and,
feeling rather queer, was about to ask *She* if we could rise,
when suddenly what at first I took to be a baboon came
hopping round the fire, and was instantly met upon the
other side by a lion, or rather a human being dressed in a
lion's skin. Then came a goat, then a man wrapped in an
ox's hide, with the horns wobbling about in a ludicrous
way. After him followed a blesbok, then an impala, then a
koodoo, then more goats, and many other animals, including a girl sewn up in the shining scaly hide of a boa con-
strictor, several yards of which trailed along the ground
behind her. When all the beasts had collected they began
to dance about in a lumbering, unnatural fashion, and to
imitate the sounds produced by the respective animals they
represented, till the whole air was alive with roars and
bleating and the hissing of snakes. This went on for a
long time, till, getting tired of the pantomime, I asked
Ayesha if there would be any objection to Leo and myself
walking round to inspect the human torches, and, as she
had nothing to say against it, we started, striking round to
the left. After looking at one or two of the flaming bodies,
we were about to return, thoroughly disgusted with the
grotesque weirdness of the spectacle, when our attention
was attracted by one of the dancers, a particularly active
leopard, that had separated itself from its fellow-beasts,
and was whisking about in our immediate neighborhood,

but gradually drawing into a spot where the shadow was darkest, equidistant between two of the flaming mummies. Drawn by curiosity, we followed it, when suddenly it darted past us into the shadows beyond, and as it did so erected itself and whispered, "Come," in a voice that we both recognized as that of Ustane. Without waiting to consult me Leo turned and followed her into the outer darkness, and I, feeling sick enough at heart, went after them. The leopard crawled on for about fifty paces—a sufficient distance to be quite beyond the light of the fire and torches—and then Leo came up with it, or, rather, with Ustane.

"Oh, my lord," I heard her whisper, "so I have found thee! Listen. I am in peril of my life from *'She-who-must-be-obeyed.'* Surely the Baboon has told thee how she drove me from thee? I love thee, my lord, and thou art mine according to the custom of the country. I saved thy life! My lion, wilt thou cast me off now?"

"Of course not," ejaculated Leo; "I have been wondering whither thou hadst gone. Let us go and explain matters to the Queen."

"Nay, nay, she would slay us. Thou knowest not her power—the Baboon there, he knoweth, for he saw. Nay, there is but one way: if thou wilt cleave to me, thou must flee with me across the marshes even now, and then perchance we may escape."

"For heaven's sake, Leo," I began, but she broke in.

"Nay, listen not to him. Swift—be swift—death is in the air we breathe. Even now, mayhap, *She* heareth us," and without more ado she proceeded to back her arguments by throwing herself into his arms. As she did so the leopard's head slipped from her hair, and I saw the three white fingermarks upon it, gleaming faintly in the starlight. Once more, realizing the desperate nature of our position, I was about to interpose, for I knew that Leo was not too strong-minded where women were concerned, when—oh, horror!—I heard a little silvery laugh behind me. I turned round, and there was *She* herself, and with her Billali and two male mutes. I gasped and nearly sank to the ground, for I knew that such a situation must result in some dreadful tragedy, of which it seemed exceedingly probable to me that I should be the first victim. As for Ustane, she untwined her arms and covered her eyes with her hands, while Leo, not knowing the full terror of the position, merely colored up, and looked as foolish as a man caught in such a trap would naturally do.

20 ◆

Triumph

THEN FOLLOWED a moment of the most painful silence that I ever endured. It was broken by Ayesha, who addressed herself to Leo.

"Nay, now my lord and guest," she said in her softest tones, which yet had the ring of steel about them, "look not so bashful. Surely the sight was a pretty one—the leopard and the lion!"

"Oh, hang it all!" said Leo in English.

"And thou, Ustane," she went on, "surely I should have passed thee by had not the light fallen on the white across thy hair," and she pointed to the bright edge of the rising moon which was now appearing above the horizon. "Well, well! The dance is done—see, the tapers have burned down, and all things end in silence and in ashes. So thou thoughtest it a fit time for love, Ustane, my servant—and I, dreaming not that I could be disobeyed, thought thee already far away."

"Play not with me," moaned the wretched woman; "slay me, and let there be an end."

"Nay, why? It is not well to go so swift from the hot lips of love down to the cold mouth of the grave," and she made a motion to the mutes, who instantly stepped up and caught the girl by either arm. With an oath Leo sprang upon the nearest, and hurled him to the ground, and then stood over him with his face set, and his fist ready.

Again Ayesha laughed. "It was well thrown, my guest;

257

thou hast a strong arm for one who so late was sick. But now out of thy courtesy I pray thee let that man live and do my bidding. He shalt not harm the girl; the night air grows chill, and I would welcome her in mine own place. Surely she whom thou dost favor shall be favored of me also."

I took Leo by the arm, and pulled him from the prostrate mute, and he, half bewildered, obeyed the pressure. Then we all set out for the cave across the plateau, where a pile of white human ashes was all that remained of the fire that had lit the dancing, for the dancers had vanished.

In due course we gained Ayesha's boudoir—all too soon it seemed to me, having a sad presage of what was to come lying heavy on my heart.

Ayesha seated herself upon her cushions, and, having dismissed Job and Billali, by signs bade the mutes tend the lamps and retire, all save one girl, who was her favorite personal attendant. We three remained standing, the unfortunate Ustane a little to the left of the rest of us.

"Now, O Holly," Ayesha began, "how came it that thou who didst hear my words bidding this evildoer"—and she pointed to Ustane—"to go from hence—thou at whose prayer I did weakly spare her life—how came it, I say, that thou wast a sharer in what I saw tonight? Answer, and for thine own sake, I say, speak all the truth, for I am not minded to hear lies upon this matter!"

"It was by accident, O Queen," I answered. "I knew naught of it."

"I do believe thee, O Holly," she answered coldly, "and well it is for thee that I do—then does the whole guilt rest upon her."

"I do not find any guilt therein," broke in Leo. "She is not another man's wife, and it appears that she has married me according to the custom of this awful place, so who is the worse? Anyway, madam," he went on, "whatever she has done I have done too, so if she is to be punished let me be punished also; and I tell thee," he went on, working himself up into a fury, "that if thou biddest one of those deaf and dumb villains to touch her again I will tear him to pieces!" And he looked as though he meant it.

Ayesha listened in icy silence, and made no remark. When he had finished, however, she addressed Ustane.

"Hast thou aught to say, woman? Thou silly straw, thou feather, who didst think to float towards thy passion's petty ends, even against the great wind of my will! Tell me, for I fain would understand. Why didst thou this thing?"

And then I think I saw the most tremendous exhibition of moral courage and intrepidity that it is possible to conceive. For the poor doomed girl, knowing what she had to expect at the hands of her terrible queen, knowing, too, from bitter experience how great was her adversary's power, yet gathered herself together, and out of the very depths of her despair drew materials to defy her.

"I did it, O *She*," she answered, drawing herself up to the full of her stately height, and throwing back the panther skin from her head, "because my love is stronger than the grave. I did it because my life without this man whom my heart chose would be but a living death. Therefore did I risk my life, and now that I know that it is forfeit to thine anger, yet am I glad that I did risk it, and pay it away in the risking, ay, because he embraced me once, and told me that he loved me yet."

Here Ayesha half rose from her couch, and then sank down again.

"I have no magic," went on Ustane, her rich voice ringing strong and full, ` and I am not a queen, nor do I live forever, but a woman's heart is heavy to sink through waters, however deep, O Queen, and a woman's eyes are quick to see, even through thy veil, O Queen!

"Listen: I know it, thou dost love this man thyself, and therefore wouldst thou destroy me who stand across thy path. Ay, I die—I die, and go into the darkness, nor know I whither I go. But this I know. There is a light shining in my breast, and by that light, as by a lamp, I see the truth, and the future that I shall not share unroll itself before me like a scroll. When first I knew my lord"—and she pointed to Leo—"I knew also that death would be the bridal gift he gave me—it rushed upon me of a sudden, but I turned not back, being ready to pay the price, and, behold, death is here! And now, even as I knew that, so do I, standing on the steps of doom, know that thou shalt not reap the profits of thy crime. Mine he is, and, though thy beauty shine like a sun among the stars, mine shall he remain for thee. Never here in this life shall he look thee in the eyes and call thee spouse. Thou too art doomed, I see"—and her voice rang like the cry of an inspired prophetess—"ah, I see—"

Then came an answering cry of mingled rage and terror. I turned my head. Ayesha had risen, and was standing with her outstretched hand pointing at Ustane, who had suddenly stopped speaking. I gazed at the poor woman, and as I gazed there came upon her face that same woeful, fixed expression of terror that I had seen once before when she had broken out into her wild chant. Her eyes grew large, her nostrils dilated, and her lips blanched.

Ayesha said nothing, she made no sound, she only drew herself up, stretched out her arm, and, her tall veiled frame quivering like an aspen leaf, appeared to look fixedly at her victim. Even as she did so Ustane put her hands to her head, uttered one piercing scream, turned round twice, and then fell backwards with a thud—prone upon the floor. Both Leo and myself rushed to her—she was stone dead— blasted into death by some mysterious electric agency or overwhelming will-force whereof the dread *She* had command.

For a moment Leo did not quite realize what had happened. But when he did, his face was awful to see. With a savage oath he rose from beside the corpse, and, turning, literally sprang at Ayesha. But she was watching, and, seeing him come, stretched out her hand again, and he went staggering back towards me, and would have fallen, had I not caught him. Afterwards he told me that he felt as though he had suddenly received a violent blow in the chest, and, what is more, felt utterly cowed, as if all the manhood had been taken out of him.

Then Ayesha spoke. "Forgive me, my guest," she said softly, addressing him, "if I have shocked thee with my justice."

"Forgive thee, thou fiend," roared poor Leo, wringing his hands in his rage and grief. "Forgive thee, thou murderess! By heaven I will kill thee if I can!"

"Nay, nay," she answered in the same soft voice, "thou dost not understand—the time has come for thee to learn. *Thou* art my love, my Kallikrates, my Beautiful, my Strong! For two thousand years, Kallikrates, have I waited for *thee*, and now at length thou hast come back to me; and as for this woman"—pointing to the corpse—"she stood between me and thee, and therefore have I removed her, Kallikrates."

"It is an accursed lie!" said Leo. "My name is not Kallikrates! I am Leo Vincey; my ancestor was Kallikrates—at least, I believe he was."

"Ah, thou sayest it—thine ancestor was Kallikrates, and thou, even thou, art Kallikrates reborn, come back—and mine own dear lord!"

"I am not Kallikrates, and as for being thy lord, or having aught to do with thee, I had sooner be the lord of a fiend from hell, for she would be better than thou."

"Sayest thou so—sayest thou so, Kallikrates? Nay, but thou hast not seen me for so long a time that no memory remains. Yet am I very fair, Kallikrates!"

"I hate thee, murderess, and I have no wish to see thee. What is it to me how fair thou art? I hate thee, I say."

"Yet within a very little space shalt thou creep to my knee, and swear that thou dost love me," answered Ayesha, with a sweet, mocking laugh. "Come, there is no time like the present time, here before this dead girl who loved thee, let us put it to the proof.

"Look now on me, Kallikrates!" and with a sudden motion she shook her gauzy covering from her, and stood forth in her low kirtle and her snaky zone, in her glorious radiant beauty and her imperial grace, rising from her wrappings, as it were, like Venus from the wave, or Galatea from her marble, or a beatified spirit from the tomb. She stood forth, and fixed her deep and glowing eyes upon Leo's eyes, and I saw his clenched fists unclasp, and his set and quivering features relax beneath her gaze. I saw his wonder and astonishment grow into admiration, and then into fascination, and the more he struggled the more I saw the power of her dread beauty fasten on him and take possession of his senses, drugging them, and drawing the heart out of him. Did I not know the process? Had not I, who was twice his age, gone through it myself? Was I not going through it afresh even then, although her sweet and passionate gaze was not for me? Yes, alas, I was! Alas, that I should have to confess that at that very moment I was rent by mad and furious jealousy. I could have flown at him, shame upon me! The woman had confounded and almost destroyed my moral sense, as she was bound to confound all who looked upon her superhuman loveliness. But—I do not quite know how—I got the better of myself, and once more turned to see the climax of the tragedy.

"Oh, great heaven!" gasped Leo, "art thou a woman?"

"A woman in truth—in very truth—and thine own spouse, Kallikrates!" she answered, stretching out her rounded ivory arms towards him, and smiling, ah, so sweetly!

He looked and looked, and slowly I perceived that he was drawing nearer to her. Suddenly his eye fell upon the corpse of poor Ustane, and he shuddered and stopped.

"How can I?" he said hoarsely. "Thou art a murderess; she loved me."

Observe, he was already forgetting that he had loved her.

"It is naught," she murmured, and her voice sounded as sweet as the night wind passing through the trees. "It is naught at all. If I have sinned, let my beauty answer for my sin. If I have sinned, it is for love of thee: let my sin, therefore, be put away and forgotten." And once more she stretched out her arms and whispered *"Come,"* and then in another few seconds it was over. I saw him struggle— I saw him even turn to fly; but her eyes drew him more strongly than iron bonds, and the magic of her beauty and concentrated will and passion entered into him and overpowered him—ay, even there, in the presence of the body of the woman who had loved him well enough to die for him. It sounds horrible and wicked enough, but he cannot be blamed too much, and be sure his sin will find him out. The temptress who drew him into evil was more than human, and her beauty was greater than the loveliness of the daughters of men.

I looked up again, and now her perfect form lay in his arms, and her lips were pressed against his own; and thus, with the corpse of his dead love for an altar, did Leo Vincey plight his troth to her red-handed murderess—plight it forever and a day. For those who sell themselves into a like dominion, paying down the price of their own honor, and throwing their soul into the balance to sink the scale to the level of their lusts, can hope for no deliverance here or hereafter. As they have sown, so shall they reap and reap, even when the poppy flowers of passion have withered in their hands, and their harvest is but bitter tares, garnered in satiety.

Suddenly, with a snakelike motion, she seemed to slip from his embrace, and then again broke out into her low laugh of triumphant mockery.

"Did I not tell thee that within a little space thou wouldst creep to my knee, O Kallikrates? And surely the space has not been a great one!"

Leo groaned in shame and misery; for though he was overcome and stricken down, he was not so lost as to be unaware of the depth of the degradation to which he had sunk. On the contrary, his better nature rose up in arms against his fallen self, as I saw clearly enough later on.

Ayesha laughed again, and then quickly veiled herself, and made a sign to the girl mute, who had been watching the whole scene with curious startled eyes. The girl left, and presently returned, followed by two male mutes, to whom the Queen made another sign. Thereon they all three seized the body of poor Ustane by the arms, and dragged it heavily down the cavern and away through the curtains at the end. Leo watched it for a little while, and then covered his eyes with his hand, and it too, to my excited fancy, seemed to watch us as it went.

"There passes the dead past," said Ayesha solemnly, as the curtains shook and fell back into their places, when the ghastly procession had vanished behind them. And then, with one of those extraordinary transitions of which I have already spoken, she again threw off her veil, and broke out, after the ancient and poetic fashion of the dwellers in Arabia,[1] into a paean of triumph or epithalamium, which, wild and beautiful as it was, is exceedingly difficult to render into English, and ought by rights to be sung to the music of a cantata, rather than written and read. It was divided into two parts—one descriptive or definitive, and the other personal; and, as nearly as I can remember, ran as follows:

> *Love is like a flower in the desert.*
> *It is like the aloe of Arabia that blooms but once and dies; it blooms in the salt emptiness of Life, and the brightness of its beauty is set upon the waste as a star is set upon a storm.*
> *It hath the sun above that is the spirit, and above it blows the air of its divinity.*

[1] Among the ancient Arabians the power of poetic declamation, either in verse or prose, was held in the highest honor and esteem, and he who excelled in it was known as "Khâteb" or Orator. Every year a general assembly was held at which the rival poets repeated their compositions, when those poems which were judged to be the best were, so soon as the knowledge of the art of writing became general, inscribed on silk in letters of gold, and publicly exhibited, being known as "Al Modhahabât," or golden verses. In the poem given above by Mr. Holly, Ayesha evidently followed the traditional poetic manner of her people, which was to embody their thoughts in a series of somewhat disconnected sentences, each remarkable for its beauty and the grace of its expression.—EDITOR.

> At the echoing of a step, Love blooms, I say; I say Love
> blooms, and bends her beauty down to him who pass-
> eth by.
>
> He plucketh it, yea, he plucketh the red cup that is full
> of honey, and beareth it away; away across the desert,
> away till the flower be withered, away till the desert be
> done.
>
> There is only one perfect flower in the wilderness of Life.
> That flower is Love!
>
> There is only one fixed star in the mists of our wandering.
> That star is Love!
>
> There is only one hope in our despairing night.
> That hope is Love!
>
> All else is false. All else is shadow moving upon water.
> All else is wind and vanity.
>
> Who shall say what is the weight or the measure of Love?
>
> It is born of the flesh, it dwelleth in the spirit. From each
> doth it draw its comfort.
>
> For beauty it is as a star.
>
> Many are its shapes, but all are beautiful, and none know
> where the star rose, or the horizon where it shall set.

Then, turning to Leo, and laying her hand upon his
shoulder, she went on in a fuller and more triumphant
tone, speaking in balanced sentences that gradually grew
and swelled from idealized prose into pure and majestic
verse:

> Long have I loved thee, oh, my love; yet has my love not
> lessened.
>
> Long have I waited for thee, and behold my reward is at
> hand—is here!
>
> Far away I saw thee once, and thou wast taken from me.
>
> Then in a grave sowed I the seed of patience, and shone
> upon it with the sun of hope, and watered it with tears
> of repentance, and breathed on it with the breath of my

knowledge. And now, lo! it hath sprung up, and borne
fruit. Lo! out of the grave hath it sprung. Yea, from
among the dry bones and ashes of the dead.
I have waited and my reward is with me.
I have overcome Death, and Death brought back to me
him that was dead.
Therefore do I rejoice, for fair is the future.
Green are the paths that we shall tread across the ever-
lasting meadows.
The hour is at hand. Night hath fled away into the valleys.
The dawn kisseth the mountain tops.
Soft shall we lie, my love, and easy shall we go.
Crowned shall we be with the diadem of kings.
Worshiping and wonder-struck, all peoples of the world,
Blinded shall fall before our beauty and our might.
From time unto times shall our greatness thunder on,
Rolling like a chariot through the dust of endless days.
Laughing shall we speed in our victory and pomp,
Laughing like the Daylight as he leaps along the hills.
Onward, still triumphant, to a triumph ever new!
Onward, in our power, to a power unattained!
Onward, never weary, clad with splendor for a robe!
Till accomplished be our fate, and the night is rushing
down.

She paused in her strange and most thrilling allegorical
chant, of which I am, unfortunately, only able to give the
burden, and that feebly enough, and then said, "Perchance
thou dost not believe my word, Kallikrates—perchance thou
thinkest that I do delude thee, and that I have not lived
these many years, and that thou hast not been born again
to me. Nay, look not so—put away that pale cast of doubt,
for oh be sure herein can error find no foothold! Sooner
shall the suns forget their course and the swallow miss
her nest, than my soul shall swear a lie and be led astray

from thee, Kallikrates. Blind me, take away mine eyes, and let the darkness utterly fence me in, and still mine ears would catch the tone of thine unforgotten voice, striking more loud against the portals of my sense than can the call of brazen-throated clarions: stop up mine hearing also, and let a thousand touch me on the brow, and I would name thee out of all: yea, rob me of every sense, and see me stand deaf and blind, and dumb, and with nerves that cannot weigh the value of a touch, yet would my spirit leap within me like a quickening child and cry unto my heart, behold Kallikrates! Behold, thou watcher, the watches of thy night are ended! Behold, thou who seekest in the night season, thy morning Star ariseth."

She paused awhile and then continued, "But stay, if thy heart is yet hardened against the mighty truth and thou dost require a further pledge of that which thou dost find too deep to understand, even now shall it be given to thee, and to thee also, O my Holly. Bear each one of you a lamp, and follow after me whither I shall lead you."

Without stopping to think—indeed, speaking for myself, I had almost abandoned the function in circumstances under which to think seemed to be absolutely useless, since thought fell hourly helpless against a black wall of wonder—we took the lamps and followed her. Going to the end of her "boudoir," she raised a curtain and revealed a little stair of the sort that was so common in these dim caves of Kôr. As we hurried down the stair I observed that the steps were worn in the center to such an extent that some of them had been reduced from seven and a half inches, at which I guessed their original height, to about three and a half. Now, all the other steps that I had seen in the caves had been practically unworn, as was to be expected, seeing that the only traffic which ever passed upon them was that of those who bore a fresh burden to the tomb. Therefore this fact struck my notice with that curious force with which little things do strike us when our minds are absolutely overwhelmed by a sudden rush of powerful sensations; beaten flat, as it were, like a sea beneath the first burst of a hurricane, so that every little object on the surface starts into an unnatural prominence.

At the bottom of the staircase I stood and stared at the worn steps, and Ayesha, turning, saw me.

"Wonderest thou whose are the feet that have worn away the rock, my Holly?" she asked. "They are mine— even mine own light feet! I can remember when these stairs were fresh and level, but for two thousand years and more have I gone down hither day by day, and see, my sandals have worn out the solid rock!"

I made no answer, but I do not think that anything that I had heard or seen brought home to my limited understanding so clear a sense of this being's overwhelming antiquity as that hard rock hollowed out by her soft white feet. How many millions of times must she have passed up and down that stair to bring about such a result?

The stair led to a tunnel, and a few paces down the tunnel was one of the usual curtain-hung doorways, a glance at which told me that it was the same where I had been a witness of that terrible scene by the leaping flame. I recognized the pattern of the curtain, and the sight of it brought the whole event vividly before my eyes, and made me tremble even at its memory. Ayesha entered the tomb (for it was a tomb), and we followed her—I, for one, rejoicing that the mystery of the place was about to be cleared up, and yet afraid to face its solution.

The Dead and Living Meet

"See now the place where I have slept for these two thousand years," said Ayesha, taking the lamp from Leo's hand and holding it above her head. Its rays fell upon a little hollow in the floor, where I had seen the leaping flame, but the fire was out now. They fell upon the white form stretched there beneath its wrappings upon its bed of stone, upon the fretted carving of the tomb, and upon another shelf of stone opposite the one on which the body lay, and separated from it by the breadth of the cave.

"Here," went on Ayesha, laying her hand upon the rock, "here have I slept night by night for all these generations, with but a cloak to cover me. It did not become me that I should lie soft when my spouse yonder"—and she pointed to the rigid form—"lay stiff in death. Here night by night have I slept in his cold company—till, thou seest, this thick slab, like the stairs down which we passed, has worn thin with the tossing of my form——so faithful have I been to thee even in thy space of sleep, Kallikrates. And now, mine own, thou shalt see a wonderful thing—living, thou shalt behold thyself dead—for well have I tended thee during all these years, Kallikrates. Art thou prepared?"

We made no answer, but gazed at each other with frightened eyes, the whole scene was so dreadful and so solemn. Ayesha advanced, and laid her hand upon the corner of the shroud, and once more spoke.

"Be not affrighted," she said; "though the thing seem wonderful to thee—all we who live have thus lived before; nor is the very shape that holds us a stranger to the sun! Only we know it not, because memory writes no record, and earth hath gathered in the earth she lent us, for none have saved our glory from the grave. But I, by my arts and by the arts of those dead men of Kôr which I have learned, have held thee back, O Kallikrates, from the dust, that the waxen stamp of beauty on thy face should ever rest before mine eye. 'Twas a mask that memory might fill, serving to fashion out thy presence from the past, and give it strength to wander in the habitations of my thought, clad in a mummery of life that stayed my appetite with visions of dead days.

"Behold now, let the Dead and Living meet! Across the gulf of Time they still are one. Time hath no power against Identity, though sleep the merciful hath blotted out the tablets of our mind, and with oblivion sealed the sorrows that else would hound us from life to life, stuffing the brain with gathered griefs till it burst in the madness of uttermost despair. Still are they one, for the wrappings of our sleep shall roll away as thunderclouds before the wind; the frozen voices of the past shall melt in music like mountain snows beneath the sun; and the weeping and the laughter of the lost hours shall be heard once more most sweetly echoing up the cliffs of immeasurable time.

"Ay, the sleep shall roll away, and the voices shall be heard, when down the completed chain, whereof our each existence is a link, the lightning of the Spirit hath passed to work out the purpose of our being; quickening and fusing those separated days of life, and shaping them to a staff whereon we may safely lean as we wend to our appointed fate.

"Therefore, have no fear, Kallikrates, when thou—living, and but lately born—shalt look upon thine own departed self, who breathed and died so long ago. I do but turn one page in thy Book of Being, and show thee what is writ thereon.

"*Behold!*"

With a sudden motion she drew the shroud from the cold form, and let the lamplight play upon it. I looked, and then shrank back terrified; since, say what she might in explanation, the sight was an uncanny one—for her explanations were beyond the grasp of our finite minds, and when they were stripped from the mists of vague esoteric philosophy, and brought into conflict with the cold and horrifying fact, did not do much to break its force. For there, stretched upon the stone bier before us, robed in white and perfectly preserved, was what appeared to be the body of Leo Vincey. I stared from Leo, standing *there* alive, to Leo lying *there* dead, and could see no difference; except, perhaps, that the body on the bier looked older. Feature for feature they were the same, even down to the crop of little golden curls, which was Leo's most uncommon beauty. It even seemed to me, as I looked, that the expression on the dead man's face resembled that which I had sometimes seen upon Leo's when he was plunged into profound sleep. I can only sum up the closeness of the resemblance by saying that I never saw twins so exactly similar as that dead and living pair.

I turned to see what effect was produced upon Leo by this sight of his dead self, and found it to be one of partial stupefaction. He stood for two or three minutes staring and said nothing, and when at last he spoke it was only to ejaculate, "Cover it up and take me away."

"Nay, wait, Kallikrates," said Ayesha, who, standing

with the lamp raised above her head, flooding with its light her own rich beauty and the cold wonder of the death-clothed form upon the bier, resembled an inspired sibyl rather than a woman, as she rolled out her majestic sentences with a grandeur and a freedom of utterance which I am, alas, quite unable to reproduce.

"Wait; I would show thee something, that no tittle of my crime may be hidden from thee. Do thou, O Holly, open the garment on the breast of the dead Kallikrates, for perchance my lord may fear to touch himself."

I obeyed with trembling hands. It seemed a desecration and an unhallowed thing to touch that sleeping image of the live man by my side. Presently his broad chest was bare, and there upon it, right over the heart, was a wound, evidently inflicted with a spear.

"Thou seest, Kallikrates," she said. "Know then that it was *I* who slew thee: in the Place of Life *I* gave thee death. I slew thee because of the Egyptian Amenartas, whom thou didst love, for by her wiles she held thy heart, and her I could not smite as but now I smote the woman, for she was too strong for me. In my haste and bitter anger I slew thee, and now for all these days have I lamented thee, and waited for thy coming. And thou hast come, and none can stand between thee and me, and of a truth now for death I will give thee life—not life eternal, for that none can give, but life and youth that shall endure for thousands upon thousands of years, and with it pomp, and power, and wealth, and all things that are good and beautiful, such as have been to no man before thee, nor shall be to any man who comes after. And now one thing more, and thou shalt rest and make ready for the day of thy new birth. Thou seest this body, which was thine own. For all these centuries it hath been my cold comfort and my companion, but now I need it no more, for I have thy living presence, and it can but serve to stir up memories of that which I would fain forget. Let it therefore go back to the dust from which I held it.

"Behold! I have prepared against this happy hour!" and going to the other shelf, or stone ledge, which, she said, had served her for a bed, she took from it a large vitrified double-handed vase, the mouth of which was tied up with a bladder. This she loosed, and then, having bent down and gently kissed the white forehead of the dead man, she undid the vase, and sprinkled its contents carefully over the form, taking, I observed, the greatest precautions against any drop of them touching us or herself, and then poured out what remained of the liquid upon the chest and head. Instantly a dense vapor arose, and the cave was filled with choking fumes that prevented us from seeing anything while the deadly acid (for I presume it was some tremendous preparation of that sort) did its work. From the spot where the body lay came a fierce fizzing and cracking sound, which ceased, however, before the fumes had cleare i away. At last they were all gone, except a little cloud that still hung over the corpse. In a couple of minutes more this too had vanished, and, wonderful as it may seem, it is a fact that on the stone bench that had supported the mortal remains of the ancient Kallikrates for so many centuries there was now nothing to be seen but a few handfuls of smoking white powder. The acid had utterly destroyed the body, and even in places eaten into the stone.

Ayesha stooped down, and, taking a handful of this powder in her grasp, threw it into the air, saying at the same time, in a voice of calm solemnity, "Dust to dust! The past to the past! The dead to the dead! Kallikrates is dead, and is born again!"

The ashes floated noiselessly to the rocky floor, and we stood in awed silence and watched them fall, too overcome for words.

"Now leave me," she said, "and sleep if ye may. I must watch and think, for tomorrow night we go hence, and the time is long since I trod the path that we must follow."

Accordingly we bowed and left her.

As we passed to our own apartment I peeped into Job's sleeping place, to see how he fared, for he had gone away just before our interview with the murdered Ustane, quite prostrated by the terrors of the Amahagger festivity. He was sleeping soundly, good honest fellow that he was, and I rejoiced to think that his nerves, which, like those of most uneducated people, were far from strong, had been spared the closing scenes of this dreadful day. Then we entered our own chamber, and here at last poor Leo, who, ever since he had looked upon that frozen image of his living self, had been in a state not far removed from stupefaction, burst out into a torrent of grief. Now that he was no longer in the presence of the dread *She*, his sense of the awfulness of all that had happened, and more especially of the wicked murder of Ustane, who was bound to him by ties so close, broke upon him like a storm, and lashed him into an agony of remorse and terror which was painful to witness. He cursed himself—he cursed the hour when we had first seen the writing on the sherd, which was being so mysteriously verified, and bitterly he cursed his own weakness. Ayesha he dared not curse—who dared speak evil of such a woman, whose consciousness for aught we knew was watching us at the very moment?

"What am I to do, old fellow?" he groaned, resting his head against my shoulder in the extremity of his grief. "I let her be killed—not that I could help that, but within five minutes I was kissing her murderess over her body. I am a degraded brute, but I cannot resist that"—and here his voice sank—"that awful sorceress. I know I shall do it again tomorrow; I know that I am in her power for always; if I never saw her again I should never think of anybody else during all my life; I must follow her as a needle follows a magnet; I would not go away now if I could; I could not leave her, my legs would not carry me, but my mind is still clear enough, and in my mind I hate her—at least, I think so. It is all so horrible; and that—that body! What can I make of it? It was *me!* I am sold into bondage, old fellow, and she will take my soul as the price of herself!"

Then, for the first time, I told him that I was in a but very little better position; and I am bound to say that, notwithstanding his own infatuation, he had the decency to sympathize with me. Perhaps he did not think it worth while being jealous, realizing that he had no cause so far as the lady was concerned. I went on to suggest that we should try to run away, but we soon rejected the project as futile, and, to be perfectly honest, I do not believe that either of us would really have left Ayesha even if some superior power had suddenly offered to convey us from these gloomy caves and set us down in Cambridge. We could no more have left her than a moth can leave the light that destroys it. We were like confirmed opium eaters: in our moments of reason we well knew the deadly nature of our pursuit, but we certainly were not prepared to abandon its terrible delights.

No man who once had seen *She* unveiled, and heard the music of her voice, and drunk in the bitter wisdom of her words, would willingly give up the sight for a whole sea of placid joys. How much more, then, was this likely to be so when, as in Leo's case, to put myself out of the question, this extraordinary creature declared her utter and absolute devotion, and gave what appeared to be proofs of its having lasted for some two thousand years?

No doubt she was a wicked person, and no doubt she had murdered Ustane when she stood in her path, but then she was very faithful, and by a law of nature man is apt to think but lightly of a woman's crimes, especially if that woman be beautiful, and the crime be committed for the love of him.

And then for the rest, when had such a chance ever come to a man before as that which now lay in Leo's hand? True, in uniting himself to this dread woman, he would place his life under the influence of a mysterious creature of evil tendencies,[1] but then that would be likely

---

[1] After some months of consideration of this statement I am bound to confess that I am not quite satisfied of its truth. It is perfectly true that Ayesha committed a murder, but I shrewdly suspect that, were we endowed with the same absolute power, and if we had the same tremendous interest at stake, we should be very apt to do likewise under parallel circumstances. Also, it must be remembered that she looked on it as an execution for disobedience under a system which made the slightest disobedience punishable by death. Putting aside this question of the murder, her evildoing resolves itself into the expression of views and the acknowledgment of motives which are contrary to our preaching if not to our practice. Now at first sight this might be fairly taken as a proof of an evil nature, but when we come to consider the great antiquity of the individual it becomes doubtful if it was anything more than the natural cynicism which arises from age and bitter experience, and the possession of extraordinary powers of observation. It is a well-known fact that very often, putting the period of boyhood out of the question, the older we grow the more cynical and hardened we get, indeed, many of us are only saved by timely death from utter moral petrifaction if not moral corruption. No one will deny that a young man is on the average better than an old one, for he is without that experience of the order of things that in certain thoughtful dispositions can hardly fail to produce cynicism, and that disregard of acknowledged methods and established custom which we call evil. Now the oldest man upon the earth was but a babe compared to Ayesha, and the wisest man upon the earth was not one-third as wise. And the fruit of her wisdom was this, that there was but one thing worth living for, and that was Love in its highest sense, and to gain that good thing she was not prepared to stop at trifles. This is really the sum of her

enough to happen to him in any ordinary marriage. On the other hand, however, no ordinary marriage could bring him such awful beauty—for awful is the only word that can describe it—such divine devotion, such wisdom, and command over the secrets of nature, and the place and power that they must win, or lastly the royal crown of unending youth, if indeed she could give that. No, on the whole, it is not wonderful that though Leo was plunged in bitter shame and grief, such as any gentleman would have felt under the circumstances, he was not ready to entertain the idea of running away from his extraordinary fortune.

My own opinion is that he would have been mad if he had done so. But then I confess that my statement on the matter must be accepted with qualifications. I am in love with Ayesha myself to this day, and I would rather have been the object of her affection for one short week than that of any other woman in the world for a whole lifetime. And let me add that if anybody who doubts this statement, and thinks me foolish for making it, could have seen Ayesha draw her veil and flash out in beauty on his gaze, his view would exactly coincide with my own. Of course, I am speaking of any *man*. We never had the advantage of a lady's opinion of Ayesha, but I think it quite possible that she would have regarded the Queen with dislike, would have expressed her disapproval in some more or less pointed manner, and ultimately have got herself blasted.

For two hours or more Leo and I sat with shaken nerves and frightened eyes, and talked over the miraculous events through which we were passing. It seemed like a dream

---

evil doings, and it must be remembered on the other hand that whatever may be thought of them she had some virtues developed to a degree very uncommon in either sex—constancy, for instance.—L. H. H.

or a fairy tale, instead of the solemn, sober fact. Who would have believed that the writing on the potsherd was not only true, but that we should live to verify its truth, and that we two seekers should find her who was sought, patiently awaiting our coming in the tombs of Kôr? Who would have thought that in the person of Leo this mysterious woman should, as she believed, discover the being whom she awaited from century to century, and whose former earthly habitation she had till this very night preserved? But so it was. In the face of all we had seen it was difficult for us as ordinary reasoning men any longer to doubt its truth, and therefore at last, with humble hearts and a deep sense of the impotence of human knowledge, and the insolence of its assumption that denies that which it has no experience of to be possible, we laid ourselves down to sleep, leaving our fates in the hands of that watching Providence which had thus chosen to allow us to draw the veil of human ignorance, and reveal to us for good or evil some glimpse of the possibilities of life.

22 ♦

Job Has a Presentiment

It was nine o'clock on the following morning when Job, who still looked scared and frightened, came in to call me, and at the same time breathe his gratitude at finding us alive in our beds, which it appeared was more than he had expected. When I told him of the awful end of poor Ustane he was even more grateful at our survival, and much shocked, though Ustane had been no favorite of his, or he of hers, for the matter of that. She had called him "pig" in bastard Arabic, and he had called her "hussy" in good English, but these amenities were forgotten in the face of the catastrophe that had overwhelmed her at the hands of her queen.

"I don't want to say anything as mayn't be agreeable, sir," said Job, when he had finished exclaiming at my tale, "but it's my opinion that that there *She* is the Old Gentleman himself, or perhaps his wife, if he has one, which I suppose he has, for he couldn't be so wicked all by himself. The Witch of Endor was a fool to her, sir: bless you, she would make no more of raising every gentleman in the Bible out of these here beastly tombs than I should of growing cress on an old flannel. It's a country of devils, this is, sir, and she's the master one of the lot; and if ever we get out of it it will be more than I expect to do. I don't see no way out of it. That witch isn't likely to let a fine young man like Mr. Leo go."

"Come," I said, "at any rate she saved his life."

"Yes, and she'll take his soul to pay for it. She'll make him a witch, like herself. I say it's wicked to have anything to do with those sort of people. Last night, sir, I lay awake and read in my little Bible that my poor old mother gave me about what is going to happen to sorceresses and them sort till my hair stood on end. Lord, how the old lady would stare if she saw where her Job had got to!"

"Yes, it's a queer country, and a queer people too, Job," I answered with a sigh, for, though I am not superstitious like Job, I admit to a natural shrinking (which will not bear investigation) from the things that are above Nature.

"You are right, sir," he answered, "and if you won't think me very foolish, I should like to say something to you now that Mr. Leo is out of the way"—Leo had got up early and gone for a stroll—"and that is that I know it is the last country as ever I shall see in this world. I had a dream last night, and I dreamed that I saw my old father with a kind of nightshirt on him, something like these folks wear when they want to be in particular full-dress, and a bit of that feathery grass in his hand, which he may have gathered on the way, for I saw lots of it yesterday about three hundred yards from the mouth of this beastly cave.

" 'Job,' he said to me, solemn like, and yet with a kind of satisfaction shining through him, more like a Methody parson when he has sold a neighbor a marked horse for a sound one and cleared twenty pounds by the job than anything I can think on—'Job, time's up, Job; but I never did expect to have to come and hunt you out in this 'ere place, Job. Such ado as I have had to nose you up; it wasn't friendly to give your poor old father such a run, let alone that a wonderful lot of bad characters hail from this place Kôr.' "

"Regular cautions," I suggested.

"Yes, sir—of course, sir, that's just what he said they was—'cautious, downright scorchers,' sir—and I'm sure I don't doubt it, seeing what I know of them and their hot-potting ways," went on Job sadly. "Anyway, he was sure that time was up, and went away saying that we should see more than we cared for of each other soon, and I suppose he was a-thinking of the fact that Father and I never could hit it off together for longer nor three days, and I dare say that things will be similar when we meet again."

"Surely," I said, "you don't think that you are going to die because you dreamed you saw your old father; if one dies because one dreams of one's father, what happens to a man who dreams of his mother-in-law?"

"Ah, sir, you're laughing at me," said Job; "but, you see, you didn't know my old father. If it had been anybody else—my Aunt Mary, for instance, who never made much of a job—I should not have thought so much of it; but my father was that idle, which he shouldn't have been with seventeen children, that he would never have put himself out to come here just to see the place. No, sir; I know that he meant business. Well, sir, I can't help it; I suppose every man must go some time or other, though it is a hard thing to die in a place like this, where Christian burial isn't to be had for its weight in gold. I've tried to be a good man, sir, and do my duty honest, and if it wasn't for the supercilus kind of way in which Father carried on last night—a sort of sniffing at me as it were, as though he hadn't no opinion of my references and testimonials—I should feel easy enough in my mind. Anyway, sir, I've been a good servant to you and Mr. Leo, bless him! Why, it seems but the other day that I used to lead him about the streets with a penny whip;

and if ever you get out of this place—which, as Father didn't allude to you, perhaps you may—I hope you will think kindly of my whitened bones, and never have anything more to do with Greek writing on flower pots, sir, if I may make so bold as to say so."

"Come, come, Job," I said seriously, "this is all nonsense, you know. You mustn't be silly enough to go getting such ideas into your head. We've lived through some queer things, and I hope that we may go on doing so."

"No, sir," answered Job, in a tone of conviction that jarred on me unpleasantly, "it isn't nonsense. I'm a doomed man, and I feel it, and a wonderful uncomfortable feeling it is, sir, for one can't help wondering how it's going to come about. If you are eating your dinner you think of poison and it goes against your stomach, and if you are walking along these dark rabbit burrows you think of knives, and Lord, don't you just shiver about the back! I ain't particular, sir, provided it's sharp, like that poor girl, who, now that she's gone, I am sorry to have spoke hard on, though I don't approve of her morals in getting married, which I considered too quick to be decent. Still, sir," and poor Job turned a shade paler as he said it, "I do hope it won't be that hot-pot game."

"Nonsense," I broke in angrily, "nonsense!"

"Very well, sir," said Job, "it isn't my place to differ from you, sir, but if you happen to be going anywhere, sir, I should be obliged if you could manage to take me with you, seeing that I shall be glad to have a friendly face to look at when the time comes, just to help one through, as it were. And now, sir, I'll be getting the breakfast," and he went, leaving me in a very uncomfortable state of mind. I was deeply attached to old Job, who was one of the best and most honest men I have ever had to

do with in any class of life, and really more of a friend than
a servant, and the mere idea of anything happening to him
brought a lump into my throat. Beneath all his ludicrous
talk I could see that he himself was quite convinced that
something was going to happen, and though in most cases
these convictions turn out to be utter moonshine—and
this particular one especially was to be amply accounted
for by the gloomy and unaccustomed surroundings in which
its victim was placed—still it did more or less carry a chill
to my heart, as any dread that is obviously a genuine object
of belief is apt to do, however absurd the belief may be.
Presently the breakfast arrived, and with it Leo, who had
been taking a walk outside the cave—to clear his mind, he
said—and very glad I was to see both, for they gave me a
respite from my gloomy thoughts. After breakfast we went
for another walk, and watched some of the Amahagger
sowing a plot of ground with the grain from which they
make their beer. This they did in Scriptural fashion—a
man with a bag made of goat's hide fastened round his
waist walking up and down the plot and scattering the
seed as he went. It was a positive relief to see one of these
dreadful people do anything so homely and pleasant as
sow a field, perhaps because it seemed to link them, as it
were, with the rest of humanity.

As we were returning Billali met us, and informed us
that it was *She*'s pleasure that we should wait upon her,
and accordingly we entered her presence, not without trepi-
dation, for Ayesha was certainly an exception to the rule.
Familiarity with her might and did breed passion and
wonder and horror, but it certainly did *not* breed contempt.

We were as usual shown in by the mutes, and after these
had retired Ayesha unveiled, and once more bade Leo
embrace her, which, notwithstanding his heart-searchings

of the previous night, he did with more alacrity and fervor than in strictness courtesy required.

She laid her white hand on his head, and looked him fondly in the eyes. "Dost thou wonder, my Kallikrates," she said, "when thou shalt call me all thine own, and when we shall of a truth be for one another and to one another? I will tell thee. First, must thou be even as I am, not immortal indeed, for that I am not, but so cased and hardened against the attacks of Time that his arrows shall glance from the armor of thy vigorous life as the sunbeams glance from water. As yet I may not mate with thee, for thou and I are different, and the very brightness of my being would burn thee up, and perchance destroy thee. Thou couldst not even endure to look upon me for too long a time lest thine eyes should ache, and thy senses swim, and therefore"—with a little coquettish nod—"shall I presently veil myself again." (This by the way she did not do.) "No: listen, thou shalt not be tried beyond endurance, for this very evening, an hour before the sun goes down, shall we start hence, and by tomorrow's dark, if all goes well, and the road is not lost to me, which I pray it may not be, shall we stand in the place of Life, and thou shalt bathe in the fire, and come forth glorified, as no man ever was before thee, and then, Kallikrates, shalt thou call me wife, and I will call thee husband."

Leo muttered something in answer to this astonishing statement, I do not know what, and she laughed a little at his confusion, and went on.

"And thou, too, O Holly; on thee also will I confer this boon, and then of a truth shalt thou be an evergreen tree, and this will I do—well, because thou hast pleased me, Holly, for thou art not altogether a fool, like most of the sons of men, and because, though thou hast a school of philosophy as full of nonsense as those of the old days, yet hast thou not forgotten how to turn a pretty phrase about a lady's eyes."

"Hullo, old fellow!" whispered Leo, with a return of his old cheerfulness. "Have you been paying compliments? I should never have thought it of you!"

"I thank thee, O Ayesha," I replied, with as much dignity as I could command, "but if there be such a place as thou dost describe, and if in this strange place there may be found a fiery virtue that can hold off Death when he comes to pluck us by the hand, yet would I none of it. For me, O Ayesha, the world has not proved so soft a nest that I would lie in it forever. A stony-hearted mother is our earth, and stones are the bread she gives her children for their daily food. Stones to eat and bitter water for their thirst, and stripes for tender nurture. Who would endure this for many lives? Who would so load up his back with memories of lost hours and loves, and of his neighbor's sorrows that he cannot lessen, and wisdom that brings not consolation? Hard is it to die, because our delicate flesh doth shrink back from the worm it will not feel, and from that unknown which the winding sheet doth curtain from our view. But harder still, to my fancy, would it be to live on, green in the leaf and fair, but dead and rotten at the core, and feel that other secret worm of recollection gnawing ever at the heart."

"Bethink thee, Holly," she said; "yet doth long life and strength and beauty beyond measure mean power and all things that are dear to man."

"And what, O Queen," I answered, "are those things that are dear to man? Are they not bubbles? Is not ambition but an endless ladder by which no height is ever climbed till the last unreachable rung is mounted? For height leads on to height, and there is no resting place upon them, and rung doth grow upon rung, and there is no limit to the number. Doth not wealth satiate and become nauseating, and no longer serve to satisfy or pleasure, or to buy an hour's ease of mind? And is there any end to wisdom that we may hope to reach it? Rather, the more we learn shall we not thereby be able only to better compass out our ignorance? Did we live ten thousand years could we hope to solve the secrets of the suns, and of the space beyond the suns, and of the Hand that hung them in the heavens? Would not our wisdom be but as a gnawing hunger calling our consciousness day by day to a knowledge of the empty craving of our souls? Would it not be but as a light in one of these great caverns, that though bright it burn, and brighter yet, doth but the more serve to show the depths of the gloom around it? And what good thing is there beyond that we may gain by length of days?"

"Nay, my Holly, there is love—love which makes all things beautiful, and doth breathe divinity into the very dust we tread. With love shall life roll gloriously on from year to year, like the voice of some great music that hath power to hold the hearer's heart poised on eagle's wings above the sordid shame and folly of the earth."

"It may be so," I answered; "but if the loved one prove a broken reed to pierce us, or if the love be loved in vain—what then? Shall a man grave his sorrows upon a stone when he hath but need to write them on the water? Nay, O *She*, I will live my day and grow old with my generation, and die my appointed death, and be forgotten. For I do hope for an immortality to which the little span that perchance thou canst confer will be but as a finger's length laid against the measure of the great world; and, mark this: the immortality to which I look, and which my faith doth promise to me, shall be free from the bonds that here must tie my spirit down. For, while the flesh endures, sorrow and evil and the scorpion whips of sin must endure also; but when the flesh hath fallen from us, then shall the spirit shine forth clad in the brightness of eternal good, and for its common air shall breathe so rare an ether of most noble thoughts, that the highest aspiration of our manhood, or the purest incense of a maiden's prayer, would prove too earthly gross to float therein."

"Thou lookest high," answered Ayesha, with a little laugh, "and speakest clearly as a trumpet and with no uncertain sound. And yet methinks that but now didst thou talk of 'that Unknown' from which the winding sheet doth curtain us. But perchance, thou seest with the eye of Faith, gazing on this brightness that is to be, through the painted glass of thy imagination. Strange are the pictures of the future that mankind can thus draw with this brush of faith and this many-colored pigment of imagination! Strange, too, that no one of them doth agree with another! I could tell thee—but there, what is the use? Why rob a fool of his bauble? Let it pass, and I pray, O Holly, that when thou dost feel old age creeping slowly towards thyself, and the confusion of senility making havoc in thy brain, thou mayest not bitterly regret that thou didst cast away the imperial boon I would have given to thee. But so it hath ever been; man can never be content with that which his hand can pluck. If a lamp be in his reach to light him through the darkness, he must needs cast it down because it is no star. Happiness danceth ever a pace before him, like the marsh fires in the swamps, and he must catch the fire, and he must hold the star! Beauty is naught to him, because there are lips more honey-sweet; and wealth is naught, because others can weigh him down with heavier shekels; and fame is naught, because there have been greater men than he. Thyself thou saidst it, and I turn thy words against thee. Well, thou dreamest that thou shalt pluck the star. I believe it not, and I think thee a fool, my Holly, to throw away the lamp."

I made no answer, for I could not—especially before Leo—tell her that since I had seen her face I knew that it would always be before my eyes, and that I had no wish to prolong an existence which must always be haunted and tortured by her memory, and by the last bitterness of unsatisfied love. But so it was, and so, alas, is it to this hour!

"And now," went on *She*, changing her tone and the subject together, "tell me, my Kallikrates, for as yet I know it not, how came ye to seek me here? Yesternight thou didst say that Kallikrates—him whom thou sawest— was thine ancestor. How was it? Tell me—thou dost not speak overmuch!"

Thus adjured, Leo told her the wonderful story of the casket and of the potsherd that, written on by his ancestress, the Egyptian Amenartas, had been the means of guiding us to her. Ayesha listened intently, and, when he had finished, spoke to me.

"Did I not tell thee one day, when we did talk of good and evil, O Holly—it was when my beloved lay so ill— that out of good came evil, and out of evil good—that they who sowed knew not what the crop should be, nor he who struck where the blow should fall? See, now: this Egyptian Amenartas, this royal child of the Nile who hated me, and whom even now I hate, for in a way she did prevail against me—see, now, she herself hath been the very means to bring her lover to mine arms! For her sake I slew him, and now, behold, through her he hath come back to me!

She would have done me evil, and sowed her seeds that I might reap tares, and behold she hath given me more than all the world can give, and there is a strange square for thee to fit into thy circle of good and evil, O Holly!

"And so," she went on after a pause, "and so she bade her son destroy me if he might, because I slew his father. And thou, my Kallikrates, art the father, and in a sense thou art likewise the son; and wouldst thou avenge thy wrong, and the wrong of that far-off mother of thine upon me, O Kallikrates? See,"—and she slid to her knees, and drew the white corsage still farther down her ivory bosom— "see, here beats my heart, and there by thy side is a knife, heavy, and long, and sharp, the very knife to slay an erring woman with. Take it now, and be avenged. Strike, and strike home! So shalt thou be satisfied, Kallikrates, and go through life a happy man, because thou hast paid back the wrong, and obeyed the mandate of the past."

He looked at her, and then stretched out his hand and lifted her to her feet.

"Rise, Ayesha," he said sadly; "well thou knowest that I cannot strike thee, no, not even for the sake of her whom thou slewest but last night. I am in thy power, and a very slave to thee. How can I kill thee? Sooner should I slay myself."

"Almost dost thou begin to love me, Kallikrates," she answered, smiling. "And now tell me of thy country—'tis a great people, is it not? With an empire like that of Rome! Surely thou wouldst return thither, and it is well, for I mean not that thou shouldst dwell in these caves of Kôr. Nay, when once thou art even as I am, we will go hence— fear not but that I shall find a path—and then shall we cross to this England of thine, and live as it becometh us to live. Two thousand years have I waited for the day when I should see the last of these hateful caves and this gloomy-visaged folk, and now it is at hand, and my heart bounds up to meet it like a child's towards its holiday. For thou shalt rule this England—"

"But we have a queen already," broke in Leo hastily.

"It is naught, it is naught," said Ayesha; "she can be overthrown."

At this we both broke out into an exclamation of dismay, and explained that we should as soon think of overthrowing ourselves.

"But here is a strange thing," said Ayesha in astonishment; "a queen whom her people love! Surely the world must have changed since I have dwelt in Kôr."

Again we explained that it was the character of monarchs that had changed, and that the one under whom we lived was venerated and beloved by all right-thinking people in her vast realms. Also, we told her that real power in our country rested in the hands of the people, and that we were in fact ruled by the votes of the lower and least educated classes of the community.

"Ah," she said, "a democracy—then surely there is a tyrant, for I have long since seen that democracies, having no clear will of their own, in the end set up a tyrant, and worship him."

"Yes," I said, "we have our tyrants."

"Well," she answered resignedly, "we can at any rate destroy these tyrants, and Kallikrates shall rule the land."

I instantly informed Ayesha that in England "blasting" was not an amusement that could be indulged in with impunity, and that any such attempt would meet with the consideration of the law and probably end upon a scaffold.

"The law," she laughed with scorn, "the law! Canst thou not understand, O Holly, that I am above the law, and so shall my Kallikrates be also? All human law will be to us as the north wind to a mountain. Does the wind bend the mountain, or the mountain the wind?

"And now leave me, I pray thee, and thou too, my own Kallikrates, for I would get me ready against our journey, and so must ye both, and your servant also. But bring no great quantity of things with thee, for I trust that we shall be but three days gone. Then shall we return hither, and I will make a plan whereby we can bid farewell forever to these sepulchers of Kôr. Yes, surely thou mayst kiss my hand!"

So we went, I, for one, meditating deeply on the awful nature of the problem that now opened out before us. The terrible *She* had evidently made up her mind to go to England, and it made me absolutely shudder to think what would be the result of her arrival there. What her powers were I knew, and I could not doubt but that she would exercise them to the full. It might be possible to control her for a while, but her proud, ambitious spirit would be certain to break loose and avenge itself for the long centuries of its solitude. She would, if necessary, and if the power of her beauty did not unaided prove equal to the occasion, blast her way to any end she set before her, and as she could not die, and for aught I knew could not even be killed,[2] what was there to stop her? In the end she would, I had little doubt, assume absolute rule over the British dominions, and probably over the whole earth, and, though I was sure that she would speedily make ours the

[2] I regret to say that I was never able to ascertain if *She* was invulnerable against the accidents of life. Presumably this was so, else some misadventure would have been sure to put an end to her in the course of so many centuries. True, she offered to let Leo slay her, but very probably this was only an experiment to try his temper and mental attitude towards her. Ayesha never gave way to impulse without some valid object.—L. H. H.

most glorious and prosperous empire that the world has ever seen, it would be at the cost of a terrible sacrifice of life.

The whole thing sounded like a dream or some extraordinary invention of a speculative brain, and yet it was a fact—a wonderful fact—of which the whole world would soon be called on to take notice. What was the meaning of it all? After much thinking I could only conclude that this wonderful creature, whose passion had kept her for so many centuries chained, as it were, and comparatively harmless, was now about to be used by Providence as a means to change the order of the world, and possibly, by the building up of a power that could no more be rebelled against or questioned than the decrees of Fate, to change it materially for the better.

23 ♦

The Temple of Truth

OUR PREPARATIONS did not take us very long. We put a change of clothing apiece and some spare boots into my Gladstone bag, also we took our revolvers and an express rifle each, together with a good supply of ammunition, a precaution to which, under Providence, we subsequently owed our lives over and over again. The rest of our gear, together with our heavy rifles, we left behind us.

A few minutes before the appointed time we once more attended in Ayesha's boudoir, and found her also ready, her dark cloak thrown over her winding sheet like wrappings.

"Are ye prepared for the great venture?" she said.

"We are," I answered, "though for my part, Ayesha, I have no faith in it."

"Ah, my Holly," she said, "thou art of a truth like those old Jews—of whom the memory vexes me so sorely—unbelieving, and hard to accept that which they have not known. But thou shalt see; for unless my mirror yonder lies"—and she pointed to the font of crystal water—"the path is yet open as it was of old time. And now let us start upon the new life which shall end—who knoweth where?"

"Ah," I echoed, "who knoweth where?" and we passed down into the great central cave, and out into the light of day. At the mouth of the cave we found a single litter with six bearers, all of them mutes, waiting, and with them I was relieved to see our old friend Billali, for whom I had conceived a sort of affection. It appeared that, for reasons not necessary to explain at length, Ayesha had thought it best that, with the exception of herself, we should proceed on foot, and this we were nothing loath to do, after our long confinement in these caves, which, however suitable they might be for sarcophagi—a singularly inappropriate word, by the way, for these particular tombs, which certainly did not consume the bodies given to their keeping—were depressing habitations for breathing mortals like ourselves. Either by accident or by the orders of *She*, the space in front of the cave where we had beheld that awful dance was perfectly clear of spectators. Not a soul was to be seen, and consequently I do not believe that our departure was known to anybody, except perhaps the mutes who waited on *She*, and they were, of course, in the habit of keeping what they saw to themselves.

In a few minutes' time we were stepping out sharply across the great cultivated plain or lake bed, framed like a vast emerald in its setting of frowning cliff, and had another opportunity of wondering at the extraordinary nature of the site chosen by these old people of Kôr for their capital, and at the marvelous amount of labor, ingenuity, and engineering skill that must have been brought into requisition by the founders of the city to drain so huge a sheet of water, and to keep it clear of subsequent accumulations. It is, indeed, so far as my experience goes, an unequaled instance of what man can do in the face of nature, for in my opinion such achievements as the Suez Canal or even the Mont Cenis Tunnel do not approach this ancient undertaking in magnitude and grandeur of conception.

When we had been walking for about half an hour, enjoying ourselves exceedingly in the delightful cool which about this time of the day always appeared to descend upon

the great plain of Kôr, and which in some degree atoned for
the want of any land or sea breeze—for all wind was kept off
by the rocky mountain wall—we began to get a clear view of
what Billali had informed us were the ruins of the great
city. And even from that distance we could see how wonderful those ruins were, a fact which with every step we
took became more evident. The city was not very large if
compared to Babylon or Thebes, or other cities of remote
antiquity; perhaps its outer wall contained some twelve
square miles of ground, or a little more. Nor had the walls,
so far as we could judge when we reached them, been
very high, probably not more than forty feet, which was
about their present height where they had not through
the sinking of the ground, or some such cause, fallen into
ruin. The reason of this, no doubt, was that the people
of Kôr, being protected from any outside attack by far
more tremendous ramparts than any that the hand of man
could rear, only required them for show and to guard
against civil discord. But on the other hand they were as
broad as they were high, built entirely of dressed stone,
hewn, no doubt, from the vast caves, and surrounded by a
great moat about sixty feet in width, some reaches of
which were still filled with water. About ten minutes before
the sun finally sank we reached this moat, and passed
down and through it, clambering across what evidently were
the piled-up fragments of a great bridge in order to do so,
and then with some little difficulty up the slope of the wall
to its summit. I wish that it lay within the power of my
pen to give some idea of the grandeur of the sight that then
met our view. There, all bathed in the red glow of the
sinking sun, were miles upon miles of ruins—columns,
temples, shrines, and the palaces of kings, varied with
patches of green bush. Of course, the roofs of these build-

ings had long since fallen into decay and vanished, but owing to the extreme massiveness of the style of building, and to the hardness and durability of the rock employed, most of the party walls and great columns still remained standing.[1]

Straight before us stretched away what had evidently been the main thoroughfare of the city, for it was very wide, wider than the Thames Embankment, and regular. Being, as we afterwards discovered, paved, or rather built, throughout of blocks of dressed stone, such as were employed in the walls, it was but little overgrown even now with grass and shrubs that could get no depth of soil to live in. What had been the parks and gardens, on the contrary, were now dense jungle. Indeed, it was easy even from a distance to trace the course of the various roads by the burnt-up appearance of the scanty grass that grew upon them. On either side of this great thoroughfare were vast blocks of ruins, each block, generally speaking, being separated from its neighbor by a space of what had once, I suppose, been garden ground, but was now dense and tangled bush. They were all built of the same colored stone, and most of them had pillars, which was as much as we could make out in the fading light as we passed swiftly up the main road, which I believe I am right in saying no living foot had pressed for thousands of years.[2]

[1] In connection with the extraordinary state of preservation of these ruins after so vast a lapse of time—at least six thousand years—it must be remembered that Kôr was not burned or destroyed by an enemy or an earthquake, but deserted, owing to the action of a terrible plague. Consequently the houses were left unharmed; also, the climate of the plain is remarkably fine and dry, and there is very little rain or wind; as a result of which these relics have only to contend against the unaided action of time, which works but slowly upon such massive blocks of masonry.—L. H. H.

[2] Billali told me that the Amahagger believe that the site of the city is haunted, and could not be persuaded to enter it upon any consideration. Indeed, I could see that he himself did not at all like doing so, and was only

Presently we came to an enormous pile, which we rightly took to be a temple covering at least four acres of ground, and apparently arranged in a series of courts, each one enclosing another of smaller size, on the principle of a Chinese nest of boxes, which were separated one from the other by rows of huge columns. And, while I think of it, I may as well state a remarkable thing about the shape of these columns, which resembled none that I have ever seen or heard of, being fashioned with a kind of waist in the center, and swelling out above and below. At first we thought that this shape was meant to roughly symbolize or suggest the female form, as was a common habit amongst the ancient religious architects of many creeds. On the following day, however, as we went up the slopes of the mountain, we discovered a large quantity of the most stately-looking palms, of which the trunks grew exactly in this shape, and I have now no doubt but that the first designer of these columns drew his inspiration from the graceful bends of those very palms, or rather of their ancestors, which then, some eight or ten thousand years ago, as now, beautified the slopes of the mountain that had once formed the shores of the volcanic lake.

At the façade of this huge temple, which, I should imagine, is almost as large as that of El-Karnac, at Thebes, some of the largest columns, which I measured, being between eighteen to twenty feet in diameter at the base, by about seventy feet in height, our little procession was halted, and Ayesha descended from her litter.

---

consoled by the reflection that he was under the direct protection of *She*. It struck Leo and myself as very curious that a people which has no objection to living amongst the dead, with whom their familiarity has perhaps bred contempt, and even using their bodies for purposes of fuel, should be terrified at approaching the habitations that these very departed had occupied when alive. After all, however, it is only a savage inconsistency.—L. H. H.

"There used to be a spot here, Kallikrates," she said to Leo, who had run up to help her down, "where one might sleep. Two thousand years ago did thou and I and that Egyptian asp rest therein, but since then have I not set foot here, nor any man, and perchance it has fallen," and, followed by the rest of us, she passed up a vast flight of broken and ruined steps into the outer court, and looked round into the gloom. Presently she seemed to recollect, and, walking a few paces along the wall to the left, halted.

"It is here," she said, and at the same time beckoned to the two mutes, who were loaded with provisions and our little belongings, to advance. One of them came forward, and, producing a lamp, lit it from his brazier (for the Amahagger when on a journey nearly always carried with them a little lighted brazier, from which to provide fire). The tinder of this brazier was made of broken fragments of mummy carefully damped, and, if the admixture of moisture was properly managed, this unholy compound would smolder away for hours.[3] As soon as the lamp was lit we entered the place before which Ayesha had halted. It turned out to be a chamber hollowed in the thickness of the wall, and, from the fact of there still being a massive stone table in it, I should think that it had probably served as a living room, perhaps for one of the doorkeepers of the great temple.

Here we stopped, and after cleaning the place out and making it as comfortable as circumstances and the darkness would permit, we ate some cold meat, at least Leo, Job, and I did, for Ayesha, as I think I have said elsewhere, never touched anything except cakes of flour, fruit, and water.

---

[3] After all, we are not much in advance of the Amahagger in these matters. "Mummy," that is, pounded ancient Egyptian, is, I believe, a pigment much used by artists, and especially by those of them who direct their talents to the reproduction of the works of the old masters.—EDITOR.

While we were still eating, the moon, which was at her full, rose above the mountain wall, and began to flood the place with silver.

"Wot ye why I have brought you here tonight, my Holly?" said Ayesha, leaning her head upon her hand and watching the great orb as she rose, like some heavenly queen, above the solemn pillars of the temple. "I brought you—nay, it is strange, but knowest thou, Kallikrates, that thou liest at this moment upon the very spot where thy dead body lay when I bore thee back to those caves of Kôr so many years ago? It all returns to my mind now. I can see it, and horrible is it to my sight!" and she shuddered.

Here Leo jumped up and hastily changed his seat. However the reminiscence might affect Ayesha, it clearly had few charms for him.

"I brought you," went on Ayesha presently, "that ye might look upon the most wonderful sight that ever the eye of man beheld—the full moon shining over ruined Kôr. When ye have done your eating—I would that I could teach thee to eat naught but fruit, Kallikrates, but that will come after thou hast laved in the fire, once I, too, ate flesh like a brute beast—when ye have done we will go out, and I will show you this great temple and the God whom men once worshiped therein."

Of course we got up at once, and started. And here again my pen fails me. To give a string of measurements and details of the various courts of the temple would only be wearisome, supposing that I had them, and yet I know not how I am to describe what we saw, magnificent as it was even in its ruin, almost beyond the power of realization. Court upon dim court, row upon row of mighty pillars—some of them (especially at the gateways) sculptured from pedestal to capital—space upon space of empty

chambers that spoke more eloquently to the imagination
than any crowded streets. And over all, the dead silence
of the dead, the sense of utter loneliness, and the brooding
spirit of the Past! How beautiful it was, and yet how drear!
We did not dare to speak aloud. Ayesha herself was awed
in the presence of an antiquity compared to which even
her length of days was but a little thing; we only whispered,
and our whispers seemed to run from column to column,
till they were lost in the quiet air. Bright fell the moonlight
on pillar and court and shattered wall, hiding all their rents
and imperfections in its silver garment, and clothing their
hoar majesty with the peculiar glory of the night. It was
a wonderful sight to see the full moon looking down on the
ruined fane of Kôr. It was a wonderful thing to think for
how many thousands of years the dead orb above and
the dead city below had gazed thus upon each other, and
in the utter solitude of space poured forth each to each
the tale of their lost life and long-departed glory. The white
light fell, and minute by minute the quiet shadows crept
across the grass-grown courts like the spirits of old priests
haunting the habitations of their worship—the white light
fell, and the long shadows grew till the beauty and grandeur of the scene and the untamed majesty of its present
Death seemed to sink into our very souls, and speak more
loudly than the shouts of armies concerning the pomp
and splendor that the grave had swallowed, and even memory had forgotten.

"Come," said Ayesha, after we had gazed and gazed, I
know not for how long, "and I will show you the stony
flower of Loveliness and Wonder's very crown, if yet it
stands to mock time with its beauty and fill the heart of
man with longing for that which is behind the veil," and,
without waiting for an answer, she led us through two

more pillared courts into the inner shrine of the old fane.

And there, in the center of the inmost court, which might have been some fifty yards square, or a little more, we stood face to face with what is perhaps the grandest allegorical work of art that the genius of her children has ever given to the world. For in the exact center of the court, placed upon a thick square slab of rock, was a huge round ball of dark stone, some forty feet in diameter, and standing on the ball was a colossal winged figure of a beauty so entrancing and divine that when I first gazed upon it, illuminated and shadowed as it was by the soft light of the moon, my breath stood still, and for an instant my heart ceased its beating.

The statue was hewn from marble so pure and white that even now, after all those ages, it shone as the moonbeams danced upon it, and its height was, I should say, a trifle under twenty feet. It was the winged figure of a woman of such marvelous loveliness and delicacy of form that the size seemed rather to add to than to detract from its so human and yet more spiritual beauty. She was bending forward and poising herself upon her half-spread wings as though to preserve her balance as she leaned. Her arms were outstretched like those of some woman about to embrace one she dearly loved, while her whole attitude gave an impression of the tenderest beseeching. Her perfect and most gracious form was naked, save—and here came the extraordinary thing—the face, which was thinly veiled, so that we could only trace the marking of her features. A gauzy veil was thrown round and about the head, and of its two ends one fell down across her left breast, which was outlined beneath it, and one, now broken, streamed away upon the air behind her.

"Who is she?" I asked, as soon as I could take my eyes off the statue.

"Canst thou not guess, O Holly?" answered Ayesha. "Where then is thy imagination? It is Truth standing on the World, and calling to its children to unveil her face. See what is writ upon the pedestal. Without doubt it is taken from the book of the scriptures of these men of Kôr," and she led the way to the foot of the statue, where an inscripiton of the usual Chinese-looking hieroglyphics was so deeply graven as to be still quite legible, at least to Ayesha. According to her translation it ran thus:

> "Is there no man that will draw my veil and look upon my face, for it is very fair? Unto him who draws my veil shall I be, and peace will I give him, and sweet children of knowledge and good works."
>
> And a voice cried, "Through all those who seek after thee desire thee, behold! Virgin art thou, and Virgin shalt thou go till Time be done. No man is there born of woman who may draw thy veil and live, nor shall be. By Death only can thy veil be drawn, oh Truth!"
>
> And Truth stretched out her arms and wept, because those who sought her might not find her, nor look upon her face to face.

"Thou seest," said Ayesha, when she had finished translating, "Truth was the goddess of the people of old Kôr, and to her they built their shrines, and her they sought; knowing that they should never find, still sought they."

"And so," I added sadly, "do men seek to this very hour, but they find not; and, as this scripture saith, nor shall they; for in Death only is Truth found."

Then with one more look at this veiled and spiritualized

loveliness—which was so perfect and so pure that one might almost fancy that the light of a living spirit shone through the marble prison to lead man on to high and ethereal thoughts—this poet's dream of beauty frozen into stone, which I never shall forget while I live, though I find myself so helpless when I attempt to describe it, we turned and went back through the vast moonlit courts to the spot whence we had started. I never saw the statue again, which I the more regret, because on the great ball of stone representing the world whereon the figure stood, lines were drawn that probably, had there been light enough, we should have discovered to be a map of the universe as it was known to the people of Kôr. It is at any rate suggestive of some scientific knowledge that these long-dead worshipers of Truth had recognized the fact that the globe is round.

24 ♦

Walking the Plank

NEXT DAY the mutes woke us before the dawn; and by the time that we had got the sleep out of our eyes, and gone through a perfunctory wash at a spring which still welled up into the remains of a marble basin in the center of the north quadrangle of the vast outer court, we found *She* standing by the litter ready to start, while old Billali and the two bearer mutes were busy collecting the baggage. As usual, Ayesha was veiled like the marble Truth (by the way, I wonder if she originally got the idea of covering up her beauty from that statue?). I noticed, however, that she seemed very depressed, and had none of that proud and buoyant bearing which would have betrayed her among a thousand women of the same stature, even if they had been veiled like herself. She looked up as we came—for her head was bowed—and greeted us. Leo asked her how she had slept.

"Ill, my Kallikrates," she answered, "ill. This night have strange and hideous dreams come creeping through my brain, and I know not what they may portend. Almost do I feel as though some evil overshadowed me; and yet how can evil touch me? I wonder," she went on with a sudden outbreak of womanly tenderness, "I wonder if, should aught happen to me, so that I slept awhile and left thee waking, thou wouldst think gently of me? I wonder, my Kallikrates, if thou wouldst tarry till I came again, as for so many centuries I have tarried for thy coming?"

305

Then, without waiting for an answer, she went on: "Come, let us be setting forth, for we have far to go, and before another day is born in yonder blue should we stand in the place of Life."

In another five minutes we were once more on our way through the vast ruined city, which loomed at us on either side in the gray dawning in a way that was at once grand and oppressive. Just as the first ray of the rising sun shot like a golden arrow athwart this storied desolation we gained the farther gateway of the outer wall, and having given one more glance at the hoar and pillared majesty through which we had passed, and (with the exception of Job, for whom ruins had no charms) breathed a sigh of regret that we had not had more time to explore it, passed through the great moat, and on to the plain beyond.

As the sun rose so did Ayesha's spirits, till by breakfast-time they had regained their normal level, and she laughingly set down her previous depression to the associations of the spot where she had slept.

"These barbarians declare that Kôr is haunted," she said, "and of a truth I do believe their saying, for never did I know so ill a night save once. I remember it now. It was on that very spot when thou didst lie dead at my feet, Kallikrates. Never will I visit it again; it is a place of evil omen."

After a very brief halt for breakfast we pressed on with such good will that by two o'clock in the afternoon we were at the foot of the vast wall of rock that formed the lip of the volcano, and which at this point towered up precipitously above us for fifteen hundred or two thousand feet. Here we halted, certainly not to my astonishment, for I did not see how it was possible that we should go any farther.

"Now," said Ayesha, as she descended from her litter, "doth our labor but commence, for here do we part with these men, and henceforward must we bear ourselves." And then, addressing Billali: "Do thou and these slaves remain here, and abide our coming. By tomorrow at the midday shall we be with thee—if not, wait."

Billali bowed humbly, and said that her august bidding should be obeyed if they stopped there till they grew old.

"And this man, O Holly," said *She*, pointing to Job; "best is it that he should tarry also, for if his heart be not high and his courage great, perchance some evil might overtake him. Also, the secrets of the place whither we go are not fit for common eyes."

I translated this to Job, who instantly and earnestly entreated me, almost with tears in his eyes, not to leave him behind. He said he was sure that he could see nothing worse than he had already seen, and that he was terrified to death at the idea of being left alone with those "dumb folk," who, he thought, would probably take the opportunity to hot-pot him.

I translated what he said to Ayesha, who shrugged her shoulders, and answered, "Well, let him come, it is naught to me; on his own head be it, and he will serve to bear the lamp and this," and she pointed to a narrow plank, some sixteen feet in length, which had been bound above the long bearing pole of her hammock, as I had thought to make the curtains spread out better, but, as it now appeared, for some unknown purpose connected with our extraordinary undertaking.

Accordingly, the plank, which, though tough, was very light, was given to Job to carry, and also one of the lamps. I slung the other onto my back, together with a spare jar of oil, while Leo loaded himself with the provisions and

some water in a kid's skin. When this was done *She* bade
Billali and the six bearer mutes to retreat behind a grove
of flowering magnolias about a hundred yards away, and
remain there under pain of death till we had vanished.
They bowed humbly, and went, and, as he departed, old
Billali gave me a friendly shake of the hand, and whispered
that he had rather that it was I than he who was going on this wonderful expedition with *"She-who-must-be-
obeyed,"* and upon my word I felt inclined to agree with
him. In another minute they were gone, and then, having
briefly asked us if we were ready, Ayesha turned, and gazed
up the towering cliff.

"Goodness me, Leo," I said, "surely we are not going to
climb that precipice!"

Leo shrugged his shoulders, being in a condition of
half-fascinated, half-expectant mystification, and as he did
so, Ayesha with a sudden move began to climb the cliff,
and of course we had to follow her. It was perfectly marvelous to see the ease and grace with which she sprang from
rock to rock, and swung herself along the ledges. The
ascent was not, however, so difficult as it seemed, although
there were one or two nasty places where it did not do to
look behind you, the fact being that the rock still sloped
here, and was not absolutely precipitous as it was higher
up. In this way we, with no great labor, mounted to the
height of some fifty feet above our last standing place, the
only really troublesome thing to manage being Job's board,
and in doing so drew some fifty or sixty paces to the left
of our starting point, for we went up like a crab, sideways.
Presently we reached a ledge, narrow enough at first, but
which widened as we followed it, and moreover sloped
inwards like the petal of a flower, so that as we followed it
we gradually got into a kind of rut or fold of rock that grew

deeper and deeper, till at last it resembled a Devonshire lane in stone, and hid us perfectly from the gaze of anybody on the slope below, if there had been anybody to gaze. This lane (which appeared to be a natural formation) continued for some fifty or sixty paces, and then suddenly ended in a cave, also natural, running at right angles to it. I am sure that it was a natural cave, and not hollowed by the hand of man, because of its irregular and contorted shape and course, which gave it the appearance of having been blown bodily in the mountain by some frightful eruption of gas following the line of the least resistance. All the caves hollowed by the ancients of Kôr, on the contrary, were cut out with the most perfect regularity and symmetry. At the mouth of this cave Ayesha halted, and bade us light the two lamps, which I did, giving one to her and keeping the other myself. Then, taking the lead, she advanced down the cavern, picking her way with great care, as indeed it was necessary to do, for the floor was most irregular —strewn with boulders like the bed of a stream, and in some places pitted with deep holes, in which it would have been easy to break one's leg.

This cavern we pursued for twenty minutes or more, it being, so far as I could form a judgment—owing to its numerous twists and turns no easy task—about a quarter of a mile long.

At last, however, we halted at its farther end, and while I was still trying to pierce the gloom a great gust of air came tearing down it, and extinguished both the lamps.

Ayesha called to us, and we crept up to her, for she was a little in front, and were rewarded with a view that was positively appalling in its gloom and grandeur. Before us was a mighty chasm in the black rock, jagged and torn and splintered through it in a far past age by some awful convulsion of Nature, as though it had been cleft by stroke upon stroke of the lightning. This chasm, which was bounded by a precipice on the hither, and presumably, though we could not see it, on the farther side also, may have measured any width across, but from its darkness I do not think that it can have been very broad. It was impossible to make out much of its outline, or how far it ran, for the simple reason that the point where we were standing was so far from the upper surface of the cliff, at least fifteen hundred or two thousand feet, that only a very dim light struggled down to us from above. The mouth of the cavern that we had been following gave onto a most curious and tremendous spur of rock, which jutted out in midair into the gulf before us, for a distance of some fifty yards, coming to a sharp point at its termination, and resembling nothing that I can think of so much as the spur upon the leg of a cock in shape. This huge spur was attached only to the parent precipice at its base, which was, of course, enormous, just as the cock's spur is attached to its leg. Otherwise it was utterly unsupported.

"Here must we pass," said Ayesha. "Be careful lest giddiness overcome you, or the wind sweep you into the gulf beneath, for of a truth it hath no bottom." And, without giving us any further time to get scared, she started walking along the spur, leaving us to follow her as best we might. I was next to her, then came Job, painfully dragging his plank, while Leo brought up the rear. It was a wonderful sight to see this intrepid woman gliding fearlessly along that dreadful place. For my part, when I had gone but a very few yards, what between the pressure of the air and the awful sense of the consequences that a slip would entail, I found it necessary to go down on my hands and knees and crawl, and so did the other two.

But Ayesha never condescended to this. On she went, leaning her body against the gusts of wind, and never seeming to lose her head or her balance.

In a few minutes we had crossed some twenty paces of this awful bridge, which got narrower at every step, and then all of a sudden a great gust came tearing along the gorge. I saw Ayesha lean herself against it, but the strong draft got under her dark cloak, and tore it from her, and away it went down the wind flapping like a wounded bird. It was dreadful to see it go, till it was lost in the blackness. I clung to the saddle of rock, and looked round, while the great spur vibrated with a humming sound beneath us, like a living thing. The sight was a truly awesome one. There we were poised in the gloom between earth and heaven. Beneath us were hundreds upon hundreds of feet of emptiness that gradually grew darker, till at last it was absolutely black, and at what depth it ended is more than I can guess. Above were space upon space of giddy air, and far, far away a line of blue sky. And down this vast gulf upon which we were pinnacled the great draft dashed and roared, driving clouds and misty wreaths of vapor before it, till we were nearly blinded, and utterly confused.

The whole position was so tremendous and so absolutely unearthly that I believe it actually lulled our sense of terror, but to this hour I often see it in my dreams, and wake up covered with cold perspiration at its mere fantasy.

"On! On!" cried the white form before us, for now the cloak had gone *She* was robed in white, and looked more like a spirit riding down the gale than a woman. "On, or ye will fall and be dashed to pieces. Keep your eyes fixed upon the ground, and closely hug the rock."

We obeyed her, and crept painfully along the quivering path, against which the wind shrieked and wailed as it shook it, causing it to murmur like a vast tuning fork. On we went, I do not know for how long, only gazing round now and again, when it was absolutely necessary, until at last we saw that we were on the very tip of the spur, a slab of rock, little larger than an ordinary table, that throbbed and jumped like any over-engined steamer. There we lay on our stomachs, clinging to the ground, and looked about us, while Ayesha stood leaning out against the wind, down which her long hair streamed, and, absolutely heedless of the hideous depth that yawned beneath, pointed before her. Then we saw why the narrow plank, which Job and I had painfully dragged along between us, had been provided. Before us was an empty space, on the other side of which was something, as yet we could not see what, for here—either owing to the shadow of the opposite cliff, or from some other cause—the gloom was that of night.

"We must wait awhile," called Ayesha; "soon there will be light."

At the moment I could not imagine what she meant. How could more light than there was ever come to this dreadful spot? While I was still debating in my mind, suddenly, like a great sword of flame, a beam from the setting sun pierced the Stygian gloom, and smote upon the point of rock whereon we lay, illumining Ayesha's lovely form with an unearthly splendor. I only wish that I could describe the wild and marvelous beauty of that sword of fire, laid across the darkness and rushing mist wreaths of the gulf. How it got there I do not to this moment know, but I presume that there was some cleft or hole in the opposing cliff, through which it pierced when the setting orb was in a direct line therewith. All I can say is that the effect was the most wonderful that I ever saw.

Right through the heart of the darkness that flaming sword was stabbed, and where it lay there was the most surpassingly vivid light, so vivid that even at a distance one could see the grain of the rock, while, outside of it— yes, within a few inches of its keen edge—was naught but clustering shadows.

And now, by this ray of light, for which *She* had been waiting, and timed our arrival to meet, knowing that at this season for thousands of years it had always struck thus at sunset, we saw what was before us. Within eleven or twelve feet of the very tip of the tonguelike rock whereon we stood there arose, presumably from the far bottom of the gulf, a sugarloaf-shaped cone, of which the summit was exactly opposite to us. But had there been a summit only it would not have helped us much, for the nearest point of its circumference was some forty feet from where we were. On the lip of this summit, however, which was circular and hollow, rested a tremendous flat stone, some- thing like a glacier stone—perhaps it was one, for all I know to the contrary—and the end of this stone approached to within twelve feet or so of us. This huge boulder was nothing more or less than a gigantic rocking stone, ac- curately balanced upon the edge of the cone or miniature crater, like a half-crown on the rim of a wine glass; for, in the fierce light that played upon it and us, we could see it oscillating in the gusts of wind.

"Quick!" said Ayesha. "The plank—we must cross while the light endures; presently it will be gone."

"Oh, Lord, sir!" groaned Job. "Surely she don't mean us to walk across that there place on that there thing," as in obedience to my direction he pushed the long board towards me.

"That's it, Job," I hallooed in ghastly merriment, though

the idea of walking the plank was no pleasanter to me than to him.

I pushed the board on to Ayesha, who deftly ran it across the gulf so that one end of it rested on the rocking stone, the other remaining on the extremity of the trembling spur. Then, placing her foot upon it to prevent it from being blown away, she turned to me.

"Since last I was here, O Holly," she called, "the support of the moving stone hath lessened somewhat, so that I am not sure if it will bear our weight or no. Therefore will I cross the first, because no harm will come unto me," and, without further ado, she trod lightly but firmly across the frail bridge, and in another second was standing safe upon the heaving stone.

"It is safe," she called. "See, hold thou the plank! I will stand on the farther side of the stone so that it may not overbalance with your greater weights. Now come, O Holly, for presently the light will fail us."

I struggled to my knees, and if ever I felt sick in my life I felt sick then, and I am not ashamed to say that I hesitated and hung back.

"Surely thou art not afraid," called this strange creature in a lull of the gale, from where she stood, poised like a bird on the highest point of the rocking stone. "Make then way for Kallikrates."

This settled me; it is better to fall down a precipice and die than be laughed at by such a woman; so I clenched my teeth, and in another instant I was on that horrible, narrow, bending plank, with bottomless space beneath and around me. I have always hated a great height, but never before did I realize the full horrors of which such a position is capable. Oh, the sickening sensation of that yielding board resting on the two moving supports. I grew dizzy, and thought that I must fall; my spine *crept*; it seemed to me that I was falling, and my delight at finding myself sprawling upon that stone, which rose and fell beneath me like a boat in a swell, cannot be expressed in words. All I know is that briefly, but earnestly enough, I thanked Providence for preserving me so far.

Then came Leo's turn, and, though he looked rather queer, he came across like a rope dancer. Ayesha stretched out her hand to clasp his own, and I heard her say, "Bravely done, my love—bravely done! The old Greek spirit lives in thee yet!"

And now only poor Job remained on the farther side of the gulf. He crept up to the plank, and yelled out, "I can't do it, sir. I shall fall into that beastly place."

"You must," I remember saying with inappropriate facetiousness, "you must, Job, it's as easy as catching flies." I suppose that I said it to satisfy my conscience, because although the expression conveys a wonderful idea of facility, as a matter of fact I know no more difficult operation in the whole world than catching flies—that is, in warm weather, unless, indeed, it is catching mosquitoes.

"I can't, sir—I can't, indeed."

"Let the man come, or let him stop and perish there. See, the light is dying! In a moment it will be gone!" said Ayesha.

I looked. She was right. The sun was passing below the level of the hole or cleft in the precipice through which the ray reached us.

"If you stop there, Job, you will die alone," I called; "the light is going."

"Come, be a man, Job," roared Leo; "it's quite easy."

Thus adjured, the miserable Job, with a most awful yell, precipitated himself face downwards on the plank—he did

not dare, small blame to him, to try to walk it, and commenced to draw himself across in little jerks, his poor legs
hanging down on either side into the nothingness beneath.

His violent jerks at the frail board made the great stone,
which was only balanced on a few inches of rock, oscillate
in a most sickening manner, and, to make matters worse,
when he was halfway across, the flying ray of lurid light
suddenly went out, just as though a lamp had been extinguished in a curtained room, leaving the whole howling
wilderness of air black with darkness.

"Come on, Job, for God's sake!" I shouted in an agony
of fear, while the stone, gathering motion with every swing,
rocked so violently that it was difficult to hang on to it.
It was a truly awful position.

"Lord have mercy on me!" cried poor Job from the
darkness. "Oh, the plank's slipping!" and I heard a violent
struggle, and thought that he was gone.

But at that moment his outstretched hand, clasping in
agony at the air, met my own, and I hauled—ah, how I
did haul, putting out all the strength that it has pleased
Providence to give me in such abundance—and to my joy
in another minute Job was gasping on the rock beside me.
But the plank! I felt it slip, and heard it knock against
a projecting knob of rock, and it was gone.

"Great Heavens!" I exclaimed. "How are we going to get
back?"

"I don't know," answered Leo out of the gloom. "Sufficient to the day is the evil thereof. I am thankful enough
to be here."

But Ayesha merely called to me to take her hand and
creep after her.

25 ♦

The Spirit of Life

I DID as I was bid, and in fear and trembling felt myself guided over the edge of the stone. I sprawled my legs out, but could touch nothing.

"I am going to fall!" I gasped.

"Nay, let thyself go, and trust to me," answered Ayesha.

Now, if the position is considered, it will be easily understood that this was a greater demand upon my confidence than was justified by my knowledge of Ayesha's character. For all I knew she might be in the very act of consigning me to a horrible doom. But in life we sometimes have to lay our faith upon strange altars, and so it was now.

"Let thyself go!" she cried, and, having no choice, I did.

I felt myself slide a pace or two down the sloping surface of the rock, and then pass into the air, and the thought flashed through my brain that I was lost. But no! In another instant my feet struck against a rocky floor, and I felt that I was standing on something solid, and out of reach of the wind, which I could hear singing away overhead. As I stood there thanking Heaven for these small mercies, there was a slip and a scuffle, and down came Leo alongside of me.

"Hullo, old fellow!" he called out. "Are you there? This is getting interesting, is it not?"

Just then, with a terrific yell, Job arrived right on top of us, knocking us both down. By the time that we had struggled to our feet again Ayesha was standing among us, and bidding us light the lamps, which fortunately remained uninjured, as also did the spare jar of oil.

I got out my box of Bryant and May's wax matches, and they struck as merrily there, in that awful place, as they could have done in a London drawing room.

In a couple of minutes both the lamps were alight; and a curious scene they revealed. We were huddled together in a rock chamber, some ten feet square, and scared enough we looked; that is, except Ayesha, who was standing calmly with her arms folded, and waiting for the lamps to burn up. The chamber appeared to be partly natural and partly hollowed out of the top of the cone. The roof of the natural part was formed of the swinging stone, and that of the back part of the chamber, which sloped downwards, was hewn from the live rock. For the rest, the place was warm and dry—a perfect haven of rest compared to the giddy pinnacle above, and the quivering spur that shot out to meet it in midair.

"So!" said *She*. "Safely have we come, though once I feared that the rocking stone would fall with you, and precipitate you into the bottomless deeps beneath, for I do believe that the cleft goeth down to the very womb of the world. The rock whereon the stone resteth hath crumbled beneath the swinging weight. And now that he"—nodding towards Job, who was sitting on the floor, feebly wiping his forehead with a red cotton pocket handkerchief—"whom they rightly call the 'Pig,' for as a pig is he stupid, hath let fall the plank, it will not be easy to return across the gulf, and to that end must I make a plan. But now rest awhile, and look upon this place. What think ye that it is?"

"We know not," I answered.

"Wouldst thou believe, O Holly, that once a man did

choose this airy nest for a daily habitation, and did here endure for many years; leaving it only but one day in every twelve to seek food and water and oil that the people brought, more than he could carry, and laid as an offering in the mouth of the tunnel through which we passed hither?"

We looked up wonderingly, and she continued, "Yet so it was. There was a man—Noot, he named himself—who, though he lived in the latter days, had all of the wisdom of the sons of Kôr. A hermit was he, and a philosopher, and skilled in the secrets of Nature, and he it was who discovered the Fire that I shall show you, which is Nature's blood and life, and also that he who bathed therein, and breathed thereof, should live while Nature lives. But like unto thee, O Holly, this man, Noot, would not turn his knowledge to account. Ill, he said, was it for man to live, for man was born to die. Therefore did he tell his secret to none, and therefore did he come and live here, where the seeker after Life must pass, and was revered of the Amahagger of the day as holy, and a hermit. And when first I came to this country—knowest thou how I came, Kallikrates? Another time will I tell thee, it is a strange tale—I heard of this philosopher, and waited for him when he came to fetch his food, and returned with him hither, though greatly did I fear to tread the gulf. Then did I beguile him with my beauty and my wit, and flatter him with my tongue, so that he led me down and showed me the Fire, and told me the secrets of the Fire, but he would not suffer me to step therein, and, fearing lest he should slay me, I refrained, knowing that the man was very old, and soon would die. And I returned, having learned from him all that he knew of the wonderful Spirit of the World, and that was much, for the man was wise and very ancient, and by purity and abstinence, and the contemplations of his innocent mind, had worn thin the veil between that which we see and the great invisible truths, the whisper of whose wings at times we hear as they sweep through the gross air of the world. Then—it was but a very few days after—I met thee, my Kallikrates, who hadst wandered hither with the beautiful Egyptian Amenartas, and I learned to love for the first and last time, once and forever, so that it entered into my mind to come hither with thee, and receive the gift of Life for thee and me. Therefore came we, with that Egyptian who would not be left behind, and, behold, we found the old man Noot lying but newly dead. *There* he lay, and his white beard covered him like a garment,"—and she pointed to a spot near where I was sitting —"but surely he hath long since crumbled into dust, and the wind hath borne his ashes hence."

Here I put out my hand and felt in the dust, and presently my fingers touched something. It was a human tooth, very yellow, but sound. I held it up and showed it to Ayesha, who laughed.

"Yes," she said, "it is his without a doubt. Behold what remaineth of Noot and the wisdom of Noot—one little tooth! And yet that man had all life at his command, and for his conscience's sake would have none of it. Well, he lay there newly dead, and we descended whither I shall lead you, and then, gathering up all my courage, and courting death that I might perchance win so glorious a crown of life, I stepped into the flames, and behold, life such as ye can never know until ye feel it also flowed into me, and I came forth undying, and lovely beyond imagining. Then did I stretch out mine arms to thee, Kallikrates, and bid thee take thine immortal bride, and behold, as I spoke, thou, blinded by my beauty, didst turn from me, and throw thine arms about the neck of Amenartas. And then a great fury filled me, and made me mad, and I seized the javelin that thou didst bear, and stabbed thee, so that there, at my very feet, in the place of Life, thou didst groan and go down into death. I knew not then that I had strength to slay with mine eyes and by the power of my will, therefore in my madness slew I with the javelin.[1]

"And when thou wast dead, ah, I wept, because I was undying and thou wast dead. I wept there in the place of Life so that had I been mortal any more my heart had surely broken. And she, the swart Egyptian—she cursed me by her gods. By Osiris did she curse me and by Isis, by Nephthys and by Hekt, by Sekhet, the lion-headed, and by Set, calling down evil on me, evil and everlasting desolation. Ah! I can see her dark face now lowering o'er me like a storm, but she could not hurt me, and I—I know not if I could hurt her. I did not try; it was naught to me then; so together we bore thee hence. And afterwards I sent her —the Egyptian—away through the swamps, and it seems that she lived to bear a son and to write the tale that should lead thee, her husband, back to me, her rival and thy murderess.

"Such is the tale, my love, and now is the hour at hand that shall set a crown upon it. Like all things on the earth,

[1] It will be observed that Ayesha's account of the death of Kallikrates differs materially from that written on the potsherd by Amenartas. The writing on the sherd says, "Then in her rage did she smite him *by her magic,* and he died." We never ascertained which was the correct version, but it will be remembered that the body of Kallikrates had a spear wound in the breast, which seems conclusive, unless, indeed, it was inflicted after death. Another thing that we never ascertained was *how* the two women—*She* and the Egyptian Amenartas—managed to bear the corpse of the man they both loved across the dread gulf and along the shaking spur. What a spectacle the two d stracted creatures must have presented in their grief and loveliness as they toiled along that awful place with the dead man between them! Probably, however, the passage was easier then.—L. H. H.

it is compounded of evil and of good—more of evil than of good, perchance; and writ in letters of blood. It is the truth; naught have I hidden from thee, Kallikrates. And now one thing before the final moment of thy trial. We go down into the presence of Death, for Life and Death are very near together, and—who knoweth?—that might happen which should separate us for another space of waiting. I am but a woman, and no prophetess, and I cannot read the future. But this I know—for I learned it from the lips of the wise man Noot—that my life is but prolonged and made more bright. It cannot live for aye. Therefore, before we go, tell me, oh Kallikrates, that of a truth thou dost forgive me, and dost love me from thy heart. See, Kallikrates: much evil have I done—perchance it was evil but two nights gone to strike that girl who loved thee cold in death—but she disobeyed me and angered me, prophesying misfortune to me, and I smote. Be careful when power comes to thee also, lest thou too shouldst smite in thine anger or thy jealousy, for unconquerable strength is a sore weapon in the hands of erring man. Yea, I have sinned—out of the bitterness born of a great love have I sinned—but yet do I know the good from the evil, nor is my heart altogether hardened. Thy love, O Kallikrates, shall be the gate of my redemption, even as aforetime my passion was the path down which I ran to evil. For deep love unsatisfied is the hell of noble hearts and a portion for the accursed, but love that is mirrored back more perfect from the soul of our desired doth fashion wings to lift us above ourselves, and make us what we might be. Therefore, Kallikrates, take me by the hand, and lift my veil with no more fear than though I were some peasant girl, and not the wisest and most beauteous woman in this wide world, and look me in the eyes, and tell me that thou dost forgive me with all thine heart, and that with all thine heart thou dost worship me."

She paused, and the strange tenderness in her voice seemed to hover round us like a memory. I know that the sound of it moved me more even than her words, it was so very human—so very womanly. Leo, too, was strangely touched. Hitherto he had been fascinated against his better judgment, something as a bird is fascinated by a snake, but now I think that all this passed away, and he realized that he really loved this strange and glorious creature, as, alas! I loved her also. At any rate, I saw his eyes fill with tears, and he stepped swiftly to her and undid the gauzy veil, and then took her by the hand, and, gazing into her deep eyes, said aloud, "Ayesha, I love thee with all my heart, and so far as forgiveness is possible I forgive thee the death of Ustane. For the rest, it is between thee and thy Maker; I know naught of it. I only know that I love thee as I never loved before, and that I will cleave to thee to the end."

"Now," answered Ayesha, with proud humility, "now when my lord doth speak thus royally and give with so free a hand, it cannot become me to lag behind in words, and be beggared of my generosity. Behold!"—and she took his hand and placed it upon her shapely head, and then bent herself slowly down till one knee for an instant touched the ground—"Behold! In token of submission do I bow me to my lord! Behold!"—and she kissed him on the lips—"In token of my wifely love do I kiss my lord. Behold!"—and she laid her hand upon his heart—"By the sin I sinned, by my lonely centuries of waiting wherewith it was wiped out, by the great love wherewith I love, and by the Spirit —the Eternal Thing that doth beget all life, from whom it ebbs, to whom it doth return again—I swear:

"I swear, even in this first most holy hour of completed

womanhood, that I will abandon Evil and cherish Good. I swear that I will be ever guided by thy voice in the straightest path of Duty. I swear that I will eschew Ambition, and through all my length of endless days set Wisdom over me as a guiding star to lead me unto Truth and a knowledge of the Right. I swear also that I will honor and will cherish thee, Kallikrates, who hast been swept by the wave of time back into my arms, ay, till the very end, come it soon or late. I swear—nay, I will swear no more, for what are words? Yet shalt thou learn that Ayesha hath no false tongue.

"So I have sworn, and thou, my Holly, art witness to my oath. Here, too, are we wed, my husband, with the gloom for bridal canopy—wed till the end of all things; here do we write our marriage vows upon the rushing winds which shall bear them up to heaven, and round and continually round this rolling world.

"And for a bridal gift I crown thee with my beauty's starry crown, and enduring life, and wisdom without measure, and wealth that none can count. Behold! The great ones of the earth shall creep about thy feet, and their fair women shall cover up their eyes because of the shining glory of thy countenance, and their wise ones shall be abased before thee. Thou shalt read the hearts of men as an open writing, and hither and thither shalt thou lead them as thy pleasure listeth. Like that old Sphinx of Egypt shalt thou sit aloft from age to age, and ever shall they cry to thee to solve the riddle of thy greatness that doth not pass away, and ever shalt thou mock them with thy silence!

"Behold! Once more I kiss thee, and by that kiss I give to thee dominion over sea and earth, over the peasant in his hovel, over the monarch in his palace halls, and cities crowned with towers, and those who breathe therein.

Where'er the sun shakes out his spears, and the lonesome waters mirror up the moon, where'er storms roll, and Heaven's painted bows arch in the sky—from the pure North clad in snows, across the middle spaces of the world, to where the amorous South, lying like a bride upon her blue couch of seas, breathes in sighs made sweet with the odor of myrtles—there shall thy power pass and thy dominion find a home. Nor sickness, nor icy-fingered fear, nor sorrow, and pale waste of form and mind hovering ever o'er humanity, shall so much as shadow thee with the shadow of their wings. As a God shalt thou be, holding good and evil in the hollow of thy hand, and I, even I, I humble myself before thee. Such is the power of Love, and such is the bridal gift I give unto thee, Kallikrates, beloved of Rā, my Lord and Lord of All.

"And now it is done, and come storm, come shine, come good, come evil, come life, come death, it never, never can be undone. For, of a truth, that which is, is, and, being done, is done for aye, and cannot be altered. I have said— Let us hence, that all things may be accomplished in their order." And, taking one of the lamps, she advanced towards the end of the chamber that was roofed in by the swaying stone, where she halted.

We followed her, and perceived that in the wall of the cone there was a stair, or, to be more accurate, that some projecting knobs of rock had been so shaped as to form a good imitation of a stair. Down this Ayesha began to climb, springing from step to step, like a chamois, and after her we followed with less grace. When we had descended some fifteen or sixteen steps we found that they ended in a tremendous rocky slope, running first outwards and then inwards—like the slope of an inverted cone, or tunnel. The slope was very steep, and often precipitous, but it was nowhere impassable, and by the light of the lamps we went down it with no great difficulty, though it was gloomy work enough traveling on thus, no one of us knew whither, into the dead heart of a volcano. As we went, however, I took the precaution of noting our route as well as I could; and this was not difficult, owing to the extraordinary and most fantastic shape of the rocks that were strewn about, many of which in that dim light looked more like the grim faces carven upon medieval gargoyles than ordinary boulders.

For a long period we traveled on thus, half an hour I should say, till, after we had descended for many hundreds of feet, I perceived that we were reaching the point of the inverted cone. In another minute we were there, and found that at the very apex of the funnel was a passage, so low and narrow that we had to stoop as we crept along it in Indian file. After some fifty yards of this creeping, the passage suddenly widened into a cave, so huge that we could see neither the roof nor the sides. We only knew that it was a cave by the echo of our tread and the perfect quiet of the heavy air. On we went for many minutes in absolute awed silence, like lost souls in the depths of Hades, Ayesha's white and ghostlike form flitting in front of us, till once more the cavern ended in a passage which opened into a second cavern much smaller than the first. Indeed, we could clearly make out the arch and stony banks of this second cave, and, from their rent and jagged appearance, discovered that, like the first long passage down which we had passed through the cliff before we reached the quivering spur, it had to all appearance been torn in the bowels of the rock by the terrific force of some explosive gas. At length this cave ended in a third passage, through which gleamed a faint glow of light.

I heard Ayesha give a sigh of relief as this light dawned upon us.

"It is well," she said; "prepare to enter the very womb of the Earth, wherein she doth conceive the Life that ye see brought forth in man and beast—ay, and in every tree and flower."

Swiftly she sped along, and after her we stumbled as best we might, our hearts filled like a cup with mingled dread and curiosity. What were we about to see? We passed down the tunnel; stronger and stronger the light beamed, reaching us in great flashes like the rays from a lighthouse, as one by one they are thrown wide upon the darkness of the waters. Nor was this all, for with the flashes came a soul-shaking sound like that of thunder and of crashing trees. Now we were through it, and—oh heavens!

We stood in a third cavern, some fifty feet in length by perhaps as great a height, and thirty wide. It was carpeted with fine white sand, and its walls had been worn smooth by the action of I know not what. The cavern was not dark like the others, it was filled with a soft glow of rose-colored light, more beautiful to look on than anything that can be conceived. But at first we saw no flashes, and heard no more of the thunderous sound. Presently, however, as we stood in amaze, gazing at the wonderful sight, and wondering whence the rosy radiance flowed, a dread and beautiful thing happened. Across the far end of the cavern, with a grinding and crashing noise—a noise so dreadful and awe-inspiring that we all trembled, and Job actually sank to his knees—there flamed out an awful cloud or pillar of fire, like a rainbow many-colored, and like the lightning bright. For a space, perhaps forty seconds, it flamed and roared thus, turning slowly round and round, and then by degrees the terrible noise ceased, and with the fire it passed away—

I know not where—leaving behind it the same rosy glow that we had first seen.

"Draw near, draw near!" cried Ayesha with a voice of thrilling exultation. "Behold the very Fountain and Heart of Life as it beats in the bosom of the great world. Behold the substance from which all things draw their energy, the bright Spirit of the Globe, without which it cannot live, but must grow cold and dead as the dead moon. Draw near, and wash you in the living flames, and take their virtue into your poor frames in all its virgin strength—not as it now feebly glows within your bosoms, filtered thereto through all the fine strainers of a thousand intermediate lives, but as it is here in the very fount and seat of earthly Being."

We followed her through the rosy glow up to the head of the cave, till at last we stood before the spot where the great pulse beat and the great flame passed. And as we went we became sensible of a wild and splendid exhilaration, of a glorious sense of such a fierce intensity of Life that the most buoyant moments of our strength seemed flat and tame and feeble beside it. It was the mere effluvium of the flame, the subtle ether that it cast off as it passed, working on us, and making us feel strong as giants and swift as eagles.

We reached the head of the cave, and gazed at each other in the glorious glow, and laughed aloud—even Job laughed, and he had not laughed for a week—in the lightness of our hearts and the divine intoxication of our brains. I know that I felt as though all the varied genius of which the human intellect is capable had descended upon me. I could have spoken in blank verse of Shakespearean beauty, all sorts of great ideas flashed through my mind; it was as though the bonds of my flesh had been loosened, and left the spirit free to soar to the empyrean of its native power.

The sensations that poured in upon me are indescribable. I seemed to live more keenly, to reach to a higher joy, and sip the goblet of a subtler thought than ever it had been my lot to do before. I was another and most glorified self, and all the avenues of the Possible were for a space laid open to the footsteps of the Real.

Then, suddenly, while I rejoiced in this splendid vigor of a new-found self, from far, far away there came a dreadful muttering noise that grew and grew to a crash and a roar, which combined in itself all that is terrible and yet splendid in the possibilities of sound. Nearer it came, and nearer yet, till it was close upon us, rolling down like all the thunder wheels of heaven behind the horses of the lightning. On it came, and with it came the glorious blinding cloud of many-colored light, and stood before us for a space, turning, as it seemed to us, slowly round and round, and then, accompanied by its attendant pomp of sound, passed away I know not whither.

So astonishing was the wondrous sight that one and all of us, save *She*, who stood up and stretched her hands towards the fire, sank down before it, and hid our faces in the sand.

When it was gone, Ayesha spoke.

"Now, Kallikrates," she said, "the mighty moment is at hand. When the great flame comes again thou must stand in it. First throw aside thy garments, for it will burn them, though thee it will not hurt. Thou must stand in the flame while thy senses will endure, and when it embraces thee suck the fire down into thy very heart, and let it leap and play around thy every part, so that thou lose no moiety of its virtue. Hearest thou me, Kallikrates?"

"I hear thee, Ayesha," answered Leo, "but, of a truth—I am no coward—but I doubt me of that raging flame. How know I that it will not utterly destroy me, so that I lose myself and lose thee also? Nevertheless will I do it," he added.

Ayesha thought for a minute, and then said, "It is not wonderful that thou shouldst doubt. Tell me, Kallikrates: if thou seest me stand in the flame and come forth unharmed, wilt thou enter also?"

"Yes," he answered, "I will enter even if it slay me. I have said that I will enter now."

"And that will I also," I cried.

"What, my Holly!" She laughed aloud. "Methought that thou wouldst naught of length of days. Why, how is this?"

"Nay, I know not," I answered, "but there is that in my heart that calleth to me to taste of the flame, and live."

"It is well," she said. "Thou art not altogether lost in folly. See now, I will for the second time bathe me in this living bath. Fain would I add to my beauty and my length of days if that be possible. If it be not possible, at the least it cannot harm me.

"Also," she continued, after a momentary pause, "is there another and a deeper cause why I would once again dip me in the flame. When first I tasted of its virtue full was my heart of passion and of hatred of that Egyptian Amenartas, and therefore, despite my strivings to be rid thereof, have passion and hatred been stamped upon my soul from that sad hour to this. But now it is otherwise. Now is my mood a happy mood, and filled am I with the purest part of thought, and so would I ever be. Therefore, Kallikrates, will I once more wash and make me pure and clean, and yet more fit for thee. Therefore also, when thou dost in turn stand in the fire, empty all thy heart of evil, and let sweet contentment hold the balance of thy mind. Shake loose thy spirit's wings, and take thy stand upon the utter verge of holy contemplation; ay, dream upon thy mother's kiss, and turn thee towards the vision of the highest good that hath ever swept on silver wings across the silence of thy dreams. For from the germ of what thou art in that dread moment shall grow the fruit of what thou shalt be for all unreckoned time.

"Now prepare thee, prepare! Even as though thy last hour were at hand, and thou wast about to cross to the land of shadows, and not through the gates of glory into the realms of Life made beautiful. Prepare, I say!"

26 ◆

What We Saw

THEN CAME a few moments' pause, during which Ayesha seemed to be gathering up her strength for the fiery trial, while we clung to each other, and waited in utter silence.

At last, from far far away, came the first murmur of sound, which grew and grew till it began to crash and bellow in the distance. As she heard it, Ayesha swiftly threw off her gauzy wrapping, loosened the golden snake from her kirtle, and then, shaking her lovely hair about her like a garment, beneath its cover slipped the kirtle off and replaced the snaky belt around her and outside the masses of falling hair. There she stood before us as Eve might have stood before Adam, clad in nothing but her abundant locks, held round her by the golden band; and no words of mine can tell how sweet she looked—and yet how divine. Nearer and nearer came the thunder wheels of fire, and as they came she pushed one ivory arm through the dark masses of her hair and flung it round Leo's neck.

"Oh, my love, my love!" she murmured. "Wilt thou ever know how I have loved thee?" And she kissed him on the forehead, and then went and stood in the pathway of the flame of Life.

There was, I remember, to my mind something very touching about her words and that kiss upon the forehead.

332

It was like a mother's kiss, and seemed to convey a benediction with it.

On came the crashing, rolling noise, and the sound thereof was as the sound of a forest being swept flat by a mighty wind, and then tossed up by it like so much grass, and thundered down a mountainside. Nearer and nearer it came; now flashes of light, forerunners of the revolving pillar of flame, were passing like arrows through the rosy air; and now the edge of the pillar itself appeared. Ayesha turned towards it, and stretched out her arms to greet it. On it came very slowly, and lapped her round with flame. I saw the fire run up her form. I saw her lift it with both hands as though it were water, and pour it over her head. I even saw her open her mouth and draw it down into her lungs, and a dread and wonderful sight it was.

Then she paused, and stretched out her arms, and stood there quite still, with a heavenly smile upon her face, as though she were the very Spirit of the Flame.

The mysterious fire played up and down her dark and rolling locks, twining and twisting itself through and around them like threads of golden lace; it gleamed upon her ivory breast and shoulder, from which the hair had slipped aside; it slid along her pillared throat and delicate features, and seemed to find a home in the glorious eyes that shone and shone, more brightly even than the spiritual essence.

Oh, how beautiful she looked there in the flame! No angel out of heaven could have worn a greater loveliness. Even now my heart faints before the recollection of it, as she stood and smiled at our awed faces, and I would give half my remaining time upon this earth to see her once like that again.

But suddenly—more suddenly than I can describe—a

kind of change came over her face, a change which I could not define or explain on paper, but none the less a change. The smile vanished, and in its place there came a dry, hard look; the rounded face seemed to grow pinched, as though some great anxiety were leaving its impress upon it. The glorious eyes, too, lost their light, and, as I thought, the form its perfect shape and erectness.

I rubbed my eyes, thinking that I was the victim of some hallucination, or that the refraction from the intense light produced an optical delusion; and, as I did so, the flaming pillar slowly twisted and thundered off whithersoever it passes to in the bowels of the great earth, leaving Ayesha standing where it had been.

As soon as it was gone, she stepped forward to Leo's side—it seemed to me that there was no spring in her step —and stretched out her hand to lay it on his shoulder. I gazed at her arm. Where was its wonderful roundness and beauty? It was getting thin and angular. And her face— by heaven!—*her face was growing old before my eyes!* I suppose that Leo saw it also; certainly he recoiled a step or two.

"What is it, my Kallikrates?" she said, and her voice— what was the matter with those deep and thrilling notes? They were quite high and cracked.

"Why, what is it—what is it?" she said confusedly. "I feel dazed. Surely the quality of the fire hath not altered. Can the principle of Life alter? Tell me, Kallikrates, is there aught wrong with my eyes? I see not clear," and she put her hand to her head and touched her hair—and oh, *horror of horrors!*—it all fell upon the floor.

"Oh, *look! Look! Look!*" shrieked Job, in a shrill falsetto of terror, his eyes nearly dropping out of his head, and foam upon his lips. "*Look! Look! Look!* She's shriveling up!

She's turning into a monkey!" And down he fell upon the ground, foaming and gnashing in a fit.

True enough—I faint even as I write it in the living presence of that terrible recollection—she *was* shriveling up; the golden snake that had encircled her gracious form slipped over her hips and to the ground; smaller and smaller she grew; her skin changed color, and in place of the perfect whiteness of its luster it turned dirty brown and yellow, like an old piece of withered parchment. She felt at her head: the delicate hand was nothing but a claw now, a human talon like that of a badly preserved Egyptian mummy, and then she seemed to realize what kind of change was passing over her, and she shrieked—ah, she shrieked!—she rolled upon the floor and shrieked!

Smaller she grew, and smaller yet, till she was no larger than a baboon. Now the skin was puckered into a million wrinkles, and on the shapeless face was the stamp of unutterable age. I never saw anything like it; nobody ever saw anything like the frightful age that was graven on that fearful countenance, no bigger now than that of a two-month-old child, though the skull remained the same size, or nearly so; and let all men pray to God they never may, if they wish to keep their reason.

At last she lay still, or only feebly moving. She, who but two minutes before had gazed upon us the loveliest, noblest, most splendid woman the world has ever seen, she lay still before us, near the masses of her own dark hair, no larger than a big monkey, and hideous—ah, too hideous for words. And yet, think of this—at that very moment I thought of it—it was the *same* woman!

She was dying: we saw it, and thanked God—for while she lived she could feel, and what must she have felt? She raised herself upon her bony hands, and blindly gazed around her, swaying her head slowly from side to side as a tortoise does. She could not see, for her whitish eyes were covered with a horny film. Oh, the horrible pathos of the sight! But she could still speak.

"Kallikrates," she said in husky, trembling notes. "Forget me not, Kallikrates. Have pity on my shame; I shall come again, and shall once more be beautiful, I swear it—it is true! Oh—h—h—" And she fell upon her face, and was still.

On the very spot where more than twenty centuries before she had slain Kallikrates the priest, she herself fell down and died.

Overcome with the extremity of horror, we too fell on the sandy floor of that dread place, and swooned away.

I know not how long we remained thus. Many hours, I suppose. When at last I opened my eyes, the other two were still outstretched upon the floor. The rosy light yet beamed like a celestial dawn, and the thunder wheels of the Spirit of Life yet rolled upon their accustomed track, for as I awoke the great pillar was passing away. There, too, lay the hideous little monkey frame, covered with crinkled yellow parchment, that once had been the glorious She. Alas! it was no hideous dream—it was an awful and unparalleled fact!

What had happened to bring this shocking change about? Had the nature of the life-giving Fire changed? Did it, perhaps, from time to time send forth an essence of Death instead of an essence of Life? Or was it that the frame once charged with its marvelous virtue could bear no more, so that were the process repeated—it mattered not at what lapse of time—the two impregnations neutralized each other, and left the body on which they acted as it was before it ever came into contact with the very essence of life? This, and this alone, would account for the sudden and terrible aging of Ayesha, as the whole length of her two thousand years took effect upon her. I have not the slightest doubt myself but that the frame now lying before me was just what the frame of a woman would be if by any extraordinary means life could be preserved in her till she at length died at the age of two-and-twenty centuries.

But who can tell what had happened? There was the fact. Often since that awful hour I have reflected that it requires no great stretch of imagination to see the finger of Providence in the matter. Ayesha locked up in her living tomb waiting from age to age for the coming of her lover worked but a small change in the order of the World. But Ayesha strong and happy in her love, clothed in immortal youth and godlike beauty, and the wisdom of the centuries, would have revolutionized society, and even perchance have changed the destiny of Mankind. Thus she opposed herself against the eternal Law, and, strong though she was, by it was swept back to nothingness—swept back with shame and hideous mockery!

For some minutes I lay faintly turning these terrors over in my mind, while my physical strength came back to me, which it quickly did in that buoyant atmosphere. Then I bethought me of the others, and staggered to my feet, to see if I could arouse them. But first I took up Ayesha's kirtle and the gauzy scarf with which she had been wont to hide her dazzling loveliness from the eyes of men, and, averting my head so that I might not look upon it, covered up that dreadful relic of the glorious dead, that shocking epitome of human beauty and human life. I did this hurriedly, fearing lest Leo should recover, and see it again.

Then, stepping over the perfumed masses of dark hair that lay upon the sand, I stooped down by Job, who was lying upon his face, and turned him over. As I did so his arm fell back in a way that I did not like, and which sent a chill through me, and I glanced sharply at him. One look was enough. Our old and faithful servant was dead. His nerves, already shattered by all he had seen and under-gone, had utterly broken down beneath this last dire sight, and he had died of terror, or in a fit brought on by terror. One had only to look at his face to see it.

It was another blow; but perhaps it may help people to understand how overwhelmingly awful was the experience through which we had passed—we did not feel it much at the time. It seemed quite natural that the poor old fellow should be dead. When Leo came to himself, which he did with a groan and trembling of the limbs about ten minutes afterwards, and I told him that Job was dead, he merely said, "Oh!" And, mind you, this was from no heartlessness, for he and Job were much attached to each other; and he often talks of him now with the deepest regret and affection. It was only that his nerves would bear no more. A harp can give out but a certain quantity of sound, however heavily it is smitten.

Well, I set myself to recovering Leo, who, to my infinite relief, I found was not dead, but only fainting, and in the end I succeeded, as I have said, and he sat up; and then I saw another dreadful thing. When we entered that awful place his curling hair had been of the ruddiest gold; now it was turning gray, and by the time we gained the outer air it was snow-white. Besides, he looked twenty years older.

"What is to be done, old fellow?" he said in a hollow, dead sort of voice, when his mind had cleared a little, and a recollection of what had happened forced itself upon it.

"Try and get out, I suppose," I answered; "that is, unless

you would like to go in there," and I pointed to the column of fire that was once more rolling by.

"I would go in if I were sure that it would kill me," he said with a little laugh. "It was my cursed hesitation that did this. If I had not been doubtful she might never have tried to show me the road. But I am not sure. The fire might have the opposite effect upon me. It might make me immortal; and, old fellow, I have not the patience to wait a couple of thousand years for her to come back again as she did for me. I had rather die when my hour comes— and I should fancy that it isn't far off either—and go my ways to look for her. Do you go in if you like."

But I merely shook my head, my excitement was as dead as ditchwater, and my distaste for the prolongation of my mortal span had come back upon me more strongly than ever. Besides, we neither of us knew what the effects of the fire might be. The result upon *She* had not been of an encouraging nature, and of the exact causes that produced that result we were, of course, ignorant.

"Well, my boy," I said, "we cannot stop here till we go the way of those two," and I pointed to the little heap under the white garment and to the stiffening corpse of poor Job. "If we are going we had better go. But, by the way, I expect that the lamps have burned out," and I took one up and looked at it, and sure enough it had.

"There is some more oil in the vase," said Leo indifferently, "if it is not broken, at least."

I examined the vessel in question—it was intact. With a trembling hand I filled the lamps—luckily there was still some of the linen wick unburned. Then I lit them with one of our wax matches. While I did so we heard the pillar of fire approaching once more as it went on its never ending journey, if, indeed, it was the same pillar that passed and repassed in a circle.

"Let's see it come once more," said Leo; "we shall never look upon its like again in this world."

It seemed a bit of idle curiosity, but somehow I shared it, and so we waited till, turning slowly round upon its own axis, it had flamed and thundered by; and I remember wondering for how many thousands of years this same phenomenon had been taking place in the bowels of the earth, and for how many more thousands it would continue to take place. I wondered also if any mortal eyes would ever again mark its passage, or any mortal ears be thrilled and fascinated by the swelling volume of its majestic sound. I do not think that they will. I believe that we are the last human beings who will ever see that unearthly sight. Presently it had gone, and we too turned to go.

But before we did so we each took Job's cold hand in ours and shook it. It was a rather ghastly ceremony, but it was the only means in our power of showing our respect to the faithful dead and of celebrating his obsequies. The heap beneath the white garment we did not uncover. We had no wish to look upon that terrible sight again. But we went to the pile of rippling hair that had fallen from her in the agony of that hideous change which was worse than a thousand natural deaths, and each of us drew from it a shining lock, and these locks we still have, the sole memento that is left to us of Ayesha as we knew her in the fullness of her grace and glory. Leo pressed the perfumed hair to his lips.

"She called to me not to forget her," he said hoarsely, "and swore that we should meet again. By heaven! I never will forget her. Here I swear that, if we live to get out of this, I will not for all my days have anything to say to another living woman, and that wherever I go I will wait for her as faithfully as she waited for me."

"Yes," I thought to myself, "if she comes back as beautiful as we knew her. But supposing she came back like that!" [1]

Well, and then we went. We went, and left those two in the presence of the very well and spring of Life, but gathered to the cold company of Death. How lonely they looked as they lay there, and how ill assorted! That little heap had been for two thousand years the wisest, loveliest, proudest creature—I can hardly call her woman—in the whole universe. She had been wicked, too, in her way; but, alas, such is the frailty of the human heart, her wickedness had not detracted from her charm. Indeed, I am by no means certain that it did not add to it. It was after all of a grand order, there was nothing mean or small about Ayesha.

And poor Job, too! His presentiment had come true, and there was an end of him. Well, he has a strange burial place—no Norfolk hind ever had a stranger, or ever will; and it is something to lie in the same sepulcher with the poor remains of the imperial *She.*

We looked our last upon them and the indescribable rosy glow in which they lay, and then with hearts far too heavy for words we left them, and crept thence broken-down men —so broken down that we even renounced the chance of practically immortal life, because all that made life valuable had gone from us, and we knew even then that to prolong our days indefinitely would only be to prolong our sufferings. For we felt—yes, both of us—that having once

---

[1] What a terrifying reflection it is, by the way, that nearly all our deep love for women who are not our kindred depends—at any rate, in the first instance—upon their personal appearance. If we lost them, and found them again dreadful to look on, though otherwise they were the very same, should we still love them?—L. H. H.

looked Ayesha in the eyes, we could not forget her forever and ever while memory and identity remained. We both loved her now and for always, she was stamped and carven on our hearts, and no other woman or interest could ever raze that splendid die. And I—there lies the sting—I had and have no right to think thus of her. As she told me, I was naught to her, and never shall be through the unfathomed depth of Time, unless, indeed, conditions alter, and a day comes at last when two men may love one woman, and all three be happy in the fact. It is the only hope of my broken-heartedness, and a rather faint one. Beyond it I have nothing. I have paid down this heavy price, all that I am worth here and hereafter, and that is my sole reward. With Leo it is different, and often and often I bitterly envy him his happy lot, for if *She* was right, and her wisdom and knowledge did not fail her at the last, which, arguing from the precedent of her own case, I think most unlikely, he has some future to look forward to. But I have none, and yet—mark the folly and the weakness of the human heart, and let him who is wise learn wisdom from it—yet I would not have it otherwise. I mean that I am content to give what I have given and must always give, and take in payment those crumbs that fall from my mistress's table, the memory of a few kind words, the hope one day in the far undreamed future of a sweet smile or two of recognition, a little gentle friendship, and a little show of thanks for my devotion to her—and Leo.

If that does not constitute true love, I do not know what does, and all I have to say is that it is a very bad state of mind for a man on the wrong side of middle age to fall into.

27 ♦

We Leap

WE PASSED through the caves without trouble, but when we came to the slope of the inverted cone two difficulties stared us in the face. The first of these was the laborious nature of the ascent, and the next the extreme difficulty of finding our way. Indeed, had it not been for the mental notes that I had fortunately taken of the shape of various rocks, etc., I am sure that we never should have managed it at all, but have wandered about in the dreadful womb of the volcano—for I suppose it must once have been something of the sort—until we died of exhaustion and despair. As it was we went wrong several times, and once nearly fell into a huge crack or crevasse. It was terrible work creeping about in the dense gloom and awful stillness from boulder to boulder, and examining it by the feeble light of the lamps to see if I could recognize its shape. We rarely spoke—our hearts were too heavy for speech—we simply stumbled about, falling sometimes and cutting ourselves, in a rather dogged sort of way. The fact was that our spirits were utterly crushed, and we did not greatly care what happened to us. Only we felt bound to try and save our lives while we could, and indeed a natural instinct prompted us to it. So for some three or four hours, I should think—I cannot tell exactly how long, for we had no watch left that would go—we blundered on. During the last two hours we were completely lost, and I began to fear that we had got

343

into the funnel of some subsidiary cone, when at last I suddenly recognized a very large rock which we had passed in descending but a little way from the top. It is a marvel that I should have recognized it, and, indeed, we had already passed it going at right angles to the proper path, when something about it struck me, and I turned back and examined it in an idle sort of way, and, as it happened, this proved our salvation.

After this we gained the rocky natural stair without much further trouble, and in due course found ourselves back in the little chamber where the benighted Noot had lived and died.

But now a fresh terror stared us in the face. It will be remembered that owing to Job's fear and awkwardness, the plank upon which we had crossed from the huge spur to the rocking stone had been whirled off into the tremendous gulf below.

How were we to cross without the plank?

There was only one answer—we must try and *jump* it, or else stop there till we starved. The distance in itself was not so very great, between eleven and twelve feet I should think, and I have seen Leo jump over twenty when he was a young fellow at college; but then, think of the conditions. Two weary, worn-out men, one of them on the wrong side of forty, a rocking stone to take off from, a trembling point of rock some few feet across to land upon, and a bottomless gulf to be cleared in a raging gale! It was bad enough, God knows, but when I pointed out these things to Leo, he put the whole matter in a nutshell by replying that, merciless as the choice was, we must choose between the certainty of a lingering death in the chamber and the risk of a swift one in the air. Of course, there was no arguing against this, but one thing was clear, we could not attempt that leap in the dark; the only thing to do was to wait for the ray of light which pierced through the gulf at sunset. How near to or how far from sunset we might be, neither of us had the faintest notion; all we did know was that when at last the light came it would not endure more than a couple of minutes at the outside, so that we must be prepared to meet it. Accordingly, we made up our minds to creep onto the top of the rocking stone and lie there in readiness. We were the more easily reconciled to this course by the fact that our lamps were once more nearly exhausted—indeed, one had gone out bodily, and the other was jumping up and down as the flame of a lamp does when the oil is done. So, by the aid of its dying light, we hastened to crawl out of the little chamber and clamber up the side of the great stone.

As we did so the light went out.

The difference in our position was a sufficiently remarkable one. Below, in the little chamber, we had only heard the roaring of the gale overhead—here, lying on our faces on the swinging stone, we were exposed to its full force and fury, as the great draft drew first from this direction and then from that, howling against the mighty precipice and through the rocky cliffs like ten thousand despairing souls. We lay there hour after hour in terror and misery of mind so deep that I will not attempt to describe it, and listened to the wild storm voices of that Tartarus, as, set to the deep undertone of the spur opposite against which the wind hummed like some awful harp, they called to each other from precipice to precipice. No nightmare dreamed by man, no wild invention of the romancer, can ever equal the living horror of that place, and the weird crying of those voices of the night, as we clung like shipwrecked mariners to a raft, and tossed on the black, unfathomed wilderness of air. Fortunately the temperature was not a low one—indeed, the wind was warm—or we should have perished. So we clung and listened, and while we were stretched out upon the rock a thing happened which was so curious and suggestive in itself, though doubtless a mere coincidence, that, if anything, it added to, rather than deducted from, the burden on our nerves.

It will be remembered that when Ayesha was standing on the spur, before we crossed to the stone, the wind tore her cloak from her, and whirled it away into the darkness of the gulf, we could not see whither. Well—I hardly like to tell the story; it is so strange. As we lay there upon the rocking stone, this very cloak came floating out of the black space, like a memory from the dead, and fell on Leo —so that it covered him nearly from head to foot. We could not at first make out what it was, but soon discovered by its feel, and then poor Leo, for the first time, gave way, and I heard him sobbing there upon the stone. No doubt the cloak had been caught upon some pinnacle of the cliff, and was thence blown hither by a chance gust; but still, it was a most curious and touching incident.

Shortly after this, suddenly, without the slightest previous warning, the great red knife of light came stabbing the darkness through and through—struck the swaying stone on which we were, and rested its sharp point upon the spur opposite.

"Now for it," said Leo, "now or never."

We rose and stretched ourselves, and looked at the cloud wreaths stained the color of blood by that red ray as they tore through the sickening depths beneath, and then at the empty space between the swaying stone and the quivering rock, and, in our hearts, despaired, and prepared for death. Surely we could not clear it—desperate though we were.

"Who is to go first?" said I.

"Do you, old fellow," answered Leo. "I will sit upon the other side of the stone to steady it. You must take as much run as you can, and jump high; and God have mercy on us, say I."

I acquiesced with a nod, and then I did a thing I had never done since Leo was a little boy. I turned and put my arm round him, and kissed him on the forehead. It sounds rather French, but as a fact I was taking my last farewell of a man whom I could not have loved more if he had been my own son twice over.

"Good-by, my boy," I said, "I hope that we shall meet again, wherever it is that we go to."

The fact was I did not expect to live another two minutes.

Next I retreated to the far side of the rock, and waited till one of the chopping gusts of wind got behind me, and then, commending my soul to God, I ran the length of the huge stone, some three- or four-and-thirty feet, and sprang wildly out into the dizzy air. Oh, the sickening terrors that I felt as I launched myself at that little point of rock, and the horrible sense of despair that shot through my brain as I realized that I had *jumped short!* But so it was, my feet never touched the point, they went down into space, only my hands and body came in contact with it. I gripped at it with a yell, but one hand slipped, and I swung right round, holding by the other, so that I faced the stone from which I had sprung. Wildly I stretched up with my left hand, and this time managed to grasp a knob of rock, and there I hung in the fierce red light, with thousands of feet of empty air beneath me. My hands were holding to either side of the under part of the spur, so that its point was touching my head. Therefore, even if I could have found the strength, I could not pull myself up. The most that I could do would be to hang for about a minute, and then drop down, down into the bottomless pit. If any man can imagine a more hideous position, let him speak! All I know is that the torture of that half minute nearly turned my brain.

I heard Leo give a cry, and then suddenly saw him in midair springing up and out like a chamois. It was a splendid leap that he took under the influence of his terror and despair, clearing the horrible gulf as though it were nothing, and, landing well onto the rocky point, he threw himself upon his face, to prevent his pitching off into the depths. I felt the spur above me shake beneath the shock of his impact, and as it did so I saw the huge rocking stone, which had been violently depressed by him as he sprang, fly back when relieved of his weight till, for the first time during all these centuries, it got beyond its balance, and fell with a most awful crash right into the rocky chamber which had once served the philosopher Noot for a hermitage, as I have no doubt, forever hermetically sealing the passage that leads to the place of Life with some hundreds of tons of rock.

All this happened in a second, and curiously enough, notwithstanding my terrible position, I noted it involuntarily, as it were. I even remember thinking that no human being would go down that dread path again.

Next instant I felt Leo seize me by the right wrist with both hands. By lying flat on the point of rock he could just reach me.

"You must let go and swing yourself clear," he said in a

calm and collected voice, "and then I will try and pull you up, or we will both go together. Are you ready?"

By way of answer I let go, first with my left hand and then with the right, and swayed out as a consequence clear of the overshadowing rock, my weight hanging upon Leo's arms. It was a dreadful moment. He was a very powerful man, I knew, but would his strength be equal to lifting me up till I could get a hold on the top of the spur, when owing to his position he had so little purchase?

For a few seconds I swung to and fro, while he gathered himself for the effort, and then I heard his sinews cracking above me, and felt myself lifted up as though I were a little child, till I got my left arm round the rock, and my chest was resting on it. The rest was easy; in two or three more seconds I was up, and we were lying panting side by side, trembling like leaves, and with the cold perspiration of terror pouring from our skins.

And then, as before, the light went out like a lamp.

For perhaps a half hour we lay thus without speaking a word, and then at length began to creep along the great spur as best we might in the dense gloom. As we drew towards the face of the cliff, however, from which the spur sprang out like a spike from a wall, the light increased, though only a very little, for it was night overhead. After that the gusts of wind decreased, and we got along rather better, and at last reached the mouth of the first cave or tunnel. But now a fresh trouble stared us in the face: our oil was gone, and the lamps were, no doubt, crushed to powder beneath the fallen rocking stone. We were even without a drop of water to stay our thirst, for we had drunk the last in the chamber of Noot. How were we to see to make our way through this last boulder-strewn tunnel?

Clearly all that we could do was to trust to our sense

of feeling, and attempt the passage in the dark, so in we crept, fearing that if we delayed to do so our exhaustion would overcome us, and we should probably lie down and die where we were.

Oh, the horrors of that last tunnel! The place was strewn with rocks, and we fell over them, and knocked ourselves up against them till we were bleeding from a score of wounds. Our only guide was the side of the cavern, which we kept touching, and so bewildered did we grow in the darkness that we were several times seized with the terrifying thought that we had turned, and were traveling the wrong way. On we went, feebly, and still more feebly, for hour after hour, stopping every few minutes to rest, for our strength was spent. Once we fell asleep, and, I think, must have slept for some hours, for, when we woke, our limbs were quite stiff, and the blood from our blows and scratches had caked, and was hard and dry upon our skin. Then we dragged ourselves on again, till at last, when despair was entering into our hearts, we once more saw the light of day, and found ourselves outside the tunnel in the rocky fold on the outer surface of the cliff that, it will be remembered, led into it.

It was early morning—that we could tell by the feel of the sweet air and the look of the blessed sky, which we had never hoped to see again. It was, so near as we knew, an hour after sunset when we entered the tunnel, so it followed that it had taken us the entire night to crawl through that dreadful place.

"One more effort, Leo," I gasped, "and we shall reach the slope where Billali is, if he hasn't gone. Come, don't give way," for he had cast himself upon his face. He got up, and, leaning on each other, we got down that fifty feet or so of cliff—somehow, I have not the least notion how.

I only remember that we found ourselves lying in a heap at the bottom, and then once more began to drag ourselves along on our hands and knees towards the grove where *She* had told Billali to wait her rearrival, for we could not walk another foot. We had not gone fifty yards in this fashion when suddenly one of the mutes emerged from some trees on our left, through which, I presume, he had been taking a morning stroll, and came running up to see what sort of strange animals we were. He stared, and stared, and then held up his hands in horror, and nearly fell to the ground. Next, he started off as hard as he could for the grove some two hundred yards away. No wonder that he was horrified at our appearance, for we must have been a shocking sight. To begin, Leo, with his golden curls turned a snowy white, his clothes nearly rent from his body, his worn face and his hands a mass of bruises, cuts, and blood-encrusted filth, was a sufficiently alarming spectacle, as he painfully dragged himself along the ground, and I have no doubt that I was little better to look on. I know that two days afterwards when I looked at my face in some water I scarcely recognized myself. I have never been famous for beauty, but there was something beside ugliness stamped upon my features that I have never got rid of until this day, something resembling that wild look with which a startled person wakes from deep sleep more than anything else that I can think of. And really it is not to be wondered at. What I do wonder at is that we escaped at all with our reason.

Presently, to my intense relief, I saw old Billali hurrying towards us, and even then I could scarcely help smiling at the expression of consternation on his dignified countenance.

"Oh, my Baboon, my Baboon!" he cried. "My dear son,

is it indeed thee and the Lion? Why, his mane that was ripe as corn is white like the snow. Whence come ye? And where is the Pig, and where too 'She-who-must-be-obeyed'?"

"Dead, both dead," I answered; "but ask no questions; help us, and give us food and water, or we too shall die before thine eyes. Seest thou not that our tongues are black for want of water? How can we talk, then?"

"Dead!" he gasped. "Impossible. She who never dies—dead, how can it be?" and then, perceiving, I think, that his face was being watched by the mutes who had come running up, he checked himself, and motioned to them to carry us to the camp, which they did.

Fortunately when we arrived some broth was boiling on the fire, and with this Billali fed us, for we were too weak to feed ourselves, thereby I firmly believe saving us from death by exhaustion. Then he bade the mutes wash the blood and grime from us with wet cloths, and after that we were laid down upon piles of aromatic grass, and instantly fell into the dead sleep of absolute exhaustion of mind and body.

28 ♦

Over the Mountain

THE NEXT THING I recollect is a feeling of the most dreadful stiffness, and a sort of vague idea passing through my half-awakened brain that I was a carpet that had just been beaten. I opened my eyes, and the first thing they fell on was the venerable countenance of our old friend Billali, who was seated by the side of the improvised bed upon which I was sleeping, and thoughtfully stroking his long beard. The sight of him at once brought back to my mind a recollection of all that we had recently passed through, which was accentuated by the vision of poor Leo lying opposite to me, his face knocked almost to a jelly, and his beautiful crowd of curls turned from yellow to white,[1] and I shut my eyes again and groaned.

"Thou hast slept long, my Baboon," said old Billali.

"How long, my father?" I asked.

"A round of the sun and a round of the moon, a day and a night hast thou slept, and the Lion also. See, he sleepeth yet."

"Blessed is sleep," I answered, "for it swallows up recollection."

"Tell me," he said, "what hath befallen ye, and what is this strange story of the death of *She* who dieth not. Bethink thee, my son: if this be true, then is thy danger

---

[1] Curiously enough, Leo's hair has lately been to some extent regaining its color—that is to say, it is now a yellowish gray—and I am not without hopes that it will in time come quite right.—L. H. H.

353

and the danger of the Lion very great—nay, almost is the
pot red wherewith ye shall be potted, and the stomachs of
those who shall eat ye are already hungry for the feast.
Knowest thou not that these Amahagger, my children,
these dwellers in the caves, hate ye? They hate ye as
strangers, they hate ye more because of their brethren
whom *She* put to the torment for your sake. Assuredly,
if once they learn that there is naught to fear from Hiya,
from the terrible One-who-must-be-obeyed, they will slay
ye by the pot. But let me hear thy tale, my poor Baboon."

Thus adjured, I set to work and told him—not everything, indeed, for I did not think it desirable to do so, but
sufficient for my purpose, which was to make him understand that *She* was really no more, having fallen into some
fire, and, as I put it—for the real thing would have been
incomprehensible to him—been burned up. I also told him
some of the horrors we had undergone in effecting our
escape, and these produced a great impression on him.
But I clearly saw that he did not believe in the report of
Ayesha's death. He believed indeed that we thought that
she was dead, but his explanation was that it had suited
her to disappear for a while. Once, he said, in his father's
time, she had done so for twelve years, and there was a
tradition in the country that many centuries back no one
had seen her for a whole generation, when she suddenly
reappeared, and destroyed a woman who had assumed the
position of queen. I said nothing to this, but only shook
my head sadly. Alas! I knew too well that Ayesha would
appear no more, or at any rate that Billali would never see
her again.

"And now," concluded Billali, "what wouldst thou do,
my Baboon?"

"Nay," I said, "I know not, my father. Can we not escape from this country?"

He shook his head.

"It is very difficult. By Kôr ye cannot pass, for ye would be seen, and as soon as those fierce ones found that ye were alone, well"—and he smiled significantly, and made a movement as though he were placing a hat on his head—"but there is a way over the cliff whereof I once spake to thee, where they drive the cattle out to pasture. Then beyond the pastures are three days' journey through the marshes, and after that I know not, but I have heard that seven days' journey from thence is a mighty river, which floweth to the black water. If ye could come thither, perchance ye might escape, but how can ye come thither?"

"Billali," I said, "once, thou knowest, I did save thy life. Now pay back the debt, my father, and save me mine and my friend's, the Lion's. It shall be a pleasant thing for thee to think of when thine hour comes, and something to set in the scale against the evildoing of thy days, if perchance thou hast done any evil. Also, if thou be right, and if *She* doth but hide herself, surely when she comes again she shall reward thee."

"My son the Baboon," answered the old man, "think not that I have an ungrateful heart. Well do I remember how thou didst rescue me when those dogs stood by to see me drown. Measure for measure will I give thee, and if thou canst be saved, surely I will save thee. Listen: by dawn tomorrow be prepared, for litters shall be here to bear ye away across the mountains, and through the marshes beyond. This will I do, saying that it is the word of *She* that it be done, and he who obeyeth not the word of *She* food is he for the hyenas. Then when ye have crossed the marshes, ye must strike with your own hands, so that perchance, if good fortune go with you, ye may live to come to that black water whereof ye told me. And now, see, the Lion wakes, and ye must eat the food I have made ready for you."

Leo's condition when once he was fairly aroused proved not to be so bad as might have been expected from his appearance, and we both of us managed to eat a hearty meal, which indeed we needed sadly enough. After this we limped down to the spring and bathed, and then came back and slept again till evening, when we once more ate enough for five. Billali was all that day, no doubt making arrangements about litters and bearers, for we were awakened in the middle of the night by the arrival of a considerable number of men in the little camp.

At dawn the old man himself appeared, and told us that he had by using *She*'s dreaded name, though with some difficulty, succeeded in getting the necessary men and two guides to conduct us across the swamps, and that he urged us to start at once, at the same time announcing his intention of accompanying us so as to protect us against treachery. I was much touched by this act of kindness on the part of that wily old barbarian towards two utterly defenseless strangers. A three—or in his case, for he would have to return, six—days' journey through those deadly swamps was no light undertaking for a man of his age, but he consented to do it cheerfully in order to promote our safety. It shows that even among those dreadful Amahagger—who are certainly with their gloom and their devilish and ferocious rites by far the most terrible savages that I ever heard of—there are people with kindly hearts. Of course self-interest may have had something to do with it. He may have thought that *She* would suddenly reappear and demand an account of us at his hands, but still, allowing for all deductions, it was a great deal more than we could expect under the circumstances, and I can only say that I shall for as long as I live cherish a most affectionate remembrance of my nominal parent, old Billali.

Accordingly, after swallowing some food, we started in the litters, feeling, so far as our bodies went, wonderfully like our old selves after our long rest and sleep. I must leave the condition of our minds to the imagination.

Then came a terrible pull up the cliff. Sometimes the ascent was natural, more often it was a zigzag roadway cut, no doubt, in the first instance by the old inhabitants of Kôr. The Amahagger say they drive their spare cattle over it once a year to pasture outside; all I know is that those cattle must be uncommonly active on their feet. Of course the litters were useless here, so we had to walk.

By midday, however, we reached the great flat top of that mighty wall of rock, and grand enough the view was from it, with the plain of Kôr, in the center of which we could clearly make out the pillared ruins of the Temple of Truth to the one side, and the boundless and melancholy marsh on the other. This wall of rock, which had no doubt once formed the lip of the crater, was about a mile and a half thick, and still covered with clinker. Nothing grew there, and the only thing to relieve our eyes were occasional pools of rainwater (for rain had lately fallen) wherever there was a little hollow. Over the flat crest of this mighty rampart we went, and then came the descent, which, if not so difficult a matter as the getting up, was still sufficiently breakneck, and took us till sunset. That night, however, we camped in safety upon the mighty slopes that rolled away to the marsh beneath.

On the following morning, about eleven o'clock, began our dreary journey across those awful seas of swamps which I have already described.

For three whole days, through stench and mire, and the all-prevailing flavor of fever, did our bearers struggle along, till at length we came to open rolling ground quite uncultivated, and mostly treeless, but covered with game of all sorts, which lies beyond that most desolate, and without guides utterly impracticable, district. And here on the following morning we bade farewell, not without some regret, to old Billali, who stroked his white beard and solemnly blessed us.

"Farewell, my son the Baboon," he said, "and farewell to thee too, O Lion. I can do no more to help you. But if ever ye come to your country, be advised, and venture no more into lands that ye know not, lest ye come back no more, but leave your white bones to mark the limit of your journeyings. Farewell once more; often shall I think of you, nor wilt thou forget me, my Baboon, for though thy face is ugly thy heart is true." And then he turned and went, and with him went the tall and sullen-looking bearers, and that was the last that we saw of the Amahagger. We watched them winding away with the empty litters like a procession bearing dead men from a battle, till the mists from the marsh gathered round them and hid them, and then, left utterly desolate in the vast wilderness, we turned and gazed around us and at each other.

Three weeks or so before four men had entered the marshes of Kôr, and now two of us were dead, and the other two had gone through adventures and experiences so strange and terrible that death himself hath not a more fearful countenance. Three weeks—and only three weeks! Truly time should be measured by events, and not by the lapse of hours. It seemed like thirty years since we saw the last of our whaleboat.

"We must strike out for the Zambesi, Leo," I said, "but God knows if we shall ever get there."

Leo nodded—he had become very silent of late—and we started with nothing but the clothes we stood in, a compass, our revolvers and express rifles, and about two hundred rounds of ammunition, and so ended the history of our visit to the ancient ruins of mighty and imperial Kôr.

As for the adventures that subsequently befell us, strange and varied as they were, I have, after deliberation, determined not to record them here. In these pages I have only tried to give a short and clear account of an occurrence which I believe to be unprecedented, and this I have done, not with a view to immediate publication, but merely to put on paper while they are yet fresh in our memories the details of our journey and its result, which will, I believe, prove interesting to the world if ever we determine to make them public. This, as at present advised, we do not intend should be done during our joint lives.

For the rest, it is of no public interest, resembling as it does the experience of more than one Central African traveler. Suffice it to say that we did, after incredible hardships and privations, reach the Zambesi, which proved to be about a hundred and seventy miles south of where Billali left us. There we were for six months imprisoned by a savage tribe, who believed us to be supernatural beings, chiefly on account of Leo's youthful face and snow-white hair. From these people we ultimately escaped, and, crossing the Zambesi, wandered off southwards, where, when on the point of starvation, we were sufficiently fortunate to fall in with a half-caste Portuguese elephant hunter who had followed a troop of elephants farther inland than he had ever been before. This man treated us most hospitably, and ultimately through his assistance we, after innumerable sufferings and adventures, reached Delagoa Bay, more than eighteen months from the time when we emerged from the marshes of Kôr, and the very next day managed to catch one of the steamboats that run round the Cape to England. Our journey home was a prosperous one, and we set our foot on the quay at Southampton exactly two years from the date of our departure upon our wild and seemingly ridiculous quest, and I now write these last words with Leo leaning over my shoulder in my old room in my college, the very same into which some two-and-twenty years ago my poor friend Vincey came stumbling on the memorable night of his death, bearing the iron chest with him.

And that is the end of this history so far as it concerns science and the outside world. What its end will be as regards Leo and myself is more than I can guess at. But we feel that is not reached yet. A story that began more than two thousand years ago may stretch a long way into the dim and distant future.

Is Leo really a reincarnation of the ancient Kallikrates of whom the inscription tells? Or was Ayesha deceived by some strange hereditary resemblance? The reader must form his own opinion on this as on many other matters. I have mine, which is that she made no such mistake.

Often I sit alone at night, staring with the eyes of the mind into the blackness of unborn time, and wondering in what shape and form the great drama will be finally developed, and where the scene of its next act will be laid. And when that *final* development ultimately occurs, as I have no doubt it must and will occur, in obedience to a fate that never swerves and a purpose that cannot be altered, what will be the part played therein by that beautiful Egyptian Amenartas, the princess of the royal race of the Pharaohs, for the love of whom the priest Kallikrates broke his vows to Isis, and, pursued by the inexorable vengeance of the outraged goddess, fled down the coast of Libya to meet his doom at Kôr?

KING ◆

SOLOMON'S

MINES

Introduction

Now THAT this book is printed, and about to be given to the world, the sense of its shortcomings, both in style and contents, weighs very heavily upon me. As regards the latter, I can only say that it does not pretend to be a full account of everything we did and saw. There are many things connected with our journey into Kukuanaland which I should have liked to dwell upon at length, and which have, as it is, been scarcely alluded to. Among these are the curious legends which I collected about the chain armor that saved us from destruction in the great battle of Loo, and also about the "silent ones" or colossi at the mouth of the stalactite cave. Again, if I had given way to my own impulses I should have liked to go into the differences, some of which are to my mind very suggestive, between the Zulu and Kukuana dialects. Also, a few pages might profitably have been given up to the consideration of the indigenous flora and fauna of Kukuanaland.[1] Then there remains the most interesting subject—which, as it is, has been only incidentally alluded to—of the magnificent system of military organization in force in that country, which is, in my opinion, much superior to that inaugurated by Chaka in Zululand, inasmuch as it permits of even more rapid mobilization, and does not necessitate the employment of the pernicious system of forced celibacy. And,

[1] I discovered eight varieties of antelope with which I was previously totally unacquainted, and many new species of plants, for the most part of the bulbous tribe.—A. Q.

3

lastly, I have scarcely touched on the domestic and family customs of the Kukuanas, many of which are exceedingly quaint, or on their proficiency in the art of smelting and welding metals. This last they carry to considerable perfection, of which a good example is to be seen in their "tollas," or heavy throwing knives, the backs of these knives being made of hammered iron, and the edges of beautiful steel welded with great skill onto the iron backs. The fact of the matter is that I thought (and so did Sir Henry Curtis and Captain Good) that the best plan would be to tell the story in a plain, straightforward manner, and leave these matters to be dealt with subsequently in whatever way may ultimately appear to be desirable. In the meanwhile I shall, of course, be delighted to give any information in my power to anybody interested in such things.

And now it only remains for me to offer my apologies for my blunt way of writing. I can only say in excuse for it that I am more accustomed to handle a rifle than a pen, and cannot make any pretense to the grand literary flights and flourishes which I see in novels—for I sometimes like to read a novel. I suppose they—the flights and flourishes—are desirable, and I regret not being able to supply them; but at the same time I cannot help thinking that simple things are always the most impressive, and books are easier to understand when they are written in plain language, though I have perhaps no right to set up an opinion on such a matter. "A sharp spear," runs the Kukuana saying, "needs no polish," and on the same principle I venture to hope that a true story, however strange it may be, does not require to be decked out in fine words.

ALLAN QUATERMAIN

I Meet Sir Henry Curtis

It is a curious thing that at my age—fifty-five last birth-day—I should find myself taking up a pen to try and write a history. I wonder what sort of a history it will be when I have done it, if I ever come to the end of the trip! I have done a good many things in my life, which seems a long one to me, owing to my having begun so young, per-haps. At an age when other boys are at school I was earn-ing my living as a trader in the old Colony. I have been trading, hunting, fighting, or mining ever since. And yet it is only eight months ago that I made my pile. It is a big pile now I have got it—I don't yet know how big—but I don't think I would go through the last fifteen or sixteen months again for it; no, not if I knew that I should come out safe at the end, pile and all. But then, I am a timid man, and don't like violence, and am pretty sick of adven-ture. I wonder why I am going to write this book; it is not in my line. I am not a literary man, though very devoted to the Old Testament and also to the *Ingoldsby Legends.* Let me try and set down my reasons, just to see if I have any.

First reason: Because Sir Henry Curtis and Captain John Good asked me to.

Second reason: Because I am laid up here at Durban with the pain and trouble in my left leg. Ever since that confounded lion got hold of me I have been liable to it, and its being rather bad just now makes me limp more than ever. There must be some poison in a lion's teeth, otherwise how is it that when your wounds are healed they break out again, generally, mark you, at the same time of year that you got your mauling? It is a hard thing, when one has shot sixty-five lions, as I have in the course of my life, that the sixty-sixth should chew your leg like a quid of tobacco. It breaks the routine of the thing, and, putting other considerations aside, I am an orderly man and don't like that. This is by the way.

Third reason: Because I want my boy Harry, who is over there at the hospital in London studying to become a doctor, to have something to amuse him and keep him out of mischief for a week or so. Hospital work must sometimes pall and get rather dull, for even of cutting up dead bodies there must come satiety, and as this history won't be dull, whatever else it may be, it may put a little life into things for a day or two while he is reading it.

Fourth reason and last: Because I am going to tell the strangest story that I know of. It may seem a queer thing to say, especially considering that there is no woman in it—except Foulata. Stop, though, there is Gagaoola, if she was a woman and not a fiend. But she was a hundred at least, and therefore not marriageable, so I don't count her. At any rate, I can safely say that there is not a *petticoat* in the whole history. Well, I had better come to the yoke. It's a stiff place, and I feel as though I were bogged up to the axle. But "sutjes, sutjes," as the Boers say (I'm sure I don't know how they spell it), softly does it. A strong team will come through at last, that is if they ain't too poor. You will never do anything with poor oxen. Now, to begin.

I, Allan Quatermain, of Durban, Natal, Gentleman, make oath and say— That's how I began my deposition before the magistrate about poor Khiva's and Ventvögel's sad deaths; but somehow it doesn't seem quite the right way to begin a book. And, besides, am I a gentleman? What is a gentleman? I don't quite know, and yet I have had to do with niggers—no, I'll scratch that word "niggers" out, for I don't like it— I've known natives who *are*, and so you'll say, Harry, my boy, before you're done with this tale, and I have known mean whites with lots of money and fresh out from home, too, who *ain't*. Well, at any rate I was born a gentleman, though I've been nothing but a poor traveling trader and hunter all my life. Whether I have remained so I know not; you must judge of that. Heaven knows I've tried. I've killed many men in my time, but I have never slain wantonly or stained my hand in innocent blood, only in self-defense. The Almighty gave us our lives, and I suppose he meant us to defend them; at least I have always acted on that, and I hope it won't be brought up against me when my clock strikes. There, there; it is a cruel and a wicked world, and, for a timid man, I have been mixed up in a deal of slaughter. I can't tell the rights of it, but at any rate I have never stolen, though I once cheated a Kaffir out of a herd of cattle. But then, he had done me a dirty turn, and it has troubled me ever since into the bargain.

Well, it's eighteen months or so ago since I first met Sir Henry Curtis and Captain Good, and it was in this way. I had been up elephant hunting beyond Bamangwato, and had had bad luck. Everything went wrong that trip, and to top up with I got the fever badly. So soon as I was well enough I trekked down to the diamond fields, sold such ivory as I had, and also my wagon and oxen, discharged my hunters, and took the post cart to the Cape. After spending a week in Cape Town, finding that they overcharged me at the hotel, and having seen everything there was to see, including the botanical gardens, which seem to me likely to confer a great benefit on the country, and the new Houses of Parliament, which I expect will do nothing of the sort, I determined to go on back to Natal by the *Dunkeld*, then lying in the docks waiting for the *Edinburgh Castle* due in from England. I took my berth and went aboard, and that afternoon the Natal passengers from the *Edinburgh Castle* transhipped, and we weighed anchor and put out to sea.

Among the passengers who came on board there were two who excited my curiosity. One, a man of about thirty, was one of the biggest-chested and longest-armed men I ever saw. He had yellow hair, a big yellow beard, clear-cut features, and large gray eyes set deep into his head. I never saw a finer-looking man, and somehow he reminded me of an ancient Dane. Not that I know much of ancient Danes, though I remember a modern Dane who did me out of ten pounds; but I remember once seeing a picture of some of those gentry, who, I take it, were a kind of white Zulus. They were drinking out of big horns, and their long hair hung down their backs, and as I looked at my friend standing there by the companion ladder, I thought that if he only let his hair grow a bit, put one of those chain shirts onto those great shoulders of his, and gave him a battle-ax and a horn mug, he might have sat as a model for that picture. And, by the way, it is a curious thing, and just shows how the blood will show out, I found out afterwards that Sir Henry Curtis, for that was the big man's name, was of Danish blood.[1] He also reminded me strongly of somebody else, but at that time I could not remember who it was.

The other man, who stood talking to Sir Henry, was of

[1] Mr. Quatermain's ideas about ancient Danes seem to be rather confused; we have always understood that they were dark-haired people. Probably he was thinking of Saxons.—EDITOR.

quite a different cut. I suspected at once that he was a naval officer. I don't know why, but it is difficult to mistake a navy man. I have gone on shooting trips with several of them in the course of my life, and they have always been just the best and bravest and nicest fellows I ever met, though given to the use of profane language.

I asked, a page or two back, what is a gentleman? I'll answer it now: a Royal Navy officer is, in a general sort of a way, though, of course, there may be a black sheep among them here and there. I fancy it is just the wide sea and the breath of God's winds that washes their hearts and blows the bitterness out of their minds and makes them what men ought to be. Well, to return, I was right again; I found out that he *was* a naval officer, a lieutenant of thirty-one, who, after seventeen years' service, had been turned out of her majesty's employ with the barren honor of a commander's rank, because it was impossible that he should be promoted. This is what people who serve the queen have to expect: to be shot out into the cold world to find a living just when they are beginning to really understand their work, and to get to the prime of life. Well, I suppose they don't mind it, but for my part I had rather earn my bread as a hunter. One's half-pence are as scarce, perhaps, but you don't get so many kicks. His name, I found out—by referring to the passengers' list—was Good—Captain John Good. He was broad, of medium height, dark, stout, and rather a curious man to look at. He was so very neat and so very clean shaved, and he always wore an eyeglass in his right eye. It seemed to grow there, for it had no string, and he never took it out except to wipe it. At first I thought he used to sleep in it, but I afterwards found that this was a mistake. He put it in his trousers pocket when he went to bed, together with his false teeth, of which he had two beautiful sets that have often, my own being none of the best, caused me to break the Tenth Commandment. But I am anticipating.

Soon after we had got under way evening closed in, and brought with it very dirty weather. A keen breeze sprang up off land, and a kind of aggravated Scotch mist soon drove everybody from the deck. And as for that *Dunkeld*, she is a flat-bottomed punt, and, going up light as she was, she rolled very heavily. It almost seemed as though she would go right over, but she never did. It was quite impossible to walk about, so I stood near the engines, where it was warm, and amused myself with watching the pendulum, which was fixed opposite to me, swinging slowly backward and forward as the vessel rolled, and marking the angle she touched at each lurch.

"That pendulum's wrong; it is not properly weighted," suddenly said a voice at my shoulder somewhat testily. Looking round I saw the naval officer I had noticed when the passengers came aboard.

"Indeed; now what makes you think so?" I asked.

"Think so. I don't think at all. Why there"—as she righted herself after a roll—"if the ship had really rolled to the degree that thing pointed to then she would never have rolled again, that's all. But it is just like these merchant skippers, they always are so confoundedly careless."

Just then the dinner bell rang, and I was not sorry, for it is a dreadful thing to have to listen to an officer of the Royal Navy when he gets onto that subject. I know only one worse thing, and that is to hear a merchant skipper express his candid opinion of officers of the Royal Navy.

Captain Good and I went down to dinner together, and there we found Sir Henry Curtis already seated. He and Captain Good sat together, and I sat opposite to them.

The captain and I soon got into talk about shooting and what not, he asking me many questions, and I answering as well as I could. Presently he got onto elephants.

"Ah, sir," called out somebody who was sitting near me, "you've got to the right man for that; hunter Quatermain should be able to tell you about elephants if anybody can."

Sir Henry, who had been sitting quite quiet listening to our talk, started visibly.

"Excuse me, sir," he said, leaning forward across the table, and speaking in a low, deep voice, a very suitable voice, it seemed to me, to come out of those great lungs. "Excuse me, sir, but is your name Allan Quatermain?"

I said it was.

The big man made no further remark, but I heard him mutter, "Fortunate," into his beard.

Presently dinner came to an end, and as we were leaving the saloon Sir Henry came up and asked me if I would come into his cabin and smoke a pipe. I accepted, and he led the way to the *Dunkeld* deck cabin, and a very good cabin it was. It had been two cabins, but when Sir Garnet, or one of those big swells, went down the coast in the *Dunkeld* they had knocked away the partition and never put it up again. There was a sofa in the cabin, and a little table in front of it. Sir Henry sent the steward for a bottle of whisky, and the three of us sat down and lit our pipes.

"Mr. Quatermain," said Sir Henry Curtis, when the steward had brought the whisky and lit the lamp, "the year before last, about this time, you were, I believe, at a place called Bamangwato, to the north of the Transvaal."

"I was," I answered, rather surprised that this gentleman should be so well acquainted with my movements, which were not, so far as I was aware, considered of general interest.

"You were trading there, were you not?" put in Captain Good in his quick way.

"I was. I took up a wagonload of goods and made a camp outside the settlement, and stopped till I had sold them."

Sir Henry was sitting opposite to me in a Madeira chair, his arms leaning on the table. He now looked up, fixing his large gray eyes full upon my face. There was a curious anxiety in them, I thought.

"Did you happen to meet a man called Neville there?"

"Oh, yes; he outspanned alongside of me for a fortnight, to rest his oxen before going on to the interior. I had a letter from a lawyer, a few months back, asking me if I knew what had become of him, which I answered to the best of my ability at the time."

"Yes," said Sir Henry, "your letter was forwarded to me. You said in it that the gentleman called Neville left Bamangwato in the beginning of May, in a wagon, with a driver, a voorlooper, and a Kaffir hunter called Jim, announcing his intention of trekking, if possible, as far as Inyati, the extreme trading post in the Matabele country, where he would sell his wagon and proceed on foot. You also said that he did sell his wagon, for, six months afterwards, you saw the wagon in the possession of a Portuguese trader, who told you that he had bought it at Inyati from a white man whose name he had forgotten, and that the white man, with a native servant, had started off for the interior on a shooting trip, he believed."

"Yes."

Then came a pause.

"Mr. Quatermain," said Sir Henry suddenly, "I suppose you know or can guess nothing more of the reasons of my —of Mr. Neville's journey to the northward, or as to what point that journey was directed?"

"I heard something," I answered, and stopped. The subject was one which I did not dare to discuss.

Sir Henry and Captain Good looked at each other, and Captain Good nodded.

"Mr. Quatermain," said the former, "I am going to tell you a story, and ask your advice, and perhaps your assistance. The agent who forwarded me your letter told me that I might implicitly rely upon it, as you were," he said, "well known and universally respected in Natal, and especially noted for your discretion."

I bowed, and drank some whisky-and-water to hide my confusion, for I am a modest man; and Sir Henry went on.

"Mr. Neville was my brother."

"Oh," I said, starting; for now I knew who Sir Henry had reminded me of when I first saw him. His brother was a much smaller man and had a dark beard, but, now I thought of it, he possessed eyes of the same shade of gray and with the same keen look in them, and the features, too, were not unlike.

"He was," went on Sir Henry, "my only and younger brother, and till five years ago I do not suppose we were ever a month away from each other. But just about five years ago a misfortune befell us, as sometimes does happen in families. We had quarreled bitterly, and I behaved very unjustly to my brother in my anger." Here Captain Good nodded his head vigorously to himself. The ship gave a big roll just then, so that the looking glass, which was fixed opposite us to starboard, was for a moment nearly over our heads, and as I was sitting with my hands in my pockets and staring upward, I could see him nodding like anything.

"As I dare say you know," went on Sir Henry, "if a man dies intestate, and has no property but land—real property it is called in England—it all descends to his eldest son. It so happened that just at the time when we quarreled our father died intestate. He had put off making his will until it was too late. The result was that my brother, who had not been brought up to any profession, was left without a penny. Of course it would have been my duty to provide for him, but at the time the quarrel between us was so bitter that I did not—to my shame I say it"—and he sighed deeply—"offer to do anything. It was not that I grudged him anything, but I waited for him to make advances, and he made none. I am sorry to trouble you with all this, Mr. Quatermain, but I must, to make things clear; eh, Good?"

"Quite so, quite so," said the captain. "Mr. Quatermain will, I am sure, keep this history to himself."

"Of course," said I, for I rather pride myself on my discretion.

"Well," went on Sir Henry, "my brother had a few hundred pounds to his account at the time, and without saying anything to me he drew out this paltry sum, and, having adopted the name of Neville, started off for South Africa in the wild hope of making a fortune. This I heard afterwards. Some three years passed, and I heard nothing of my brother, though I wrote several times. Doubtless the letters never reached him. But as time went on I grew more and more troubled about him. I found out, Mr. Quatermain, that blood is thicker than water."

"That's true," said I, thinking of my boy Harry.

"I found out, Mr. Quatermain, that I would have given half my fortune to know that my brother George, the only relation I have, was safe and well, and that I should see him again."

"But you never did, Curtis," jerked out Captain Good, glancing at the big man's face.

"Well, Mr. Quatermain, as time went on I became more

and more anxious to find out if my brother was alive or dead, and, if alive, to get him home again. I set inquiries on foot, and your letter was one of the results. So far as it went it was satisfactory, for it showed that till lately George was alive; but it did not go far enough. So, to cut a long story short, I made up my mind to come out and look for him myself, and Captain Good was so kind as to come with me."

"Yes," said the captain; "nothing else to do, you see. Turned out by my lords of the admiralty to starve on half pay. And now, perhaps, sir, you will tell us what you know or have heard of the gentleman called Neville."

2 ♦

The Legend of Solomon's Mines

"WHAT WAS it that you heard about my brother's journey at Bamangwato?" said Sir Henry, as I paused to fill my pipe before answering Captain Good.

"I heard this," I answered, "and I have never mentioned it to a soul till today. I heard that he was starting for Solomon's Mines."

"Solomon's Mines!" ejaculated both my hearers at once. "Where are they?"

"I don't know," I said; "I know where they are said to be. I once saw the peaks of the mountains that border them, but there was a hundred and thirty miles of desert between me and them, and I am not aware that any white man ever got across it, save one. But perhaps the best thing I can do is tell you the legend of Solomon's Mines as I know it, you passing your word not to reveal anything I tell you without my permission. Do you agree to that? I have my reasons for asking it."

Sir Henry nodded, and Captain Good replied, "Certainly, certainly."

"Well," I began, "as you may guess, in a general way elephant hunters are a rough set of men, and don't trouble themselves with much beyond the facts of life and the ways of Kaffirs. But here and there you meet a man who takes the trouble to collect traditions from the natives, and tries

16

to make out a little piece of the history of this dark land. It was such a man as this who first told me the legend of Solomon's Mines, now a matter of nearly thirty years ago. It was when I was on my first elephant hunt in the Matabele country. His name was Evans, and he was killed next year, poor fellow, by a wounded buffalo, and lies buried near the Zambesi Falls. I was telling Evans one night, I remember, of some wonderful workings I had found while hunting koodoo and eland in what is now the Lydenburg district of the Transvaal. I see they have come across these workings again lately in prospecting for gold, but I knew of them years ago. There is a great wide wagon road cut out of the solid rock, and leading to the mouth of the working or gallery. Inside the mouth of this gallery are stacks of gold quartz piled up ready for crushing, which shows that the workers, whoever they were, must have left in a hurry, and about twenty paces in the gallery is built across, and a beautiful bit of masonry it is.

"'Ay,' said Evans, 'but I will tell you a queerer thing than that,' and he went on to tell me how he had found in the far interior a ruined city, which he believed to be the Ophir of the Bible—and, by the way, other more learned men have said the same long since poor Evans's time. I was, I remember, listening open-eared to all these wonders, for I was young at the time, and this story of an ancient civilization, and of the treasure which those old Jewish or Phoenician adventurers used to extract from a country long since lapsed into the darkest barbarism, took a great hold upon my imagination, when suddenly he said to me, 'Lad, did you hear of the Suliman Mountains up to the northwest of the Mashukulumbwe country?' I told him I never had. 'Ah, well,' he said, 'that was where Solomon really had his mines—his diamond mines, I mean.'

" 'How do you know that?' I asked.

" 'Know it? Why, what is "Suliman" but a corruption of Solomon?[1] And, besides, an old isanusi [witch doctor] up in the Manica country told me all about it. She said that the people who lived across those mountains were a branch of the Zulus, speaking a dialect of Zulu, but finer and bigger men even; that there lived among them great wizards, who had learned their art from white men when "all the world was dark," and who had the secret of a wonderful mine of "bright stones." '

"Well, I laughed at this story at the time, though it interested me, for the diamond fields were not discovered then, and poor Evans went off and got killed, and for twenty years I never thought any more of the matter. But just twenty years afterwards—and that is a long time, gentlemen; an elephant hunter does not often live for twenty years at his business—I heard something more definite about Suliman's Mountains and the country which lies beyond them. I was up beyond the Manica country at a place called Sitanda's Kraal, and a miserable place it was, for one could get nothing to eat there, and there was but little game about. I had an attack of fever, and was in a bad way generally, when one day a Portugee arrived with a single companion—a half-breed. Now I know your Delagoa Portugee well. There is no greater devil unhung, in a general way, battening as he does upon human agony and flesh in the shape of slaves. But this was quite a different type of man to the low fellows I had been accustomed to meet; he reminded me more of the polite dons I have read about. He was tall and thin, with large dark eyes and curling gray mustache. We talked together a little, for he could speak broken English, and I understood a little Portugee, and he

[1] Suliman is the Arabic form of Solomon.—EDITOR.

told me that his name was José Silvestre, and that he had a place near Delagoa Bay; and when he went on next day, with his half-breed companion, he said, 'Good-by,' taking off his hat quite in the old style. 'Good-by, señor,' he said; 'if ever we meet again I shall be the richest man in the world, and I will remember you.' I laughed a little—I was too weak to laugh much—and watched him strike out for the great desert to the west, wondering if he was mad, or what he thought he was going to find there.

"A week passed, and I got the better of my fever. One evening I was sitting on the ground in front of the little tent I had with me, chewing the last leg of a miserable fowl I had bought from a native for a bit of cloth worth twenty fowls, and staring at the hot, red sun sinking down into the desert, when suddenly I saw a figure, apparently that of a European, for it wore a coat, on the slope of the rising ground opposite to me, about three hundred yards away. The figure crept along on its hands and knees, then it got up and staggered along a few yards on its legs, only to fall and crawl along again. Seeing that it must be somebody in distress, I sent one of my hunters to help him, and presently he arrived, and who do you suppose it turned out to be?"

"José Silvestre, of course," said Captain Good.

"Yes, José Silvestre, or rather his skeleton and a little skin. His face was bright yellow with bilious fever, and his large, dark eyes stood nearly out of his head, for all his flesh had gone. There was nothing but yellow, parchment-like skin, white hair, and the gaunt bones sticking up beneath.

"'Water! For the sake of Christ, water!' he moaned. I saw that his lips were cracked, and his tongue, which protruded between them, was swollen and blackish.

"I gave him water with a little milk in it, and he drank

it in great gulps, two quarts or more, without stopping. I would not let him have any more. Then the fever took him again, and he fell down and began to rave about Suliman's Mountains, and the diamonds, and the desert. I took him into the tent and did what I could for him, which was little enough; but I saw how it must end. About eleven o'clock he got quieter, and I lay down for a little rest and went to sleep. At dawn I woke again, and saw him in the half light sitting up, a strange, gaunt form, and gazing out towards the desert. Presently the first ray of the sun shot right across the wide plain before us till it reached the far-away crest of one of the tallest of the Suliman Mountains, more than a hundred miles away.

" 'There it is!' cried the dying man in Portuguese, stretching out his long, thin arm, 'but I shall never reach it, never. No one will ever reach it!'

"Suddenly he paused, and seemed to take a resolution. 'Friend.' he said, turning towards me, 'are you there? My eyes grow dark.'

" 'Yes,' I said; 'yes, lie down now, and rest.'

" 'Ay,' he answered, 'I shall rest soon; I have time to rest —all eternity. Listen, I am dying! You have been good to me. I will give you the paper. Perhaps you will get there if you can live through the desert, which has killed my poor servant and me.'

"Then he groped in his shirt and brought out what I thought was a Boer tobacco pouch of the skin of the Swart-vet-pens [sable antelope]. It was fastened with a little strip of hide, what we call a rimpi, and this he tried to untie, but could not. He handed it to me. 'Untie it,' he said. I did so, and extracted a bit of torn yellow linen, on which something was written in rusty letters. Inside was a paper.

"Then he went on feebly, for he was growing weak: 'The

paper has it all, that is on the rag. It took me years to read. Listen: my ancestor, a political refugee from Lisbon and one of the first Portuguese who landed on these shores, wrote that when he was dying on those mountains which no white foot ever pressed before or since. His name was José da Silvestra, and he lived three hundred years ago. His slave, who waited for him on this side the mountains, found him dead, and brought the writing home to Delagoa. It has been in the family ever since, but none have cared to read it till at last I did. And I have lost my life over it, but another may succeed, and become the richest man in the world—the richest man in the world. Only give it to no one; go yourself!' Then he began to wander again, and in an hour it was all over.

"God rest him! He died very quietly, and I buried him deep, with big boulders on his breast; so I do not think that the jackals can have dug him up. And then I came away."

"Ay, but the document," said Sir Henry, in a tone of deep interest.

"Yes, the document; what was in it?" added the captain.

"Well, gentlemen, if you like I will tell you. I have never showed it to anybody yet except my dear wife, who is dead, and she thought it was all nonsense, and a drunken old Portuguese trader who translated it for me, and had forgotten all about it next morning. The original rag is at my home in Durban, together with poor Don José's translation, but I have the English rendering in my pocketbook, and a facsimile of the map, if it can be called a map. Here it is."

I, José da Silvestra, who am now dying of hunger in the little cave where no snow is on the north side of the nipple of the southernmost of the two mountains I have named Sheba's Breasts, write this in the year 1590 with a cleft bone upon a remnant of my raiment, my blood being the

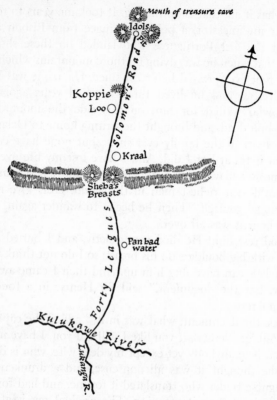

ink. If my slave should find it when he comes, and should bring it to Delagoa, let my friend [name illegible] bring the matter to the knowledge of the king, that he may send an army which, if they live through the desert and the mountains, and can overcome the brave Kukuanes and their devilish arts, to which end many priests should be brought, will make him the richest king since Solomon. With my own eyes have I seen the countless diamonds stored in Solomon's treasure chamber behind the white

Death; but through the treachery of Gagool the witch-finder I might bring nought away, scarcely my life. Let him who comes follow the map, and climb the snow of Sheba's left breast till he comes to the nipple, on the north side of which is the great road Solomon made, from whence three days' journey to the King's Place. Let him kill Gagool. Pray for my soul. Farewell.

JOSÉ DA SILVESTRA[2]

When I had finished reading the above and shown the copy of the map, drawn by the dying hand of the old don with his blood for ink, there followed a silence of astonishment.

"Well," said Captain Good, "I have been round the world twice, and put in at most ports, but may I be hung if I ever heard a yarn like that out of a storybook, or in it either, for the matter of that."

"It's a queer story, Mr. Quatermain," said Sir Henry. "I suppose you are not hoaxing us? It is, I know, sometimes thought allowable to take a greenhorn in."

"If you think that, Sir Henry," I said, much put out, and pocketing my paper, for I do not like to be thought one of

[2] Eu José da Silvestra que estou morrendo de fome ná pequena cova onde não ha neve ao lado norte do bico mais ao sul das duas montanhas que chamei seio de Sheba; escrevo isto no anno 1590; escrevo isto com um pedaço d' ôsso n' um farrapo de minha roupa e com sangue meu por tinta; se o meu escravo dér com isto quando venha ao levar para Lourenzo Marquez, que o meu amigo [———] leve a cousa ao conhecimento d' El Rei, para que possa mandar um exercito que, se desfiler pelo deserto e pelas montanhas e mesmo sobrepujar os bravos Kukuanes e suas artes diabolicas, pelo que se deviam trazer muitos padres Fara o Rei mais rico depois de Salomão. Com meus proprios olhos vé os di amantes sem conto guardados nas camaras do thesouro de Salomão a traz da morte branca, mas pela traição de Gagoal a feiticeira achadora, nada poderia levar, e apenas a minha vida. Quem vier siga o mappa e trepe pela neve de Sheba peito à esquerda até chegar ao bico, do lado norte do qual está a grande estrada do Salomão por elle feita, donde ha tres dias de journada até ao Palacio do Rei. Mate Gagoal. Reze por minha alma. Adeos.

JOSÉ DA SILVESTRA

those silly fellows who consider it witty to tell lies, and who are forever boasting to newcomers of extraordinary hunting adventures which never happened, "why there is an end of the matter," and I rose to go.

Sir Henry laid his large hand upon my shoulder. "Sit down, Mr. Quatermain," he said, "I beg your pardon; I see very well you do not wish to deceive us, but the story sounded so extraordinary that I could hardly believe it."

"You shall see the original map and writing when we reach Durban," I said, somewhat mollified; for really, when I came to consider the matter, it was scarcely wonderful that he should doubt my good faith. "But I have not told you about your brother. I knew the man Jim who was with him. He was a Bechuana by birth, a good hunter, and, for a native, a very clever man. The morning Mr. Neville was starting, I saw Jim standing by my wagon and cutting up tobacco on the disselboom.

" 'Jim,' said I, 'where are you off to this trip? Is it elephants?'

" 'No, Baas,' he answered, 'we are after something worth more than ivory.'

" 'And what might that be?' I said; for I was curious. 'Is it gold?'

" 'No, Baas, something worth more than gold,' and he grinned.

"I did not ask any more questions, for I did not like to lower my dignity by seeming curious, but I was puzzled. Presently Jim finished cutting his tobacco.

" 'Baas,' said he.

"I took no notice.

" 'Baas,' said he again.

" 'Eh, boy, what is it?' said I.

" 'Baas, we are going after diamonds.'

" 'Diamonds! Why, then, you are going in the wrong direction; you should head for the fields.'

" 'Baas, have you ever heard of Suliman's Berg?' (Solomon's Mountains.)

" 'Ay!'

" 'Have you ever heard of the diamonds there?'

" 'I have heard a foolish story, Jim.'

" 'It is no story, Baas. I once knew a woman who came from there, and got to Natal with her child. She told me; she is dead now.'

" 'Your master will feed the *Assvögels* [vultures], Jim, if he tries to reach Suliman's country, and so will you, if they can get any pickings off your worthless old carcass,' said I.

"He grinned. 'Mayhap, Baas. Man must die; I'd rather like to try a new country myself; the elephants are getting worked out about here.'

" 'Ah, my boy,' I said, 'you wait till the "pale old man" [death] gets a grip of your yellow throat, and then we'll hear what sort of a tune you sing.'

"Half an hour after that I saw Neville's wagon move off. Presently Jim came running back. 'Good-by, Baas,' he said. 'I didn't like to start without bidding you good-by, for I dare say you are right, and we shall never come back again.'

" 'Is your master really going to Suliman's Berg, Jim, or are you lying?'

" 'No,' says he; 'he is going. He told me he was bound to make his fortune somehow, or try to; so he might as well try the diamonds.'

" 'Oh!' said I. 'Wait a bit, Jim; you will take a note to your master, Jim, and promise not to give it to him until you reach Inyati?' (which was some hundred miles off).

" 'Yes,' said he.

"So I took a scrap of paper and wrote on it, 'Let him who comes . . . climb the snow of Sheba's left breast till he comes to the nipples, on the north side of which is the great road Solomon made.'

" 'Now, Jim,' I said, 'when you give this to your master, tell him he had better follow the advice implicitly. You are not to give it to him now, because I don't want him back asking me questions which I won't answer. Now be off, you idle fellow, the wagon is nearly out of sight.'

"Jim took the note and went, and that is all I know about your brother, Sir Henry; but I am much afraid—"

"Mr. Quatermain," said Sir Henry, "I am going to look for my brother; I am going to trace him to Suliman's Mountains, and over them, if necessary, until I find him, or until I know that he is dead. Will you come with me?"

I am, as I think I have said, a cautious man, indeed, a timid one, and I shrank from such an idea. It seemed to me that to start on such a journey would be to go to certain death, and, putting other things aside, as I had a son to support, I could not afford to die just then.

"No, thank you, Sir Henry, I think I had rather not," I answered. "I am too old for wild-goose chases of that sort, and we should only end up like my poor friend Silvestre. I have a son dependent on me, so cannot afford to risk my life."

Both Sir Henry and Captain Good looked very disappointed.

"Mr. Quatermain," said the former, "I am well off, and I am bent upon this business. You may put the remuneration for your services at whatever figure you like, in reason, and it shall be paid over to you before we start. Moreover, I will, before we start, arrange that in the event of anything

happening to us or to you, your son shall be suitably provided for. You will see from this how necessary I think
your presence. Also, if by any chance we should reach this
place, and find diamonds, they shall belong to you and
Good equally. I do not want them. But of course the
chance is as good as nothing, though the same thing would
apply to any ivory we might get. You may pretty well make
your own terms with me, Mr. Quatermain; of course I
shall pay all expenses."

"Sir Henry," said I, "this is the most liberal offer I ever
had, and one not to be sneezed at by a poor hunter and
trader. But the job is the biggest I ever came across, and
I must take time to think it over. I will give you my answer
before we get to Durban."

"Very good," answered Sir Henry, and then I said good
night and turned in, and dreamed about poor, long-dead
Silvestre and the diamonds.

3 ♦

Umbopa Enters Our Service

It takes from four to five days, according to the vessel and the state of the weather, to run up from the Cape to Durban. Sometimes, if the landing is bad at East London, where they have not yet got that wonderful harbor they talk so much of and sink such a mint of money in, one is delayed for twenty-four hours before the cargo boats can get out to take the goods off. But on this occasion we had not to wait at all, for there were no breakers on the bar to speak of, and the tugs came out at once with their long strings of ugly, flat-bottomed boats, into which the goods were bundled with a crash. It did not matter what they were, over they went, slap-bang! Whether they were china or woolen goods they met with the same treatment. I saw one case containing four dozen bottles of champagne smashed all to bits, and there was the champagne fizzing and boiling about in the bottom of the dirty cargo boat. It was a wicked waste, and so evidently the Kaffirs in the boat thought, for they found a couple of unbroken bottles, and knocking the tops off drank the contents. But they had not allowed for the expansion caused by the fizz in the wine, and feeling themselves swelling, rolled about in the bottom of the boat, calling out that the good liquor was "tagati" (bewitched). I spoke to them from the vessel, and told them that it was the white man's strongest medicine, and that they were as good as dead men. They went onto the shore in a very great fright, and I do not think they will touch champagne again.

Well, all the time we were running up to Natal I was thinking over Sir Henry Curtis's offer. We did not speak any more on the subject for a day or two, though I told them many hunting yarns, all true ones. There is no need to tell lies about hunting, for so many curious things happen within the knowledge of a man whose business it is to hunt; but this is by the way.

At last, one beautiful evening in January, which is our hottest month, we steamed along the coast of Natal, expecting to make Durban Point by sunset. It is a lovely coast all along from East London, with its red sandhills and wide sweeps of vivid green, dotted here and there with Kaffir kraals, and bordered by a ribbon of white surf which spouts up in pillars of foam where it hits the rocks. But just before you get to Durban there is a peculiar richness about it. There are the deep kloofs cut in the hills by the rushing rains of centuries, down which the rivers sparkle; there is the deepest green of the bush, growing as God planted it, and the other greens of the mealie gardens and the sugar patches, while here and there a white house, smiling out at the placid sea, puts a finish and gives an air of homeliness to the scene. For to my mind, however beautiful a view may be, it requires the presence of man to make it complete, but perhaps that is because I have lived so much in the wilderness, and therefore know the value of civilization, though, to be sure, it drives away the game. The Garden of Eden, no doubt, was fair before man was, but I always think it must have been fairer when Eve was walking about it. But we had miscalculated a little, and the sun was well down before we dropped anchor off the Point, and heard the gun which told the good folk that the English mail was in. It was too late to think of getting over the bar that night, so we went down comfortably to dinner, after seeing the mail carried off in the lifeboat.

When we came up again the moon was up, and shining so brightly over sea and shore that she almost paled the quick, large flashes from the lighthouse. From the shore floated sweet spicy odors that always remind me of hymns and missionaries, and in the windows of the houses on the Berea sparkled a hundred lights. From a large brig lying near came the music of the sailors as they worked at getting the anchor up to be ready for the wind. Altogether it was a perfect night, such a night as you get only in southern Africa, and it threw a garment of peace over everybody as the moon threw a garment of silver over everything. Even the great bulldog belonging to a sporting passenger seemed to yield to the gentle influences, and, giving up yearning to come to close quarters with the baboon in a cage on the fo'c'stle, snored happily in the door of the cabin, dreaming, no doubt, that he had finished him, and happy in his dream.

We all—that is, Sir Henry Curtis, Captain Good, and myself—went and sat by the wheel, and were quiet for a while.

"Well, Mr. Quatermain," said Sir Henry presently, "have you been thinking about my proposals?"

"Ay," echoed Captain Good, "what do you think of them, Mr. Quatermain? I hope you are going to give us the pleasure of your company as far as Solomon's Mines, or wherever the gentleman you knew as Neville may have got to."

I rose and knocked out my pipe before I answered. I had not made up my mind, and wanted the additional moment to complete it. Before the burning tobacco had fallen into the sea it was completed; just that little extra second did the trick. It is often the way when you have been bothering a long time over a thing.

"Yes, gentlemen," I said, sitting down again, "I will go, and by your leave I will tell you why and on what terms. First, for the terms which I ask.

"1. You are to pay all expenses, and any ivory or other valuables we may get is to be divided between Captain Good and myself.

"2. That you pay me £500 for my service on the trip before we start, I undertaking to serve you faithfully till you choose to abandon the enterprise, or till we succeed, or disaster overtakes us.

"3. That before we start you execute a deed agreeing in the event of my death or disablement, to pay my boy Harry, who is studying medicine over there in London at Guy's Hospital, a sum of £200 a year for five years, by which time he ought to be able to earn a living for himself. That is all, I think, and I dare say you will say quite enough, too."

"No," answered Sir Henry, "I accept them gladly. I am bent upon this project, and would pay more than that for your help, especially considering the peculiar knowledge you possess."

"Very well. And now that I have made my terms I will tell you my reasons for making up my mind to go. First of all, gentlemen, I have been observing you both for the last few days, and if you will not think me impertinent I will say that I like you, and think that we shall come up well to the yoke together. That is something, let me tell you, when one has a long journey like this before one.

"And now as to the journey itself, I tell you flatly, Sir Henry and Captain Good, that I do not think it probable that we can come out of it alive, that is, if we attempt to cross the Suliman Mountains. What was the fate of the old Don de Silvestra three hundred years ago? What was the fate of his descendant twenty years ago? What has been your brother's fate? I tell you frankly, gentlemen, that as their fate was so I believe ours will be."

I paused to watch the effect of my words. Captain Good looked a little uncomfortable; but Sir Henry's face did not change. "We must take our chance," he said.

"You may perhaps wonder," I went on, "why, if I think this, I, who am, as I told you, a timid man, should undertake such a journey. It is for two reasons. First, I am a fatalist, and believe that my time is appointed to come quite independently of my own movements, and that if I am to go to Suliman Mountains to be killed, I shall go there and shall be killed there. God Almighty, no doubt, knows his mind about me, so I need not trouble on that point. Secondly, I am a poor man. For nearly forty years I have hunted and traded, but I have never made more than a living. Well, gentlemen, I don't know if you are aware that the average life of an elephant hunter from the time he takes to the trade is from four to five years. So you see I have lived through about seven generations of my class, and I should think that my time cannot be far off, anyway. Now, if anything were to happen to me in the ordinary course of business, by the time my debts were paid there would be nothing left to support my son Harry while he was getting in the way of earning a living, whereas now he would be provided for for five years. There is the whole affair in a nutshell."

"Mr. Quatermain," said Sir Henry, who had been giving me the most serious attention, "your motives for undertaking an enterprise which you believe can only end in disaster reflect a great deal of credit on you. Whether or not you are right, time and the event, of course, alone can show. But whether you are right or wrong, I may as well tell you at once that I am going through with it to the end, sweet or bitter. If we are going to be knocked on the head, all that I have to say is that I hope we shall get a little shooting first—eh, Good?"

"Yes, yes," put in the captain. "We have all three of us been accustomed to face danger, and hold our lives in our hands in various ways, so it is no good turning back now."

"And now I vote we go down to the saloon and take an observation, just for luck, you know." And we did—through the bottom of a tumbler.

Next day we went ashore, and I put Sir Henry and Captain Good up at the little shanty I have on the Berea, and which I call my home. There are only three rooms and a kitchen in it, and it is built of green brick with a galvanized iron roof, but there is a good garden, with the best loquot trees in it that I know, and some nice young mangoes, of which I hope great things. The curator of the botanical gardens gave them to me. It is looked after by an old hunter of mine, named Jack, whose thigh was so badly broken by a buffalo cow in Sikukunïs country that he will never hunt again. But he can potter about and garden, being a Griqua by birth. You can never get your Zulu to take much interest in gardening. It is a peaceful art, and peaceful arts are not in his line.

Sir Henry and Good slept in a tent pitched in my little grove of orange trees at the end of the garden (for there was no room for them in the house), and what with the smell of the bloom and the sight of the green and golden fruit—for in Durban you will see all three on the tree to-gether—I dare say it is a pleasant place enough (for we have few mosquitoes here unless there happens to come an unusually heavy rain).

Well, to get on—for unless I do you will be tired of my story before ever we fetch up at Suliman's Mountains— having once made up my mind to go, I set about making the necessary preparations. First I got the deed from Sir Henry, providing for my boy in case of accidents. There was some little difficulty about getting this legally executed, as Sir Henry was a stranger here, and the property to be charged was over the water; but it was ultimately got over with the help of a lawyer, who charged £20 for the job—a price that I thought outrageous. Then I got my check for £500. Having paid this tribute to my bump of caution, I bought a wagon and a span of oxen on Sir Henry's behalf, and beauties they were. It was a twenty-two-foot wagon with iron axles, very strong, very light, and built through-out of stink-wood. It was not quite a new one, having been to the diamond fields and back, but in my opinion it was all the better for that, for one could see that the wood was well seasoned. If anything is going to give in a wagon, or if there is green wood in it, it will show out on the first trip. It was what we call a "half-tented" wagon—that is to say, it was only covered in over the after twelve feet, leav-ing all the front part free for the necessaries we had to carry with us. In this after part was a hide "cartle," or bed, on which two people could sleep, also racks for rifles, and many other little conveniences. I gave £125 for it, and think it was cheap at the price. Then I bought a beautiful team of twenty "salted" Zulu oxen, which I had had my eye on for a year or two. Sixteen oxen are the usual number for a team, but I had four extra to allow for casualties. These Zulu oxen are small and light, not more than half the size of the Africander oxen, which are generally used for transport purposes; but they will live where the Africander will starve, and with a light load will make five miles a day better going, being quicker and not so liable to get footsore. What is more, this lot were thoroughly "salted"—that is, they had worked all over South Africa, and so had become proof (comparatively speaking) against red water, which so frequently destroys whole teams of oxen when they get onto strange "veldt" (grass country). As for "lung sick," which is a dreadful form of pneumonia, very prevalent in this country, they had all been inoculated against it. This is done by cutting a slit in the tail of an ox, and binding in a piece of the diseased lung of an animal which has died of the sickness. The result is that the ox sickens, takes the disease in a mild form, which causes its tail to drop off, as a rule about a foot from the root, and becomes proof against future attacks. It seems cruel to rob the animal of his tail, especially in a country where there are so many flies, but it is better to sacrifice the tail and keep the ox than to lose both tail and ox, for a tail without an ox is not much good except to dust with. Still it does look odd to trek along behind twenty stumps, where there ought to be tails. It seems as though Nature had made a trifling mistake, and stuck the stern ornaments of a lot of prize bull-dogs onto the rumps of the oxen.

Next came the question of provisioning and medicines, one which required the most careful consideration, for what one had to do was to avoid lumbering the wagon up, and yet take everything absolutely necessary. Fortunately, it turned out that Good was a bit of a doctor, having at some period in his previous career managed to pass through a course of medical and surgical instruction, which he had more or less kept up. He was not, of course, qualified, but he knew more about it than many a man who could write

M.D. after his name, as we found out afterwards, and he had a splendid traveling medicine chest and a set of instruments. While we were at Durban he cut off a Kaffir's big toe in a way which it was a pleasure to see. But he was quite flabbergasted when the Kaffir, who had sat stolidly watching the operation, asked him to put on another, saying that a "white one" would do at a pinch.

There remained, when these questions were satisfactorily settled, two further important points for consideration, namely, that of arms and that of servants. As to the arms I cannot do better than put down a list of those we finally decided on from among the ample store that Sir Henry had brought with him from England, and those which I had. I copy it from my pocketbook, where I made the entry at the time:

"Three heavy breechloading double-eight elephant guns, weighing about fifteen pounds each, with a charge of eleven drams of black powder." Two of these were by a well-known London firm, most excellent makers, but I do not know by whom mine, which was not so highly finished, was made. I had used it on several trips, and shot a good many elephants with it, and it had always proved a most superior weapon, thoroughly to be relied on.

"Three double .500 expresses, constructed to carry a charge of six drams," sweet weapons, and admirable for medium-sized game, such as eland or sable antelope, or for men, especially in an open country and with the semihollow bullet.

"One double No. 12 central-fire Keeper's shotgun, full choke both barrels." This gun proved of the greatest service to us afterwards in shooting game for the pot.

"Three Winchester repeating rifles (not carbines)," spare guns.

"Three single-action Colt's revolvers, with the heavier pattern of cartridge."

This was our total armament, and the reader will doubtless observe that the weapons of each class were of the same make and caliber, so that the cartridges were interchangeable, a very important point. I make no apology for detailing it at length, for every experienced hunter will know how vital a proper supply of guns and ammunition is to the success of an expedition.

Now as to the men who were to go with us. After much consultation we decided that their number should be limited to five, namely, a driver, a leader, and three servants.

The driver and leader I got without much difficulty, two Zulus, named respectively Goza and Tom; but the servants were a more difficult matter. It was necessary that they should be thoroughly trustworthy and brave men, as in a business of this sort our lives might depend upon their conduct. At last I secured two, one a Hottentot called Ventvögel ("Wind-bird"), and one a little Zulu named Khiva, who had the merit of speaking English perfectly. Ventvögel I had known before; he was one of the most perfect "spoorer" (game trackers) I ever had to do with, and tough as whipcord. He never seemed to tire. But he had one failing, so common with his race, drink. Put him within reach of a bottle of grog and you could not trust him. But as we were going beyond the region of grogshops this little weakness of his did not so much matter.

Having got these two men I looked in vain for a third to suit my purpose, so we determined to start without one, trusting to luck to find a suitable man on our way up-country. But on the evening before the day we had fixed for our departure the Zulu Khiva informed me that a man was waiting to see me. Accordingly, when we had done dinner, for we were at table at the time, I told him to bring him in. Presently a very tall, handsome-looking man, somewhere about thirty years of age, and very light-colored for a Zulu, entered, and, lifting his knob stick by way of salute, squatted himself down in the corner on his haunches and sat silent. I did not take any notice of him for a while, for it is a great mistake to do so. If you rush into conversation at once a Zulu is apt to think you a person of little dignity or consideration. I observed, however, that he was a "keshla" (ringed man), that is, that he wore on his head the black ring, made of a species of gum polished with fat and worked in with the hair, usually assumed by Zulus on attaining a certain age or dignity. Also, it struck me that his face was familiar to me.

"Well," I said at last, "what is your name?"

"Umbopa," answered the man, in a slow, deep voice.

"I have seen your face before."

"Yes; the Inkoosi [chief] saw my face at the place of the Little Hand [Isandhlwana] the day before the battle."

Then I remembered. I had been one of Lord Chelmsford's guides in that unlucky Zulu war, and had had the good fortune to leave the camp in charge of some wagons the day before the battle. While I had been waiting for the cattle to be inspanned I had fallen into conversation with this man, who held some small command among the native auxiliaries, and he had expressed to me his doubts of the safety of the camp. At the time I had told him to hold his tongue, and leave such matters to wiser heads; but afterwards I thought of his words.

"I remember," I said; "what is it you want?"

"It is this, Macumazahn [that is my Kaffir name, and means the man who gets up in the middle of the night; or, in vulgar English, he who keeps his eyes open], I hear that you go on a great expedition far into the north with the white chiefs from over the water. Is it a true word?"

"It is."

"I hear that you go even to the Lukanga River, a moon's journey beyond the Manica country. Is this so also, Macumazahn?"

"Why do you ask whither we go? What is it to thee?" I answered suspiciously, for the objects of our journey had been kept a dead secret.

"It is this, O white men, that if indeed you travel so far I would travel with you."

There was a certain assumption of dignity in the man's mode of speech, and especially in his use of the words "O white men," instead of "O inkoosis" (chiefs), which struck me.

"You forget yourself a little," I said. "Your words come out unawares. That is not the way to speak. What is your name, and where is your kraal? Tell us, that we may know with whom we have to deal."

"My name is Umbopa. I am of the Zulu people, yet not of them. The house of my tribe is in the far north; it was left behind when the Zulus came down here a 'thousand years ago,' long before Chaka reigned in Zululand. I have no kraal. I have wandered for many years. I came from the north as a child to Zululand. I was Cetywayo's man in the Nkomabakosi regiment. I ran away from Zululand and came to Natal because I wanted to see the white man's ways. Then I served against Cetywayo in the war. Since then I have been working in Natal. Now I am tired, and would go north again. Here is not my place. I want no money, but I am a brave man, and am worth my place and meat. I have spoken."

I was rather puzzled at this man and his way of speech.

It was evident to me from his manner that he was in the main telling the truth, but he was somehow different from the ordinary run of Zulus, and I rather mistrusted his offer to come without pay. Being in a difficulty, I translated his words to Sir Henry and Good, and asked them their opinion. Sir Henry told me to ask him to stand up. Umbopa did so, at the same time slipping off the long military greatcoat he wore, and revealing himself naked except for the moocha round his middle and a necklace of lions' claws. He certainly was a magnificent-looking man; I never saw a finer native. Standing about six foot three high, he was broad in proportion, and very shapely. In that light, too, his skin looked scarcely more than dark, except here and there where deep, black scars marked old assegai wounds. Sir Henry walked up to him and looked into his proud, handsome face.

"They make a good pair, don't they?" said Good; "one as big as the other."

"I like your looks, Mr. Umbopa, and I will take you as my servant," said Sir Henry in English.

Umbopa evidently understood him, for he answered in Zulu, "It is well," and then, with a glance at the white man's great stature and breadth, "we are men, you and I."

4 ♦

An Elephant Hunt

Now I DO not propose to narrate at full length all the incidents of our long journey up to Sitanda's Kraal, near the junction of the Lukanga and Kalukwe rivers, a journey of more than a thousand miles from Durban, the last three hundred or so of which, owing to the frequent presence of the dreadful tsetse fly, whose bite is fatal to all animals except donkeys and men, we had to make on foot.

We left Durban at the end of January, and it was in the second week of May that we camped near Sitanda's Kraal. Our adventures on the way were many and various, but as they were of the sort which befall every African hunter, I shall not—with one exception to be presently detailed—set them down here, lest I should render this history too wearisome.

At Inyati, the outlying trading station in the Matabele country, of which Lobengula (a great scoundrel) is king, we with many regrets parted from our comfortable wagon. Only twelve oxen remained to us out of the beautiful span of twenty which I had bought at Durban. One we had lost from the bite of a cobra, three had perished from the want of water, one had been lost, and the other three had died from eating the poisonous herb called tulip. Five more sickened from this cause, but we managed to cure them with doses of an infusion made by boiling down the tulip leaves. If administered in time this is a very effective anti-

41

dote. The wagon and oxen we left in the immediate charge of Goza and Tom, the driver and leader, both of them trustworthy boys, requesting a worthy Scotch missionary who lived in this wild place to keep an eye to it. Then, accompanied by Umbopa, Khiva, Ventvögel, and half a dozen bearers whom we hired on the spot, we started off on foot upon our wild quest. I remember we were all a little silent on the occasion of that departure, and I think that each of us was wondering if we should ever see that wagon again; for my part, I never expected to. For a while we tramped on in silence, till Umbopa, who was marching in front, broke into a Zulu chant about how some brave men, tired of life and the tameness of things, started off into a great wilderness to find new things or die, and how, lo and behold, when they had got far into the wilderness, they found it was not a wilderness at all, but a beautiful place full of young wives and fat cattle, of game to hunt and enemies to kill.

Then we all laughed and took it for a good omen. He was a cheerful savage, was Umbopa, in a dignified sort of way, when he had not got one of his fits of brooding, and had a wonderful knack of keeping one's spirits up. We all got very fond of him.

And now for the one adventure I am going to treat myself to, for I do heartily love a hunting yarn.

About a fortnight's march from Inyati we came across a peculiarly beautiful bit of fairly-watered wooded country. The kloofs in the hills were covered with dense bush, idoro bush, as the natives call it, and in some places with the wacht-een-beche (wait-a-little) thorn, and there were great quantities of the beautiful machabell tree, laden with refreshing yellow fruit with enormous stones. This tree is the elephant's favorite food, and there were not wanting signs that the great brutes were about, for not only was their spoor frequent, but in many places the trees were broken down and even uprooted. The elephant is a destructive feeder.

One evening, after a long day's march, we came to a spot of peculiar loveliness. At the foot of a bush-clad hill was a dry riverbed, in which, however, were to be found pools of crystal water all trodden round with the hoofprints of game. Facing this hill was a parklike plain, where grew clumps of flat-topped mimosa, varied with occasional glossy-leaved machabells, and all round was the great sea of pathless, silent bush.

As we emerged into this riverbed path we suddenly started a troop of tall giraffes, who galloped, or, rather, sailed off, with their strange gait, their tails screwed up over their backs, and their hoofs rattling like castanets. They were about three hundred yards from us, and therefore practically out of shot, but Good, who was walking ahead and had an express loaded with solid ball in his hand, could not resist, but upped gun and let drive at the last, a young cow. By some extraordinary chance the ball struck it full on the back of the neck, shattering the spinal column, and that giraffe went rolling head over heels just like a rabbit. I never saw a more curious thing.

"Curse it!" said Good—for I am sorry to say he had a habit of using strong language when excited—contracted no doubt, in the course of his nautical career. "Curse it, I've killed him."

"Ou, Bougwan," ejaculated the Kaffirs; "Ou! Ou!"

They called Good "Bougwan" ("Glass Eye") because of his eyeglass.

"Oh, 'Bougwan'!" reechoed Sir Henry and I; and from that day Good's reputation as a marvelous shot was established, at any rate among the Kaffirs. Really he was a bad one, but whenever he missed we overlooked it for the sake of that giraffe.

Having set some of the "boys" to cut off the best of the giraffe meat, we went to work to build a "scherm" near one of the pools about a hundred yards to the right of it. This is done by cutting a quantity of thorn bushes and laying them in the shape of a circular hedge. Then the space enclosed is smoothed, and dry tambouki grass, if obtainable, is made into a bed in the center, and a fire or fires lighted.

By the time the scherm was finished the moon was coming up, and our dinner of giraffe steaks and roasted marrowbones was ready. How we enjoyed those marrowbones, though it was rather a job to crack them! I know no greater luxury than giraffe marrow, unless it is elephant's heart, and we had that on the morrow. We ate our simple meal, pausing at times to thank Good for his wonderful shot, by the light of the full moon, and then we began to smoke and yarn, and a curious picture we must have made squatted there round the fire. I, with my short grizzled hair sticking up straight, and Sir Henry with his yellow locks, which were getting rather long, were rather a contrast, especially as I am thin and short and dark, weighing only nine stone and a half, and Sir Henry is tall and broad and fair, and weighs fifteen. But perhaps the most curious-looking of the three, taking all the circumstances of the case into consideration, was Captain John Good, R.N. There he sat upon a leather bag, looking just as though he had come in from a comfortable day's shooting in a civilized country, absolutely clean, tidy, and well dressed. He had on a shooting suit of brown tweed, with a hat to match, and neat gaiters. He was, as usual, beautifully shaven, his eyeglass and his false teeth appeared to be in perfect order, and altogether he was the neatest man I ever had to do with in the wilderness. He even had on a collar, of which he had a supply, made of white gutta-percha.

"You see, they weigh so little," he said to me innocently, when I expressed my astonishment at the fact; "I always liked to look like a gentleman."

Well, there we all sat yarning away in the beautiful moonlight, and watching the Kaffirs a few yards off sucking their intoxicating "daccha" in a pipe of which the mouthpiece was made of the horn of an eland, till they one by one rolled themselves up in their blankets and went to sleep by the fire, that is, all except Umbopa, who sat a little apart (I noticed he never mixed much with the other Kaffirs), his chin resting on his hand, apparently thinking deeply.

Presently, from the depths of the bush behind us came a loud "Woof! Woof!" "That's a lion," said I, and we all started up to listen. Hardly had we done so, when from the pool, about a hundred yards off, came the strident trumpeting of an elephant. "Unkungunklovo! Unkungunklovo!" ("Elephant! Elephant!") whispered the Kaffirs; and a few minutes afterwards we saw a succession of vast shadowy forms moving slowly from the direction of the water towards the bush. Up jumped Good, burning for slaughter, and thinking, perhaps, that it was as easy to kill elephant as he had found it to shoot giraffe, but I caught him by the arm and pulled him down.

"It's no good," I said, "let them go."

"It seems that we are in a paradise of game. I vote we stop here a day or two, and have a go at them," said Sir Henry presently.

I was rather surprised, for hitherto Sir Henry had always been for pushing on as fast as possible, more especially since we had ascertained at Inyati that about two years ago an Englishman of the name of Neville *had* sold his wagon there, and gone on upcountry; but I suppose his hunter instincts had got the better of him.

Good jumped at the idea, for he was longing to have a go at those elephants; and so, to speak the truth, did I, for it went against my conscience to let such a herd as that escape without having a pull at them.

"All right, my hearties," said I. "I think we want a little recreation. And now let's turn in, for we ought to be off by dawn, and then perhaps we may catch them feeding before they move on."

The others agreed, and we proceeded to make preparations. Good took off his clothes, shook them, put his eyeglass and his false teeth into his trousers pocket, and, folding them all up neatly, placed them out of the dew under a corner of his mackintosh sheet. Sir Henry and I contented ourselves with rougher arrangements, and were soon curled up in our blankets and dropping off into the dreamless sleep that rewards the traveler.

Going, going, go— What was that?

Suddenly, from the direction of the water came a sound of violent scuffling, and next instant there broke upon our ears a succession of the most awful roars. There was no mistaking what they came from; only a lion could make such a noise as that. We all jumped up and looked towards the water, in the direction of which we saw a confused mass, yellow and black in color, staggering and struggling towards us. We seized our rifles, and, slipping on our veldtschoons (shoes made of untanned hide), ran out of the scherm towards it. By this time it had fallen, and was rolling over and over on the ground, and by the time we reached it, it struggled no longer, but was quite still.

And this was what it was. On the grass there lay a sable antelope bull—the most beautiful of all the African antelopes—quite dead, and transfixed by its great curved horns was a magnificent black-maned lion, also dead. What had happened, evidently, was this. The sable antelope had come down to drink at the pool, where the lion—no doubt the same we had heard—had been lying in wait. While the antelope was drinking the lion had sprung upon him, but was received upon the sharp, curved horns and transfixed. I once saw the same thing happen before. The lion, unable to free himself, had torn and beaten at the back and neck of the bull, which, maddened with fear and pain, had rushed on till it dropped dead.

As soon as we had sufficiently examined the dead beasts we called the Kaffirs, and between us managed to drag their carcasses up to the scherm. Then we went in and lay down, to wake no more till dawn.

With the first light we were up and making ready for the fray. We took with us the three eight-bore rifles, a good supply of ammunition, and our large water bottles filled with weak, cold tea, which I have always found the best stuff to shoot on. After swallowing a little breakfast we started, Umbopa, Khiva, and Ventvögel accompanying us. The other Kaffirs we left, with instructions to skin the lion and the sable antelope, and cut up the latter.

We had no difficulty in finding the broad elephant trail, which Ventvögel, after examination, pronounced to have been made by between twenty and thirty elephants, most of them full-grown bulls. But the herd had moved on some way during the night, and it was nine o'clock, and already very hot, before, from the broken trees, bruised leaves and bark, and smoking dung, we knew we could not be far off them.

Presently we caught sight of the herd, numbering, as Ventvögel had said, between twenty and thirty, standing in a hollow, having finished their morning meal, and flapping their great ears. It was a splendid sight.

They were about two hundred yards from us. Taking a handful of dry grass, I threw it into the air to see how the wind was; for if once they winded us I knew they would be off before we could get a shot. Finding that, if anything, it blew from the elephants to us, we crept stealthily on, and, thanks to the cover, managed to get within forty yards or so of the great brutes. Just in front of us and broadside on stood three splendid bulls, one of them with enormous tusks. I whispered to the others that I would take the middle one; Sir Henry covered the one to the left, and Good the bull with the big tusks.

"Now," I whispered.

Boom! Boom! Boom! went the three heavy rifles, and down went Sir Henry's elephant, dead as a hammer, shot right through the heart. Mine fell onto its knees, and I thought he was going to die, but in another moment he was up and off, tearing along straight past me. As he went I gave him the second barrel in his ribs, and this brought him down in good earnest. Hastily slipping in two fresh cartridges, I ran up close to him, and a ball through the brain put an end to the poor brute's struggles. Then I turned to see how Good had fared with the big bull, which I had heard screaming with rage and pain as I gave mine its quietus. On reaching the captain I found him in a great state of excitement. It appeared that on receiving the bullet the bull had turned and come straight for his assailant, who had barely time to get out of his way, and then charged blindly on past him, in the direction of our encampment. Meanwhile the herd had crashed off in wild alarm in the other direction.

For a while we debated whether to go after the wounded bull or follow the herd, and finally decided for the latter alternative, and departed thinking that we had seen the last of those big tusks. I have often wished since that we had. It was easy work to follow the elephants, for they had left a trail like a carriage road behind them, crushing down the thick bush in their furious flight as though it were tambouki grass.

But to come up with them was another matter, and we had struggled on under a broiling sun for over two hours before we found them. They were, with the exception of one bull, standing together, and I could see, from their unquiet way and the manner in which they kept lifting their trunks to test the air, that they were on the lookout for mischief. The solitary bull stood fifty yards or so this side of the herd, over which he was evidently keeping sentry, and about sixty yards from us. Thinking that he would see or wind us, and that it would probably start them all off again if we tried to get nearer, especially as the ground was rather open, we all aimed at this bull and, at my whispered word, fired. All three shots took effect, and down he went, dead. Again the herd started on, but, unfortunately for them, about a hundred yards farther on was a nullah, or dried water track, with steep banks, a place very much resembling the one the Prince Imperial was killed in in Zululand. Into this the elephants plunged, and when we reached the edge we found them struggling in wild confusion to get up the other bank, and filling the air with their screams, and trumpeting as they pushed one another aside in their selfish panic, just like so many human beings. Now was our opportunity, and, firing away as quick as we could load, we killed five of the poor beasts, and no doubt should have bagged the whole herd had they not suddenly given up their attempts to climb the bank and rushed headlong down the nullah. We were too tired to follow them, and perhaps also a little sick of slaughter, eight elephants being a pretty good bag for one day.

So, after we had rested a little and the Kaffirs had cut out the hearts of two of the dead elephants for supper, we started homeward, very well pleased with ourselves, having made up our minds to send the bearers on the morrow to chop out the tusks.

Shortly after we had passed the spot where Good had wounded the patriarchal bull we came across a herd of eland, but did not shoot at them, as we had already plenty of meat. They trotted past us, and then stopped behind a little patch of bush about a hundred yards away and wheeled round to look at us. As Good was anxious to get a near view of them, never having seen an eland close, he handed his rifle to Umbopa, and, followed by Khiva, strolled up to the patch of bush. We sat down and waited for him, not sorry of the excuse for a little rest.

The sun was just going down in its reddest glory, and Sir Henry and I were admiring the lovely scene, when suddenly we heard an elephant scream, and saw its huge and charging form with uplifted trunk and tail silhouetted against the great red globe of the sun. Next second we saw something else, and that was Good and Khiva tearing back towards us with the wounded bull (for it was he) charging after them. For a moment we did not dare to fire—though it would have been little use if we had at that distance—for fear of hitting one of them, and the next a dreadful thing happened: Good fell a victim to his passion for civilized dress. Had he consented to discard his trousers and gaiters as we had, and hunt in a flannel shirt and a pair of veldtschoons, it would have been all right, but as it was his trousers cumbered him in that desperate race, and presently, when he was about sixty yards from us, his boot, polished by the dry grass, slipped, and down he went on his face right in front of the elephant.

We gave a gasp, for we knew he must die, and ran as hard as we could towards him. In three seconds it had ended, but not as we thought. Khiva, the Zulu boy, had seen his master fall, and, brave lad that he was, had turned and flung his assegai straight into the elephant's face. It stuck in his trunk.

With a scream of pain the brute seized the poor Zulu, hurled him to the earth, and, placing his huge foot onto his body about the middle, twined his trunk round his upper part and *tore him in two*.

We rushed up, mad with horror, and fired again and again, and presently the elephant fell upon the fragments of the Zulu.

As for Good, he got up and wrung his hands over the brave man who had given his life to save him; and myself, though an old hand, I felt a lump in my throat. Umbopa stood and contemplated the huge dead elephant and the mangled remains of poor Khiva.

"Ah, well," he said presently, "he is dead, but he died like a man."

5 ◆

Our March into the Desert

WE HAD KILLED nine elephants, and it took us two days to cut out the tusks and get them home and bury them carefully in the sand under a large tree, which made a conspicuous mark for miles round. It was a wonderfully fine lot of ivory. I never saw a better, averaging as it did between forty and fifty pounds a tusk. The tusks of the great bull that killed poor Khiva scaled one hundred and seventy pounds the pair, as nearly as we could judge.

As for Khiva himself, we buried what remained of him in an ant-bear hole, together with an assegai to protect himself with on his journey to a better world. On the third day we started on, hoping that we might one day return to dig up our buried ivory, and in due course, after a long and wearisome tramp, and many adventures which I have not space to detail, reached Sitanda's Kraal, near the Lukanga River, the real starting-point of our expedition. Very well do I recollect our arrival at that place. To the right was a scattered native settlement with a few stone cattle kraals and some cultivated lands down by the water, where these savages grew their scanty supply of grain, and beyond it great tracts of waving veldt covered with tall grass, over which herds of the smaller game were wandering. To the left was the vast desert. This spot appeared to be the outpost of the fertile country, and it would be difficult to say to what natural causes such an abrupt

52

change in the character of the soil was due. But so it was. Just below our encampment flowed a little stream, on the farther side of which was a stony slope, the same down which I had twenty years before seen poor Silvestre creeping back after his attempt to reach Solomon's Mines, and beyond that slope began the waterless desert covered with a species of karoo shrub. It was evening when we pitched our camp, and the great fiery ball of the sun was sinking into the desert, sending glorious rays of many-colored light flying over all the vast expanse. Leaving Good to superintend the arrangement of our little camp, I took Sir Henry with me, and we walked to the top of the slope opposite and gazed out across the desert. The air was very clear, and far, far away I could distinguish the faint blue outlines, here and there capped with white, of the great Suliman Berg.

"There," I said, "there is the wall of Solomon's Mines, but God knows if we shall ever climb it."

"My brother should be there, and if he is I shall reach him somehow," said Sir Henry, in that tone of quiet confidence which marked the man.

"I hope so," I answered, and turned to go back to the camp, when I saw that we were not alone. Behind us, also gazing earnestly towards the far-off mountains, was the great Zulu, Umbopa.

The Zulu spoke when he saw that I had observed him, but addressed himself to Sir Henry, to whom he had attached himself.

"Is it to that land that thou wouldst journey, Incubu [a native word meaning, I believe, an elephant, and the name given to Sir Henry by the Kaffirs]?" he said, pointing towards the mountains with his broad assegai.

I asked him sharply what he meant by addressing his master in that familiar way. It is very well for natives to have a name for one among themselves, but it is not decent that they should call one by their heathenish appellations to one's face. The man laughed a quiet little laugh which angered me.

"How dost thou know that I am not the equal of the inkoosi I serve?" he said. "He is of a royal house, no doubt; one can see it in his size and in his eye; so, mayhap, am I. At least I am as great a man. Be my mouth, O Macumazahn, and say my words to the Inkoosi, Incubu, my master, for I would speak to him and to thee."

I was angry with the man, for I am not accustomed to be talked to in that way by Kaffirs, but somehow he impressed me, and besides I was curious to know what he had to say, so I translated, expressing my opinion at the same time that he was an impudent fellow, and that his swagger was outrageous.

"Yes, Umbopa," answered Sir Henry, "I would journey there."

"The desert is wide and there is no water; the mountains are high and covered with snow, and man cannot say what is beyond them, behind the place where the sun sets; how shalt thou come thither, Incubu, and wherefore dost thou go?"

I translated again.

"Tell him," answered Sir Henry, "that I go because I believe that a man of my blood, my brother, has gone there before me, and I go to seek him."

"That is so, Incubu; a man I met on the road told me that a white man went out into the desert two years ago towards those mountains with one servant, a hunter. They never came back."

"How do you know it was my brother?" asked Sir Henry.

"Nay, I know not. But the man, when I asked what the white man was like, said that he had your eyes and a black beard. He said, too, that the name of the hunter with him was Jim, that he was a Bechuana hunter and wore clothes."

"There is no doubt about it," said I; "I knew Jim well."

Sir Henry nodded. "I was sure of it," he said. "If George set his mind upon a thing he generally did it. It was always so from his boyhood. If he meant to cross the Suliman Berg he has crossed it, unless some accident has overtaken him, and we must look for him on the other side."

Umbopa understood English, though he rarely spoke it.

"It is a far journey, Incubu," he put in, and I translated his remark.

"Yes," answered Sir Henry, "it is far. But there is no journey upon this earth that a man may not make if he sets his heart to it. There is nothing, Umbopa, that he cannot do, there are no mountains he may not climb, there are no deserts he cannot cross, save a mountain and a desert of which you are spared the knowledge, if love leads him, and he holds his life in his hand counting it as nothing, ready to keep it or to lose it as Providence may order."

I translated.

"Great words, my father," answered the Zulu (I always called him a Zulu, though he was not really one), "great, swelling words, fit to fill the mouth of a man. Thou art right, my father Incubu. Listen! What is life? It is a feather; it is the seed of the grass, blown hither and thither, sometimes multiplying itself and dying in the act, sometimes carried away into the heavens. But if the seed be good and heavy it may perchance travel a little way on the road it will. It is well to try and journey one's road and to fight with the air. Man must die. At the worst he can but die a little sooner. I will go with thee across the desert and over the mountains, unless perchance I fall to the ground on the way, my father."

He paused awhile, and then went on with one of those strange bursts of rhetorical eloquence which Zulus sometimes indulge in, and which, to my mind, full as they are of vain repetitions, show that the race is by no means devoid of poetic instinct and of intellectual power.

"What is life? Tell me, O white men, who are wise, who know the secrets of the world, and the world of stars, and the world that lies above and round the stars; who flash their words from afar without a voice; tell me, white men, the secret of our life—whither it goes and whence it comes!

"Ye cannot answer; ye know not. Listen, I will answer. Out of the dark we came, into the dark we go. Like a storm-driven bird at night we fly out of the Nowhere; for a moment our wings are seen in the light of the fire, and, lo, we are gone again into the Nowhere. Life is nothing. Life is all. It is the hand with which we hold off death. It is the glowworm that shines in the nighttime and is black in the morning; it is the white breath of the oxen in winter; it is the little shadow that runs across the grass and loses itself at sunset."

"You are a strange man," said Sir Henry, when he ceased.

Umbopa laughed. "It seems to me that we are much alike, Incubu. Perhaps I seek a brother over the mountains."

I looked at him suspiciously. "What dost thou mean?" I asked. "What dost thou know of the mountains?"

"A little; a very little. There is a strange land there, a land of witchcraft and beautiful things; a land of brave people and of trees and streams and white mountains and of a great white road. I have heard of it. But what is the good of talking? It grows dark. Those who live to see will see."

Again I looked at him doubtfully. The man knew too much.

"Ye need not fear me, Macumazahn," he said, interpreting my look. "I dig no holes for ye to fall in. I make no plots. If ever we cross those mountains behind the sun, I will tell what I know. But death sits upon them. Be wise, and turn back. Go and hunt elephant. I have spoken."

And without another word he lifted his spear in salutation and returned towards the camp, where shortly afterwards we found him cleaning a gun like any other Kaffir.

"That is an odd man," said Sir Henry.

"Yes," answered I, "too odd by half. I don't like his little ways. He knows something, and won't speak out. But I suppose it is no use quarreling with him. We are in for a curious trip, and a mysterious Zulu won't make much difference one way or another."

Next day we made our arrangements for starting. Of course it was impossible to drag our heavy elephant rifles and other kit with us across the desert, so, dismissing our bearers, we made an arrangement with an old native who had a kraal close by to take care of them till we returned. It went to my heart to leave such things as those sweet tools to the tender mercies of an old thief, of a savage whose greedy eyes I could see gloating over them. But I took some precautions.

First of all I loaded all the rifles, and informed him that

if he touched them they would go off. He instantly tried the experiment with my eight-bore, and it did go off, and blew a hole right through one of his oxen, which were just then being driven up to the kraal, to say nothing of knocking him head over heels with the recoil. He got up considerably startled, and not at all pleased at the loss of the ox, which he had the impudence to ask me to pay for, and nothing would induce him to touch them again.

"Put the live devils up there in the thatch," he said, "out of the way, or they will kill us all."

Then I told him that if, when we came back, one of those things was missing I would kill him and all his people by witchcraft; and if we died and he tried to steal the things, I would come and haunt him and turn his cattle mad and his milk sour till life was a weariness, and make the devils in the guns come out and talk to him in a way he would not like, and generally gave him a good idea of judgment to come. After that he swore he would look after them as though they were his father's spirit. He was a very superstitious old Kaffir and a great villain.

Having thus disposed of our superfluous gear we arranged the kit we five—Sir Henry, Good, myself, Umbopa, and the Hottentot Ventvögel—were to take with us on our journey. It was small enough, but do what we would we could not get it down under about forty pounds a man. This is what it consisted of:

The three express rifles and two hundred rounds of ammunition.

The two Winchester repeating rifles (for Umbopa and Ventvögel), with two hundred rounds of cartridge.

Three Colt revolvers and sixty rounds of cartridge.

Five Cochrane's water bottles, each holding four pints.

Five blankets.

Twenty-five pounds' weight of biltong (sun-dried game flesh).

Ten pounds' weight of best mixed beads for gifts.

A selection of medicine, including an ounce of quinine, and one or two small surgical instruments.

Our knives, a few sundries, such as a compass, matches, a pocket filter, tobacco, a trowel, a bottle of brandy, and the clothes we stood in.

This was our total equipment, a small one, indeed, for such a venture, but we dared not attempt to carry more. As it was, that load was a heavy one per man to travel across the burning desert with, for in such places every additional ounce tells upon one. But try as we would we could not see our way to reducing it. There was nothing but what was absolutely necessary.

With great difficulty, and by the promise of a present of a good hunting knife each, I succeeded in persuading three wretched natives from the village to come with us for the first stage, twenty miles, and to carry each a large gourd holding a gallon of water. My object was to enable us to refill our water bottles after the first night's march, for we determined to start in the cool of the night. I gave out to these natives that we were going to shoot ostriches, with which the desert abounded. They jabbered and shrugged their shoulders, and said we were mad and should perish of thirst, which I must say seemed very probable; but being desirous of obtaining the knives, which were almost unknown treasures up there, they consented to come, having probably reflected that, after all, our subsequent extinction would be no affair of theirs.

All next day we rested and slept, and at sunset ate a hearty meal of fresh beef washed down with tea, the last, as Good sadly remarked, we were likely to drink for many a long day. Then, having made our final preparations, we lay down and waited for the moon to rise. At last, about nine o'clock, up she came in all her chastened glory, flooding the wild country with silver light, and throwing a weird sheen on the vast expanse of rolling desert before us, which looked as solemn and quiet and as alien to man as the star-studded firmament above. We rose up, and in a few minutes were ready, and yet we hesitated a little, as human nature is prone to hesitate on the threshold of an irrevocable step. We three white men stood there by ourselves. Umbopa, assegai in hand and the rifle across his shoulders, a few paces ahead of us, looked out fixedly across the desert; the three hired natives, with gourds of water, and Ventvögel were gathered in a little knot behind.

"Gentlemen," said Sir Henry presently, in his low, deep voice, "we are going on about as strange a journey as men can make in this world. It is very doubtful if we can succeed in it. But we are three men who will stand together for good or for evil to the last. And now before we start let us for a moment pray to the Power who shapes the destinies of men, and who ages since has marked out our paths, that it may please him to direct our steps in accordance with his will."

Taking off his hat, he, for the space of a minute or so, covered his face with his hands, and Good and I did likewise.

I do not say that I am a first-rate praying man; few hunters are; and as for Sir Henry, I never heard him speak like that before, and only once since, though deep down in his heart I believe he is very religious. Good, too, is pious, though very apt to swear. Anyhow, I do not think I ever, excepting on one single occasion, put in a better

prayer in my life than I did during that minute, and somehow I felt the happier for it. Our future was so completely unknown, and I think the unknown and the awful
always bring a man nearer to his Maker.

"And now," said Sir Henry, "trek."

So we started.

We had nothing to guide ourselves by except the distant mountains and old José da Silvestra's chart, which,
considering that it was drawn by a dying and half dis-
traught man on a fragment of linen three centuries ago,
was not a very satisfactory sort of thing to work on. Still,
such as it was, our sole hope of success depended on it. If
we failed in finding that pool of bad water which the old
don had marked as being situated in the middle of the
desert, about sixty miles from our starting point and as far
from the mountains, we must in all probability perish
miserably of thirst. And to my mind the chances of our
finding it in that great sea of sand and karoo scrub seemed
almost infinitesimal. Even supposing Da Silvestra had
marked it right, what was there to prevent its having been
generations ago dried up by the sun, or trampled in by
game, or filled with drifting sand?

On we tramped silently as shades through the night and
in the heavy sand. The karoo bushes caught our shins and
retarded us, and the sand got into our veldtschoons and
Good's shooting boots, so that every few miles we had to
stop and empty them; but still the night was fairly cool,
though the atmosphere was thick and heavy, giving a sort
of creamy feel to the air, and we made fair progress. It
was very still and lonely there in the desert, oppressively
so indeed. Good felt this, and once began to whistle "The
Girl I Left Behind Me," but the notes sounded lugubrious
in that vast place, and he gave it up. Shortly afterwards

a little incident occurred which, though it made us jump at the time, gave rise to a laugh. Good, as the holder of the compass, which, being a sailor, of course he thoroughly understood, was leading, and we were toiling along in single file behind him, when suddenly we heard the sound of an exclamation, and he vanished. Next second there arose all round us a most extraordinary hubbub—snorts, groans, wild sounds of rushing feet. In the faint light, too, we could descry dim, galloping forms half hidden by wreaths of sand. The natives threw down their loads and prepared to bolt, but, remembering that there was nowhere to bolt to, cast themselves upon the ground and howled out that it was the devil. As for Sir Henry and myself, we stood amazed; nor was our amazement lessened when we perceived the form of Good careering off in the direction of the mountains, apparently mounted on the back of a horse and halloing like mad. In another second he threw up his arms, and we heard him come to the earth with a thud. Then I saw what had happened: we had stumbled right on to a herd of sleeping quagga, onto the back of one of which Good had actually fallen, and the brute had naturally enough got up and made off with him. Singing out to the others that it was all right, I ran towards Good, much afraid lest he should be hurt, but to my great relief found him sitting in the sand, his eyeglass still fixed firmly in his eye, rather shaken and very much startled, but not in any way injured.

After this we traveled on without any further misadventure till after one o'clock, when we called a halt, and having drunk a little water—not much, for water was precious—and rested for half an hour, started on again.

On, on we went, till at last the east began to blush like the cheek of a girl. Then there came faint rays of primrose light that changed presently to golden bars, through which the dawn glided out across the desert. The stars grew pale and paler still, till at last they vanished; the golden moon waxed wan, and her mountain ridges stood out clear against her sickly face like the bones on the face of a dying man; then came spear upon spear of glorious light flashing far away across the boundless wilderness, piercing and firing the veils of mist till the desert was draped in a tremulous golden glow, and it was day.

Still we did not halt, though by this time we should have been glad enough to do so, for we knew that when once the sun was fully up it would be almost impossible for us to travel in it. At length, about six o'clock, we spied a little pile of rocks rising out of the plain, and to this we dragged ourselves. As luck would have it, here we found an overhanging slab of rock carpeted beneath with smooth sand, which afforded a most grateful shelter from the heat. Underneath this we crept, and having drunk some water each and eaten a bit of biltong, we lay down and were soon sound asleep.

It was three o'clock in the afternoon before we woke, to find our three bearers preparing to return. They had already had enough of the desert, and no number of knives would have tempted them to come a step farther. So we had a hearty drink, and, having emptied our water bottles, filled them up again from the gourds they had brought with them, and then watched them depart on their twenty miles' tramp home.

At half-past four we also started on. It was lonely and desolate work, for, with the exception of a few ostriches, there was not a single living creature to be seen on all the vast expanse of sandy plain. It was evidently too dry for game, and, with the exception of a deadly-looking cobra or two, we saw no reptiles. One insect, however, was abundant, and that was the common or house fly. There they came, "not as single spies, but in battalions," as I think the Old Testament says somewhere. He is an extraordinary animal, is the house fly. Go where you will you find him, and so it must always have been. I have seen him enclosed in amber which must, I was told, have been half a million years old, looking exactly like his descendant of today, and I have little doubt that when the last man on the earth lies dying he will be buzzing round—if that event should happen to occur in summer—watching for an opportunity to settle on his nose.

At sunset we halted, waiting for the moon to rise. At ten she came up beautiful and serene as ever, and, with one halt about two o'clock in the morning, we trudged wearily on through the night, till at last the welcome sun put a period to our labors. We drank a little and flung ourselves down, thoroughly tired out, on the sand, and were soon all asleep. There was no need to set a watch, for we had nothing to fear from anybody or anything in that vast, untenanted plain. Our only enemies were heat, thirst, and flies, but far rather would I have faced any danger from man or beast than that awful trinity. This time we were not so lucky as to find a sheltering rock to guard us from the glare of the sun, with the result that about seven o'clock we woke up experiencing the exact sensations one would attribute to a beefsteak on a gridiron. We were literally being baked through and through. The burning sun seemed to be sucking our very blood out of us. We sat up and gasped.

"Phew!" said I, grabbing at the halo of flies which buzzed cheerfully round my head. The heat did not affect them.

"My word," said Sir Henry.

"It *is* hot!" said Good.

It was hot, indeed, and there was not a bit of shelter to be had. Look where we would there was no rock or tree; nothing but an unending glare, rendered dazzling by the hot air which danced over the surface of the desert as it does over a red-hot stove.

"What is to be done?" asked Sir Henry. "We can't stand this for long."

We looked at each other blankly.

"I have it," said Good; "we must dig a hole and get into it, and cover ourselves with the karoo bushes."

It did not seem a very promising suggestion, but at least it was better than nothing, so we set to work, and, with the trowel we had brought with us and our hands, succeeded in about an hour in delving out a patch of ground about ten feet long by twelve wide to the depth of two feet. Then we cut a quantity of low scrub with our hunting knives, and, creeping into the hole, pulled it over us all, with the exception of Ventvögel, on whom, being a Hottentot, the sun had no particular effect. This gave us some slight shelter from the burning rays of the sun, but the heat in that amateur grave can be better imagined than described. The Black Hole of Calcutta must have been a fool to it; indeed, to this moment, I do not know how we lived through the day. There we lay panting, and every now and again moistening our lips from our scanty supply of water. Had we followed our inclinations we should have finished off all we had in the first two hours, but we had to exercise the most rigid care, for if our water failed us we knew that we must quickly perish miserably.

But everything has an end, if only you live long enough to see it, and somehow that miserable day wore on towards evening. About three o'clock in the afternoon we determined that we could stand it no longer. It would be better to die walking than to be slowly killed by heat and thirst in that dreadful hole. So, taking each of us a little drink from our fast diminishing supply of water, now heated to about the same temperature as a man's blood, we staggered on.

We had now covered some fifty miles of desert. If my reader will refer to the rough copy and translation of old Da Silvestra's map, he will see that the desert is marked as being forty leagues across, and the "pan bad water" is set down as being about in the middle of it. Now, forty leagues is one hundred and twenty miles; consequently, we ought at the most to have been within twelve or fifteen miles of the water, if any really existed.

Through the afternoon we crept slowly and painfully along, scarcely doing more than a mile and a half an hour. At sunset we again rested, waiting for the moon, and, after drinking a little, managed to get some sleep.

Before we lay down Umbopa pointed out to us a slight and indistinct hillock on the flat surface of the desert about eight miles away. At the distance it looked like an ant hill, and as I was dropping off to sleep I fell to wondering what it could be.

With the moon we started on again, feeling dreadfully exhausted, and suffering tortures from thirst and prickly heat. Nobody who has not felt it can know what we went through. We no longer walked, we staggered, now and again falling from exhaustion, and being obliged to call a halt every hour or so. We had scarcely energy left in us to speak. Up to now Good had chatted and joked, for he was a merry fellow; .but now he had not a joke left in him.

At last, about two o'clock, utterly worn out in body and

mind, we came to the foot of this queer hill, or sand koppie, which did at first sight resemble a gigantic ant heap about a hundred feet high, and covering at the base nearly a morgen (two acres) of ground.

Here we halted, and, driven by our desperate thirst, sucked down our last drops of water. We had but half a pint a head, and we could each have drunk a gallon.

Then we lay down. Just as I was dropping off to sleep I heard Umbopa remark to himself in Zulu, "If we cannot find water we shall all be dead before the moon rises tomorrow."

I shuddered, hot as it was. The near prospect of such an awful death is not pleasant, but even the thought of it could not keep me from sleeping.

Water! Water!

IN TWO HOURS' time, about four o'clock, I woke up. As soon as the first heavy demand of bodily fatigue had been satisfied, the torturing thirst from which I was suffering asserted itself. I could sleep no more. I had been dreaming that I was bathing in a running stream with green banks, and trees upon them, and I awoke to find myself in that arid wilderness, and to remember that, as Umbopa had said, if we did not find water that day we must certainly perish miserably. No human creature could live long without water in that heat. I sat up and rubbed my grimy face with my dry and horny hands. My lips and eyelids were stuck together, and it was only after some rubbing and with an effort that I was able to open them. It was not far from dawn, but there was none of the bright feel of dawn in the air, which was thick with a hot murkiness I cannot describe. The others were still sleeping. Presently it began to grow light enough to read, so I drew out a little pocket copy of the *Ingoldsby Legends* I had brought with me, and read the "Jackdaw of Rheims." When I got to where

> *A nice little boy held a golden ewer,*
> *Embossed, and filled with water as pure*
> *As any that flows between Rheims and Namur,*

I literally smacked my cracked lips, or, rather, tried to smack them. The mere thought of that pure water made me mad. If the cardinal had been there with his bell, book, and candle, I would have whipped in and drunk his water up, yes, even if he had already filled it with the suds of soap worthy of washing the hands of the pope, and I knew that the whole concentrated curse of the Catholic Church should fall upon me for so doing. I almost think I must have been a little light-headed with thirst and weariness and want of food; for I fell to thinking how astonished the cardinal and his nice little boy and the jackdaw would have looked to see a burned-up, brown-eyed, grizzled-haired little elephant hunter suddenly bound in and put his dirty face into the basin and swallow every drop of the precious water. The idea amused me so that I laughed, or rather cackled, aloud, which woke the others up, and they began to rub *their* dirty faces and get *their* gummed-up lips and eyelids apart.

As soon as we were all well awake, we fell to discussing the situation, which was serious enough. Not a drop of water was left. We turned the water bottles upside down and licked the tops, but it was a failure; they were as dry as a bone. Good, who had charge of the bottle of brandy, got it out and looked at it longingly; but Sir Henry promptly took it away from him, for to drink raw spirit would only have been to precipitate the end.

"If we do not find water we shall die," he said.

"If we can trust to the old don's map there should be some about," I said; but nobody seemed to derive much satisfaction from that remark, it was so evident that no great faith could be put in the map. It was now gradually growing light, and as we sat blankly staring at each other I observed the Hottentot Ventvögel rise and begin to walk about with his eyes on the ground. Presently he stopped short and, uttering a guttural exclamation, pointed to the earth.

"What is it?" we exclaimed, and simultaneously rose and went to where he was standing pointing at the ground.

"Well," I said, "it is pretty fresh springbok spoor; what of it?"

"Sprinbucks do not go far from water," he answered in Dutch.

"No," I answered, "I forgot; and thank God for it."

This little discovery put new life into us; it is wonderful how, when one is in a desperate position, one catches at the slightest hope, and feels almost happy in it. On a dark night a single star is better than nothing.

Meanwhile, Ventvögel was lifting his snub nose, and sniffing the hot air for all the world like an old impala ram who scents danger. Presently he spoke again.

"I *smell* water," he said.

Then we felt quite jubilant, for we knew what a wonderful instinct these wild-bred men possess.

Just at that moment the sun came up gloriously and revealed so grand a sight to our astonished eyes that for a moment or two we forgot even our thirst.

For there, not more than forty or fifty miles from us, glittering like silver in the early rays of the morning sun, were Sheba's breasts; and stretching away for hundreds of miles on each side of them was the great Suliman Berg. Now that I, sitting here, attempt to describe the extraordinary grandeur and beauty of that sight, language seems to fail me. I am impotent even before its memory. There, straight before us, were two enormous mountains, the like of which are not, I believe, to be seen in Africa, if, indeed, there are any other such in the world, measuring each at least fifteen thousand feet in height, standing not more than a dozen miles apart, connected by a precipitous cliff of rock, and towering up in awful white solemnity straight into the sky. These mountains standing thus, like the pillars of a gigantic gateway, are shaped exactly like a woman's breasts. Their bases swelled gently up from the plain, looking, at that distance, perfectly round and smooth; and on the top of each was a vast round hillock covered with snow, exactly corresponding to the nipple on the female breast. The stretch of cliff which connected them appeared to be some thousand feet in height, and perfectly precipitous, and on each side of them, as far as the eye could reach, extended similar lines of cliff, broken only here and there by flat, table-topped mountains, something like the world-famed one at Cape Town—a formation, by the way, very common in Africa.

To describe the grandeur of the whole view is beyond my powers. There was something so inexpressibly solemn and overpowering about those huge volcanoes—for doubtless they are extinct volcanoes—that it fairly took our breath away. For a while the morning lights played upon the snow and the brown and swelling masses beneath, and then, as though to veil the majestic sight from our curious eyes, strange mists and clouds gathered and increased around them, till presently we could only trace their pure and gigantic outline swelling ghostlike through the fleecy envelope. Indeed, as we afterwards discovered, they were normally wrapped in this curious gauzy mist, which doubtless accounted for our not having made them out more clearly before.

Scarcely had the mountains vanished into cloud-clad privacy before our thirst—literally a burning question—reasserted itself.

It was all very well for Ventvögel to say he smelled water, but look which way we would we could see no signs of it. So far as the eye could reach there was nothing but arid, sweltering sand and karoo scrub. We walked round the hillock and gazed about anxiously on the other side, but it was the same story, not a drop of water was to be seen; there was no indication of a pan, a pool, or a spring.

"You are a fool," I said angrily to Ventvögel; "there is no water."

But still he lifted his ugly snub nose and sniffed.

"I smell it, Baas," he answered; "it is somewhere in the air."

"Yes," I said, "no doubt it is in the clouds, and about two months hence it will fall and wash our bones."

Sir Henry stroked his yellow beard thoughtfully. "Perhaps it is on the top of the hill," he suggested.

"Rot," said Good. "Who ever heard of water being found on the top of a hill?"

"Let us go and look," I put in, and hopelessly enough we scrambled up the sandy sides of the hillock, Umbopa leading. Presently he stopped as though he were petrified.

"Nanzia manzie!" ("Here is water!") he cried with a loud voice.

We rushed up to him, and there, sure enough, in a deep cup or indentation on the very top of the sand koppie, was an undoubted pool of water. How it came to be in such a strange place we did not stop to inquire, nor did we hesitate at its black and uninviting appearance. It was water, or a good imitation of it, and that was enough for us. We gave a bound and a rush, and in another second were all down on our stomachs sucking up the uninviting fluid as though it were nectar fit for the gods. Heavens, how we did drink! Then, when we had done drinking, we tore off our clothes and sat down in it, absorbing the moisture through our parched skins. You, my reader, who have only to turn on a couple of taps and summon "hot" and "cold" from an unseen, vasty boiler, can have little idea of the luxury of that muddy wallow in brackish, tepid water.

After a while we arose from it, refreshed indeed, and fell to on our biltong, of which we had scarcely been able to touch a mouthful for twenty-four hours, and ate our fill. Then we smoked a pipe, and lay down by the side of that blessed pool under the overhanging shadow of the bank and slept till midday.

All that day we rested there by the water, thanking our stars that we had been lucky enough to find it, bad as it was, and not forgetting to render a due share of gratitude to the shade of the long-departed Da Silvestra, who had corked it down so accurately on the tail of his shirt. The wonderful thing to us was that it should have lasted so long, and the only way that I can account for it is by the supposition that it is fed by some spring deep down in the sand.

Having filled both ourselves and our water bottles as full as possible, in far better spirits we started off again with the moon. That night we covered nearly five-and-twenty miles, but, needless to say, found no more water, though we were lucky enough on the following day to get a little shade behind some ant heaps. When the sun rose and, for a while, cleared away the mysterious mists, Suliman's Berg and the two majestic breasts, now only about twenty miles off, seemed to be towering right above us, and looked grander than ever. At the approach of evening we started on again, and, to cut a long story short, by daylight next morning found ourselves upon the lowest slopes of Sheba's left breast, for which we had been steadily steering. By this time our water was again exhausted and we were suffering severely from thirst, nor indeed could we see any chance of relieving it till we reached the snow line, far, far above us. After resting an hour or two, driven to it by our torturing thirst, we went on again, toiling painfully in the burning heat up the lava slopes, for we found that the huge base of the mountain was composed entirely of lava beds belched out in some far-past age.

By eleven o'clock we were utterly exhausted, and were, generally speaking, in a very bad way indeed. The lava clinker, over which we had to make our way, though comparatively smooth compared with some clinker I have heard of, such as that on the island of Ascension, for instance, was yet rough enough to make our feet very sore, and this, together with our other miseries, had pretty well finished us. A few hundred yards above us were some large lumps of lava, and towards these we made with the intention of lying down beneath their shade. We reached them, and to our surprise, so far as we had a capacity for surprise left in us, on a little plateau or ridge close by we saw that the lava was covered with a dense green growth. Evidently soil formed from decomposed lava had rested there, and in due course had become the receptacle of seeds deposited by birds. But we did not take much further interest in the green growth, for one cannot live on grass, like Nebuchadnezzar. That requires a special dispensation of Providence and peculiar digestive organs. So we sat down under the rocks and groaned, and I, for one, heartily wished that we had never started on this fool's errand. As we were sitting there I saw Umbopa get up and hobble

.off towards the patch of green, and a few minutes afterwards, to my great astonishment, I perceived that usually uncommonly dignified individual dancing and shouting like a maniac, and waving something green. Off we all scrambled towards him as fast as our wearied limbs would carry us, hoping that he had found water.

"What is it, Umbopa, son of a fool?" I shouted in Zulu.

"It is food and water, Macumazahn," and again he waved the green thing.

Then I saw what he had got. It was a melon. We had hit upon a patch of wild melons, thousands of them, and dead ripe.

"Melons!" I yelled to Good, who was next me; and in another second he had his false teeth fixed in one.

I think we ate about six each before we had done, and, poor fruit as they were, I doubt if I ever thought anything nicer.

But melons are not very satisfying, and when we had satisfied our thirst with their pulpy substance, and set a stock to cool by the simple process of cutting them in two and setting them end on in the hot sun to get cold by evaporation, we began to feel exceedingly hungry. We had still some biltong left, but our stomachs turned from biltong, and, besides, we had to be very sparing of it, for we could not say when we should get more food. Just at this moment a lucky thing happened. Looking towards the desert I saw a flock of about ten large birds flying straight towards us.

"Skit, Baas, skit!" ("Shoot, Master, Shoot!") whispered the Hottentot, throwing himself on his face, an example which we all followed.

Then I saw that the birds were a flock of pauw (bustards), and that they would pass within fifty yards of my

head. Taking one of the repeating Winchesters, I waited
till they were nearly over us, and then jumped onto my
feet. On seeing me the pauw bunched up together, as I
expected they would, and I fired two shots straight into
the thick of them, and, as luck would have it, brought one
down, a fine fellow, which weighed about twenty pounds.
In half an hour we had a fire made of dry melon stalks, and
he was toasting over it, and we had such a feed as we had
not had for a week. We ate that pauw—nothing was left
of him but his bones and his beak—and felt not a little the
better afterwards.

That night we again went on with the moon, carrying as
many melons as we could with us. As we got higher up we
found the air got cooler and cooler, which was a great relief to us, and at dawn, so far as we could judge, were not
more than about a dozen miles from the snow line. Here
we found more melons, so had no longer any anxiety about
water, for we knew that we should soon get plenty of snow.
But the ascent had now become very precipitous, and we
made but slow progress, not more than a mile an hour. Also
that night we ate our last morsel of biltong. As yet, with
the exception of the pauw, we had seen no living thing on
the mountain, nor had we come across a single spring or
stream of water, which struck us as very odd, considering
all the snow above us, which must we thought melt sometimes. But as we afterwards discovered, owing to some
cause which it is quite beyond my power to explain, all the
streams flowed down upon the north side of the mountains.

We now began to grow very anxious about food. We
had escaped death by thirst, but it seemed probable that
it was only to die of hunger. The events of the next three
miserable days are best described by copying the entries
made at the time in my notebook.

"21st May.—Started 11:00 A.M., finding the atmosphere quite cold enough to travel by day, carrying some watermelons with us. Struggled on all day, but saw no more melons, having, evidently, passed out of their district. Saw no game of any sort. Halted for the night at sundown, having had no food for many hours. Suffered much during the night from cold.

"22d.—Started at sunrise again, feeling very faint and weak. Only made five miles all day; found some patches of snow of which we ate, but nothing else. Camped at night under the edge of a great plateau. Cold bitter. Drank a little brandy each, and huddled ourselves together, each wrapped up in our blanket to keep ourselves alive. Are now suffering frightfully from starvation and weariness. Thought that Ventvögel would have died during the night.

"23d.—Struggled forward once more as soon as the sun was well up, and had thawed our limbs a little. We are now in a dreadful plight, and I fear that unless we get food this will be our last day's journey. But little brandy left. Good, Sir Henry, and Umbopa bear up wonderfully, but Ventvögel is in a very bad way. Like most Hottentots, he cannot stand cold. Pangs of hunger not so bad, but have a sort of numb feeling about the stomach. Others say the same. We are now on a level with the precipitous chain, or wall of lava, connecting the two breasts, and the view is glorious. Behind us the great glowing desert rolls away to the horizon, and before us lies mile upon mile of smooth, hard snow almost level, but swelling gently upward, out of the center of which the nipple of the mountain, which appears to be some miles in circumference, rises about four thousand feet into the sky. Not a living thing is to be seen. God help us, I fear our time has come."

And now I will drop the journal, partly because it is not

very interesting reading, and partly because what follows requires perhaps rather more accurate telling.

All that day (the twenty-third of May) we struggled slowly on up the incline of snow, lying down from time to time to rest. A strange, gaunt crew we must have looked, as, laden as we were, we dragged our weary feet over the dazzling plain, glaring round us with hungry eyes. Not that there was much use in glaring, for there was nothing to eat. We did not do more than seven miles that day. Just before sunset we found ourselves right under the nipple of Sheba's left breast, which towered up thousands of feet into the air above us, a vast, smooth hillock of frozen snow. Bad as we felt, we could not but appreciate the wonderful scene, made even more wonderful by the flying rays of light from the setting sun, which here and there stained the snow blood red, and crowned the towering mass above us with a diadem of glory.

"I say," gasped Good presently, "we ought to be somewhere near the cave the old gentleman wrote about."

"Yes," said I, "if there is a cave."

"Come, Quatermain," groaned Sir Henry, "don't talk like that; I have every faith in the don; remember the water. We shall find the place soon."

"If we don't find it before dark we are dead men, that is all about it," was my consolatory reply.

For the next ten minutes we trudged on in silence, when suddenly Umbopa, who was marching along beside me, wrapped up in his blanket and with a leather belt strapped so tight round his stomach, to "make his hunger small," as he said, that his waist looked like a girl's, caught me by the arm.

"Look!" he said, pointing towards the springing slope of the nipple.

I followed his glance, and perceived, some two hundred yards from us, what appeared to be a hole in the snow.

"It is the cave," said Umbopa.

We made the best of our way to the spot, and found, sure enough, that the hole was the mouth of a cave, no doubt the same as that of which Da Silvestra wrote. We were none too soon, for just as we reached shelter the sun went down with startling rapidity, leaving the whole place nearly dark. In these latitudes there is but little twilight. We crept into the cave, which did not appear to be very big, and, huddling ourselves together for warmth, swallowed what remained of our brandy—barely a mouthful each—and tried to forget our miseries in sleep. But this the cold was too intense to allow us to do. I am convinced that at that great altitude the thermometer cannot have been less than fourteen or fifteen degrees below freezing point. What this meant to us, enervated as we were by hardship, want of food, and the great heat of the desert, my reader can imagine better than I can describe. Suffice it to say that it was something as near death from exposure as I have ever felt. There we sat hour after hour through the bitter night, feeling the frost wander round and nip us now in the finger, now in the foot, and now in the face. In vain did we huddle up closer and closer; there was no warmth in our miserable, starved carcasses. Sometimes one of us would drop into an uneasy slumber for a few minutes, but we could not sleep long, and perhaps it was fortunate, for I doubt if we should ever have waked again. I believe it was only by force of will that we kept ourselves alive at all.

Not very long before dawn I heard the Hottentot Ventvögel, whose teeth had been chattering all night like castanets, give a deep sigh, and then his teeth stopped chattering. I did not think anything of it at the time, concluding that he had gone to sleep. His back was resting against mine, and it seemed to grow colder and colder, till at last it was like ice.

At length the air began to grow gray with light, then swift golden arrows came flashing across the snow, and at last the glorious sun peeped up above the lava wall and looked in upon our half-frozen forms and upon Ventvögel, sitting there among us *stone dead*. No wonder his back had felt cold, poor fellow. He had died when I heard him sigh, and was now almost frozen stiff. Shocked beyond measure, we dragged ourselves from the corpse (strange, the horror we all have of the companionship of a dead body), and left it still sitting there, with its arms clasped round its knees.

By this time the sunlight was pouring its cold rays (for here they were cold) straight in at the mouth of the cave. Suddenly I heard an exclamation of fear from someone, and turned my head down the cave.

And this was what I saw. Sitting at the end of it, for it was not more than twenty feet long, was another form, of which the head rested on the chest and the long arms hung down. I stared at it, and saw that it too was a *dead man*, and, what was more, a white man.

The others saw it, too, and the sight proved too much for our shattered nerves. One and all we scrambled out of the cave as fast as our half-frozen limbs would allow.

7 ♦

Solomon's Road

OUTSIDE the cave we halted, feeling rather foolish.

"I am going back," said Sir Henry.

"Why?" asked Good.

"Because it has struck me that—what we saw—may be my brother."

This was a new idea, and we re-entered the cave to put it to the proof. After the bright light outside our eyes, weak as they were with staring at the snow, could not for a while pierce the gloom of the cave. Presently, however, we grew accustomed to the semidarkness, and advanced to the dead form.

Sir Henry knelt down and peered into its face.

"Thank God," he said with a sigh of relief, "it is not my brother."

Then I went and looked. The corpse was that of a tall man in middle life, with aquiline features, grizzled hair, and a long black mustache. The skin was perfectly yellow, and stretched tightly over the bones. Its clothing, with the exception of what seemed to be the remains of a pair of woolen hose, had been removed, leaving the skeleton-like frame naked. Round the neck hung a yellow ivory crucifix. The corpse was frozen perfectly stiff.

"Who on earth can it be?" said I.

"Can't you guess?" asked Good.

I shook my head.

"Why, the old don, José da Silvestra, of course—who else?"

"Impossible!" I gasped. "He died three hundred years ago."

"And what is there to prevent his lasting for three thousand years in this atmosphere, I should like to know?" asked Good. "If only the air is cold enough, flesh and blood will keep as fresh as New Zealand mutton forever, and Heaven knows it is cold enough here. The sun never gets in here; no animal comes here to tear or destroy. No doubt his slave, of whom he speaks on the map, took off his clothes and left him. He could not have buried him alone. Look here," he went on, stooping down and picking up a queer-shaped bone scraped at the end into a sharp point, "here is the 'cleft bone' that he used to draw the map with."

We gazed astonished for a moment, forgetting our own miseries in the extraordinary and, as it seemed to us, semi-miraculous sight.

"Ay," said Sir Henry, "and here is where he got his ink from," and he pointed to a small wound on the dead man's left arm. "Did ever man see such a thing before?"

There was no longer any doubt about the matter, which I confess, for my own part, perfectly appalled me. There he sat, the dead man, whose directions, written some ten generations ago, had led us to this spot. There in my own hand was the rude pen with which he had written them, and there round his neck was the crucifix his dying lips had kissed. Gazing at him my imagination could reconstruct the whole scene: the traveler dying of cold and starvation, and yet striving to convey the great secret he had discovered to the world; the awful loneliness of his death, of which the evidence sat before us. It even seemed to me that I could trace in his strongly marked features a likeness to those of my poor friend Silvestre, his descendant, who had died twenty years ago in my arms, but perhaps that was fancy. At any rate, there he sat, a sad memento of the fate that so often overtakes those who would penetrate into the unknown; and there probably he will still sit, crowned with the dread majesty of death, for centuries yet unborn, to startle the eyes of wanderers like ourselves, if any such should ever come again to invade his loneliness. The thing overpowered us, already nearly done to death as we were with cold and hunger.

"Let us go," said Sir Henry in a low voice; "stay, we will give him a companion," and, lifting up the dead body of the Hottentot Ventvögel, he placed it near that of the old don. Then he stooped down and with a jerk broke the rotten string of the crucifix round his neck, for his fingers were too cold to attempt to unfasten it. I believe that he still has it. I took the pen, and it is before me as I write—sometimes I sign my name with it.

Then, leaving those two, the proud white man of a past age and the poor Hottentot, to keep their eternal vigil in the midst of the eternal snows, we crept out of the cave into the welcome sunshine and resumed our path, wondering in our hearts how many hours it would be before we were even as they are.

When we had gone about half a mile we came to the edge of the plateau, for the nipple of the mountain did not rise out of its exact center, though from the desert side it seemed to do so. What lay below us we could not see, for the landscape was wreathed in billows of morning mist. Presently, however, the higher layers of mist cleared a little, and revealed, some five hundred yards beneath us, at the end of a long slope of snow, a patch of green grass, through which a stream was running. Nor was this all. By the stream, basking in the morning sun, stood and lay a group of from ten to fifteen *large antelopes*—at that distance we could not see exactly what they were.

The sight filled us with an unreasoning joy. There was food in plenty if only we could get it. But the question was how to get it. The beasts were fully six hundred yards off, a very long shot, and one not to be depended on when one's life hung on the results.

Rapidly we discussed the advisability of trying to stalk the game, but finally reluctantly dismissed it. To begin with, the wind was not favorable, and further, we should be certain to be perceived, however careful we were, against the blinding background of snow which we should be obliged to traverse.

"Well, we must have a try from where we are," said Sir Henry. "Which shall it be, Quatermain, the repeating rifles or the expresses?"

Here again was a question. The Winchester repeaters— of which we had two, Umbopa carrying poor Ventvögel's as well as his own—were sighted up to a thousand yards, whereas the expresses were only sighted to three hundred and fifty, beyond which distance shooting with them was more or less guesswork. On the other hand, if they did hit, the express bullets, being expanding, were much more likely to bring the game down. It was a knotty point, but I made up my mind that we must risk it and use the expresses.

"Let each of us take the buck opposite to him. Aim well at the point of the shoulder, and high up," said I; "and Umbopa, do you give the word, so that we may all fire together."

Then came a pause, each man aiming his level best, as indeed one is likely to do when one knows that life itself depends upon the shot.

"Fire!" said Umbopa in Zulu, and at almost the same instant the three rifles rang out loudly; three clouds of smoke hung for a moment before us, and a hundred echoes went flying away over the silent snow. Presently the smoke cleared, and revealed—oh, joy!—a great buck lying on its back and kicking furiously in its death agony. We gave a yell of triumph; we were saved, we should not starve. Weak as we were, we rushed down the intervening slope of snow, and in ten minutes from the time of firing, the animal's heart and liver were lying smoking before us. But now a new difficulty arose; we had no fuel, and therefore could make no fire to cook them at. We gazed at each other in dismay.

"Starving men must not be fanciful," said Good; "we must eat raw meat."

There was no other way out of the dilemma, and our gnawing hunger made the proposition less distasteful than it would otherwise have been. So we took the heart and liver and buried them for a few minutes in a patch of snow to cool them off. Then we washed them in the ice-cold water of the stream, and lastly ate them greedily. It sounds horrible enough, but, honestly, I never tasted anything so good as that raw meat. In a quarter of an hour we were changed men. Our life and our vigor came back to us, our feeble pulses grew strong again, and the blood went coursing through our veins. But, mindful of the results of over-feeding on starving stomachs, we were careful not to eat too much, stopping while we were still hungry.

"Thank God!" said Sir Henry. "That brute has saved our lives. What is it, Quatermain?"

I rose and went to look at the antelope, for I was not certain. It was about the size of a donkey, with large, curved horns. I had never seen one like it before, the species was

new to me. It was brown with faint red stripes and a thick
coat. I afterwards discovered that the natives of that wonderful country called the species "inco." It was very rare,
and only found at a great altitude, where no other game
would live. The animal was fairly shot high up in the
shoulder, though whose bullet it was that brought it down
we could not, of course, discover. I believe that Good,
mindful of his marvelous shot at the giraffe, secretly set it
down to his own prowess, and we did not contradict him.

We had been so busy satisfying our starving stomachs
that we had hitherto not found time to look about us. But
now, having set Umbopa to cut off as much of the best
meat as we were likely to be able to carry, we began to inspect our surroundings. The mist had now cleared away,
for it was eight o'clock, and the sun had sucked it up, so
we were able to take in all the country before us at a glance.
I know not how to describe the glorious panorama which
unfolded itself to our enraptured gaze. I have never seen
anything like it before, nor shall, I suppose, again.

Behind and over us towered Sheba's snowy breasts, and
below, some five thousand feet beneath where we stood, lay
league on league of the most lovely champaign country.
Here were dense patches of lofty forest, there a great river
wound its silvery way. To the left stretched a vast expanse
of rich, undulating veldt, on which we could just make out
countless herds of game or cattle, at that distance we could
not tell which. This expanse appeared to be ringed in by a
wall of distant mountains. To the right the country was
more or less mountainous, that is, solitary hills stood up
from its level, with stretches of cultivated lands between,
among which we could distinctly see groups of dome-shaped
huts. The landscape lay before us like a map, in which rivers
flashed like silver snakes, and Alplike peaks crowned with

wildly twisted snow wreaths rose in solemn grandeur, while over all was the glad sunlight and the wide breath of Nature's happy life.

Two curious things struck us as we gazed. First, that the country before us must lie at least five thousand feet higher than the desert we had crossed, and, secondly, that all the rivers flowed from south to north. As we had painful reason to know, there was no water at all on the southern side of the vast range on which we stood, but on the northern side were many streams, most of which appeared to unite with the great river we could trace winding away farther than we could follow it.

We sat down for a while and gazed in silence at this wonderful view. Presently Sir Henry spoke.

"Isn't there something on the map about Solomon's Great Road?" he said.

I nodded, my eyes still looking out over the far country.

"Well, look; there it is!" and he pointed a little to our right.

Good and I looked accordingly, and there, winding away towards the plain, was what appeared to be a wide turnpike road. We had not seen it at first because it, on reaching the plain, turned behind some broken country. We did not say anything, at least not much; we were beginning to lose the sense of wonder. Somehow it did not seem particularly unnatural that we should find a sort of Roman road in this strange land. We accepted the fact, that was all.

"Well," said Good, "it must be quite near us if we cut off to the right. Hadn't we better be making a start?"

This was sound advice, and so soon as we had washed our faces and hands in the stream we acted on it. For a mile or so we made our way over boulders and across patches of snow, till suddenly, on reaching the top of the little rise, there lay the road at our feet. It was a splendid road cut out of the solid rock, at least fifty feet wide, and apparently well kept; but the odd thing about it was that it seemed to begin there. We walked down and stood on it, but one single hundred paces behind us, in the direction of Sheba's breasts, it vanished, the whole surface of the mountain being strewed with boulders interspersed with patches of snow.

"What do you make of that, Quatermain?" asked Sir Henry.

I shook my head, I could make nothing of it.

"I have it!" said Good. "The road no doubt ran right over the range and across the desert on the other side, but the sand of the desert has covered it up, and above us it has been obliterated by some volcanic eruption of molten lava."

This seemed a good suggestion; at any rate, we accepted it, and proceeded down the mountain. It was a very different business traveling along downhill on that magnificent pathway with full stomachs, to what it had been traveling uphill over the snow quite starved and almost frozen. Indeed, had it not been for melancholy recollections of poor Ventvögel's sad fate, and of that grim cave where he kept company with the old don, we should have been positively cheerful, notwithstanding the sense of unknown dangers before us. Every mile we walked the atmosphere grew softer and balmier, and the country before us shone with a yet more luminous beauty. As for the road itself, I never saw such an engineering work, though Sir Henry said that the great road over the St. Gothard in Switzerland was very like it. No difficulty had been too great for the Old World engineer who designed it. At one place we came to a great ravine three hundred feet broad and at least a hundred deep. This vast gulf was actually filled in, apparently with huge blocks of dressed stone, with arches pierced at the bottom for a waterway, over which the road went sublimely on. At another place it was cut in zigzags out of the side of a precipice five hundred feet deep, and in a third it tunneled right through the base of an intervening ridge a space of thirty yards or more.

Here we noticed that the sides of the tunnel were covered with quaint sculptures, mostly of mailed figures driving chariots. One, which was exceedingly beautiful, represented a whole battle scene with a convoy of captives being marched off in the distance.

"Well," said Sir Henry, after inspecting this ancient work of art, "it is very well to call this Solomon's Road, but my humble opinion is that the Egyptians have been here before Solomon's people ever set a foot on it. If that isn't Egyptian handiwork, all I have to say is it is very like it."

By midday we had advanced sufficiently far down the mountain to reach the region where wood was to be met with. First we came to scattered bushes which grew more and more frequent, till at last we found the road winding through a vast grove of silver trees similar to those which are to be seen on the slopes of Table Mountain at Cape Town. I had never before met with them in all my wanderings, except at the Cape, and their appearance here astonished me greatly.

"Ah!" said Good, surveying these shining-leaved trees with evident enthusiasm. "Here is lots of wood, let us stop and cook some dinner; I have about digested that raw meat."

Nobody objected to this, so leaving the road, we made our way to a stream which was babbling away not far off, and soon had a goodly fire of dry boughs blazing. Cutting off some substantial hunks from the flesh of the inco which we had brought with us, we proceeded to toast them on the ends of sharp sticks, as one sees the Kaffirs do, and ate them with relish. After filling ourselves, we lit our pipes and gave ourselves up to enjoyment, which, compared to the hardships we had recently undergone, seemed almost heavenly.

The brook, of which the banks were clothed with dense masses of a gigantic species of maidenhair fern interspersed with feathery tufts of wild asparagus, babbled away merrily at our side, the soft air murmured through the leaves of the silver trees, doves cooed around, and bright-winged birds flashed like living gems from bough to bough. It was like Paradise.

The magic of the place, combined with the overwhelming sense of dangers left behind and of the promised land reached at last, seemed to charm us into silence. Sir Henry and Umbopa sat conversing in a mixture of broken English and Kitchen Zulu in a low voice, but earnestly enough, and I lay, with my eyes half shut, upon that fragrant bed of fern and watched them. Presently I missed Good, and looked to see what had become of him. As I did so I observed him sitting by the bank of the stream, in which he had been bathing. He had nothing on but his flannel shirt, and, his natural habits of extreme neatness having reasserted themselves, was actively employed in making a most elaborate toilet. He had washed his gutta-percha collar, thoroughly shaken out his trousers, coat, and waistcoat, and was now folding them up neatly till he was ready to put them on, shaking his head sadly as he did so over the numerous rents and tears in them which had naturally resulted from our frightful journey. Then he took his boots, scrubbed them over with a handful of fern, and finally

rubbed them over with a piece of fat which he had carefully saved from the inco meat, till they looked, comparatively speaking, respectable. Having inspected them judi-
ciously through his eyeglass, he put them on and began
a fresh operation. From a little bag he carried he produced
a pocketcomb in which was fixed a tiny looking glass, and
in this surveyed himself. Apparently he was not satisfied,
for he proceeded to do his hair with great care. Then came
a pause while he again contemplated the effect; still it was
not satisfactory. He felt his chin, on which was now the
accumulated scrub of a ten days' beard. "Surely," thought
I, "he is not going to try and shave." But so it was. Taking
the piece of fat with which he had greased his boots, he
washed it carefully in the stream. Then, diving again into
the bag, he brought out a little pocket razor with a guard
to it, such as are sold to people afraid of cutting themselves,
or to those about to undertake a sea voyage. Then he vigorously scrubbed his face and chin with the fat and began.
But it was evidently a painful process, for he groaned very
much over it, and I was convulsed with inward laughter as
I watched him struggling with that stubbly beard. It seemed
so very odd that a man should take the trouble to shave
himself with a piece of fat in such a place and under such
circumstances. At last he succeeded in getting the worst of
the scrub off the right side of his face and chin, when
suddenly I, who was watching, became aware of a flash of
light that passed just by his head.

Good sprang up with a profane exclamation (if it had
not been a safety razor he would certainly have cut his
throat), and so did I, without the exclamation, and this
was what I saw. Standing there, not more than twenty
paces from where I was, and ten from Good, was a group
of men. They were very tall and copper-colored, and some

of them wore great plumes of black feathers and short cloaks of leopard skins; this was all I noticed at the moment. In front of them stood a youth of about seventeen, his hand still raised and his body bent forward in the attitude of a Grecian statue of a spear thrower. Evidently the flash of light had been a weapon, and he had thrown it.

As I looked an old, soldierly-looking man stepped forward out of the group, and, catching the youth by the arm, said something to him. Then they advanced upon us.

Sir Henry, Good, and Umbopa had by this time seized their rifles and lifted them threateningly. The party of natives still came on. It struck me that they could not know what rifles were, or they would not have treated them with such contempt.

"Put down your guns!" I hallooed to the others, seeing that our only chance of safety lay in conciliation. They obeyed, and, walking to the front, I addressed the elderly man who had checked the youth.

"Greeting," I said in Zulu, not knowing what language to use. To my surprise I was understood.

"Greeting," answered the man, not, indeed, in the same tongue, but in a dialect so closely allied to it that neither Umbopa nor myself had any difficulty in understanding it. Indeed, as we afterwards found out, the language spoken by this people was an old-fashioned form of the Zulu tongue, bearing about the same relationship to it that the English of Chaucer does to the English of the nineteenth century.

"Whence come ye?" he went on. "What are ye? And why are the faces of three of ye white, and the face of the fourth as the face of our mothers' sons?" and he pointed to Umbopa. I looked at Umbopa as he said it, and it flashed across me that he was right. Umbopa's face was like the faces of the men before me; so was his great form. But I had no time to reflect on this coincidence.

"We are strangers, and come in peace," I answered, speaking very slow, so that he might understand me, "and this man is our servant."

"Ye lie," he answered, "no strangers can cross the mountains where all things die. But what do your lies matter; if ye are strangers then ye must die, for no strangers may live in the land of the Kukuanas. It is the king's law. Prepare then to die, O strangers!"

I was slightly staggered at this, more especially as I saw the hands of some of the party of men steal down to their sides, where hung on each what looked to me like a large and heavy knife.

"What does that beggar say?" asked Good.

"He says we are going to be scragged," I answered grimly.

"Oh, Lord," groaned Good, and, as was his way when perplexed, put his hand to his false teeth, dragging the top set down and allowing them to fly back to his jaw with a snap. It was a most fortunate move, for next second the dignified crowd of Kukuanas gave a simultaneous yell of horror, and bolted back some yards.

"What's up?" said I.

"It's his teeth," whispered Sir Henry excitedly. "He moved them. Take them out, Good, take them out!"

He obeyed, slipping the set into the sleeve of his flannel shirt.

In another second curiosity had overcome fear, and the men advanced slowly. Apparently they had now forgotten their amiable intentions of doing for us.

"How is it, O strangers," asked the old man solemnly, "that the teeth of the man"—(pointing to Good, who had nothing on but a flannel shirt, and had only half finished his shaving)—"whose body is clothed, and whose legs are bare, who grows hair on one side of his sickly face and not on the other, and who has one shining and transparent eye, move of themselves, coming away from the jaws and returning of their own will?"

"Open your mouth," I said to Good, who promptly curled up his lips and grinned at the old gentleman like an angry dog, revealing to their astonished gaze two thin red lines of gum as utterly innocent of ivories as a newborn elephant. His audience gasped.

"Where are his teeth?" they shouted. "With our eyes we saw them."

Turning his head slowly and with a gesture of ineffable contempt, Good swept his hand across his mouth. Then he grinned again, and lo! there were two rows of lovely teeth.

The young man who had flung the knife threw himself down on the grass and gave vent to a prolonged howl of terror; and as for the old gentleman, his knees knocked together with fear.

"I see that ye are spirits," he said falteringly; "did ever man born of woman have hair on one side of his face and not on the other, or a round and transparent eye, or teeth which moved and melted away and grew again? Pardon us, O my lords."

Here was luck indeed, and, needless to say, I jumped at the chance.

"It is granted," I said, with an imperial smile. "Nay, ye shall know the truth. We come from another world, though we are men such as ye; we come," I went on, "from the biggest star that shines at night."

"Oh! Oh!" groaned the chorus of astonished aborigines.

"Yes," I went on, "we do, indeed," and I again smiled benignly as I uttered that amazing lie. "We come to stay with you a little while, and bless you by our sojourn. Ye will see, O friends, that I have prepared myself by learning your language."

"It is so, it is so," said the chorus.

"Only, my lord," put in the old gentleman, "thou hast learned it very badly."

I cast an indignant glance at him and he quailed.

"Now, friends," I continued, "ye might think that after so long a journey we should find it in our hearts to avenge such a reception, mayhap to strike cold in death the impious hand that—that, in short—threw a knife at the head of him whose teeth come and go."

"Spare him, my lords," said the old man in supplication; "he is the king's son, and I am his uncle. If anything befalls him his blood will be required at my hands."

"Yes, that is certainly so," put in the young man with great emphasis.

"You may perhaps doubt our power to avenge," I went on, heedless of this byplay. "Stay, I will show you. Here, you dog and slave"—addressing Umbopa in a savage tone—"give me the magic tube that speaks"; and I tipped a wink towards my express rifle.

Umbopa rose to the occasion, and with something as nearly resembling a grin as I have ever seen on his dignified face, handed me the rifle.

"It is here, O lord of lords," he said with a deep obeisance.

Now, just before I asked for the rifle I had perceived a little klipspringer antelope standing on a mass of rock about seventy yards away, and determined to risk a shot at it.

"Ye see that buck," I said, pointing the animal out to the party before me. "Tell me, is it possible for man, born of woman, to kill it from here with a noise?"

"It is not possible, my lord," answered the old man.

"Yet shall I kill it," I said quietly.

The old man smiled. "That my lord cannot do," he said.

I raised the rifle, and covered the buck. It was a small animal, and one which one might well be excused for missing, but I knew that it would not do to miss.

I drew a deep breath, and slowly pressed on the trigger. The buck stood still as stone.

Bang! Thud! The buck sprang into the air and fell on the rock dead as a doornail.

A groan of terror burst from the group before us.

"If ye want meat," I remarked coolly, "go fetch that buck."

The old man made a sign and one of his followers departed, and presently returned bearing the klipspringer. I noticed, with satisfaction, that I had hit it fairly behind the shoulder. They gathered round the poor creature's body, gazing at the bullet hole in consternation.

"Ye see," I said, "I do not speak empty words."

There was no answer.

"If ye yet doubt our power," I went on, "let one of ye go stand upon that rock, that I may make him as this buck."

None of them seemed at all inclined to take the hint, till at last the king's son spoke.

"It is well said. Do thou, my uncle, go stand upon the rock. It is but a buck that the magic has killed. Surely it cannot kill a man."

The old gentleman did not take the suggestion in good part. Indeed, he seemed hurt.

"No, no!" he ejaculated hastily. "My old eyes have seen

enough. These are wizards, indeed. Let us bring them to the king. Yet if any should wish a further proof, let *him* stand upon the rock, that the magic tube may speak with him."

There was a most general and hasty expression of dissent.

"Let not good magic be wasted on our poor bodies," said one, "we are satisfied. All the witchcraft of our people cannot show the like of this."

"It is so," remarked the old gentleman in a tone of intense relief; "without any doubt it is so. Listen, children of the stars, children of the shining eye and the movable teeth, who roar out in thunder and slay from afar. I am Infadoos, son of Kafa, once king of the Kukuana people. This youth is Scragga."

"He nearly scragged me," murmured Good.

"Scragga, son of Twala, the great king—Twala, husband of a thousand wives, chief and lord paramount of the Kukuanas, keeper of the great road, terror of his enemies, student of the Black Arts, leader of a hundred thousand warriors: Twala the One-eyed, the Black, the Terrible."

"So," said I superciliously, "lead us then to Twala. We do not talk with low people and underlings."

"It is well, my lords, we will lead you, but the way is long. We are hunting three days' journey from the place of the king. But let my lords have patience, and we will lead them."

"It is well," I said carelessly. "All time is before us, for we do not die. We are ready; lead on. But Infadoos, and thou, Scragga, beware! Play us no tricks, make for us no snares, for before your brains of mud have thought of them we shall know them and avenge them. The light from the transparent eye of him with the bare legs and the half-haired face [Good] shall destroy you, and go through your

land; his vanishing teeth shall fix themselves fast in you
and eat you up, you and your wives and children; the magic
tubes shall talk with you loudly, and make you as sieves.
Beware!"

This magnificent address did not fail of its effect; indeed,
it was hardly needed, so deeply were our friends already impressed with our powers.

The old man made a deep obeisance, and murmured the
word "Koom, Koom," which I afterwards discovered was
their royal salute, corresponding to the Bayéte of the Zulus,
and, turning, addressed his followers. These at once proceeded to lay hold of all our goods and chattels, in order
to bear them for us, excepting only the guns, which they
would on no account touch. They even seized Good's
clothes, which were, as the reader may remember, neatly
folded up beside him.

He at once made a dive for them, and a loud altercation
ensued.

"Let not my lord of the transparent eye and the melting
teeth touch them," sad the old man. "Surely his slaves
shall carry the things."

"But I want to put 'em on!" roared Good in nervous
English.

Umbopa translated.

"Nay, my lord," put in Infadoos, "would my lord cover
up his beautiful white legs"—although he was so dark Good
had a singularly white skin—"from the eyes of his servants?
Have we offended my lord that he should do such a thing?"

Here I nearly exploded with laughing; and meanwhile,
one of the men started on with the garments.

"Damn it!" roared Good. "That black villain has got my
trousers."

"Look here, Good," said Sir Henry, "you have appeared

in this country in a certain character, and you must live up
to it. It will never do for you to put on trousers again.
Henceforth you must live in a flannel shirt, a pair of boots,
and an eyeglass."

"Yes," I said, "and with whiskers on one side of your
face and not on the other. If you change any of these things
they will think that we are impostors. I am very sorry for
you, but, seriously, you must do it. If once they begin to
suspect us, our lives will not be worth a brass farthing."

"Do you really think so?" said Good gloomily.

"I do indeed. Your 'beautiful white legs' and your eyeglass are now *the* feature of our party, and, as Sir Henry
says, you must live up to them. Be thankful that you have
got your boots on, and that the air is warm."

Good sighed, and said no more, but it took him a fortnight to get accustomed to his attire.

We Enter Kukuanaland

ALL THAT afternoon we traveled on along the magnificent roadway, which headed steadily in a northwesterly direction. Infadoos and Scragga walked with us, but their followers marched about one hundred paces ahead.

"Infadoos," I said at length, "who made this road?"

"It was made, my lord, of old time, none knew how or when, not even the wise woman, Gagool, who has lived for generations. We are not old enough to remember its making. None can make such roads now, but the king lets no grass grow upon it."

"And whose are the writings on the walls of the caves through which we have passed on the road?" I asked, referring to the Egyptian-like sculptures we had seen.

"My lord, the hands that made the road wrote the wonderful writings. We know not who wrote them."

"When did the Kukuana race come into this country?"

"My lord, the race came down here like the breath of a storm ten thousand thousand moons ago, from the great lands which lie there beyond," and he pointed to the north. "They could travel no farther, so say the old voices of our fathers that have come down to us, the children, and so says Gagool, the wise woman, the smeller-out of witches, because of the great mountains which ring in the land," and he pointed to the snow-clad peaks. "The country, too, was good, so they settled here and grew strong and power-
100

ful, and now our numbers are like the sea sand, and when Twala the king calls up his regiment their plumes cover the plain as far as the eye of man can reach."

"And if the land is walled in with mountains, who is there for the regiments to fight with?"

"Nay, my lord, the country is open there," and again he pointed towards the north, "and now and again war-riors sweep down upon us in clouds from a land we know not, and we slay them. It is the third part of the life of a man since there was a war. Many thousands died in it, but we destroyed those who came to eat us up. So, since then there has been no war."

"Your warriors must grow weary of resting on their spears."

"My lord, there was one war, just after we destroyed the people that came down upon us, but it was a civil war— dog eat dog."

"How was that?"

"My lord, the king, my half-brother, had a brother born at the same birth and of the same woman. It is not our custom, my lord, to let twins live; the weakest must always die. But the mother of the king hid away the weakest child, which was born the last, for her heart yearned over it, and the child is Twala the king. I am his younger brother born of another wife."

"Well?"

"My lord, Kafa, our father, died when we came to man-hood, and my brother Imotu was made king in his place, and for a space reigned and had a son by his favorite wife. When the babe was three years old, just after the great war, during which no man could sow or reap, a famine came upon the land, and the people murmured because of the famine, and looked round like a starved lion for something to rend. Then it was that Gagool, the wise and terrible woman, who does not die, proclaimed to the people, saying, 'The king Imotu is no king.' And at the time Imotu was sick with a wound, and lay in his hut not able to move.

"Then Gagool went into a hut and led out Twala, my half-brother, and the twin brother of the king, whom she had hidden since he was born among the caves and rocks, and, stripping the moocha off his loins, showed the people of the Kukuanas the mark of the sacred snake coiled round his waist, wherewith the eldest son of the king is marked at birth, and cried out loud, 'Behold, your king, whom I have saved for you even to this day!' And the people, being mad with hunger and altogether bereft of reason and the knowledge of truth, cried out, '*The king! The king!*' but I knew that it was not so, for Imotu, my brother, was the elder of the twins, and was the lawful king. And just as the tumult was at its height Imotu the king, though he was very sick, came crawling from his hut holding his wife by the hand, and followed by his little son Ignosi [The Lightning].

" 'What is this noise?' he asked. 'Why cry ye *The king! The king!*'

"Then Twala, his own brother, born of the same woman and in the same hour, ran to him, and, taking him by the hair, stabbed him through the heart with his knife. And the people, being fickle, and ever ready to worship the rising sun, clapped their hands and cried, '*Twala is king!* Now we know that Twala is king!' "

"And what became of his wife and her son Ignosi? Did Twala kill them too?"

"Nay, my lord. When she saw that her lord was dead she seized the child with a cry, and ran away. Two days afterwards she came to a kraal very hungry, and none would give her milk or food, now that her lord the king was dead, for all men hate the unfortunate. But at nightfall a little child, a girl, crept out and brought her to eat, and she blessed the child, and went on towards the mountains with her boy before the sun rose again, where she must have perished, for none have seen her since, nor the child Ignosi."

"Then if this child Ignosi had lived, he would be the true king of the Kukuana people?"

"That is so, my lord; the sacred snake is round his middle. If he lives he is the king; but alas! he is long dead."

"See, my lord," and he pointed to a vast collection of huts surrounded with a fence, which was in its turn surrounded by a great ditch, that lay on the plain beneath us. "That is the kraal where the wife of Imotu was last seen with the child Ignosi. It is there that we shall sleep tonight, if, indeed," he added doubtfully, "my lords sleep at all upon this earth."

"When we are among the Kukuanas, my good friend Infadoos, we do as the Kukuanas do," I said majestically, and I turned round suddenly to address Good, who was tramping along sullenly behind, his mind fully occupied with unsatisfactory attempts to keep his flannel shirt from flapping up in the evening breeze, and to my astonishment butted into Umbopa, who was walking along immediately behind me, and had very evidently been listening with the greatest interest to my conversation with Infadoos. The expression on his face was most curious, and gave the idea of a man who was struggling with partial success to bring something long ago forgotten back into his mind.

All this while we had been pressing on at a good rate down towards the undulating plain beneath. The mountains we had crossed now loomed high above us, and

Sheba's breasts were modestly veiled in diaphanous wreaths of mist. As we went on the country grew more and more lovely. The vegetation was luxuriant without being tropical; the sun was bright and warm, but not burning, and a gracious breeze blew softly along the odorous slopes of the mountains. And, indeed, this new land was little less than an earthly paradise; in beauty, in natural wealth, and in climate I have never seen its like. The Transvaal is a fine country, but it is nothing to Kukuanaland.

So soon as we started, Infadoos had dispatched a runner on to warn the people of the kraal, which, by the way, was in his military command, of our arrival. This man had departed at an extraordinary speed, which Infadoos had informed me he would keep up all the way, as running was an exercise much practiced among his people.

The result of this message now became apparent. When we got within two miles of the kraal we could see that company after company of men was issuing from its gates and marching towards us.

Sir Henry laid his hand upon my arm, and remarked that it looked as though we were going to meet with a warm reception. Something in his tone attracted Infadoos' attention.

"Let not my lords be afraid," he said hastily, "for in my breast there dwells no guile. This regiment is one under my command, and comes out by my orders to greet you."

I nodded easily, though I was not quite easy in my mind. About half a mile from the gates of the kraal was a long stretch of rising ground sloping gently upward from the road, and on this the companies formed. It was a splendid sight to see them, each company about three hundred strong, charging swiftly up the slope, with flashing spears and waving plumes, and taking their appointed place. By

the time we came to the slope twelve such companies, or
in all three thousand six hundred men, had passed out and
taken up their positions along the road.

Presently we came to the first company, and were able
to gaze in astonishment on the most magnificent set of
men I have ever seen. They were all men of mature age,
mostly veterans of about forty, and not one of them was
under six feet in height, while many were six feet three
or four. They wore upon their heads heavy black plumes
of sacaboola feathers, like those which adorned our guides.
Round their waists and also beneath the right knee were
bound circlets of white ox tails, and in their left hands
were round shields about twenty inches across. These
shields were very curious. The framework consisted of an
iron plate beaten out thin, over which was stretched milk-
white ox hide. The weapons that each man bore were simple, but most effective, consisting of a short and very heavy
two-edged spear with a wooden shaft, the blade being about
six inches across at the widest part. These spears were not
used for throwing, but, like the Zulu "bangwan," or stabbing assegai, were for close quarters only, when the wound
inflicted by them was terrible. In addition to these bang-
wans each man also carried three large and heavy knives,
each knife weighing about two pounds. One knife was
fixed in the ox-tail girdle, and the other two at the back of
the round shield. These knives, which are called "tollas"
by the Kukuanas, take the place of the throwing assegai of
the Zulus. A Kukuana warrior can throw them with great
accuracy at a distance of fifty yards, and it is their custom
on charging to hurl a volley of them at the enemy as they
come to close quarters.

Each company stood like a collection of bronze statues
till we were opposite to it, when, at a signal given by its

commanding officer, who, distinguished by a leopard-skin cloak, stood some paces in front, every spear was raised into the air, and from three hundred throats sprang forth with a sudden roar the royal salute of *"Koom!"* Then, when we had passed, the company formed behind us and followed us towards the kraal, till at last the whole regiment of the "Grays" (so called from their white shields), the crack corps of the Kukuana people, was marching behind us with a tread that shook the ground.

At length, branching off from Solomon's Great Road, we came to the wide fosse surrounding the kraal, which was at least a mile round and fenced with a strong palisade of piles formed of the trunks of trees. At the gateway this fosse was spanned by a primitive drawbridge which was let down by the guard to allow us to pass in. The kraal was exceedingly well laid out. Through the center ran a wide pathway intersected at right angles by other pathways so arranged as to cut the huts into square blocks, each block being the quarters of a company. The huts were dome-shaped, and built, like those of the Zulus, of a framework of wattle beautifully thatched with grass; but, unlike the Zulu huts, they had doorways through which one could walk. Also, they were much larger, and surrounded with a veranda about six feet wide, beautifully paved with pow-dered lime trodden hard. All along each side of the wide pathway that pierced the kraal were ranged hundreds of women, brought out by curiosity to look at us. These women are, for a native race, exceedingly handsome. They are tall and graceful, and their figures are wonderfully fine. The hair, though short, is rather curly than woolly, the fea-tures are frequently aquiline, and the lips are not unpleas-antly thick, as is the case in most African races. But what struck us most was their exceeding quiet, dignified air. They

were as well bred in their way as the habitués of a fashion-
able drawing room, and in this respect differ from Zulu
women, and their cousins, the Masai, who inhabit the district behind Zanzibar. Their curiosity had brought them
out to see us, but they allowed no rude expression of wonder or savage criticism to pass their lips as we trudged wearily in front of them. Not even when old Infadoos with a
surreptitious motion of the hand pointed out the crowning
wonder of poor Good's "beautiful white legs," did they allow the feeling of intense admiration which evidently mastered their minds to find expression. They fixed their dark
eyes upon their snowy loveliness, and that was all. But this
was quite enough for Good, who is modest by nature.

When we got to the center of the kraal Infadoos halted
at the door of a large hut, which was surrounded at a distance by a circle of smaller ones.

"Enter, sons of the stars," he said in a magniloquent
voice, "and deign to rest awhile in our humble habitations.
A little food shall be brought to you, so that ye shall have
no need to draw your belts tight from hunger; some honey
and some milk, and an ox or two, and a few sheep; not
much, my lords, but still a little food."

"It is good," said I. "Infadoos, we are weary with traveling through realms of air; now let us rest."

Accordingly we entered into the hut, which we found
amply prepared for our comfort. Couches of tanned skins
were spread for us to rest on, and water was placed for us
to wash in.

Presently we heard a shouting outside, and, stepping to
the door, saw a line of damsels bearing milk and roasted
mealies and honey in a pot. Behind there were some youths
driving a fat young ox. We received the gifts, and then one
of the young men took the knife from his girdle and dex-

terously cut the ox's throat. In ten minutes it was dead, skinned, and cut up. The best of the meat was then cut off for us, and the rest I, in the name of our party, presented to the warriors round us, who took it off and distributed the "white men's gift."

Umbopa set to work, with the assistance of an extremely prepossessing young woman, to boil our portion in a large earthenware pot over a fire which was built outside the hut, and when it was nearly ready we sent a message to Infadoos, and asked him, and Scragga the king's son, to join us.

Presently they came, and, sitting down upon little stools, of which there were several about the hut (for the Kukuanas do not in general squat upon their haunches like the Zulus), helped us to get through our dinner. The old gentleman was most affable and polite, but it struck us that the young one regarded us with suspicion. He had, together with the rest of the party, been overawed by our white appearance and by our magic properties; but it seemed to me that on discovering that we ate, drank, and slept like other mortals, his awe was beginning to wear off and be replaced by a sullen suspicion, which made us feel rather uncomfortable.

In the course of our meal Sir Henry suggested to me that it might be well to try and discover if our hosts knew anything of his brother's fate, or if they had ever seen or heard of him; but, on the whole, I thought that it would be wiser to say nothing of the matter at that time.

After supper we filled our pipes and lit them, a proceeding which filled Infadoos and Scragga with astonishment. The Kukuanas were evidently unacquainted with the divine uses of tobacco smoke. The plant was grown among them extensively; but, like the Zulus, they only used it for snuff, and quite failed to identify it in its new form.

Presently I asked Infadoos when we were to proceed on our journey, and was delighted to learn that preparations had been made for us to leave on the following morning, messengers having already left to inform Twala, the king, of our coming. It appeared that Twala was at his principal place, known as Loo, making ready for the great annual feast which was held in the first week of June. At this gathering all the regiments, with the exception of certain detachments left behind for garrison purposes, were brought up and paraded before the king, and the great annual witch hunt, of which more by and by, was held.

We were to start at dawn; and Infadoos, who was to accompany us, expected that we should, unless we were detained by accident or by swollen rivers, reach Loo on the night of the second day.

When they had given us this information our visitors bade us good night; and, having arranged to watch turn and turn about, three of us flung ourselves down and slept the sweet sleep of the weary, while the fourth sat up on the lookout for possible treachery.

9 ♦

Twala, the King

It will not be necessary for me to detail at length the incidents of our journey to Loo. It took two good days' traveling along Solomon's Great Road, which pursued its even course right into the heart of Kukuanaland. Suffice it to say that as we went the country seemed to grow richer and richer, and the kraals, with their wide surrounding belts of cultivation, more and more numerous. They were all built upon the same principles as the first one we had reached, and were guarded by ample garrisons of troops. Indeed, in Kukuanaland, as among the Germans, the Zulus, and the Masai, every able-bodied man is a soldier, so that the whole force of the nation is available for its wars, offensive or defensive. As we traveled along we were overtaken by thousands of warriors hurrying up to Loo to be present at the great annual review and festival, and a grander series of troops I never saw. At sunset on the second day we stopped to rest awhile upon the summit of some heights over which the road ran, and there, on a beautiful and fertile plain before us, was Loo itself. For a native town it was an enormous place, quite five miles round, I should say, with outlying kraals jutting out from it, which served on grand occasions as cantonments for the regiments, and a curious horseshoe-shaped hill, with which we were destined to become better acquainted, about two miles to the north. It was beautifully situated, and through the center of the kraal, dividing it into two portions, ran a river, which appeared to be bridged at several places, the same, perhaps, that we had seen from the slopes of Sheba's breasts. Sixty or seventy miles away three great snow-capped mountains, placed like the points of a triangle, started up out of the level plain. The conformation of these mountains was unlike that of Sheba's breasts, being sheer and precipitous, instead of smooth and rounded.

Infadoos saw us looking at them and volunteered a remark:

"The road ends there," he said, pointing to the mountains, known among the Kukuanas as the "Three Witches."

"Why does it end?" I asked.

"Who knows?" he answered with a shrug. "The mountains are full of caves, and there is a great pit between them. It is there that the wise men of old time used to go to get whatever it was they came to this country for, and it is there now that our kings are buried in the Place of Death."

"What was it they came for?" I asked eagerly.

"Nay, I know not. My lords who come from the stars should know," he answered, with a quick look. Evidently he knew more than he chose to say.

"Yes," I went on, "you are right; in the stars we know many things. I have heard, for instance, that the wise men of old came to those mountains to get bright stones, pretty playthings, and yellow iron."

"My lord is wise," he answered coldly. "I am but a child and cannot talk with my lord on such things. My lord must speak with Gagool the old, at the king's place, who is wise even as my lord," and he turned away.

As soon as he was gone I turned to the others and pointed out the mountains. "There are Solomon's diamond mines," I said.

Umbopa was standing with them, apparently plunged in one of the fits of abstraction which were common to him, and caught my words.

"Yes, Macumazahn," he put in, in Zulu, "the diamonds are surely there, and you shall have them, since you white men are so fond of toys and money."

"How dost thou know that, Umbopa?" I asked sharply, for I did not like his mysterious ways.

He laughed. "I dreamed it in the night, white men," and then he too turned upon his heel and went.

"Now what," said Sir Henry, "is our black friend at? He knows more than he chooses to say, that is clear. By the way, Quatermain, has he heard anything of—of my brother?"

"Nothing; he has asked everyone he has got friendly with, but they all declare no white man has ever been seen in the country before."

"Do you suppose he ever got here at all?" suggested Good. "We have only reached the place by a miracle; is it likely he could have reached it at all without the map?"

"I don't know," said Sir Henry gloomily, "but somehow I think that I shall find him."

Slowly the sun sank, and then suddenly darkness rushed down on the land like a tangible thing. There was no breathing place between the day and the night, no soft transformation scene, for in these latitudes twilight does not exist. The change from day to night is as quick and as absolute as the change from life to death. The sun sank and the world was wreathed in shadows. But not for long, for see, in the east there is a glow, then a bent edge of silver light, and at last the full bow of the crescent moon peeps above the plain and shoots its gleaming arrows far and wide, filling the earth with a faint refulgence, as the glow of a good man's deeds shines for a while upon his little world after his sun has set, lighting the faint-hearted travelers who follow on towards a fuller dawn.

We stood and watched the lovely sight, while the stars grew pale before this chastened majesty, and felt our hearts lifted up in the presence of a beauty we could not realize, much less describe. Mine has been a rough life, my reader, but there are a few things I am thankful to have lived for, and one of them is to have seen that moon rise over Kuku-analand. Presently our meditations were broken in upon by our polite friend Infadoos.

"If my lords are ready we will journey on to Loo, where a hut is made ready for my lords tonight. The moon is now bright, so that we shall not fall on the way."

We assented, and in an hour's time were at the outskirts of the town, of which the extent, mapped out as it was by thousands of campfires, appeared absolutely endless. Indeed, Good, who was always fond of a bad joke, christened it "Unlimited Loo." Presently we came to a moat with a drawbridge, where we were met by the rattling of arms and the hoarse challenge of a sentry. Infadoos gave some password that I could not catch, which was met with a salute, and we passed on through the central street of the great grass city. After nearly half an hour's tramp past endless lines of huts, Infadoos at last halted at the gate of a little group of huts which surrounded a small courtyard of powdered limestone, and informed us that these were to be our "poor" quarters.

We entered, and found that a hut had been assigned to each of us. These huts were superior to any which we had yet seen, and in each was a most comfortable bed made of tanned skins spread upon mattresses of aromatic grass. Food, too, was ready for us, and as soon as we had washed ourselves with water, which stood ready in earthenware jars, some young women of handsome appearance brought us roasted meat and mealie cobs daintily served on wooden platters, and presented it to us with deep obeisances.

We ate and drank, and then, the beds having by our request been all moved into one hut, a precaution at which the amiable young ladies smiled, we flung ourselves down to sleep, thoroughly wearied out with our long journey.

When we woke, it was to find that the sun was high in the heavens, and that the female attendants, who did not seem to be troubled by any false shame, were already standing inside the hut, having been ordered to attend and help us to "make ready."

"Make ready, indeed," growled Good; "when one has only a flannel shirt and a pair of boots, that does not take long. I wish you would ask them for my trousers."

I asked accordingly, but was informed that those sacred relics had already been taken to the king, who would see us in the forenoon.

Having, somewhat to their astonishment and disappointment, requested the young ladies to step outside, we proceeded to make the best toilet that the circumstances admitted of. Good even went the length of again shaving the right side of his face; the left, on which now appeared a very fair crop of whiskers, we impressed upon him he must on no account touch. As for ourselves, we were contented with a good wash and combing our hair. Sir Henry's yellow locks were now almost down to his shoulders, and he looked more like an ancient Dane than ever, while my grizzled scrub was fully an inch long, instead of half an inch, which in a general way I considered my maximum length.

By the time that we had eaten our breakfast and smoked a pipe, a message was brought to us by no less a personage than Infadoos himself that Twala, the king, was ready to see us, if we would be pleased to come.

We remarked in reply that we should prefer to wait until the sun was a little higher, we were yet weary with our journey, etc. It is always well, when dealing with uncivilized people, not to be in too great a hurry. They are apt to mistake politeness for awe or servility. So, although we were quite as anxious to see Twala as Twala could be to see us, we sat down and waited for an hour, employing the interval in preparing such presents as our slender stock of goods permitted—namely, the Winchester rifle which had been used by poor Ventvögel, and some beads. The rifle and ammunition we determined to present to his royal highness, and the beads were for his wives and courtiers. We had already given a few to Infadoos and Scragga, and found that they were delighted with them, never having seen anything like them before. At length we declared that we were ready, and, guided by Infadoos, started off to the levée, Umbopa carrying the rifle and the beads.

After walking a few hundred yards we came to an enclosure, something like that which surrounded the huts that had been allotted to us, only fifty times as big. It could not have been less than six or seven acres in extent. All round the outside fence was a row of huts, which were the habitations of the king's wives. Exactly opposite the gateway, on the farther side of the open space, was a very large hut, which stood by itself, in which his majesty resided. All the rest was open ground; that is to say, it would have been open had it not been filled by company after company of warriors, who were mustered there to the number of seven or eight thousand. These men stood still as statues as we advanced through them, and it would be impossible to give an idea of the grandeur of the spectacle which they presented, in their waving plumes, their glancing spears, and iron-backed ox-hide shields.

The space in front of the large hut was empty, but before it were placed several stools. On three of these, at a sign from Infadoos, we seated ourselves, Umbopa standing behind us. As for Infadoos, he took up a position by the door of the hut. So we waited for ten minutes or more in the midst of a dead silence, but conscious that we were the object of the concentrated gaze of some eight thousand pairs of eyes. It was a somewhat trying ordeal, but we carried it off as best we could. At length the door of the hut opened, and a gigantic figure, with a splendid tigerskin karross flung over its shoulders, stepped out, followed by the boy Scragga, and what appeared to us to be a withered-up monkey wrapped in a fur cloak. The figure seated itself upon a stool, Scragga took his stand behind it, and the withered-up monkey crept on all fours into the shade of the hut and squatted down.

Still there was silence.

Then the gigantic figure slipped off the karross and stood up before us, a truly alarming spectacle. It was that of an enormous man with the most entirely repulsive countenance we had ever beheld. The lips were as thick as a Negro's, the nose was flat, it had but one gleaming black eye (for the other was represented by a hollow in the face), and its whole expression was cruel and sensual to a degree. From the large head rose a magnificent plume of white ostrich feathers, the body was clad in a shirt of shining chain armor, while round the waist and right knee was the usual garnish of white ox tails. In the right hand was a huge spear. Round the neck was a thick torque of gold, and bound onto the forehead was a single enormous uncut diamond.

Still there was silence; but not for long. Presently the figure, whom we rightly guessed to be the king, raised the great spear in his hand. Instantly eight thousand spears were raised in answer, and from eight thousand throats rang out the royal salute of *"Koom!"* Three times this was repeated, and each time the earth shook with the noise, which can only be compared to the deepest notes of thunder.

"Be humble, O people," piped out a thin voice which seemed to come from the monkey in the shade; "it is the king."

"It is the king," boomed out eight thousand throats, in answer. *"Be humble, O people; it is the king!"*

Then there was silence again—dead silence. Presently, however, it was broken. A soldier on our left dropped his shield, which fell with a clatter on the limestone flooring.

Twala turned his one cold eye in the direction of the noise.

"Come hither, thou," he said in a voice of thunder.

A fine young man stepped out of the ranks, and stood before him.

"It was thy shield that fell, thou awkward dog. Wilt thou make me a reproach in the eyes of strangers from the stars? What hast thou to say?"

And then we saw the poor fellow turn pale under his dusky skin.

"It was by chance, O calf of the black cow," he murmured.

"Then it is a chance for which thou must pay. Thou hast made me foolish; prepare for death."

"I am the king's ox," was the low answer.

"Scragga," roared the king, "let me see how thou canst use thy spear. Kill me this awkward dog."

Scragga stepped forward with an ill-favored grin, and lifted his spear. The poor victim covered his eyes with his hand and stood still. As for us, we were petrified with horror.

Once, twice, he waved the spear and then struck—ah, God!—right home—the spear stood out a foot behind the soldier's back. He flung up his hands and dropped dead. From the multitude rose something like a murmur; it rolled round and round, and died away. The tragedy was finished—there lay the corpse—and we had not yet realized that it had been enacted. Sir Henry sprang up and swore a great oath, then, overpowered by the sense of silence, sat down again.

"The thrust was a good one," said the king; "take him away."

Four men stepped out of the ranks, and, lifting the body of the murdered man, carried it away.

"Cover up the bloodstains, cover them up," piped out the thin voice from the monkey-like figure; "the king's word is spoken, the king's doom is done."

Thereupon a girl came forward from behind the hut, bearing a jar filled with powdered lime, which she scattered over the red mark, blotting it from sight.

Sir Henry meanwhile was boiling with rage at what had happened; indeed, it was with difficulty that we could keep him still.

"Sit down, for heaven's sake," I whispered; "our lives depend on it."

He yielded and remained quiet.

Twala sat still until the traces of the tragedy had been removed, then he addressed us.

"White people," he said, "who come hither, whence I know not, and why I know not, greeting."

"Greeting, Twala, King of the Kukuanas," I answered.

"White people, whence come ye, and what seek ye?"

"We come from the stars, ask us not how. We come to see this land."

"Ye come from far to see a little thing. And that man with ye," pointing to Umbopa, "does he too come from the stars?"

"Even so; there are people of thy color in the heavens above; but ask not of matters too high for thee, Twala, the King."

"Ye speak with a loud voice, people of the stars," Twala answered, in a tone which I scarcely liked. "Remember that the stars are far off, and ye are here. How if I make ye as him whom they bare away?"

I laughed out loud, though there was little laughter in my heart.

"O King," I said, "be careful; walk warily over hot stones, lest thou shouldst burn thy feet; hold the spear by the handle, lest thou shouldst cut thy hands. Touch but one hair of our heads, and destruction shall come upon thee. What, have not these"—pointing to Infadoos and Scragga (who, young villain that he was, was employed in cleaning the blood of the soldier off his spear)—"told thee what manner of men we are? Hast thou ever seen the like of us?" and I pointed to Good, feeling quite sure that he had never seen anybody before who looked in the least like *him* as he then appeared.

"It is true, I have not," said the king.

"Have they not told thee how we strike with death from afar?" I went on.

"They have told me, but I believe them not. Let me see you kill. Kill me a man among those who stand yonder"— and he pointed to the opposite side of the kraal—"and I will believe."

"Nay," I answered; "we shed no blood of man except in just punishment; but if thou wilt see, bid thy servants drive in an ox through the kraal gates, and before he has run twenty paces I will strike him dead."

"Nay," laughed the king, "kill me a man, and I will believe."

"Good, O King, so be it," I answered coolly; "do thou walk across the open space, and before thy feet reach the gate thou shalt be dead; or, if thou wilt not, send thy son Scragga" (whom at that moment it would have given me much pleasure to shoot).

On hearing this suggestion Scragga gave a sort of howl, and bolted into the hut.

Twala frowned majestically; the suggestion did not please him.

"Let a young ox be driven in," he said.

Two men at once departed, running swiftly.

"Now, Sir Henry," said I, "do you shoot. I want to show this ruffian that I am not the only magician of the party."

Sir Henry accordingly took the express, and made ready.

"I hope I shall make a good shot," he groaned.

"You must," I answered. "If you miss with the first barrel, let him have the second. Sight for one hundred and fifty yards, and wait till the beast turns broadside on."

Then came a pause, till presently we caught sight of an ox running straight for the kraal gate. It came on through the gate, and then, catching sight of the vast concourse of people, stopped stupidly, turned round, and bellowed.

"Now's your time," I whispered.

Up went the rifle.

Bang! Thud! And the ox was kicking on his back, shot in the ribs. The semihollow bullet had done its work well, and a sigh of astonishment went up from the assembled thousands.

I turned coolly round. "Have I lied, O King?"

"Nay, white man, it is a truth," was the somewhat awed answer.

"Listen, Twala," I went on. "Thou hast seen. Now know we come in peace, not in war. See here" and I held up the Winchester repeater, "here is a hollow staff that shall enable you to kill even as we kill, only this charm I lay upon it, thou shalt kill no man with it. If thou liftest it against a man, it shall kill thee. Stay, I will show thee. Bid a man step forty paces and place the shaft of a spear in the ground so that the flat blade looks towards us."

In a few seconds it was done.

"Now, see, I will break the spear."

Taking a careful sight, I fired. The bullet struck the flat of the spear and broke the blade into fragments.

Again the sigh of astonishment went up.

"Now, Twala"—handing him the rifle—"this magic tube we give to thee, and by and by I will show thee how to use it; but beware how thou usest the magic of the stars against a man of earth," and I handed him the rifle. He took it very gingerly, and laid it down at his feet. As he did so I observed the wizened, monkey-like figure creeping up from the shadow of the hut. It crept on all fours, but when it reached the place where the king sat it rose upon its feet, and, throwing the furry covering off its face, revealed a most extraordinary and weird countenance. It was (apparently) that of a woman of great age, so shrunken that in size it was no larger than that of a year-old child, and was made up of a collection of deep, yellow wrinkles. Set in the wrinkles was a sunken slit that represented the mouth, beneath which the chin curved outward to a point. There was no nose to speak of; indeed, the whole countenance might have been taken for that of a sun-dried corpse had it not been for a pair of large black eyes, still full of fire and intelligence, which gleamed and played under the snow-white eyebrows and the projecting parchment-colored skull, like jewels in a charnel house. As for the skull itself, it was perfectly bare, and yellow in hue, while its wrinkled scalp moved and contracted like the hood of a cobra.

The figure to whom this fearful countenance, which caused a shiver of fear to pass through us as we gazed on it, belonged stood still for a moment, and then suddenly projected a skinny claw armed with nails nearly an inch long, and laid it on the shoulder of Twala, the king, and began to speak in a thin, piercing voice.

"Listen, O King! Listen, O people! Listen, O mountains and plains and rivers, home of the Kukuana race! Listen, O skies and sun, O rain and storm and mist! Listen, all things that live and must die! Listen, all dead things that must live again—again to die! Listen, the spirit of life is in me, and I prophesy. I prophesy! I prophesy!"

The words died away in a faint wail, and terror seemed to seize upon the hearts of all who heard them, including ourselves. The old woman was very terrible.

"*Blood! Blood! Blood!* Rivers of blood; blood everywhere. I see it, I smell it, I taste it—it is salt; it runs red upon the ground, it rains down from the skies.

"*Footsteps! Footsteps! Footsteps!* The tread of the white man coming from afar. It shakes the earth; the earth trembles before her master.

"Blood is good, the red blood is bright; there is no smell like the smell of new-shed blood. The lions shall lap it and roar, the vultures shall wash their wings in it and shriek in joy.

"I am old! I am old! I have seen much blood; but I shall see more ere I die, and be merry. How old am I, think ye? Your fathers knew me, and their fathers knew me, and their fathers' fathers. I have seen the white man, and know his desires. I am old, but the mountains are older than I. Who made the great road, tell me? Who wrote in pictures on the rocks, tell me? Who reared up the three silent ones yonder, who gaze across the pit, tell me?" (And she pointed towards the three precipitous mountains we had noticed on the previous night.)

"Ye know not, but I know. It was a white people who were before ye were, who shall be when ye are not, who shall eat ye up and destroy ye. Yea! Yea! Yea!

"And what came they for, the white ones, the terrible ones, the skilled in magic and all learning, the strong, the unswerving? What is that bright stone upon thy forehead, O King? Whose hands made the iron garments upon thy breast, O King? Ye know not, but I know. I the old one, I the wise one, I the Isanusi [Witch Doctress]!"

Then she turned her bald, vulture head towards us.

"What seek ye, white men of the stars? Ah, yes, of the stars! Do ye seek a lost one? Ye shall not find him here. He is not here. Never for ages upon ages has a white foot pressed this land; never but once, and he left it but to die. Ye come for bright stones; I know it—I know it; ye shall find them when the blood is dry; but shall ye return whence ye came, or shall ye stop with me? Ha, ha, ha!

"And thou, thou with the dark skin and the proud bearing"—pointing her skinny finger at Umbopa—"who art *thou*, and what seekest *thou*? Not stones that shine; not yellow metal that gleams; that thou leavest to 'white men from the stars.' Methinks I know thee; methinks I can smell the smell of the blood in thy veins. Strip off the girdle—"

Here the features of this extraordinary creature became convulsed, and she fell to the ground foaming in an epileptic fit and was carried off into the hut.

The king rose up, trembling, and waved his hand. Instantly the regiments began to file off, and in ten minutes, save for ourselves, the king, and a few attendants, the great space was left clear.

"White people," he said, "it passes in my mind to kill ye. Gagool has spoken strange words. What say ye?"

I laughed. "Be careful, O King, we are not easy to slay. Thou hast seen the fate of the ox; wouldst thou be as the ox?"

The king frowned. "It is not well to threaten a king."

"We threaten not, we speak what is true. Try to kill us, O King, and learn."

The great man put his hand to his forehead.

"Go in peace," he said at length. "Tonight is the great dance. Ye shall see it. Fear not that I shall set a snare for ye. Tomorrow I shall think."

"It is well, O King," I answered unconcernedly, and then, accompanied by Infadoos, we rose and went back to our kraal.

10 ♦

The Witch Hunt

ON REACHING our hut, I motioned to Infadoos to enter with us.

"Now, Infadoos," I said, "we would speak with thee."

"Let my lords say on."

"It seems to us, Infadoos, that Twala, the king, is a cruel man."

"It is so, my lords. Alas, the land cries out with his cruelties. Tonight ye will see. It is the great witch hunt, and many will be smelled out as wizards and slain. No man's life is safe. If the king covets a man's cattle or a man's life, or if he fears a man that he should excite a rebellion against him, then Gagool, whom ye saw, or some of the witch-finding women whom she has taught, will smell that man out as a wizard, and he will be killed. Many will die before the moon grows pale tonight. It is ever so. Perhaps I too shall be killed. As yet I have been spared, because I am skilled in war and beloved by the soldiers; but I know not how long I shall live. The land groans at the cruelties of Twala, the king; it is wearied of him and his red ways."

"Then why is it, Infadoos, that the people do not cast him down?"

"Nay, my lords, he is the king, and if he were killed Scragga would reign in his place, and the heart of Scragga is blacker than the heart of Twala, his father. If Scragga

were king the yoke upon our neck would be heavier than
the yoke of Twala. If Imotu had never been slain, or if
Ignosi, his son, had lived, it had been otherwise; but they
are both dead."

"How know you that Ignosi is dead?" said a voice behind us. We looked round with astonishment to see who
spoke. It was Umbopa.

"What meanest thou, boy?" asked Infadoos. "Who told
thee to speak?"

"Listen, Infadoos," was the answer, "and I will tell
thee a story. Years ago the king Imotu was killed in this
country, and his wife fled with the boy Ignosi. Is it not
so?"

"It is so."

"It was said that the woman and the boy died upon
the mountains. Is it not so?"

"It is even so."

"Well, it came to pass that the mother and the boy
Ignosi did not die. They crossed the mountains, and were
led by a tribe of wandering desert men across the sands
beyond, till at last they came to water and grass and trees
again."

"How knowest thou?"

"Listen. They traveled on and on, many months' journey, till they reached a land where a people called the
Amazulu, who too are of the Kukuana stock, live by war,
and with them they tarried many years, till at length the
mother died. Then the son, Ignosi, again became a wan-
derer, and went on into a land of wonders, where white
people live, and for many more years learned the wisdom
of the white people."

"It is a pretty story," said Infadoos incredulously.

"For many years he lived there working as a servant

and a soldier, but holding in his heart all that his mother
had told him of his own place, and casting about in his
mind to find how he might get back there to see his own
people and his father's house before he died. For many
years he lived and waited, and at last the time came, as it
ever comes to him who can wait for it, and he met some
white men who would seek this unknown land, and joined
himself to them. The white men started and journeyed
on and on, seeking for one who is lost. They crossed the
burning desert, they crossed the snow-clad mountains, and
reached the land of the Kukuanas, and there they met
thee, O Infadoos."

"Surely thou art mad to talk thus," said the astonished
old soldier.

"Thou thinkest so; see, I will show thee, O my uncle.
I am Ignosi, rightful king of the Kukuanas!"

Then, with a single movement, he slipped off the moocha
round his middle, and stood naked before us.

"Look," he said; "what is this?" and he pointed to the
mark of a great snake tattooed in blue round his middle,
its tail disappearing in its open mouth just above where
the thighs are set into the body.

Infadoos looked, his eyes starting nearly out of his head,
and then fell upon his knees.

"*Koom! Koom!*" he ejaculated. "It is my brother's son;
it is the king."

"Did I not tell thee so, my uncle? Rise; I am not yet
the king, but with thy help, and with the help of these
brave white men, who are my friends, I shall be. But the
old woman Gagool was right; the land shall run with blood
first, and hers shall run with it, for she killed my father
with her words, and drove my mother forth. And now,
Infadoos, choose thou. Wilt thou put thy hands between

my hands and be my man? Wilt thou share the dangers that lie before me, and help me to overthrow this tyrant and murderer, or wilt thou not? Choose thou?"

The old man put his hand to his head and thought. Then he rose, and, advancing to where Umbopa, or rather Ignosi, stood, knelt before him and took his hand.

"Ignosi, rightful king of the Kukuanas, I put my hand between thy hands, and am thy man till death. When thou wast a babe I dandled thee upon my knee; now shall my old arm strike for thee and freedom."

"It is well, Infadoos; if I conquer, thou shalt be the greatest man in the kingdom after the king. If I fail, thou canst only die, and death is not far off for thee. Rise, my uncle.

"And ye, white men, will ye help me? What have I to offer ye! The white stones, if I conquer and you can find them, ye shall have as many as ye can carry hence. Will that suffice ye?"

I translated this remark.

"Tell him," answered Sir Henry, "that he mistakes an Englishman. Wealth is good, and if it comes in our way we will take it; but a gentleman does not sell himself for wealth. But, speaking for myself, I say this: I have always liked Umbopa, and so far as in me lies will stand by him in this business. It will be very pleasant to me to try and square matters with that cruel devil, Twala. What do you say, Good, and you, Quatermain?"

"Well," said Good, "to adopt the language of hyperbole, in which all these people seem to indulge, you can tell him that a row is surely good, and warms the cockles of the heart, and that, so far as I am concerned, I'm his boy. My only stipulation is that he allow me to wear trousers."

I translated these answers.

"It is well, my friends," said Ignosi, late Umbopa; "and what say you, Macumazahn; art thou too with me, old hunter, cleverer than a wounded buffalo?"

I thought awhile and scratched my head.

"Umbopa, or Ignosi," I said, "I don't like revolutions. I am a man of peace, and a bit of a coward"—(here Umbopa smiled)—"but, on the other hand, I stick to my friends, Ignosi. You have stuck to us and played the part of a man, and I will stick to you. But, mind you, I am a trader, and have to make my living; so I accept your offer about those diamonds, in case we should ever be in a position to avail ourselves of it. Another thing: we came, as you know, to look for Incubu's [Sir Henry's] lost brother. You must help us to find him."

"That will I do," answered Ignosi. "Stay, Infadoos; by the sign of the snake round my middle, tell me the truth. Has any white man to thy knowledge set his foot within the land?"

"None, O Ignosi."

"If any white man had been seen or heard of, wouldst thou have known it?"

"I should certainly have known."

"Thou hearest, Incubu?" said Ignosi to Sir Henry. "He has not been here."

"Well, well," said Sir Henry, with a sigh; "there it is; I suppose he never got here. Poor fellow, poor fellow! So it has all been for nothing. God's will be done."

"Now for business," I put in, anxious to escape from a painful subject. "It is very well to be a king by right divine, Ignosi, but how dost thou propose to become a king indeed?"

"Nay, I know not. Infadoos, hast thou a plan?"

"Ignosi, son of the lightning," answered his uncle, "to-night is the great dance and witch hunt. Many will be smelled out and perish, and in the hearts of many others there will be grief and anguish and anger against the king Twala. When the dance is over, then will I speak to some of the great chiefs, who in turn, if I can win them over, shall speak to their regiments. I shall speak to the chiefs softly at first, and bring them to see that thou art indeed the king, and I think that by tomorrow's light thou shalt have twenty thousand spears at thy command. And now must I go and think and hear and make ready. After the dance is done I will, if I am yet alive, and we are all alive, meet thee here, and we will talk. At the best there will be war."

At this moment our conference was interrupted by the cry that messengers had come from the king. Advancing to the door of the hut, we ordered that they should be admitted, and presently three men entered, each bearing a shining shirt of chain armor and a magnificent battle-ax.

"The gifts of my lord, the king, to the white men from the stars!" exclaimed a herald who had come with them.

"We thank the king," I answered; "withdraw."

The men went, and we examined the armor with great interest. It was the most beautiful chain work we had ever seen. A whole coat fell together so closely that it formed a mass of links scarcely too big to be covered with both hands.

"Do you make these things in this country, Infadoos?" I asked. "They are very beautiful."

"Nay, my lord; they come down to us from our fore-fathers. We know not who made them, and there are but few left. None but those of royal blood may wear them. They are magic coats through which no spear can pass. He who wears them is well-nigh safe in the battle. The king is well pleased or much afraid, or he would not have sent them. Wear them tonight, my lords."

The rest of the day we spent quietly resting and talking over the situation, which was sufficiently exciting. At last the sun went down, the thousand watch fires glowed out, and through the darkness we heard the tramp of many feet and the clashing of hundreds of spears, as the regiments passed to their appointed places to be ready for the great dance. About ten the full moon came up in splendor, and as we stood watching her ascent Infadoos arrived, clad in full war toggery, and accompanied by a guard of twenty men to escort us to the dance. We had already, as he recommended, donned the shirts of chain armor which the king had sent us, putting them on under our ordinary clothing, and finding to our surprise that they were neither very heavy nor uncomfortable. These steel shirts, which had evidently been made for men of a very large stature, hung somewhat loosely upon Good and myself, but Sir Henry's fitted his magnificent frame like a glove. Then, strapping our revolvers round our waists, and taking the battle-axes which the king had sent with the armor in our hands, we started.

On arriving at the great kraal where we had that morning been interviewed by the king, we found that it was closely packed with some twenty thousand men arranged in regiments round it. The regiments were in turn divided into companies, and between each company was a little path to allow free passage to the witch finders to pass up and down. Anything more imposing than the sight that was presented by this vast and orderly concourse of armed men it is impossible for one to conceive. There they stood perfectly silent, and the moonlight poured its light upon the forest of their raised spears, upon their majestic forms, waving plumes, and the harmonious shading of their various-colored shields. Wherever we looked was line upon line of set faces surmounted by range upon range of glittering spears.

"Surely," I said to Infadoos, "the whole army is here?"

"Nay, Macumazahn," he answered, "but a third part of it. One third part is present at this dance each year, another third part is mustered outside in case there should be trouble when the killing begins, ten thousand more garrison the outposts round Loo, and the rest watch at the kraals in the country. Thou seest it is a very great people."

"They are very silent," said Good; and, indeed, the intense stillness among such a vast concourse of living men was almost overpowering.

"What says Bougwan?" asked Infadoos.

I translated.

"Those over whom the shadow of death is hovering are silent," he answered grimly.

"Will many be killed?"

"Very many."

"It seems," I said to the others, "that we are going to assist at a gladiatorial show arranged regardless of expense."

Sir Henry shivered, and Good said that he wished that we could get out of it.

"Tell me," I asked Infadoos, "are we in danger?"

"I know not, my lords—I trust not; but do not seem afraid. If ye live through the night all may go well. The soldiers murmur against the king."

All this while we had been advancing steadily towards the center of the open space, in the midst of which were placed some stools. As we proceeded we perceived another small party coming from the direction of the royal hut.

"It is the king, Twala, and Scragga his son, and Gagool

the old, and see, with them are those who slay," and he pointed to a little group of about a dozen gigantic and savage-looking men, armed with spears in one hand and heavy kerries in the other.

The king seated himself upon the center stool, Gagool crouched at his feet, and the others stood behind.

"Greeting, white lords," he cried as we came up; "be seated, waste not the precious time—the night is all too short for the deeds that must be done. Ye come in a good hour, and shall see a glorious show. Look round, white lords; look round," and he rolled his one wicked eye from regiment to regiment. "Can the stars show ye such a sight as this? See how they shake in their wickedness, all those who have evil in their hearts and fear the judgment of 'Heaven above.'"

"*Begin! Begin!*" cried out Gagool in her thin, piercing voice. "The hyenas are hungry, they howl for food. *Begin! Begin!*" Then for a moment there was intense stillness, made horrible by a presage of what was to come.

The king lifted his spear, and suddenly twenty thousand feet were raised, as though they belonged to one man, and brought down with a stamp upon the earth. This was repeated three times, causing the solid ground to shake and tremble. Then from a far point of the circle a solitary voice began a wailing song, of which the refrain ran something as follows:

"*What is the lot of man born of woman?*"

Back came the answer rolling out from every throat in that vast company:

"*Death!*"

Gradually, however, the song was taken up by company after company, till the whole armed multitude were singing it, and I could no longer follow the words, except in so far as they appeared to represent various phases of human passions, fears, and joys. Now it seemed to be a love song, now a majestic swelling war chant, and last of all a death dirge, ending suddenly in one heartbreaking wail that went echoing and rolling away in a volume of blood-curdling sound.

Again the silence fell upon the place, and again it was broken by the king's lifting up his hand. Instantly there was a pattering of feet, and from out of the masses of the warriors strange and awful figures came running towards us. As they drew near we saw that they were those of women, most of them aged, for their white hair, ornamented with small bladders taken from fish, streamed out behind them. Their faces were painted in stripes of white and yellow; down their backs hung snake skins, and round their waists rattled circlets of human bones, while each held in her shriveled hand a small forked wand. In all there were ten of them.

When they arrived in front of us they halted, and one of them, pointing with her wand towards the crouching figure of Gagool, cried out: "Mother, old mother, we are here."

"Good! Good! Good!" piped out that aged iniquity. "Are your eyes keen, Isanusis [Witch Doctresses], ye seers in dark places?"

"Mother, they are keen."

"Good! Good! Good! Are your ears open, Isanusis, ye who hear words that come not from the tongue?"

"Mother, they are open."

"Good! Good! Good! Are your senses awake, Isanusis —can ye smell blood, can ye purge the land of the wicked ones who compass evil against the king and against their neighbors? Are ye ready to do the justice of 'Heaven above,' ye whom I have taught, who have eaten of the bread of my wisdom and drunk of the water of my magic?"

"Mother, we can."

"Then go! Tarry not, ye vultures; see the slayers"—pointing to the ominous group of executioners behind—"make sharp their spears; the white men from afar are hungry to see. Go."

With a wild yell the weird party broke away in every direction, like fragments from a shell, and, the dry bones round their waists rattling as they ran, made direct for various points of the dense human circle. We could not watch them all, so fixed our eyes upon the Isanusi nearest us. When she came within a few paces of the warriors, she halted and began to dance wildly, turning round and round with an almost incredible rapidity, and shrieking out sentences such as: "I smell him, the evildoer!" "He is near, he who poisoned his mother!" "I hear the thoughts of him who thought evil of the king!"

Quicker and quicker she danced, till she lashed herself into such a frenzy of excitement that the foam flew in flecks from her gnashing jaws, her eyes seemed to start from her head, and her flesh to quiver visibly. Suddenly she stopped dead, and stiffened all over, like a pointer dog when he scents game, and then with outstretched wand began to creep stealthily towards the soldiers before her. It seemed to us that as she came their stoicism gave way, and that they shrank from her. As for ourselves, we followed her movements with a horrible fascination. Presently, still creeping and crouching like a dog, she was before them. Then she stopped and pointed, and then again crept on a pace or two.

Suddenly the end came. With a shriek she sprang in and touched a tall warrior with the forked wand. Instantly two of his comrades, those standing immediately next to him, seized the doomed man, each by one arm, and advanced with him towards the king.

He did not resist, but we saw that he dragged his limbs as though they were paralyzed, and his fingers, from which the spear had fallen, were as limp as those of a man newly dead.

As he came, two of the villainous executioners stepped forward to meet him. Presently they met, and the executioners turned round towards the king as though for orders.

"*Kill!*" said the king.

"*Kill!*" squeaked Gagool.

"*Kill!*" re-echoed Scragga, with a hollow chuckle.

Almost before the words were uttered, the horrible deed was done. One man had driven his spear into the victim's heart, and, to make assurance doubly sure, the other had dashed out his brains with his great club.

"*One,*" counted Twala, the king, just like a black Madame Defarge, as Good said, and the body was dragged a few paces away and stretched out.

Hardly was this done before another poor wretch was brought up, like an ox to the slaughter. This time we could see, from the leopard-skin cloak, that the man was a person of rank. Again the awful syllables were spoken, and the victim fell dead.

"*Two,*" counted the king.

And so the deadly game went on, till some hundred bodies were stretched in rows behind us. I have heard of the gladiatorial shows of the Caesars, and of the Spanish bullfights, but I take the liberty of doubting if they were either of them half as horrible as this Kukuana witch hunt. Gladiatorial shows and Spanish bullfights, at any rate, contributed to the public amusement, which certainly was not the case here. The most confirmed sensation-monger would fight shy of sensation if he knew that it was well on the cards that he would, in his own proper person, be the subject of the next "event."

Once we rose and tried to remonstrate, but were sternly repressed by Twala.

"Let the law take its course, white men. These dogs are magicians and evildoers; it is well that they should die," was the only answer vouchsafed to us.

About midnight there was a pause. The witch finders gathered themselves together, apparently exhausted with their bloody work, and we thought that the whole performance was done with. But it was not so, for presently, to our surprise, the old woman, Gagool, rose from her crouching position, and, supporting herself with a stick, staggered off into the open space. It was an extraordinary sight to see this frightful, vulture-headed old creature, bent nearly double with extreme age, gather strength by degrees till at last she rushed about almost as actively as her ill-omened pupils. To and fro she ran, chanting to herself, till suddenly she made a dash at a tall man standing in front of one of the regiments, and touched him. As she did so a sort of groan went up from the regiment, which he evidently commanded. But all the same two of its members seized him and brought him up for execution. We afterwards learned that he was a man of great wealth and importance, being, indeed, a cousin of the king's.

He was slain, and the king counted one hundred and three. Then Gagool again sprang to and fro, gradually drawing nearer and nearer to ourselves.

"Hang me if I don't believe she is going to try her games on us," ejaculated Good in horror.

"Nonsense!" said Sir Henry.

As for myself, as I saw that old fiend dancing nearer and nearer, my heart positively sank into my boots. I glanced behind us at the long rows of corpses, and shivered.

Nearer and nearer waltzed Gagool, looking for all the world like an animated crooked stick, her horrid eyes gleaming and glowing with a most unholy luster.

Nearer she came, and nearer yet, every pair of eyes in that vast assemblage watching her movements with intense anxiety. At last she stood still and pointed.

"Which is it to be?" asked Sir Henry to himself.

In a moment all doubts were set at rest, for the old woman had rushed in and touched Umbopa, now Ignosi, on the shoulder.

"I smell him out!" she shrieked. "Kill him, kill him, he is full of evil; kill him, the stranger, before blood flows for him. Slay him, O King."

There was a pause, which I instantly took advantage of.

"O King," I called out, rising from my seat, "this man is the servant of thy guests, he is their dog; whosoever sheds the blood of our dog sheds our blood. By the sacred law of hospitality I claim protection for him."

"Gagool, mother of the witch doctors, has smelled him out; he must die, white men," was the sullen answer.

"Nay, he shall not die," I replied; "he who tries to touch him shall die indeed."

"Seize him!" roared Twala to the executioners, who stood round red to the eyes with the blood of their victims.

They advanced towards us, and then hesitated. As for Ignosi, he raised his spear, and raised it as though determined to sell his life dearly.

"Stand back, ye dogs," I shouted, "if ye would see tomorrow's light. Touch one hair of his head and your king dies," and I covered Twala with my revolver. Sir Henry and Good also drew their pistols, Sir Henry pointing his at the leading executioner, who was advancing to carry out the sentence, and Good taking a deliberate aim at Gagool.

Twala winced perceptibly, as my barrel came in a line with his broad chest.

"Well," I said, "what is it to be, Twala?"

Then he spoke.

"Put away your magic tubes," he said; "ye have adjured me in the name of hospitality, and for that reason, but not from fear of what ye can do, I spare him. Go in peace."

"It is well," I answered unconcernedly; "we are weary of slaughter, and would sleep. Is the dance ended?"

"It is ended," Twala answered sulkily. "Let these dogs"—pointing to the long rows of corpses—"be flung out to the hyenas and the vultures," and he lifted his spear.

Instantly the regiments began in perfect silence to defile off through the kraal gateway, a fatigue party only remaining behind to drag away the corpses of those who had been sacrificed.

Then we too rose, and, making our salaam to his majesty, which he hardly deigned to acknowledge, departed to our kraal.

"Well," said Sir Henry, as we sat down, having first lit a lamp of the sort used by the Kukuanas, of which the wick is made of the fiber of a species of palm leaf and the oil of clarified hippopotamus fat, "well, I feel uncommonly inclined to be sick."

"If I had any doubts about helping Umbopa to rebel against that infernal blackguard," put in Good, "they are gone now. It was as much as I could do to sit still while that slaughter was going on. I tried to keep my eyes shut, but they would open just at the wrong time. I wonder where Infadoos is. Umbopa, my friend, you ought to be grateful to us; your skin came near to having an air hole made in it."

"I am grateful, Bougwan," was Umbopa's answer, when I had translated, "and I shall not forget. As for Infadoos, he will be here by and by. We must wait."

So we lit our pipes and waited.

11 ◆

We Give a Sign

FOR A LONG while—two hours, I should think—we sat there in silence, for we were too overwhelmed by the recollection of the horrors we had seen to talk. At last, just as we were thinking of turning in—for already there were faint streaks of light in the eastern sky—we heard the sound of steps. Then came the challenge of the sentry who was posted at the kraal gate, which was apparently answered, though not in an audible tone, for the steps came on; and in another second Infadoos had entered the hut, followed by some half a dozen stately-looking chiefs.

"My lords," he said, "I have come, according to my word. My lords and Ignosi, rightful king of the Kukuanas, I have brought with me these men," pointing to the row of chiefs, "who are great men among us, having each one of them the command of three thousand soldiers, who live but to do their bidding, under the king's. I have told them of what I have seen, and what my ears have heard. Now let them also see the sacred snake round thee, and hear thy story, Ignosi, that they may say whether or no they will make cause with thee against Twala the king."

For answer, Ignosi again stripped off his girdle and exhibited the snake tattooed around him. Each chief in turn drew near and examined it by the dim light of the lamp, and without saying a word passed on to the other side.

141

Then Ignosi resumed his moocha and, addressing them, repeated the history he had detailed in the morning.

"Now ye have heard, chiefs," said Infadoos, when he had done, "what say ye; will ye stand by this man and help him to his father's throne, or will ye not? The land cries out against Twala, and the blood of the people flows like the waters in spring. Ye have seen tonight. Two other chiefs there were with whom I had it in my mind to speak, and where are they now? The hyenas howl over their corpses. Soon will ye be as they are if ye strike not. Choose, then, my brothers."

The eldest of the six men, a short, thick-set warrior with white hair, stepped forward a pace and answered,

"Thy words are true, Infadoos; the land cries out. My own brother is among those who died tonight; but this is a great matter, and the thing is hard to believe. How know we that if we lift our spears it may not be for an impostor? It is a great matter, I say, and none may see the end of it. For of this be sure, blood will flow in rivers before the deed is done; many will still cleave to the king, for men worship the sun that still shines bright in the heavens, and not that which has not risen. These white men from the stars, their magic is great, and Ignosi is under the cover of their wing. If he be indeed the rightful king, let them give us a sign, and let the people have a sign, that all may see. So shall men cleave to us, knowing that the white man's magic is with them."

"Ye have the sign of the snake," I answered.

"My lord, it is not enough. The snake may have been placed there since the man's birth. Show us a sign. We will not move without a sign."

The others gave a decided assent, and I turned in perplexity to Sir Henry and Good, and explained the situation.

"I think I have it," said Good exultingly; "ask them to give us a moment to think."

I did so, and the chiefs withdrew. As soon as they were gone, Good went to the little box in which his medicines were, unlocked it, and took out a notebook, in the front of which was an almanac. "Now, look here, you fellows, isn't tomorrow the fourth of June?"

We had kept a careful note of the days, so were able to answer that it was.

"Very good; then here we have it—'4 June, total eclipse of the sun commences at 11:15 Greenwich time, visible in these islands, *Africa*, etc.' There's a sign for you. Tell them that you will darken the sun tomorrow."

The idea was a splendid one; indeed, the only fear about it was a fear lest Good's almanac might be incorrect. If we made a false prophecy on such a subject, our prestige would be gone forever, and so would Ignosi's chance of the throne of the Kukuanas.

"Suppose the almanac is wrong?" suggested Sir Henry to Good, who was busily employed in working out something on the flyleaf of the book.

"I don't see any reason to suppose anything of the sort," was his answer. "Eclipses always come up to time; at least, that is my experience of them, and it especially states that it will be visible in Africa. I have worked out the reckonings as well as I can without knowing our exact position; and I make out that the eclipse should begin here about one o'clock tomorrow, and last till half-past two. For half an hour or more there should be total darkness."

"Well," said Sir Henry, "I suppose we had better risk it."

I acquiesced, though doubtfully, for eclipses are queer cattle to deal with, and sent Umbopa to summon the chiefs back.

Presently they came, and I addressed them thus: "Great men of the Kukuanas, and thou, Infadoos, listen. We are not fond of showing our powers, since to do so is to interfere with the course of nature, and plunge the world into fear and confusion; but as this matter is a great one, and as we are angered against the king because of the slaughter we have seen, and because of the act of the Isanusi Gagool, who would have put our friend Ignosi to death, we have determined to do so, and to give such a sign as all men may see. Come thither," and I led them to the door of the hut and pointed to the fiery ball of the rising sun. "What see ye there?"

"We see the rising sun," answered the spokesman of the party.

"It is so. Now tell me, can any mortal man put out that sun, so that night comes down on the land at midday?"

The chief laughed a little. "No, my lord, that no man can do. The sun is stronger than man who looks on him."

"Ye say so. Yet I tell you that this day, one hour after midday, will we put out that sun for a space of an hour, and darkness shall cover the earth, and it shall be for a sign that we are indeed men of honor, and that Ignosi is indeed the king of the Kukuanas. If we do this thing will it satisfy ye?"

"Yea, my lords," answered the old chief with a smile, which was reflected on the faces of his companions; "*if* ye do this thing we will be satisfied indeed."

"It shall be done: we three, Incubu the Elephant, Bougwan the clear-eyed, and Macumazahn, who watches in the night, have said it, and it shall be done. Dost thou hear, Infadoos?"

"I hear, my lord, but it is a wonderful thing that ye

promise, to put out the sun, the father of all things, who shines forever."

"Yet shall we do it, Infadoos."

"It is well, my lords. Today, a little after midday, will Twala send for my lords to witness the girls dance, and one hour after the dance begins shall the girl whom Twala thinks the fairest be killed by Scragga, the king's son, as a sacrifice to the silent stone ones, who sit and keep watch by the mountains yonder," and he pointed to the three strange-looking peaks where Solomon's Road was supposed to end. "Then let my lords darken the sun, and save the maiden's life, and the people will indeed believe."

"Ay," said the old chief, still smiling a little, "the people will believe, indeed."

"Two miles from Loo," went on Infadoos, "there is a hill curved like the new moon, a stronghold, where my regiment, and three other regiments which these men command, are stationed. This morning we will make a plan whereby other regiments, two or three, may be moved there also. Then, if my lords can indeed darken the sun, in the darkness I will take my lords by the hand and lead them out of Loo to this place, where they shall be safe, and thence can we make war upon Twala, the king."

"It is good," said I. "Now leave us to sleep awhile and make ready our magic."

Infadoos rose, and, having saluted us, departed with the chiefs.

"My friends," said Ignosi, as soon as they were gone, "can ye indeed do this wonderful thing, or were ye speaking empty words to the men?"

"We believe that we can do it, Umbopa—Ignosi, I mean."

"It is strange," he answered, "and had ye not been Englishmen I would not have believed it; but English 'gentlemen' tell no lies. If we live through the matter, be sure I will repay ye!"

"Ignosi," said Sir Henry, "promise me one thing."

"I will promise, Incubu, my friend, even before I hear it," answered the big man with a smile. "What is it?"

"This: that if you ever come to be king of this people you will do away with the smelling out of witches such as we have seen last night; and that the killing of men without trial shall not take place in the land."

Ignosi thought for a moment, after I had translated this, and then answered: "The ways of black people are not as the ways of white men, Incubu, nor do we hold life so high as ye. Yet will I promise it. If it be in my power to hold them back, the witch finders shall hunt no more, nor shall any man die the death without judgment."

"That's a bargain, then," said Sir Henry; "and now let us get a little rest."

Thoroughly wearied out, we were soon sound asleep, and slept till Ignosi woke us about eleven o'clock. Then we got up, washed, and ate a hearty breakfast, not knowing when we should get any more food. After that we went outside the hut and stared at the sun, which we were distressed to observe presented a remarkably healthy appearance, without a sign of an eclipse anywhere about it.

"I hope it will come off," said Sir Henry doubtfully. "False prophets often find themselves in painful positions."

"If it does not, it will soon be up with us," I answered mournfully; "for so sure as we are living men, some of those chiefs will tell the whole story to the king, and then there will be another sort of eclipse, and one that we shall not like."

Returning to the hut, we dressed ourselves, putting on the mail shirts which the king had sent us as before. Scarcely had we done so when a messenger came from Twala to bid us to the great annual "dance of girls" which was about to be celebrated.

Taking our rifles and ammunition with us, so as to have them handy in case we had to fly, as suggested by Infadoos, we started boldly enough, though with inward fear and trembling. The great space in front of the king's kraal presented a very different appearance from what it had done on the previous evening. In the place of the grim ranks of serried warriors were company after company of Kukuana girls, not overdressed, so far as clothing went, but each crowned with a wreath of flowers, and holding a palm leaf in one hand and a tall white lily (the arum) in the other. In the center of the open space sat Twala, the king, with old Gagool at his feet, attended by Infadoos, the boy Scragga, and about a dozen guards. There were also present about a score of chiefs, among whom I recognized most of our friends of the night before.

Twala greeted us with much apparent cordiality, though I saw him fix his one eye viciously on Umbopa.

"Welcome, white men from the stars," he said; "this is a different sight from what your eyes gazed on by the light of last night's moon, but it is not so good a sight. Girls are pleasant, and were it not for such as these"—and he pointed round him—"we should none of us be here today; but men are better. Kisses and the tender words of women are sweet, but the sound of the clashing of men's spears, and the smell of men's blood, are sweeter far! Would ye have wives from among our people, white men? If so, choose the fairest here, and ye shall have them, as many as ye will," and he paused for an answer.

As the prospect did not seem to be without attractions to Good, who was, like most sailors, of a susceptible nature, I, being elderly and wise, and foreseeing the endless complications that anything of the sort would involve (for women bring trouble as surely as the night follows the day), put in a hasty answer.

"Thanks, O King, but we white men wed only with white women like ourselves. Your maidens are fair, but they are not for us!"

The king laughed. "It is well. In our land there is a proverb which says, 'Woman's eyes are always bright, whatever the color,' and another which says, 'Love her who is present, for be sure she who is absent is false to thee,' but perhaps these things are not so in the stars. In a land where men are white all things are possible. So be it, white men, the girls will not go begging! Welcome again; and welcome, too, thou black one; if Gagool here had had her way thou wouldst have been stiff and cold now. It is lucky that thou, too, camest from the stars; ha, ha!"

"I can kill thee before thou killest me, O King," was Ignosi's calm answer, "and thou shalt be stiff before my limbs cease to bend."

Twala started. "Thou speakest boldly, boy," he replied angrily; "presume not too far."

"He may well be bold in whose lips are truth. The truth is a sharp spear which flies home and fails not. It is a message from 'the stars,' O King!"

Twala scowled, and his one eye gleamed fiercely, but he said nothing more.

"Let the dance begin," he cried, and next second the flower-crowned girls sprang forward in companies, singing a sweet song and waving the delicate palms and white flowers. On they danced, now whirling round and round, now meeting in mimic warfare, swaying, eddying here and there, coming forward, falling back in an ordered confusion delightful to witness. At last they paused, and a beautiful young woman sprang out of the ranks and began to pirouette in front of us with a grace and vigor which would have put most ballet girls to shame. At length she fell back exhausted, and another took her place, then another and another, but none of them, either in grace, skill, or personal attractions, came up to the first.

At length the king lifted his hand.

"Which think ye the fairest, white men?" he asked.

"The first," said I unthinkingly. Next second I regretted it, for I remembered that Infadoos had said that the fairest woman was offered as a sacrifice.

"Then is my mind as your minds, and my eyes as your eyes. She is the fairest; and a sorry thing it is for her, for she must die!"

"*Ay, must die!*" piped out Gagool, casting a glance from her quick eyes in the direction of the poor girl, who, as yet ignorant of the awful fate in store for her, was standing some twenty yards off in front of a company of girls, engaged in nervously picking a flower from her wreath to pieces, petal by petal.

"Why, O King?" said I, restraining my indignation with difficulty. "The girl has danced well and pleased us; she is fair, too; it would be hard to reward her with death."

Twala laughed as he answered, "It is our custom, and the figures who sit in stone yonder"—and he pointed towards the three distant peaks—"must have their due. Did I fail to put the fairest girl to death today misfortune would fall upon me and my house. Thus runs the prophecy of my people: 'If the king offer not a sacrifice of a fair girl on the day of the dance of maidens to the old ones who sit and

watch on the mountains, then shall he fall and his house.'
Look ye, white men, my brother who reigned before me
offered not the sacrifice, because of the tears of the woman,
and he fell, and his house, and I reign in his stead. It is
finished; she must die!" Then, turning to the guards: "Bring
her hither; Scragga, make sharp thy spear."

Two of the men stepped forward, and as they did so
the girl, for the first time realizing her impending fate,
screamed aloud and turned to fly. But the strong hands
caught her fast, and brought her, struggling and weeping,
up before us.

"What is thy name, girl?" piped Gagool. "What! wilt
thou not answer; shall the king's son do his work at once?"

At this hint Scragga, looking more evil than ever, advanced a step and lifted his great spear, and as he did so I
saw Good's hand creep to his revolver. The poor girl
caught the glint of the cold steel through her tears, and it
sobered her anguish. She ceased struggling, but merely
clasped her hands convulsively, and stood shuddering from
head to foot.

"See," cried Scragga in high glee, "she shrinks from the
sight of my little plaything even before she has tasted it,"
and he tapped the broad blade of the spear.

"If I ever get the chance, you shall pay for that, you
young hound!" I heard Good mutter beneath his breath.

"Now that thou art quiet, give us thy name, my dear.
Come, speak up, and fear not," said Gagool in mockery.

"Oh, mother," answered the girl in trembling accents,
"my name is Foulata, of the house of Suko. Oh, mother,
why must I die? I have done no wrong!"

"Be comforted," went on the old woman in her hateful
tone of mockery. "Thou must die, indeed, as a sacrifice to

the old ones who sit yonder"—and she pointed to the peaks —"but it is better to sleep in the night than to toil in the daytime; it is better to die than to live, and thou shalt die by the royal hand of the king's own son."

The girl Foulata wrung her hands in anguish, and cried out aloud: "Oh, cruel; and I so young! What have I done that I should never again see the sun rise out of the night, or the stars come following on his track in the evening: that I should no more gather the flowers when the dew is heavy, or listen to the laughing of the waters! Woe is me, that I shall never see my father's hut again, nor feel my mother's kiss, nor tend the kid that is sick! Woe is me, that no lover shall put his arm around me and look into my eyes, nor shall men children be born of me! Oh, cruel, cruel!" and again she wrung her hands and turned her tear-stained, flower-crowned face to heaven, looking so lovely in her despair—for she was indeed a beautiful woman— that it would assuredly have melted the hearts of any one less cruel than the three fiends before us. Prince Arthur's appeal to the ruffians who came to blind him was not more touching than this savage girl's.

But it did not move Gagool or Gagool's master, though I saw signs of pity among the guard behind and on the faces of the chiefs; and as for Good, he gave a sort of snort of indignation, and made a motion as though to go to her. With all a woman's quickness, the doomed girl interpreted what was passing in his mind, and with a sudden movement flung herself before him, and clasped his "beautiful white legs" with her hands.

"Oh, white father from the stars!" she cried. "Throw over me the mantle of thy protection; let me creep into the shadow of thy strength, that I may be saved. Oh, keep me from these cruel men and from the mercies of Gagool!"

"All right, my hearty, I'll look after you," sang out Good, in nervous Saxon. "Come, get up, there's a good girl," and he stooped and caught her hand.

Twala turned and motioned to his son, who advanced with his spear lifted.

"Now's your time," whispered Sir Henry to me; "what are you waiting for?"

"I am waiting for the eclipse," I answered; "I have had my eye on the sun for the last half hour, and I never saw it look healthier."

"Well, you must risk it now or the girl will be killed. Twala is losing patience."

Recognizing the force of the argument, having cast one more despairing look at the bright face of the sun, for never did the most ardent astronomer with a theory to prove await a celestial event with such anxiety, I stepped, with all the dignity I could command, between the prostrate girl and the advancing spear of Scragga.

"King," I said; "this shall not be; we will not tolerate such a thing; let the girl go in safety."

Twala rose from his seat in his wrath and astonishment, and from the chiefs and serried ranks of girls, who had slowly closed in upon us in anticipation of the tragedy, came a murmur of amazement.

"*Shall not be*, thou white dog, who yaps at the lion in his cave; *shall not be!* Art thou mad? Be careful lest this chicken's fate overtake thee and those with thee. How canst thou prevent it? Who art thou, that thou standest between me and my will? Withdraw, I say. Scragga, kill her. Ho, guards! Seize these men."

At his cry armed men came running swiftly from behind the hut, where they had evidently been placed beforehand.

Sir Henry, Good, and Umbopa ranged themselves alongside of me and lifted their rifles.

"Stop!" I shouted boldly, though at the moment my heart was in my boots. "Stop! We, the white men from the stars, say that it shall not be. Come but one pace nearer and we will put out the sun and plunge the land in darkness. Ye shall taste of our magic."

My threat produced an effect; the men halted, and Scragga stood still before us, his spear lifted.

"Hear him! Hear him!" piped Gagool: "Hear the liar who says he will put out the sun like a lamp. Let him do it and the girl shall be spared. Yes, let him do it, or die with the girl, he and those with him."

I glanced up at the sun, and, to my intense joy and relief, saw that we had made no mistake. On the edge of its brilliant surface was a faint rim of shadow.

I lifted my hand solemnly towards the sky, an example which Sir Henry and Good followed, and quoted a line or two of the *Ingoldsby Legends* at it in the most impressive tones I could command. Sir Henry followed suit with a verse out of the Old Testament, while Good addressed the king of day in a volume of the most classical bad language that he could think of.

Slowly the dark rim crept on over the blazing surface, and as it did so I heard a deep gasp of fear rise from the multitude around.

"Look, O King! Look, Gagool! Look, chiefs and people and women, and see if the white men from the stars keep their word, or if they be but empty liars!

"The sun grows dark before your eyes; soon there will be night—ay, night in the noontime. Ye have asked for a sign; it is given to ye. Grow dark, O sun! Withdraw thy light, thou bright one; bring the proud heart to the dust, and eat up the world with shadows."

A groan of terror rose from the onlookers. Some stood petrified with fear, others threw themselves upon their knees and cried out. As for the king, he sat still and turned pale beneath his dusky skin. Only Gagool kept her courage.

"It will pass," she cried; "I have seen the like before; no man can put out the sun; lose not heart; sit still—the shadow will pass."

"Wait, and ye shall see," I replied, hopping with excitement.

"Keep it up, Good; I can't remember any more poetry. Curse away, there's a good fellow."

Good responded nobly to the tax upon his inventive faculties. Never before had I the faintest conception of the breadth and depth and height of a naval officer's objurgatory powers. For ten minutes he went on without stopping, and he scarcely ever repeated himself.

Meanwhile the dark ring crept on. Strange and unholy shadows encroached upon the sunlight, an ominous quiet filled the place, the birds chirped out frightened notes and then were still; only the cocks began to crow.

On, yet on, crept the ring of darkness; it was now more than half over the reddening orb. The air grew thick and dusky. On, yet on, till we could scarcely see the fierce faces of the group before us. No sound now rose from the spectators, and Good stopped swearing.

"The sun is dying—the wizards have killed the sun," yelled out the boy Scragga at last. "We shall all die in the dark," and, animated by fear or fury, or both, he lifted his spear and drove it with all his force at Sir Henry's broad chest. But he had forgotten the mail shirts that the king had given us, and which we wore beneath our clothing. The steel rebounded harmless, and before he could repeat the blow Sir Henry had snatched the spear from his hand and sent it straight through him. He dropped dead.

At the sight, and driven mad with fear at the gathering gloom, the companies of girls broke up in wild confusion and ran screeching for the gateways. Nor did the panic stop there. The king himself, followed by the guards, some of the chiefs, and Gagool, who hobbled away after them with marvelous alacrity, fled for the huts, so that in another minute or so ourselves, the would-be victim, Foulata, Infadoos, and some of the chiefs who had interviewed us on the previous night were left alone upon the scene with the dead body of Scragga.

"Now, chiefs," I said, "we have given you the sign. If ye are satisfied, let us fly swiftly to the place ye spoke of. The charm cannot now be stopped. It will work for an hour. Let us take advantage of the darkness."

"Come," said Infadoos, turning to go, an example which was followed by the awed chiefs, ourselves, and the girl Foulata, whom Good took by the hand.

Before we reached the gate of the kraal the sun went out altogether.

Holding each other by the hand, we stumbled on through the darkness.

12 ♦

Before the Battle

LUCKILY for us, Infadoos and the chiefs knew all the pathways of the great town perfectly, so that, notwithstanding the intense gloom, we made fair progress.

For an hour or more we journeyed on, till at length the eclipse began to pass, and that edge of the sun which had disappeared the first became again visible. In another five minutes there was sufficient light to see our whereabouts, and we then discovered that we were clear of the town of Loo, and approaching a large, flat-topped hill, measuring some two miles in circumference. This hill, which was of a formation very common in southern Africa, was not very high; indeed, its greatest elevation was not more than two hundred feet, but it was shaped like a horseshoe, and its sides were rather precipitous and strewn with boulders. On the grass tableland at the top was ample camping ground, which had been utilized as a military cantonment of no mean strength. Its ordinary garrison was one regiment of three thousand men, but as we toiled up the steep side of the hill in the returning daylight we perceived that there were many more warriors than that upon it.

Reaching the tableland at last, we found crowds of men huddled together in the utmost consternation at the natural phenomenon which they were witnessing. Passing through these without a word, we gained a hut in the center of the ground, where we were astonished to find two men waiting, laden with our few goods and chattels, which, of course, we had been obliged to leave behind in our hasty flight.

"I sent for them," explained Infadoos; "also for these," and he lifted up Good's long-lost trousers.

With an exclamation of rapturous delight Good sprang at them, and instantly proceeded to put them on.

"Surely my lord will not hide his beautiful white legs!" exclaimed Infadoos regretfully.

But Good persisted, and once only did the Kukuana people get the chance of seeing his beautiful legs again. Good is a very modest man. Henceforward they had to satisfy their esthetic longings with one whisker, his transparent eye, and his movable teeth.

Still gazing with fond remembrance at Good's trousers, Infadoos next informed us that he had summoned the regiments to explain to them fully the rebellion which was decided on by the chiefs, and to introduce to them the rightful heir to the throne, Ignosi.

In half an hour the troops, in all nearly twenty thousand men, constituting the flower of the Kukuana army, were mustered on a large, open space, to which we proceeded. The men were drawn up in three sides of a dense square, and presented a magnificent spectacle. We took our station on the open side of the square, and were speedily surrounded by all the principal chiefs and officers.

These, after silence had been proclaimed, Infadoos proceeded to address. He narrated to them in vigorous and graceful language—for, like most Kukuanas of high rank, he was a born orator—the history of Ignosi's father, how he had been basely murdered by Twala, the king, and his wife and child driven out to starve. Then he pointed out how the land suffered and groaned under Twala's cruel rule, instancing the proceedings of the previous night, when, under pretense of their being evildoers, many of the noblest in the land had been hauled forth and cruelly done to death. Next he went on to say that the white lords from the stars, looking down on the land, had perceived its trouble, and determined, at great personal inconvenience, to alleviate its lot; how they had accordingly taken the real king of the country, Ignosi, who was languishing in exile, by the hand and led him over the mountains; how they had seen the wickedness of Twala's doings, and for a sign to the wavering, and to save the life of the girl Foulata, had actually, by the exercise of their high magic, put out the sun and slain the young fiend, Scragga; and how they were prepared to stand by them, and assist them to overthrow Twala, and set up the rightful king, Ignosi, in his place.

He finished his discourse amid a murmur of approbation, and then Ignosi stepped forward and began to speak. Having reiterated all that Infadoos, his uncle, had said, he concluded a powerful speech in these words: "O chiefs, captains, soldiers, and people, ye have heard my words. Now must ye make choice between me and him who sits upon my throne, the uncle who killed his brother, and hunted his brother's child forth to die in the cold and the night. That I am indeed the king these"—pointing to the chiefs—"can tell ye, for they have seen the snake about my middle. If I were not the king, would these white men be on my side, with all their magic? Tremble, chiefs, captains, soldiers, and people! Is not the darkness they have brought upon the land to confound Twala, and cover our flight, yet before your eyes?"

"It is," answered the soldiers.

"I am the king; I say to ye, I am the king," went on Ignosi, drawing up his great stature to its full, and lifting his broad-bladed battle-ax above his head. "If there be any man among ye who says that it is not so, let him stand forth, and I will fight him now, and his blood shall be a red token that I tell ye true. Let him stand forth, I say," and he shook the great ax till it flashed in the sunlight.

As nobody seemed inclined to respond to this heroic version of "Dilly, Dilly, come and be killed," our late henchman proceeded with his address.

"I am indeed the king, and if ye do stand by my side in the battle, if I win the day ye shall go with me to victory and honor. I will give ye oxen and wives, and ye shall take place of all the regiments; and if ye fall I will fall with ye.

"And behold, this promise do I give ye, that when I sit upon the seat of my fathers, bloodshed shall cease in the land. No longer shall ye cry for justice to find slaughter, no longer shall the witch finder hunt ye out so that ye be slain without a cause. No man shall die save he who offendeth against the laws. The 'eating up' of your kraals shall cease; each shall sleep secure in his own hut and fear not, and justice shall walk blind throughout the land. Have ye chosen, chiefs, captains, soldiers, and people?"

"We have chosen, O King," came back the answer.

"It is well. Turn your heads and see how Twala's messengers go forth from the great town, east and west, and north and south, to gather a mighty army to slay me and ye, these my friends and my protectors. Tomorrow, or perchance the next day, will he come with all who are faithful to him. Then shall I see the man who is indeed my man, the man who fears not to die for his cause; and I tell ye he shall not be forgotten in the time of spoil. I have spoken, O chiefs, captains, soldiers, and people. Now go to your huts and make you ready for war."

There was a pause, and then one of the chiefs lifted his

hand, and out rolled the royal salute, "*Koom!*" It was a sign that the regiments accepted Ignosi as their king. Then they marched off in battalions.

Half an hour afterwards we held a council of war, at which all the commanders of regiments were present. It was evident to us that before very long we should be attacked in overwhelming force. Indeed, from our point of vantage on the hill we could see troops mustering, and messengers going forth from Loo in every direction, doubtless to summon regiments to the king's assistance. We had on our side about twenty thousand men, composed of seven of the best regiments in the country. Twala had, so Infadoos and chiefs calculated, at least thirty to thirty-five thousand on whom he could rely at present assembled in Loo, and they thought that by midday on the morrow he would be able to gather another five thousand or more to his aid. It was, of course, possible that some of his troops would desert and come over to us, but it was not a contingency that could be reckoned on. Meanwhile, it was clear that active preparations were being made to subdue us. Already strong bodies of armed men were patrolling round and round the foot of the hill, and there were other signs of a coming attack.

Infadoos and the chiefs, however, were of opinion that no attack would take place that night, which would be devoted to preparation and to the removal by every possible means of the moral effect produced upon the minds of the soldiery by the supposed magical darkening of the sun. The attack would be on the morrow, they said, and they proved to be right.

Meanwhile, we set to work to strengthen the position as much as possible. Nearly the entire force was turned out, and in two hours which yet remained to sundown wonders were done. The paths up the hill—which was rather a sanitarium than a fortress, being used generally as the camping place of regiments suffering from recent service in unhealthy portions of the country—were carefully blocked with masses of stones, and every other possible approach was made as impregnable as time would allow. Piles of boulders were collected at various spots to be rolled down upon an advancing enemy, stations were appointed to the different regiments, and every other preparation which our joint ingenuity could suggest was taken.

Just before sundown we perceived a small company of men advancing towards us from the direction of Loo, one of whom bore a palm leaf in his hand as a sign that he came as a herald.

As he came, Ignosi, Infadoos, one or two chiefs, and ourselves went down to the foot of the mountain to meet him. He was a gallant-looking fellow, with the regulation leopard-skin cloak.

"Greeting!" he cried, as he came near. "The king's greeting to those who make unholy war against the king; the lion's greeting to the jackals who snarl around his heels."

"Speak," I said.

"These are the king's words. Surrender to the king's mercy ere a worse thing befall ye. Already the shoulder has been torn from the black bull, and the king drives him bleeding about the camp." [1]

"What are Twala's terms?" I asked, for curiosity.

"His terms are merciful, worthy of a great king. These are the words of Twala, the one-eyed, the mighty, the husband of a thousand wives, lord of the Kukuanas, keeper of the Great Road, beloved of the strange ones who sit in

[1] This cruel custom is not confined to the Kukuanas, but is by no means uncommon among African tribes on the occasion of the outbreak of war or any other important public event.—A. Q.

silence at the mountains yonder [the Three Witches], calf of the black cow, elephant whose tread shakes the earth, terror of the evildoer, ostrich whose feet devour the desert, huge one, black one, wise one, king from generation to generation! these are the words of Twala: 'I will have mercy and be satisfied with a little blood. One in every ten shall die, the rest shall go free; but the white man Incubu, who slew Scragga, my son, and Infadoos, my brother, who brews rebellion against me, these shall die by torture as an offering to the silent ones.' Such are the merciful words of Twala."

After consulting with the others a little I answered him in a loud voice, so that the soldiers might hear, thus: "Go back, thou dog, to Twala, who sent thee, and say that we, Ignosi, veritable king of the Kukuanas, Incubu, Bougwan, and Macumazahn, the wise white ones from the stars who make dark the sun, Infadoos, of the royal house, and the chiefs, captains, and people here gathered, make answer and say, 'That we will not surrender; that before the sun has twice gone down Twala's corpse shall stiffen at Twala's gate, and Ignosi, whose father Twala slew, shall reign in his stead.' Now go, ere we whip thee away, and beware how ye lift a hand against such as we."

The herald laughed loud. "Ye frighten not men with such swelling words," he cried out. "Show yourselves as bold tomorrow, O ye who darken the sun. Be bold, fight, and be merry, before the crows pick your bones till they are whiter than your faces. Farewell; perhaps we may meet in the fight; wait for me, I pray, white men." And with this shaft of sarcasm he retired, and almost immediately the sun sank.

That night was a busy one for us, for, as far as was possible by the moonlight, all preparations for the morrow's fight were continued. Messengers were constantly coming and going from the place where we sat in council. At last, about an hour after midnight, everything that could be done was done, and the camp, save for the occasional challenge of a sentry, sank into sleep. Sir Henry and I, accompanied by Ignosi and one of the chiefs, descended the hill and made the round of the vedettes. As we went, suddenly, from all sorts of unexpected places, spears gleamed out in the moonlight, only to vanish again as we uttered the password. It was clear to us that none were sleeping at their posts. Then we returned, picking our way through thousands of sleeping warriors, many of whom were taking their last earthly rest.

The moonlight flickered along their spears, and played upon their features and made them ghastly; the chilly night wind tossed their tall and hearselike plumes. There they lay in wild confusion, with arms outstretched and twisted limbs; their stern, stalwart forms looking weird and unhuman in the moonlight.

"How many of these do you suppose will be alive at this time tomorrow?" asked Sir Henry.

I shook my head and looked again at the sleeping men, and to my tired and yet excited imagination it seemed as though death had already touched them. My mind's eye singled out those who were sealed to slaughter, and there rushed in upon my heart a great sense of the mystery of human life, and an overwhelming sorrow at its futility and sadness. Tonight these thousands slept their healthy sleep; tomorrow they, and many others with them, ourselves perhaps among them, would be stiffening in the cold; their wives would be widows, their children fatherless, and their place know them no more forever. Only the old moon would shine serenely on, the night wind would stir the grasses, and the wide earth would take its happy rest, even as it did eons before these were, and will do eons after they have been forgotten.

Yet man dies not while the world, at once his mother and his monument, remains. His name is forgotten, indeed, but the breath he breathed yet stirs the pine tops on the mountains, the sound of the words he spoke yet echoes on through space; the thoughts his brain gave birth to we have inherited today; his passions are our cause of life; the joys and sorrows that he felt are our familiar friends—the end from which he fled aghast will surely overtake us also.

Truly the universe is full of ghosts; not sheeted, churchyard spectres, but the inextinguishable and immortal elements of life, which, having once been, can never *die*, though they blend and change and change again forever.

All sorts of reflections of this sort passed through my mind—for as I get older I regret to say that a detestable habit of thinking seems to be getting a hold on me—while I stood and stared at those grim yet fantastic lines of warriors sleeping, as their saying goes, "upon their spears."

"Curtis," I said to Sir Henry, "I am in a condition of pitiable funk."

Sir Henry stroked his yellow beard and laughed as he answered, "I've heard you make that sort of remark before, Quatermain."

"Well, I mean it now. Do you know, I very much doubt if one of us will be alive tomorrow night. We shall be attacked in overwhelming force, and it is exceedingly doubtful if we can hold this place."

"We'll give a good account of some of them, at any rate. Look here, Quatermain, the business is a nasty one, and one with which, properly speaking, we ought not to be mixed up; but we are in for it, so we must make the best of it.

Speaking personally, I had rather be killed fighting than any other way, and now that there seems little chance of finding my poor brother, it makes the idea easier to me. But fortune favors the brave, and we may succeed. Anyway, the slaughter will be awful, and as we have a reputation to keep up, we shall have to be in the thick of it."

Sir Henry made this last remark in a mournful voice, but there was a gleam in his eye which belied it. I have a sort of idea that Sir Henry Curtis actually likes fighting.

After this we went and slept for a couple of hours.

Just about dawn we were awakened by Infadoos, who came to say that great activity was to be observed in Loo, and that parties of the king's skirmishers were driving in our vedettes.

We got up and dressed ourselves for the fray, each putting on his chain-armor shirt, for which at the present juncture we felt exceedingly thankful. Sir Henry went the whole length about the matter, and dressed himself like a native warrior. "When you are in Kukuanaland, do as the Kukuanas do," he remarked as he drew the shining steel over his broad shoulders, which it fitted like a glove. Nor did he stop there. At his request, Infadoos had provided him with a complete set of war uniform. Round his throat he fastened the leopard-skin cloak of a commanding officer, on his brows he bound the plume of black ostrich feathers worn only by generals of high rank, and round his center a magnificent moocha of white ox tails. A pair of sandals, a leglet of goat's hair, a heavy battle-ax with a rhinoceros-horn handle, a round iron shield covered with white ox hide, and the regulation number of tollas, or throwing knives, made up his equipment, to which, however, he added his revolver. The dress was, no doubt, a savage one; but I am bound to say I never saw a finer sight than Sir

Henry Curtis presented in this guise. It showed off his magnificent physique to the greatest advantage, and when Ignosi arrived, presently, arrayed in similar costume, I thought to myself that I never before saw two such splendid men. As for Good and myself, the chain armor did not suit us nearly so well. To begin with, Good insisted upon keeping on his trousers, and a stout, short gentleman with an eyeglass, and one half of his face shaved, arrayed in a mail shirt carefully tucked into a very seedy pair of corduroys, looks more striking than imposing. As for myself, my chain shirt being too big for me, I put it on over all my clothes, which caused it to bulge out in a somewhat ungainly fashion. I discarded my trousers, however, determined to go into battle with bare legs, in order to be the lighter in case it became necessary to retire quickly, retaining only my veldtschoons. This, a spear, a shield, which I did not know how to use, a couple of tollas, a revolver, and a huge plume, which I pinned into the top of my shooting hat in order to give a bloodthirsty finish to my appearance, completed my modest equipment. In addition to all these articles, of course, we had our rifles, but as ammunition was scarce, and they would be useless in case of a charge, we had arranged to have them carried behind us by bearers.

As soon as we had equipped ourselves we hastily swallowed some food, and then started out to see how things were progressing. At one point in the tableland of the mountain there was a little koppie of brown stone, which served for the double purpose of headquarters and a conning tower. Here we found Infadoos surrounded by his own regiment, the Grays, which was undoubtedly the finest in the Kukuana army, and the same which we had first seen at the outlying kraal. This regiment, now three thousand five hundred strong, was being held in reserve, and the men were lying down on the grass in companies, and watching the king's forces creep out of Loo in long, antlike columns. There seemed to be no end to those columns—three in all, and each numbering at least eleven or twelve thousand men.

As soon as they were clear of the town, they formed up. Then one body marched off to the right, one to the left, and the third came slowly on towards us.

"Ah," said Infadoos, "they are going to attack us on three sides at once."

This was rather serious news, for as our position on the top of the mountain, which was at least a mile and a half in circumference, was an extended one, it was important to us to concentrate our comparatively small defending force as much as possible. But, as it was impossible for us to dictate in what way we should be attacked, we had to make the best of it, and accordingly sent orders to the various regiments to prepare to receive the separate onslaughts.

13 ♦

The Attack

SLOWLY, and without the slightest appearance of haste, or excitement, the three columns crept on. When within about five hundred yards of us, the main or center column halted at the root of a tongue of open plain which ran up into the hill, to enable the other two to circumvent our position, which was shaped more or less in the form of a horseshoe, the two points being towards the town of Loo, their object being, no doubt, that the threefold assault should be delivered simultaneously.

"Oh, for a gatling!" groaned Good, as he contemplated the serried phalanxes beneath us. "I would clear the plain in twenty minutes."

"We have not got one, so it is no use yearning for it; but suppose you try a shot, Quatermain. See how near you can go to that tall fellow who appears to be in command. Two to one you miss him, and an even sovereign, to be honestly paid if ever we get out of this, that you don't drop the ball within ten yards."

This piqued me, so, loading the express with solid ball, I waited till my friend walked some ten yards out from his force, in order to get a better view of our position, accompanied only by an orderly, and then, lying down and resting the express upon a rock, I covered him. The rifle, like all expresses, was only sighted to three hundred and fifty yards,

so, to allow for the drop in trajectory, I took him halfway
down the neck, which ought, I calculated, to find him in
the chest. He stood quite still and gave me every opportunity, but whether it was the excitement or the wind, or the
fact of the man being a long shot, I don't know, but this
was what happened. Getting dead on, as I thought, a fine
sight, I pressed, and when the puff of smoke had cleared
away I, to my disgust, saw my man standing unharmed,
while his orderly, who was at least three paces to the left,
was stretched upon the ground, apparently dead. Turning
swiftly, the officer I had aimed at began to run towards his
force, in evident alarm.

"Bravo, Quatermain!" sang out Good. "You've frightened him."

This made me very angry, for if possible to avoid it, I
hate to miss in public. When one can only do one thing
well, one likes to keep up one's reputation in that thing.
Moved quite out of myself at my failure, I did a rash thing.
Rapidly covering the general as he ran, I let drive with the
second barrel. The poor man threw up his arms and fell
forward on his face. This time I had made no mistake; and
—I say it as a proof of how little we think of others when
our own pride or reputation is in question—I was brute
enough to feel delighted at the sight.

The regiments who had seen the feat cheered wildly at
this exhibition of the white man's magic, which they took
as an omen of success, while the force to which the general
had belonged—which, indeed, as we afterwards ascertained,
he had commanded—began to fall back in confusion. Sir
Henry and Good now took up their rifles and began to fire,
the latter industriously "browning" the dense mass before
him with a Winchester repeater, and I also had another

shot or two, with the result that, so far as we could judge, we put some eight or ten men *hors de combat* before they got out of range.

Just as we stopped firing there came an ominous roar from our far right, then a similar roar from our left. The two other divisions were engaging us.

At the sound the mass of men before us opened out a little, and came on towards the hill up the spit of bare grassland at a slow trot, singing a deep-throated song as they advanced. We kept up a steady fire from our rifles as they came, Ignosi joining in occasionally, and accounted for several men, but of course produced no more effect upon that mighty rush of armed humanity than he who throws pebbles does on the advancing wave.

On they came, with a shout and the clashing of spears; now they were driving in the outposts we had placed among the rocks at the foot of the hill. After that the advance was a little slower, for, though as yet we had offered no serious opposition, the attacking force had to come uphill, and came slowly to save their breath. Our first line of defense was about halfway up the side, our second fifty yards farther back, while our third occupied the edge of the plain.

On they came, shouting their war cry, *"Twala! Twala! Chielé! Chielé!"* ("Twala! Twala! Smite! Smite!"). *"Ignosi! Ignosi! Chielé! Chielé!"* answered our people. They were quite close now, and the tollas began to flash backward and forward, and now with an awful yell the battle closed in.

To and fro swayed the mass of struggling warriors, men falling thick as leaves in an autumn wind; but before long the superior weight of the attacking force began to tell, and our first line of defense was slowly pressed back, till it merged into the second. Here the struggle was very fierce, but again our people were driven back and up, till at length, within twenty minutes of the commencement of the fight, our third line came into action.

But by this time the assailants were much exhausted, and had, besides, lost many men killed and wounded, and to break through that third impenetrable hedge of spears proved beyond their powers. For a while the dense mass of struggling warriors swung backward and forward in the fierce ebb and flow of battle, and the issue was doubtful. Sir Henry watched the desperate struggle with a kindling eye, and then without a word he rushed off, followed by Good, and flung himself into the hottest of the fray. As for myself, I stopped where I was.

The soldiers caught sight of his tall form as he plunged into the battle, and there rose a cry of, *"Nanzia Incubu!"* ("Here is the Elephant!") *"Chielé! Chielé!"*

From that moment the issue was no longer in doubt. Inch by inch, fighting with desperate gallantry, the attacking force was pressed back down the hillside, till at last it retreated upon its reserves in something like confusion. At that moment, too, a messenger arrived to say that the left attack had been repulsed, and I was just beginning to congratulate myself that the affair was over for the present, when, to our horror, we perceived our men who had been engaged in the right defense being driven towards us across the plain, followed by swarms of the enemy, who had evidently succeeded at this point.

Ignosi, who was standing by me, took in the situation at a glance, and issued a rapid order. Instantly the reserve regiment round us (the Grays) extended itself.

Again Ignosi gave a word of command, which was taken up and repeated by the captains, and in another second, to my intense disgust, I found myself involved in a furious onslaught upon the advancing foe. Getting as much as I could behind Ignosi's huge frame, I made the best of a bad job, and toddled along to be killed, as though I liked it. In a minute or two—the time seemed all too short to me—we were plunging through the flying groups of our men, who at once began to re-form behind us, and then I am sure I do not know what happened. All I can remember is a dreadful rolling noise of the meeting of shields, and the sudden apparition of a huge ruffian, whose eyes seemed literally to be starting out of his head, making straight at me with a bloody spear. But—I say it with pride—I rose to the occasion. It was an occasion before which most people would have collapsed once and for all. Seeing that if I stood where I was I must be done for, I, as the horrid apparition came, flung myself down in front of him so cleverly that, being unable to stop himself, he took a header right over my prostrate form. Before he could rise again I had risen and settled the matter from behind with my revolver.

Shortly after this somebody knocked me down, and I remember no more of the charge.

When I came to I found myself back at the koppie, with Good bending over me with some water in a gourd.

"How do you feel, old fellow?" he asked anxiously.

I got up and shook myself before answering.

"Pretty well, thank you," I answered.

"Thank heaven! When I saw them carry you in I felt quite sick; I thought you were done for."

"Not this time, my boy. I fancy I only got a rap on the head, which knocked me out of time. How has it ended?"

"They are repulsed at every point for the time. The loss is dreadfully heavy; we have lost quite two thousand killed and wounded, and they must have lost three. Look, there's a sight!" and he pointed to long lines of men advancing by fours. In the center of, and being borne by, each group of four was a kind of hide tray, of which a Kukuana force always carried a quantity, with a loop for a handle at each corner. On these trays—and their number seemed endless— lay wounded men, who as they arrived were hastily examined by the medicine men, of whom ten were attached to each regiment. If the wound was not of a fatal character the sufferer was taken away and attended to as carefully as circumstances would allow. But if, on the other hand, the wounded man's condition was hopeless, what followed was very dreadful, though doubtless it was the truest mercy. One of the doctors, under pretense of carrying out an examination, swiftly opened an artery with a sharp knife, and in a minute or two the sufferer expired painlessly. There were many cases that day in which this was done. In fact, it was done in most cases when the wound was in the body, for the gash made by the entry of the enormously broad spears used by the Kukuanas generally rendered recovery hopeless. In most cases the sufferers were already unconscious, and in others the fatal "nick" of the artery was done so swiftly and painlessly that they did not seem to notice it. Still, it was a ghastly sight, and one from which we were glad to escape; indeed, I never remember one which affected me more than seeing those gallant soldiers thus put out of pain by the red-handed medicine men, except, indeed, on an occasion when, after an attack, I saw a force of Swazis burying their hopelessly wounded *alive*.

Hurrying from this dreadful scene to the farther side of the koppie, we found Sir Henry (who still held a bloody battle-ax in his hand), Ignosi, Infadoos, and one or two of the chiefs in deep consultation.

"Thank heaven, here you are, Quatermain! I can't make out what Ignosi wants to do. It seems that, though we have

beaten off the attack, Twala is now receiving large reinforce-
ments, and is showing a disposition to invest us, with a
view of starving us out."

"That's awkward."

"Yes; especially as Infadoos says that the water supply
has given out."

"My lord, that is so," said Infadoos; "the spring cannot
supply the wants of so great a multitude, and is failing
rapidly. Before night we shall all be thirsty. Listen, Macumazahn. Thou art wise, and hast doubtless seen many
wars in the lands from whence thou camest—that is if,
indeed, they make wars in the stars. Now tell us, what shall
we do? Twala has brought up many fresh men to take the
place of those who have fallen. But Twala has learned a
lesson; the hawk did not think to find the heron ready; but
our beak has pierced his breast; he will not strike at us
again. We, too, are wounded, and he will wait for us to die;
he will wind himself round us like a snake round a buck,
and fight the fight of 'sit down.' "

"I hear you," I said.

"So, Macumazahn, thou seest we have no water here,
and but a little food, and we must choose between these
three things—to languish like a starving lion in his den, or
to strive to break away towards the north, or"—and here
he rose and pointed towards the dense mass of our foes—
"to launch ourselves straight at Twala's throat. Incubu, the
great warrior—for today he fought like a buffalo in a net,
and Twala's soldiers went down before his axe like corn
before the hail; with these eyes I saw it—Incubu says
'charge,' but the Elephant is ever prone to charge. Now
what says Macumazahn, the wily old fox, who has seen
much and loves to bite his enemy from behind? The last
word is in Ignosi, the king, for it is a king's right to speak

of war; but let us hear thy voice, O Macumazahn, who watchest by night, and the voice too of him of the transparent eye."

"What sayest thou, Ignosi?"

"Nay, my father," answered our quondam servant, who now, clad as he was in the full panoply of savage war, looked every inch a warrior king, "do thou speak, and let me, who am but a child in wisdom beside thee, hearken to thy words."

Thus abjured, I, after taking hasty counsel with Good and Sir Henry, delivered my opinion briefly to the effect, that, being trapped, our best chance, especially in view of the failure of our water supply, was to initiate an attack upon Twala's forces, and then I recommended that the attack should be delivered at once, "before our wounds grew stiff," and also before the sight of Twala's overpowering force caused the hearts of our soldiers "to wax small like fat before a fire." Otherwise, I pointed out, some of the captains might change their minds, and, making peace with Twala, desert to him, or even betray us into his hands.

This expression of opinion seemed, on the whole, to be favorably received; indeed, among the Kukuanas my utterances met with a respect which has never been accorded to them before or since. But the real decision as to our course lay with Ignosi, who, since he had been recognized as rightful king, could exercise the almost unbounded rights of sovereignty, including, of course, the final decision on matters of generalship, and it was to him that all eyes were now turned.

At length, after a pause, during which he appeared to be thinking deeply, he spoke:

"Incubu, Macumazahn, and Bougwan, brave white men, and my friends; Infadoos, my uncle, and chiefs; my heart is fixed. I will strike at Twala this day, and set my fortunes on the blow, ay, and my life; my life and your lives also. Listen: thus will I strike. Ye see how the hill curves round like the half moon, and how the plain runs like a green tongue towards us within the curve?"

"We see," I answered.

"Good; it is now midday, and the men eat and rest after the toil of battle. When the sun has turned and traveled a little way towards the dark, let thy regiment, my uncle, advance with one other down to the green tongue. And it shall be that when Twala sees it he shall hurl his force at it to crush it. But the spot is narrow, and the regiments can come against thee one at a time only, so shall they be destroyed one by one, and the eyes of all Twala's army shall be fixed upon a struggle the like of which has not been seen by living man. And with thee, my uncle, shall go Incubu, my friend, that when Twala sees his battle-ax flashing in the first rank of the Grays his heart may grow faint. And I will come with the second regiment, that which follows thee, so that if ye are destroyed, as it may happen, there may yet be a king left to fight for; and with me shall come Macumazahn the wise."

"It is well, O King," said Infadoos, apparently contemplating the certainty of the complete annihilation of his regiment with perfect calmness. Truly these Kukuanas are a wonderful people. Death has no terrors for them when it is incurred in the course of duty.

"And while the eyes of the multitude of Twala's regiments are thus fixed upon the fight," went on Ignosi, "behold, one third of the men who are left alive to us" (*i.e.*, about six thousand) 'shall creep along the right horn of the hill and fall upon the left flank of Twala's force, and one third shall creep along the left horn and fall upon Twala's right flank. And when I see that the horns are ready to toss Twala, then will I, with the men who are left to me, charge home in Twala's face, and if fortune goes with us the day will be ours, and before Night drives her horses from the mountains to the mountains we shall sit in peace at Loo. And now let us eat and make ready; and, Infadoos, do thou prepare, that the plan be carried out; and stay, let my white father, Bougwan, go with the right horn, that his shining eye may give courage to the men."

The arrangements for the attack thus briefly indicated were set in motion with a rapidity that spoke well for the perfection of the Kukuana military system. Within little more than an hour rations had been served out to the men and devoured, the three divisions were formed, the plan of attack explained to the leaders, and the whole force— with the exception of a guard left with the wounded—now numbering about eighteen thousand men in all, was ready to be put in motion.

Presently Good came up and shook hands with Sir Henry and myself.

"Good-by, you fellows," he said, "I am off with the right wing, according to orders; and so I have come to shake hands in case we should not meet again, you know," he added significantly.

We shook hands in silence, and not without the exhibition of as much emotion as Englishmen are wont to show.

"It is a queer business," said Sir Henry, his deep voice shaking a little, "and I confess I never expect to see tomorrow's sun. As far as I can make out, the Grays, with whom I am to go, are to fight until they are wiped out in order to enable the wings to slip round unawares and outflank Twala. Well, so be it; at any rate, it will be a man's death! Good-by, old fellow. God bless you! I hope you will pull through and live to collar the diamonds; but if you do, take my advice and don't have anything more to do with pretenders!"

In another second Good had wrung us both by the hand and gone; and then Infadoos came up and led off Sir Henry to his place in the forefront of the Grays, while, with many misgivings, I departed with Ignosi to my station in the second attacking regiment.

14 ♦

The Last Stand of the Grays

IN A FEW more minutes the regiments destined to carry out the flanking movements had tramped off in silence, keeping carefully under the lee of the rising ground in order to conceal the movement from the keen eyes of Twala's scouts.

Half an hour or more was allowed to elapse between the setting out of the horns or wings of the army before any movement was made by the Grays and the supporting regiment, known as the Buffaloes, and which were destined to bear the brunt of the battle.

Both of these regiments were almost perfectly fresh, and of full strength, the Grays having been in reserve in the morning, and having lost but a small number of men in sweeping back that part of the attack which had proved successful in breaking the line of defense on the occasion when I charged with them and got knocked silly for my pains. As for the Buffaloes, they had formed the third line of defense on the left, and as the attacking force at that point had not succeeded in breaking through the second, had scarcely come into action at all.

Infadoos, who was a wary old general, and knew the absolute importance of keeping up the spirits of his men on the eve of such a desperate encounter, employed the pause in addressing his own regiment, the Grays, in poetical language; in explaining to them the honor that they were receiving in being put thus in the forefront of the battle, and in having the great white warrior from the stars to fight with them in their ranks, and in promising large rewards of cattle and promotion to all who survived in the event of Ignosi's arms being successful.

I looked down the long lines of waving black plumes and stern faces beneath them, and sighed to think that within one short hour most, if not all, of those magnificent veteran warriors, not a man of whom was under forty years of age, would be laid dead or dying in the dust. It could not be otherwise; they were being condemned, with that wise recklessness of human life that marks the great general, and often saves his forces and attains his ends, to certain slaughter, in order to give the cause and the remainder of the army a chance of success. They were foredoomed to die, and they knew it. It was to be their task to engage regiment after regiment of Twala's army on the narrow strip of green beneath us, till they were exterminated, or till the wings found a favorable opportunity for their onslaught. And yet they never hesitated, nor could I detect a sign of fear upon the face of a single warrior. There they were—going to certain death, about to quit the blessed light of day forever, and yet able to contemplate their doom without a tremor. I could not, even at that moment, help contrasting their state of mind with my own, which was far from comfortable, and breathing a sigh of envy and admiration. Never before had I seen such an absolute devotion to the idea of duty, and such a complete indifference to its bitter fruits.

"Behold your king!" ended old Infadoos, pointing to Ignosi. "Go fight and fall for him, as is the duty of brave men, and cursed and shameful forever be the name of him who shrinks from death for his king, or who turns his back to his enemy. Behold your king! Chiefs, captains, and soldiers; now do your homage to the sacred snake, and then follow on, that Incubu and I may show ye the road to the heart of Twala's forces."

There was a moment's pause, then suddenly there rose from the serried phalanxes before us a murmur, like the distant whisper of the sea, caused by the gentle tapping of the handles of six thousand spears against their holders' shields. Slowly it swelled, till its growing volume deepened and widened into a roar of rolling noise that echoed like thunder against the mountains, and filled the air with heavy waves of sound. Then it decreased and slowly died away into nothing, and suddenly out crashed the royal salute.

Ignosi, I thought to myself, might well be a proud man that day, for no Roman emperor ever had such a salutation from gladiators "about to die."

Ignosi acknowledged this magnificent act of homage by lifting his battle-ax, and then the Grays filed off in a triple-line formation, each line containing about one thousand fighting men, exclusive of officers. When the last line had gone some five hundred yards, Ignosi put himself at the head of the Buffaloes, who were drawn up in a similar three-line formation, and gave the word to march, and off we went, I, needless to say, uttering the most heartfelt prayers that I might come out of that job with a whole skin. Many a queer position have I found myself in, but never before in one quite so unpleasant as the present, or one in which my chance of coming off safe was so small.

By the time that we reached the edge of the plateau the Grays were already halfway down the slope ending in the tongue of grassland that ran up into the bend of the mountain, something as the frog of a horse's foot runs up into the shoe. The excitement in Twala's camp on the plain beyond was very great, and regiment after regiment was starting forward at a long swinging trot in order to reach the root of the tongue of land before the attacking force could emerge into the plain of Loo.

This tongue of land, which was some three hundred yards in depth, was, even at its root or widest part, not more than three hundred and fifty paces across, while at its tip it scarcely measured ninety. The Grays, who, in passing down the side of the hill and on to the tip of the tongue, had formed in column, on reaching the spot where it broadened out again reassumed their triple-line formation, and halted dead.

Then we—that is, the Buffaloes—moved down the tip of the tongue and took our stand in reserve, about one hundred yards behind the last line of the Grays, and on slightly higher ground. Meanwhile, we had leisure to observe Twala's entire force, which had evidently been reinforced since the morning attack, and could not now, notwithstanding their losses, number less than forty thousand, moving swiftly up towards us. But as they drew near the root of the tongue they hesitated, having discovered that only one regiment could advance into the gorge at a time, and that there, some seventy yards from the mouth of it, unassailable except in front, on account of the high walls of boulder-strewn ground on either side, stood the famous regiment of Grays, the pride and glory of the Kukuana army, ready to hold the way against their forces as the three Romans once held the bridge against thousands. They hesitated, and finally stopped their advance; there was no eagerness to cross spears with those three lines of grim warriors who stood so firm and ready. Presently, however, a tall general, with the customary headdress of nodding ostrich plumes, came running up, attended by a group of chiefs and orderlies, being, I thought, none other than Twala himself, and gave an order, and the first regiment raised a shout, and charged up towards the Grays, who remained perfectly still and silent until the attacking troops were within forty yards, and a volley of tollas, the throwing knives, came rattling among their ranks.

Then suddenly, with a bound and a roar, they sprang forward with uplifted spears, and the two regiments met in deadly strife. Next second the roll of the meeting shields came to our ears like the sound of thunder, and the whole plain seemed to be alive with flashes of light reflected from the stabbing spears. To and fro swung the heaving mass of struggling, stabbing humanity, but not for long. Suddenly the attacking lines seemed to grow thinner, and then with a slow, long heave the Grays passed over them, just as a great wave heaves up and passes over a sunken ridge. It was done; that regiment was completely destroyed, but the Grays had but two lines left now; a third of their number were dead.

Closing up shoulder to shoulder once more, they halted in silence and awaited attack; and I was rejoiced to catch sight of Sir Henry's yellow beard as he moved to and fro, arranging the ranks. So he was yet alive!

Meanwhile, we moved up onto the ground of the encounter, which was cumbered by about four thousand prostrate human beings, dead, dying, and wounded, and literally stained red with blood. Ignosi issued an order, which was rapidly passed down the ranks, to the effect that none of the enemy's wounded were to be killed, and, so far as we could see, this order was scrupulously carried out. It would have been a shocking sight, if we had had time to think of it.

But now a second regiment, distinguished by white plumes, kilts, and shields, was moving up to the attack of the two thousand remaining Grays, who stood waiting in the same ominous silence as before, till the foe was within forty yards or so, when they hurled themselves with irresistible force upon them. Again there came the awful roll of the meeting shields, and as we watched, the grim tragedy repeated itself. But this time the issue was left longer in doubt; indeed, it seemed for a while almost impossible that the Grays should again prevail. The attacking regiment, which was one formed of young men, fought with the utmost fury, and at first seemed by sheer weight to be driving the veterans back. The slaughter was something awful, hundreds falling every minute; and from among the shouts of the warriors and the groans of the dying, set to the clashing music of meeting spears, came a continuous hissing undertone of "S'gee, s'gee," the note of triumph of each victor as he passed his spear through and through the body of his fallen foe.

But perfect discipline and steady and unchanging valor can do wonders, and one veteran soldier is worth two young ones, as soon became apparent in the present case. For just as we thought that it was all up with the Grays, and were preparing to take their place so soon as they made room by being destroyed, I heard Sir Henry's deep voice ringing out above the din, and caught a glimpse of his circling battle-ax as he waved it high above his plumes. Then came a change; the Grays ceased to give; they stood still as a rock, against which the furious waves of spearmen broke again and again, only to recoil. Presently they began to move again—forward this time; as they had no firearms there was no smoke, so we could see it all. Another minute and the onslaught grew fainter.

"Ah, they are *men* indeed; they will conquer again,"

called out Ignosi, who was grinding his teeth with excitement at my side. "See, it is done!"

Suddenly, like puffs of smoke from the mouth of a cannon, the attacking regiment broke away in flying groups, their white headdresses streaming behind them in the wind, and left their opponents victors, indeed, but, alas! no more a regiment. Of the gallant triple line, which forty minutes before had gone into action three thousand strong, there remained at most some six hundred blood-bespattered men; the rest were underfoot. And yet they cheered and waved their spears in triumph, and then, instead of falling back upon us as we expected, they ran forward, for a hundred yards or so, after the flying groups of foemen, took possession of a gently rising knoll of ground, and, resuming the old triple formation, formed a threefold ring round it. And then, thanks be to God, standing on the top of a mound for a minute, I saw Sir Henry, apparently unharmed, and with him our old friend Infadoos. Then Twala's regiments rolled down upon the doomed band, and once more the battle closed in.

As those who read this history will probably long ago have gathered, I am, to be honest, a bit of a coward, and certainly in no way given to fighting, though, somehow, it has often been my lot to get into unpleasant positions, and to be obliged to shed men's blood. But I have always hated it, and kept my own blood as undiminished in quantity as possible, sometimes by a judicious use of my heels. At this moment, however, for the first time in my life, I felt my bosom burn with martial ardor. Warlike fragments from the *Ingoldsby Legends*, together with numbers of sanguinary verses from the Old Testament, sprang up in my brain like mushrooms in the dark; my blood, which hitherto had been half-frozen with horror, went beating through my veins, and there came upon me a savage desire to kill and spare not. I glanced round at the serried ranks of warriors behind us, and somehow, all in an instant, began to wonder if my face looked like theirs. There they stood, their heads craned forward over their shields, the hands twitching, the lips apart, the fierce features instinct with the hungry lust of battle, and in the eyes a look like the glare of a bloodhound when he sights his quarry.

Only Ignosi's heart seemed, to judge from his comparative self-possession, to all appearance, to beat as calmly as ever beneath his leopard-skin cloak, though even *he* still kept on grinding his teeth. I could stand it no longer.

"Are we to stand here till we put out roots, Umbopa—Ignosi, I mean—while Twala swallows our brothers yonder?" I asked.

"Nay, Macumazahn," was the answer; "see, now is the ripe moment; let us pluck it."

As he spoke a fresh regiment rushed past the ring upon the little mound, and, wheeling round, attacked it from the hither side.

Then, lifting his battle-ax, Ignosi gave the signal to advance, and, raising the Kukuana battle cry, the Buffaloes charged home with a rush like the rush of the sea.

What followed immediately on this it is out of my power to tell. All I can remember is a wild yet ordered rushing that seemed to shake the ground; a sudden change of front and forming up on the part of the regiment against which the charge was directed; then an awful shock, a dull roar of voices, and a continuous flashing of spears, seen through a red mist of blood.

When my mind cleared I found myself standing inside the remnant of the Grays near the top of the mound, and just behind no less a person than Sir Henry himself. How I got there I had, at the moment, no idea, but Sir Henry afterwards told me that I was borne up by the first furious charge of the Buffaloes almost to his feet, and then left, as they in turn were pressed back. Thereon he dashed out of the circle and dragged me into it.

As for the fight that followed, who can describe it? Again and again the multitudes surged up against our momentarily lessening circle, and again and again we beat them back.

> *The stubborn spearsmen still made good*
> *The dark impenetrable wood;*
> *Each stepping where his comrade stood*
> *The instant that he fell . . .*

as I think the *Ingoldsby Legends* beautifully puts it.

It was a splendid thing to see those brave battalions come on time after time over the barriers of their dead, sometimes holding corpses before them to receive our spear thrusts, only to leave their own corpses to swell the rising piles. It was a gallant sight to see that sturdy old warrior, Infadoos, as cool as though he were on parade, shouting out orders, taunts, and even jests, to keep up the spirit of his few remaining men, and then, as each charge rolled up, stepping forward to wherever the fighting was thickest, to bear his share in repelling it. And yet more gallant was the vision of Sir Henry, whose ostrich plumes had been shorn off by a spear stroke, so that his long yellow hair streamed out in the breeze behind him. There he stood, the great Dane, for he was nothing else, his hands, his ax, and his armor all red with blood, and none could live before his stroke. Time after time I saw it come sweeping down, as some great warrior ventured to give him battle, and as he struck he shouted, *"Oh-hoy! Oh-hoy!"* like his Berserkir forefathers, and the blow went crashing through shield and spear, through headdress, hair, and skull, till at last none would of their own will come near the great white "tagati" (wizard), who killed and failed not.

But suddenly there rose a cry of *"Twala, y' Twala,"* and out of the press sprang forward none other than the gigantic one-eyed king himself, also armed with battle-ax and shield, and clad in chain armor.

"Where art thou, Incubu, thou white man, who slew Scragga, my son—see if thou canst kill me!" he shouted, and at the same time hurled a tolla straight at Sir Henry, who, fortunately, saw it coming, and caught it on his shield, which transfixed it, so that it remained wedged in the iron plate behind the hide.

Then, with a cry, Twala sprang forward straight at him, and with his battle-ax struck him such a blow upon the shield that the mere force and shock of it brought Sir Henry, strong man as he was, down upon his knees.

But at the time the matter went no further, for at that instant there rose from the regiments pressing round us something like a shout of dismay, and on looking up I saw the cause.

To the right and to the left the plain was alive with the plumes of charging warriors. The outflanking squadrons had come to our relief. The time could not have been better chosen. All Twala's army had, as Ignosi had predicted would be the case, fixed their attention on the bloody struggle which was raging round the remnant of the Grays and the Buffaloes, who were now carrying on a battle of their own at a little distance, which two regiments had formed the chest of our army. It was not until the horns were about to close upon them that they had dreamed of their approach. And now, before they could even assume a proper formation for defense, the outflanking Impis had leaped, like greyhounds, on their flanks.

In five minutes the fate of the battle was decided. Taken on both flanks, and dismayed by the awful slaughter inflicted upon them by the Grays and Buffaloes, Twala's regiments broke into flight, and soon the whole plain between us and Loo was scattered with groups of flying soldiers, making good their retreat. As for the forces that had so recently surrounded us and the Buffaloes, they melted away as though by magic, and presently we were left standing there like a rock from which the sea has retreated. But what a sight it was! Around us the dead and dying lay in heaped-up masses, and of the gallant Grays their remained alive but ninety-five men. More than two thousand nine hundred had fallen in this one regiment, most of them never to rise again.

"Men," said Infadoos calmly, as between the intervals of binding up a wound in his arm he surveyed what remained to him of his corps, "ye have kept up the reputation of your regiment, and this day's fighting will be spoken of by our children's children." Then he turned round and shook Sir Henry Curtis by the hand. "Thou art a great man, Incubu," he said simply; "I have lived a long life among warriors, and known many a brave one, yet have I never seen a man like thee."

At this moment the Buffaloes began to march past our position on the road to Loo, and as they did so a message was brought to us from Ignosi requesting Infadoos, Sir Henry, and myself to join him. Accordingly, orders having been issued to the remaining men of the Grays to employ themselves in collecting the wounded, we joined Ignosi, who informed us that he was pressing on to Loo to complete the victory by capturing Twala, if that should be possible. Before we had gone far we suddenly discovered the figure of Good sitting on an ant heap about one hundred paces from us. Close beside him was the body of a Kukuana.

"He must be wounded," said Sir Henry anxiously. As he made the remark, an untoward thing happened. The dead body of the Kukuana soldier, or rather what had appeared to be his dead body, suddenly sprang up, knocked Good head over heels off the ant heap, and began to spear him. We rushed forward in terror, and as we drew near we saw the brawny warrior making dig after dig at the prostrate Good, who at each prod jerked all his limbs into the air. Seeing us coming, the Kukuana gave one final most vicious dig, and with a shout of "Take that, wizard," bolted off. Good did not move, and we concluded that our poor comrade was done for. Sadly we came towards him, and were astonished to find him pale and faint indeed, but with a serene smile upon his face, and his eyeglass still fixed in his eye.

"Capital armor this," he murmured, on catching sight of our faces bending over him. "How sold he must have been," and then he fainted. On examination we discovered that he had been seriously wounded in the leg by a tolla in the course of the pursuit, but that the chain armor had prevented his last assailant's spear from doing anything more than bruise him badly. It was a merciful escape. As nothing could be done for him at the moment, he was placed on one of the wicker shields used for the wounded, and carried along with us.

On arriving before the nearest gate of Loo we found one of our regiments watching it in obedience to orders received from Ignosi. The remaining regiments were in the same way watching the other exits to the town. The officer in command of this regiment coming up, saluted Ignosi as king, and informed him that Twala's army had taken refuge in the town, whither Twala himself had also escaped, but that he thought they were thoroughly demoralized, and would surrender. Thereupon Ignosi, after taking counsel with us, sent forward heralds to each gate ordering the defenders to open, and promising on his royal word life and forgiveness to every soldier who laid down his arms. The message was not without its effect. Presently, amid the shouts and cheers of the Buffaloes, the bridge was dropped across the fosse, and the gates upon the farther side flung open.

Taking due precautions against treachery, we marched on into the town. All along the roadways stood dejected warriors, their heads drooping and their shields and spears at their feet, who, as Ignosi passed, saluted him as king. On we marched, straight to Twala's kraal. When we reached the great space, where a day or two previously we had seen the review and the witch hunt, we found it deserted. No, not quite deserted, for there, on the farther side, in front of his hut, sat Twala himself, with but one attendant—Gagool.

It was a melancholy sight to see him seated there, his battle-ax and shield by his side, his chin upon his mailed breast, with but one old crone for companion, and, notwithstanding his cruelties and misdeeds, a pang of compassion shot through me as I saw him thus "fallen from his high estate." Not a soldier of all his armies, not a courtier out of the hundreds who had cringed round him, not even a solitary wife, remained to share his fate or halve the bitterness of his fall. Poor savage! He was learning the lesson that fate teaches to most who live long enough, that the eyes of mankind are blind to the discredited, and that he who is defenseless and fallen finds few friends and little mercy. Nor, indeed, in this case did he deserve any.

Filing through the kraal gate, we marched straight across the open space to where the ex-king sat. When within about fifty yards the regiment was halted, and, accompanied only by a small guard, we advanced towards him, Gagool reviling us bitterly as we came. As we drew near, Twala, for the first time, lifted up his plumed head, and fixed his one eye, which seemed to flash with suppressed fury almost as brightly as the great diadem bound round his forehead, upon his successful rival—Ignosi.

"Hail, O King!" he said with bitter mockery. "Thou who hast eaten of my bread, and now by the aid of the white man's magic hast seduced my regiments and defeated mine army, hail! What fate hast thou for me, O King?"

"The fate thou gavest to my father, whose throne thou hast sat on these many years!" was the stern answer.

"It is well. I will show thee how to die, that thou mayest remember it against thine own time. See, the sun sinks in blood," and he pointed with his red battle-ax towards the fiery orb now going down; "it is well that my sun should sink with it. And now, O King! I am ready to die, but I crave the boon of the Kukuana royal house[1] to die fighting. Thou canst not refuse it, or even those cowards who fled today will hold thee shamed."

"It is granted. Choose—with whom wilt thou fight? Myself, I cannot fight with thee, for the king fights not except in war."

Twala's somber eye ran up and down our ranks, and I

[1] It is a law among the Kukuanas that no man of the royal blood can be put to death unless by his own consent, which is, however, never refused. He is allowed to choose a succession of antagonists, to be approved by the king, with whom he fights until one of them kills him.

felt, as for a moment it rested on myself, that the position had developed a new horror. What if he chose to begin by fighting *me?* What chance should I have against a desperate savage six feet five high, and broad in proportion? I might as well commit suicide at once. Hastily I made up my mind to decline the combat, even if I were hooted out of Kukuanaland as a consequence. It is, I think, better to be hooted than to be quartered with a battle-ax.

Presently he spoke.

"Incubu, what sayest thou, shall we end what we began today, or shall I call thee coward, white—even to the liver?"

"Nay," interposed Ignosi hastily; "thou shalt not fight with Incubu."

"Not if he is afraid," said Twala.

Unfortunately Sir Henry understood this remark, and the blood flamed up into his cheeks.

"I will fight him," he said; "he shall see if I am afraid."

"For God's sake," I entreated, "don't risk your life against that of a desperate man. Anybody who saw you today will know that you are not a coward."

"I will fight him," was the sullen answer. "No living man shall call me a coward. I am ready now!" and he stepped forward and lifted his ax.

I wrung my hands over this absurd piece of Quixotism; but if he was determined on fighting, of course I could not stop him.

"Fight not, my white brother," said Ignosi, laying his hand affectionately on Sir Henry's arm; "thou hast fought enough, and if aught befell thee at his hands it would cut my heart in twain."

"I will fight, Ignosi," was Sir Henry's answer.

"It is well, Incubu; thou art a brave man. It will be

a good fight. Behold, Twala, the Elephant is ready for thee."

The ex-king laughed savagely, and stepped forward and faced Curtis. For a moment they stood thus, and the setting sun caught their stalwart frames and clothed them both in fire. They were a well-matched pair.

Then they began to circle round each other, their battle-axes raised.

Suddenly Sir Henry sprang forward and struck a fearful blow at Twala, who stepped to one side. So heavy was the stroke that the striker half overbalanced himself, a circumstance of which his antagonist took a prompt advantage. Circling his heavy battle-ax round his head, he brought it down with tremendous force. My heart jumped into my mouth; I thought the affair was already finished. But no; with a quick upward movement of the left arm Sir Henry interposed his shield between himself and the ax, with the result that its outer edge was shorn clean off, the ax falling on his left shoulder, but not heavily enough to do any serious damage. In another second Sir Henry got in another blow, which was also received by Twala upon his shield. Then followed blow upon blow, which were, in turn, either received upon the shield or avoided. The excitement grew intense; the regiment which was watching the encounter forgot its discipline, and, drawing near, shouted and groaned at every stroke. Just at this time, too, Good, who had been laid upon the ground by me, recovered from his faint, and sitting up, perceived what was going on. In an instant he was up, and, catching hold of my arm, hopped about from place to place on one leg, dragging me after him, yelling out encouragements to Sir Henry.

"Go it, old fellow!" he cried. "That was a good one! Give it him amidships," and so on.

Presently Sir Henry, having caught a fresh stroke upon his shield, hit out with all his force. The stroke cut through Twala's shield and through the tough chain armor behind it, gashing him in the shoulder. With a yell of pain and fury Twala returned the stroke with interest, and, such was his strength, sheared right through the rhinoceros-horn handle of his antagonist's battle-ax, strengthened as it was with bands of steel, wounding Curtis in the face.

A cry of dismay rose from the Buffaloes as our hero's broad ax head fell to the ground; and Twala, again raising his weapon, flew at him with a shout. I shut my eyes. When I opened them again, it was to see Sir Henry's shield lying on the ground, and Sir Henry himself with his great arms twined round Twala's middle. To and fro they swung, hugging each other like bears, straining with all their mighty muscles for dear life and dearer honor. With a supreme effort Twala swung the Englishman clean off his feet, and down they came together, rolling over and over on the lime paving, Twala striking out at Curtis' head with the battle-ax, and Sir Henry trying to drive the tolla he had drawn from his belt through Twala's armor.

It was a mighty struggle and an awful thing to see.

"Get his ax!" yelled Good; and perhaps our champion heard him.

At any rate, dropping the tolla, he made a grab at the ax, which was fastened to Twala's wrist by a strip of buffalo hide, and, still rolling over and over, they fought for it like wildcats, drawing their breath in heavy gasps. Suddenly the hide string burst, and then, with a great effort, Sir Henry freed himself, the weapon remaining in his grasp. Another second and he was up on his feet, the red blood streaming from the wound in his face, and so was Twala. Drawing the heavy tolla from his belt, he staggered straight at Curtis and struck him upon the breast. The blow came home true and strong, but whoever it was made that chain armor understood his art, for it withstood the steel. Again Twala struck out with a savage yell, and again the heavy knife rebounded and Sir Henry went staggering back. Once more Twala came on, and as he came our great Englishman gathered himself together, and, swinging the heavy ax round his head, hit at him with all his force. There was a shriek of excitement from a thousand throats, and, behold! Twala's head seemed to spring from his shoulders, and then fell and came rolling and bounding along the ground towards Ignosi, stopping just at his feet. For a second the corpse stood upright, the blood spouting in fountains from the severed arteries; then with a dull crash it fell to the earth, and the gold torque from the neck went rolling away across the pavement. As it did so Sir Henry, overpowered by faintness and loss of blood, fell heavily across it.

In a second he was lifted up, and eager hands were pouring water on his face. Another minute, and the great gray eyes opened wide.

He was not dead.

Then I, just as the sun sank, stepping to where Twala's head lay in the dust, unloosed the diamond from the dead brows and handed it to Ignosi.

"Take it," I said, "lawful king of the Kukuanas."

Ignosi bound the diadem upon his brows, and then advancing placed his foot upon the broad chest of his headless foe and broke out into a chant, or rather a paean of victory, so beautiful, and yet so utterly savage, that I despair of being able to give an adequate idea of it. I once heard a scholar with a fine voice read aloud from the Greek poet Homer, and I remember that the sound of the rolling lines seemed to make my blood stand still. Ignosi's chant, uttered as it was in a language as beautiful and sonorous as the old Greek, produced exactly the same effect on me, although I was exhausted with toil and many emotions.

"Now," he began, "now is our rebellion swallowed up in victory, and our evildoing justified by strength.

"In the morning the oppressors rose up and shook themselves; they bound on their plumes and made them ready for war.

"They rose up and grasped their spears: the soldiers called to the captains, 'Come, lead us'—and the captains cried to the king, 'Direct thou the battle.'

"They rose up in their pride, twenty thousand men, and yet a twenty thousand.

"Their plumes covered the earth as the plumes of a bird cover her nest; they shook their spears and shouted, yea, they hurled their spears into the sunlight; they lusted for the battle and were glad.

"They came up against me; their strong ones came running swiftly to crush me; they cried, 'Ha! Ha! He is as one already dead.'

"Then breathed I on them, and my breath was as the breath of a storm, and lo! they were not.

"My lightnings pierced them; I licked up their strength with the lightning of my spears; I shook them to the earth with the thunder of my shouting.

"They broke—they scattered—they were gone as the mists of the morning.

"They are food for the crows and the foxes, and the place of battle is fat with their blood.

"Where are the mighty ones who rose up in the morning?

"Where are the proud ones who tossed their plumes and cried, 'He is as one already dead'?

"They bow their heads, but not in sleep; they are stretched out, but not in sleep.

"They are forgotten; they have gone into the blackness, and shall not return; yea, others shall lead away their wives, and their children shall remember them no more.

"And I—I—the king—like an eagle have I found my eyrie.

"Behold! Far have I wandered in the nighttime, yet have I returned to my little ones at the daybreak.

"Creep ye under the shadow of my wings, O people, and I will comfort ye, and ye shall not be dismayed.

"Now is the good time, the time of spoil.

"Mine are the cattle in the valleys, the virgins in the kraals are mine also.

"The winter is overpast, the summer is at hand.

"Now shall Evil cover up her face, and prosperity shall bloom in the land like a lily.

"Rejoice, rejoice, my people! Let all the land rejoice in that the tyranny is trodden down, in that I am the king."

He paused, and out of the gathering gloom there came back the deep reply: "Thou art the king."

Thus it was that my prophecy to the herald came true, and within the forty-eight hours Twala's headless corpse was stiffening at Twala's gate.

15 ♦

Good Falls Sick

AFTER THE fight was ended Sir Henry and Good were carried into Twala's hut, where I joined them. They were both utterly exhausted by exertion and loss of blood, and, indeed, my own condition was little better. I am very wiry, and can stand more fatigue than most men, probably on account of my light weight and long training; but that night I was fairly done up, and, as is always the case with me when exhausted, that old wound the lion gave me began to pain me. Also, my head was aching violently from the blow I had received in the morning, when I was knocked senseless. Altogether, a more miserable trio than we were that evening it would have been difficult to discover; and our only comfort lay in the reflection that we were exceedingly fortunate to be there to feel miserable, instead of being stretched dead upon the plain, as so many thousands of brave men were that night, who had risen well and strong in the morning. Somehow, with the assistance of the beautiful Foulata, who, since we had been the means of saving her life, had constituted herself our handmaiden, and especially Good's, we managed to get off the chain shirts, which had certainly saved the lives of two of us that day, when we found that the flesh underneath was terribly bruised, for, though the steel links had prevented the weapons from entering, they had not prevented them from bruising. Both Sir Henry and Good were a mass of

199

bruises, and I was by no means free. As a remedy Foulata brought us some pounded green leaves with an aromatic odor, which, when applied as a plaster, gave us considerable relief. But though the bruises were painful, they did not give us such anxiety as Sir Henry's and Good's wounds. Good had a hole right through the fleshy part of his "beautiful white leg," from which he had lost a great deal of blood; and Sir Henry had a deep cut over the jaw, inflicted by Twala's battle-ax. Luckily Good was a very decent surgeon, and as soon as his small box of medicines was forthcoming, he, having thoroughly cleansed the wounds, managed to stitch up first Sir Henry's and then his own pretty satisfactorily, considering the imperfect light given by the primitive Kukuana lamp in the hut. Afterwards he plentifully smeared the wounds with some antiseptic ointment, of which there was a pot in the little box, and we covered them with the remains of a pocket-handkerchief which we possessed.

Meanwhile Foulata had prepared us some strong broth, for we were too weary to eat. This we swallowed, and then threw ourselves down on the piles of magnificent karrosses, or fur rugs, which were scattered about the dead king's great hut. By a very strange instance of the irony of fate, it was on Twala's own couch, and wrapped in Twala's own particular karross, that Sir Henry, the man who had slain him, slept that night.

I say slept; but after that day's work sleep was indeed difficult. To begin with, in very truth the air was full

> Of farewells to the dying
> And mournings for the dead.

From every direction came the sound of the wailing of women whose husbands, sons, and brothers had perished in the fight. No wonder that they wailed, for over twenty thousand men, or nearly a third of the Kukuana army, had been destroyed in that awful struggle. It was heart-rending to lie and listen to their cries for those who would never return; and it made one realize the full horror of the work done that day to further man's ambition. Towards midnight, however, the ceaseless crying of the women grew less frequent, till at length the silence was only broken at intervals of a few minutes by a long, piercing howl that came from a hut in our immediate rear, and which I afterwards discovered proceeded from Gagool wailing for the dead king, Twala.

After that I got a little fitful sleep, only to wake from time to time with a start, thinking that I was once more an actor in the terrible events of the last twenty-four hours. Now I seemed to see that warrior, whom my hand had sent to his last account, charging at me on the mountain top; now I was once more in that glorious ring of Grays, which made its immortal stand against all Twala's regiments, upon the little mound; and now again I saw Twala's plumed and gory head roll past my feet with gnashing teeth and glaring eye. At last, somehow or other, the night passed away; but when dawn broke I found that my companions had slept no better than myself. Good, indeed, was in a high fever, and very soon afterwards began to grow light-headed, and also, to my alarm, to spit blood, the result, no doubt, of some internal injury inflicted by the desperate efforts made by the Kukuana warrior on the previous day to get his big spear through the chain armor. Sir Henry, however, seemed pretty fresh, notwithstanding the wound on his face, which made eating difficult and laughter an impossibility, though he was so sore and stiff that he could scarcely stir.

About eight o'clock we had a visit from Infadoos, who

seemed but little the worse—tough old warrior that he was—for his exertions on the previous day, though he informed us he had been up all night. He was delighted to see us, though much grieved at Good's condition, and shook hands cordially; but I noticed that he addressed Sir Henry with a kind of reverence, as though he were something more than man; and, indeed, as we afterwards found out, the great Englishman was looked on throughout Kukuanaland as a supernatural being. No man, the soldiers said, could have fought as he fought, or could, at the end of a day of such toil and bloodshed, have slain Twala, who, in addition to being the king, was supposed to be the strongest warrior in Kukuanaland, in single combat, sheering through his bull-neck at a stroke. Indeed, that stroke became proverbial in Kukuanaland, and any extraordinary blow or feat of strength was thenceforth known as "Incubu's blow."

Infadoos told us also that all Twala's regiments had submitted to Ignosi, and that like submissions were beginning to arrive from chiefs in the country. Twala's death at the hands of Sir Henry had put an end to all further chance of disturbance; for Scragga had been his only son, and there was no rival claimant left alive.

I remarked that Ignosi had swum to the throne through blood. The old chief shrugged his shoulders. "Yes," he answered; "but the Kukuana people can only be kept cool by letting the blood flow sometimes. Many were killed, indeed, but the women were left, and others will soon grow up to take the places of the fallen. After this the land will be quiet for a while."

Afterwards, in the course of the morning, we had a short visit from Ignosi, on whose brows the royal diadem was now bound. As I contemplated him advancing with kingly dignity, an obsequious guard following his steps, I could not help recalling to my mind the tall Zulu who had presented himself to us at Durban some few months back, asking to be taken into our service, and reflecting on the strange revolutions of the wheel of fortune.

"Hail, O King!" I said, rising.

"Yes, Macumazahn. King at last, by the grace of your three right hands," was the ready answer.

All was, he said, going on well; and he hoped to arrange a great feast in two weeks' time, in order to show himself to the people.

I asked him what he had settled to do with Gagool.

"She is the evil genius of the land," he answered, "and I shall kill her, and all the witch doctors with her! She has lived so long that none can remember when she was not old, and always she it is who has trained the witch hunters, and made the land evil in the sight of the heavens above."

"Yet she knows much," I replied; "it is easier to destroy knowledge, Ignosi, than to gather it."

"It is so," he said, thoughtfully. "She, and she only, knows the secret of the Three Witches yonder, whither the great road runs, where the kings are buried, and the silent ones sit."

"Yes, and the diamonds are. Forget not thy promise, Ignosi; thou must lead us to the mines, even if thou hast to spare Gagool alive to show the way."

"I will not forget, Macumazahn, and I will think on what thou sayest."

After Ignosi's visit I went to see Good, and found him quite delirious. The fever from his wound seemed to have taken a firm hold of his system, and to be complicated by an internal injury. For four or five days his condition was most critical; indeed, I firmly believe that had it not been for Foulata's indefatigable nursing he must have died.

Women are women, all the world over, whatever their color. Yet somehow it seemed curious to watch this dusky beauty bending night and day over the fevered man's couch, and performing all the merciful errands of the sickroom as swiftly, gently, and with as fine an instinct as a trained hospital nurse. For the first night or two I tried to help her, and so did Sir Henry so soon as his stiffness allowed him to move, but she bore our interference with impatience, and finally insisted upon our leaving him to her, saying that our movements made him restless, which I think was true. Day and night she watched and tended him, giving him his only medicine, a native cooling drink made of milk, in which was infused the juice of the bulb of a species of tulip, and keeping the flies from settling on him. I can see the whole picture now as it appeared night after night by the light of our primitive lamp, Good tossing to and fro, his features emaciated, his eyes shining large and luminous, and jabbering nonsense by the yard; and seated on the ground by his side, her back resting against the wall of the hut, the soft-eyed, shapely Kukuana beauty, her whole face, weary as it was, animated by a look of infinite compassion—or was it something more than compassion?

For two days we thought that he must die, and crept about with heavy hearts. Only Foulata would not believe it. "He will live," she said.

For three hundred yards or more around Twala's chief hut, where the sufferer lay, there was silence; for by the king's order all who lived in the habitations behind it had, except Sir Henry and myself, been removed, lest any noise should come to the sick man's ear. One night, it was the

fifth night of his illness, as was my habit I went across to
see how he was getting on before turning in for a few
hours.

I entered the hut carefully. The lamp placed upon the
floor showed the figure of Good, tossing no more, but lying quite still.

So it had come at last! And in the bitterness of my heart
I gave something like a sob.

"Hush—h—h!" came from the patch of dark shadow
behind Good's head.

Then, creeping closer, I saw that he was not dead, but
sleeping soundly, with Foulata's tapered fingers clasped
tightly in his poor white hand. The crisis had passed, and
he would live. He slept like that for eighteen hours; and
I scarcely like to say it, for fear I should not be believed,
but during that entire period did that devoted girl sit by
him, fearing that if she moved and drew away her hand
it would wake him. What she must have suffered from
cramp, stiffness, and weariness, to say nothing of want of
food, nobody will ever know; but it is a fact that, when
at last he woke, she had to be carried away—her limbs
were so stiff that she could not move them.

After the turn had once been taken, Good's recovery
was rapid and complete. It was not till he was nearly
well that Sir Henry told him of all he owed to Foulata;
and when he came to the story of how she sat by his side
for eighteen hours, fearing lest by moving she should
wake him, the honest sailor's eyes filled with tears. He
turned and went straight to the hut where Foulata was
preparing the midday meal (we were back in our old
quarters now), taking me with him to interpret in case he
could not make his meaning clear to her, though I am
bound to say she understood him marvelously as a rule

considering how extremely limited was his foreign vocabulary.

"Tell her," said Good, "that I owe her my life, and that I will never forget her kindness."

I interpreted, and under her dark skin she actually seemed to blush.

Turning to him with one of those swift and graceful motions that in her always reminded me of the flight of a wild bird, she answered softly, glancing at him with her large brown eyes, "Nay, my lord; my lord forgets! Did he not save *my* life, and am I not my lord's handmaiden?"

It will be observed that the young lady appeared to have entirely forgotten the share which Sir Henry and myself had had in her preservation from Twala's clutches. But that is the way of women! I remember my dear wife was just the same. I retired from that little interview sad at heart. I did not like Miss Foulata's soft glances, for I knew the fatal amorous propensities of sailors in general, and Good in particular.

There are two things in the world, as I have found it, which cannot be prevented: you cannot keep a Zulu from fighting, or a sailor from falling in love upon the slightest provocation!

It was a few days after this last occurrence that Ignosi held his great "indaba" (council), and was formally recognized as king by the "indunas" (head men) of Kukuanaland. The spectacle was a most imposing one, including, as it did, a great review of troops. On this day the remaining fragment of the Grays were formally paraded, and in the face of the army thanked for their splendid conduct in the great battle. To each man the king made a large present of cattle, promoting them one and all to the rank of officers in the new corps of Grays which was in process of formation. An order was also promulgated throughout the length and breadth of Kukuanaland that, while we honored the country with our presence, we three were to be greeted with the royal salute, to be treated with the same ceremony and respect that was by custom accorded to the king, and the power of life and death was publicly conferred upon us. Ignosi, too, in the presence of his people, reaffirmed the promises that he had made, to the effect that no man's blood should be shed without trial, and that witch hunting should cease in the land.

When the ceremony was over we waited upon Ignosi, and informed him that we were now anxious to investigate the mystery of the mines to which Solomon's Road ran, asking him if he had discovered anything about them.

"My friends," he answered, "this have I discovered. It is there that the three great figures sit, who here are called the Silent Ones, and to whom Twala would have offered the girl, Foulata, as a sacrifice. It is there, too, in a great cave deep in the mountain, that the kings of the land are buried; there ye shall find Twala's body, sitting with those who went before him. There, too, is a great pit which, at some time, long dead men dug out, mayhap for the stones ye speak of, such as I have heard men in Natal speak of at Kimberley. There, too, in the Place of Death is a secret chamber, known to none but the king and Gagool. But Twala, who knew it, is dead, and I know it not, nor know I what is in it. But there is a legend in the land that once, many generations gone, a white man crossed the mountains, and was led by a woman to the secret chamber and shown the wealth, but before he could take it she betrayed him, and he was driven by the king of the day back to the mountains, and since then no man has entered the chamber."

"The story is surely true, Ignosi, for on the mountains we found the white man," I said.

"Yes, we found him. And now I have promised ye that if ye can find that chamber, and the stones are there—"

"The stone upon thy forehead proves that they are there," I put in, pointing to the great diamond I had taken from Twala's dead brows.

"Mayhap; if they are there," he said, "ye shall have as many as ye can take hence—if, indeed, ye would leave me, my brothers."

"First we must find the chamber," said I.

"There is but one who can show it to thee—Gagool."

"And if she will not?"

"Then shall she die," said Ignosi sternly. "I have saved her alive but for this. Stay, she shall choose," and, calling to a messenger, he ordered Gagool to be brought.

In a few minutes she came, hurried along by two guards, whom she was cursing as she walked.

"Leave her," said the king to the guards.

As soon as their support was withdrawn the withered old bundle, for she looked more like a bundle than anything else, sank into a heap on the floor, out of which her two bright, wicked eyes gleamed like a snake's.

"What will ye with me, Ignosi?" she piped. "Ye dare not touch me. If ye touch me I will blast ye as ye sit. Beware of my magic."

"Thy magic could not save Twala, old she wolf, and it cannot hurt me," was the answer. "Listen: I will this of thee, that thou reveal where is the chamber where are the shining stones."

"Ha, ha!" she piped. "None know but I, and I will

never tell thee. The white devils shall go hence empty-handed."

"Thou wilt tell me. I will make thee tell me."

"How, O King?" Thou art great, but can thy power wring the truth from a woman?"

"It is difficult, yet will I do it."

"How, O King?"

"Nay, thus; if thou tellest not thou shalt slowly die."

"Die!" she shrieked in terror and fury. "Ye dare not touch me—man, ye know not who I am. How old think ye am I? I knew your fathers, and your fathers' fathers' fathers. When the country was young I was here, when the country grows old I shall still be here. I cannot die unless I be killed by chance, for none dare slay me."

"Yet will I slay thee. See, Gagool, mother of evil, thou art so old thou canst no longer love thy life. What can life be to such a hag as thee, who hast no shape, nor form, nor hair, nor teeth—hast naught, save wickedness and evil eyes? It will be mercy to slay thee, Gagool."

"Thou fool," shrieked the old fiend, "thou accursed fool, thinkest thou that life is sweet only to the young? It is not so, and naught thou knowest of the heart of man to think it. To the young, indeed, death is sometimes welcome, for the young can feel. They love and suffer, and it wrings them to see their beloved pass to the land of shadows. But the old feel not, they love not, and, ha, ha! they laugh to see another go out into the dark; ha, ha! they laugh to see the evil that is done under the sun. All they love is life, the warm, warm sun, and the sweet, sweet air. They are afraid of the cold; afraid of the cold and the dark, ha, ha, ha!" and the old hag writhed on the ground in ghastly merriment.

"Cease thine evil talk and answer me," said Ignosi angrily. "Wilt thou show the place where the stones are, or wilt thou not? If thou wilt not, thou diest, even now," and he seized a spear and held it over her.

"I will not show it; thou darest not kill me, darest not. He who slays me will be accursed forever."

Slowly Ignosi brought down the spear till it pricked the prostrate heap of rags.

With a wild yell she sprang to her feet, and then again fell and rolled upon the floor.

"Nay; I will show it. Only let me live, let me sit in the sun and have a bit of meat to suck, and I will show thee."

"It is well. I thought I should find a way to reason with thee. Tomorrow shalt thou go with Infadoos and my white brothers to the place, and beware how thou failest, for if thou showest it not, then shalt thou slowly die. I have spoken."

"I will not fail, Ignosi. I always keep my word: *ha, ha, ha!* Once a woman showed the place to a white man before, and behold evil befell him," and here her wicked eyes glinted. "Her name was Gagool, too. Perchance I was that woman."

"Thou liest," I said, "that was ten generations gone."

"Mayhap, mayhap; when one lives long one forgets. Perhaps it was my mother's mother who told me; surely her name was Gagool, also. But mark, ye will find in the place where the bright playthings are a bag of hide full of stones. The man filled that bag, but he never took it away. Evil befell him, I say; evil befell him! Perhaps it was my mother's mother who told me. It will be a merry journey—we can see the bodies of those who died in the battle as we go. Their eyes will be gone by now, and their ribs will be hollow. Ha, ha, ha!"

16 ♦

The Place of Death

It was already dark on the third day after the scene described in the previous chapter, when we camped in some huts at the foot of the Three Witches. Our party consisted of our three selves and Foulata, who waited on us—especially on Good—Infadoos, Gagool, who was borne along in a litter, inside which she could be heard muttering and cursing all day long, and a party of guards and attendants. The mountains, or rather the three peaks of the mountains, for the whole mass evidently consisted of a solitary upheaval, were, as I have said, in the form of a triangle, of which the base was towards us, one peak being on our right, one on our left, and one straight in front of us. Never shall I forget the sight afforded by those three towering peaks in the early sunlight of the following morning. High, high above us, up into the blue air, soared their twisted snow wreaths. Beneath the snow the peaks were purple with heath, and so were the wild moors that ran up the slopes towards them. Straight before us the white ribbon of Solomon's Great Road stretched away uphill to the foot of the center peak, about five miles from us, and then stopped. This was its terminus.

I had better leave the feelings of intense excitement with which we set out on our march that morning to the imagination of those who read this history. At last we were drawing near to the wonderful mines that had been the cause of the miserable death of the old Portuguese don, three centuries ago, of my poor friend, his ill-starred descendant, and also, as we feared, of George Curtis, Sir Henry's brother. Were we destined, after all that we had gone through, to fare any better? Evil befell them, as that old fiend, Gagool, said; would it also befall us? Somehow, as we were marching up that last stretch of beautiful road, I could not help feeling a little superstitious about the matter, and so, I think, did Good and Sir Henry.

For an hour and a half or more we tramped on up the heather-fringed road, going so fast in our excitement that the bearers with Gagool's hammock could scarcely keep pace with us, and its occupant piped out to us to stop.

"Go more slowly, white men," she said, projecting her hideous, shriveled countenance between the curtains, and fixing her gleaming eyes upon us. "Why will ye run to meet the evil that shall befall ye, ye seekers after treasure?" and she laughed that horrible laugh which always sent a cold shiver down my back, and which for a while took the enthusiasm out of us.

However, on we went, till we saw bfore us, and between ourselves and the peak, a vast circular hole with sloping sides, three hundred feet or more in depth, and quite half a mile round.

"Can't you guess what this is?" I said to Sir Henry and Good, who were staring in astonishment down into the awful pit before us.

They shook their heads.

"Then it is clear that you have never seen the diamond mines at Kimberley. You may depend on it that this is Solomon's diamond mine; look there," I said, pointing to the stiff blue clay which was yet to be seen among the grass and bushes which clothed the sides of the pit, "the formation is the same. I'll be bound that if we went down there we should find 'pipes' of soapy, brecciated rock. Look, too," and I pointed to a series of worn, flat slabs of rock which were placed on a gentle slope below the level of a water-course which had in some past age been cut out of the solid rock. "If those are not tables once used to wash the 'stuff,' I'm a Dutchman."

At the edge of this vast hole, which was the pit marked on the old don's map, the great road branched into two and circumvented it. In many places this circumventing road was built entirely of vast blocks of stone, apparently with the object of supporting the edges of the pit and pre-venting falls of reef. Along this road we pressed, driven by curiosity to see what the three towering objects were which we could discern from the hither side of the great hole. As we got nearer we perceived that they were colossi of some sort or another, and rightly conjectured that these were the three "Silent Ones" that were held in such awe by the Kukuana people. But it was not until we got quite close that we recognized the full majesty of these "Silent Ones."

There, upon huge pedestals of dark rock, sculptured in unknown characters, twenty paces between each, and look-ing down the road which crossed some sixty miles of plain to Loo, were three colossal seated forms—two males and one female—each measuring about twenty feet from the crown of the head to the pedestal.

The female form, which was nude, was of great though severe beauty, but unfortunately the features were injured by centuries of exposure to the weather. Rising from each side of her head were the points of a crescent. The two male colossi were, on the contrary, draped, and presented a terrifying cast of features, especially the one to our right, which had the face of a devil. That to our left was serene in countenance, but the calm upon it was dreadful. It was the calm of inhuman cruelty, the cruelty, Sir Henry remarked, that the ancients attributed to beings potent for good, who could yet watch the sufferings of humanity, if not with rejoicing, at least without suffering themselves. The three formed a most awe-inspiring trinity, as they sat there in their solitude and gazed out across the plain forever. Contemplating these "Silent Ones," as the Kukuanas called them, an intense curiosity again seized us to know whose were the hands that had shaped them, who was it that had dug the pit and made the road. While I was gazing and wondering, it suddenly occurred to me (being familiar with the Old Testament) that Solomon went astray after strange gods, the names of three of whom I remembered —"Ashtoreth the goddess of the Zidonians, Chemosh the god of the Moabites, and Milcom the god of the children of Ammon"—and I suggested to my companions that the three figures before us might represent these false divinities.

"Hum," said Sir Henry, who was a scholar, having taken a high degree in classics at college, "there may be something in that; Ashtoreth of the Hebrews was the Astarte of the Phoenicians, who were the great traders of Solomon's time. Astarte, who afterwards was the Aphrodite of the Greeks, was represented with horns like the half-moon, and there on the brow of the female figure are distinct horns. Perhaps these colossi were designed by some Phoenician official who managed the mines. Who can say?"

Before we had finished examining these extraordinary relics of remote antiquity, Infadoos came up, and, having saluted the "Silent Ones" by lifting his spear, asked us if we intended entering the "Place of Death" at once, or if we would wait till after we had taken food at midday. If we were ready to go at once, Gagool had announced her willingness to guide us. As it was not more than eleven o'clock, we—driven to it by a burning curiosity—announced our intention of proceeding at once, and I suggested that, in case we should be detained in the cave, we should take some food with us. Accordingly Gagool's litter was brought up, and that lady herself assisted out of it; and meanwhile Foulata, at my request, stored some biltong together with a couple of gourds of water, in a reed basket. Straight in front of us, at a distance of some fifty paces from the backs of the colossi, rose a sheer wall of rock, eighty feet or more in height, that gradually sloped up till it formed the base of the lofty snow-wreathed peak which soared up into the air three thousand feet above us. As soon as she was clear of her hammock Gagool cast one evil grin upon us, and then, leaning on a stick, hobbled off towards the sheer face of the rock. We followed her till we came to a narrow portal solidly arched, that looked like the opening of a gallery of a mine.

Here Gagool was waiting for us, still with that evil grin upon her horrid face.

"Now, white men from the stars," she piped; "great warriors, Incubu, Bougwan, and Macumazahn the wise, are ye ready? Behold, I am here to do the bidding of my lord the king, and to show ye the store of bright stones."

"We are ready," I said.

"Good! Good! Make strong your hearts to bear what ye shall see. Comest thou too, Infadoos, who betrayed thy master?"

Infadoos frowned as he answered; "Nay, I come not; it is not for me to enter there. But thou, Gagool, curb thy tongue, and beware how thou dealest with my lords. At thy hands will I require them, and if a hair of them be hurt, Gagool, be thou fifty times a witch, thou shalt die. Hearest thou?"

"I hear, Infadoos; I know thee, thou didst ever love big words; when thou wast a babe I remember thou didst threaten thine own mother. That was but the other day. But fear not, fear not; I live but to do the bidding of the king. I have done the bidding of many kings, Infadoos, till in the end they did mine. Ha, ha! I go to look upon their faces once more, and Twala's, too! Come on, come on, here is the lamp," and she drew a great gourd full of oil, and fitted with a rush wick, from under her fur cloak.

"Art thou coming, Foulata?" asked Good in his villainous Kitchen Kukuana, in which he had been improving himself under that lady's tuition.

"I fear, my lord," the girl answered timidly.

"Then give me the basket."

"Nay, my lord, whither thou goest, there will I go also."

"The deuce you will!" thought I to myself; "that will be rather awkward if ever we get out of this."

Without further ado Gagool plunged into the passage, which was wide enough to admit of two walking abreast, and quite dark, we following her voice as she piped to us to come on, in some fear and trembling, which was not allayed by the sound of a sudden rush of wings.

"Hullo! what's that?" hulloed Good. "Somebody hit me in the face."

"Bats," said I; "on you go."

When we had, as far as we could judge, gone some fifty paces we perceived that the passage was growing faintly light. Another minute, and we stood in the most wonderful place that the eyes of living man ever lit on.

Let the reader picture to himself the hall of the vastest

cathedral he ever stood in, windowless, indeed, but dimly lighted from above (presumably by shafts connected with the outer air and driven in the roof, which arched away a hundred feet above our heads), and he will get some idea of the size of the enormous cave in which we stood, with the difference that this cathedral designed of nature was loftier and wider than any built by man. But its stupendous size was the least of the wonders of the place, for, running in rows adown its length were gigantic pillars of what looked like ice, but were, in reality, huge stalactites. It is impossible for me to convey any idea of the overpowering beauty and grandeur of these pillars of white spar, some of which were not less than twenty feet in diameter at the base, and sprang up in lofty and yet delicate beauty sheer to the distant roof. Others again were in process of formation. On the rock floor there was in these cases what looked, Sir Henry said, exactly like a broken column in an old Grecian temple, while high above, depending from the roof, the point of a huge icicle could be dimly seen. And even as we gazed we could hear the process going on, for presently with a tiny splash a drop of water would fall from the far-off icicle onto the column below. On some columns the drops only fell once in two or three minutes, and in these cases it would form an interesting calculation to discover how long, at that rate of dripping, it would take to form a pillar, say eighty feet high by ten in diameter. That the process was, in at least one instance, incalculably slow, the following instance will suffice to show. Cut on one of these pillars we discovered a rude likeness of a mummy, by the head of which sat what appeared to be one of the Egyptian gods, doubtless the handiwork of some Old-World laborer in the mine. This work of art was executed at about the natural height at which an idle fellow, be he Phoenician workman or British cad, is in the habit of trying to immortalize himself at the expense of nature's masterpieces, namely, about five feet from the ground; yet at the time that we saw it, which *must* have been nearly three thousand years after the date of the execution of the drawing, the column was only eight feet high, and was still in process of formation, which gives a rate of growth of a foot to a thousand years, or an inch and a fraction to a century. This we knew because, as we were standing by it, we heard a drop of water fall.

Sometimes the stalactites took strange forms, presumably where the dropping of the water had not always been on the same spot. Thus, one huge mass, which must have weighed a hundred tons or so, was in the form of a pulpit, beautifully fretted over outside with what looked like lace. Others resembled strange beasts, and on the sides of the cave were fanlike ivory tracings, such as the frost leaves upon a pane.

Out of the vast main aisle there opened here and there smaller caves, exactly, Sir Henry said, as chapels open out of great cathedrals. Some were large, but one or two—and this is a wonderful instance of how Nature carries out her handiwork by the same unvarying laws, utterly irrespective of size—were tiny. One little nook, for instance, was no larger than an unusually big doll's house, and yet it might have been the model of the whole place, for the water dropped, the tiny icicles hung, and the spar columns were forming in just the same way.

We had not time, however, to examine this beautiful place as thoroughly as we should have liked to do, for unfortunately Gagool seemed to be indifferent to stalactites, and only anxious to get her business over. This annoyed me the more, as I was particularly anxious to discover, if possible, by what system the light was admitted into the place, and whether it was by the hand of man or of nature that this was done; also if it had been used in any way in ancient times, as seemed probable. However, we consoled ourselves with the idea that we would examine it thoroughly on our return, and followed on after our uncanny guide.

On she led us, straight to the top of the vast and silent cave, where we found another doorway, not arched as the first was, but square at the top, something like the doorways of Egyptian temples.

"Are ye prepared to enter the Place of Death?" asked Gagool, evidently with a view to making us feel uncomfortable.

"Lead on, Macduff," said Good solemnly, trying to look as though he was not at all alarmed, as indeed did we all except Foulata, who caught Good by the arm for protection.

"This is getting rather ghastly," said Sir Henry, peeping into the dark doorway. "Come on, Quatermain—*seniores priores*. Don't keep the old lady waiting!" and he politely made way for me to lead the van, for which I inwardly did not bless him.

Tap, tap went old Gagool's stick down the passage, as she trotted along, chuckling hideously; and, still overcome by some unaccountable presentiment of evil, I hung back.

"Come, get on, old fellow," said Good, "or we shall lose our fair guide."

Thus adjured, I started down the passage, and after about twenty paces found myself in a gloomy apartment some forty feet long by thirty broad and thirty high, which in some past age had evidently been hollowed, by hand labor, out of the mountain. This apartment was not nearly so well lighted as the vast stalactite ante-cave, and at the first glance all I could make out was a massive stone table running its length, with a colossal white figure at its head, and life-sized white figures all round it. Next I made out a brown thing, seated on the table in the center, and in another moment my eyes grew accustomed to the light, and I saw what all these things were, and I was tailing out of it as hard as my legs would carry me. I am not a nervous man, in a general way, and very little troubled with superstitions, of which I have lived to see the folly; but I am free to own that that sight quite upset me, and had it not been that Sir Henry caught me by the collar and held me, I do honestly believe that in another five minutes I should have been outside that stalactite cave, and that the promise of all the diamonds in Kimberley would not have induced me to enter it again. But he held me tight, so I stopped because I could not help myself. But next second his eyes got accustomed to the light, too, and he let go of me and began to mop the perspiration off his forehead. As for Good, he swore feebly, and Foulata threw her arms round his neck and shrieked.

Only Gagool chuckled loud and long.

It *was* a ghastly sight. There at the end of the long stone table, sat *Death* himself, shaped in the form of a colossal human skeleton, fifteen feet or more in height. High above his head he held the spear, as though in the act of striking; one bony hand rested on the stone table before him, in the position a man assumes on rising from his seat, while his frame was bent forward so that the vertebrae of the neck and the grinning, gleaming skull projected towards us and fixed its hollow eye places upon us, the jaws a little open, as though it were about to speak.

"Great heavens!" said I faintly, at last. "What can it be?"

"And what are *those things?*" said Good, pointing to the white company round the table.

"And what on earth is *that thing?*" said Sir Henry, pointing to the brown creature seated on the table.

"Hee, hee, hee!" laughed Gagool. "To those who enter the Hall of the Dead, evil comes. Hee, hee, hee! Ha, ha!"

"Come Incubu, brave in battle, come and see him thou slewest," and the old creature caught his coat in her skinny fingers, and led him away towards the table. We followed. Presently she stopped and pointed at the brown object seated on the table. Sir Henry looked, and started back with an exclamation; and no wonder, for there seated, quite naked, on the table, the head which Sir Henry's battle-ax had shorn from the body resting on its knees, was the gaunt corpse of Twala, last king of the Kukuanas. Yes, there, the head perched upon the knees, it sat in all its ugliness, the vertebrae projecting a full inch above the level of the shrunken flesh of the neck, for all the world like a black double of Hamilton Tighe.[1] Over the whole surface of the corpse there was gathered a thin, glassy film, which made its appearance yet more appalling, and for which we were, at the moment, quite unable to account, till we presently observed that from the roof of the chamber the water fell steadily—*drip, drip, drip!*—onto the neck of the corpse, from whence it ran down over the entire surface, and finally escaped into the rock through a tiny hole in the table. Then I guessed what it was—*Twala's body was being transformed into a stalactite.*

[1] Now haste ye, my handmaidens, haste and see
How he sits there and glowers with his head on his knee.

A look at the white forms seated on the stone bench that ran round that ghastly board confirmed this view. They were human forms, indeed, or rather had been human forms; now they were *stalactites*. This was the way in which the Kukuana people had from time immemorial preserved their royal dead. They petrified them. What the exact system was, if there was any beyond placing them for a long period of years under the drip, I never discovered, but there they sat, iced over and preserved forever by the siliceous fluid. Anything more awe-inspiring than the spectacle of this long line of departed royalties, wrapped in a shroud of ice-like spar, through which the features could be dimly made out (there were twenty-seven of them, the last being Ignosi's father), and seated round that inhospitable board, with Death himself for a host, it is impossible to imagine. That the practice of thus preserving their kings must have been an ancient one is evident from the number, which, allowing for an average reign of fifteen years, would, supposing that every king who reigned was placed here—an improbable thing, as some are sure to have perished in battle far from home—fix the date of its commencement at four and a quarter centuries back. But the colossal Death who sits at the head of the board is far older than that, and, unless I am much mistaken, owes his origin to the same artist who designed the three colossi. He was hewn out of a single stalactite, and, looked at as a work of art, was most admirably conceived and executed. Good, who understood anatomy, declared that, so far as he could see, the anatomical design of the skeleton was perfect down to the smallest bones.

My own idea is that this terrific object was a freak of fancy on the part of some Old-World sculptor, and that its presence had suggested to the Kukuanas the idea of placing their royal dead under its awful presidency. Or perhaps it was placed there to frighten away any marauders who might have designs upon the treasure chamber beyond. I cannot say. All I can do is to describe it as it is, and the reader must form his own conclusion.

Such, at any rate, was the white Death and such were the white dead!

17 ♦

Solomon's Treasure Chamber

WHILE WE had been engaged in getting over our fright, and in examining the grisly wonders of the place, Gagool had been differently occupied. Somehow or other —for she was marvelously active when she chose—she had scrambled onto the great table and made her way to where our departed friend Twala was placed under the drip, to see, suggested Good, how he was "pickling," or for some dark purpose of her own. Then she came hobbling back, stopping now and again to address a remark (the tenor of which I could not catch) to one or other of the shrouded forms, just as you or I might greet an old acquaintance. Having gone through this mysterious and horrible ceremony, she squatted herself down on the table immediately under the white Death, and began, so far as I could make out, to offer up prayers to it. The spectacle of this wicked old creature pouring out supplications (evil ones, no doubt) to the archenemy of mankind was so uncanny that it caused us to hasten our inspection.

"Now, Gagool," said I in a low voice—somehow one did not dare to speak above a whisper in that place—"lead us to the chamber."

The old creature promptly scrambled down off the table.

"My lords are not afraid?" she said, leering up into my face.

"Lead on."

"Good, my lords," and she hobbled round to the back of the great Death. "Here is the chamber; let my lords light the lamp, and enter," and she placed the gourd full of oil upon the floor, and leaned herself against the side of the cave. I took out a match, of which we still had a few in a box, and lit the rush wick, and then looked for the doorway, but there was nothing before us but the solid rock. Gagool grinned. "The way is there, my lords."

"Do not jest with us," I said sternly.

"I jest not, my lords. See!" and she pointed at the rock.

As she did so, on holding up the lamp we perceived that a mass of stone was slowly rising from the floor and vanishing into the rock above, where doubtless there was a cavity prepared to receive it. The mass was of the width of a good-sized door, about ten feet high and not less than five feet thick. It must have weighed at least twenty or thirty tons, and was clearly moved upon some simple balance principle, probably the same as that upon which the opening and shutting of an ordinary modern window is arranged. How the principle was set in motion, of course none of us saw; Gagool was careful to avoid that; but I have little doubt that there was some very simple lever, which was moved ever so little by pressure on a secret spot, thereby throwing additional weight onto the hidden counterbalances, and causing the whole huge mass to be lifted from the ground. Very slowly and gently the great stone raised itself, till at last it had vanished altogether, and a dark hole presented itself to us in the place which it had filled.

Our excitement was so intense, as we saw the way to Solomon's treasure chamber at last thrown open, that I for one began to tremble and shake. Would it prove a hoax after all, I wondered, or was old Da Silvestra right? And were there vast hoards of wealth stored in that dark place, hoards which would make us the richest men in the whole world? We should know in a minute or two.

"Enter, white men from the stars," said Gagool, advancing into the doorway, "but first hear your servant, Gagaoola the old. The bright stones that ye will see were dug out of the pit over which the Silent Ones are set, and stored here, I know not by whom. But once has this place been entered since the time that those who stored the stones departed in haste, leaving them behind. The report of the treasure went down among the people who lived in the country from age to age, but none knew where the chamber was, nor the secret of the door. But it happened that a white man reached this country from over the mountains, perchance he too came 'from the stars,' and was well received of the king of the day. He it is who sits yonder," and she pointed to the fifth king at the table of the dead. "And it came to pass that he and a woman of the country who was with him came to this place, and that by chance the woman learned the secret of the door—a thousand years might ye search, but ye should never find it. Then the white man entered with the woman and found the stones, and filled with stones the skin of a small goat, which the woman had with her to hold food. And as he was going from the chamber he took up one more stone, a large one, and held it in his hand." Here she paused.

"Well," I asked, breathless with interest, as we all were, "what happened to Da Silvestra?"

The old hag started at the mention of the name.

"How knowest thou the dead man's name?" she asked sharply. And then, without waiting for an answer, she went on, "None knew what happened; but it came about that the white man was frightened, for he flung down the goatskin with the stones, and fled out with only the one stone in his hand, and that the king took, and it is the stone that thou, Macumazahn, didst take from Twala's brow."

"Have none entered here since?" I asked, peering again down the dark passage.

"None, my lords. Only the secret of the door hath been kept, and every king hath opened it, though he hath not entered. There is a saying, that those who enter there will die within a moon, even as the white man died in the cave upon the mountain, where ye found him, Macumazahn. Ha, ha! Mine are true words."

Our eyes met as she said it, and I turned sick and cold. How did the old hag know all these things?

"Enter, my lords. If I speak truth the goatskin with the stones will lie upon the floor; and if there is truth as to whether it is death to enter here, that will ye learn afterwards. Ha, ha, ha!" And she hobbled through the doorway, bearing the light with her; but I confess that once more I hesitated about following.

"Oh, confound it all!" said Good. "Here goes. I am not going to be frightened by that old devil." And, followed by Foulata, who, however, evidently did not at all like the job, for she was shivering with fear, he plunged into the passage after Gagool—an example which we quickly followed.

A few yards down the passage, in the narrow way hewn out of the living rock, Gagool had paused, and was waiting for us.

"See, my lords," she said, holding the light before her, "those who stored the treasure here fled in haste, and bethought them to guard against any who should find the secret of the door, but had not the time," and she pointed to large square blocks of stone, which had, to the height of two courses (about two feet three), been placed across the passage with a view to walling it up. Along the side of the passage were similar blocks ready for use, and, most curious of all, a heap of mortar and a couple of trowels, which, so far as we had time to examine them, appeared to be of a similar shape and make to those used by workmen of this day.

Here Foulata, who had throughout been in a state of great fear and agitation, said that she felt faint and could go no farther, but would wait there. Accordingly we set her down on the unfinished wall, placing the basket of provisions by her side, and left her to recover.

Following the passage for about fifteen paces farther, we suddenly came to an elaborately painted wooden door. It was standing wide open. Whoever was last there had either not had the time, or had forgotten to shut it.

Across the threshold lay a skin bag, formed of a goatskin, that appeared to be full of pebbles.

"Hee, hee, white men," sniggered Gagool, as the light from the lamp fell upon it. "What did I tell ye, that the white man who came here fled in haste, and dropped the woman's bag—behold it!"

Good stooped down and lifted it. It was heavy and jingled.

"By Jove! I believe it's full of diamonds," he said in an awed whisper; and, indeed, the idea of a small goatskin full of diamonds is enough to awe anybody.

"Go on," said Sir Henry impatiently. "Here, old lady, give me the lamp," and, taking it from Gagool's hand, he stepped through the doorway and held it high above his head.

We pressed in after him, forgetful, for the moment, of

the bag of diamonds, and found ourselves in Solomon's treasure chamber.

At first, all that the somewhat faint light given by the lamp revealed was a room hewn out of the living rock, and apparently not more than ten feet square. Next there came into sight, stored one on the other as high as the roof, a splendid collection of elephant tusks. How many of them there were we did not know, for of course we could not see how far they went back, but there could not have been less than the ends of four or five hundred tusks of the first quality visible to our eyes. There, alone, was enough ivory before us to make a man wealthy for life. Perhaps, I thought, it was from this very store that Solomon drew his material for his "great throne of ivory," of which there was not the like made in any kingdom.

On the opposite side of the chamber were about a score of wooden boxes, something like Martini-Henry ammunition boxes, only rather larger, and painted red.

"There are the diamonds!" cried I. "Bring the light."

Sir Henry did so, holding it close to the top box, of which the lid, rendered rotten by time even in that dry place, appeared to have been smashed in, probably by Da Silvestra himself. Pushing my hand through the hole in the lid I drew it out full, not of diamonds, but of gold pieces, of a shape that none of us had seen before, and with what looked like Hebrew characters stamped upon them.

"Ah!" I said, replacing the coin, "we shan't go back empty-handed, anyhow. There must be a couple of thousand pieces in each box, and there are eighteen boxes. I suppose it was the money to pay the workmen and merchants."

"Well," put in Good, "I think that is the lot; I don't

see any diamonds, unless the old Portuguese put them all into this bag."

"Let my lords look yonder where it is darkest, if they would find the stones," said Gagool, interpreting our looks. "There my lords will find a nook, and three stone chests in the nook, two sealed and one open."

Before interpreting this to Sir Henry, who had the light, I could not resist asking how she knew these things, if no one had entered the place since the white man, generations ago.

"Ah, Macumazahn, who watchest by night," was the mocking answer, "ye who live in the stars, do ye not know that some have eyes that can see through rock?"

"Look in that corner, Curtis," I said, indicating the spot Gagool had pointed out.

"Hullo, you fellows," he said, "here's a recess. Great heavens! Look here."

We hurried up to where he was standing in a nook, something like a small bow window. Against the wall of this recess were placed three stone chests, each about two feet square. Two were fitted with stone lids; the lid of the third rested against the side of the chest, which was open.

"*Look!*" he repeated hoarsely, holding the lamp over the open chest. We looked, and for a moment could make nothing out, on account of a silvery sheen that dazzled us. When our eyes got used to it we saw that the chest was three quarters full of uncut diamonds, most of them of considerable size. Stooping, I picked some up. Yes, there was no mistake about it, there was the unmistakable soapy feel about them.

I fairly gasped as I dropped them.

"We are the richest men in the whole world," I said. "Monte Cristo is a fool to us."

"We shall flood the market with diamonds," said Good.

"Got to get them there first," suggested Sir Henry.

And we stood with pale faces and stared at each other, with the lantern in the middle, and the glimmering gems below, as though we were conspirators about to commit a crime, instead of being, as we thought, the three most fortunate men on earth.

"Hee, hee, hee!" went old Gagool behind us, as she flitted about like a vampire bat. "There are the bright stones that ye love, white men, as many as ye will; take them, run them through your fingers, *eat* of them, hee, hee! *Drink* of them, ha, ha!"

There was something so ridiculous at that moment to my mind in the idea of eating and drinking diamonds that I began to laugh outrageously, an example which the others followed, without knowing why. There we stood and shrieked with laughter over the gems which were ours, which had been found for *us* thousands of years ago by the patient delvers in the great hole yonder, and stored for *us* by Solomon's long-dead overseer, whose name, perchance, was written in the characters stamped on the faded wax that yet adhered to the lids of the chest. Solomon never got them, nor David, nor Da Silvestra, nor anybody else. *We* had got them; there before us were millions of pounds' worth of diamonds, and thousands of pounds' worth of gold and ivory, only waiting to be taken away.

Suddenly the fit passed off, and we stopped laughing.

"Open the other chests, white men," croaked Gagool, "there are surely more therein. Take your fill, white lords!"

Thus adjured, we set to work to pull up the stone lids on the other two, first—not without a feeling of sacrilege —breaking the seals that fastened them.

Hoorah! They were full too, full to the brim; at least the

second one was; no wretched Da Silvestra had been filling goatskins out of that. As for the third chest, it was only about a fourth full, but the stones were all picked ones, none less than twenty carats, and some of them as large as pigeon eggs. Some of these biggest ones, however, we could see by holding them up to the light, were a little yellow, "off colored," as they call it at Kimberley.

What we did *not* see, however, was the look of fearful malevolence that old Gagool favored us with as she crept, crept like a snake, out of the treasure chamber and down the passage towards the massive door of solid rock.

Hark! Cry upon cry comes ringing up the vaulted path. It is Foulata's voice!

"Oh, Bougwan! Help! Help! The rock falls!"

"Leave go, girl!"

"Help! Help! She has stabbed me!"

By now we are running down the passage, and this is what the light from the lamp falls on. The door of rock is slowly closing down; it is not three feet from the floor. Near it struggle Foulata and Gagool. The red blood of the former runs to her knee, but still the brave girl holds the old witch, who fights like a wildcat. Ah! She is free! Foulata falls, and Gagool throws herself on the ground, to twist herself like a snake through the crack of the closing stone. She is under—ah, God! Too late! Too late! The stone nips her, and she yells in agony. Down, down it comes, all the thirty tons of it, slowly pressing her old body against the rock below. Shriek upon shriek, such as we never heard, then a long, sickening *crunch*, and the door was shut just as we, rushing down the passage, hurled ourselves against it.

It was all done in four seconds.

Then we turned to Foulata. The poor girl was stabbed in the body, and could not, I saw, live long.

"Ah, Bougwan, I die!" gasped the beautiful creature. "She crept out—Gagool; I did not see her, I was faint—and the door began to fall; then she came back, and was looking up the path—and I saw her come in through the slowly falling door, and caught her and held her, and she stabbed me, and I *die*, Bougwan."

"Poor girl! Poor girl!" Good cried; and then, as he could do nothing else, he fell to kissing her.

"Bougwan," she said, after a pause, "is Macumazahn there? It grows so dark, I cannot see."

"Here I am, Foulata."

"Macumazahn, be my tongue for a moment, I pray thee, for Bougwan cannot understand me, and before I go into the darkness—I would speak a word."

"Say on, Foulata, I will render it."

"Say to my lord, Bougwan, that—I love him, and that I am glad to die because I know that he cannot cumber his life with such as me, for the sun cannot mate with the darkness, nor the white with the black.

"Say that at times I have felt as though there were a bird in my bosom, which would one day fly hence and sing elsewhere; even now, though I cannot lift my hand, and my brain grows cold, I do not feel as though my heart were dying; it is so full of love that could live a thousand years, and yet be young. Say that if I live again, mayhap I shall see him in the stars, and that—I will search them all, though perchance I should there still be black and he would —still be white. Say—nay, Macumazahn, say no more, save that I love—Oh, hold me closer, Bougwan, I cannot feel thine arms— *Oh! Oh!*"

"She is dead—she is dead!" said Good, rising in grief, the tears running down his honest face.

"You need not let that trouble you, old fellow," said Sir Henry.

"Eh!" said Good. "What do you mean?"

"I mean that you will soon be in a position to join her. *Man, don't you see that we are buried alive?*"

Until Sir Henry uttered these words, I do not think the full horror of what had happened had come home to us, preoccupied as we were with poor Foulata's death. But now we understood. The ponderous mass of rock had closed, probably forever, for the only brain which knew its secret was crushed to powder beneath it. This was a door that none could hope to force with anything short of dynamite in large quantities. And we were the wrong side of it!

For a few minutes we stood horrified there over the corpse of Foulata. All the manhood seemed to have gone out of us. The first shock of this idea of the slow and miserable end that awaited us was overpowering. We saw it all now; that fiend Gagool had planned this snare for us from the first. It would have been just the jest that her evil mind would have rejoiced in, the idea of the three white men, whom, for some reason of her own, she had always hated, slowly perishing of thirst and hunger in the company of the treasure they had coveted. I saw the point of that sneer of hers about eating and drinking the diamonds now. Perhaps somebody had tried to serve the poor old don in the same way, when he abandoned the skin full of jewels.

"This will never do," said Sir Henry hoarsely; "the lamp will soon go out. Let us see if we can't find the spring that works the rocks."

We sprang forward with desperate energy, and, standing in a bloody ooze, began to feel up and down the door and the sides of the passage. But no knob or spring could we discover.

"Depend on it," I said, "it does not work from the inside; if it did Gagool would not have risked trying to crawl underneath the stone. It was the knowledge of this that made her try to escape at all hazard, curse her."

"At all events," said Sir Henry with a hard little laugh, "retribution was swift; hers was almost as awful an end as ours is likely to be. We can do nothing with the door; let us go back to the treasure room." We turned and went, and as we did so I perceived by the unfinished wall across the passage the basket of food which poor Foulata had carried. I took it up and brought it with me back to that accursed treasure chamber that was to be our grave. Then we went back and reverently bore in Foulata's corpse, laying it on the floor by the boxes of coin.

Next we seated ourselves, leaning our backs against the three stone chests of priceless treasures.

"Let us divide the food," said Sir Henry, "so as to make it last as long as possible." Accordingly we did so. It would, we reckoned, make four infinitesimally small meals for each of us; enough, say, to support life for a couple of days. Besides the biltong, there were two gourds of water, each holding about a quart.

"Now," said Sir Henry, "let us eat and drink, for tomorrow we die."

We each ate a small portion of the biltong, and drank a sip of water. We had, needless to say, but little appetite, though we were sadly in need of food, and felt better after swallowing it. Then we got up and made a systematic examination of the walls of our prison house, in the faint hope of finding some means of exit, sounding them and the floor carefully.

There was none. It was not probable that there would be one to a treasure chamber.

The lamp began to burn dim. The fat was nearly exhausted.

"Quatermain," said Sir Henry, "what is the time—your watch goes?"

I drew it out and looked at it. It was six o'clock; we had entered the cave at eleven.

"Infadoos will miss us," I suggested. "If we do not return tonight he will search for us in the morning, Curtis."

"He may search in vain. He does not know the secret of the door, nor even where it is. No living person knew it yesterday, except Gagool. Today no one knows it. Even if he found the door he could not break it down. All the Kukuana army could not break through five feet of living rock. My friends, I see nothing for it but to bow ourselves to the will of the Almighty. The search for treasure has brought many to a bad end; we shall go to swell their number."

The lamp grew dimmer yet.

Presently it flared up and showed the whole scene in strong relief, the great mass of white tusks, the boxes full of gold, the corpse of poor Foulata stretched before them, the goatskin full of treasure, the dim glimmer of the diamonds, and the wild, wan faces of us three white men seated there awaiting death by starvation.

Suddenly it sank, and expired.

After a while he gave it up, and came back very thirsty, and had to have some water. After that we gave up yelling, as it encroached on the supply of water.

So we all sat down once more against our chests of useless diamonds in that dreadful inaction which was one of the hardest circumstances of our fate; and I am bound to say that, for my part, I gave way in despair. Laying my head against Sir Henry's broad shoulder, I burst into tears; and I think I heard Good gulping on the other side, and swearing hoarsely at himself for doing so.

Ah, how good and brave that great man was! Had we been two frightened children, and he our nurse, he could not have treated us more tenderly. Forgetting his own share of miseries, he did all he could to soothe our broken nerves, telling stories of men who had been in somewhat similar circumstances and miraculously escaped; and when these failed to cheer us, pointing out how, after all, it was only anticipating an end that must come to us all, that it would soon be over, and that death from exhaustion was a merciful one (which is not true). Then, in a diffident sort of a way, as I had once before heard him do, he suggested that we should throw ourselves on the mercy of a higher Power, which, for my part, I did with great vigor.

His is a beautiful character, very quiet, but very strong.

And so somehow the day went as the night had gone (if, indeed, one can use the terms where all was densest night), and when I lit a match to see the time it was seven o'clock.

Once more we ate and drank, and as we did so an idea occurred to me.

"How is it," said I, "that the air in this place keeps fresh? It is thick and heavy, but it is perfectly fresh."

"Great heavens!" said Good, starting up, "I never

thought of that. It can't come through the stone door, for it is airtight, if ever a door was. It must come from somewhere. If there were no current of air in the place we should have been stifled when we first came in. Let us have a look."

It was wonderful what a change this mere spark of hope wrought in us. In a moment we were all three groping about the place on our hands and knees, feeling for the slightest indication of a draft. Presently my ardor received a check. I put my hand on something cold. It was poor Foulata's dead face.

For an hour or more we went on feeling about, till at last Sir Henry and I gave it up in despair, having got considerably hurt by constantly knocking our heads against tusks, chests, and the sides of the chamber. But Good still persevered, saying, with an approach to cheerfulness, that it was better than doing nothing.

"I say, you fellows," he said presently, in a constrained sort of voice, "come here."

Needless to say we scrambled over towards him quick enough.

"Quatermain, put your hand here where mine is. Now, do you feel anything?"

"I *think* I feel air coming up."

"Now listen." He rose and stamped upon the place and a flame of hope shot up in our hearts. *It rang hollow.*

With trembling hands I lit a match. I had only three left, and we saw that we were in the angle of the far corner of the chamber, a fact that accounted for our not having noticed the hollow ring of the place during our former exhaustive examination. As the match burned we scrutinized the spot. There was a join in the solid rock floor, and— great heavens!—there, let in level with rock, was a stone ring. We said no word; we were too excited, and our hearts beat too wildly with hope to allow us to speak. Good had a knife, at the back of which was one of those hooks that are made to extract stones from horses' hoofs. He opened it, and scratched away at the ring with it. Finally he got it under, and levered away gently for fear of breaking the hook. The ring began to move. Being of stone, it had not got set fast in all the centuries it had lain there, as would have been the case had it been of iron. Presently it was upright. Then he got his hands into it and tugged with all his force, but nothing budged.

"Let me try," I said impatiently, for the situation of the stone, right in the angle of the corner, was such that it was impossible for two to pull at once. I got hold and strained away, but with no results.

Then Sir Henry tried and failed.

Taking the hook again, Good scratched all around the cracks where we felt the air coming up.

"Now, Curtis," he said, "tackle on, and put your back into it; you are as strong as two. Stop," and he took off a stout black silk handkerchief, which, true to his habits of neatness, he still wore, and ran it through the ring. "Quatermain, get Curtis round the middle and pull for dear life when I give the word. *Now!*"

Sir Henry put out all his enormous strength, and Good and I did the same, with such power as nature had given us.

"Heave! Heave! It's giving," gasped Sir Henry; and I heard the muscles of his great back cracking. Suddenly there came a parting sound, then a rush of air, and we were all on our backs on the floor with a great flagstone on top of us. Sir Henry's strength had done it, and never did muscular power stand a man in better stead.

"Light a match, Quatermain," he said, as soon as we had picked ourselves up and got one breath; "carefully now."

I did so, and there before us was—God be praised—the *first step of a stone stair.*

"Now what is to be done?" asked Good.

"Follow the stair, of course, and trust to Providence."

"Stop!" said Sir Henry. "Quatermain, get the bit of biltong and the water that is left; we may want them."

I went creeping back to our place by the chests for that purpose, and as I was coming away an idea struck me. We had not thought much of the diamonds for the last twenty-four hours or so; indeed, the idea of diamonds was nauseating, seeing what they had entailed upon us; but, thought I, I may as well pocket a few in case we ever should get out of this ghastly hole. So I just stuck my fist into the first chest and filled all the available pockets of my shooting coat, topping up—this was a happy thought—with a couple of handfuls of big ones out of the third chest.

"I say, you fellows," I sang out, "won't you take some diamonds with you? I've filled my pockets."

"Oh, hang the diamonds!" said Sir Henry. "I hope that I may never see another."

As for Good, he made no answer. He was, I think, taking a last farewell of all that was left of the poor girl who loved him so well. And, curious as it may seem to you, my reader, sitting at home at ease and reflecting on the vast, indeed, the immeasurable, wealth which we were thus abandoning, I can assure you that if you had passed some twenty-eight hours with next to nothing to eat and drink in that place, you would not have cared to cumber yourself with diamonds while plunging down into the unknown bowels of the earth, in the wild hope of escape from an agonizing death. If it had not, from the habits of a lifetime, become a sort of second nature with me never to leave anything worth having behind if there was the slightest chance of my being able to carry it away, I am sure I should not have bothered to fill my pockets.

"Come on, Quatermain," said Sir Henry, who was already standing on the first step of the stone stair. "Steady, I will go first."

"Mind where you put your feet; there may be some awful hole underneath," said I.

"Much more likely to be another room," said Sir Henry, as he slowly descended, counting the steps as he went.

When he got to "fifteen" he stopped. "Here's the bottom," he said. "Thank goodness! I think it's a passage. Come on down."

Good descended next, and I followed last, and on reaching the bottom lit one of the two remaining matches. By its light we could just see that we were standing in a narrow tunnel, which ran right and left at right angles to the staircase we had descended. Before we could make out any more the match burned my fingers and went out. Then arose the delicate question of which way to turn. Of course it was impossible to know what the tunnel was or where it ran to, and yet to turn one way might lead us to safety, and the other to destruction. We were utterly perplexed, till suddenly it struck Good that when I had lit the match the draft of the passage blew the flame to the left.

"Let us go against the draft," he said; "air draws inward, not outward."

We took this suggestion, and, feeling along the wall with our hands, while trying the ground before at every step, we departed from that accursed treasure chamber on our terrible quest. If ever it should be entered again by living man, which I do not think it will be, he will find a token of our presence in the open chests of jewels, the empty lamp, and the white bones of poor Foulata.

When we had groped our way for about a quarter of an hour along the passage it suddenly took a sharp turn, or else was bisected by another, which we followed, only in course of time to be led into a third. And so it went on for some hours. We seemed to be in a stone labyrinth which led nowhere. What all these passages are, of course I cannot say, but we thought that they must be the ancient workings of a mine, of which the various shafts traveled hither and thither as the ore led them. This is the only way in which we could account for such a multitude of passages.

At length we halted, thoroughly worn out with fatigue, and with that hope deferred which maketh the heart sick, and ate up our poor remaining piece of biltong, and drank our last sup of water, for our throats were like lime kilns. It seemed to us that we had escaped Death in the darkness of the chamber only to meet him in the darkness of the tunnels.

As we stood, once more utterly depressed, I thought I caught a sound, to which I called the attention of the others. It was very faint and very far off, but it *was* a sound, a faint, murmuring sound, for the others heard it too, and no words can describe the blessedness of it after all those hours of utter, awful stillness.

"By heavens! It's running water," said Good. "Come on."

Off we started again in the direction from which the faint murmur seemed to come, groping our way as before along the rocky walls. As we went it got more and more audible, till at last it seemed quite loud in the quiet. On, yet on; now we could distinctly make out the unmistakable swirl of rushing water. And yet how could there be running water in the bowels of the earth? Now we were quite near to it, and Good, who was leading swore that he could smell it.

"Go gently, Good," said Sir Henry, "we must be close."

Splash! And a cry from Good.

He had fallen in.

"Good! Good! Where are you?" we shouted in terrified distress. To our intense relief, an answer came back in a choky voice.

"All right; I've got hold of a rock. Strike a light to show me where you are."

Hastily I lit the last remaining match. Its faint gleam discovered to us a dark mass of water running at our feet. How wide it was we could not see, but there, some way out, was the dark form of our companion hanging on to a projecting rock.

"Stand clear to catch me," sang out Good. "I must swim for it."

Then we heard a splash and a great struggle. Another minute and he had grabbed at and caught Sir Henry's outstretched hand, and we had pulled him up high and dry into the tunnel.

"My word!" he said, between his gasps, "that was touch and go. If I hadn't caught that rock, and known how to swim, I should have been done. It runs like a millrace, and I could feel no bottom."

It was clear that this would not do; so after Good had rested a little, and we had drunk our fill from the water of the subterranean river, which was sweet and fresh, and washed our faces, which sadly needed it, as well as we could, we started from the banks of this African Styx, and began to retrace our steps along the tunnel, Good dripping unpleasantly in front of us. At length we came to another tunnel leading to our right.

"We may as well take it," said Sir Henry wearily; "all roads are alike here; we can only go on till we drop."

Slowly, for a long, long while, we stumbled, utterly weary, along this new tunnel, Sir Henry leading now.

Suddenly he stopped, and we bumped up against him.

"Look!" he whispered. "Is my brain going, or is that light?"

We stared with all our eyes, and there, yes, there, far ahead of us, was a faint glimmering spot, no larger than a cottage windowpane. It was so faint that I doubt if any eyes except those which, like ours, had for days seen nothing but blackness could have perceived it at all.

With a sort of gasp of hope we pushed on. In five minutes there was no longer any doubt: it *was* a patch of faint light. A minute more and a breath of real live air was fanning us. On we struggled. All at once the tunnel narrowed. Sir Henry went on his knees. Smaller yet it grew, till it was only the size of a large fox's earth—it was *earth* now, mind you; the rock had ceased.

A squeeze, a struggle, and Sir Henry was out, and so was Good, and so was I, and there above us were the blessed stars, and in our nostrils was the sweet air; then suddenly something gave, and we were all rolling over and over and over through grass and bushes and soft, wet soil.

I caught at something and stopped. Sitting up, I hulloed lustily. An answering shout came from just below, where Sir Henry's wild career had been stopped by some level ground. I scrambled to him, and found him unhurt, though breathless. Then we looked for Good. A little way off we found him, too, jammed in a forked root. He was a good deal knocked about, but soon came to.

We sat down together there on the grass, and the revul-

sion of feeling was so great that I really think we cried for
joy. We had escaped from that awful dungeon, that was
so near to becoming our grave. Surely some merciful Power
must have guided our footsteps to the jackal hole at the
termination of the tunnel (for that is what it must have
been). And see, there on the mountains, the dawn we had
never thought to look upon again was blushing rosy red.

Presently the gray light stole down the slopes, and we
saw that we were at the bottom, or, rather, nearly at the
bottom of the vast pit in front of the entrance to the cave.
Now we could make out the dim forms of the three colossi
who sat upon its verge. Doubtless those awful passages,
along which we had wandered the livelong night, had originally been, in some way, connected with the great diamond
mine. As for the subterranean river in the bowels of the
mountain, heaven only knows what it was, or whence it
flows, or whither it goes. I, for one, have no anxiety to trace
its course.

Lighter it grew, and lighter yet. We could see each
other now, and such a spectacle as we presented I have
never set eyes on before or since. Gaunt-cheeked, hollow-
eyed wretches, smeared all over with dust and mud, bruised,
bleeding, the long fear of imminent death yet written on
our countenances, we were, indeed, a sight to frighten the
daylight. And yet it is a solemn fact that Good's eyeglass
was still fixed in Good's eye. I doubt whether he had ever
taken it out at all. Neither the darkness, nor the plunge
in the subterranean river, nor the roll down the slope, had
been able to separate Good and his eyeglass.

Presently we rose, fearing that our limbs would stiffen
if we stopped there longer, and commenced with slow and
painful steps to struggle up the sloping sides of the great

pit. For an hour or more we toiled steadfastly up the blue clay, dragging ourselves on by the help of the roots and grasses with which it was clothed.

At last it was done, and we stood on the great road, on the side of the pit opposite to the colossi.

By the side of the road, a hundred yards off, a fire was burning in front of some huts, and round the fire were figures. We made towards them, supporting one another, and halting every few paces. Presently, one of the figures rose, saw us, and fell onto the ground, crying out for fear.

"Infadoos, Infadoos! It is us, thy friends."

We rose; he ran to us, staring wildly, and still shaking with fear.

"Oh, my lords, my lords, it is indeed you come back from the dead—come back from the dead!"

And the old warrior flung himself down before us, and clasped Sir Henry's knees, and wept aloud for joy.

19 ♦

Ignosi's Farewell

TEN DAYS from that eventful morning found us once more in our old quarters at Loo; and, strange to say, but little the worse for our terrible experience, except that my stubbly hair came out of that cave about three shades grayer than it went in, and that Good never was quite the same after Foulata's death, which seemed to move him very greatly. I am bound to say that, looking at the thing from the point of view of an oldish man of the world, I consider her removal a fortunate occurrence, since, otherwise, complications would have been sure to ensue. The poor creature was no ordinary native girl, but a person of great, I had almost said stately, beauty, and of considerable refinement of mind. But no amount of beauty or refinement could have made an entanglement between Good and herself a desirable occurrence; for, as she herself put it, "The sun cannot mate with the darkness, nor the white with the black."

I need hardly state that we never again penetrated into Solomon's treasure chamber. After we had recovered from our fatigue, a process which took us forty-eight hours, we descended into the great pit in the hope of finding the hole by which we had crept out of the mountain, but with no success. To begin with, rain had fallen, and obliterated our spoor; and what is more, the sides of the vast pit were full of ant bear and other holes. It was impossible to say to

249

which of these we owed our salvation. We also, on the day before we started back to Loo, made a further examination of the wonders of the stalactite cave, and, drawn by a kind of restless feeling, even penetrated once more into the Chamber of the Dead; and, passing beneath the spear of the white Death, gazed, with sensations which it would be quite impossible for me to describe, at the mass of rock which had shut us off from escape, thinking, the while, of the priceless treasures beyond, of the mysterious old hag whose flattened fragments lay crushed beneath it, and of the fair girl of whose tomb it was the portal. I say gazed at the "rock," for examine as we would we could find no traces of the join of the sliding door; nor, indeed, could we hit upon the secret, now utterly lost, that worked it, though we tried for an hour or more. It was certainly a marvelous bit of mechanism, characteristic, in its massive and yet inscrutable simplicity, of the age which produced it; and I doubt if the world has another such to show.

At last we gave it up in disgust; though, if the mass had suddenly risen before our eyes, I doubt if we should have screwed up courage to step over Gagool's mangled remains and once more enter the treasure chamber, even in the sure and certain hope of unlimited diamonds. And yet I could have cried at the idea of leaving all that treasure, the biggest treasure probably that has ever in the world's history been accumulated in one spot. But there was no help for it. Only dynamite could force its way through five feet of solid rock. And so we left it. Perhaps, in some remote unborn century, a more fortunate explorer may hit upon the "Open Sesame," and flood the world with gems. But, myself, I doubt it. Somehow, I seem to feel that the millions of pounds' worth of gems that lie in the three stone coffers will never shine round the neck of an earthly beauty. They and Foulata's bones will keep cold company till the end of all things.

With a sigh of disappointment we made our way back, and next day started for Loo. And yet it was really very un- grateful of us to be disappointed; for, as the reader will remember, I had, by a lucky thought, taken the precaution to fill the pockets of my old shooting coat with gems be- fore we left our prison house. A good many of these fell out in the course of our roll down the side of the pit, in- cluding most of the big ones, which I had crammed in on the top. But, comparatively speaking, an enormous quantity still remained, including eighteen large stones ranging from about one hundred to thirty carats in weight. My old shoot- ing coat still held enough treasure to make us all, if not millionaires, at least exceedingly wealthy men, and yet to keep enough stones each to make the three finest sets of gems in Europe. So we had not done so badly.

On arriving at Loo we were most cordially received by Ignosi, whom we found well, and busily engaged in con- solidating his power and reorganizing the regiments which had suffered most in the great struggle with Twala.

He listened with breathless interest to our wonderful story; but when we told him old Gagool's frightful end, he grew thoughtful.

"Come hither," he called to a very old "induna" (coun- cilor), who was sitting with others in a circle round the king, but out of earshot. The old man rose, approached, saluted, and seated himself.

"Thou art old," said Ignosi.

"Ay, my lord the king!"

"Tell me, when thou wast little, didst thou know Ga- gaoola, the witch doctress?"

"Ay, my lord the king!"

"How was she then—young, like thee?"

"Not so, my lord the king! She was even as now; old and dried, very ugly, and full of wickedness."

"She is no more; she is dead."

"So, O King! then is a curse taken from the land."

"Go!"

"*Koom!* I go, black puppy, who tore out the old dog's throat. *Koom!*"

"Ye see, my brothers," said Ignosi, "this was a strange woman, and I rejoice that she is dead. She would have let ye die in the dark place, and mayhap afterwards she had found a way to slay me, as she found a way to slay my father and set up Twala, whom her heart loved, in his place. Now go on with the tale; surely there never was the like!"

After I had narrated all the story of our escape, I, as we had agreed between ourselves that I should, took the opportunity to address Ignosi as to our departure from Kukuanaland.

"And now, Ignosi, the time has come for us to bid thee farewell, and start to seek once more our own land. Behold, Ignosi, with us thou camest a servant, and now we leave thee a mighty king. If thou art grateful to us, remember to do even as thou didst promise: to rule justly, to respect the law, and to put none to death without a cause. So shalt thou prosper. Tomorrow, at break of day, Ignosi, wilt thou give us an escort who shall lead us across the mountains? Is it not so, O King?"

Ignosi covered his face with his hands for a while before answering.

"My heart is sore," he said at last; "your words split my heart in twain. What have I done to ye, Incubu, Macumazahn, and Bougwan, that ye should leave me desolate?

Ye who stood by me in rebellion and battle, will ye leave me in the day of peace and victory? What will ye—wives? Choose from out the land! A place to live in? Behold, the land is yours as far as you can see. The white man's houses? Ye shall teach my people how to build them. Cattle for beef and milk? Every married man shall bring ye an ox or a cow. Wild game to hunt? Does not the elephant walk through my forests, and the river horse sleep in the reeds? Would ye make war? My impis [regiments] wait your word. If there is anything more that I can give, that will I give ye."

"Nay, Ignosi, we want not these things," I answered; "we would seek our own place."

"Now do I perceive," said Ignosi bitterly, and with flashing eyes, "that it is the bright stones that ye love more than me, your friend. Ye have the stones; now would ye go to Natal and across the black water and sell them, and be rich, as it is the desire of a white man's heart to be. Cursed for your sake be the stones, and curse he who seeks them. Death shall it be to him who sets foot in the Place of Death to seek them. I have spoken, white men; ye can go."

I laid my hand upon his arm. "Ignosi," I said, "tell us, when thou didst wander in Zululand, and among the white men in Natal, did not thine heart turn to the land thy mother told thee of, thy native land, where thou didst see the light, and play when thou wast little, the land where thy place was?"

"It was even so, Macumazahn."

"Then thus do our hearts turn to our land and to our own place."

Then came a pause. When Ignosi broke it, it was in a different voice.

"I do perceive that thy words are, now as ever, wise and full of reason, Macumazahn; that which flies in the air loves not to run along the ground; the white man loves not to live on the level of the black. Well, ye must go, and leave my heart sore, because ye will be as dead to me, since from where ye will be no tidings can come to me.

"But listen, and let all the white men know my words. No other white man shall cross the mountains, even if any may live to come so far. I will see no traders with their guns and rum. My people shall fight with the spear and drink water, like their forefathers before them. I will have no praying men to put fear of death into men's hearts, to stir them up against the king, and make a path for the white men who follow to run on. If a white man comes to my gates I will send him back; if a hundred come, I will push them back; if an army comes, I will make war on them with all my strength, and they shall not prevail against me. None shall ever come for the shining stones; no, not an army, for if they come I will send a regiment and fill up the pit, and break down the white columns in the caves and fill them with rocks, so that none can come even to that door of which ye speak, and whereof the way to move it is lost. But for ye three, Incubu, Macumazahn, and Bougwan, the path is always open; for behold, ye are dearer to me than aught that breathes.

"And ye would go. Infadoos, my uncle and my induna, shall take thee by the hand and guide thee, with a regiment. There is, as I have learned, another way across the mountains that he shall show ye. Farewell, my brothers, brave white men. See me no more, for I have no heart to bear it. Behold, I make a decree, and it shall be published from the mountains to the mountains: your names, Incubu, Macumazahn, and Bougwan, shall be as the names of dead kings, and he who speaks them shall die.[1] So shall your memory be preserved in the land forever.

"Go, now, ere my eyes rain tears like a woman's. At times when ye look back down the path of life, or when ye are old and gather yourselves together to crouch before the fire, because the sun has no more heat, ye will think of how we stood shoulder to shoulder in that great battle that thy wise words planned, Macumazahn; of how thou wast the point of that horn that galled Twala's flank, Bougwan; whilst thou stoodst in the ring of the Grays, Incubu, and men went down before thine ax like corn before a sickle; ay, and of how thou didst break the wild bull's [Twala's] strength, and bring his pride to dust. Fare ye well forever, Incubu, Macumazahn, and Bougwan, my lords and my friends."

He rose, looked earnestly at us for a few seconds, and then threw the corner of his karross over his head, so as to cover his face from us.

We went in silence.

Next day at dawn we left Loo, escorted by our old friend Infadoos, who was heartbroken at our departure, and the regiment of Buffaloes. Early as the hour was, all the main street of the town was lined with multitudes of people, who gave us the royal salute as we passed at the head of the regiment, while the women blessed us as having rid the land of Twala, throwing flowers before us as we went. It really was very affecting, and not the sort of thing one is accustomed to meet with from natives.

---

[1] This extraordinary and negative way of showing intense respect is by no means unknown among African people, and the result is that if, as is usual, the name in question has a significance, the meaning has to be expressed by an idiom or another word. In this way a memory is preserved for generations, or until the new word supplants the old one.

One very ludicrous incident occurred, however, which I rather welcomed, as it gave us something to laugh at.

Just before we got to the confines of the town a pretty young girl, with some beautiful lilies in her hand, came running forward and presented them to Good (somehow they all seemed to like Good; I think his eyeglass and solitary whisker gave him a fictitious value), and then said she had a boon to ask.

"Speak on."

"Let my lord show his servant his beautiful white legs, that his servant may look on them, and remember them all her days, and tell of them to her children; his servant has traveled four days' journey to see them, for the fame of them has gone throughout the land."

"I'll be hanged if I do!" said Good excitedly.

"Come, come, my dear fellow," said Sir Henry, "you can't refuse to oblige a lady."

"I won't," said Good, obstinately; "it is positively indecent."

However, in the end he consented to draw up his trousers to the knee, amidst notes of rapturous admiration from all the women present, especially the gratified young lady, and in this guise he had to walk till we got clear of the town.

Good's legs will, I fear, never be so greatly admired again. Of his melting teeth, and even of his "transparent eye," they wearied more or less, but of his legs, never.

As we traveled, Infadoos told us that there was another pass over the mountains, to the north of the one followed by Solomon's Great Road, or rather that there was a place where it was possible to climb down the wall of cliff that separated Kukuanaland from the desert, and was broken by the towering shapes of Sheba's breasts. It appeared, too,

that rather more than two years previously a party of Kukuana hunters had descended this path into the desert in
search of ostriches, whose plumes were much prized among
them for war headdresses, and that in the course of their
hunt they had been led far from the mountains, and were
much troubled by thirst. Seeing, however, trees on the
horizon, they made towards them, and discovered a large
and fertile oasis of some miles in extent, and plentifully
watered. It was by way of this oasis that he suggested that
we should return, and the idea seemed to us a good one, as
it appeared that we should escape the rigors of the mountain pass, and as some of the hunters were in attendance
to guide us to the oasis, from which, they stated, they could
perceive more fertile spots far away in the desert.[2]

Traveling easily, on the night of the fourth day's journey we found ourselves once more on the crest of the
mountains that separate Kukuanaland from the desert,
which rolled away in sandy billows at our feet, and about
twenty-five miles to the north of Sheba's breasts.

At dawn on the following day we were led to the commencement of a precipitous descent, by which we were to
descend the precipice, and gain the desert two thousand
and more feet below.

Here we bade farewell to that true friend and sturdy old
warrior, Infadoos, who solemnly wished all good upon us,

[2] It often puzzled all of us to understand how it was possible that
Ignosi's mother, bearing the child with her, should have survived the
dangers of the journey across the mountains and the desert, dangers which
so nearly proved fatal to ourselves. It has since occurred to me, and I
give the idea to the reader for what it is worth, that she must have taken
this second route, and wandered out like Hagar into the desert. If she
did so, there is no longer anything inexplicable about the story, since she
may well, as Ignosi himself related, have been picked up by some ostrich
hunters before she or the child were exhausted, and led by them to the
oasis, and thence by stages to the fertile country, and so on by slow degrees southward to Zululand.—A. Q.

and nearly wept with grief. "Never, my lords," he said, "shall mine old eyes see the like of ye again. Ah! The way that Incubu cut his men down in the battle! Ah! For the sight of that stroke with which he swept off my brother Twala's head! It was beautiful—beautiful! I may never hope to see such another, except perchance in happy dreams."

We were very sorry to part from him; indeed, Good was so moved that he gave him as a souvenir—what do you think?—an *eyeglass.* (Afterwards we discovered that it was a spare one.) Infadoos was delighted, foreseeing that the possession of such an article would enormously increase his prestige, and after several vain attempts actually succeeded in screwing it into his own eye. Anything more incongruous than the old warrior with an eyeglass I never saw. Eyeglasses don't go well with leopard-skin cloaks and black ostrich plumes.

Then, having seen that our guides were well laden with water and provisions, and having received a thundering farewell salute from the Buffaloes, we wrung the old warrior's hand, and began our downward climb. A very arduous business it proved to be, but somehow that evening we found ourselves at the bottom without accident.

"Do you know," said Sir Henry that night, as we sat by our fire and gazed up at the beetling cliffs above us, "I think that there are worse places than Kukuanaland in the world, and that I have spent unhappier times than the last month or two, though I have never spent such queer ones. Eh, you fellows?"

"I almost wish I were back," said Good with a sigh.

As for myself, I reflected that all's well that ends well; but in the course of a long life of shaves I never had such shaves as those I had recently experienced. The thought of that battle still makes me feel cold all over, and as for our experience in the treasure chamber—!

Next morning we started on a toilsome march across the desert, having with us a good supply of water carried by our five guides, and camped that night in the open, starting again at dawn on the morrow.

By midday of the third day's journey we could see the trees of the oasis of which the guides spoke, and by an hour before sundown we were once more walking upon grass and listening to the sound of running water.

20 ◆

Found

AND NOW I come to perhaps the strangest thing that
happened to us in all that strange business, and one which
shows how wonderfully things are brought about.

I was walking quietly along, some way in front of the
other two, down the banks of the stream which ran from
the oasis till it was swallowed up in the hungry desert
sands, when suddenly I stopped and rubbed my eyes, as
well I might. There, not twenty yards in front, placed in
a charming situation, under the shade of a species of fig-
tree, and facing the stream, was a cosy hut, built more
or less on the Kaffir principle of grass and withes, only with
a full-length door instead of a bee hole.

"What the dickens," said I to myself, "can a hut be
doing here!" Even as I said it, the door of the hut opened,
and there limped out of it a *white man* clothed in skins,
and with an enormous black beard. I thought that I must
have got a touch of the sun. It was impossible. No hunter
ever came to such a place as this. Certainly no hunter
would ever settle in it. I stared and stared, and so did the
other man, and just at that juncture Sir Henry and Good
came up.

"Look here, you fellows," I said, "is that a white man,
or am I mad?"

Sir Henry looked, and Good looked, and then all of a
260

sudden the lame white man with the black beard gave a great cry, and came hobbling towards us. When he got close he fell down in a sort of faint.

With a spring Sir Henry was by his side.

"Great Powers!" he cried. "*It is my brother George!*"

At the sound of the disturbance another figure, also clad in skins, emerged from the hut with a gun in his hand, and came running towards us. On seeing me he too gave a cry.

"Macumazahn," he hulloed, "don't you know me, Baas? I'm Jim, the hunter. I lost the note you gave me to give to the Baas, and we have been here nearly two years." And the fellow fell at my feet and rolled over and over, weeping for joy."

"You careless scoundrel!" I said. "You ought to be well hided."

Meanwhile the man with the black beard had recovered and got up, and he and Sir Henry were pump-handling away at each other, apparently without a word to say. But whatever they had quarreled about in the past (I suspect it was a lady, though I never asked), it was evidently forgotten now.

"My dear old fellow," burst out Sir Henry at last, "I thought that you were dead. I have been over Solomon's Mountains to find you, and now I come across you perched in the desert, like an old *Aasvögel* [vulture]."

"I tried to go over Solomon's Mountains nearly two years ago," was the answer, spoken in the hesitating voice of a man who has had little recent opportunity of using his tongue, "but when I got here, a boulder fell on my leg and crushed it, and I have been able to go neither forward nor back."

Then I came up. "How do you do, Mr. Neville?" I said. "Do you remember me?"

"Why," he said, "isn't it Quatermain, eh, and Good, too? Hold on a minute, you fellows, I am getting dizzy again. It is all so very strange, and, when a man has ceased to hope, so very happy."

That evening, over the campfire, George Curtis told us his story, which, in its way, was almost as eventful as our own, and amounted, briefly, to this. A little short of two years before, he had started from Sitanda's Kraal, to try and reach the mountains. As for the note I had sent him by Jim, that worthy had lost it, and he had never heard of it till today. But, acting upon information he had received from the natives, he made, not for Sheba's breasts, but for the ladder-like mountains down which we had just come, which was clearly a better route than that marked out in old Don Silvestra's plan. In the desert he and Jim suffered great hardships, but finally they reached this oasis, where a terrible accident befell George Curtis. On the day of their arrival he was sitting by the stream, and Jim was extracting the honey from the nest of a stingless bee, which is to be found in the desert, on the top of the bank immediately above him. In so doing he loosed a great boulder of rock, which fell upon George Curtis's right leg, crushing it frightfully. From that day he had been so dreadfully lame that he had found it impossible to go either forward or back, and had preferred to take the chances of dying on the oasis to the certainty of perishing in the desert.

As for food, however, they had got on pretty well, for they had a good supply of ammunition, and the oasis was frequented, especially at night, by large quantities of game, which came thither for water. These they shot, or trapped in pitfalls, using their flesh for food and, after their clothes wore out, their hides for covering.

"And so," he ended, "we have lived for nearly two years,

like a second Robinson Crusoe and his man Friday, hoping against hope that some natives might come here and help us away, but none have come. Only last night we settled that Jim should leave me and try to reach Sitanda's Kraal and get assistance. He was to go tomorrow, but I had little hope of ever seeing him back again. And now *you*, of all the people in the world, *you* who I fancied had long ago forgotten all about me, and were living comfortably in old England, turn up in a promiscuous way and find me where you least expected. It is the most wonderful thing I ever heard of, and the most merciful, too."

Then Sir Henry set to work and told him the main facts of our adventures, sitting till late into the night to do it.

"By Jove!" he said, when I showed him some of the diamonds. "Well, at least you have got something for your pains, besides my worthless self."

Sir Henry laughed. "They belong to Quatermain and Good. It was part of the bargain that they should share any spoils there might be."

This remark set me thinking, and, having spoken to Good, I told Sir Henry that it was our unanimous wish that he should take a third share of the diamonds, or, if he would not, that his share should be handed to his brother, who had suffered even more than ourselves on the chance of getting them. Finally, we prevailed upon him to consent to this arrangement, but George Curtis did not know of it till some time afterwards.

And here, at this point, I think I shall end this history. Our journey across the desert back to Sitanda's Kraal was most arduous, especially as we had to support George Curtis, whose right leg was very weak indeed, and continually throwing out splinters of bone; but we did accomplish it, somehow, and to give its details would only be to reproduce much of what happened to us on the former occasion.

Six months from the date of our rearrival at Sitanda's, where we found our guns and other goods quite safe, though the old scoundrel in charge was much disgusted at our surviving to claim them, saw us all once more safe and sound at my little place on the Berea, near Durban, where I am now writing, and whence I bid farewell to all who have accompanied me throughout the strangest trip I ever made in the course of a long and varied experience.

Just as I had written the last word a Kaffir came up my avenue of orange trees, with a letter in a cleft stick, which he had brought from the post. It turned out to be from Sir Henry, and, as it speaks for itself, I give it in full.

Brayley Hall, Yorkshire

My Dear Quatermain,

I sent you a line a few mails back to say that the three of us, George, Good, and myself, fetched up all right in England. We got off the boat at Southampton, and went up to town. You should have seen what a swell Good turned out the very next day, beautifully shaved, frock coat fitting like a glove, brand-new eyeglass, etc., etc. I went and walked in the park with him, where I met some people I know, and at once told them the story of his "beautiful white legs."

He is furious, especially as some ill-natured person has printed it in a society paper.

To come to business, Good and I took the diamonds to Streeter's to be valued, as we arranged, and I am really afraid to tell you what they put them at, it seems so enormous. They say that of course it is more or less guess-work, as such stones have never to their knowledge been put on the market in anything like such quantities. It appears that they are (with the exception of one or two of the largest) of the finest water, and equal in every way to the best Brazilian stones. I asked them if they would buy them, but they said it was beyond their power to do so, and recommended us to sell by degrees, for fear we should flood the market. They offer, however, a hundred and eighty thousand for a small portion of them.

You must come home, Quatermain, and see about these things, especially if you insist upon making the magnificent present of the third share, which does *not* belong to me, to my brother George. As for Good, he is *no good*. His time is too much occupied in shaving, and other matters connected with the vain adorning of his body. But I think he is still down on his luck about Foulata. He told me that since he had been home he hadn't seen a woman to touch her, either as regards her figure or the sweetness of her expression.

I want you to come home, my dear old comrade, and buy a place near here. You have done your day's work, and have lots of money now, and there is a place for sale quite close which would suit you admirably. Do come; the sooner the better; you can finish writing the story of our adventures on board ship. We have refused to tell the story till it is written by you, for fear that we shall not be believed. If you start on receipt of this you will reach here by Christmas, and I book you to stay with me for that. Good is coming, and George, and so, by the way, is your boy Harry (there's a bribe for you). I have had him down for a week's shooting, and like him. He is a cool young hand; he shot me in the leg, cut out the pellets, and then remarked upon the advantage of having a medical student in every shooting-party.

Good-bye, old boy; I can't say any more, but I know that you will come, if it is only to oblige your sincere friend,

Henry Curtis

P.S.—The tusks of the great bull that killed poor Khiva have now been put up in the hall here, over the pair of buffalo-horns you gave me, and look magnificent; and the ax with which I chopped off Twala's head is stuck up over my writing-table. I wish we could have managed to bring away the coats of chain armor.   H.C.

Today is Tuesday. There is a steamer going on Friday, and I really think I must take Curtis at his word, and sail by her for England, if it is only to see my boy Harry and see about the printing of this history, which is a task I do not like to trust to anybody else.

MODERN LIBRARY GIANTS

A series of sturdily bound and handsomely printed, full-sized library editions of books formerly available only in expensive sets. These volumes contain from 600 to 1,400 pages each.

THE MODERN LIBRARY GIANTS REPRESENT A SELECTION OF THE WORLD'S GREATEST BOOKS

G76 ANDERSEN & GRIMM: *Tales*
G74 AUGUSTINE, ST.: *The City of God*
G58 AUSTEN, JANE: *Complete Novels*
G70 BLAKE, WILLIAM & DONNE, JOHN: *Complete Poetry*
G2 BOSWELL, JAMES: *Life of Samuel Johnson*
G17 BROWNING, ROBERT: *Poems and Plays*
G14 BULFINCH: *Mythology* (Illustrated)
G35 BURY, J. B.: *A History of Greece*
G13 CARLYLE, THOMAS: *The French Revolution*
G28 CARROLL, LEWIS: *Complete Works*
G15 CERVANTES: *Don Quixote* (Illustrated)
G33 COLLINS, WILKIE: *The Moonstone* and *The Woman in White*
G27 DARWIN, CHARLES: *Origin of Species* and *The Descent of Man*
G43 DEWEY, JOHN: *Intelligence in the Modern World: John Dewey's Philosophy*
G70 DONNE, JOHN & BLAKE, WILLIAM: *Complete Poetry*
G36 DOSTOYEVSKY, FYODOR: *The Brothers Karamazov*
G60 DOSTOYEVSKY, FYODOR: *The Idiot*
G51 ELIOT, GEORGE: *Best-Known Novels*
G41 FARRELL, JAMES T.: *Studs Lonigan*
G82 FAULKNER, WILLIAM: *The Faulkner Reader*
G39 FREUD, SIGMUND: *The Basic Writings*
G6
G7 } GIBBON, EDWARD: *The Decline and Fall of the Roman Empire*
G8   (Complete in three volumes)
G25 GILBERT & SULLIVAN: *Complete Plays*
G76 GRIMM & ANDERSEN: *Tales*
G37 HAWTHORNE, NATHANIEL: *Compl. Novels & Selected Tales*
G78 HOLMES, OLIVER WENDELL: *The Mind and Faith of Justice Holmes*
G19 HOMER: *Complete Works*
G3 HUGO, VICTOR: *Les Miserables*
G18 IBSEN, HENRIK: *Eleven Plays*
G11 JAMES, HENRY: *Short Stories*
G52 JOYCE, JAMES: *Ulysses*
G4 KEATS & SHELLEY: *Complete Poems*
G24 LAMB, CHARLES: *The Complete Works and Letters*
G20 LINCOLN, ABRAHAM: *The Life and Writings of Abraham Lincoln*
G84 MANN, THOMAS: *Stories of Three Decades*
G26 MARX, KARL: *Capital*
G57 MELVILLE, HERMAN: *Selected Writings*
G38 MURASAKA, LADY: *The Tale of Genji*
G30 MYERS, GUSTAVUS: *History of the Great American Fortunes*
G34 NIETZSCHE, FRIEDRICH: *The Philosophy of Nietzsche*

G88   O'HARA, JOHN: 49 Stories
G55   O'NEILL, EUGENE: Nine Plays
G68   PAINE, TOM: Selected Work
G86   PASTERNAK, BORIS: Doctor Zhivago
G5   PLUTARCH: Lives (The Dryden Translation)
G40   POE, EDGAR ALLAN: Complete Tales and Poems
G29   PRESCOTT, WILLIAM H.: The Conquest of Mexico and The
          Conquest of Peru
G62   PUSHKIN: Poems, Prose and Plays
G65   RABELAIS: Complete Works
G12   SCOTT, SIR WALTER: The Most Popular Novels (Quentin
          Durward, Ivanhoe & Kenilworth)
G4   SHELLEY & KEATS: Complete Poems
G32   SMITH, ADAM: The Wealth of Nations
G61   SPAETH, SIGMUND: A Guide to Great Orchestral Music
G91   SPENSER, EDMUND: Selected Poetry
G75   STEVENSON, ROBERT LOUIS: Selected Writings
G53   SUE, EUGENE: The Wandering Jew
G42   TENNYSON: The Poems and Plays
G23   TOLSTOY, LEO: Anna Karenina
G1   TOLSTOY, LEO: War and Peace
G49   TWAIN, MARK: Tom Sawyer and Huckleberry Finn
G50   WHITMAN, WALT: Leaves of Grass
G83   WILSON, EDMUND: The Shock of Recognition

                    MISCELLANEOUS

G77   An Anthology of Famous American Stories
G54   An Anthology of Famous British Stories
G67   Anthology of Famous English and American Poetry
G81   An Encyclopedia of Modern American Humor
G47   The English Philosophers from Bacon to Mill
G16   The European Philosophers from Descartes to Nietzsche
G31   Famous Science-Fiction Stories
G85   Great Ages and Ideas of the Jewish People
G89   Great Classical Myths
G72   Great Tales of Terror and the Supernatural
G9   Great Voices of the Reformation
G87   Medieval Epics
G48   The Metropolitan Opera Guide
G46   A New Anthology of Modern Poetry
G69   One Hundred and One Years' Entertainment
G90   Philosophies of Art and Beauty: Readings in Aesthetics from
          Plato to Heidegger
G21   Sixteen Famous American Plays
G63   Sixteen Famous British Plays
G71   Sixteen Famous European Plays
G45   Stoic and Epicurean Philosophers
G22   Thirty Famous One-Act Plays
G66   Three Famous Murder Novels, Before the Fact, Francis Iles,
          Trent's Last Case, E. C. Bentley, The House of the Arrow,
          A. E. W. Mason
G10   Twelve Famous Plays of the Restoration and Eighteenth Cen-
          tury (1660–1820) Dryden, Congreve, Wycherley, Gay, etc.
G56   The Wisdom of Catholicism
G59   The Wisdom of China and India
G79   The Wisdom of Israel